At the head of th
harder-fighting C
Light Cavalry, a y
Army captain was
famous characters
his small build, mo ppearance, and
quiet manner, he could strike when least
expected with the raging fury of a Texas
twister and leave destruction as great as
any whirlwind in his wake.

His name was Dusty Fog . . .

Also available from Corgi Books:

J.T. EDSON OMNIBUS VOLUME 2

Revised list of J.T. EDSON *titles in chronological and categorical sequence:*

Ole Devil Hardin series

YOUNG OLE DEVIL
OLE DEVIL AND THE CAPLOCKS
OLE DEVIL AND THE MULE TRAIN
OLE DEVIL AT SAN JACINTO
GET URREA

The Civil War series

COMANCHE
THE START OF THE LEGEND }*
How Belle Boyd Became The Rebel Spy }
YOU'RE IN COMMAND NOW, MR. FOG
THE BIG GUN
UNDER THE STARS AND BARS
THE FASTEST GUN IN TEXAS
A MATTER OF HONOUR
KILL DUSTY FOG!
THE DEVIL GUN
THE COLT AND THE SABRE
THE REBEL SPY
THE BLOODY BORDER
BACK TO THE BLOODY BORDER

The Floating Outfit series

THE YSABEL KID
.44 CALIBRE MAN
A HORSE CALLED MOGOLLON
GOODNIGHT'S DREAM
FROM HIDE AND HORN
SET TEXAS BACK ON HER FEET
THE HIDE AND TALLOW MEN
THE HOODED RIDERS
QUIET TOWN
TRAIL BOSS
WAGONS TO BACKSIGHT
TROUBLED RANGE
SIDEWINDER
RANGELAND HERCULES
McGRAW'S INHERITANCE
THE HALF BREED
WHITE INDIANS
THE WILDCATS
THE BAD BUNCH
THE FAST GUN
CUCHILO
A TOWN CALLED YELLOWDOG
TRIGGER FAST
THE MAKING OF A LAWMAN
THE TROUBLE BUSTERS
DECISION FOR DUSTY FOG
DIAMONDS, EMERALDS, CARDS AND COLTS
THE CODE OF DUSTY FOG
THE GENTLE GIANT
SET A-FOOT
THE LAW OF THE GUN
THE PEACEMAKERS
TO ARMS! TO ARMS! IN DIXIE
HELL IN THE PALO DURO
GO BACK TO HELL
THE SOUTH WILL RISE AGAIN
THE QUEST FOR BOWIE'S BLADE
BEGUINAGE
BEGUINAGE IS DEAD
MASTER OF TRIGGERNOMETRY
THE RUSHERS
BUFFALO ARE COMING
THE FORTUNE HUNTERS
RIO GUNS
GUN WIZARD
THE TEXAN
OLD MOCCASINS ON THE TRAIL
MARK COUNTER'S KIN
THE RIO HONDO KID
OLE DEVIL'S HANDS AND FEET
WACO'S DEBT

The Floating Outfit series cont'd

THE HARD RIDERS
THE FLOATING OUTFIT
APACHE RAMPAGE
THE RIO HONDO WAR
THE MAN FROM TEXAS
GUNSMOKE THUNDER
THE SMALL TEXAN
THE TOWN TAMERS
RETURN TO BACKSIGHT
TERROR VALLEY
GUNS IN THE NIGHT

Waco series

WACO'S BADGE
SAGEBRUSH SLEUTH
ARIZONA RANGER
WACO RIDES IN
THE DRIFTER
DOC LEROY, M.D.
HOUND DOG MAN

Calamity Jane series

CALAMITY, MARK AND BELLE
COLD DECK, HOT LEAD
THE BULL WHIP BREED
TROUBLE TRAIL
THE COW THIEVES
THE HIDE AND HORN SALOON
CUT ONE, THEY ALL BLEED
CALAMITY SPELLS TROUBLE
WHITE STALLION, RED MARE
THE REMITTANCE KID
THE WHIP AND THE WAR LANCE
THE BIG HUNT

Waxahachie Smith series

NO FINGER ON THE TRIGGER
SLIP GUN
CURE THE TEXAS FEVER*

Alvin Dustine 'Cap' Fog series

YOU'RE A TEXAS RANGER, ALVIN FOG
RAPIDO CLINT
THE JUSTICE OF COMPANY 'Z'
'CAP' FOG, TEXAS RANGER, MEET MR. J.G. REEDER
THE RETURN OF RAPIDO CLINT AND MR. J.G. REEDER

The Rockabye County series

THE SIXTEEN DOLLAR SHOOTER
THE LAWMEN OF ROCKABYE COUNTY
THE SHERIFF OF ROCKABYE COUNTY
THE PROFESSIONAL KILLERS
THE ¼ SECOND DRAW
THE DEPUTIES
POINT OF CONTACT
THE OWLHOOT
RUN FOR THE BORDER
BAD HOMBRE

Bunduki series

BUNDUKI
BUNDUKI AND DAWN
SACRIFICE FOR THE QUAGGA GOD
FEARLESS MASTER OF THE JUNGLE

Miscellaneous titles

J.T.'S HUNDREDTH
J.T.'S LADIES
J.T.'S LADIES RIDE AGAIN
MORE J.T.'S LADIES
IS-A-MAN
WANTED! BELLE STARR
SLAUGHTER'S WAY
TWO MILES TO THE BORDER
BLONDE GENIUS (*Written in collaboration with Peter Clawson*)

** Title awaiting publication at Corgi Books*

J.T. EDSON
Omnibus Volume 1

comprising:

YOU'RE IN COMMAND NOW, MR. FOG

KILL DUSTY FOG!

THE DEVIL GUN

CORGI BOOKS

J.T. EDSON OMNIBUS VOLUME 1
A CORGI BOOK 0 552 13602 6

THE DEVIL GUN originally published in Great Britain by Brown Watson Ltd.

PRINTING HISTORY – YOU'RE IN COMMAND NOW, MR. FOG
Corgi edition published 1973
Corgi edition reprinted 1978

PRINTING HISTORY – KILL DUSTY FOG!
Corgi edition published 1970
Corgi edition reissued 1973
Corgi edition reprinted 1978

PRINTING HISTORY – THE DEVIL GUN
Corgi edition published 1968
Corgi edition reprinted 1968
Corgi edition reissued 1971
Corgi edition reprinted 1979

Corgi Omnibus edition published 1990

Corgi Books are published by Transworld Publishers Ltd., 61–63 Uxbridge Road, Ealing, London W5 5SA, in Australia by Transworld Publishers (Australia) Pty. Ltd., 15–23 Helles Avenue, Moorebank, NSW 2170, and in New Zealand by Transworld Publishers (N.Z.) Ltd., Cnr. Moselle and Waipareira Avenues, Henderson, Auckland.

Printed and bound in Great Britain by
Cox & Wyman Ltd., Reading, Berks.

You're In Command Now, Mr Fog

Author's note: *This book is in response to numerous readers' requests for details of Dusty Fog's early life.*

For Bob and Sue, mine host and hostess at the White Lion Hotel, Melton Mowbray; who are sufficiently strong-willed, blast them, to keep me on 'Slim-Lines' when necessary

Part One

THE BATTLE OF MARTIN'S MILL

CHAPTER ONE

ALTHOUGH the blue-uniformed sharpshooter sitting on a branch of the big old chestnut tree did not realize it, he was soon to cause the United States' Army of Arkansas to lose the vitally important Battle of Martin's Mill. That he brought this about would not result from incompetence. His selection of the target would be basically correct. The trouble was that he would fire too soon.

Being an ambitious professional soldier, who had adopted his specialized but frequently dangerous type of work as a means of gaining rapid promotion, the sharpshooter – in future wars the term would be changed to 'sniper' – wanted to carry out his duties in the most efficient manner possible. By doing so, he hoped to earn Colonel Middleton's approbation and maybe gain the elevation in rank that he desired.

Dispatched to carry out a routine scouting mission, he had not at first seen any hope of turning it to his advantage. In fact, he had believed that circumstances were preventing him from being with his outfit at a time when there should have been numerous opportunities to display his talents favourably to his superiors. While he had been searching the woodland, he had found himself cut off from his companions and there was clearly soon to be a battle.

From his place in the tree, he scanned – with the help of the Sharps Model of 1859 rifle's barrel-long telescopic sight

– the terrain over which the battle would be fought. Annoyance and disappointment ate at him. It seemed that he was fated to remain on the side-line. Unless something unexpected was to happen, he would be unable to do anything to further the Union's cause or to increase his hopes of obtaining promotion.

An increasing sense of frustration assailed him. In his hands he held one of the finest, most powerful, far-shooting and accurate breech-loading rifles available at that period. With it, he had been trained to the point where he could be relied upon to drive a .52 bullet into a man's chest at range of half a mile. Using a ball of soft lead, carefully shaped for its deadly purpose, such a wound was certain to incapacitate its recipient even if it did not kill him outright.

Knowing the capability of his weapon, he had chosen his point of vantage wisely on becoming aware of his predicament. The branch upon which he was seated was so massive and steady that there was no motion from it to disturb his aim. The foliage offered adequate all-round concealment, but there were sufficient gaps and openings for him to have an excellent field of vision. The full panorama of the battle-ground was spread like a map before him. All he needed was targets upon which he could practise his art.

Occupying their hastily-constructed defensive system, the remainder of the sharpshooter's regiment – the 18th 'Wisconsin' Heavy Infantry – lined their long-barrelled Springfield U.S. Model of 1861 rifle-muskets. They were ready to defend the bridge across the Ouachita River against the much larger force of Confederate State's infantry and cavalry which had made its appearance and were massing for an assault.

Behind the trench lines, exposed to the sharpshooter's view by virtue of their positions, three enormous Vandenburg Volley Guns had been trained and loaded by their crews. Each Vandenburg had ninety-one separate .50 calibre barrels. When fired simultaneously, their bullets would sweep the terrain in front of the muzzle like the charge from a gigantic shotgun.

So the ugly, awkward, multi-barrelled weapons could easily prove to be a decisive factor in the forthcoming fight. They might have been damned and cursed bitterly during the march, but they were going to have a far-reaching effect on that part of the War Between The States which was being waged in Arkansas. Their presence amongst the buildings of Martin's Mill and the adjacent small hamlet did much to nullify the advantage in numbers held by the Rebels.

As on the other, better-publicized battle-fronts in the East, the Federal soldiers had the Army of the Confederate States in retreat. Being a hard-bitten realist, the sharpshooter disregarded such blindly patriotic notions as one Yankee being equal to three Johnny Rebs. Nor did he subscribe to the more religiously-inspired idea that the Good Lord was favouring the Northern cause. He accepted that superior numbers, industrial potential, technology and economics – although he would not have understood such words and would have expressed himself in more simple terms – were the chief causes of the Union's successes.

What was more, in Arkansas – no matter what rumour claimed to be happening elsewhere – the retreat was anything but a rout that had the Rebels in full flight. In fact, they were pulling back in an orderly, well-organized manner. All of their equipment and supplies were being moved towards the Ouachita River, with infantry, cavalry and artillery ably covering the withdrawal. They were effectively preventing the pursuing Union soldiers from coming even within long cannon-shot of the valuable convoy, which hardly seemed to be the actions of defeated, fleeing men.

There had recently been a change in the command of the Confederate States Army of Arkansas and North Texas. By all accounts, the new general – Ole Devil Hardin was his name – had considerable ability as a fighting man and tactician. He was playing hell with 'Cussing' Culver's often repeated boast that the Union troops would 'push those bastard-born Texas sons-of-bitches right back into their lice-infested State and make them regret the day when they first heard the word "Secession" '.

While Hardin had been unable to prevent his men from falling back, it was clear to the sharpshooter that he had them doing considerable 'pushing' on their own account. The fact was that they were just about retreating in their own good time. If they once got all their gear across the Ouachita, they would be in a fine position to prevent the Yankees from following.

Yes sir. Ole Devil Hardin was a foxy son-of-a-bitch. The way in which he had gone about shifting his supplies to safety had given proof of his shrewd tactical sense and planning ability. At first it had seemed that he intended to follow the obvious course of crossing the Ouachita near Arkadelphia. To prevent this, Culver had dispatched two cavalry regiments from his pursuing Army. After they had gone, it became obvious that Hardin had swung the column upstream.

Luckily, somebody – the sharpshooter did not credit General Culver with possessing the necessary intelligence or military knowledge – had made a shrewd guess at the supply column's destination. There was a bridge at Martin's Mill that would be capable of standing up to the heavy flow of traffic. Hardin was intending, having misled his enemies, to go over the river by the bridge. The 18th 'Wisconsin' Heavy Infantry Regiment, a half-battery of Vandenburg Volley Guns and three companies of the Long Island Lancers had been dispatched with orders to travel at their best speed and prevent the Rebels from crossing.

To the sharpshooter's way of thinking, the easiest and most effective means of carrying out their orders would have been to destroy the bridge; which could easily have been done by a smaller party. However, it seemed that General Culver had decided the bridge would be useful to his Army as they advanced to conquer Texas. So he had stated that it could only be destroyed if it was certain to fall into the enemies' hands.

Basically, Culver's plan had been good. He wanted to halt the supply column until he could bring up the full strength of his command. Then he hoped to crush the majority of military opposition in Arkansas and leave the way open for him to continue with the invasion of Northern Texas.

On either side of the trail that led to the bridge, the land rose for over a mile in a gentle, fairly even and completely open slope. Apart from the stumps of cut-down trees, it offered no shelter and could only be traversed in plain view of the defenders. There was an area of wooded land – the tree in which he sat was on the edge of it – extending at an angle from beyond the rim to join the trees and bushes which fringed the river far upstream of the bridge. It would not allow the enemy to move in close and launch an undetected flank attack. There was a similar formation on the eastern side, but even farther away from the trail, and the woods on that bank were much more open.

Any assault by the Rebels would have to be made straight down the slope, head-on to the waiting infantry, concealed Lancers and possibly unsuspected Vandenburg Volley Guns.

All in all, the situation still had much to favour the sharpshooter's party. Maybe the Rebels' advance guard had arrived way ahead of time, but they still had to make their attack across the open ground and under fire.

Suddenly it became apparent that the presence of the Vandenburgs was not unsuspected. However, their positions were causing the Rebels to attempt the counter battery work from the required direction.

Travelling at a gallop, limbered for draught, a battery of four twelve-pounder mountain howitzers* swung into sight from behind the mass of the Rebels' force. Taking advantage of the favourable nature of the terrain, they had the short-barrelled, light-weight weapons mounted on the carriages instead of being broken down into the various components and carried on the horses' pack saddles. Towed by a single

* The officially recommended number of guns in a battery was six, but that figure could rarely be made available in the Confederate States' Army.

horse, each howitzer could be moved at a swifter pace than when transported on the packs and made ready for action in a shorter time.

The Rebel artillerymen looked to be members of an efficient, well-commanded outfit. At a signal from the tall, slim, moderately handsome, dark-haired captain who led them, each chief-of-piece guided the horse which was hauling his howitzer in a tight circle. They halted with the muzzles pointing towards the village. Something over half a mile separated them from the nearest trench, which meant that they were reasonably safe from the defenders' rifle fire. However, with less than half that distance between them and the sharpshooter, they were within range of his Sharps.

In the absence of a specific target, a sharpshooter was expected to pick off the enemy's officers and deprive the enlisted men of leadership at crucial moments. There was one serious disadvantage to him taking such action. He had climbed the tree in the first place to try to ascertain the full strength of the enemy, hoping to take the news to his commanding officer. While it offered a steady base from which to do accurate shooting, he could not leave it in a hurry. Nor could he rejoin his regiment without making a lengthy detour. Each shot he fired would render his position more likely to be located and it would not be long before men were dispatched to hunt him down.

Besides which, the battery could be more effectively silenced by the Long Island Lancers. When preparing the defences, Colonel Middleton had concealed his cavalrymen in the woods fringing the upstream side of the river and had arranged the Vandenburgs accordingly. His gamble had paid off. Wanting to deal with the multi-barrelled guns as quickly as possible, the Rebel battery had taken up a position from which they could see their targets. By doing so, they had placed themselves in front of – although some distance from – where the Lancers were hidden.

Maybe the fly-slicers* were only a volunteer outfit, commanded by scent-smelling New York dudes and armed with

* Fly-slicers: derogatory name for cavalrymen.

nothing better than steel tipped wooden sticks, but there were one hundred and fifty of them against the battery's thirty-six or so. Given odds like that, the Lancers ought to be able to crush the howitzers' crews by sheer weight of numbers and far more quickly than a single rifle could do it. Nor would there be sufficient time for the Rebel cavalry on the rim to intervene, providing that the Lancers launched their attack immediately.

Sure enough, the Lancers were moving into the open.

If the sharpshooter killed the artillery captain—

Movements in the woodland, about a quarter of a mile from the chestnut tree, caught the corner of the sharpshooter's eye. Turning his head for a precautionary closer look, he was handed one hell of a shock.

Three riders were sitting their horses at the edge of the trees!

They were not alone!

Others were behind them!

Just how many more, the sharpshooter could not see. He was, however, shrewd enough to make a fairly accurate deduction.

One thing he knew for sure.

The uniforms worn by the new arrivals told him, without any question, that they were *not* members of the Federal Government's Army of Arkansas.

Studying the trio, the sharpshooter made them out to be a pair of very young lieutenants – a shavetail and a full-blown luff – and an older captain. Which implied there was at least a whole company of Confederate States' cavalry at their backs, fifty to seventy men that would be. Not just ordinary leather bumpers either, but an outfit that had already won themselves considerable acclaim as hard-fighting and very capable soldiers.

Of the three officers, the captain struck the sharpshooter as being the only one to be contended with. Tall, square-shouldered, ramrod erect on his saddle, he had a ruddy face and the hard, unsmiling features of a parade ground martinet. He looked like a German, one of the kind who called themselves 'Prussians'. In the sharpshooter's experience, they were most unimaginative, stiff-backed, bow-necked officers with copies of the various *Manuals of Regulations* bracing their spines. Yet he knew better than to sell such men short when it came to making war, for they had been trained in such matters practically from birth. Given a military problem, they would be able to come up with an answer and it was frequently the right one.

Every inch of the captain's uniform was as stipulated in the Army of the Confederate States' *Manual of Dress Regulations.* He wore a white Jeff Davis campaign hat, with its brim down and unadorned by the plume of feathers many officers on both sides sported. In front, on the centre of the crown, was a badge formed from a silver five-pointed star in a circle. That circle would bear a laurel wreath motif and the centre of the star was embossed with the letters TLC.

Not that the sharpshooter could make out the embellishments. He was familiar with the hat badge of the Texas Light Cavalry.

Closed at the neck, the captain's stand-up collar carried the triple, three-inch long, half-inch wide strips of gold which denoted his rank. The double breasted jacket had twin rows of seven buttons. Two strands of gold braid were formed into a 'chicken guts' Austrian knot at the cuffs of the sleeves and the skirt extended correctly to half-way between the hip and the knee. Yellow-striped riding breeches ended in Hessian boots that still retained something of what must, on more suitable occasions, have been an almost mirror-like shine. The same attention had been given to his weapon belt – which the sharpshooter was willing to bet had once been fastened by a U.S. Army's buckle. It supported a sabre on the left and a revolver in a butt-forward, closed topped holster at the right. His saddle was an officer's issue McClellan, again most likely stemming from the days before he had seceded from the Union and ridden South.

Everything about the captain suggested tough, capable military efficiency. He would be fully aware of the danger to the battery and, most likely, was already formulating the means to protect the howitzers.

Neither of the junior officers appealed to the sharpshooter as being worthy of consideration on that score. From their appearances, they were a pair of rich young sprouts who had been handed their commissions because of the wealth and influence wielded by their families. In general, their uniforms followed that of the captain. Probably it was at his insistence that they stuck so closely to what was required by the *Dress Regulations*. It was unlikely that either had much military training, or control over the enlisted men.

The shavetail matched the captain in height, with wide shoulders and a build that hinted at strength. Tilted back on his head, the Jeff Davis hat exposed rumpled, untidy, curly, fiery red hair. There was something cheerfully pugnacious about his freckled, ruggedly handsome young face. It suggested that he possessed a reckless, impulsive nature. Only one bar graced a collar that would most likely have been open had he been permitted to follow his inclinations. Likewise, his 'chicken guts' were formed from a single braid.

Still only in his late teens, the second-lieutenant looked like a hot-head who would not be over-fond of discipline, nor well-versed in military strategy. He sat his big brown horse with the easy grace of a natural rider, afork a low-horned, double-girthed saddle that was definitely not an official Government issue.

Apparently the luff was somebody important's favourite son, or nephew. The sharpshooter could imagine no other reason to account for him having attained that rank. In age, he would probably match that of the shavetail – a young eighteen, at most – but he was nowhere such a fine physical specimen.

Although no more than five foot six inches in height, the luff had a sturdy enough figure. It might, the sharpshooter told himself, be more the result of a tailor's efforts than natural. Dusty blond hair showed from under his Jeff Davis hat and his tanned face was fairly good looking. However, nothing suggested to the Yankee watcher that other than family connections had pinned the second gold strip to his collar. He too used one of these hefty and – to the sharpshooter's Eastern-raised eyes – unusual saddles. Like the shavetail, he looked completely at ease on the back of the large bay gelding. Which proved little. Most rich kids, particularly down South, were taught to ride early and given ample opportunities to improve their equestrian skills.

The trio remained in cover, studying the open ground and taking notice of all that developed. At first, their attention was directed at the mountain battery and they appeared to be discussing it. While the shavetail and the captain talked, the short-grown luff continued to dart around what the watcher regarded as being nervous and anxious glances. So, not surprisingly, it was he who first observed the appearance of the Long Island Lancers and he drew his companions' attention to them.

Directing the telescopic sight at the captain's face, the sharpshooter saw that he was speaking. He appeared to be telling the first lieutenant to go somewhere, then addressed the shavetail. Most likely he would be making arrangements to lead his men to the battery's rescue. In which case, he must be stopped. A surprise attack from the flank might easily throw the Lancers into confusion. Freshly recruited back East, as yet untried in combat, armed with what the sharpshooter – and many better-informed, senior soldiers – regarded as hopelessly obsolete and antiquated weapons, they were such an uncertain element that he felt disinclined to rely upon their stability when they came under fire. Especially against the well-led, battle-hardened veterans of the Texas Light Cavalry.

Excitement filled the sharpshooter as he laid his sights on the captain's head. Here was his chance to take a significant part in the battle. By killing the captain, he would put that undersized luff in command. That would ensure the destruction of the battery, allowing the Vandenburgs to do their work without interruption.

Satisfied that he was laying the foundations of his promotion, the sharpshooter squeezed the trigger. He felt the hard thrust of the recoil against his left shoulder and the swirling gasses from the detonated powder momentarily obscured the target. Not that he doubted he had held true. His shooting instincts reassured him that he had aimed correctly. Sure enough, as the smoke was wafted away in the breeze, he saw the captain pitching from the saddle. The campaign hat had been torn off by the bullet and the captain's skull was a bloody ruin. There was no doubt that he had been killed instantly.

A crackling and crashing amongst the bushes not far from the chestnut tree caused the sharpshooter to look away from his victim. Bursting into view, glaring upwards, was a tall, lean, Indian-dark corporal of the Texas Light Cavalry. He was on foot, but moving with a deadly purpose that was menacing in the extreme. Skidding to a halt, he snapped the butt of his Henry rifle upwards, sighting straight at the sharpshooter's hiding place.

Even as the Yankee soldier tried to work the triggerguard lever as a preliminary to reloading, flames spiked wickedly from the Henry's muzzle. Slashing through the foliage, a flat-nosed ·44 calibre bullet ploughed into his left breast. Letting the rifle slip through his fingers, he followed it as it fell out of the tree. He was dead before his body struck the ground. So he never learned how he had made the mistake that would cause the Union Army to lose the Battle of Martin's Mill.

CHAPTER TWO

'HERE comes good old Doug – Captain Staunce and his boys,' announced Second Lieutenant Charles William Henry Blaze, whose ever-untidy, fiery thatch of hair had affixed to him the sobriquet 'Red', pointing to the mountain battery. 'They can sure handle those wheel-guns.'

The change in the wording of Red's first sentence had been brought about by a belated recollection of how his Company's commanding officer regarded over-familiarity between the various grades of rank. Having caught the cold glare of disapproval darted his way by the captain, he had revised his comment and made it more acceptable.

Despite the alteration, Captain Otto von Hertz continued to scowl. A young man like Mr. Blaze would never have been permitted to attain officer's status in the Prussian Army, especially in the cavalry. In von Hertz's opinion, the red head lacked the necessary aptitude to control the enlisted men, or to maintain discipline. He was far too lax and easy-going in his ways for that, despite being a member of one of the trio of Texas families whose money had recruited, equipped and organized the regiment in which von Hertz was serving.

The Prussian had to admit that the majority of the Fogs, Blazes and Hardins in the Texas Light Cavalry were capable and efficient officers, if somewhat unorthodox in many of their methods. Von Hertz's second-in-command was one of that number.

In spite of First Lieutenant Dustine Edward Marsden Fog's lack of formal military training and background, von Hertz considered him to have the makings of a very good officer and soldier. The small Texan had already proven himself capable of handling men and appeared to have gained the respect of the hardbitten veterans of Company 'C'. All in all, he was a much more satisfactory subordinate than the captain had expected at their first meeting.

'I hope they can handle them well enough,' von Hertz answered, turning his gaze to the howitzers. 'The Vandenburgs will tear the infantry to pieces unless they are silenced.'

Several years of living in the United States had failed to remove completely the harsh, Teutonic timbre from Captain von Hertz's voice. Nor could he ever obliterate the suggestion that he was consciously forcing himself to speak in what he would always regard as a foreign language. In moments of stress, he had been known to revert explosively to his native German; which was mighty disconcerting to the majority of the Texans under his command. They spoke only English, with maybe some Spanish, or an Indian dialect thrown in.

All through the years in which he had served, first in the Federal then the Confederate States' Armies, von Hertz had regretted that he could not drill the men under his command to the rigidly disciplined precision attained by German soldiers. He had managed to instil some military training into the members of Company 'C' and could count on them to carry out his orders. It was not enough for his own satisfaction, but ought to be adequate whilst carrying out the duty to which they had been assigned.

While his cousin and von Hertz watched the battery dashing to a position from which it could bombard the Vandenburgs, First Lieutenant Dusty Fog was subjecting the whole area to a thorough scrutiny. In particular, he studied the woodland fringing the river. That was where the counter-measures against the howitzers could be expected to make an appearance. Soon, too, he would be going there to carry out a delicate, difficult and dangerous mission. So he wished to form an impression of what he might be headed into.

The sharpshooter would have been amazed if he had known the nature of the assignment which had been given to that small, insignificant-seeming youngster.

A quarter of a mile was not a distance over which a detailed examination of a person could be made, even with the aid of a powerful telescopic sight. So the sharpshooter had missed much that would have been informative about Dusty Fog's appearance. Nor was the soldier given to forming a deep analysis of character. He tended to allow his first impressions to rule his judgment. If he had been a more perceptive man, he might have reached a very different opinion regarding the short first lieutenant and been less likely to think of him as a 'luff', the highly derogatory term for one of his rank.

There was an air of command about Dusty Fog which would have been obvious to more discerning eyes than those of the sharpshooter. Young, but already blooded in battle, Dusty Fog was ready, willing and able to accept responsibility. Nor was his attitude born out of a cocky, arrogant, over-inflated self-importance which had been sponsored by the knowledge that he had powerful family connections and influence behind him. He had none of the bombast that often came when a small, very young man found himself in a position of authority over his physical superiors. Instead, he carried himself with the undefinable assurance of one who had been born with the gift of leadership.

If the sharpshooter had taken the trouble to look, think and deduce, instead of dismissing Dusty as a 'luff', there were many pointers to his true potential. The horse was one. Almost seventeen hands, it was a blaze-faced bay gelding which showed power, speed and spirit in its every line. Only a strong, exceptionally capable rider could handle such a mount. Dusty occupied its Texas range saddle in a relaxed effortless manner that emphasized he was in complete command. Yet his control had not been established by cruelty, or imposed by such heavy-handed dominance that the animal no longer had a will of its own.

What the watcher in the chestnut tree took to be anxiety and nervousness, as the small Texan continually scanned the surrounding terrain, was no more than natural caution mingled with an awareness of various possibilities. Dusty was searching for anything that might interfere with the plans that his uncle, General Ole Devil Hardin, had made for capturing and holding the bridge until the supply column had crossed. Wishing to avoid drawing attention to Martin's Mill, Ole Devil had not caused it to be guarded. Instead, he had been counting on taking the Yankees by surprise; but had not left that to chance.

Presented with the duty of scouting the area the previous afternoon, von Hertz had assigned the task to two of the half-a-dozen Prussian-born soldiers who had served with him in the United States' Army before accompanying him to the South at the start of the War Between The States. There were, Dusty had considered, several men better suited to carry out the duty. His opinion had not been sought and, when he had hinted at it, von Hertz had claimed that none of the Texans – experienced Indian fighters though they undoubtedly were – possessed the military training to form a correct assessment of the situation. The two men had returned with what, on the face of it, had been adequate information.

According to von Hertz's scouts, the citizens of Martin's Mill had fled and left the hamlet unoccupied when the enemy had made an appearance. A battalion of Lancers had accompanied the 18th 'Wisconsin' Heavy Infantry and the three Vandenburg Volley Guns, but had taken an almost immediate departure in the direction from which they had come. Following their orders to the letter, the scouts had returned as soon as they had seen the Yankees taking up defensive positions on the northern side of the river.

It would have been better, Dusty had believed, if the scouts had displayed more initiative and less blind obedience to orders. One of them should have continued to keep the Yankees under observation, while the other returned with the information they had already gathered. Instead, they had followed the captain's instructions to the letter and without having attempted to think for themselves.

Fortunately, von Hertz had agreed with Dusty on one

point. The departure of the Lancers did not necessarily mean that they could be discounted as a factor. Suspecting that there might be scouts watching them, they might have been playing tricky. After giving the impression that they had left, they could easily have doubled back after dark and concealed themselves ready to take cards once the fighting began.

If Dusty had been in command of Company 'C', he would have chosen men used to thinking for themselves and told them to—

'Everything is ready for you to carry out your assignment, Mr. Fog?' von Hertz inquired, diverting the small Texan's thoughts from the men he would have selected for the scouting mission and the discretionary instructions he would have given to them.

'Yes, sir,' Dusty replied.

'Corporal Cotton hasn't returned, I see,' the captain went on coldly.

'No, sir,' Dusty admitted and glanced to where a short, white-haired, old corporal and six private soldiers sat their horses some feet away from the remainder of the Company. 'I've told Corporal Hassle to come with me if Kiowa's not back in time.'

'You should have consulted with me before sending Cotton to scout the woods!' von Hertz protested indignantly. 'I'm most displeased that you did not.'

'Yes, sir,' Dusty said, in a flat, expressionless tone.

'There was no need to send him,' von Hertz went on. 'Even if the Yankees had sent men up here to keep watch, they would already have returned to say that our force was coming.'

From the rim of the slope came the ringing notes of bugles and the rapid rolling thunder of drums. Formed up in their companies, enlisted men's bayonets and officers' swords twinkling brightly in the mid-morning sun, the 1st 'Arkansas' Rifle Regiment were commencing the assault. They intended to advance in three waves, each comprised of two companies, at two hundred yards intervals. On the flanks of the leading wave, which would bear the brunt of the attack, rode the supporting companies supplied by the Texas Light Cavalry.

At the sight and sounds of activity from the main body, von Hertz's words came to an abrupt halt. Although the captain and Red Blaze turned their eyes to the rim, Dusty continued to keep the wooded land along the northern bank of the river under observation.

'It's sure lucky those folks ran out of Martin's Mill before the Yankees arrived.' Red remarked. 'They'd've hobbled us good if some of them'd stayed in their homes.'

'We couldn't have allowed them to influence our action,' von Hertz pointed out. 'They would have had to take—'

'Just like we figured, sir,' Dusty interrupted, pointing to where the blue-clad riders were emerging. 'The Lancers did come back, all of them.'

'So they did,' von Hertz agreed, following the direction indicated by the small Texan. 'And we are ready for them. You may go and attend to your duty, Mr. Fog. Good luck.'

'Yo!' Dusty replied instantly, giving the cavalryman's traditional assent to the receipt of an order.

If the sharpshooter had refrained from firing for another minute, or even thirty seconds, Dusty Fog would have ridden away and been delayed in – maybe prevented from – taking command of the Company. The mission upon which he was about to embark had considerable urgency and was so important that he had set his horse into motion as soon as the single word had left his lips.

However, acting as he believed in the best interests of the Union, the sharpshooter selected that moment to complete his pressure on the Sharps' trigger and turned loose the bullet.

On the point of addressing Red, von Hertz took the bullet in his temple. Killed instantly, he was slammed sideways and lost his seat on the saddle. Alarmed by its rider's actions, the horse snorted and plunged forward. In death, von Hertz's left hand had tightened on the reins. So, although he was pitched lifeless to the ground, his grasp prevented the animal from running away and being seen by the enemy.

'What the—?' Red ejaculated.

Any further words were chopped off by the brown gelding moving restlessly in response to the behaviour of von Hertz's startled horse. Deftly Red regained control of his mount and swung his gaze to his cousin.

Halting his bay, Dusty twisted his torso and stared in the direction from which the shot had come. His left hand flashed across to the flap of the close-topped holster on the right of his belt. Being unable to locate the enemy sharpshooter, he did not attempt to complete his draw. Nor, apparently, was there any need for him to do so.

'Kiowa's got the bastard!' Red guessed, when the second shot – obviously from a different weapon – sounded. 'It's lucky you sent him on that *pasear*, Cousin Dusty.'

'Not lucky enough!' Dusty growled, looking down. Hearing the startled exclamations and sounds of movement which arose from the enlisted men, he swung his attention towards them. A hard, commanding note came to his Texas drawl as he raised his voice, 'Quieten it down, damn you. Keep them back and silent, you sergeants!'

Barked-out orders from the sergeants brought about the effect desired by Dusty. While the men looked about them, searching for further enemies, they fell silent and remained in their ranks. Their concern on that score was relieved by the sound of Corporal Kiowa Cotton's voice reaching their ears.

'He's cashed and there ain't no more of them!'

Accompanied by the Company's sandy-haired. good-looking young guidon carrier and the stocky, older bugler, Sergeant Major Goering galloped forward. The bulky warrant officer sprang from his saddle and knelt at von Hertz's side. One glance told him all that he needed to know. The captain was no longer able to command Company 'C'; but there was still a vitally important duty to be carried out. So his eyes lifted towards the Company's second-in-command.

Goering had never been unduly worried about who was

placed above him in the chain of command. *Befehl ist befehl*, orders are orders, was a dictum deeply ingrained by his long years of military service. It was for the officer to make the decision on what line of action was to be taken, while Goering saw to it that his superior's wishes were carried out. However, he understood the importance of their mission and realized how high the price of failure would be.

Things could, Goering admitted to himself, be worse, Although First Lieutenant Fog lacked experience, he had the makings of a very good officer. While small, he was anything but a puny weakling. He could wield a sabre – mounted or on foot – with the best in the regiment and was the finest shot Goering had ever seen, being able to use a revolver equally well with either hand. When the occasion had demanded it, he had demonstrated bare-handed fighting techniques – learned, it was said, from General Hardin's Japanese servant – which rendered larger and stronger men helpless in his grasp.

However, the sergeant major wondered if Mr. Fog would be able to cope with the great responsibility that had been thrust upon him by Captain von Hertz's death?

Fortunately, the Company's line of action had already been decided by von Hertz when planning how to deal with the Lancers.

'The captain's dead!' Goering announced and came to his feet. Snapping into a brace as smartly as if he had been on a formal parade, he saluted and went on, 'You're in command now, Mr. Fog!'

That was one detail of which Dusty did not require to be reminded. Not only had he reached a similar conclusion, he was considering all that being left in command entailed. Yet, on the face of it, there should have been no need for him to think about how to deal with the situation.

When making arrangements to recapture the bridge, Colonel Harvey Barnett – commanding the 1st Arkansas Rifle Regiment and the assault force – had taken the danger of the Lancers' intervention into consideration. Their duty would be to nullify any attempt to bring the Vandenburgs under counter-battery fire. So he had sent Company 'C' to take up a position from which they could dash out and defend the mountain howitzers if necessary, or participate in the main attack if the need to do so did not arise.

When it had been pointed out that Company 'C' would be opposed by a force three times its size, von Hertz had declared that he was confident he could deal with the Lancers. He would offset the disparity in numbers by taking advantage of his men's superior weapons and employ a *caracole*, preventing a head-on clash that would favour the larger party. Wishing to retain as many men as possible to be thrown against the 'Wisconsins'[2] defences, Barnett had given his consent to von Hertz's arrangements.

Looking at the battery, Dusty discovered that Captain Douglas St. John Staunce did not intend to rely solely upon the cavalry to protect his howitzers. He had reduced each piece's crew to three men and formed up the remainder, under the command of Sergeant Major Smalley, in a fighting line between the battery and the Lancers. Even the horse-holders had been called upon to take part in the defensive duty, leaving the animals to fend for themselves.

Dusty sucked in a deep breath as he noticed the latter point. Aware of how much depended upon his howitzers being able to silence the Vandenburgs, Staunce was leaving himself without the means of retreat. Once the fighting started, the horses were certain to stampede and he would not be able to use them to haul his little guns to safety. It was clearly a case of root, hog, or die, for the men of the battery – especially if Company 'C' should fail to halt their attackers.

From examining the artillerymen and their howitzers, Dusty returned his gaze to the Lancers. They were already assembled in three waves as they emerged from concealment. Each line was formed of one company, with its officers at the front and in the centre of it. However, the waves were so close that the heads of the officers' horses were almost touching the rumps of the preceding company's mounts. Nor did they appear to be rectifying the situation.

Studying the close proximity of the Lancers' three companies, Dusty could visualize one major objection to attacking them in the manner suggested by his dead superior.

The *caracole* was one of the earliest manoeuvres to have been developed for use by cavalry carrying firearms. When charging to engage an approaching enemy, instead of meeting them head-on, the party performing the *caracole* would divide itself into two groups. Turning outwards, each section would gallop around their opponent's flanks and attack from the rear.

Under certain circumstances, a *caracole* could be a devastatingly effective tactic. It was especially useful when performed against men armed with swords or lances.*

'Shall I tell the men to move out, Mr. Fog?' Goering prompted.

'Yes,' Dusty confirmed. 'Column of twos.'

'It might be as well if I warned them we'll be doing a *caracole*, sir,' the sergeant major remarked, in polite, deferential tones.

'Don't tell them that!' Dusty snapped.

'It would be better for them to know what we're going to do,' Goering insisted, without waiting for the small Texan to continue with an explanation.

'I'm not gainsaying it, sergeant major,' Dusty replied. 'But we're not using a *caracole*.'

'Captain von Hertz said that was how—!' Goering reminded.

'The captain's dead,' Dusty interrupted. 'And, like you said, *I'm* in command now. Is that understood, sergeant major?'

'Yo!' affirmed Goering, stiffening even more into his rigid parade-ground brace. Holding his voice flatly emotionless, he went on, 'May I ask the lieutenant's intentions, sir?'

'We'll form into echelon as we leave the trees, Dusty explained, watching the sergeant major's face. 'Then we'll

* How effective a caracole could be is described in *Sidewinder*.

ride forward until we're between the battery and the Lancers. When we're there, I'll give the order to turn right and we'll charge straight at them.

Before swinging his gaze towards the mass of the Lancers, Goering's features showed a mixture of surprise and alarm. Red Blaze displayed no such misgivings. Instead, he let out a low whoop of approval.

'Yeeah! That's what I wanted to hear, Cousin Dusty!'

Neither Dusty nor Goering gave any indication that they had heard the redhead's words. Instead, their eyes met and seemed to be locked in a struggle for domination. After a couple of seconds, Goering lowered his gaze.

'They have us outnumbered, sir,' the sergeant major warned.

'I know that,' Dusty conceded. 'But my way is the only one that will stop them reaching the howitzers. There's no time to argue, or to hold a debate, sergeant major. Carry out my orders.'

For a moment Goering seemed to be on the verge of continuing his protests. Instead, his eyes flickered to the Lancers and back in Dusty's direction. Years of living under military discipline had their effect, backed by an instinctive feeling that the young officer was acting as he believed for the best. Certainly time was not available for a discussion on the matter.

'Yo!' Goering said, saluting and turning to mount his horse.

'You'll take over my detail, Cousin Red,' Dusty ordered, as Goering rode towards the enlisted men.

'Me!' Red yelped, realizing that to obey would cause him to miss out on what he figured would be a real good fight.

'You,' Dusty agreed. 'It has to be done and, way things've turned out, I can't do it. So you'll have to take my place.'

'I don't have a knife with me,' Red remarked hopefully.

'Take mine,' Dusty offered, drawing the Russell-Barlow clasp-knife from his breeches' pocket and holding it out. 'Company "A's" detail aren't likely to get through, the woods're too open on that side of the bridge. Happen you handle it the way I told you I aimed to, you'll likely get by.'

'I'll give her a whirl anyways,' Red promised, sounding resigned, and pocketed the knife. 'You figure you're playing it right, going for them head-on?'

'I figure I'm right,' Dusty declared. 'If I am, you've got to stop them blowing up the bridge.'

'Count on me to try,' Red grinned, deciding that his new assignment had possibilities of action and danger that would in some measure compensate for him missing the forthcoming battle with the Lancers. 'Good luck, Cousin Dusty.'

'And to you,' Dusty replied.

'Likely we'll both need it,' Red drawled. 'See you on the bridge.'

Watching Red join the corporal and six men of the special detail, Dusty could hear Goering passing on his orders to the remainder of the Company. So the small Texan turned his gaze once more to the open land. Everything he could see reaffirmed his belief that he had made the right decision. There was, he knew, one major objection to using the *caracole* in the prevailing conditions. So he had selected what he felt sure was the only way for his outnumbered force to give the mountain battery adequate protection.

There were also, Dusty realized, desperate risks involved.

He would be leading his men into a conflict with odds of at least three to one against them. What was more, he was disregarding the method by which his older, more experienced – now dead – superior officer had planned to deal with the situation. If Dusty was wrong and failed, the future of the Confederate States Army of Arkansas and North Texas would be placed in jeopardy.

Everything depended upon how much faith the men of Company 'C' had in their new commanding officer.

If they trusted his judgment, they would follow him.

Ever since Dusty had joined Company 'C', he had worked to earn the respect and confidence of its members. The next few minutes would show whether or not he had succeeded. Dusty thought of some of the events which, he hoped, would have helped him to gain the approbation of the men fate had placed under his command.

Part Two

THE MAKING OF A LEADER

CHAPTER THREE

DESPITE Sergeant Billy Jack's gloomy predictions on being given the assignment, he had reached Arkadelphia – seat of Clark County, Arkansas – without having been waylaid, captured, or killed by marauding Yankees. His horse had failed to throw and roll on him, there had been no lightning to strike him, nor had any of the numerous other disasters occurred that he had envisaged when discussing his mission before leaving the headquarters of the Texas Light Cavalry. Of course, he told himself with doleful satisfaction, he still had to locate the two replacement officers and twenty-four volunteers whom he had been sent to find and deliver to the regiment.

Slouching on the saddle of his powerful dun gelding, Billy Jack looked like a dejected and ill-used stork. A kepi, bearing the silver star-in-a-circle badge of the Texas Light Cavalry, perched at what – in almost any other person – would have been a jaunty angle on the back of his head. A prominent Adam's apple combined with a receding chin and thin face to give him almost miserable, careworn aspect. Tall, lanky, his rawboned, angular frame did little to set off a uniform that showed signs of the journey which he was making. He had on a waist-long tunic, yet the three chevrons on the sleeves seemed almost out of place, taken with his general appearance. About his waist hung a Western-style gunbelt, with 1860 Army Colts in the tied-down, open topped holsters. Yellow-striped riding breeches and Hessian boots served to emphasize the thinness of his legs. All in all, he did not appear to be the kind of man to hold rank of sergeant in a tough, fighting cavalry regiment.

With his horse ambling leisurely along the main street, Billy Jack wondered what kind of officers Lieutenants Fog and Blaze would develop into. He had a strong personal interest in the matter. Recently graduated from Judge Blaze's small military academy – down at Polveroso City, Rio Hondo County, Texas – they were coming to his Company and one of them was sure to become his immediate superior. So he hoped that they would prove to be satisfactory. On the face of it, there had originally seemed a better than fair chance that they might.

If the former youngster was anything like his father, Major Hondo Fog, he ought to turn into a damned good fighting cavalry leader and should be an asset to Company 'C'. Mr. Blaze already had two older brothers in the Texas Light Cavalry and they were rapidly carving names for themselves as courageous, capable and efficient officers. Billy Jack hoped that the latest arrival from the Blaze family would come up to his brothers' standards.

Trouble was that they might not come up to the high standards set by their kinsmen. Events certainly appeared to be pointing in that direction. They had been expected to arrive in Little Rock, with the twenty-four volunteers they were escorting, a week back. Needing the men, and wanting to train them before sending them into action, Colonel Blaze had dispatched Billy Jack with orders to locate them. Taking the route over which they were supposed to be travelling, Billy Jack had arrived at Arkadelphia without finding any trace of them.

Most of the evidence pointed to the two young officers having lost their way. Which did not say much for their abilities. All they had had to do was follow the route taken by Colonel Jubal Early's herders when delivering herds of cattle to help feed the Army of Arkansas and North Texas. That would have brought them to Arkadelphia and, once they had crossed the Ouachita River, there was a well-defined trail to Little Rock.

If Mr. Fog and Mr. Blaze could not follow such an obvious line of march, they would be of little use to Company 'C'.

Thinking sombrely about the two young officers. Billy Jack found himself approaching the Clinton Hotel. There were, he noticed, eight horses standing hitched to the rail outside the building. Six carried McClellan saddles and had Enfield single-shot carbines in their boots. The other pair, a big, blaze-faced bay and an equally large brown gelding were much finer animals. Each bore a good quality Texas range rig, like the one on Billy Jack's dun, with a bed roll lashed to the cantle. More significantly, each of them had a coiled rope and a sabre dangling on either side of its saddle's low horn.

In passing, then turning alongside the two horses, Billy Jack observed that there was a Henry rifle in the bay's saddleboot and the brown carried a Spencer carbine. He found the weapons less interesting than the animals' brands. The bay was marked with the letters 'O' and 'D', placed so close together that their edges touched. On the rump of the brown had been burned a pair of 'B's'.

'OD Connected and Double B,' the sergeant translated, swinging to the ground and securing the dun's reins to the hitching rail. 'Must be them, but where're the enlisted men at? Likely they've all deserted 'n' I'll get blamed for it.

With that mournful sentiment concluded, Billy Jack crossed the sidewalk. Passing through the hotels open front doors, he found its lobby deserted. He was strolling towards the reception desk, meaning to see if he could obtain information about the owners of the two horses, when he heard voices from the barroom.

'I've come to fetch you bunch out to the herd,' a young-sounding, well-educated Texas drawl was declaring. 'And I'm not about to go back without you.'

'That's the way of it, huh?' demanded a set of harsh,

rasping tones which Billy Jack believed he recognized. 'Well, Eli, Trug, Japhet, Lou 'n' Toby here's all of a mind with me, sonny. We don't take kind to no frying-size civilian delivering such messages from officer-boys.'

'We don't even take no notice when he sends *corporals* to fetch us,' stated a second familiar voice. 'But we'll not hold you coming again' you, happen you shows you're sorry by setting up the drinks.'

'That's what's knowed as an old Army custom, half-portion,' continued a third speaker, making the sergeant even more certain he knew some of the men in the barroom. 'In times of war, all civilians has to buy us fighting soldiers drinks when we asks for 'em.'

'Are *you* bunch *fighting* soldiers?' inquired the Texas drawl, every word suggesting that such a thing was highly unlikely.

'Just what do *you* reckon we are?' demanded the first of the familiar voices, throbbing with menace.

Having an idea of what might be happening, or likely to happen in the near future, Billy Jack approached the barroom. Its door was wide open and allowed him an excellent all-round view of the interior. What he saw confirmed that he did know some of the occupants and was correct in his assumptions of what they were planning to do.

Watched by the fat, bald-headed, grinning, elderly bartender, half a dozen soldiers were moving to form a loose circle around a civilian. Clad in kepis, with tunics that were unbuttoned to display dirty undershirts, riding breeches and boots, the soldiers were long-haired, unshaven and dishevelled. The bands around their hats, the stand-up collars and cuffs of their tunics and the stripes on the legs of their breeches were buff in colour. Although all wore weapon belts, only the burly corporal, who was standing directly in front of the civilian, had a holstered revolver.

Recognizing Corporal 'Bully' Chatswen and the five enlisted men, Billy Jack could see that they were going to indulge in a favourite pastime. It was called 'jostling'. Gathering around a potential victim, they would taunt and harass him in the hope that he would be goaded into attacking one of them. Once that happened, the rest would watch and enjoy the fight – or help if it seemed likely that their companion was getting beaten.

There had been an occasion, in this same barroom, when Chatswen and is companions had selected Billy Jack for their victim. He doubted whether they would have forgotten how their 'jostling' had been turned into a painful disaster, due to his unexpected ability to defend himself and the fortuitous arrival of four more members of Company 'C'.

Possibly Chatswen's party had profited from that unfortunate and painful experience. While they had apparently not given up 'jostling', they had at least grown more discriminating in their selection of a victim. From all appearances, their current potential recipient hardly seemed capable of producing any serious or dangerous resistance.

Standing with his back to Billy Jack, confronted and almost dwarfed by the bulky, black-haired Corporal Chatswen, the civilian was no more than five foot six inches in height. He had no hat and his hair was a dusty blond colour. The scarlet silk bandana, tight rolled and knotted about his throat, black and white calfskin vest, grey shirt, brown trousers, with their cuffs turned back and hanging outside high heeled boots, were the working clothes of a Texas cowhand.

Although Billy Jack could not see the small Texan's face, his general appearance and the references made to his youth by the soldiers suggested that he was much younger as well as smaller and lighter than his tormentors. Yet, despite the fact that he did not appear to be armed in any way, he displayed little concern over their threatening attitudes or the fact that they were surrounding him. Probably, the sergeant concluded, the cowhand did not appreciate his peril. Certainly his response to Chatswen's challenging question was not that of a frightened young man.

'From what I've seen of you,' the Texan drawled, in tones as gentle as the first menacing whispers of a blue norther storm blowing up. 'You're what I've heard are called "too-fars".'

At that moment, Billy Jack noticed the second of the room's doors was slowly easing open. He could not see who, or what, might be at the other side and the continuation of the conversation diverted his attention back to the speakers.

'"Too-fars"?' repeated Chatswen, looking puzzled. 'Just what the hell're "too-fars"?'

'Fellers who're too far forward to wash and shave,' answered the small Texan, apparently oblivious of Trug moving to stand behind him. 'But too far away from the fighting to get shot at.'

Billy Jack decided that although the blond had shown a shrewd judgment of the soldiers' characters, he could not be considered a person of tact, diplomacy, or even of good sense. There was little else that the youngster could have said which would have been more likely to bring Chatswen's wrath down upon him. Serving in the Commissary General's Department, the corporal and his five companions had never seen active duty. They were employed to collect and complete the delivery of the cattle which Colonel Jubal Early's trail crews had driven from Texas. Their work was of considerable importance to the Confederate States' war effort, but that did not alter the fact of them never having engaged in combat with the enemy. So they strenuously resented any comments on the matter; especially when such were made by a small, insignificant-looking civilian.

'And you figure's me 'n' the boys're these-here "too-fars"?' Chatswen challenged, while his companions rumbled menacingly.

'That's what I figure,' confirmed the Texan, apparently glancing to where Eli had moved forward from between Japhet and Lou. Or he could, Billy Jack realized, have been looking at the partially open side door beyond the three soldiers. 'And nothing I've seen of you yet's come close to making me think I *might* not be right about it.'

'You hear that, Hervey?' Chatswen said to the bartender. 'This short-grown runt's disrespecting us.'

'That's what he's doing, Billy,' agreed the fat, bald

civilian. 'Nobody'd blame you should you get riled about it.'

'So that's the way it goes, huh?' drawled the small Texan, without looking at the bartender. 'I figured it would be something like that. All right, I'm through asking. Let's have you out of here and on your horses—'

'Boy!' Chatswen interrupted, advancing and reaching with a ham-like right hand towards the diminutive – in comparison with his own bulk – young figure. 'I'm going to teach you some respect—'

Billy Jack found himself on the horns of a dilemma over what, if any, action he should take. Being in Arkadelphia on official business, he had no desire to become involved in a barroom brawl. Especially when the bartender invariably backed up the excuses of his good customers. Yet the sergeant could hardly stand by and watch a fellow-Texan – no matter how undiplomatic or rash – being assaulted by the larger, heavier soldiers.

To intervene, however, would invite painful repercussions. There was little love lost between the men of the Texas Light Cavalry and Chatswen's bunch. Secure in the knowledge that Hervey would support their stories in the event of an inquiry, the six men would resist any orders that Billy Jack might attempt to give to them. Instead, they would turn part of their wrath on him. That meant he would have to take them on with only such small help as the young blond could muster. There was no other assistance available.

Confident in the advantages granted by his extra size and weight, Chatswen saw no call for caution. Probably, on realizing that he had bitten off a whole heap more than he could chew, the runty beef-head* would attempt to jump backwards or try to run away. In either event, Trug was positioned so as to cut off his retreat.

Deciding to use his Colts as a means of enforcing his demands, Billy Jack dropped his hands to the butts as he stepped into the barroom. The other door was thrown open, but the sergeant's attention was held by Chatswen and the blond.

* Beef-head: derogatory name for a Texan.

Instead of retreating in an attempt to avoid being caught by the corporal's reaching fist, the small Texan moved swiftly to meet him. Chatswen's brain failed to react swiftly enough to assess and counter such an unexpected development. Up flashed the blond's left hand. The corporal felt his right wrist grasped with surprising strength and it was jerked forward. Nor did that end his misfortunes. Spreading his feet apart and bowing his knees, the Texan darted his right hand between Chatswen's thighs and took hold of the slack seat of his breeches.

Just what was happening, neither Billy Jack, Chatswen or the other soldiers could have said. Continuing to move with such speed that the corporal had no opportunity to resist, the small Texan ducked his head under the captured arm and tilted Chatswen's bulky torso across his shoulders. With a surging heave that told of considerable muscular power behind it, the blond straightened his legs. Elevating the amazed corporal from the floor, he pivoted and, lowering his head, pitched Chatswen into the advancing Trug's arms. Letting out mutually startled yells, the two men toppled to the floor in a tangled heap.

Like Billy Jack, who had halted with his Colts still in leather and mouth open but not emitting any words, the remaining soldiers were frozen into immobility by what they had seen. Possibly only the sergeant was aware of another element about to enter the game.

Tall, well-built, about the same age as the small blond, a second cowhand entered. He came through the side door, grinning delightedly as he darted swiftly across the room. Bare-headed and unarmed, he had untidy, fiery red hair and a freckled, pugnaciously handsome face.

Amazed by what he had seen happen to Chatswen, the bartender failed to give a warning of the newcomer's presence. Not that his omission left the soldiers in complete ignorance of the danger. The red-head made his presence felt swiftly enough.

Coming from behind the unsuspecting Japhet and Lou, the red-head bounded into the gap between them. He threw open his arms, enfolding their necks from the rear and clamping home in a determined, forceful manner.

'Dusty!' whooped the newcomer, swinging up his feet and bringing his full weight to bear on the two soldiers.

Thrusting forward, the red-head's high-heeled boots thudded into the centre of Eli's back and he was sent hurtling in the small Texan's direction. Flailing wildly with his arms, Eli bore down rapidly upon the blond. The soldier was big and brawny enough to have come off best in the event of a collision, but such a fortunate result was denied to him.

In turning to throw Chatswen at Trug, the small Texan had allowed Billy Jack to see his face. Tanned, grey-eyed, not too bad looking, the features put the sergeant in mind of somebody and supplied a clue to the blond's identity. That wrestling throw, too, was much like one Billy Jack had seen performed by Ole Devil Hardin's servant, a smallish, smiling man who claimed to hail from some place called 'Nippon'. That too was suggestive of who the young cowhand might be.

All of which was driven from the sergeant's thoughts as he watched Eli hurtling on a collision course for the short youngster. Even as the sergeant prepared to deliver a warning, he saw that the blond had heard and understood the red-head's shouted work.

Turning fast, the blond stepped to the left sufficiently far to avoid being struck by the rushing soldier. Nor did he restrict his attentions to mere evasion. Knotting his right hand, he threw a punch. Watching the hand sink almost wrist-deep into Eli's ample belly, Billy Jack could nearly sympathize with his agony-filled gurgling croak as he folded over. Blundering onwards, clutching at his mid-section as he moaned and gasped for breath, Eli reached the bar and collapsed, retching, by it.

Taken by surprise by the red-head's unexpected intervention, Japhet and Lou had not been able to resist. His weight caused them to bend forward and he retained his hold on their necks. Bracing himself on spread-apart feet and leaning backwards, he exerted his strength to prevent them from straightening up and getting free.

'Now this pair, Cousin Dusty!' the red-haired youngster called.

Almost as if working to a preconceived plan, the blond ignored the stricken Eli and darted towards the entangled trio. Bounding from the floor, he propelled his feet against the tops of Lou's and Japhet's heads. At the moment of impact, displaying superb timing, the red-head released his hold and the assaulted pair went reeling backwards. They landed on their rumps at practically the same moment, then flopped supine with dazed, glassy-eyed expressions on their unprepossessing faces.

'I thought I said for you to throw down on them with your Colts—' the blond said as he alighted from the bounding kick which had once more reminded Billy Jack of a trick used by Tommy Okasi.

Looking like a man waking from a nightmare, Toby stared from one to another of his companions. Although Chatswen and Trug had rolled apart, neither had yet succeeded in rising. From all appearances, the remainder of the party were no longer actively interested in the affair. That, Toby decided, put matters in his hands. Figuring to uphold his bunch's reputation for toughness – and to take the cowhands by surprise – he lumbered rapidly in their direction. Being a slugger, who relied on brawn instead of skill, he was basing his attack's success on a bull-like rush. It should, he concluded, be easy. Having felled Lou and Japhet in that sneaky, tricky way, the cowhands were talking to each other and not watching him.

'Shucks, don't be a spoilsport, Cous—' the red-head protested, then glanced towards Toby. 'Look out!'

Once again the youngsters displayed a teamwork which Billy Jack watched with admiration. Spinning swiftly, the blond stepped aside to avoid being struck by the heavier man. Advancing, the red-head moved in the opposite direction when level with his cousin. Unable to halt in time, Toby started to pass between them and his big hands grasped empty air. Out flashed two fists, their knuckles connecting on each side of Toby's jaw. The soldier's eyes glazed and, carried forward by his impetus, he kept moving until his knees buckled and deposited him face down on the floor.

Paying no greater attention to Toby than he had to his other victims, the small blond swung to face Chatswen as the corporal lurched erect.

'I sent my corporals into town last night with a message for you,' the Texan said quietly, shaking and working the fingers of the hand that had struck Toby's jaw. 'You got them into a fight, beat them up and sent word that I should come myself. So I'm here.'

'You bastard!' Chatswen bellowed, so furious that he failed to understand the full implications of what he was hearing. Instead, he hurled himself bodily at the small blond. 'I'll fix your wag—!'

Having allowed his Colts to settle back in their holsters, on being satisfied that the young Texans did not require that kind of assistance. Billy Jack had remained in the doorway. Leaning his shoulder against the jamb. he watched Chatswen bearing down massively upon the shorter cowhand.

Exactly what happened after that the sergeant could not be certain. Once again the blond caught the corporal by an arm, pivoted and Chatswen sailed almost gracefully over his shoulder. Landing on a table, Chatswen's weight collapsed it and he was dumped on to the floor. Muttering profane threats, he rose and rushed at his tormentor.

While Billy Jack had no liking for Chatswen, he felt nearly sorry as he watched the corporal receive one hell of a thrashing. Not only did the small Texan know a number of wrestling throws and holds which more than off-set his lack of size, he was remarkably strong and could use his fists with devastating effectiveness. When Chatswen received a final series of crashing punches that tumbled him limply into a corner, he had been as thoroughly beaten as had any of his 'jostling' victims.

Leaving his cousin to deal with the corporal, the red-head had taken on Trug. To Billy Jack, it seemed that the taller cowhand was delighted with the opportunity of a fight. They were evenly matched in size and weight, but the Texan was younger, fitter and more skilful. So, although he took some punishment himself and was far less spectacular in his methods, he handed out nearly as painful a battering.

'What happened to my corporals last night?' the blond demanded, crossing to the bar after glancing in Billy Jack's direction.

'They come in and started getting all uppy with Bully and the boys—' the bartender began, trying to repay the soldiers for the business they had put his way.

'*They* started it, huh?' the blond grunted.

'You might say that,' Hervey agreed, feeling uneasy as cold grey eyes seemed to be boring into his inner thoughts.

'It's not likely I would, being raised to speak the truth,' interrupted the blond.

'Are you saying I'm lying,' Hervey demanded, sounding a whole heap tougher and indignant than he felt.

'Let's put it you're just being loyal to good customers,' drawled the blond. 'You all right, Cousin Red?'

'*Bueno*, Cousin Dusty,' grinned the red head, dabbing at his bloody nose with a bandana. 'I'll go fetch our hats and gunbelts.'

'You do that,' the blond confirmed and turned his attention back to the bartender. 'Get those yahoos on their feet. Tell them to meet me down at the livery barn in half an hour. If they're longer than that, I'll come back and fetch them – and, mister, if that happens, I'll not be coming peaceable.'

'Bully and the boys won't like me telling them that,' Hervey objected, wondering how one so young and small could make him feel uneasy.

'Tell them I'll be waiting at the barn and they can take it up with me there,' ordered the blond and swung to face Billy Jack. 'Howdy, sergeant. I reckon you might be looking for me.'

'Likely, sir,' Billy Jack admitted, snapping into a brace and saluting. 'Unless I'm wrong, which I admit I most times am, you'll be Lieutenant Fog.'

CHAPTER FOUR

'THEY'RE coming, Mr. Fog,' Sergeant Billy Jack announced dolefully, while his lean features registered what seemed to be considerable alarm and despondency. 'Only I don't reckon it's 'cause they've figured out who you are and're all respectful of your rank.'

'Maybe not,' Dusty Fog drawled, also glancing overtly to where Corporal Chatswen's detail were approching. They were leading their horses and the enlisted men held the Enfield carbines which had previously been in the saddle-boots, while the flap of the corporal's holster was open and tucked back. 'Don't let on we've seen them.'

'Yo!' Billy Jack assented and swung his gaze to where Red Blaze was standing the last of half a dozen empty whisky bottles on the top rail of an unused corral. 'We could allus mount up and ride to the herd for help.'

'I'd sooner stop here and see what they're planning to do,' Dusty replied, having realized just how little of the sergeant's attitude and general line of speech was genuine. 'You never know, we might all get ourselves killed and save the Yankees the trouble of doing it.'

'I ain't likely to be *that* lucky,' Billy Jack protested dismally. 'It'll only be you'n' Mr. Blaze's dies and I'll have to go back 'n' tell Captain von Hertz I couldn't carry out his orders.'

'Well now,' Dusty grinned. 'I sure wouldn't want *you* to have to do that. So we'll see if we can sort of dissuade these "too-fars" from abusing us.'

'I surely hope we can,' Billy Jack admitted, in tones which implied that he felt it was highly unlikely. 'Now if them bottles was full—'

'It'd be a sinful shame and wasteful of good whisky,' Dusty finished.

'Never knowed Harvey selled any *good* whisky,' Billy Jack objected, wondering just what the small young officer had had in mind when asking him to obtain the six empty bottles before they had left the hotel.

Having donned the gunbelt and hat which Red had collected from the hall outside the barroom's side door, Dusty had accompanied his cousin and the sergeant to the rendezvous he had designated to the bartender.

The livery barn was situated on the edge of town. Leaving the horses – Billy Jack had been correct in his assumption of who owned them – outside the main building, Dusty had led the way to the empty corral. There he had requested that Red should stand the bottles on the side of the fence farthest away from the town. Grinning at the mystified expression on the sergeant's face, the red-head had complied. Ignoring Billy Jack's obvious puzzlement, Dusty had continued with his explanation of what had led up to the confrontation at the Clinton Hotel.

Given the acting rank of first lieutenant, Dusty had been put in command of a party of recruits on their way to join the Texas Light Cavalry. As they had ridden north, they had come across Colonel Jubal Early of the Commissary General's Department. The colonel had just purchased a herd of cattle for delivery to the Army of Arkansas and North Texas, but had wished to take up an offer of an even larger bunch made by a rancher in Denton County. Knowing that most of the recruits had been cowhands, Dusty had offered to drive the herd to Arkadelphia. Doing so would delay the party's arrival at Little Rock, but he had believed that he was acting for the best. Early had accepted, with the proviso that one of his experienced sergeants should accompany the cattle. An accident while crossing the Red River had deprived Dusty of the sergeant's services, but he had been successful in handling the trail drive without the expert's advice.

Reaching the Arkadelphia area the previous night, Dusty had bedded the herd down a couple of miles from the town. The cattle had been restless, so he and Red had remained with them. Knowing that a party from the Commissary General's Department were to take charge of the cattle at that point, Dusty had sent the two youngsters he had appointed acting corporals to carry word of their arrival. The corporals had located Chatswen's detail, who were drinking at the Clinton Hotel. On hearing Dusty's message, Chatswen had 'jostled' the corporals and provoked a fight. He had then sent back the beaten Texans with a message to the effect that Lieutenant Fog should come in and tell Chatswen himself and not send wet-behind-the-ears underlings.

'I reckon he figured that he was dealing with a couple of fuzz-faced, inexperienced shavetails and could get away with it,' Dusty had commented. 'Or he allowed to say he'd never said any such thing and could count on that fat bartender to back up any lies he told.'

'Hervey'd do that for sure,' Billy Jack had conceded.

Realizing that he could not overlook such a flagrant disrespect of his authority, Dusty had been determined to take action. When Chatswen's detail had not reached the herd by about ten o'clock in the morning, he had gone to find them accompanied by Red.

'I reckoned that those yahoos wouldn't show too much respect for a young lieutenant, especially one who wasn't in their outfit,' Dusty had explained. 'So I knew that I'd get no place walking in and flashing my collar bars. That's why I'm wearing my civilians clothes.'

At the hotel, following the plan formulated by Dusty during the ride to town, Red had taken Dusty's gunbelt and hat, while Dusty had entered the barroom Red had taken up his position outside the second door. The red-head was supposed to make his appearance and, using his Colts to enforce his demand, compel the enlisted men to stand aside while Dusty had dealt with Chatswen. That had not appealed to Red's ebullient nature and, seeing how the men had positioned themselves around Dusty, he had taken the opportunity to shed his own weapons and take a more active part in the scheme.

During the walk from the hotel, Billy Jack had warned Dusty that the soldiers were unlikely to forget, or forgive, the humiliation and punishment they had received. They were, the sergeant had continued, likely to come looking for evens. In which case, having failed with their fists, they might conclude to call the next play with guns. Much to Billy Jack's surprise, Dusty had appeared to be inclined to overlook the possibility. Red Blaze had declared cheerfully that everything was liable to work out fine.

Having noticed the menacing attitudes and held weapons of the approaching men, Billy Jack felt that he had guessed correctly about how they planned to take their revenge. However, he also had a suspicion that Mr. Fog was not only aware of the danger, but had something in mind to circumvent it.

'All set, Cousin Dusty,' Red announced cheerily. 'Don't them blasted "too-fars" look all mean 'n' ornery, though?'

'That they do,' Dusty admitted, showing just as little sign of knowing that Chatswen's detail were drawing nearer and fanning into a line. 'Reckon this's going to work, Cousin Red?'

'Happen it don't, I'll never speak to you again,' Red grinned. 'What do you think, Billy Jack?'

'That I don't know what to think,' the sergeant groaned, looking worried and not a little afraid. 'I'll be pleased when it's all over. Happen I live through it, that is.'

'Don't you get killed before I've finished,' Dusty said. 'That's an order.'

With that, the small Texan started to walk across the corral towards the bottle-decorated fence. Billy Jack's panic-stricken aspect departed and he divided his attention between watching Dusty and covertly keeping the soldiers under observation. He noticed that Chatswen's party were also watching the young blond and appeared puzzled by what they were seeing.

Halting when he was about twenty-one feet from the fence, Dusty stood on spread-apart, slightly bent legs. At the same instant, his hands flashed inwards. Crossing, they swept the bone-handled Colts from the carefully-designed holsters. Thumbing back the hammers and slipping his forefingers into the triggerguards only *after* the barrels had cleared leather, Dusty aimed from waist level and by instinctive alignment. Just three-quarters of a second after his hands' first movements, flame licked out of the muzzles of the Colts and their detonations came almost as a single sound.

With the exception of Red, who was aware of his cousin's ambidextrous ability, the watching men believed that Dusty had only fired once. Startled exclamations rose from Chatswen's detail when the bottles at each end of the line disintegrated simultaneously. Even Billy Jack, who was no slouch when it came to handling a brace of Army Colts, was impressed by the small Texan's lightning speed and double-handed accuracy. Nor did the display end there.

Cocking each Colt as its seven-and-a-half inch 'Civilian Model' barrel* reached the height of its recoil, Dusty turned the muzzles inwards. Without raising the revolvers higher or taking more careful sight, he continued to throw lead. As the Colts roared, the bottles shattered and he never missed. On destroying the final pair, he twirled the weapons on his trigger-fingers and returned them to their holsters almost as swiftly as they had emerged.

Turning, Dusty strolled to where Red and Billy Jack were standing side by side. If the lanky sergeant's face was showing admiration, it was nothing to the expressions being exhibited by the other soldiers. All had come to a halt and were staring in alarmed, awe-filled amazement.

As if becoming aware for the first time of Chatswen's detail being around, Dusty swung towards them. His eyes went to the carbines, dropped briefly at the opened flap of the corporal's holster, then lifted and raked the men's faces.

* Colt 1860 Army revolvers intended for sale to the military had eight inch barrels.

Not one of them would meet the cold scrutiny. Even Chatswen lowered his head to hide his confusion and uncertainty.

'Are you expecting trouble from the Yankees, corporal?' Dusty demanded, walking closer to the soldiers.

'Huh?' Chatswen ejaculated, jerking up his face and staring in a puzzled manner at the small Texan.

Except that Dusty no longer seemed small, or insignificant. In some mysterious manner, he appeared to have grown until he bettered the corporal in size.

'I said are you expecting trouble with the Yankees?' Dusty repeated.

'What Yankees?' Chatswen wanted to know.

'If there aren't any, why the hell are your men carrying their carbines?' Dusty snapped. 'And why isn't your holster flap fastened down?'

'I—' Chatswen began.

'Are there any Yankees hereabout, sergeant?' Dusty asked over his shoulder, without taking his gaze from the soldiers.

'Nary a one's I knows about, *Lieutenant* Fog, sir,' Billy Jack answered, guessing correctly how Dusty wanted the reply to be worded.

'I reckon we can take your word on that,' Dusty drawled and stared hard at Chatswen. 'Don't you, corporal?'

For a moment the burly non-com did not reply. Clearly Hervey had been telling the truth, when he had claimed that the short-grown – or *very big* – blond son-of-a-bitch was an officer. Which put an entirely different complexion on the matter, despite Chatswen's assertions that not even a blasted officer could treat him in such a fashion and live to boast about it.

'Yeah,' the corporal finally agreed, knowing that doing so was backing down and eating crow. 'I reckon we can.'

'I might accept "mister" from a man I respected,' Dusty said in that gentle, yet terribly menacing fashion his voice could adopt. 'But the likes of you call me "sir".'

'I reckon we can – sir,' Chatswen repeated, when it

became obvious that the small Texan was awaiting such a response.

'Boot those carbines and get ready to move out,' Dusty told the enlisted men. 'I've wasted too much damned time on you already.'

Glancing from side to side, Chatswen watched his men obeying with alacrity. He knew that he would receive no backing from them, even if he had contemplated taking up the small Texan's unspoken but very real challenge.

'Corporal,' Dusty said. 'I've better things to do with my time than to start asking what happened last night. There's a herd of five hundred head waiting for you. I want to hand it over and attend to more important duties.'

'Yes – sir,' Chatswen replied, hurriedly adding the honorific when Dusty frowned at its omission. 'We'll come right away, sir.'

'Just one thing, corporal,' Dusty went on. 'If I should ever hear of you pulling a game like this again, I'll have you and every man concerned transfered to my Company. And then, soldier, I'll make you wish you'd never been born.'

Staring at the *big* young blond, Chatswen and the other enlisted men knew that they were hearing a warning which it would pay them to heed. There was no bombast in the officer's voice, only a chillingly menacing promise. Something warned them that he might have the necessary influence to carry out his threat. A variety of throbbing aches, caused by the injuries inflicted in the fight, gave emphasis to their belief that service under his command would be anything but pleasant. Certainly it would be far more hazardous and harder work than their present occupations.

'Yes, sir,' Chatswen muttered, making the only comment he felt would be appropriate, acceptable, or safe, under the circumstances.

Watching the incident, Billy Jack refrained from showing the delight he was feeling. Unless he missed his guess, Mr. Fog was going to turn out as good an officer as his father. While still inexperienced, he had already displayed a sound knowledge of how to handle men.

Many young officers, faced with Mr. Fog's predicament, might have been at a loss to figure out what to do for the best. It would have been all too easy for him to have gone about handling Chatswen's bunch in the wrong manner. He could have tried to use his insignias of rank and the powers which he imagined were automatically granted to him by the *Manual of Field Regulations*, expecting them to ensure the soldiers' obedience.

Realizing just how little actual authority the *Manual of Field Regulations* and his badges of rank gave to a very young, newly appointed lieutenant – especially when dealing with men who did not belong to his regiment – Mr. Fog had guessed correctly that he must depend upon the strength of his personality.

Instead of attempting to pull rank, the small Texan had faced the recalcitrant soldiers while dressed as a civilian. He had then established a physical superiority – which they could appreciate and understand far better than any display of *Manual*-backed attempts at authority – in no uncertain manner. What was more, he had been aware that his victims might wish to take the matter even further. So he had arranged for them to witness his expert handling of firearms and had averted what might easily have ended in gunsmoke and corpses.

Although satisfied with Dusty's potential as an officer and a leader, Billy Jack still experienced misgivings regarding Red Blaze.

The red-head was brave enough, tough and a good hand in a fist fight; but he was also reckless and more than a mite foolhardy. That had been proven by the way he had changed Mr. Fog's plans for dealing with Chatswen. By disregarding his cousin's arrangements, Mr. Blaze might have caused them to become the victims, instead of them emerging as the victors.

Such a failure would have lessened, if it had not completely destroyed, any chance of the pair becoming effective officers. Once the story of their failure had made the rounds, it would have been difficult – maybe even impossible – for them to earn the respect of the Texas Light Cavalry's hard-bitten veterans.

So Billy Jack considered that Mr. Blaze would need far longer than Mr. Fog to develop into a satisfactory officer. The red-head would probably come to be well liked, but he would need to mature before he was respected and accepted as a leader. Perhaps, the sergeant told himself – and, for once, his regret was genuine – Mr. Blaze would never make it.

CHAPTER FIVE

'COLONEL BLAZE allowed's I should come and fetch—' Sergeant Billy Jack began as he rode with Lieutenants Fog and Blaze towards the herd of cattle. Then he revised his words into a more tactful form. 'I should tell you he wants the recruits getting to the regiment as fast as possible.'

'You near on said, "I should come and fetch you pair, so's you don't get lost",' Red grinned.

'Now that wouldn't've been polite of me, Mr. Blaze,' the lanky sergeant protested. 'Which I'm allus *real* polite to anybody's out-ranks me.'

'Even to green shavetails?' Dusty inquired.

'*Especially* to green shavetails, sir,' Billy Jack affirmed. 'That's 'cause I'm a good, loyal soldier – and scared they'd get mean and have me busted if I wasn't polite to them.'

Throwing a glance at his cousin, Dusty could see that Red was aware of the tribute being paid to them. By answering in such a manner, Billy Jack was showing his respect and approval.

During the ride from Arkadelphia. Dusty Fog had continued to impress Billy Jack with his potential for making an officer. With Chatswen's detail following about a hundred yards to their rear, the three Texans had talked as they kept their mounts moving at a steady trot. All the questions asked by Dusty had been to the point and showed that he possessed a fair appreciation of the conditions prevailing at that time in Arkansas.

From general matters, Dusty had turned the conversation to the Texas Light Cavalry and, in particular, Company 'C'. At first he had restricted himself to tactical duties, with Red injecting questions regarding the possibility of frequently 'locking horns with the Yankees'. After listening to some of the usual enlisted men's grouches, Dusty had drawn Billy Jack into commenting upon the man who would be his immediate superior.

With a frankness which surprised him, when he came to consider it later, Billy Jack had described Captain Otto von Hertz's character and personality.

'I surely hopes's how you young gents've got uniforms just like it says in the *Manual of Dress Regulations*,' the sergeant had said, after stating that von Hertz was a stickler for discipline, military protocol – although he did not use those exact words – and training, but also well-versed in all aspects of cavalry warfare.

'That we have,' Red had admitted wryly. 'The collar on my jacket's like to cut my head off under my chin, way it is when it's fastened.'

'You'll have to take a chance that it don't happen and keep it fastened, Mr. Blaze,' Billy Jack had warned. 'Cause that's how Cap'n von Hertz wants it.'

'Your gunbelt and saddle's not *Regulation*, sergeant,' Dusty had pointed out.

'I ain't gainsaying it, sir,' Billy Jack had replied. 'But that's only 'cause we don't have enough of the *Regulation* kind, and the cap'n's not happy about it.'

'Looks like we'll be able to go on wearing our belts, Cousin Dusty,' Red had announced, showing satisfaction until Billy Jack had demolished it.

'I wouldn't count on that, Mr. Blaze,' the sergeant had said. 'He'll expect you-all, being officers 'n' gentlemen, to wear the right kind of belts even if you don't sit McClellan saddles.'

'Whee-dogie!' Red had ejaculated. 'I can see me and Cap'n Hertz—'

'Captain *von* Hertz,' Billy Jack had corrected. 'He's tolerable set on having folks use that there "*von*", whatever it be.'

'Well all right,' Red had grinned. 'I can't see Captain *von Hertz* and me getting on too good unless one of us changes our ways. Which I'm too old, ornery and set in 'em for it to be me.'

That and similar cheerfully irrelevant remarks had done little to make Billy Jack revise his opinion regarding Red's possibilities as an officer. From other parts of the conversation, it had become obvious that the red-head hero-worshipped his smaller cousin and was satisfied that Dusty Fog could do no wrong. In fact, Billy Jack had guesed that it was Red's blind faith in the small Texan's capability, as much as a genuine enjoyment of being involved in a fight, which had led him to revise the plan for dealing with Chatswen's detail at the hotel.

Billy Jack noticed, as they drew nearer to the herd, that its bed-ground had been selected with care and showed a shrewd appreciation of the kind of precautions required to ensure its safety.

The cattle were being held close to the banks of a small stream, in a location which offered them water and good grazing. With those needs filled so adequately, they would settle down and show less inclination towards drifting away. The nearest clump of trees was at least half a mile away and there were neither ravines nor draws – that might harbour and conceal wild animals or hostile human beings – close by. Any attempt at stealing, or merely stampeding, the five hundred head of half-wild longhorn steers would have been detected and countered before it could have been put into effect, even during the night.

A corporal and four soldiers, wearing the uniforms of the Texas Light Cavalry were riding herd on the cattle. According to Dusty, there had been eight men on duty through the hours of darkness, positioned so that nobody could have approached the herd without being seen or heard. Until that morning, all such work had been carried out in civilian clothing. Wishing to avoid any further delays in joining the regiment, Dusty had ordered the change to military attire so that his party would be ready to move off as soon as they had turned the herd over to the men from the Commissary General's Department.

Galloping up, the corporal saluted Dusty and reported that everything was satisfactory with the herd. He had a bruised face and threw a scowl towards Chatswen's detail. However, it changed to a more cheerful look as he observed the burly non-com's equally battered features.

Telling Red to attend to handing over the herd, Dusty accompanied Billy Jack to the recruits' camp. Everything had been made ready for them to resume their journey. The young soldiers' gear was packed, their horses saddled and standing ground-hitched ready to be mounted. A team was hitched to the chuck wagon and the fire had been doused. There was none of the litter all too often seen when a soldiers' camp was being broken up.

Looking about him, Billy Jack could find no fault with the location of the camp-site. It was on the bank of the stream, about a quarter of a mile above the herd and between the cattle and the nearest clump of trees. At that distance, the soldiers would not have needed to worry about the normal camp's noises spooking the steers, but could have reached the animals swiftly in an emergency. All in all, it gave the sergeant yet another example of Mr. Fog's competence.

Turning his head to make some comment to the small Texan, Billy Jack found that he was looking at a horse that was tied by its reins to the chuck wagon's tailgate. The sergeant had noticed the animal, mainly because it was not with the others and apparently needed securing to something instead of being prevented from straying by merely having its reins dangling free.

Now that Billy Jack's attention had been drawn to the horse, a big roan gelding, he detected other differences.

Obviously the recruits had fetched along their own mounts on enlistment. The ground-hitched animals were typically range-bred stock. Not one topped fifteen hands and the majority lacked four inches of that height, but they looked agile, wiry, packed with vitality and endurance. Each carried a low horned, double girthed – a Texan rarely used the word 'cinch' because of its Spanish connotations – saddle with a sabre and coiled rope dangling from it.

Bigger, more powerful, the roan by the chuck wagon had one piece reins and not the two separate strands mostly used by Texans. Its light, high-horned saddle had a centrally-fitted girth and the leathers of the covered stirrups passed over the seat. No self-respecting son of the Lone Star State would be caught sitting such a Spanish-looking saddle.

Only one of the recruits was in sight. Lounging with a shoulder against the side of the wagon, he was tall, lean, with a hard, savage, Indian-dark cast of features that suggested mixed blood. As Dusty and Billy Jack rode up, he straightened and spoke over his shoulder.

Going closer, the sergeant discovered that the remainder of the party were beyond the wagon, gathered around a tall, black-clad civilian. However, at the dark soldier's words, a good-looking, sandy-haired youngster – whose sleeves bore the chevrons of a corporal – swung away from his companions. His blackened left eye, swollen top lip and bruised right cheek implied that he had been the second of Chatswen's victims. Billy Jack noticed that he did not appear to be surprised, on glancing towards the herd, to find that Mr. Fog had succeeded in returning with its new attendants. Halting as Dusty and Billy Jack dismounted, he threw up a smart salute.

'Everything's ready for us to pull out, Mr. Fog,' the corporal stated, then nodded towards the cattle. 'He allowed he'd come, happen you went for him.'

'Why sure,' Dusty agreed. 'This here's Sergeant Billy Jack. He'll be showing us the way to the regiment. Sergeant, let me present Corporal Sandy McGraw.'

'Howdy, corporal,' Billy Jack responded, extending his right hand.

'Glad to know you, sergeant,' Sandy McGraw replied.

'Who's the caller?' Dusty inquired, after they had shaken hands.

'The Reverend Hotchkiss, from Arkadelphia,' Sandy answered. 'He just now rode up and wants for us to go to some prayer meeting he's holding in town tonight.'

'What did you tell him?' Dusty asked.

'That he'd have to wait until you came back for an answer,' Sandy replied.

Before any more could be said, the civilian had turned and was walking away from the soldiers. He would not be more than in his late thirties and had a tanned, unsmiling face under a round-topped black hat of the style much favoured by preachers of various denominations. His jacket, vest, shirt, cravat and trousers were pretty much what a small town's parson might wear. Even his Wellington leg-boots were not unexpected, or unusual, items of attire. He most likely visited the country-dwelling members of his flock on horseback. However, he walked with a slightly swaggering gait that would have seemed more natural in a cavalry soldier than a man of the cloth.

'Good day, sergeant,' greeted the civilian, in a Southern but not an Arkansas' drawl. He had given Dusty just one quick glance before devoting his attention to Billy Jack. 'You've a fine body of young men here. Has your officer stayed out at the herd?'

'Nope,' Billy Jack replied, looking and sounding at his most miserable and dejected as he stared at the speaker. 'This here's Lieutenant Fog.'

Following the direction indicated by the sergeant, the civilian gave Dusty a much longer scrutiny. Hotchkiss seemed unwilling to believe his ears. Studying the excellent condition of the camp, he frowned in a puzzled manner as if unable to reconcile such evidence of discipline with the short, insignificant figure in the dress of a working cowhand. Then he swung a glance at Billy Jack, but found no enlightenment in the lanky sergeant's appearance. Once more his eyes returned to Dusty and he realized that he was not acting in a polite, or even tactful manner.

'I'm sorry, Mr. Fog,' the civilian said. 'I didn't realize who you were. My name's Hotchkiss and I've come to extend an invitation for you and your men to attend a little prayer meeting and social evening we're holding in town tonight.'

'You-all must've took over from the regular preacher real recent, Mr. Hotchkiss,' Billy Jack injected.

'I haven't taken over officially as yet, sergeant,' the civilian replied. 'But I'm the Reverend Deane's nephew and he's asked me to replace him when he retires at the end of the month.'

'I hadn't heard he was retiring,' Billy Jack stated, being puzzled by the other's appearance.

'It's not been announced yet,' Hotchkiss answered evenly. 'But he's wanting to quit. His health isn't too good.' With that, he looked pointedly away from his interrogator. 'Can I expect you and your men tonight, Mr. Fog?'

'Well now, sir,' Dusty said hesitantly, glancing at Billy Jack as if seeking approval and advice. When none came, he continued, "I'm sorry, but we won't be able to come. Will we, sergeant?'

'Nope,' Billy Jack agreed, surprised by the change which had come over the small Texan.

'May I ask why not?' Hotchkiss said, addressing Dusty.

'We'll be moving out as soon as I've changed my clothes, sir,' Dusty explained. 'Serg – I'll be starting as soon as I'm back in uniform.'

Watching Dusty, Billy Jack was at a loss to understand the way in which his confident manner had changed. He seemed uncertain and anything but the competent young officer who had so impressed the sergeant during the ride from town.

'Ah yes,' Hotchkiss said, nodding his head. 'You'll be moving the cattle again.'

'Not us, sir,' Dusty corrected. 'I've done my part of the delivery. Men from the Commissary General's Department are looking to them now.'

'Surely that leaves you free to bring your men to the meeting?' Hotchkiss stated. 'The town's ladies would be delighted to see you and your voices would be of great assistance in the hymn-singing.'

'I'm sorry, sir,' Dusty insisted, having thrown another swift look at Billy Jack. 'My orders are to get to my regiment as quickly as possible. I hope to be fifteen miles closer to Little Rock by nightfall.'

'The cattle couldn't cover that much distance, could they?' Hotchkiss asked.

'No, sir,' Dusty admitted. 'But there's no reason why they should.'

'You won't be escorting them any further?'

'Not us, sir. They're headed for our main supply depot at Pine Bluff.'

'Without your party to guard them?' Hotchkiss said, sounding puzzled.

'Shucks, sir,' Dusty affirmed. 'There's no need for us, or anybody else, to guard them. The Yankees wouldn't dare to come this far behind our lines. Corporal Chatswen's got five good men to help him and we'd be wasting our time if we went along.'

Although Billy Jack did not show it, he was growing alarmed and concerned by the trend of the conversation. As it had progressed, Mr. Fog had started to diminish in the sergeant's estimation. After having observed what he had believed to be so many sterling qualities in the small Texan, it was disappointing to hear him speaking to a stranger in such a frank, indiscreet even, fashion. Especially after Billy Jack had given an oblique warning that the civilian was not the regular preacher from Arkadelphia.

There was something about Hotchkiss that disturbed Billy Jack. It was not just his claim to be a preacher, but something deeper. Perhaps it was his bearing and attitude, or the hard look about the tanned face. None of them suggested that he was a man of peace, or the kind who would be content to stagnate in a small town like Arkadelphia. He would, Billy Jack considered, be more likely to try to take an active part in the War.

What if Hotchkiss should be taking a more active part in the War – but on the side of the Union?

Both the North and the South made use of spies in the other's territory, or so Billy Jack had heard. There could hardly be a better way for one to conceal his identity than by acting as the preacher in a small town. Such a man would be almost above suspicion and was ideally situated to obtain information. The frank way in which Mr. Fog had answered Hotchkiss's questions had been proof of the latter point.

'Sergeant,' Dusty said, cutting through Billy Jack's thoughts. 'Go and make sure everything's ready for us to move out.'

'Yo!' the sergeant replied. 'Maybe—.'

'Do I have to have every order debated?' Dusty yelped, sounding more like an indignant schoolboy whose assumed authority was challenged than the capable young officer who had dealt with Chatswen's detail.

'No, sir,' Billy Jack said, barely concealing his annoyance. 'You don't.'

'Wait here, San – corporal,' Dusty said, as Sandy made as if to follow Billy Jack. Then he looked at Hotchkiss and smiled. 'I reckon I could think up a good reason for us to stay and attend your meeting, sir.'

Alarm and disappointment showed on Sandy's face. Not only was he eager to reach the Texas Light Cavalry, attending a church social was hardly his idea of how to spend a night in town. The emotions changed to surprise. He had sensed that the sergeant disapproved of Mr. Fog for some reason and suddenly realized what had caused it. However, having known the small Texan for longer than Billy Jack had, Sandy had developed considerable faith in his judgment. If Mr. Fog allowed that the preacher was all right, Sandy accepted his summation without question. For all that, the offer he had just heard came as a surprise.

'Wouldn't that be contrary to your orders?' Hotchkiss asked, showing less enthusiasm than Sandy would have expected.

'Well—' Dusty said hesitantly. 'Well, sort of—'

'A lot more than just "sort of", I'd say,' Hotchkiss interrupted sternly.

'Shucks,' Dusty answered, lowering his head and shuffling his feet. 'We wouldn't be missed and I'd think up some story for why we were late arriving.'

'I couldn't permit *that*!' Hotchkiss declared. 'It would be almost like starting out on a lie. When I came here, I didn't realize the urgency of your orders. If I had known, I wouldn't have invited you.'

'It'd work out all right, sir—,' Dusty began.

'Whether it would or not, I can't let it happen,' protested the civilian. 'And it wouldn't do me any good for my congregation to know I'd allowed you to go against your orders.'

'You're right, I reckon,' Dusty admitted, a trifle sulkily.

'You *know* I am,' Hotchkiss barked. 'Perhaps we'll be able to entertain you and your men at a later date, when you'll be free to come. Until then, I'll wish you a safe journey to Pine Bluff!'

'Little Rock, sir,' Dusty corrected. 'It's the herd that's headed for Pine Bluff. Can I offer you a meal, or anything, sir?'

'No, thank you,' Hotchkiss refused. 'I won't do anything to delay you. Good afternoon, Mr. Fog, corporal. I wish you both every success for the future. Remember, always fight the good fight and the Lord will be strong for you.'

'I'll do just that, sir,' Dusty promised. '*Adios!*'

Still feeling puzzled and a mite annoyed by what he regarded as Mr. Fog's failure to maintain the high standard of capability, Billy Jack watched Hotchkiss walk towards the chuck wagon. Unfastening the big roan's reins, the man swung into the saddle and rode away.

Frowning, Billy Jack wondered if he should not have insisted upon continuing questioning Hotchkiss, or have demanded proof of his identity. Then he thought that maybe he was allowing his disappointment in Mr. Fog to cause his imagination to run away with him. Certainly the preacher in Arkadelphia was an old man and could be figuring on retiring. In which case, he was likely to try to have a deserving kinsman come to replace him. Yet Hotchkiss had not seemed all he should be and he could sure ride a horse real well.

Thinking back to the conversation during the ride from town, Billy Jack recollected having told Mr. Fog, on being asked, that the Yankees had never tried to interfere with the herds of cattle. There did not seem to be any reason why they should be starting right now.

Billy Jack decided that there was nothing to worry over. However, he figured that he had better warn Mr. Fog about the dangers of talking so freely with strangers. It was a pity that the young officer should have made such a potentially dangerous mistake after having behaved so admirably up to then. At least, Billy Jack consoled himself, there had been no real harm done by the small Texan's indiscretion.

Urging his horse to a trot, Hotchkiss headed towards the herd of cattle. After he had covered about a hundred yards, he shook his head in amused disgust.

'That stupid peckerwood* son-of-a-bitch,' the black-dressed man said to himself, thinking of the way in which the small Texan had given him all the information he would require. 'It looks like we're not the only Army that gives commissions to fool kids because their folks know somebody important. I almost wish he was going with the herd, so that he could see how easy he's made things for us when we take it.'

* Peckerwood: derogatory name for a Confederate supporter.

CHAPTER SIX

As Captain Stratford Hotchkiss rode through the darkness towards the camp of the men who were now handling the herd of cattle, he was still feeling amused by the ease with which he had tricked the small Texan into helping him. The information that he had been given was of the greatest value. It was making his assignment so much easier than he had hoped might happen.

When Sergeant Leps had returned from making a scout the previous night, telling how adequately the cattle were being watched over and protected, Hotchkiss had wondered if he could carry out his attempt to take them from the Rebels. Clearly somebody with the escort had known the most suitable precautions to take against such an eventuality.

Deciding to discover the strength and weakness of the escort, Hotchkiss had visited their camp. His mission was being undertaken in civilian clothing and he had along attire suitable for him to pose as a preacher from Arkadelphia. Fortunately, he had discovered the name of the town's real preacher. At first, he had doubted that he would learn anything. The smart, alert young soldiers and the condition of the camp had hinted at experienced leadership of a high quality.

Only that skinny-gutted, miserable-looking sergeant had not accepted Hotchkiss as being genuine. He was either suspicious, or more careful than his immediate superior. For a time Hotchkiss had been uneasy, for he knew nothing more about the Reverend Deane than the name and his age. However, the small luff had had to assert his authority and sent away the man who might have spoiled things for Hotchkiss. After that, the ease with which the short-grown runt had supplied all the necessary information – including the size and destination of escort *and* the name and rank of the man commanding it – had come almost as an anti-climax.

For a moment, as had happened more than once since leaving the Rebels' camp, Hotchkiss found himself wondering who had been responsible for its excellent condition. Most likely it had been the lean sergeant, whom Hotchkiss suspected of being more capable than showed on the surface. The efforts of more than one enterprising and efficient soldier had been brought to nothing by the incompetence of superiors who owed their ranks to family influence rather than ability. Hotchkiss himself was, he felt, a case in point.

Having learned something about handling cattle in California, before volunteering to serve in the Union Army, Hotchkiss had seen an opportunity to put his specialized knowledge to good use.

Sent to the Army of Arkansas, Hotchkiss had found it poorly fed and demoralized. It was not a fighting force to inspire an ambitious man with confidence or hopes for a distinguished future. Then he had seen what he had believed was a good way to gain acclaim and draw attention his way. Learning that the Rebels received regular supplies of fresh beef from Texas, he had proposed that he was given men to raid and drive the cattle back to his own lines. By doing so, he would produce food for the soldiers and cause the Confederate States' Army to use men to guard the future deliveries.

Like many another man, Hotchkiss discovered that it was easier to think up a plan than to gain acceptance and official backing for it. His own colonel and General Culver had been interested, but neither was willing openly to associate himself with something that might easily fail. However, he had received grudging and qualified permission to proceed. To his annoyance, he had been compelled to use men from his own Company instead of gathering skilled help. He had selected a sergeant and eight enlisted men with farming backgrounds. While they had not had experience with trail driving, they at least know how to handle cattle.

Helped by the information so stupidly given to him, Hotchkiss was for the first time confident of success. Once he had captured and delivered the herd, he could hope for promotion and to be given a much larger, more experienced, force with which to expand his efforts.

'Looks like they've set up camp in the bushes along by the river,' Sergeant Leps remarked, pointing ahead as his horse came alongside the roan. 'That's something we hadn't figured on.'

'It won't make too much difference,' Hotchkiss replied. 'Drop back and make sure the men know I don't want any shooting. It could spook the herd and start a stampede.'

'Sneaking up on them fellers won't be easy among the bushes,' Leps objected, instead of obeying. 'We could go straight to the herd—.'

'And have the rest of the men come after and hit us, or go to Arkadelphia for help?' Hotchkiss scoffed. 'Well do it *my* way, *sergeant*. Ride up and take the men at the fire prisoner, then go along and get the night herders. That way, the Rebs won't know what's happened until the cattle don't arrive at Pine Bluff. By that time, we'll be well on our way to safety.'

'What if them fellers don't hold with your notion about no shooting?' Leps inquired.

'Let me worry about *that*, sergeant!' Hotchkiss growled. 'Go tell the men my orders.'

'Yo!' Leps answered sullenly and slowed his horse to let the rest of the party catch up.

Hotchkiss felt irritated and annoyed by his sergeant's attitude. A career soldier, Leps had little faith in the abilities of volunteer officers. He had been openly, or covertly, critical of every decision made by Hotchkiss since the start of the mission. Much of the mistrust had arisen from Hotchkiss's reticence and reluctance to take his subordinates into his confidence. Instead of telling the sergeant all his plan, he had merely given the necessary orders and reserved several vital details until they could be produced at the most advantageous moment. By doing so, he hoped to impress the men with his brilliance.

They were drawing closer to the bushes and Hotchkiss could hear the muted, startled comments from the enlisted men as Leps passed on his orders. Stopping his horse, Hotchkiss allowed the others to catch up. There was sufficient light from the stars for him to see that they were uneasy and alarmed.

'I don't reckon we can sneak up on them fellers without 'em hearing us, cap'n,' one of the privates declared, speaking quietly, and the others muttered their agreement.

'Neither do I,' Hotchkiss admitted. 'So we're not going to try.' With that he raised his voice. 'Hello the fire. Is that you, Corporal Chatswen?'

Exclamations of consternation rose from the soldiers, but the instincts for self-preservation caused them to be held down to little more than alarmed whispers. Ignoring the *sotto voce* comments, Hotchkiss held his breath in eager – and anxious – anticipation. The answer came with gratifying promptitude and suggested that he had guessed correctly when planning his moves.

'Yeah. It's me. Who're you?'

'The Reverend Hotchkiss, from Arkadelphia. I spoke to you at the herd this morning.'

'Oh sure, I remember,' called back the voice from amongst the bushes. 'You wanting something, Reverend?'

'The ladies suggested that, as you couldn't come to our meeting and they'd cooked extra food, we should fetch it out to you,' Hotchkiss replied and the low-spoken expressions of delight which came from his men were like music to his ears. They were now suitably impressed by him. 'May we bring it?'

'Fetch it ahead, Reverend,' offered the speaker.

'Remember, men!' Hotchkiss hissed. 'No shooting. Not that there's likely to be any need for it. We'll take the peckerwood bastards by surprise.'

Having delivered his statement, Hotchkiss set the roan into motion. He grinned in delight, satisfied that he had created the desired impression upon his men. After this, they would be more responsive and willing to carry out his orders without hesitation.

'Dismount!' Hotchkiss hissed, on reaching the fringe of the bushes. 'Millet, Dorst, stay with the horses. The rest of you, have your revolvers out but keep them hidden behind your backs.'

The men obeyed with a willing speed that had rarely been in evidence when previously responding to his orders. All could see the wisdom of completing the approach to the camp on foot. The horses would be a hindrance when it came to dealing with the Rebels.

Dismounting, they passed their reins to the designated pair and followed Hotchkiss into the bushes. As they moved forward, their admiration for their officer increased with every step. There was something satisfying about being able to advance boldly and have no worries over making noises that could alert and alarm an unsuspecting camp.

'Get into line once we're in the clearing,' Hotchkiss ordered in a whisper. 'And don't show your guns until I fetch mine out.'

'Sure, cap'n,' Leps hissed back and the others gave soft-spoken agreement.

Peering ahead, the men saw that their victims had made camp in a small clearing. Four Confederate soldiers were standing by the fire, facing the oncoming party but not holding weapons. Beyond them was a chuck wagon. Its team had been unhitched and was nowhere in sight. Nor, if it came to that, were the quartet's mounts. However, none of Hotchkiss's party attached any significance to the missing animals. They were all too eager to carry out their work to pay attention to apparently unimportant trifles. Each held his revolver behind his back and thought complacently of the surprise they were going to hand to their enemies.

'Good evening, gentlemen,' Hotchkiss greeted, stepping into the clearing.

'Howdy, Reverend,' Corporal Chatswen replied, but he seemed to be nervous and his eyes flickered from side to side. 'Come ahead.'

Slowing his pace, Hotchkiss allowed his men to spread into a line on either side of him. He continued to approach the fire without producing his weapon, wanting to be so close when he did that the Rebels would realize any resistance would be fatal.

Studying the four Confederate soldiers, Sergeant Leps felt a vague, disturbing sensation creeping through him. He began to realize that there was something wrong with their attitudes. They seemed strained and did not look like men awaiting a pleasant meal. What was more, every one of them kept darting glances at the bushes as if expecting to see something – or somebody.

It was some*body*!

Figures stepped swiftly from the bushes, with revolvers or Enfield carbines lining towards the Yankees. Young men wearing cadet-grey uniforms and the silver star-in-the-circle hat badges of the Texas Light Cavalry. A tall, lean, miserable-faced sergeant and a short, young first lieutenant sprang from either end of the wagon, alighting with a revolver in each hand.

That the four men by the fire had been expecting the others was proven by the rapidity of their movements. They flung themselves to the ground, leaving the newcomers a clear field of fire at the Yankees.

'Howdy, Reverend Hotchkiss,' greeted the lieutenant. 'It looks like we've got together for that meeting after all. We'll start by having you and your deacons dropping the guns.'

For a moment Hotchkiss stood as if turned to stone. Then he felt an uncontrollable fury surging inside him. All the time he had been congratulating himself upon the ease with which he had fooled the small Texan, but it was he who had been the dupe. Somehow the young blond had suspected him and had contrived to deceive him, laying a trap into which he had walked. Not just him, either. He had brought his whole force, with the exception of the horse-holders—

'Look out, cap—!' yelled a voice from the darkness, the words ending with a thudding sound and a gurgle of agony as if the speaker had been hit hard in the pit of the stomach.

Not even the horse-holders had escaped the trap!

'You bastard!' Hotchkiss screeched – and there could be

no better description of the sound which burst from his lips – snatching his revolver into view with a reckless disregard for the consequences. 'Get them!'

Catching his superior's movements from the corner of his eye, Sergeant Leps could have quite willingly shot Hotchkiss. Up to that moment, Leps had been planning to do the sensible thing and surrender. Hotchkiss's actions were about to ruin any hope of giving up peaceably.

'Fight 'em!' Leps bellowed, bringing the Colt from behind his back.

It was a foolish gesture under the circumstances. There were fifteen Texans spaced around the clearing. Young recruits, with the exception of Billy Jack, at least half of them were armed with single-shot Enfield carbines; but they had grown up handling weapons and most had fought Indians, or bad Mexicans, at some time during their lives. So they responded to the challenge with a speed and deadly purpose that was often lacking amongst newly-enlisted men from the more civilized East.

Flame erupted from the muzzles of revolvers and carbines, while the roaring of detonated black powder shattered the silence of the night. A veritable storm of lead flew across the clearing, converging upon the Yankees as they tried to bring their weapons into action.

Hotchkiss took three bullets in the body. While his revolver was still thrusting forward and unfired, they flung him to the ground.

Struck in the head by an Enfield's solitary load, Leps twirled and fell. In going down, he sent a bullet into the ground before him. It was the only powder burned by the would-be cattle-thieves.

Four more of them took lead in the opening volley. The remainder hurriedly discarded their revolvers, raised their hands and yelled that they wished to surrender.

'Hold your fire, men!' Dusty Fog shouted, refraining from releasing the hammer of his left hand Colt as its muzzle was swung from the height of its recoil and sought for a second target.

It said much for the control the small Texan had gained over his party that they responded immediately and not another shot was fired.

Returning his Colts to their holsters, Billy Jack listened for any hint that the noise had disturbed the herd. Failing to hear anything. he concluded that he had caused it to be bedded down far enough from the camp for Mr. Blaze's detail to have no worries on that account.

'You all right, Kiowa?' the sergeant yelled.

'Why sure,' answered a voice from the direction in which Hotchkiss and his men had come. 'We got their hosses and the two fellers's was left with 'em.'

'Bueno,' Dusty replied. 'Bring them in.' Then he looked at Billy Jack. 'Sergeant, see to the prisoners. Give their revolvers to some of our men who don't own one. Do what you can for the fellers who've taken lead. Are you and your men all right, Corporal Chatswen?'

'They never touched us, lieutenant,' Chatswen declared as he and his men stood up. 'You sure called the play right all along the line, sir.'

Glancing at the burly corporal in passing to commence his duties, Billy Jack hid a grin. There had been no hesitation in Chatswen's use of the honorific that time. Then the sergeant looked briefly at Dusty and a flicker of admiration passed across his face. It changed to a wry grin as he remembered his misgivings regarding Mr. Fog's actions at the camp that morning.

When Hotchkiss had ridden away, the young officer had sent Corporal McGraw and the lean, Indian-dark soldier, Kiowa Cotton, after him. They had orders to follow him, without allowing him to see them. If he did not return to Arkadelphia, they had to learn where he was going. Then Kiowa was to keep him under observation while Sandy reported back to the camp.

Realizing that Mr. Fog was once more acting in a firm, decisive and capable manner, Billy Jack had sought enlightenment. Far from blindly accepting the visitor's story, the small Texan had been suspicious of it. The young blond had not seen Hotchkiss pass while waiting for Chatswen at the livery barn, yet he should have gone by if he had so recently come from the town. The man's bearing and California saddle had proved little, to Mr. Fog's way of thinking, but something else had been more significant. On being introduced, he had called Dusty 'Mr.', which was the correct military form of address when speaking to a lieutenant. A civilian would not have been likely to know that. Tied together, the various details had suggested to the small Texan much the same possibilities as Billy Jack had considered.

There were, the young officer had decided, objections to challenging the man's veracity. If he should be genuine, he – and many of his congregation – might deeply resent the accusation and it was important for the Army to retain the goodwill of the civilian population.

On the other hand, if Hotchkiss was a spy and planning mischief against the herd, he would not be working alone. Although he would be in custody, his companions would be at liberty to continue their schemes, or escape to their own lines. Wishing to capture the whole bunch, if possible, Mr. Fog had put on an act calculated to lull Hotchkiss into a sense of false security. He had dismissed Billy Jack in that insulting manner to prevent the sergeant from reaching the point where Hotchkiss would be compelled to produce proof of his identity. Left to himself, Mr. Fog had fed the man with sufficient information to make him think he could do his work with ease.

When Mr. Blaze and Chatswen had come to report that the herd was ready to move, they had brought news. Hotchkiss had visited them and extended an invitation for the corporal and his men to attend the prayer meeting. As such a function was of no interest to him, and knowing that Mr. Fog would not approve. Chatswen had declined. So Hotchkiss had ridden off, in the direction of Arkadelphia.

Corporal McGraw had returned, afork a lathered, hand-ridden horse, after about an hour. The news which he had brought removed any lingering doubts. Once out of sight of the herd, Hotchkiss had turned south. Unaware that he was being followed, he had joined several more men – who had also worn civilian clothing – in a wood about five miles from the town. Leaving Kiowa to keep the men under observation, Sandy had returned as fast as his horse would carry him.

On hearing the corporal's news, Chatswen had stated that the men were planning to stampede the herd. Mr. Fog had not agreed, claiming that Hotchkiss would not have taken the risks involved in visiting the camp if that was all they intended. In the small Texan's opinion – although it had never been tried by the Yankees – the men hoped to steal the herd and take it to the Union's Army of Arkansas.

Not only had the small Texan been correct in his assumption, he had proved equally accurate in deciding when and how the attempt would be made. He had figured that they would strike that night, reducing the distance they would have to drive the herd to its new destination. What was more, he had believed that Hotchkiss would want to capture Chatswen's detail, rather than having them killed from an ambush. Doing the latter might allow one or more of them to escape and fetch help and the shooting was almost certain to cause a stampede. So Mr. Fog had declared that the try would be made soon after the herd was bedded down. That would allow the Yankees to move the cattle before they had become too settled. They would also have the full night in which to take the herd around and clear of Arkadelphia; where its appearance and change of route was likely to arouse unwanted interest and attention.

Having stated his conclusions, Mr. Fog had made plans to counter the attempt. Billy Jack had changed uniforms with Japhet, who was closest amongst the herders to his lanky build, and had accompanied the cattle. The chuck wagon had been taken along, to serve as a hiding place at the night camp if it should be needed. With the cattle moving, Mr. Fog and the recruits had followed at a sufficient distance for their presence to be undetected.

The precautions had paid off when, late in the afternoon,

Billy Jack had located a man engaged in scouting the herd. When sure that the escort's proximity was unsuspected by the watcher, the sergeant had selected a camp-site and bed ground which he had felt sure was ideally suited to his officer's needs.

After keeping Hotchkiss's party under observation all day, Kiowa had slipped away when their scout – it had been Sergeant Leps – returned at sundown. Visiting the herd and camp, he had delivered a warning and gone on to report to Mr. Fog. From that point, everything had followed the small Texan's plan as if all concerned were working together.

While Mr. Blaze – complaining bitterly that his cousin was pulling rank and giving him all the worst chores – had taken some of the men to protect the herd, the remainder had moved into their places of concealment and waited for the Yankees to arrive. Nothing had been left to chance. Mr. Fog had even thought of sending away the horses so that they would not be disturbed if there should be shooting.

Shaking his head in unspoken admiration, Billy Jack thought of his conjectures regarding the young officers. No matter how Mr. Blaze turned out – and the sergeant still had doubts about him – Mr. Fog sure had the making of a leader.

''Less he gets killed off afore he gets a chance to,' Billy Jack thought, reverting to his pessimistic pose – a sure sign that he believed all was going well. 'Which he could, working with an unlucky cuss like me.'

Part Three

THE MAKING OF A LEADER, cont'd.

CHAPTER SEVEN

LEANING against his long-barrelled, muzzle-loading U.S. Model of 1861 rifle musket, Private Phineas Devlin was a bitter, disgruntled and discontented soldier. He glowered through the darkness to where three glowing areas of red light marked the camp-sites of the two infantry regiments and the large remount depot that was situated in the valley's bottom below and between them. Over there, the other enlisted men of his outfit – even those guarding the horses – were eagerly awaiting the arrival of the O'Bannion's whiskey. Back across the river, in Searcy, the officers were attending a meeting and ball, enjoying themselves while Devlin stood his lonely duty. With only that damned shavetail, Crosby, as officer of the day at the camp, the sergeant of the guard might forget to come and relieve him when his time was up; especially if the whiskey arrived and was shared out.

An annoyed snort burst from the soldier. When he had enlisted in the Chicago All-Irish Volunteers, he had expected to do more exciting things than having to stand guard at night on a bridge that crossed the Little Red River in White County, Arkansas. Yet there he was, wearing his kepi, long cloak-coat over his uniform and hung about with all the paraphernalia – a bayonet in its sheath and dangling by its frog from his waist belt, water canteen, tin cup, pack, ammunition pouches and the rest – the Army figured necessary for such a task.

At any time, even without the added inducement of the O'Bannion's gift, Devlin would have felt that the guard detail was not a fitting task for a fighting man who was ready, willing and eager to be beating the devil out of his country's enemies. It seemed even more pointless under the circumstances. What fighting was being done in Arkansas at that period was taking place a good eighty miles to the south, where the Rebels were defending Little Rock. They would never dare to come so far into Union-held territory just to destroy a bridge. So guarding it, in his opinion, was a waste of time.

'And if the guarding has to be done, why the hell couldn't they have some of them damned niggers doing it?' Devlin muttered, thinking sourly about the regiment of Negro soldiers who were camped in the vicinity.

A bitter, prejudiced man who hated coloured people – and every other racial or religious group – on principle and without thought, cause or reason, Devlin could not see why his regiment should be required to perform any duties while there were members of lesser breeds available.

The sound of a horse's hooves diverted Devlin's thoughts at the point. Turning, he stared south across the bridge to where a rider was approaching from the direction of Searcy. Although the moon had not yet come up, Devlin's eyes had grown accustomed to the darkness. In a few seconds with the rider half way across the bridge, the sentry could discern that he was a soldier of some kind.

Maybe even an officer, Devlin silently warned himself. With so many from every outfit at the meeting, there was likely to be plenty of them going back and forth before the night was through.

One thing Devlin had learned early in his brief career as a soldier was that officers always expected a man on sentry duty to act in the correct military manner. So he had better do what was expected of him.

'Halt!' Devlin shouted, bringing up the rifle to hold it at waist level and, without bothering to cock back the big side-hammer, swung its muzzle to the front. 'Who goes there?'

'Friend,' answered the rider, slowing but not stopping his large, powerful mount. He had an accent that was far different from the tall, lean soldier's broad Irish brogue. 'Easy there with that rifle, mister. It's bad enough having to ride dispatch all night without getting throwed down on every damned whichways a man turns.'

Having challenged the other soldier, Devlin found himself uncertain of what he should do next. On being posted, he had received no instructions as to his conduct. However, the response implied that the rider was not an officer and so would be willing to overlook any improper behaviour.

'Come ahead slow and easy,' Devlin ordered, although the rider was continuing to advance anyway.

Drawing nearer, the rider proved to be smallish and conveyed an impression of youth. He sat his big horse with an easy, effortless grace that would have been obvious had Devlin had experience in such matters. His right hand grasped the reins, while the left for some reason was tucked into the open front of his double-breasted cloak-coat. On his head was perched a kepi with the usual crossed sabres insignia of the U.S. Cavalry across its top. The cloak-coat concealed his tunic, but the weapon belt strapped over it appeared to be of the normal pattern. So did the sabre which dangled from the pommel of a saddle that differed in several respects from the issue McClellan; but not to Devlin's inexperienced eyes. No horseman, he failed to notice that the saddle was unlike those he had seen used by various cavalry outfits. Riding breeches and Hessian boots emerged from below the cloak-coat. Despite the darkness, Devlin could make out the yellow stripes along the legs of the breeches.

'I'd be tolerable obliged happen you'd point that rifle some other way, friend,' the rider said amiably, as the muzzle of the weapon was almost touching his mount's chest. 'Or do you reckon I'm a Johnny Reb's's come all this way behind the lines to blow up the bridge?'

Although still undecided what he should do, Devlin turned aside the rifle to avoid it striking the horse. He looked up as the rider loomed above him, left hand still hidden inside the cloak-coat. Stepping backwards a couple of paces, the sentry felt a momentary alarm. There was something wrong, but he could not decide what it might be. Then he decided that he was worrying for nothing. No Rebel would be likely to act in such a relaxed, friendly manner.

'It's only me duty I'm after doing,' Devlin pointed out, returning the butt of his rifle to the ground.

'Why sure,' answered the rider, taking his hand from the front of the cloak-coat. It emerged empty. 'I don't know which of us's got the lousiest chore, friend, you or me.'

'At least you're going some place,' Devlin commented, watching the other swing from the saddle. 'I just have to stand here. and the devil of a bit of good I'm doing. Like you said, none of 'em'd dare come this far behind our lines.'

'That's for sure,' agreed the rider, releasing his reins so that they dangled in two separate strands below the horse's bit.

Ever since the other man had replied to the challenge, Devlin had noticed the way in which he spoke. There was something about it that did not seem right. His clothes, equipment and attitude appeared correct, but the voice—

Realization struck home!

'Hey!' Devlin ejaculated, retreating a further two steps and starting to raise the rifle. 'You sound like these goober-grabber* bastards who live around these parts.'

'Easy on there, friend,' the rider protested in amiable tones. He showed no alarm other than to spread his hands clear of his sides – so that it almost looked as if he meant to slap the horse's rump with the right – and showing that they were empty. 'I'm always having this same son-of-a-bitching trouble.'

'How do you mean?' Devlin inquired.

'My folks had a ranch in North Texas and I growed up there,' the rider explained. 'Only them Secessionist bastards run us out. So I joined the Army to get back at them. And now, every time I open my mouth near on, somebody takes me for a Reb.'

*** Goober-grabber: derogatory name for a native of Arkansas.**

The sentry had not been long in the Army, but he did not wish for the smaller, younger, yet clearly more experienced soldier to realize how short his period of service had been. So he did not intend to display the uncertainty he was feeling. At the back of his mind, getting stronger all the time, was the belief that the other man could not be an enemy, no matter how he talked.

'It don't cost nothing to be careful, bucko,' Devlin commented, lowering the rifle once more and adopting what he hoped would be the tone of a seasoned veteran. 'No offence meant by it.'

'None took, friend,' drawled the rider.

'You'll likely have been in Searcy for that officers' shindig,' Devlin suggested, wanting to keep the other man talking as a means of relieving his own boredom. 'What's it all about?'

'What do you reckon it's about?' countered the other.

'I'm damned if I know,' Devlin admitted. 'All our officers, 'cepting the officer of the day's there. Same with the other outfits, I'd say.'

'It is with mine,' confirmed the rider, turning to his horse and opening its near-side saddle pouch. He removed a bottle and went on, 'I got took there to run messages. So I reckoned I was entitled to help myself to something to keep the cold out. How do you feel about soldiers drinking on duty, friend?'

'That all depends on who's doing the drinking,' Devlin answered, eyeing the bottle with considerable interest.

'My pappy allus allowed it's a mortal sin for a man to drink alone – unless there's nobody else around to take a snort with him,' the rider stated, drawing the cork. 'Here, friend, help yourself to a nip. I've already had me a couple. It's a good way to keep out the miseries on a night like this.'

If Devlin had been a more observant man, he might have noticed that the bottle was still remarkably full; considering that it was supposed to have already been sampled. Instead of seeing, he accepted it and took a long drink. The liquor burned pleasantly down his throat and made him even more determined to hold the rider in conversation, so that he might be offered other drinks.

'Now that's what I call good whiskey,' Devlin declared, wiping his mouth on his right sleeve without returning the bottle. 'The luck of the Irish to you, young feller.'

'I'm having my share of it,' thought the small horseman, conscious of the bone handled Colt 1860 Army revolver which was thrust into his breeches' waistband and pressed against his right ribs. 'And so are you. If you'd been smarter, I might've had to kill you, which wouldn't have done either of us any good.'

After only six weeks with the Texas Light Cavalry, Dusty Fog was carrying out his first independent assignment.

They had been six weeks of hard work under a demanding, but fair, superior officer and constantly watched by interested, or critical, eyes. During the period, Dusty had continued to develop his ability to control larger, older, more experienced men. He had also improved his knowledge – already obtained at Judge Blaze's small military academy – of how to carry out *caracoles*, riding and manoeuvring in echelon, or the various other cavalry drills and minor tactics.

On the whole, Dusty believed that he had acquitted himself in a satisfactory manner. In addition to earning his superiors' approbation, he had already built up a basis of trust and faith in his abilities amongst the hard-bitten veterans of Company 'C'. Billy Jack's whole-hearted support, taken with the manner of Dusty's arrival at the regiment, had been of the greatest help in achieving the latter.

For preventing the loss of the herd and capturing, or killing, every member of the Union's cattle-stealing expedition, Dusty had been allowed to retain his rank of first lieutenant. That had made him second-in-command of Company 'C'.

To an equally fortunate, but less able young officer, the appointment might have been a disastrous failure. Supported by an inborn instinct for leadership, natural intelligence and the strength of his personality, Dusty had avoided the many pitfalls that threatened a man placed in his position.

Being aware of its value, he had demonstrated his ambidextrous wizardry with the two Colts and had impressed men who were fully capable of understanding the excellence of the display. In addition, he had given convincing proof of his skill as a horse-master. On two occasions, he had been compelled to prove himself physically. Each time he had taken on a bigger, stronger, heavier man and beaten him thoroughly, yet in a way that did not humiliate the loser.

Maybe the enlisted men were not yet ready to accept Dusty as fit to command the Company in action, but he was working towards the point where – if it should become necessary – they would be likely to do so. Until then, he was satisfied with the thought that he had been considered capable of carrying out an important scouting mission.

News had reached the Texas Light Cavalry of a Union Army's remount depot having been established about ten miles north of Searcy, across the Little Red River and near to the trail to Newport, the seat of Jackson County. Even more significant, if one remembered General 'Cussing' Culber's boasts regarding the future conduct of the War in Arkansas, the Yankees were commandeering every available horse and all the fodder they could lay their hands on in the territory under their control. It all suggested that Culver was making preparations for a major offensive.

Wanting further and more definite news, Colonel Blaze had decided to send out a scouting detail. It had been Company 'C's' turn to supply the men for such a task, but Captain von Hertz was required at headquarters. So the colonel had taken the opportunity to discover how Dusty would carry out one of a cavalry officer's main duties; the gathering of information from behind the enemy's lines.

On receiving his orders, Dusty had asked for permission to select the men who would accompany him. It was granted grudgingly by von Hertz, especially when the youngster had named two of the recruits he had brought from Texas. However, as Sergeant Billy Jack and three veterans were to complete the party, the captain had agreed to the arrangement.

Having made preparations which had met with Billy Jack's approval, the party had set off. They had passed through the Yankees' forward positions at night and without difficulty. Avoiding being seen by the enemy, they had travelled towards Searcy.

During the journey, the Texans had seen two parties of Yankee officers heading in the same direction. At a ford over the Bayous des Arc River, they had watched General Culver and his staff going over, then disappearing up the trail to Searcy. Clearly something of importance was going to take place in the town.

Waiting until sundown, Dusty had allowed Billy Jack and Sandy McGraw to try to enter Searcy and see what could be learned. Sandy's uncle lived in the town, which had been the reason for Dusty asking to fetch him along. The rest of the detail had pushed on to the Little Red River. They had found the bridge was guarded. By only one man, but with the possibility of reinforcements near by. He was at the northern end, which made any chance of sneaking up on him almost impossible.

Recollecting how Hotchkiss had tried to trick him and his men, Dusty had come prepared to resort to similar methods. Apart from the colours, which were not too important before the moon rose, the Armies of the North and the South wore a similar style of uniform. The cloak-coats particularly were identical in cut and line; a point which more than one Confederate cavalry raider had turned to his advantage. Only the hats were different and Dusty had been ready to deal with that. Every member of his party had brought a U.S. Cavalry kepi, taken from Yankee prisoners and held at the regiment for just such a purpose.

For the first time, Dusty had been grateful to von Hertz for insisting that his junior officers always wore the regulation pattern gunbelt. Apart from the lettering on its buckle, it was an almost exact duplicate of the Union Army's issue. Only the saddle was different, but Dusty had gambled on it going unnoticed in the darkness and when seen by an infantryman.

Having donned the kepi, Dusty had placed the Colt where its availability was concealed. Approaching the sentry, he had been ready to draw and shoot if necessary. Or, as he had drawn nearer, had hoped to merely throw down on the man and threaten him into silence. He had managed to come close enough to make the latter feasible, without needing to do it. There had been a bad moment when the sentry had become aware of his accent, but it had passed over. However, while showing his bare hands, Dusty had been neither helpless nor harmless. If his explanation had not been accepted, he had planned to slap the horse's rump. That would have caused the high-spirited animal to bound forward. Even if it had not struck the sentry, it would have distracted him for long enough to let Dustry tackle him.

When that danger had passed, Dusty had set about the business of obtaining information. He had brought the whiskey from the regiment, figuring that it might serve the kind of purpose to which he was now putting it. He had already learned that only one officer remained at the soldier's camp and felt sure that he would be told much more if he played his cards right.

Remembering his father's comments on the way to win confidence, Dusty led Devlin to talk about his grievances. By the time the sentry had taken a couple more drinks, the small Texan knew a fair amount about the formation of the Chicago All-Irish Volunteers, the quality of its officers and non-coms, and its readiness for war. After listening to the man's grouses, Dusty turned the conversation to a matter of more immediate interest.

'What do you reckon old "Cussing" Culver's come to Searcy for?' Dusty asked, knowing that the enlisted men often picked up rumours or hints of their superiors' intentions.

'You know officers,' Devlin replied, sounding disinterested. 'They're allus getting together for one thing or another and devil the thought for the likes of you and me.'

'Some of us're figuring it might mean old "Cussing's" going to have us do what he's been telling everybody he'll do, run the Rebs back to Texas.'

'Is that the way of it, do you think?' Devlin inquired and again sampled the contents of the bottle.

'It could be,' Dusty drawled, guessing that the other had neither knowledge nor thoughts on the matter and was not especially interested.

'Well, it's not before time, if that's the way of it,' Devlin sniffed. 'Just so long as we're not expected to have to keep on doing the dirty work for them damned niggers.'

'Niggers?' Dusty repeated. 'What do you mean?'

'Aren't you with them hosses in the valley?' Devlin asked.

'Nope,' Dusty replied and continued with the answer he had decided to use in the event of such a question. 'I'm in the New Jersey Dragoons. Try another lil nip, friend.'

'It's kind you are,' Devlin stated, the words being punctuated by the call of a whip-poor-will repeated twice from the southern bank of the river. 'And it's lucky you are not to be having any truck with them niggers. *Soldiers*, they calls themselves.'

Having heard the 'bird's' call, which told him that Billy Jack and Sandy had rejoined the detail, Dusty was considering taking his departure. The moon would soon be coming up and he wanted to have his men across the river before that happened. However, the reference to Negro soldiers required investigation.

'What's up with them?' Dusty inquired.

Taking another, longer drink, Devlin launched into the required explanation. A recently formed regiment of Negro infantry had travelled West with his own outfit. From the start, there had been friction between them. In addition to resenting the Negroes' assumption of equality, the members of the All-Irish Volunteers had noticed that the coloured soldiers appeared to be better armed and equipped than themselves.

'You should see them uniforms and tents 'n' everything

they've got. And every last mother's son of 'em's got a breech-loading rifle,' Devlin continued, glaring bitterly at the weapon in his left hand. 'And good Americans like us have to make do with *these* damned things. Colonel Milligan tried to make them swap with us, but them stinking soft-shells* 's is their officers – may the Devil take them all – wouldn't let it happen. Nigger-loving bastards!'

Once more Devlin raised the bottle and the level of the whiskey sank lower. Then he continued with the catalogue of his regiment's grievances against the Negro soldiers. Not only had they been allowed to use the same kind of railway cars during the first stage of the journey from the East, but their officers had insisted that they were given the first choice in accommodation.

On their arrival in White County, the two regiments had been ordered to set up camp on opposite rims overlooking the valley along which the remount deport was established. They were there to protect the horses, but when the time had come to commence the actual guard duties, the task had fallen upon the Chicago All-Irish Volunteers.

'I'll tell you, we was riled about that,' Devlin declared. 'But their colonel's got more pull than Joe Milligan. So we have to send out a full company a night to guard the horses, while them black bastards sit on their fat butts, doing nothing. I tell you, bucko, it's sick to our guts we are of them and their uppy ways. We don't let niggers act that way back home in Chicago.'

Although Dusty was not too interested in the sentry's attitude towards the Negro soldiers, he had remained in the hope of learning something useful. Having discovered the strength of the guard at the remount depot, he decided that he had exhausted the soldier's use as a source of information.

'Well, I'd best be getting on my way,' Dusty said.

'Your bottle's near on empty,' Devlin said, sounding puzzled by such an unexpected phenomena. He had reached a state of intoxication where he felt a desire to be generous,

* Soft-shell: derogatory name for a liberal-intellectual.

especially to such a sociable, friendly companion. 'Still it's my turn to get the next.'

'Do you have it with you?' Dusty inquired, turning towards his waiting horse and reaching for its trailing, split-ended reins; another pointer to his true identity that the sentry had overlooked.

'No,' admitted Devlin. 'But I'll you what to do, bucko. Are you headed for Newport?'

'Why sure,' Dusty agreed, thinking fast to decide upon an acceptable reason for visiting that town.

It was not needed.

'Then keep your eyes open for a wagon on the trail. If there's a sergeant and three fellers with it, it'll be coming to our camp,' Devlin went on, without waiting for an explanation. 'Call in on the way back and ask for Phineas Devlin, which's me, and I'll return the favour you've done me this night.'

'I don't follow you,' Dusty said, truthfully, postponing his intention of departing although the night was growing lighter.

'Isn't it the whiskey that's been given to us by the O'Bannion – a saintly man – as's coming this night?' Devlin asked and elaborated on the statement.

Being involved in recruiting the regiment, a prominent Chicago politician had offered the inducement of a regular supply of whiskey to all who joined. Not just for the officers, Devlin insisted, but sufficient to ensure that every enlisted man had his fair share. The latest consignment was on its way south from the railroad and was due to reach the camp that night.

'I sure hope it gets here safely,' Dusty drawled, an idea starting to develop in his imaginative, fertile head.

'And why shouldn't it?' Devlin demanded indignantly.

'A wagon-load of whiskey'd be mighty tempting pickings to a lot of folks,' Dusty elaborated. 'Them niggers like to take a drink or more, I've been told.'

'Just let 'em try to touch a single bottle of the blessed stuff!' Devlin growled. 'If they did that, it's little good their officers'd do 'em.'

'All the same, it's lucky their officers haven't gone to the meeting,' Dusty remarked and received the information he had hoped for.

'But they have gone,' Devlin said, a worried note creeping into his voice. 'If I thought that—'

'There's riders coming,' Dusty interrupted, swinging astride his horse.

That had been the signal agreed upon with his men. Seeing him mount, they started to ride from their places of concealment and head towards the bridge.

'Who are they?' Devlin asked, glaring across the river.

'Look like some of our boys,' Dusty answered. 'Oh hell. Lieutenant Billy Jack's with them. I'd be obliged if you'd not mention that bottle, friend.'

'That's the way of it, huh?' Devlin grunted, setting the bottle on the ground. 'Count on good old Phineas Devlin not to let a pal down.'

'Howdy, Lieutenant!' Dusty called. 'I was just asking the sentry which's the best way to Newport.'

Without replying, Billy Jack led the others to join Dusty. Realizing his own position, Devlin stood at as steady a brace as he could manage and let the Texans ride by without speaking to them; although he gave Billy Jack a salute.

'You-all sure got promoted fast, Billy Jack,' drawled Private Kiowa Cotton as the detail passed out of hearing distance of the sentry.

'Why sure,' agreed the sergeant miserably. 'And now I'm likely to get busted again.'

'Didn't you get to see Sandy's uncle?' Dusty inquired.

'I'll have to say "no" to that,' Billy Jack confessed in his most dejected fashion.

'You're busted back to sergeant,' Dusty declared, then became serious. 'What happened?'

'Found a sign fastened to a tree outside town,' Billy Jack explained. 'It said there was a curfew from sundown and anybody seen on the streets'd be shot. Streets were alive with Yankee patrols, too. You know me, I'm fearless. But I recollected you'd said you'd's soon not have the Yankees all riled up. So I concluded we'd best come and report.'

'*Bueno*,' Dusty drawled. 'I've found that there's two new regiments been moved in here. What do you make of it, sergeant?'

'Reinforcements,' Billy Jack replied. 'Now they're here, Culver's called him a council of war and's figuring how he can run us Southron boys out of Arkansas, like he's being saying he would.'

'That's about how I see it,' Dusty conceded. 'You know, sergeant, was he to lose those remounts it'd make things a whole heap harder for him.'

'And you-all're figuring on trying to make him lose them,' Billy Jack guessed looking at the small Texan.

'Let's say I'm going to see if there's a way we can do it,' Dusty corrected. 'If we can, you might even win back your promotion.'

'With my luck,' Billy Jack wailed dismally, 'we're more likely to get seen at it, catched and killed.'

'I just knew you'd be pleasured to back my play,' Dusty declared. 'It does a man real good to know he's got such brave, trusting and willing help.'

CHAPTER EIGHT

'THERE's no way's I can see for us to get at them hosses, Mr. Fog,' Billy Jack declared miserably, as he lay alongside the small Texan amongst a clump of bushes and looking into the valley. 'With the moon up and all, we're sure to be seen by the guards.'

Behind the sergeant's mournful façade lay genuine disappointment, for he had hoped that they might be able to achieve something against the Yankees' remount depot. Certainly it was a tempting target and of sufficient importance to make the taking of risks worthwhile. Unfortunately, their examination of the area did not lead Billy Jack to believe that they could hope to succeed.

'That's for sure,' Dusty conceded. 'There'd be too many of them for us to take them all out of the deal. Not counting all the extra help they could right easy call on from the camps on the rims.'

Although there was no fence surrounding the remount depot, the six large pole corrals holding the horses were adequately covered by patrolling sentries. What was more, the few areas that would have been in deep shadow were illuminated by the fires kept blazing in basket-like iron cressets. More cressets lit up the two infantry camps and the hour was far too early for many of the soldiers to have turned into their beds. The prospects looked anything but good for the small detail of Texans.

'What're you figuring on doing now, sir?' Billy Jack asked, for his companion had not sounded perturbed or disappointed.

'We may as well go back to the others,' Dusty replied, starting to rise.

'It's sure a pity we can't scatter 'em,' the sergeant went on, throwing a look into the valley as he came to his feet. 'That'd play all hell with any notions ole "Cussing" Culver's got for doing meanness to us Southron boys.'

'Why sure,' Dusty agreed.

'Maybe Kiowa and young McGraw'll have better luck with that wagon you sent 'em to look for,' Billy Jack went on, eyeing his young officer in a quizzical manner. 'Not that I'm expecting 'em to.'

'That's more like you,' Dusty drawled, directing a final glance across the valley at the camp occupied by the Negro soldiers and turning to lead the way through the bushes. 'I was getting scared you'd had an accident and was starting to look on the bright side.'

'Any time that happens, I right soon stop it,' Billy Jack assured him. 'That way I don't get the miseries so bad when things start going wrong. Which they allus do for me.'

Withdrawing cautiously to where they had left their horses concealed in a hollow, Dusty and Billy Jack mounted. They rode away from the vicinity of the valley without being seen by anybody in either of the camps. After covering about a mile, they approached a small, but thick, grove of post oaks. Billy Jack gave a fair imitation of a whip-poor-will calling twice and received a similar answer to the pre-arranged signal. Entering the grove, they could see the glow of a small fire amongst the trees. On reaching it, they found all but one of the enlisted men standing and looking in their direction.

'How'd it go, Sandy?' Dusty inquired, leaving his bay ground-hitched.

'Well, we found a place where we *could* jump the wagon, sir,' Sandy McGraw replied. 'Kiowa send me back to tell you. He's pushed on up the trail to see if it's coming.'

'It's not too good a place, huh? Dusty asked.

'Nope,' Sandy admitted. 'But it's the *only* place anywheres along the trail for over two mile, as we could see.'

'Do'you mind if I ask what's in that wagon, Mr. Fog?' one of the veteran privates put in.

'Whiskey,' Dusty drawled.

'*Whiskey!*' repeated the veteran and his voice took on a more hopeful timbre. 'Whee-dogie! Everybody's going to be real pleased with us, happen we can get it back to the regiment.'

'That's for sure,' agreed the second of the old hands. 'They'll all—'

'We're not going to try to take it back,' Dusty warned, not wanting his men to build up hopes that he must shatter.

'What you got in mind to do with it, sir?' the third veteran inquired.

'Give it to the Yankees,' Dusty answered, in a matter of fact fashion.

The time had not yet arrived when the small Texan could make startling, unexpected announcements and have them accepted by the veterans of Company 'C'. So the three older privates exchanged puzzled glances, then turned their eyes in an inquiring manner to Billy Jack. Sandy McGraw was just as baffled by Dusty's words but had greater faith in his judgment, and waited expectantly for him to continue with his explanation.

'There's some's might figure it's wasting time to take it away, happen all we intend to do is give it back to 'em, sir,' Billy Jack commented, while the three veterans muttered their agreement.

'Well, now,' Dusty said quietly, 'I wasn't exactly figuring on giving it back to the same Yankees we'll be taking it from.'

At that moment, they heard the sound of fast-moving hooves approaching.

'Sandy,' Dusty went on, giving the others no opportunity to question his last statement. 'Haul some of those branches from the fire and let the burned ends cool down. We'll need them, if Kiowa's bringing the right news.'

Once more the veterans displayed interest, but a lack of understanding. None of them had been surprised when their young officer had told them to make a fire in the centre of the grove. They knew that, in wooded country, a small fire was less likely to be seen from a distance at night than in daylight, when the smoke rising from it was noticeable.* Mr. Fog's words had implied that the fire was to serve some other purpose than making the camp more comfortable, but the veterans could not imagine what it might be.

Riding through the trees, his horse showing signs of having travelled a good distance at speed, Kiowa Cotton slipped from his saddle at the edge of the fire's glow. Dropping his reins, he slouched towards Dusty.

'It's coming, Mr. Fog,' the Indian-dark soldier announced, delivering what passed as a salute. 'Sergeant and three men riding guard, two more on the wagon. I reckon it's them. Leastwise, they all sound liquored up and Irish, way they're singing.'

'How far off are they?' Dusty wanted to know, watching Sandy drawing a couple of thick branches from the fire.

''Bout three miles, when I left 'em,' Kiowa replied. 'They're not pushing their hosses.'

'That ought to give us enough time to get everything ready,' Dusty said, half to himself. Then he turned his gaze to Billy Jack. 'Have the crossed sabres taken off those Yankee kepis, sergeant. Then I want everybody with their hands and faces black.'

'Yo!' Billy Jack agreed, but puzzlement was plain on his face.

'Tell me about this place you've got in mind for us to use when we jump the wagon, Kiowa,' Dusty requested, ignoring the muttered comments and pointed glances being directed his way as Billy Jack set the enlisted men to carrying out his order regarding the kepis.

'It's not good,' Kiowa admitted. 'But it's the only place where you could get in close enough to jump 'em, happen you're set on doing it.'

'I am,' Dusty assured him.

'It'd be easier to lay up and shoot 'em as they go by,' Kiowa pointed out. 'You couldn't get close to the trail with-

* The British Army engaged in anti-Mau-Mau terrorist patrols in the Kenya forests also took advantage of this fact.

out being seen, 'cepting at this place, but you could get to maybe a hundred yards of it.'

'I want them alive, at least some of them, if I can get them.'

'Then it'll have to be that place. There's a rise on the right of the trail, but at this place it drops straight down instead of being a slope, and the wagon has to go by along the bottom of it.'

'How high's the rim?'

'Not much higher'n the top of the wagon's cover.

'That's high enough!' Dusty enthused.

'Way the trail curves, they'd see us if we sat our hosses on the top of the wall or even back a ways from it.'

'Huh huh!' Dusty grunted. 'How're the men riding?

'Sergeant and one of them was out front, the other two flanking the wagon box, 'Kiowa replied.

'And they'd been drinking?'

'If they hadn't, they was sure trying to sound like they had.'

'*Bueno!* Dusty ejaculated and Kiowa could see that he was satisfied with what he had heard. 'I reckon we can make a stab at it.'

Wishing to avoid raising false hopes amongst his men, Dusty had kept them in ignorance of what he hoped to do until he knew that he had the means available to put the scheme into operation, Kiowa had satisfied him on that point, so he did not delay any longer before taking them into his confidence. He told them all he had learned from the sentry at the bridge and how he hoped to turn his discoveries to their advantage. Listening, the men stared at their youthful officer with a mixture of surprise and incredulity. Billy Jack, Kiowa and Sandy showed that they were interested. However, the three veteran privates were more inclined to be critical and doubtful.

'Them fellers'll see we're not Yankee infantry, even if we've got our faces and hands black,' one of the trio objected. 'Our uniforms aren't even the same colour.'

'All of the men with the wagon've been drinking,' Dusty

pointed out. 'And, happen we handle things right, it'll all be over so fast they'll not have the chance to think about how we're dressed.'

'It'll never work,' Billy Jack wailed, setting his seal of approval upon the scheme. 'We'll be seen afore they get under us. I'll bet none of us're alive comes morning.'

Watching the veterans' response to the doleful comment, Dusty was grateful for having won Billy Jack's confidence and trust. The three enlisted men looked less dubious and uncertain than they had while he was telling them of his idea. While they had been disinclined to support openly such an unconventional notion as Dusty had outlined, they had faith in their sergeant's judgment. Clearly Billy Jack considered that the scheme could work, so they were more willing to go along with it.

The preparations were made quickly. Using the charred ends of branches from the fire, the men blackened their faces and hands. While they did so, Dusty had different members of the party impersonate a coloured man's way of speaking. Selecting the most accurate, he warned them that they must sound as minstrel shows would have most likely taught men raised in the North to expect Negroes to speak. At last, wearing the unmarked kepis, but no further disguises, they mounted up and set off on their mission.

Approaching the trail, Dusty ordered his men to dismount. The horses were left in the reluctant care of the oldest veteran, while the remainder of the detail continued their advance on foot. Billy Jack, Sandy McGraw and the other two veterans each carried his coiled rope.

On reaching the top of the small cliff, Dusty could see that Kiowa had been correct in his assumption as to where an ambush would be possible. There was no other place along the trail that would have allowed them to come so close and remain undetected. Nor would there have been sufficient time for them to make hiding places. Already they could hear singing, hooves, the rumbling of wheels and creaking of leather.

Swiftly Dusty surveyed his surroundings, as he and his

men flattened on their bellies on the top of the cliff. The area was almost perfect for his needs, he decided. Below him, the wall fell perpendicular and formed the edge of the trail. Even if the wagon was at the far side, it ought to still be within leaping distance. Most likely though, with a rider on each flank, it would be travelling along the centre of the trail.

'They sure sound like they're enjoying life,' Billy Jack remarked disapprovingly, shaking loose the coils of his rope and extending its loop. 'I don't reckon they'll be too all-fired eager and watchful.'

'Or me,' Dusty agreed. 'In fact, I'm counting on just that.'

'Now me,' the sergeant declared. 'I never count on nothing going *right*.'

'Tell you what,' Dusty growled, glaring at the miserable, care-worn face. 'If you get killed because of me I'll say I'm sorry most humble.'

Despite his gloomy words, Billy Jack was studying the wagon and its escort as they came into sight. The moon was up and there was good visibility. While that would allow the Texans' blackened hands and faces to be seen clearly, it also showed all too clearly that they did not wear the uniforms of the Yankee Infantry. However, his examination of the approaching party suggested that, once again, Mr. Fog had drawn some mighty smart conclusions. If their behaviour was anything to go by, they were unlikely to be too observant.

As when Kiowa had seen them, the burly sergeant and an equally brawny private rode ahead of the wagon. The other two ranged their horses on either side of the vehicle. The sergeant and two men on the driver's box were armed with revolvers, holstered on their waist-belts, but the three mounted privates each had his long Springfield rifle resting across his knees.

'That bastard beyond the wagon's too far back for us to rope him!' Billy Jack whispered, indicating one of the pair who were riding beside the vehicle. 'You just can't trust Yankees to do nothing right.'

'That's for sure,' Dusty agreed. 'So you'd best leave him to Kiowa or me.'

'Yo!' the sergeant answered.

'Remember,' Dusty went on. 'We're coloured folks, but the kind those fellers've seen in minstrel shows. Talk like it.'

'Yoh-all can count on us to do des' that, Rastus,' promised one of the veterans, employing the type of accent and name used by such performers.

'I jes' hopes them white gennelmen appreciates what we-all's doing, Sambo,' Sandy McGraw stated, following his older companion's example.

'Hold the noise down!' Billy Jack hissed.

Silence fell amongst the Texans, but the precaution was not necessary. Every member of the Yankee party had clearly taken sufficient drinks to render him in a musical frame of mind. Their voices, raised in song, would have drowned louder noises than the watchers' quiet words and none of them were bothering to look around them in search of possible enemies.

Nearer came the wagon, with the sergeant and his companion leading the way with a blissful– or whisky-induced – disregard for anything other than the song they were bellowing. Quickly Dusty gave his final instructions for the attack.

Slowly, carefully, the Texans eased themselves into positions of greater readiness. Their attention flickered between the wagon, the riders and where Dusty and Kiowa were backing away from the rim.

Cautiously the small blond rose. With some relief, he discovered that he could see the top of the wagon's canopy although the riders were hidden by the edge of the cliff.

'Now!' Dusty hissed, thrusting himself into motion, with Kiowa on his heels.

Even as Billy Jack and the other men came to their feet, spaced far enough apart so that each would have room to spin and throw his rope, Dusty reached the rim and jumped. Still the Irishmen were not displaying any sign of hearing, or becoming aware of, the danger that was threatening them.

The small Texan landed on the canopy, feeling it give under his weight; but it held up against the pressure. Down came his second foot, on the other side of the centre bar, and he caught his balance deftly. A moment later, Kiowa alighted behind him with equal success.

Hearing and feeling the impacts of the two Texans' arrivals on top of the canopy, the man seated by the driver started to rise. Swaying from side to side, due to the influence of the whiskey he had consumed, he turned to investigate. Shock twisted at his face as he stared upwards to where Dusty and Kiowa loomed above him. Although the light of the moon clearly illuminated every detail of their appearances, only the colour of their skins attracted his attention and he drew the required conclusion. Like most members of the Chicago All-Irish Volunteers, he had a very prejudiced nature and outlook. Conditions during the journey had served to increase his already considerable intolerance and bias against Negroes. So he was willing to accept the newcomers at their face value, without thinking of other details.

'Niggers!' the soldier screeched.

Wishing to prevent the Irishman from noticing and realizing how the 'niggers' were clad, Dusty lashed around his right boot. Its toe thudded against the side of the man's head an instant after the word had left his lips. Already off balance, the kick completed the destruction of his equilibrium and he pitched sideways from the box.

Bringing his foot down from delivering the attack, Dusty teetered briefly before regaining his balance. He felt the canopy vibrate beneath him and heard an ear-splitting yell as Kiowa left it to deal with the horseman on the far side. At the same moment, the rest of the detail started to carry out their parts of the affair.

While Dusty and Kiowa were still in mid-air, Billy Jack was measuring with his eyes the distance separating him from his target. An expert with a rope, he had selected the rider farthest from the rim. Satisfied with his aim, he swung his rope in one fast whirl to the right and up over his head.

Then, causing the loop to flatten out horizontally, he sent it forward. It passed above the leading private and dropped neatly over the Yankee sergeant's head and shoulders. Twitching the loop tight, the lanky non-com jerked his Federal counterpart over the cantle of the saddle and dumped him rump-first on the hard ground.

'Get the white bastards!' howled Sandy McGraw, having been told to help plant the idea of Negroes being responsible for the attack and to leave the catching of the riders to the older men.

Like Billy Jack, the two veterans had been cowhands before enlisting in the Texas Light Cavalry. Each duplicated his hooley-ann throw* so well that all three ropes were in flight at the same time. Having a shorter distance to cover, the privates achieved equal accuracy. Snared around the neck, the soldier at the sergeant's side joined him in being unhorsed. Nor did the man on the near side of the wagon fare any better. Ensnared by a constricting coil of rope, he was plucked from his mount and deposited half-strangled and winded upon the trail.

Leaving Dusty to attend to the men on the box, Kiowa gave his attention to the rider who was beyond the reach of the ropers. He saw the man's head and torso swivelling in his direction and the mouth dropped open in amazement. Letting out a Kiowa war whoop, the Texan hurled himself from the wagon. Spreading apart his legs, he passed them on either side of the bewildered Irishman. Even if the other had intended to try to use his rifle, the opportunity was denied him.

Looking as if he was sitting on the man's lap, Kiowa bore him from his horse. They went down together, but Kiowa was expecting that it would happen. So he alighted on his feet and painlessly. Less fortunate, the Irishman smashed on to the unyielding surface. Nor did his troubles end there. Still straddling his victim, Kiowa let his rump descend with all his weight on to the man's chest. Although Kiowa was ready to continue his assault, he found that it was not

* A full description of the hooley-ann throw is given in *Trail Boss.*

necessary. The impact had already rendered the Yankee soldier unconscious.

Alarmed by the sudden disruption of what had been, up to that moment, a most pleasant and uneventful journey, the driver also started to stand up. Dusty did not give him the chance to do more than elevate his rump from the seat. Dropping to sit on the front arch of the canopy's support, he placed the sole of his right foot against the man's shoulder and shoved. Letting out a wail and dropping the reins of the four-horse team, the driver shot head-long from the box and sprawled downwards helplessly. Although the small Texan leapt after the man, it was not to continue the attack. Ignoring his victim, he ran to the heads of the two leading horses so as to get them under control and prevent any tendency to bolt.

Being dissatisfied with the part assigned to him, especially as he saw the other three men's ropes flying accurately and knew that he would not need to use his own, Sandy McGraw sought for another way to help. The solution was simple enough, if risky. Dropping his rope, he darted along the edge of the rim and leapt outwards.

Landing on the canopy, just after Dusty and Kiowa had quit it, Sandy slid recklessly from the top to the ground. The driver was struggling to rise and the youngster darted towards him as he shook his head in a dazed manner. Driving a kick against the man's temple, Sandy ended any danger of intervention from that source. However, a glance around showed that there were others requiring attention if the attack was to succeed.

'Get the white bastards, Rastus!' Billy Jack yelled, having watched Sandy's departure. 'Take that whiskey!'

'Ah'll do that, Sambo!' the young soldier answered, retaining sufficient presence of mind – despite his excitement – to respond in the correct fashion. He drew the 1860 Army Colt from its holster, but grasped it around the cylinder and with the butt ahead of his hand. 'Ah sure likes white fellers' whiskey!'

Leaping to his feet, Kiowa scooped up his victim's discarded rifle. He listened to the conversation and swung his gaze to discover where he would be most usefully employed.

The sergeant and the other point rider were now seated side by side on the trail. While the former tried to free his arms, the latter clutched wildly at the rope that was threatening to strangle him. On the rim, Billy Jack and the two privates braced themselves and kept the loops tight.

Being unable to see the last rider. Kiowa ran around the rear of the wagon. Although unhorsed, partially choked and winded the Irishman had managed to land on his feet and was jerking at the rope. Hearing Kiowa approaching the man turned. In this he was hampered by his captor manipulating the rope in a way that hindered his movements. Having no room to manoeuvre Kiowa raised the borrowed rifle above his head in both hands. Down it whipped, the butt catching the soldier on the forehead. Blood gushed from the gash it caused and its recipient reeled. For a moment the rope held him erect. Slackening his grip, the Texan allowed his captive to collapse limply.

Hurdling the man's motionless body, Kiowa ran forward. He saw that Sandy had already reached the sergeant and, delivering the base of the Colt's butt in a hammer-like blow to the top of the non-com's skull, knocked him senseless.

'You have de last one, Bones!' Sandy offered, pointing to where the remaining Yankee was struggling to rise, get free, or do anything that might save him from his companions' fates.

Advancing, while the man on the rim tugged repeatedly on the rope and kept his catch off balance, Kiowa once again used the rifle's butt. He hit the Irishman behind the head and ended all the resistance – such as it had been – from the whiskey wagon's escort.

'Good going!' Dusty praised, looking around to make sure that only his own men could hear him. Satisfied that the Yankees were all unconscious, he continued with orders. 'Sergeant, get our horses up here. Kiowa, Sandy, move those two out of the way. Then get the wagon moving.'

'It worked, Mr. Fog,' Sandy enthused as he bent to remove the rope from the sergeant's neck.

'So far,' the small Texan replied. 'But we've a fair way to go yet.'

There were, Dusty realized, still things that could go wrong; but at least the first portion of his plan had been successfully accomplished.

CHAPTER NINE

LEISURELY tossing pieces of wood into the cresset before the guard tent, the Negro sentry became aware of movement on the edge of the woodland some distance from the camp. Reaching for his Sharps breech-loading rifle, he looked to where a wagon emerged along the trail that led to Herber Springs. At first, he saw no cause for alarm. It was the usual type of four-horse vehicle used in considerable numbers by the Quartermaster Corps. However, he did not return to his work of feeding the fire. He enjoyed being in a position where he could order white people around; even if only to the extent of making one halt and submit to his questioning at a guard post.

Bringing his rifle into the ready position, the sentry prepared to challenge the driver. He was debating whether to make the approaching man halt the wagon some yards away, dismount and advance to be recognized, then he stared harder. Suddenly a feeling of superstitious fear bit at him. Although the four horses continued to walk towards the camp, the wagon's box was empty.

There was no driver!

'Hey, serge!' the sentry yelled. 'Come out here and take a look at this!'

'What's up?' was the reply from the guard tent.

'You come and see!' the sentry insisted.

Followed by the other occupants of the tent, a burly Negro sergeant strode out. None of them were armed and their eruption lacked any suggestion of military purpose or precision.

'What do you wan—?' the sergeant began, then he too saw the wagon. 'Now where the hell's that come from?'

'I dunno,' admitted the sentry. 'It just come along the trail with nobody driving it.'

'We'd best fetch it in,' the sergeant decided, while a low muttering rose from the man behind him. None of them moved, however, and his voice took on a harsher note. 'You heard me! Go fetch it in.'

'Looks like it's coming, fetched or not,' the sentry pointed out. 'Ain't no call to go and meet it.'

'I ain't in this man's Army to go fetching no wagon,' stated another of the guard, as the sergeant's eyes swung in his direction. 'Especially when they comes from nowhere, without nobody driving them.'

Seeing the lights of the camp, the experienced horses sensed that their hard day's work might soon be ended. So they kept walking towards the soldiers.

'Maybe we should get the officer-of-the-day,' suggested a third enlisted man, sensing that he might be called up to go near the mysterious wagon. 'Him being so well eddicated 'n' all, he'll know for sure what to do.'

'Where the hell is he?' demanded the sergeant, seeing that he might be able to pass the buck to his superior.

'He went down the valley,' supplied the sentry. 'Allowed that, with all their officers likely in town for the meeting, he'd best go and make sure them Mick-landers's doing their work properly. He reckons they's all likely to be sleeping if he don't watch 'em.'

None of the men thought it unusual that their officer-of-the-day should take it upon himself to check on the behaviour of the Irish sentries, nor that he would inform one of their number of his suspicions. As an aid to winning the Negroes' confidence, their officers invariably spoke disparagingly about the abilities and trustworthy qualities of white soldiers. So, although the officer-of-the-day was only accepting an invitation to have supper with his opposite number at the remount depot, he could not resist the opportunity to ingratiate himself with one of his men.

'What're we going to do about that thing, serge?' a soldier wanted to know.

The question posed a problem for its recipient. In their desire to 'prove' their beliefs in racial equality, the officers had taken their Negro sergeant major and carefully selected sergeants to the meeting in Searcy. Wishing to create a good impression, they had picked all the most responsible and capable of the non-coms. So the sergeant had nobody to whom he could turn for guidance, or who would have given the correct advice if he had asked for it. He held his own rank more on muscular prowess than intelligence or military knowledge.

While the men had been talking and the sergeant was trying to reach a decision, the wagon had continued to draw nearer. Studying it, the sergeant became aware that the reins were fastened to the brake's handle. A moment later, he noticed something familiar standing on the otherwise unoccupied box. Stepping forward, he reached towards the head of the near-side lead horse. The tired animals came to a stop. Striding by them, he detected an aroma which he identified.

'It was spirits's caused this to come here,' the sergeant announced, reaching over to take the bottle of whiskey from the driver's seat. 'But they was this kind.'

'How d'you mean,' asked the sentry, still eyeing the wagon warily.

'The driver's likely been guzzling this and fell off,' the sergeant explained, drawing the cork from the bottle and taking a long drink. 'Yes sir. I'll bet that's all's's happened.'

'Is that for-real whiskey?' the sentry inquired hopefully.

'Well now,' answered the sergeant. 'I'll just take another pull to make sure of it.'

'I'll help you make sure,' offered a soldier, running the tip of his tongue over his lips. 'Happen you're so minded.'

'Wonder what's in that wagon,' another went on, when the sergeant declined to reply.

'Take a look and find out,' suggested a third.

For a moment nobody offered to follow the suggestion. Then curiosity overrode the sentry's superstitious awe.

Resting the rifle against the side of the wagon, he scrambled on to the box. There was sufficient light from the cresset for him to see inside. The interior was packed with boxes and he was not left in doubt as to some of their contents. Several at the front had had their tops removed. He could see that they were filled with bottles or jugs of the kind used for holding whiskey.

'Look at these!' the sentry whooped, turning with a bottle in each hand. 'It's full of 'em, boys.'

Excited comments arose from the rest of the guard. Jumping to the ground, the sentry passed one bottle to a friend and opened the other.

'Maybe you'd best let me try it, Ben,' hinted the man who had offered to help the sergeant.

'You get your own,' the sentry replied. 'There's plenty more where this come from.'

'Who do you reckon it belongs to?' queried a soldier who had been silent up to that point, looking at the sergeant.

'They do say finders's keepers,' another man pointed out, watching the helpful one boarding the wagon. 'Ain't that right, serge?'

'That's what they say,' declared the non-com.

Although the sergeant could guess at who owned the whiskey – for the Irishmen had not attempted to keep its coming a secret – he refused to make his knowledge public. Like the majority of his regiment, he disliked white men and accompanying the Chicago All-Irish Volunteers had done nothing to make him change his feelings. So he had no intention of returning the consignment to its owners.

Having been granted what they chose to regard as permission, the members of the guard who were not already in possession of bottles swarmed around the wagon. Attracted by their excited shouts, more men hurried up. Hearing the news, they clamoured to be allowed to share in the fortunate arrival.

Standing just inside the fringe of the woodland, Dusty Fog, Billy Jack and the other Texans, except for Kiowa, watched what was happening.

'Looks like they're doing what we want them to,' the lanky sergeant commented, although his tones suggested that the Negroes' behaviour was a tragedy and not a successful part of their arrangements. 'Now some of their officers're sure to come, make 'em put it all back and take it to them Irish jaspers.'

'If they do,' Dusty threatened, 'I'll have something to say at the court martial.'

'What court martial?' Billy Jack inquired.

'The one I'll get you for wishing it to happen,' the small Texan explained, then became more serious. 'Anyways, I'm banking on them all, except the officer-of-the-day, being at the meeting in Searcy.'

'It's possible,' Billy Jack conceded, but contrived to imply that he did not expect it to happen. 'Any time the Commanding General comes a-visiting, every officer busts a gut trying to get to meet him. There's some's calls it "butt-licking".'

'But not you?' Dusty challenged, continuing to watch the camp.

'Me!' the sergeant yelped indignantly. 'Why Mr. Fog, sir, as if *I'd* say such a thing! I'm too loyal—'

'So you keep telling me,' Dusty drawled. 'But I notice that you always seem to know about things like that.'

'Anyways,' Billy Jack said, obviously wanting to change *that* subject. 'The officer-of-the-day'll come and make 'em give it back.'

'Or maybe a swarm of diamondbacks'll come and spook the team, so they bolt across the valley,' Dusty suggested, glancing at his sergeant.

'Knowing *my* luck, it could happen,' Billy Jack warned, wishing that he had thought of such a contingency.

'One thing I know,' Dusty declared, in tones redolent with mock resignation. 'If we get out of this alive, I'm going to find me a more cheerful sergeant.'

'That don't worry me none,' Billy Jack answered. 'With *me* along, we ain't likely to get back alive.'

Watching the Negroes boarding and unloading the

wagon, while others opened the boxes, or distributed the contents, Dusty heard chuckles from his men at Billy Jack's comment. The small Texan grinned. He knew that Billy Jack used the predictions of doom and disaster to help keep up the enlisted men's spirits, or relieve their anxieties in dangerous situations. So he had started to go along with his sergeant, realizing what good morale-boosters such conversations could be. In fact, he admitted to himself, they even helped him in times of stress.

'They're sure getting liquored up,' commented one of the veterans, a touch wistfully.

'I'd sooner we was drinking it than them,' the second old hand went on.

'All we'd've got out of it'd've been sore heads in the morning,' Billy Jack pointed out. 'This way it'll be the Yankees's gets 'em.'

'One thing's for sure,' Dusty drawled. 'Unless their officer-of-the-day arrives real soon, he'll not be able to make them obey him. Most of them'll be too drunk to take orders.'

Dusty had not based his strategy upon ideas of Negroes being naturally drunken, shiftless, or irresponsible. The Hardin, Fog and Blaze clan had never owned slaves, nor had there been any in the surrounding counties. The clan's participation in the War, on the side of the Confederacy, had been caused by a belief in the inalienable right of any State to secede from the Union if its interests and policies should prove incompatible with those of the Federal Government.*
So, until he had joined the Texas Light Cavalry in Arkansas, Dusty's contacts with coloured people had been few and, if anything, would have led him to form exactly the opposite opinion regarding their behviour.

What the small Texan had counted on was his growing

* This was the major cause of the War Between The States, although the anti-slavery issue was much enlarged upon and exploited in the North to give the white, working class population – who would have been unlikely to understand the implications of the Secessionist issue – an acceptable reason – that they would be helping to set free the poor, ill-used, down-trodden slaves – for enlisting and fighting against their countrymen.

knowledge of men; particularly men who, while serving as soldiers, found themselves away from their homes and removed from their accepted codes of social conduct.

From the sentry's comments, Dusty had deduced that he was completely biased against Negroes, but, as became a good 'one hundred and *ten* per cent'* American, would have been no less prejudiced against any other racial, or religious group.

However, Dusty had decided that the soldier's comments about the Negroes' lack of discipline and military skill might have some basis of truth. Not because they were Negroes, but through a lack of sound, experienced leadership.

Any regiment, the young lieutenant had been taught, was only as good as its officers made it. The correct kind of training and discipline, carried out by officers who had shown themselves to be capable and to know their work, or who took the right kind of interest in the enlisted men's health and welfare, was what built *esprit de corps* and turned a bunch of civilians into a fighting regiment. The Texas Light Cavalry was commanded by officers who possessed those qualities.

According to the sentry, the Negroes' white officers were 'soft shells' who had come into the Army straight from college; their commissions having been handed to them despite their lack of military abilities, because nobody else could be found to take on the task of training the coloured soldiers. That was possible, Dusty had believed, for he had heard that career officers fought shy of serving in the few volunteer regiments of Negroes that had been formed. So the Union Army's top brass might have been willing to take applicants, regardless of knowledge or aptitude.

With that in mind, Dusty had made his plans and gambled on the general lack of discipline prevalent in many volunteer outfits on both sides. Appointed through political

* The story is that, in the course of an argument with an Irishman, an Italian immigrant stated that he was one hundred per cent American. Not to be outdone, the Irishman replied that he was a one hundred and ten per cent American.

or social influence, far too many of the officers had proved lacking in the ability to control the enlisted men. Dusty had believed that this was the case with the Negroes. He had also decided that similar conditions existed amongst the Chicago All-Irish Volunteers. With the absence of most of the officers, the scheme ought to have a good chance of working.

After the arrival of the horses, Dusty had dispatched Billy Jack and the three veterans to escort Sandy with the wagon. They had orders to make the best possible speed, especially while in the vicinity of the cliff. After their companions' departure, the small Texan and Kiowa had tied up but did not gag the unconscious men. Ensuring that the knots were such that the soldiers could release themselves, after a struggle, the Texans had returned to the rim and awaited developments.

By the time the Irishmen had recovered consciousness, the wagon and riders were out of sight and beyond hearing distance. So were the Yankees' mounts, which had bolted during the excitement of the attack. From the profane and lurid comments overheard by the listening Texans, their bait had been swallowed without reservation. The Irishmen were convinced that they had been attacked by members of the Negro regiment. What was more, the furious men had sworn vengeance and, having escaped from their bonds, had started to walk as fast as they could in the direction of their camp.

Once that had happened, Dusty and Kiowa had collected their horses, which had been left at a suitable distance. Then they had separated. Kiowa was to keep the Irishmen under surveillance, while Dusty had pushed on to rejoin the rest of the detail. On his doing so, they had turned off of the trail, making a detour to avoid the Chicago All-Irish Volunteers' camp, and had crossed the valley without being seen by the occupants of the remount depot. With that accomplished, they had arranged for the driverless wagon to go to the Negroes' quarters.

While all had gone well so far, Dusty knew that complete success was still a long way from being assured. However, the prospects were constantly improving. As yet, no officer had made an appearance to investigate the commotion. The longer the arrival of someone in authority was delayed, the smaller grew his chances of being able to accomplish anything with the men.

Laughter, shouts, singing and other evidences of merriment rolled in an increasing volume from the Negroes' camp. More men, drawn from their tents by the noises, joined the milling group about the wagon. Bottles were continually being opened, sampled and passed from hand to hand.

Turning his attention to the other side of the valley, Dusty used the field glasses that he had been loaned before leaving the regiment. He could see figures gathering to look in the Negroes' direction. Even if the Irishmen could not see the wagon, they would be wondering what was causing all the excitement.

The call of a whip-poor-will, repeated twice, reached Dusty's ears from somewhere to his rear. Billy Jack replied in the same manner and, a few seconds later, Kiowa joined them.

'Those jaspers we caught should just about be at their camp, Mr. Fog,' the dark-faced soldier stated. 'They didn't see anybody on the way and, like you told me, I left 'em when they got close to the camp.'

'Then we ought to be seeing something hap—' Dusty began.

At that moment, from across the valley, came yells of anger. The men who had been watching the Negroes were turning to run into the centre of their camp, while others poured from the tents. Louder and more menacing rose the roaring of voices as the crowd grew in size.

Scanning the opposite side of the half-mile wide valley, Dusty tried to discover exactly what was happening. At that distance, even in the bright moonlight, he could not make out the figures clearly enough to hope to identify any of them. Yet he felt sure that the centre of the attraction must be his victims telling their story. Everything now depended on the reaction of their audience. More particularly, the continuation of the affair hinged upon the type of men who had gained promotion as the regiment's non-commissioned officers.

From what Devlin had told him, Dusty assumed that promotion in the Chicago All-Irish Volunteers – at least as far as the enlisted men were concerned – had been mainly on physical qualifications. Working on the principle that a non-com would need to be able to enforce his orders with his fists – regardless of other, more suitable military qualities – the colonel had selected men capable of doing it. In which case, Dusty was gambling on the non-coms being roughnecks more interested in the recovery of 'the O'Bannion's' gift than the maintenance of discipline. If the sentry had spoken the truth, the only officer in the camp was not the kind who could control the enraged soldiers.

The soldiers were scattering, making for their quarters on the run!

Although the rest of Dusty's party did not have field glasses, they could discern enough to see the latest development. The three older soldiers exchanged glances, while Sandy's face showed his disappointment at what he regarded as a sign that the rest of the plan would not work. Darting a look at Dusty, Billy Jack said nothing. The sergeant knew when *not* to make comments on failure, or gloomy predictions of mishaps.

Then the Irishmen started to reappear and assemble at the top of the slope. Through his glasses, Dusty could see the reason for their departures. Every man was carrying his firearm and had his weapon belt strapped about his waist.

'They're coming!' Sandy ejaculated, watching the mass of men pouring towards the bottom of the valley 'That's 'cause they've seen us bunch and know what we've done,' Billy Jack declared. 'Now they're coming all mean 'n' riled up to catch us.'

Detecting the undertone of relief in the sergeant's doleful voice, Dusty grinned. Billy Jack had been just as concerned as he had by the Irishmen's departure, but now realized why it had happened.

Wondering what the occupants of the remount depot were making of the new disturbance, Dusty turned his field glasses in their direction. Previous checks had shown the sentries and soldiers who would be in charge of the horses were looking towards the rims, trying to discover what all the commotion was about. There was more activity now. The sentries were deserting their posts and converging on the mass of advancing men. The remainder of the guard came from their accommodation and made for the slope. Curiosity was causing the depot's staff to accompany the other enlisted men. Three officers, one wearing a cavalryman's uniform, rushed from a tent.

There were shouted explanations, followed by bellows of rage from the men of the guard. Even the depot's staff joined in the mob, caught up by excitement and a desire to do something, anything, to relieve the boredom of their existence.

Yelling commands, the three officers ran to confront the soldiers. On strode the enlisted men. One of the infantry lieutenants, Dusty could not tell which – although he guessed, correctly, that he was from the Negro regiment – tried to draw a revolver. It was a very bad mistake, with the mood the Irishmen were in. Before the weapon was clear of its holster, several soldiers charged. Rifle butts swung and all of the officers were battered to the ground. Forwards swept the crowd, leaving the trio of motionless figures as the only human occupants of the depot.

Directing his glasses back to the Negroes' camp, Dusty saw that they had not been unaware of what was happening. Probably a number of them had suspected, or been sure, to whom the wagon had been intended to be delivered. However, it having come into their possession – and mindful of its owners' animosity towards them – they were disinclined to hand it over. Especially when the Irishmen were clearly coming in such a hostile manner to try to recover it.

Already many of the Negroes had collected their weapons

and others were hurrying to arm themselves. The sight of them standing at the top of the slope, holding their rifles, was all the inducement required by the Irishmen. Weapons on both sides were raised. Just who fired the first shot was uncertain. It could have come from either group and it was followed almost immediately by a ragged volley. Lead slashed up and down the slope, with men falling dead or wounded as some of it found its way into flesh.

'All right,' Dusty said, as the Irishmen started to take cover half-way up the slope. 'Let's go.'

With the Yankee soldiers engrossed in firing at each other, Dusty and his men made only a short detour before reaching the corrals unobserved. Working fast, they opened the gates and drove out the already disturbed and milling animals. With horses and mules bolting along the bottom of the valley, the Texans set fire to the stacks of fodder. Still without interruption from the fighting soldiers, they collected their own mounts and rode away.

'Did you ever see the beat of it?' demanded one of the veterans. 'We've not only chased off all ole "Cussing" Culver's hosses, we've got his fellers killing each other off for us.'

'That sure was slick figuring, Mr. Fog,' the second veteran went on.

'I can't see them mules going far,' Billy Jack protested. 'The Yankees'll likely get most of 'em back comes morning.'

'They won't get many of the hosses,' the third old hand pointed out. 'Most of 'em'll be headed back home.'

'I don't reckon there'll be any of the hay and grain saved,' Sandy McGraw continued, staring in frank admiration at the small Texan as he rode ahead of the detail. 'Them fellers're too busy shooting each other up to think about putting the fires out.'

'Thought you said his fool notion'd never work, Tom,' the first veteran drawled to the second, lowering his voice in the hope that Dusty would not hear.

'You didn't think it would, either,' protested the doubter.
'I ain't gainsaying it,' admitted the first speaker. 'That's one smart young feller we've got bossing us.'

Listening to the words, Dusty felt a surge of pride and satisfaction. He knew his actions that night would go a long way – once told back at the regiment – towards gaining his acceptance as a leader.

While Dusty did not know it, he had struck an even more important blow for the Confederate cause than merely scattering the remounts and destroying the fodder. He realized that the morale of the two regiments would be adversely affected for a long time to come, but did not visualize the full ramifications.

On learning of the incident, General Culver realized the delicate nature of the situation. There had been no hope of hushing it up and the respective colonels were each equally determined that his regiment should not be blamed. So Culver was compelled, reluctantly, to hold a court of inquiry in an attempt to discover what had occurred. He soon saw that there was no hope of establishing the guilt or innocence of either outfit. However, feelings were still running so high between the Irishmen and the Negroes – for both had lost a number of men – that Culver knew he must take some form of action.

Deciding on what type of measures to take had been fraught with difficulties. All the other white outfits under Culver's command tended to side with the Chicago All-Irish Volunteers and were expressing distrust of the coloured soldiers. There was one snag to Culver taking the obvious step. The Negroes' officers had important connections in the political world. So he realized that they could make a lot of trouble for him if he 'victimized' their regiment by sending it away.

Showing a flair for diplomacy, Culver solved the problem by ordering both regiments to return East; where they could 'recruit and bring themselves up to fighting strength'. While that had, at least, saved everybody's face, Culver was left with a far reduced force when he commenced his offensive and could have used the departed soldiers.

Dusty received considerable acclaim for his actions, on returning to the Texas Light Cavalry, and Kiowa Cotton was promoted to corporal for his work as a scout. During the next weeks, through the Yankees' offensive and until the Battle at Martin's Mill, the small Texan worked under Captain von Hertz's direct command and was given no further opportunity to distinguish himself. However, he had continued to hold the enlisted men's esteem.

That was to become important!

Part Four

THE BATTLE OF MARTIN'S MILL, cont'd.

CHAPTER TEN

ONCE clear of the trees, Sergeant Major Goering halted his horse and watched Company 'C' passing by. Despite his misgivings regarding Mr. Fog's decision to ignore their dead captain's plan for making the attack, he wanted to be sure that the men were adopting the echelon formation as required by the young first lieutenant. Fortunately, it was a drill that the Company had frequently carried out. So the men knew what was expected of them without needing long explanations.

Although the two columns were parallel, the men in them formed a staggered pattern. The first and second men of the right hand file rode with a distance of about three yards between their horses and the leading man of the other column positioned his mount opposite the gap. A similar formation extended along the length of the Company so that, when they turned to face the enemy, every man would have an unrestricted field of fire.

When satisfied that all was in order, the sergeant major galloped after and joined his youthful commanding officer.

Accompanied by Sandy McGraw and the bugler, Dusty Fog rode to the right of the Company's line of march. The small Texan had put aside his thoughts of the past and was concentrating on the work at hand. At his signal, the other two slowed their mounts and allowed the columns to go by.

'Tell the men to leave their revolvers holstered, sergeant major,' Dusty requested, as Goering rode up. 'I don't want any shooting until I give the word.'

'Yo!' responded the sergeant major and raised his voice to relay the order.

Dusty left Goering to attend to such details, giving his attention to other matters. Watching the Lancers urging their mounts to a gallop, the youngster wondered if he should increase his Company's pace. After at moment's thought, he decided against giving the command. He wanted to have the men under complete control, which was never easy once they started to gallop, and for the horses to be as fresh as possible when they were required to charge.

Would he be in time if he held the Company to a trot?

There certainly would not be much in it, but Dusty was gambling that they would.

The Lancers sure looked mighty impressive and menacing. Ahead of the leading wave galloped a major and two lieutenants. Unlike their men, they – and the other officers – were armed with revolvers and sabres. They had each drawn the latter weapon and were waving it while encouraging their followers. The enlisted men carried nine foot long lances, made of Norwegian fir and tipped with diamond-shaped, needle-pointed, steel tips; but had no other weapons.

That last point was one of the factors upon which Dusty was basing his strategy. Another, which he had hoped might happen, was already starting to take place. The Lancers had commenced their advance in a kind of triple echelon formation. Already the lines were growing ragged and the men had started to close together as their speed increased. Unless they opened out again, they would be badly bunched before they reached their objective.

Looking from his point of vantage higher up the slope, Dusty decided that only the captain in command of the rear company appeared to have noticed the danger. The youngster could see him yelling and signalling for his men to spread out, or drop back a short distance and regroup. Apparently the words were falling on deaf ears.

Dusty swung his gaze from the Lancers, to make an examination of the rest of the battleground.

At the mountain battery, Captain Staunce threw a glance towards the Lancers. Then he turned his attention to the four howitzers and left control of the small defensive party to his capable sergeant major. They would be an inconsiderable factor in protecting the little guns, but their presence was good for the crews' morale. The safety of the battery really depended on Company 'C' of the Texas Light Cavalry – and they would be outnumbered by around three to one.

All in all, it was a very dangerous situation. Staunce knew that the success of the Confederate attack depended on his howitzers silencing the Yankees' three Vandenburg Volley Guns. He had complete faith in his men's ability to carry out their duty, unless the Lancers prevented them from doing it. In that event, Staunce hoped he would be killed and not captured. Although he wore the uniform of a Confederate States' artillery captain, he was not a native of that country.

Not long past his twentieth birthday, Douglas St. John Staunce was the son of Britain's leading artillerist. From his father, he had learned the art of handling cannon and the War Between The States had seemed like a good opportunity for him to gain practical experience in the field. Like Staunce, the men of the battery were British. Veterans of the Crimean War, who had been disenchanted with civilian life in England, he had gathered them when a group of cotton manufacturers had financed the battery and offered him command. Trained in the British fashion of discipline backed by fair play and a sense of humour, they had become a crack outfit. Staunce knew that he could depend upon them to do their best, even without the knowledge of their fate if they should be captured.

'Fire!' Staunce barked, when each piece's gunner had reported that it was trained and ready.

Four hands tugged sharply at lanyards, causing friction

primers* to ignite and touch off the powder charges. With almost simultaneous bellows, the howitzers flung their loads into the air. Standing upwind, so as to be clear of the smoke, Staunce watched for the results of the shots. They proved to be good. Two of the shells bracketed the Vandenburg farthest from the battery, killing most of its crew when they exploded. The third and fourth shells landed close enough to the remaining Volley Guns to make the men handling them dive hurriedly for shelter.

'Reload!' Staunce yelled. 'Go to it, lads! Independent rapid fire!'

While the gunners changed the friction primers and connected the lanyards, the number two men sponged out the barrels of the pieces. They used water out of the buckets which had been transported suspended under the carriages and filled on arrival from the men's canteens. The third member of each crew dashed to the battery's two-wheeled caisson, of the type known as the 'prairie ammunition cart'. The lid of its forward chest was open and the sergeant in charge handed out 'fixed'† twelve-pounder rounds to replenish the howitzers.

Allowing his men to carry out their duties, Staunce looked towards the woods. To his relief, he found that Company 'C' was on the move. However, von Hertz was nowhere in sight. Instead young Dusty Fog appeared to be in command. Young, maybe, but Staunce did not doubt that – no matter what had happened to the captain – the cavalrymen were being led in a satisfactory manner.

Staunce did not watch the Texans for long. Satisfied that they were coming to his aid, he devoted his attention to the working of his howitzers.

Allowing half of the men to go by, with Billy Jack controlling their speed at the front and Sergeant 'Stormy' Weather bringing up the rear, Dusty and his party increased their horses' speed to match that of the rest of the Company.

* A description of how a friction primer works is given in: *The Hooded Riders*.

† 'Fixed' round: one with the cartridge bag attached to the shot.

Without waiting for orders, leaving his superior to concentrate on the tactical situation, Goering told the men opposite his party to open up a gap. That would ensure they were able to start shooting once the turn had been made.

Watching the Lancers, Dusty compared their pace to that of his men. He also gauged the distances involved and knew there would be little margin for error.

Thinking only of the relative positions of his Company, the battery and the Lancers, Dusty guided the Texans into the narrowing gap between the former and the latter. He could sense a growing tension among his men and saw that all of them were watching the Lancers. Many, especially the younger, less-experienced soldiers, were fingering the butts of their revolvers. However, so far they were showing no signs of disobeying, or anticipating his orders.

Dusty knew that the situation could easily change. If one of the anxious, or over-eager, riders should turn on the enemy prematurely, others were sure to follow his example. Only with a massed, concerted effort could Company 'C' hope to achieve anything against the Yankees' superior numbers.

Everything hinged upon how much faith the men had in Dusty's judgment.

What to do for the best was not an easy decision for a young officer, freshly thrust into command, to have to make. Especially when the future of the Confederate States' Army of Arkansas and North Texas hung precariously in the balance and his actions could easily tilt the scales in the wrong direction.

The moment had come for Company 'C' to turn and face the enemy!

'Columns right, yo!' Dusty called, reining his bay around until its head was pointing at the horse ridden by the Lancers' commanding officer.

The superb horsemanship of the Texans soon became evident. Rider after rider swung his mount to the right. While they did not make their turns like puppets coupled to a single string, they came around sufficiently in unison to form the solid body that Dusty required for his purposes.

In a few seconds, deftly controlling the restlessness caused to their horses by the mountain battery's howitzers bellowing not too far away, the twin columns that had been passing across the Lancers' front had changed into two staggered lines heading towards the blue-clad soldiers.

'Rear column forward!' Goering reminded in a booming tone, looking back across his shoulder.

Urging their horses to a faster pace, the men at the rear advanced until they filled the gaps in the front line. Without needing orders. Sandy McGraw and the bugler slowed down until they too occupied their positions in the Company. Dusty and Goering continued to stay ahead of the enlisted men, as was their right and duty. It was good for the soldiers' morale to see their superiors in front of them as they rushed to meet an enemy.

With the Company turned towards the Lancers, Dusty prepared to carry out the next part of his plan. Nodding in confirmation to the sergeant major's unasked question, he knotted the split-ended reins to his saddle's horn.

'Secure your reins!' Goering bellowed.

One of the drills carried out regularly at Colonel Blaze's instigation had been much enjoyed by the enlisted men, few of whom had bothered to consider the full perils that would be entailed by doing it in action. It was to make a charge with a weapon in each hand – they could be two revolvers, or a handgun and a sabre – while guiding the horses with knee-pressure instead of using the reins.

That was the means by which Dusty hoped to prevent the Lancers from overrunning Captain Staunce's battery.

While the Texans duplicated Dusty's actions, Goering and the other Germans – who were still using their McClelland saddles and U.S. Army bridles – merely dropped their one-piece reins over the pommels. Then they all awaited the next command, which would be to arm themselves.

It did not come!

Instead, the men of Company 'C' continued to rush with empty hands towards the mass of charging Lancers.

CHAPTER ELEVEN

RIDING alongside Second Lieutenant Charles William Henry Blaze, with the six privates following close behind, Corporal Vern Hassle could sense restlessness and tension in the air. The white-haired old timer guessed that the rest of the detail were disturbed and anxious over the change in leadership. One thought was uppermost in each of the enlisted men's minds. They would rather have been under the command of Mr. Fog while handling such a tricky, dangerous and important assignment.

Although he did not show it, Red Blaze was equally aware of the five soldiers' misgivings. He had noticed them studying him in a somewhat critical manner when he had joined them and had known why. He was popular with the enlisted men, due to his amiable nature, good humour and general disregard for strict military discipline, but he lacked his small cousin's personality and ability to inspire confidence. The detail had expected to be led by Dusty Fog and were dubious about their chances now that Red had taken charge.

As Billy Jack had surmised that day outside Arkadelphia, Red was liked by the men of Company 'C', but he had not come anywhere near to gaining the kind of respect earned by Dusty Fog. There had been too many incidents which, while amusing, were not likely to have increased his prestige as an officer.

Soon after his arrival at the regiment, Red had been told to take half of the Company on skirmishing training. All the men concerned had been veterans, with considerable practical experience in that type of duty. So Red had decided that it would be a waste of time and effort to put them through their paces. Captain von Hertz had found the party lounging at ease in a hollow, which had not enamoured him towards the young red-head.

However, after Dusty had explained that an officer must carry out orders if he expected the enlisted men to do as he told them, Red had never repeated that mistake. From then on, he had performed his duties well enough, but it had taken time for him to recover from the consequences of his misguided leniency. At first, the men had expected it to be continued. Eventually they had realized that when he gave an order, he intended to have it obeyed. Unfortunately, he had had a tendency to show in an unfavourable light on other counts. For one thing, if there was a fight when he was around, he was certain to become involved in it.

Red's willingness to shed his jacket and waive all thoughts of differences in rank if challenged or provoked had earned him a reputation – particularly as he had proved to be very adept in all aspects of rough-house brawling and more than able to hold his own in a fight – but it was not one to foster faith in his ability as a military leader. Rather he was considered as a brave, hot-headed, impulsive, if likeable youngster who occasionally said, or did, rash things on the spur of the moment and frequently regretted them later.

Despite his disappointment at having to miss out on the opportunity to side his Cousin Dusty in what ought to be a memorable fight, Red fully realized the importance of his mission. If he failed, the assault would be of little use. With the bridge over the Ouachita River destroyed, the supply column could not cross and would be trapped by the Yankee Army.

It was the first time since Red had joined the Texas Light Cavalry that he had been trusted with a task involving so much responsibility. The thought of the consequences of failure had a sobering effect upon his normally ebullient spirits. He was grimly determined that he would carry out his duty to the best of his ability.

'What d'you-all reckon's waiting for us, Mr. Blaze?' Hassle asked, having drawn certain conclusions regarding the young officer's fitness for the work ahead and wanting to try to verify them.

'A whole mess of Yankees,' Red replied.

'Any notions on where they're likely to be?' Hassle wanted to know.

'Was it me,' Red answered, I'd have vedettes spread through the woods all the way to the river, but hold the main bunch somewhere close to the middle so they're handy for getting to wherever they're needed.'

'Could be,' drawled the ancient corporal, having made much the same deduction. He was aware that the other men were gathering closer to hear what was being said and continued, 'Do you reckon we'll have enough time to keep hid in these woods, all the way down to them along the river?'

'Nope,' Red admitted. 'So we'll only keep in them until we can cut across behind the Lancers.'

As he spoke, Red surreptitiously studied the reactions of the enlisted men. The privates were all looking at Hassle and Red felt vaguely annoyed by their apparent need to seek the corporal's opinion. Then he remembered that, in the early days, the soldiers had acted in a similar manner when Dusty had made a decision.

It was, Red realized, up to him to prove that he was worthy of command. Only after he had achieved that would the men accept his decisions. He also guessed that, at that moment, how the corporal responded to his suggestion was important. The privates were looking to Hassle for guidance.

'I was hoping's you'd say that, Mr. Blaze,' the non-com declared. 'Likely them jaspers by the river'll not be expecting us to come at 'em from that way.'

Guiding his party along the fringe of the woodland, Red kept them amongst the trees. He watched the Lancers and, when he considered it safe to do so, turned at an angle down the slope. On riding into the open, he experienced a moment of uncertainty and wondered if he had appeared too soon. However, if any of the Lancers saw his detail, they gave no indication of it. Instead of a section being dispatched to intercept the eight Texans, they all continued to rush in the direction of the mountain battery.

With that particular danger having gone by, Red led his men along a line which would allow them to reach the woods fringing the river; but keeping them beyond the range of the rifles held by the foot soldiers in the trenches.

'Just look at them Lancers go,' suggested one of the detail, as they were approaching the trees. 'Anybody'd think they didn't like us Johnny Rebs, way they're taking on.'

'Our boys'll sure take the curl out of their tails,' enthused another. 'Trust Mr. Fog to see to that.'

'Wished I was with the Company,' yet a third declared.

'Now me,' remarked the first speaker, who went by the name of Wilbur and was the youngest of the enlisted men. 'I'd say we was safer away from such dangerous fellers. I'd surely hate to have one of 'em trying to poke me with his sticker.'

'That don't worry me none,' grunted the third speaker. 'They'd have to come close enough to do the sticking first. Which me 'n' my ole Army Colt'd have a whole heap to say about *that.*'

'Talking about Army Colts,' the fourth member of the detail put in. 'If I was with the Company, I'd sure's hell have mine out by now.'

Listening to the men, Red grinned tolerantly and turned his head, meaning to make a remark to Hassle. He discovered that the corporal was staring hard at the trees. Then, as if feeling Red's eyes on him, the old timer swung a cold-eyed glare around. Although the leathery features showed nothing of Hassle's thoughts, the youngster realized that he did not approve of what was going on behind them. For a moment Red was puzzled by the corporal's attitude, then he realized what was causing it.

'You bunch watch where we're headed and forget the Lancers!' Red advised coldly. 'Could be they ignored us because they *know* there's somebody waiting and watching, ready to hand us our needings.'

'Shucks,' Wilbur answered cheerfully. 'They ain't likely to

have anybody watching where the Lancers've just come from.'

'I'm not fixing to count on that,' Red warned. 'I'm a heap too young and lovable to want to get killed.'

'I'm all old, ornery 'n' ugly, but I don't want that neither,' the ancient – yet far from decrepit – corporal went on. 'So I floats my stick 'long of you, Mr. Blaze. It'd be the Yankees' way to do something real sneaky like that.'

Maybe Red's unsupported word would not have carried much weight with the enlisted men, but Hassle's agreement caused them to accept the warning. So they turned their attention to scanning the edge of the woodland in search of enemies.

When selecting men for the assignment, Dusty Fog had made certain to impress them with its full importance. He had also warned them of the possible dangers. All they had needed was for somebody to jolt those facts into their thoughts once more.

Finding that young Red Blaze – none of them thought of him as 'Mr.' – appreciated the dangers had given the men more confidence in him. He had pointed out one of the things his cousin had mentioned, but which they had forgotten. Doubtless the Yankees would have anticipated such an attempt would be made and had taken steps to prevent it. If there should be vedettes watching and more men waiting, the detail's task was anything but a sinecure. The penalty for growing unwary under those conditions could easily be death.

Taking time out from his scrutiny of the woods, Hassle glanced behind him. All the men were now watching their front and disregarding whatever might be happening between the Company and the Lancers. In the corporal's opinion, Mr. Blaze was shaping up as well as he had anticipated. All he needed was just a little hint, to show him when he was starting to go wrong. The way in which he had just responded proved that he was willing to accept advice from an older, more experienced subordinate.

'Fan out,' Red ordered, without needing the corporal to

prompt him, and drew the Spencer carbine from its boot under his left leg. 'And keep your eyes to the front, no matter what goes on behind.'

Following his own instructions, Red searched for signs of danger. When he failed to locate any, he grew uneasy. An old adage of Indian-fighting was that the time to start worrying was when you *didn't* see any of them. So he decided that he had the right to start worrying. Besides, if the Yankees did not have vedettes keeping watch, his men might regard him as an alarmist who spooked for no reason. That would cost him what little esteem he had acquired.

Standing with his back resting against the wide trunk of an oak tree, at the edge of the woodland, Private Blumfeld of the 18th 'Wisconsin' Heavy Infantry looked sleepily into the branches. That he was neglecting his duty did not bother him, for he was very tired after the long, gruelling forced march and the work of preparing defensive positions. On top of that, he felt he was wasting his time. The Lancers had ridden by his position on their way to attack the mountain battery, so he considered it extremely unlikely that any Rebels would come in his direction. To do that, they would have to cross the open country in plain sight of the Lancers and the men in the trenches.

Any attempt to out-flank the regiment's positions or prevent the destruction of the bridge, Blumfeld had repeatedly told himself, would be made by moving through the woods along the edge of the river. He considered that, if he had to be sent on picket duty, he should have been placed where he could do something useful instead of in a position where nothing was likely to happen.

Hearing the sound of hooves, Blumfeld sighed. Some of the Lancers must be returning. Maybe he had better look as if he was carrying out his duty, useless as it might be, in the correct manner. Turning, he started to step from behind the tree.

Looking idly towards the riders, Blumfeld's brain started to record details. Then it screamed a warning that something was very wrong. The horsemen, who he had assumed to be part of his regiment's cavalry screen, wore uniforms of cadet-grey and did not carry lances!

Fright lent speed to Blumfeld's limbs, for it was his first contact with the enemy. Jerking his long Springfield rifle-musket into the firing position, he sighted quickly and squeezed the trigger. To his horror, he realized that he had been seen by the riders. While the recoil's kick was still taking the barrel into the air, he sprang to his left.

'Look out, Mr. Blaze!' exclaimed Corporal Hassle, watching the Yankee emerge from behind the tree.

Even as the old timer ended his warning and swung his Henry rifle towards his shoulder, the Springfield banged. Its heavy calibre ball struck the star-in-a-circle badge, jerking Red's hat from his head. The loss of his hat and a narrow escape from death meant little to the youngster when confronted by such convincing proof that his warning to the men had been justified.

Squinting along the barrel of his repeater and allowing for the up and down motion of his horse, Hassle depressed the Henry's trigger. Flipping down, then up, the loading lever, he ejected the empty case and fed another bullet from the magazine tube to the chamber.

'You missed, Vern!' Wilbur scoffed.

'He jumped back while I was aiming,' the corporal replied. 'That ain't what I calls sport—'

There was a sudden, roaring thunder of army revolver shots. They were followed by the screams of stricken horses, the thuds of numerous heavy bodies crashing to the ground and cries of men in pain.

'Keep watching those blasted trees!' Red bellowed, despite the anxiety he was experiencing over his Cousin Dusty's safety now that the badly outnumbered Company had made contact with the enemy. 'There's sure to be more of them waiting for us.'

A faint grin creased Hassle's seamed, grim old face at the youngster's words. Mr. Blaze had said the right thing, without needing any reminding or prompting. What was more important, the enlisted men were taking heed of his warning.

There were some in Company 'C' who might have been worried, or even out-and-out alarmed, when Captain von Hertz had taken lead. The ancient corporal had not been numbered amongst them. Over the years, he had become a shrewd judge of human nature and had learned to assess character with some accuracy. So he had been willing to bet that Mr. Fog would be able to replace the dead captain and was just as capable of dealing with the Lancers.

Nor had Hassle been perturbed when Mr. Blaze had been put in charge of the detail. The shavetail might not have Mr. Fog's flair for leadership; but Hassle had believed that he would do to ride the river with, even if the water should be high among the willows. So the corporal had been willing to back Mr. Blaze's play and give him a nudge in the right direction if it was needed.

Something thudded into the tree's trunk as Blumfeld returned to his place behind it. For an instant, he was puzzled by the sound. The realization came. That white-haired old bastard had taken a shot at him and, despite being astride a fast-moving horse, had come very close to making a hit.

Panic bit at Blumfeld. A young recruit, he had not previously come under fire and found the sensation most unpleasant. What was more, he had emptied his only weapon – he did not regard his bayonet in that light – at the Texans. Reloading a Springfield was a slow, tedious process, even when one's nerves were not flurried. Even if he reloaded, he could not hope to deal with all eight riders before they reached him. Especially as each of them had been holding a Henry or a Spencer repeater. What was more, he had been given definite orders by Sergeant Lipski. If he saw any hint of enemy activity coming his way, he was to return and warn the picketing force.

Having reached that conclusion in a remarkably short time, and growing conscious of the sound of hooves coming closer, Blumfeld dropped his rifle. He tried to remain concealed by the oak tree as he started to run away.

'There he goes!' whooped one of the detail and raised his Spencer, trying to line it at the fleeing soldier.

'Don't shoot!' Red snapped. 'You're likely to need the bullets before we've finished today.'

'That's for sure,' Hassle agreed, having made no attempt to use his Henry. 'He's only the first of 'em.'

'We'll make jim-dandy targets on these horses, Vern,' Red remarked, when the man refrained from firing.

'Sure will, Mr. Blaze,' Hassle replied.

'I dearly love walking,' Red went on, slowing his big brown gelding. 'But only when I've got a horse under me to do it. All right, boys. We'll go the rest of the way on foot.'

'My ma didn't raise her favourite son to be a puddle-splasher,'* Hassle moaned, secretly delighted that Red had once again reached the right conclusion.

'You'll make a real fine one,' Red assured him and stopped the brown. The other men followed his example and he looked at the nearest of them. 'You see to the horses, Wilbur.'

'Shouldn't we just—' the soldier in question began, not relishing the idea of being given such a menial task.

'I'm not asking you to do it as a *favour*, soldier!' Red barked, modelling his tone and attitude on how he believed his Cousin Dusty would have handled a similar situation. 'I told *you* to hold the horses. Now get the hell down and see to it.'

Instead of obeying immediately, Wilbur looked at the other members of the detail. If he had hoped to see any support for his unfinished suggestion, he was disappointed. His companions were studying him with blank indifference and obviously intended to leave the issue between him and their young officer. There was just a hint of warning in Corporal Hassle's cold-eyed scrutiny, but he neither moved nor spoke.

'Hit the ground, *pronto*!' Red continued in a hard growl, glaring straight at Wilbur. He had seen the other men's reactions and knew he must bend the soldier to his will or lose all control of the detail. 'If I have to tell you again, I'll knock you out of that saddle!'

* Puddle-splasher: derogatory name for an infantryman.

Wilbur suddenly realized that Red meant every word he had said. Grim, deadly determination throbbed in his voice and showed in his normally cheerful, freckled face. Meeting the red-head's glare, Wilbur became fully aware of the change that had come over him. No longer was he the easy-going young shavetail who had frequently been in trouble with von Hertz because of his disregard for military matters. Instead, he looked mean, hard and ornery; much as Mr. Fog did when riled or crossed. What was more, Wilbur knew that Red – Mr. Blaze – was just as capable as his cousin of backing up such a threat.

Maybe Wilbur could not claim to be one of the smartest men in the Texas Light Cavalry, but he figured that he had sense enough to know when the time had come to yell 'calf-rope'* and obey orders without argument.

Watching Wilbur swinging hurriedly from his saddle, Hassle concealed a grin. The corporal had been ready, if not willing or eager, to help Red enforce the order and felt pleased that he had not been called upon to do so. It was better for all concerned that the members of the detail realized they had an officer who could and *would* make his decisions stick.

'Here, Wilbur,' Red said, in a gentler tone, as he dismounted and held out his reins. 'Let us get a head start, then come after us.'

'Yo!' answered the soldier.

'Don't get eager and crowd us too close,' Red went on. 'If you do, you could get shot. Should *that* happen, try to fall on the reins and stop the horses getting away. We'll need 'em when we've done what we came for.'

Listening to the chuckles – in which Wilbur joined – that greeted Red's comment, Hassle scored up another point in the youngster's favour. Red had asserted his authority and was now showing the right kind of attitude. There were grins as the rest of the detail joined him on the ground and handed their reins to Wilbur. Then, at Red's order, they spread out into a skirmishing line that had him and Hassle as

* 'Calf-rope': cowhands' expression for admitting surrender.

its centre. Carrying their repeaters at what bayonet fighters termed the 'high port' position, which would allow the weapons to be brought rapidly into whatever kind of use was required, they started to move into the woodland.

The unwilling horse-holder watched his companions depart, then made ready to carry out his duty. Fastening the reins of Red's gelding to his own mount's saddlehorn, he secured Hassle's to Red's in the same manner and continued until all of the animals were attached in a line.

'All right, blast you,' Wilbur said, returning to his horse and taking hold of its reins. 'Let's go slow and easy. I'd hate like hell to get shot and not fall on the reins, although that'd serve Mr. Blaze right for handing me this no good chore.'

Having delivered that sentiment, the soldier led the horses in the direction taken by his faster-moving, unencumbered companions. He grinned as he watched Red until the trees hid the youngster from sight. There was one tough young cuss and he was nowhere near as easy-going as a lot of folks imagined. Anybody who sold him short when there was a job of work to do stood a better than fair chance of wishing that such a notion had never come.

Glancing first right, then left, Red was satisfied with what he saw. Every enlisted man in the detail had been a member of the Texas Rangers before enlisting in the Army. Experienced in all aspects of fighting Indians, the Rangers' primary occupation before the War, they needed no advice on how to handle the kind of work they were doing.

Keeping roughly in line and close enough for easy communication one with another, they were picking their own routes and darting from cover to cover. As they advanced, they scanned the terrain ahead of them constantly. All had learned the importance of unceasing vigilance when stalking an enemy.

'There goes that blue-belly bastard, Mr. Blaze!' announced the soldier at Red's left, gesturing ahead with his Spencer carbine. 'I'll drop hi—'

'Leave him be, all of you!' Red commanded, watching the Yankee infantryman come briefly into view running as fast as his legs would carry him. 'There's no sense in letting his *amigos* know for sure which way we're coming.'

'Was just thinking that meself,' commented Hassle, from Red's right.

Lowering his weapon without firing, the soldier resumed his advance. The infantryman continued to run ahead of the detail. They could only see him at infrequent intervals, obtaining brief glimpses through the gaps in the bushes or between the trunks of the trees.

'Have you seen any of them yet, Vern?' Red inquired, after they had covered about a hundred yards.

'Nary a sign,' the corporal admitted, interrupting his scrutiny for a moment. 'But they're around somewheres. I feel it in me bones. Just wish I could see some of 'em. I hates surprises.'

'Trouble with you is you wants things too easy,' Red scoffed, but did not permit the levity to prevent him examining what lay ahead. 'That's the worst of fighting Indians. They don't make things hard enough, way they come a-whooping and a-hollering. So you – *Look*!'

The final exclamation burst from Red's lips as the fleeing soldier made one of his sporadic appearances. Skidding to a halt, he peered up at the foliage of a flowering dogwood tree and pointed excitedly to his rear.

'Reb's!' the soldier screeched, to all intents and purposes addressing the leaves and branches. 'They're coming, Sergeant Lipski! They're coming and'll soon be here.'

CHAPTER TWELVE

'WEAPONS, sir?' Sergeant Major Goering prompted, wondering why his young superior had not given the expected order.

Keeping his eyes fixed on the approaching Lancers, Dusty Fog thought fast before replying. If he gave permission for his men to arm themselves, he ran the risk of somebody starting to shoot long before it was advisable to open fire.

What Dusty wanted – in fact, the only thing that would serve his purpose was a volley from every member of the Company. A straggle of individual shots might inflict a few casualties, but would do nothing to halt the Lancers.

On the other hand, Dusty wanted to have his men holding their weapons before giving the order to increase speed.

There was something else for the small Texan to consider. The sight of Company 'C's' drawn weapons – especially the revolvers which every man carried – might have an unnerving effect upon the Lancers. Some, at least, would realize the inadequacy of a lance when opposed by a man with a firearm.

There was, Dusty decided, only one answer.

'Yes, sergeant major,' he said. 'But no shooting until I give the word.'

'Draw pistols and sabres!' Goering commanded in his stentorian tones. 'Hold your fire until ordered.'

Having given his consent, Dusty carried out the process of arming himself. His right hand reached for and slid the sabre from its sheath. Designed to meet his physical requirements, by the Haiman Brothers' best craftsmen and from their finest steel, the blade was two inches shorter and somewhat lighter than one of the standard issue. Dusty did not consider that to be a disadvantage. Due to his size, he found the regulation weapon cumbersome. While he could handle one adequately, if circumstances compelled him to do so,* he achieved better results with the sabre that had been made especially for him.

Crossing his body, Dusty's left hand opened the flap of the holster and he drew out the bone-handled Colt 1860 Army revolver. It belonged to a pair that had been a present from his father. He only carried the one – and used the awkward, unsatisfactory close-topped military holster – because Captain von Hertz had never approved of him wearing the more practical Western-style gunbelt with which he was already something of an expert.

Seeing that the Texans were arming themselves, the trio of officers ahead of the Lancers started shooting. As about two hundred and fifty yards separated the two parties, Dusty wondered if they were doing it for a deliberate reason. Firing from the backs of galloping horses at that range, they could hardly hope to score hits.

Maybe they had guessed Dusty's purpose and were hoping to provoke his men into a premature retaliation!

'Hold your fire!' Dusty bellowed, an instant before Goering could give a similar command. 'Don't let anybody start shooting, you sergeants!'

'That goes for you, you hame-headed yahoo!' Sergeant Weather bawled, glaring along the line at a soldier who was elevating his Colt. 'Wait for the order, god-damn it!'

Looking sheepish, the man in question lowered his weapon. It did not pay to disregard Mr. Fog's wishes, especially when Stormy Weather was helping to enforce them.

'Don't none of you go riling them Yankees by shooting at 'em!' bleated Sergeant Billy Jack at the other end of the line. 'They'll get mean if you do and I could get hurt.' His voice hardened. 'That means you-all, Jones!'

Maybe the lanky non-com's miserable, hangdog attitude

* This is proven in the 'A Convention Of War' episode of: *Under the Stars and Bars*.

might have led a stranger to forming the wrong conclusions about his character, but the man he had named was fully aware of his true potential. So Jones' obedience, and the fact that the others who heard took heed of the warning, did not stem from concern over annoying the enemy.

'At the gallop,' Goering ordered, watching and interpreting Dusty's signal correctly. 'Yo!'

Throwing a quick glance at the hamlet, as he and his men built up their mounts' gaits to a manoeuvring gallop, Dusty saw that the howitzers were continuing with their work. The central Vandenburg's carriage had a broken wheel and its muzzle pointed into the air, rendering it useless. However, the other two Volley Guns would be operable once their crews rose from having dived into cover to avoid the mountain battery's shells.

More shots were coming from the major and two lieutenants, drawing Dusty's attention back to them. Still none of their bullets had taken effect as far as he could tell. Nor had any of his men thrown off the bonds of discipline and replied in kind. Yet they were certain to be resenting being fired upon and doing nothing in return.

'Let them waste their lead, men!' Goering advised, having realized the value of the opening volley. 'Our turn will come.'

The two sergeants were also aware of what their youthful officer was hoping to achieve. So they lent their advice to Goering's and added suitable threats against anybody who failed to obey.

One hundred yards separated the converging bodies of men.

Seventy-five yards!

Fifty.

Dusty set his teeth grimly. To hold on was inviting casualties among his men and the chance that some of them would open fire before he gave the command. If only one man cut loose, others were sure to follow his example and all hope of a devastating close-range volley would be lost.

Another ten yards was diminished from the distance between the Texans and the Lancers.

The Yankee major was taking careful aim!

Flame spurted from the revolver in the major's hand. Giving a croaking cry, Goering jerked spasmodically and slid sideways from his saddle.

Like the sharpshooter earlier, the major had made the error of misjudging Dusty's potential. Believing that the burly sergeant major was responsible for Company 'C's' well-managed manoeuvring, the Lancers' commanding officer had decided that his removal would throw the Rebels into confusion.

'Hold your fire!' Dusty shouted; hating to have to give the order which delayed avenging Goering, but accepting that it must be done and that he would be more than repaid by the volley.

The Lancers had lowered their weapons into the attacking position. Steel points, looking as sharp as needles, extended before the horses in an awe-inspiring manner. They looked mighty dangerous and menacing. Especially to men who were riding with their reins lashed to the saddlehorns, guiding the horses by knee-pressure – which did not permit a great deal of fancy evasive action to be taken.

Studying the sight, Dusty could guess at the tensions rising amongst the enlisted men. If they had had less faith in him, they would have disregarded the order and started shooting.

'Take aim!' Dusty called, thrusting forward his Colt.

Before aligning his sights, the small Texan glanced left and then right. On either side, his men were pointing their revolvers in the Lancers' direction. It would, he guessed, be an impressive – maybe even frightening – sight. More than one member of the Yankees' leading company must be all too aware that he was far beyond a distance at which the weapon he held would be of any use.

'Ready!' Dusty continued, returning his gaze to the Colt's barrel. He pointed it straight at the centre of the major's chest, ignoring the flame which erupted from his target's gun-filled fist and the eerie sound of a bullet winging close by his head. 'Fire!'

Giving the word that his men had been awaiting, Dusty squeezed the Colt's trigger and the hammer pivoted forward. Propelled by the explosive force of thirty grains of powder, the .44 conical bullet spun through the rifling grooves. It belched out of the muzzle and flew unerringly to its objective.

Jolting under the impact, the major threw aside his weapons and clutched at the wound. Feeling its rider swaying, the horse swerved to the right and pitched him off its back.

Following immediately on the heels of Dusty's shot, some sixty revolvers of various types and calibres spewed out their loads in a thunderous, rolling cacophony.

From the results he saw, Dusty concluded that the majority of the Company had taken the trouble to aim before discharging their weapons. Both the lieutenants were hit and toppled from their mounts. At least ten horses were falling, flinging their riders from them. Still others had been less seriously hurt, but started rearing and plunging in pain. Possibly a dozen of the enlisted men had taken lead. In fact, the whole of the Lancers' leading rank appeared to be in some way affected by the Texans' volley.

It soon became apparent that Dusty's strategy had been correct and he was justified in his insistence that the men did not open fire until they had come to close quarters.

Having gathered together, for mutual protection and to present as imposing a front as possible to their enemies, the Lancers were ideally positioned to suffer the fullest impact of the Texans' gun-play. Although only the foremost company had taken the punishment, those who followed were thrown into confusion.

If the second and third companies had kept their distances, they could have averted much of what was coming. Instead, the excitement of the charge and a general lack of control being exercised by their officers had induced them to crowd almost to the rumps of the horses ahead of them. Even the captain commanding the rear company had failed to restrain his men.

As a result of the Lancers' undisciplined folly, a state of pandemonium resulted from the arrival of the Texans' volley. Many of the riders in the centre rank tried to swerve away, to halt even, so as to avoid trampling upon fallen companions. Others were unable to control their mounts and crashed over horses which lay on the ground. The men of the rearmost rank found themselves in much the same position.

Company 'C' had dealt the Lancers a terrible blow and their youthful commanding officer had every intention of following up their advantage. Dusty realized that he dare not allow considerations of humanity to weaken his determination. If he hesitated, their enemies would recover from the shock, regroup and continue the attack on the battery.

'Pour it into them, boys!' Dusty exhorted at the top of his voice, cocking the Colt aided by the kick of its recoil and sending its next load through the head of a survivor in the front rank.

There was no real necessity for the order. Once the enlisted men had been allowed to start shooting, they continued to do so. More lead slashed its way into the disorganized Lancers, clearing saddles in the second and third ranks. Before any of the Yankees could recover from the devastating effect of the first volley, or attain any form of cohesion, the men of the Texas Light Cavalry closed in upon them like wolves attacking a cornered herd of pronghorn antelope.

With his bay hurdling the major's body, Dusty saw a lance being thrust in his direction from the right. He responded automatically. Using the flat of the blade, so that it would not cut into and be trapped by the wood, he deflected the Norwegian fir shaft outwards. With the attack parried, he disengaged the sabre. Turning his hand so that the palm was uppermost, he lunged and sank the point deep into his assailant's chest. Confronted by the onrushing bay gelding, the Lancer's horse tried to swerve. Dusty's mount rammed the other animal with its shoulder and knocked it staggering with a force that tore the sabre from the small Texan's hand.

As the stricken soldier carried Dusty's sabre away from him, he found that another lance's head seemed to be hurtling in his direction. It was coming from the left, wielded by a wild-eyed, yelling corporal, and aimed so that it would catch the young officer in the stomach.

Although Dusty had been deprived of one weapon, he held another equally effective in his left hand. At that moment, the ambidextrous powers he had developed early in his young life – as a means of distracting attention from his small size – came in very useful. Almost as if drawn by a magnet, the Colt in his left hand turned and flame blossomed ahead of its muzzle. He had aimed instinctively and fired the only way he dared under the circumstances; at the head, in the hope of an instantaneous kill.

Back snapped the corporal's head, with blood oozing from where the left eye had been and the base of the skull shattering as the lead emerged. As the man's torso bowed to the rear, the lance's point rose slightly.

Not enough, however!

It was now directed towards the top of Dusty's chest!

What was more, the man's hand had tightened in a death grip on the shaft.

The on-rushing weapon was just as deadly as ever.

CHAPTER THIRTEEN

'GET the hell out of here, you stupid son-of-a-bitch!'

Glowering furiously through the thick foliage of the flowering dogwood tree, into which he had climbed so that he could keep an eye upon the bulk of his picket and obtain a clearer view of the surrounding woodland from above the tops of the numerous bushes, Sergeant Lipski spat out the words as if they were burning his mouth. He had taken a lot of trouble to position and conceal his men, being aware of the importance of their task, and had no desire to see all his work ruined because of Private Blumfeld's panic-induced stupidity.

When Lipski had been ordered to establish a line of look-outs, extending across the woodland to the Ouachita River and protecting the flank of the defences, he had selected his men carefully. Blumfeld should not have been with them. On reaching the dogwood tree and starting to organize his detail, the sergeant had discovered that one of his men had persuaded the inexperienced recruit to take his place.

Instead of telling Blumfeld to return, Lipski had sent him to watch from the edge of the wood. The recruit would be so close to the Lancers that there should have been no danger of him coming into contact with the enemy.

Instead of being safely out of the way, Blumfeld had come dashing back without his rifle and looking scared out of his wits. Unfortunately, he was not so frightened that he had forgotten where Lipski had told the detail he would take up his position. So he had come straight to the tree and started yelling his warning.

'But the Rebs—!' Blumfeld began, indignant at his superior's response to such important news.

'Why the hell don't you go hold their hands and fetch 'em to see where I'm at?' Lipski snarled, scanning the land behind the soldier without locating any sign of pursuit. However, he decided that Blumfeld would not have been mistaken or lying, so went on, 'Head for the bridge and warn Mr. Rosenbaum that they're coming our way.'

After Blumfeld had departed to deliver the message, Lipski glanced around and then stared once more in the direction from which the recruit had come.

The sergeant could not see what was happening beyond the trees, but his ears and knowledge of the general tactical situation enabled him to form fairly accurate conclusions. If the sound of rifles firing volleys was any indication, the Rebels' main assault was well under way. He knew that the Lancers had ridden out earlier than would have been necessary to help disrupt the attackers. That meant they had gone to silence an artillery battery brought up by the Rebs to deal with the Vandenburg Volley Guns.

From a different direction to the rifles had come the crashing of many revolvers and other noises suggesting that the Lancers had met with very stiff opposition. Going by the way that several light cannons – probably mountain howitzers, the sergeant guessed – bellowed repeatedly, although the Vandenburgs did not commence their bombardment, Lipski realized that the Lancers had either failed or been delayed in completing their duty. Maybe the massive multi-barrelled weapons had been put out of action by the shelling.

If that was the case, Lipski figured the situation was growing desperate.

Without the support of the half-battery of Vandenburgs, the 'Wisconsins' would be hard put to hold the bridge. Fortunately, Colonel Middleton had taken that possibility into consideration. Lipski remembered the colonel's orders in the event of their position becoming untenable. Instead of attempting to hold on, they were to withdraw across the river, destroy the bridge and make a long circle to rejoin their advancing army. That ought not to be too difficult, as the

Rebs would be fully occupied in trying to protect their supplies.

There was movement amongst the bushes!

Staring harder, Lipski saw a bare-headed Rebel shavetail and a short, white-haired corporal who looked as old as sin but a whole heap more spry. Other grey-uniformed fly-slicers formed a skirmishing line on either side of the pair. Not many, however. Less than ten, Lipski counted. Which meant his picket had the advantage of numbers.

If only Blumfeld had not betrayed Lipski's position, all would have been perfect.

Yet, although they were advancing carefully, the Rebels did not appear to be aware of the flowering dogwood's significance. Possibly they had not seen Blumfeld's indiscretion, even if they had heard him yelling the warning. They would know that Yankees were about, but would not have any idea of where to look.

Easing back the hammer of his Spencer rifle, Lipski raised the butt to his shoulder. There was an oak tree thirty yards in front of him. By the time the Rebs reached it, they would be within a distance at which the pickets were unlikely to miss them. Commanded by that bald-faced young officer and a decrepit old corporal, the skirmishers ought to be easy meat. Even if they should avoid being shot down in the opening attack, Lipski had another item in his favour. The Texans – their hat-badges told him to which State they belonged – had a habit of calling orders and instructions in Mexican. If they should do so on this occasion, they would betray their purpose. Lipski's corporal spoke Spanish and would be able to translate anything the Rebels said.

At Red Blaze's word, *'Look!'*, the rest of the detail had taken cover before attempting to do so. They listened to Blumfeld giving his warning and exchanged glances.

'That jasper must be kin to my wife,' Corporal Hassle commented dryly, wondering what the man in the tree was thinking about the soldier's indiscreet behaviour. 'They do say stupidity runs in families. It must be *galloping* in his'n.'

'Now me,' Red answered. 'I'm right pleased I didn't let you blood-thirsty yahooes kill him.'

'He's sure obliging, for a Yankee,' Hassle admitted and watched Blumfeld resume his flight. 'What now, Mr. Blaze?'

'We'll keep moving, what else,' Red replied. 'Go extra careful from here on, boys. But don't let on we figure there's a feller in that dogwood. Vern and I'll attend to his needings. You watch out for his *amigos*.'

Continuing their advance the Texans displayed an even greater caution. They studied every bush and tree, with the exception of the dogwood in which the Yankee sergeant was hiding, searching for traces that it might conceal an enemy. Self-preservation demanded that they tried to locate the Yankee pickets before they were exposed to the others' weapons.

Although Red failed to detect any suggestion of danger, he heard Hassle let out low grunts of satisfaction on three occasions and surmised that the corporal had been more successful. He hoped that the remainder of his party were duplicating the old timer's efforts.

Nothing happened as the Texans continued to move forward. The woods about them remained silent, except for the noises of their darting passage from one piece of shelter to the next. Not a shot was fired in their direction and nothing suggested that men might be lurking in concealment, waiting to kill them.

Scuttling to a massive old oak tree about thirty yards from the dogwood, Hassle halted with its trunk between himself and the possible source of danger. Red came to a stop alongside the old timer.

'There's some of them ahead, Mr. Blaze!' called a soldier on the left flank of the line, speaking in Spanish. 'Watch out!'

'Same this side,' continued the man at the extreme right, also using Mexican to avoid giving information to the enemy.

'They've seen some of our boys, serge!' the Spanish-speaking corporal warned, in tones which he hoped would not carry beyond Lipski's hearing.

'Somebody out there knows Mex!' the keen-eared Corporal Hassle said.

'Sounds that way,' Red agreed. 'What do you reckon, Vern. Was that Yankee playing tricky and only pretending there's somebody in that tree?'

'Nope,' the old timer replied. 'I catched just a leetle glimpse of the blue-belly son-of-a-bitch. He's squatting up there like a bluebird on its nest, only not so pretty.'

'And he's not the only one of 'em,' Red drawled.

'There's a fair slew of 'em ahead of us,' Hassle confirmed. 'Four I know about for certain and I've got suspicions on another three. Which ain't counting them's the boys say they've seen.'

'And the ones who've been smart enough to stay hid,' Red said quietly.

'Them too,' Hassle conceded. 'And I'm certain sure some of 'em's slick enough to have kept hid. It's them's'll cause us most grief.'

Red did not need reminding that to move forward without having located the majority – if not all – of the pickets would be inviting disaster. He also knew that he and his men could not stay put and play a waiting game, hoping the Yankees might run out of patience and reveal their positions.

'Let's stir things up a mite,' the youngster suggested and explained what he wanted to do.

'We'd best let the boys know for sure what you're planning, Mr. Blaze,' Hassle replied. 'Which ain't going to be easy, without letting the Yankees know at the same time. One of the sneaky bastards talks Mex.'

'He does,' Red agreed. 'I reckon you speak Comanch', Vern?'

'Some.'

'How about the rest of the boys?'

'They all hail from my neck of the *Nemenuh** country and've had dealings with the red varmints. Likely they'll speak about's much's me, only maybe not so good.'

* Nemenuh: 'The People', the Comanches' name for their nation.

'Good enough for them to understand what I want done?' Red wanted to know.

'I reckon I can get it through to 'em,' Hassle decided. 'Only could be that Yankee talks Comanch' as well as Mex.'

'You're getting to sound like Billy Jack,' Red warned. 'Way I see it, I reckon it's Spanish more than Mex he speaks. So he won't know Comanch'. We'll have to take that chance.'

Raising his voice, Hassle used the dialect of the *Tanima* – Liver Eaters – band to ascertain that the other enlisted men could understand him. Receiving their assurances that they could, he outlined Red's wishes.

'What's that, Garcia?' Sergeant Lipski called, as the old timer's voice reached him.

'I don't know,' the man in question admitted. 'It's not Spanish.'

'Stop that bellowing, damn you!' Red yelled, trying to sound impatient and annoyed. 'Let's go, there's none of the blue-bellied bastards around here.'

'I ain't sure on that, Mr. Blaze,' Hassle protested. 'The boys allow—'

'You heard me!' Red interrupted. 'There's none of them closer than the bridge. The Lancers were covering this part, with the feller we run off in case anybody came after they'd pulled out. Come on, time's a-wasting.'

With that, Red strode around the trunk of the tree. He went with an apparently reckless disregard for possible danger. For all that, he was as alert as an old buck whitetail deer which had been hunted regularly. If he had looked, he would have seen his men emerging from their places of concealment, but with the wary caution arising from greater wisdom and experience. Or so it appeared to the watching Yankees.

Cradling the Spencer's butt to his shoulder, Lipski watched the Texans moving into view. He was not surprised to see the enlisted men displaying more care than the young officer. So far as he could tell, however, they did not realize how close they were to the main body of his pickets.

Certainly the shavetail did not suspect the danger. Just as Lipski had figured, he was a hot-head. It was unlikely that such a man would pose any serious threat to the destruction of the bridge. In fact, the sergeant intended to make sure that he did not.

With the rifle's barrel turning in Red's direction, Lipski remembered the ancient corporal.

The old timer had not yet made his appearance!

That realization came just a moment too late for Lipski.

Instead of leaving the shelter of the oak tree, Hassle had peered around its trunk. From his position, he had been able to make out sufficient of the Yankee sergeant to be aware of what was happening.

'Back!' Hassle snapped, as the Spencer rifle's barrel started to move.

Instantly Red propelled himself swiftly to the rear and sideways. Nor was he a moment too soon. He heard a sharp bang from amongst the dogwood's foliage and, as a bullet ploughed home, a spurt of splinters erupted from the oak's bark about level with his head.

Stepping from his hiding place, with the Henry already lifting to his shoulder, Hassle sighted and fired in what appeared to be a single flowing motion. There was a violent flurry of movement which set the dogwood tree's leaves shaking. Then a Spencer rifle tumbled out, followed by the spasmodically jerking body of the Union infantry sergeant.

Like Red, Hassle did not linger in the open. Having fired and made his hit, he sprang rapidly for the safety offered by the sturdy trunk of the old oak tree. Two bullets hammered into it, instead of finding their billets in his body.

Many more shots sounded as the Texans and the rest of the pickets opened fire at each other. One of Red's men spun around, hit in the head and dead on his feet. Having exposed himself while he was aiming at a Yankee infantryman, he had been killed by another whose presence he had failed to detect.

With lead whistling around them from numerous places,

the Texans were driven back into hiding. It was obvious that the Yankees had set out a strong picket force.

'There's close to twenty of 'em,' Hassle computed, looking at Red. 'And more'n half of 'em's got Spencers. I'd say we're pinned down, Mr. Blaze.'

'Just like Cousin Dusty figured we might be,' Red replied. 'They got Ted.'

'He was unlucky, no more,' the corporal drawled. 'It wasn't your fault. All the boys knowed what you wanted 'em to do and that it wouldn't be easy. You took the biggest chance of all.'

'I've still got to get to the bridge,' Red declared, hiding the relief he was experiencing at Hassle's words. He had been blaming himself for the soldier getting killed. 'The woods on the other side're more open than these. So Company 'A'll' be in an even worse tight than us. So I'm open for suggestions, smart or otherwise, was they to be offered.'

'We could try rushing 'em, horns a-hooking,' Hassle said dubiously. 'Some of us'll get killed for sure, but *maybe* the others'll get through.'

'We daren't go betting on a "maybe", Vern,' Red pointed out.

'One man, moving fast and sneaky, might get down to the river, happen the rest of us keep the Yankees busy.'

'It's possible,' Red drawled.

'You fixing to call for a volunteer, Mr. Blaze?' the corporal inquired hopefully, although his summation of the youngster's character had already told him what the answer would be.

'I've already done it,' Red announced with a grin. 'And, like a dad-blasted fool, it was me who said "I'll go".'

'Try saving some of that lead!' Hassle bellowed, as the other members of the detail exchanged shots with the Yankees. Then he looked at Red and went on, 'That's the way it should be, Mr. Blaze. Are you going to handle it the way Mr. Fog was fixing to?'

'If it was good enough for Cousin Dusty, it's good enough for me.'

'You'll have to slip by any more of 'em's been staked out between here and the river.'

'Sure, unless I can get around them.'

'There's that,' Hassle conceded, ''cepting you don't have time to go too far around.'

'So I'll not go *too* far, but move faster,' Red answered.

'Are you going on foot, or as the Good Lord intended when he made us miserable sinners smart enough to catch 'n' tame hosses?'

'Like I said,' Red replied, looking around and thinking fast. 'I dearly hate walking, unless there's a horse under me doing it. And that goes double for *running*.'

'Running'll be a right good way for you to go,' Hassle admitted. 'Except I don't reckon them Yankees'll be too pleasured, happen they see you lighting out.'

'I'm not counting on letting them see me go,' Red declared. 'Tell the boys to cover me.'

While the corporal gave the necessary orders in Comanche, Red leaned his Spencer against the trunk of the tree. Removing his weapon belt, the youngster took the Colt from its holster.

'I don't want anything slowing me down,' Red told Hassle, placing the belt on the ground. 'Start cutting loose and make them think we're fixing to rush them.'

Throwing back his head, Hassle let out the kind of war-whoop used when the *Tanima* Comanche rode to attack the hated white brother. Then he thrust the Henry around the side of the tree. Sighting in the direction of one of the pickets, he threw three shots as fast as he could work the rifle's lever. The remainder of the detail, who had stopped shooting, resumed their bombardment. Instantly every picket in the vicinity, suspecting that this was the prelude of an attack, replied with hot lead.

Red waited until the exchange of fire had built up. Hoping that the attention of the Yankees was set on his men, he sank to his stomach. Hassle stepped over him, swapping the Henry for his Spencer carbine and using it from the other side of the trunk. Knowing what the corporal was trying to do, Red wriggled rapidly across the open land that separated him from a clump of bushes. At every writhing movement, he expected to feel a bullet crashing into his body, or close by, warning that his departure had been observed. It did not happen and, reaching the bushes, he rose cautiously. Hassle's ruse had worked. Being fired on with different weapons from either side of the oak, the Yankees did not know that Red had slipped away.

Keeping in concealment if possible, or running swiftly across such open spaces as came his way, Red darted rapidly through the trees. He had covered about three hundred yards when he saw Wilbur and the horses. The enlisted man was behaving sensibly, Red decided. Having heard the shooting, he had halted instead of leading the animals to where they might be seen by the Yankees.

'Turn my horse loose, Wilbur!' Red called, as he approached the soldier.

'Yo!' Wilbur replied.

To give the soldier credit, he did not for a moment think that Red was deserting their companions. Instead, he realized that the young officer was carrying out the most important part of the assignment.

Releasing his hold on his horse's bridle, the soldier sprang to set free Red's gelding. Before the youngster arrived, Wilbur had also removed Hassle's reins from the brown's saddlehorn. Running up, Red grasped the saddlehorn in his left hand and vaulted on to his mount's back. He was about to ride away when he noticed how Wilbur was staring towards the shooting. There was an almost pleading expression on the soldier's face as he swung his gaze towards his officer.

'All right,' Red said with a grin. 'Fasten up those fool critters and go help the boys.'

'*Gracias*, Mr. Blaze!' Wilbur whooped delightedly. 'Good luck.'

'Likely I'll need it,' Red answered, starting his horse moving and turning it to the south. 'You go careful. There may be more of 'em around.'

Encouraging his gelding to a fast trot, Red listened to the continuing sounds of conflict. Clearly his detail was still contriving to hold the attention of the Yankee pickets. Beyond the woods, going by the noise, the fighting was carrying on with unabated fury at the hamlet and where Company 'C' was locking horns with the Lancers.

Despite all the activity elsewhere, Red's passage through the woods proved to be uneventful. Apparently he had been fortunate enough to have selected a route which was taking him clear of any vedettes set out by the Yankee sergeant. Or they had quit their posts and moved in to help the main body of the picket. Whatever the reason, he came into sight of the Ouachita River without finding use for the Colt in his right hand.

The river lay at the foot of a fairly steep slope. Having seen nothing to disturb him, Red started to make the descent.

Raising a Spencer rifle to his shoulder, a Union Army infantryman sprang from behind a bush ahead of Red. The man was so close that he seemed unlikely to miss.

CHAPTER FOURTEEN

WITH the lance's point passing the head of his bay gelding, Dusty Fog tightened his legs' grip on the saddle and inclined his body to the right. He had to tilt himself farther than he had expected. Even then, he barely escaped being impaled. The lance's diamond-shaped head brushed his left shoulder in passing, but it did him no harm and the corporal's horse carried its lifeless burden by his mount.

Dusty found that he was still in danger. Looming up on his right, a lieutenant belonging to the Lancers' second company was turning a revolver towards him. Hanging by his legs alone, almost beyond the point of balance, Dusty was in no position to protect himself.

Wild with excitement and elation at the success of their volley, the men of Company 'C' gave no thought to being outnumbered. Already they had whittled down the odds against them and felt that victory was assured. So they charged recklessly into the fray. If it came to a point, few of them would have been able to halt, or even divert, their fast-running horses.

'Yeah! Texas Light!'

Uttering their war-yell, the Texans rushed into the Lancers' ranks. Collisions were unavoidable, but the men of Company 'C' were the better riders and came out of the impacts more successfully than their opponents. They had another advantage, being armed with weapons that could be wielded at close quarters.

Sabres swung in glistening arcs, until their blades were reddened with blood. Revolvers thundered and flung death indiscriminately at man or beast. Lances drove into flesh, or were parried to leave their wielders exposed to the would-be victims' counter-measures. Men yelled, cursed, or shrieked in pain. Struck by steel, or flying lead, horses screamed, snorted, reared high, plunged, or collapsed kicking wildly.

To the right and slightly behind Dusty, Sandy McGraw was carrying out his duty by sticking close to his commanding officer. Seeing the small Texan's predicament, the guidon carrier acted fast. Swinging up the Colt in his right hand, he thumbed off two shots as fast as he could squeeze the trigger and work the hammer. He hoped to hit the Yankee officer. Instead, the first bullet missed. The second struck the neck of the lieutenant's horse. Down went the animal, front legs buckling under it, to hurl its rider from its back. Losing his revolver, the lieutenant rolled under and was trampled by Dusty's big gelding.

Even as Sandy intervened, Dusty was grabbing for the saddlehorn with his right hand. Taking hold, he pulled and regained a more secure, upright seat on the gelding's back. A Lancer was passing on Dusty's left. Seeming to move of its own volition, the bone-handled Colt pointed and hurled a bullet into the soldier's ribs as he went by.

Then Dusty found that there was nobody in front or on either side of him. For a moment he was puzzled. Realization flooded over him. He was clear of the Lancer's shattered ranks, having cut and shot his way through them.

Looking behind him, Dusty discovered that the main force of the attack had been halted. Some of the Lancers, who had been on the ends of the ranks had avoided the confusion and continued to charge towards the battery. They were few in numbers and Sergeant Major Smalley's defending force appeared to be dealing with them in a satisfactory manner. Certainly they were not impeding the four howitzers' rate of fire.

The battery was operating independent fire now, with each diminished crew doing its best to attain the greatest speed in reloading and retraining its piece. Following the crash of the Number Four howitzer, there was a much louder than usual detonation at the hamlet.

Curving downwards, the piece's twelve-pound shell plunged into the open chest at the front end of the Vandenburg Volley Guns' solitary ammunition caisson. Ignited by the flash of the howitzer's powder charge going off, the fuse had been burning steadily during the flight. The minute spurt of flame reached the shell's half-pound burster charge at precisely – if luckily – the right moment.

Although the caisson's crew must have realized their peril, they were unable to escape. The shell exploded before any of them could attempt to spring away from the danger area. So did the mass of paper cartridges into which the missile had descended, to be followed in rapid succession by the contents of the second and third chests.

In one blinding instant of roaring sound, the whole of the three multi-barrelled weapons' ammunition supply disintegrated. Along with it went the crew of the caisson, blown into oblivion.

Several of the Texans, including Sandy McGraw and the bugler had also fought their way through the Lancers' disrupted formation. However, the majority were still battling in a wild, savage, no-quarter-asked-or-given melee. Dusty knew that he must return and support his men.

Hooking the fingers of his right hand under the off-side rein, the small Texan ignored the explosion of the caisson. He was more concerned with regaining control of his mount. Having accomplished that, he started to guide it in a half circle so that he could get back into the fight.

Riding towards the mass of struggling figures, Dusty decided that his strategy had worked. He did not allow himself to grow complacent. The fight was not yet over, nor was the safety of the battery assured. The Lancers had been hard hit by Company 'C's' opening volley and were continuing to lose men. For all that, they still had the advantage of numbers. If somebody could organize them and coordinate their efforts, they would still be a force to reckon with.

'Company "D"!' roared a voice, in an educated Northern accent. 'Company "D"! Rally around, men! Make for the guns.'

Attracted by the words, for they seemed to have sprung out of his own thoughts, Dusty sought for and located the speaker. It was the captain who had commanded the rear company; a tall, handsome, well-dressed and expensively equipped young man – but clearly one who knew his duty. He alone of the officers was trying to bring some kind of order out of the chaos. There was a chance, Dusty decided, that he might succeed if he was permitted to do so.

Although Dusty was interested by the captain's attempt to rally the Lancers, he did not permit it to hold all his attention. Which was just as well. He saw a burly, blue-clad soldier approaching to his right and was conscious of a second, on the left and to the rear, coming his way.

Hearing the shattering roar, and feeling the blast of the explosion, Colonel Middleton – commanding officer of the defending force – took his attention from the advancing Rebels. He stared for a moment at the smoking crater where the caisson had been. Then he turned his gaze to the three massive, cumbersome Volley Guns which had cost his small force so much effort and hard work during the forced march to Martin's Mill. Due to the accurate shelling, not one of them was able to operate. So, except as a morale factor, the loss of their ammunition would make little difference to the outcome of his mission.

Swinging his gaze to the Lancers, Middleton concluded that they would not be able to help him hold the Rebels away from the bridge. That was yet another point in his summation of the situation. Everything he could see told him that his position was rapidly becoming untenable.

From the beginning, Middleton had had little faith in his ability to carry out the duty in the manner which General Culver had demanded. It was, the tall, spare Infantry colonel realized, an almost classic case of too little arriving too late.

Colonel Middleton had been the first man to suspect where Ole Devil Hardin was intending to cross the Ouachita River and had suggested that an attempt be made to destroy the bridge. However, he had never expected to be given the assignment; especially with such restrictions upon his actions and so small a force at his disposal.

At a meeting of his commanding officers. Culver had agreed with Middleton as to the Rebels' destination and had given his orders. Middleton's regiment was to have the 'honour' of taking and holding the bridge, while the main force continued to 'drive' the enemy before them. According to Culver, all the 'Wisconsins' needed to do was stand fast and prevent the supply column from crossing. Backed by the half-battery of Vandenburgs and three companies of Lancers, they would – in the general's opinion – be more than a match for the Rebels' advance guard. Before any major assault could be launched, Culver had declared with his usual profanity, the rest of the Army of Arkansas would be on the scene.

Unfortunately, if not unexpectedly, things had not gone in the way General Culver had suggested. The task would have been more suitable to a cavalry regiment, supported by field artillery, but he had refused to use either. Nor would he give Middleton more men. Neither the Irish nor the Negro infantry regiments had been replaced, so Culver had claimed that he could not spare a larger force. Instead, Culver had dispatched the 'Wisconsins' with a small mounted screen of Lancers and three massive guns more appropriate to siege warfare than for rapid transportation. Apart from the difficulties of moving them, the Vandenburgs were basically a good choice for the work that had been expected. That they had failed was no fault of Colonel Middleton.

The limited time at Middleton's disposal had meant making a forced march and reaching his destination with exhausted men. They had been so tired that there had been no hope of establishing an extensive, strong defensive system, or of creating adequate protection for the Vandenburgs. On top of all the other problems, the Rebels' advance guard had come on to the scene far sooner than Culver – or even Middleton – had anticipated.

After that had happened, the whole affair had gone from bad to worse. First, although not unexpectedly, the mountain battery had moved in to counter the Vandenburgs. Then the company of Rebel cavalry had effectively prevented the Lancers from protecting the Volley Guns. Without the support of the Lancers and the half-battery, the 'Wisconsins'' position was desperate. Certainly they could not hope to carry out Culver's original idea of retaining the bridge for his own Army's use.

There was only one thing left to do, Middleton decided. He must put his alternative plan into operation. It meant abandoning Culver's scheme and might even be regarded as a deliberate disobedience of orders. For all that, Middleton believed he was acting correctly. A humane, sensible man, he could not face the prospect of causing many of his soldiers to be killed in a hopeless fight. Far better, he considered, to withdraw across the river, destroy the bridge and keep as many men as possible to fight another day.

A lesser man might have called upon his second-in-command for an opinion, perhaps even demanded that it be put in writing and witnessed. Middleton refused to do such a thing. The decision was his and his alone. So he would make it and stand by the consequences.

'Go and tell the company commanders to prepare to retire,' the colonel said, trying to keep all emotion out of his voice.

'Yes, sir,' answered the adjutant, to whom the words had been addressed, adopting an equally neutral tone. Then he hurried away to deliver the message that might lead to Middleton being court martialled when General Culver heard of it.

Finding himself between two converging enemies, Dusty Fog's mind worked at lightning speed in search of a way out of the dangerous situation. A fast-taken glance warned him that he had no hope of avoiding both attackers. So he tried to work out a solution. Of the pair, the one on the left and to the rear was the nearer, and, therefore, the more immediate threat. So he was the obvious choice to be dealt with first.

There was, Dusty decided from his examination, one small point in his favour. Coming from that angle, the man had been compelled to pass the lance across his horse's head so that its pointed extended to the left instead of being directed straight forward.

With Dusty, to think was to act. Twisting slightly to the left, he lined and fired his Colt by instinctive alignment. As he had demonstrated to Billy Jack and the men from the Commissary General's Department in Arkadelphia, he was capable of considerable accuracy with that method of shooting. Flying true, the bullet entered the soldier's left breast and ripped into his heart. Shock and pain caused him to rock backwards and his left hand tugged involuntarily at his horse's reins. The animal responded to the signal and started to swing in the direction of the pull. In doing so, it ensured that the lance was turned away from the small Texan.

'Watch ahead, Mr. Fog!' Sandy McGraw yelled, who was able to see Dusty's peril but, being so positioned, was unable to help against the man in front of his officer.

The warning had not been needed. On firing, barely waiting to see the result, Dusty returned his attention to the approaching rider. He was not a moment too soon. Aimed to take him in the lower body, the lance's steel tip had already come by the head of his bay gelding.

Once again, Dusty's ambidextrous ability came to his rescue. Up flashed his empty right hand, cupping under and elevating the shaft away from him. The soldier yelled in fury, but was unable to prevent his weapon from missing its mark. Before he could do more than register a vocal protest, the two horses had swept by each other.

The Lancer was given no opportunity to recover. Coming up unnoticed, Sandy McGraw attacked him. Wishing to conserve the three bullets remaining in his Colt, the youngster dropped forward the top of his guidon. There was a spear-head mounted on the nine foot long pole, turning it into an effective weapon. The point took the man in his ribs, sinking until the quillons of the cross-guard – fitted to prevent the spear from penetrating so deep that the flag entered the wound – halted its forward progress. It was sufficient. Knocked from the saddle by the unexpected attack, the Lancer's weight dragged him free from the tip of the guidon.

Throwing a quick glance to where his first attacker's horse was swinging away, its rider sliding off of its back, Dusty swung his gaze to where the Yankee captain was still trying to rally men.

Even as Dusty started to ride towards the captain, meaning to silence him before he achieved his intentions, the matter was taken from out of his hands. Bleeding from a sabre cut on his face, a lieutenant rushed from the melee beyond the captain. Seeing Dusty approaching, the lieutenant – who had a scared expression on his face – tried to line his Colt. Just as the officer jerked at the trigger, the captain sent his mount in the small Texan's direction. He took the bullet intended for Dusty in the centre of the back.

Shock and agony distorted the captain's face. Clutching at the pommel of his saddle, he tried to hold himself on it. Failing, he fell beneath the hooves of his killer's horse. Realizing what he had done, the lieutenant threw aside his revolver. Before he could do anything more, Sergeant Weather appeared behind him. A swing of the sergeant's sabre almost tore the officer's head from his shoulders.

Although Dusty did not know it, the killing of the captain would be an indirect cause of much trouble and bloodshed in Rio Hondo County a few years after the end of the War.*

The fighting continued for a short while longer. Having emptied his revolver, without wasting a load, Dusty quit his horse's back. He acquired a discarded sabre and helped to engage some of the dismounted Lancers.

Then it was over.

Left practically leaderless by the disposal of their officers – being armed with revolvers, they had been the Texans' first targets – and having suffered heavy losses due to the unsuitability of their archaic weapons when opposed by firearms, the Lancers were demoralized and disheartened.

* How this happened is told in: *The Rio Hondo War.*

Some, on foot and mounted, threw down their lances and raised their hands. Others, who had stayed on their horses, turned to gallop towards the hamlet. The remainder scattered and fled in all directions. Eagerly a number of the Texans took up the pursuit.

'Bugler!' Dusty shouted, looking around him.

'Yo!' answered the musician, riding up.

'Sound "Recall"!' Dusty ordered, being determined to regain control of the enlisted men.

With the notes of the 'Recall' ringing in his ears, Dusty turned his attention to the main part of the battle. The howitzers were no longer barking and he realized that he had not heard the deeper note of the Vandenburgs. Already the leading wave of the Arkansas Rifles were swarming towards the first line of trenches, with the supporting Companies of the Texas Light Cavalry preparing to dash ahead.

An examination of the village told Dusty that the Vandenburgs had all been silenced before they could be brought into use. The assault had a better than fair chance of succeeding.

Which brought up another, vitally important, matter.

Swinging his gaze towards the bridge, Dusty heard the sound of shooting from the woodland on either side of it. From what he could make out, the detail sent by Company 'A' had run into heavy opposition and would not be able to reach their objective. Due to the denser nature of the terrain, he could see nothing of what was going on upstream. Perhaps Red and his men had also been halted. If so, the Yankees would be free to destroy the bridge.

Except that, by doing it, the commanding officer of the defending force would be trapping all his men on the northern side of the Ouachita.

Men were returning in answer to the bugle's repeated summons. Among them was Sandy McGraw, leading Dusty's bay, Billy Jack, Weather and Kiowa, the latter having arrived in time to take part in the later stages of the fighting.

'The sergeant major's cashed in, Mr. Fog,' Weather said,

'Damn the luck!' Dusty growled, but forced himself to remember his duties. 'Take six men and see to the wounded and prisoners, Sergeant Weather.'

'Yo!' Weather replied, turning and gathering the nearest six soldiers to help him carry out the order.

'Sergeant Billy Jack,' Dusty went on. 'Take rank as sergeant major. Form up the Company ready to move out.'

'Yo!' reponded the lanky non-com.

Having given the orders, Dusty looked at the hamlet. Encouraged by the destruction of the multi-barrelled weapons, the attackers were springing forward at a faster pace. They were within fifty yards of the forward trenches, with the cavalry galloping before them, playing a vital part in preventing the Yankees from concentrating their fire on the slower-moving, more vulnerable foot-soldiers.

Although Company 'C' should have been joining in the assault, Dusty decided that their absence would not have any adverse effect upon the outcome. They had already provided a most useful service by protecting the mountain battery. With their horses tired from the exertions of the charge and subsequent fighting, they would not be able to form up and reach the hamlet before the issue was resolved one way or the other.

At that moment, Dusty noticed something happening which aroused his curiosity and gave him cause for speculation.

After discharging a single volley, the occupants of the forward defences sprang from their trenches. They fell back rapidly, but – as far as Dusty could determine – under the control of their officers. Certainly they did not appear to be fleeing in panic. Passing the second and third lines of trenches, they continued to run towards the river.

'We've licked 'em, Mr. Fog!' Sandy McGraw enthused, sentiments which were echoed delightedly by the other men who were forming up before their officer.

'It's not over yet,' Dusty warned.

'If they go over the river, they'll be in our neck of the woods,' the bugler pointed out. 'We'll have 'em—.'

'Not if they blow up the bridge,' Dusty corrected. 'Then they'll have a better chance of getting away than they would from this side.'

'Don't we have help coming, Mr. Fog?' Billy Jack wanted to know.

'Gaylord's Dare-Devils and the Second Texas Infantry should be on their way,' Dusty answered, an idea starting to form as he looked at the hamlet. 'Colonel Barnett sent word to them to move up here as soon as our scouts reported about the Yankees holding the crossing.'

'Then we've got the bastards trapped,' the bugler insisted.

'Not if they can destroy the bridge,' Dusty warned. 'With that done, they can be long gone before Colonel Gaylord arrives from Arkadelphia. Reload those handguns, you men. Then we're moving out.'

'Yo!' Billy Jack answered, then eyed Dusty with interest. Unless he was mistaken, the young officer had something in mind. 'You-all fixing on us going to help run the Yankees across the Ouachita?'

'Nope,' Dusty replied. 'We're going to see how Cousin Red's detail are making out. When we've done that. I've got something else for you to do, sergeant major. But I'll tell you about it on the way.'

With the thirty men available to him, Dusty rode towards the woodland into which Red's detail had disappeared. He studied what was happening at the bridge and made sure that his earlier conclusions were on the right lines. Noticing that no defensive positions had been prepared on the southern side of the river, he felt certain that the Yankees had no intention of holding the bridge from there. So they must be relying upon destroying it to halt the supply column. Possibly they were under orders to only do so as a last alternative. Maybe General Culver had hoped to retain it intact for his Army's use after defeating the Confederate force which he was pursuing.

No matter what the original idea had been, the Yankees must now be committed to destroying the bridge. If they could be prevented from doing it, Dusty believed that there was a way to avert further bloodshed.

Quietly the small Texan outlined his idea to Billy Jack, whose gloomy assertion that it would not work – because of several highly unlikely accidents – showed that it stood a good chance of succeeding.

However, everything still hinged upon whether or not Red had been able to carry out his first independent and very responsible duty.

CHAPTER FIFTEEN

ALTHOUGH the soldier's appearance came as a complete surprise to Red Blaze, it did not cause him to be frozen into immobility. Letting out a yell, he jabbed his spurs into the brown gelding's flanks. As the spirited animal bounced onwards at an increased speed, he thrust out, cocked and fired his Colt. Fast-taken and aimed by the roughest possible instinctive alignment, the shot came *very* close to making a hit and partially achieved its purpose.

Hearing the bullet splitting the air as it passed close to his left ear, the soldier ducked involuntarily. In doing so, he caused the barrel of his rifle to lower at the instant when his right forefinger was tightening on the trigger. The Spencer bellowed, but its muzzle was no longer pointing at the redhead's chest.

A violent shudder ripped through the brown gelding as the heavy calibre bullet drove into its heart. Feeling the animal's legs buckling, Red kicked his feet free from the stirrups and tossed his right leg forward over the saddlehorn. He thrust himself clear of the falling horse, contriving to alight on his feet and running. While struggling to maintain his equilibrium and avoid plunging headlong down the slope, he swung his eyes towards his would-be killer. Being armed with a Spencer repeating rifle, the man was still a potential danger.

Horror was twisting at the Yankee's features as he realized his peril. Although the horse had been shot and was dying, its momentum was carrying it in his direction. Desperately he tried to fling himself aside, but he was too slow. The stricken animal crashed into him and he screamed in agony as its weight hurled him backwards. Horse and man went down the slope together. On top, the gelding was crushing the soldier between itself and the hard, unyielding ground.

After running almost uncontrollably for some yards, Red regained control of his movements and managed to stop. He hurried to where his horse was sprawled on top of the soldier. One glance told him that both were beyond all human aid. Looking around, he found nothing to suggest that the man had companions in the immediate vicinity.

Satisfied that he was not, for the moment at least, in danger of further attempts on his life, Red continued walking. On reaching the edge of the river, he went swiftly about making his preparations. For all that, despite being fully aware of the situation's extreme urgency, he refused to let himself become flustered or to act hastily. Instead, he thought out his movements with a care that would have surprised many of his elders if they had witnessed it.

If the main body of the picket had heard the commotion, some of them might come to investigate. Possibly he would be on his way before they arrived, but he wanted to try to avoid leaving obvious indications of his intentions. What he was planning to do would be sufficiently dangerous, without him needlessly adding to the risks.

Laying the Colt on the ground, the youngster divested himself of his tunic. He retained his dark grey shirt, but sat down to remove his boots and socks. Concealing the discarded items under a bush, he patted his breeches' pocket to ensure that Dusty's Russel Barlow knife was there. If he should succeed in reaching the bridge, he would need it.

With a final look around, to make certain that he had hidden the more obvious suggestions of what he was planning to do, Red waded into the river. His feet sank into the mud, but he thrust himself on until reaching deeper water. Taking a final look up the slope and satisfying himself that he was unobserved, he dived forward to start swimming downstream. At his point of entry, a gentle curve hid the bridge from his sight. Moving towards it, he kept constantly alert for any hint that he might have been seen by the enemy.

On reaching the bend, Red swam towards the southern bank. The current had carved a deep hole at that point and, even when close to the shore, his feet could not touch the bottom. Treading the water gently, with only his head above the surface, he let himself be swept slowly onwards and soon received his first view of the bridge.

From all appearances, the tide of the battle was swinging in the Confederate States' favour. While there was fighting taking place on the fringe of the hamlet, the Yankees appeared to be pulling back from the positions.

For a few seconds, Red was puzzled by the enemies' actions. They were retiring across the bridge. Yet they were doing it in an orderly manner and not in full flight. Then he started to understand their motives and realized that, now more than ever, he must do his utmost to prevent the destruction of the bridge.

Just as Red was about to thrust himself forward at a faster rate, he recollected his Cousin Dusty's often-repeated advice. The time to study the situation was *before* one became involved in it. With that in mind, Red allowed himself to be drifted closer by the push of the current and subjected his objective to a careful scrutiny.

The bridge had been built to handle plenty of heavy traffic and was of a sturdy construction. Unlike many of its day, it was not covered over as a means of protecting its timbers from the elements. Only a low guard rail was between Red and the soldiers who were already starting to run across. It would not be of any help in preventing them from seeing him. Fortunately, Dusty had taken that into consideration when planning how he would handle the assignment. He had told Red everything and the youngster was turning that information to his own use. So he knew how he could reach the bridge, but still keep out of the Yankees' sight.

Dusty had guessed that the destructive charge would be placed where it would do most damage. Bearing that in mind, Red looked at the massive oak central support and its Y-shaped bracing struts. Sure enough, a large keg of black powder had been placed in the angle formed by the southern supporting beam.

Sucking in a deep breath, Red allowed himself to sink beneath the suface. He did not dare go closer while on the top, in case he should be seen by the men who were crossing the bridge or upon the banks. Waiting until his feet touched the bottom, he started to swim just above the swaying weeds.

Soon Red's lungs felt as if they would burst. Grimly he forced himself to go on, for he had no means of estimating how close he might be to the bridge and had no desire to make a premature appearance. To do so under the circumstances would be asking for disaster.

At last, however, lack of air drove the youngster upwards. Above him, the surface was a circle of silvery light. Then the downstream portion of it started to become straight instead of curved. That would be the side of the bridge, cutting out the light. So he ought to be close enough to escape the Yankees' notice.

Something large, black and roughly oblong appeared, growing rapidly in size as it plunged downwards.

There was a crashing splash and Red felt the sudden turbulence of the disturbed water strike him. The mysterious shape came close and the younger's hands touching clothing. Silently cursing his lousy luck, he grabbed hold of the thing and confirmed his suspicions. Apparently a soldier had seen him approaching beneath the surface and had leapt over the guard rail to attack him.

Clutching his assailant by the front of the tunic and one arm, Red tried to prevent them from rising to the surface. He could not do it. Even as they started to ascend, he wondered why the man was not struggling to escape. He soon learned the answer.

Shaking the water from his eyes and filling his lungs with air, Red stared into the attacker's face. There was little above the eyebrows but torn flesh and splintered bones. The blood, tissue and brains had been washed away after being exposed to the water when a bullet had shattered its way through the skull.

With a strangled exclamation of disgust, the youngster released his hold. He watched the corpse drifting away, then looked upwards. Luck was still on his side, for they had surfaced under the bridge.

Another body plummeted over the guard rail, on the downstream side, almost landing on the one that had handed Red such a shock. Overhead, boots stamped on the planks as the withdrawl continued.

Swimming towards the upstream central support, Red had only the smallest worries regarding the way in which he would carry out his work. They did not come from wondering how he could reach the barrel. Company 'C' had visited Martin's Mill ten days earlier, before the start of the retreat, and Dusty had studied the bridge. He had formulated his plan from memories of that examination. The answer to how one could climb the support was simple – or would have been under less trying conditions.

Whoever had designed the bridge was clearly a man skilled in his work. He had included the means by which the bottom of the structure could be examined. Iron rungs had been driven into the massive central support, extending to water-level, allowing it to be climbed with comparative ease.

The only thing wrong with that, from Red's point of view, was the way the rungs were placed. On the *outside*. Which meant that, as he climbed up, he would be in plain sight of either bank; although there was sufficient of an overhang to provide concealment from the men who were crossing the bridge.

There was a shrill scream of agony and a third body tumbled into the river. Then a fourth followed. Bobbing up and down in the wash caused by their arrival and counteracting the thrust of the current, which was fairly strong beneath the bridge, Red took rapid stock of the situation.

A moment's thought told him that things might not be quite as bad as he had first imagined. Given just a smidgin of good old Texas luck, everybody would be too engrossed with their own affairs to notice him. Or the Yankees might figure he was one of them who had been hit by a Rebel's bullet, knocked from the bridge, but not so badly hurt that he was unable to try to climb back. Sodden by their long immersion, his shirt and breeches ought to look dark enough to aid such a deception.

Of course, one of the attackers might draw a similar conclusion and take the appropriate action.

'Yes, sir,' Red told himself. 'Things aren't quite so bad. Like getting thrown by a horse and being told you've only bust *both* legs, not your neck.'

Never one to worry unduly about the future, the youngster did not let the last thought depress him. Reaching for the nearest rung, he hauled himself upwards. Nobody took any notice of him as he ascended to the point where the supporting braces spread at angles of forty-five degrees from the central post. One shove would topple the keg into the water and the job would be done.

Or would it?

Placing his hand on the keg, Red started to notice things which caused him to revise his optimistic opinion.

Firstly, the keg had been carefully covered with waterproof tarpaulin.

Secondly, the Yankees had merely rested in in the angle and had not attempt to fasten or hold it in place.

Thirdly, despite having failed to take that basic precaution, they had gone to the trouble of arranging the barrel with the fuse on the *inside* of the bridge. Doing that must have been more difficult than merely sliding it in the other way round.

Lastly, as Red discovered when he climbed higher and seated himself on the unoccupied bracing strut, the fuse appeared to have been fixed in a haphazard manner. Not because it led to the southern bank. That had only to be expected. The explosion could not be touched off until the Yankees had crossed, so must be handled from that side What had caught Red's eye was the way in which the fuse had been passed loosely through the arches of the next support. Once it had burned beyond that point, its end would fall into the water and be extinguished.

Looking closer at the fuse, Red decided that it was unlike any type of slow- or quick-match he had ever seen. Taking hold of the fuse, he found that it was stiffer and felt different too.

It must, he concluded, be one of those new-fangled wire fuses that operated from something called an electric battery. Red had heard tell of such things, although he had had no personal experience with them. So he had an idea of the device's capabilities.

Somebody on the Yankees' side had been mighty smart and tricky!

The charge had been placed so that anybody who happened to find it, most likely being in one hell of a rush to save the bridge from destruction, would have reached an erroneous conclusion. Wanting to prevent the explosion, the rescuer would have shoved the barrel from its position and counted on the river to render it harmless. Instead, the waterproof covering would have kept the charge as lethal as ever.

Wriggling through the aperture, Red sat on the stout cross beam which permitted an examination to be carried out across the width of the under-surface. He tugged at the fuse, but it refused to return through the hole into which it had been inserted.

'I'm sure pleased this's Dusty's Barlow, not mine,' Red mused as he took out and opened the knife. Gathering a loop of the wire, he sawed through it. Letting the cut end fall, he sent the barrel after it. 'That's settled their—' he went on, but some instinct caused him to look over his shoulder. His relief ended and he twisted around, muttering, 'The sneaky bastards. They've put another barrel over there!'

Continuing to grip the open knife, Red began to scramble along the inspection beam. Over his head, heavy boots pounded incessantly as men poured over the bridge to what they hoped would be safety. From the various other sounds which had been, and still were, reaching the youngster's ears, the withdrawal was costing the Yankees dearly. Four more men had toppled over the guard rail, struck down by the Confederate bullets. If the screams and cries of pain that had repeatedly rang out meant anything, others had been hit and remained on the bridge, or were carried away by their companions.

Three harsh, sharp detonations from the southern bank caused Red a moment's anxiety. Then he realized that they must be shells going off. Having silenced the Vandenburg Volley Guns, Douglas Staunce's mountain battery had switched targets and were already bombarding the soldiers who had reached the other side of the Ouachita.

How much time did Red have?

Once the last of the Yankees had completed the crossing, the electric battery would be operated. The youngster had no way of knowing how the withdrawal was progressing. Of one thing he felt certain. If the remaining barrel of powder should be detonated, it would be powerful enough to wreck the bridge; or, at best, render it unsafe for the heavy wagons of the supply column.

'And it sure's hell won't do me a whole heap of good, comes to that,' Red admitted silently. 'If only the good die young, I likely don't have long to go.'

On reaching the second central support, the youngster once more tried to draw free the fuse. As with the other, the wire must have been knotted on the inside before the lid was fixed in position. However, Red did not waste time in idle conjecture over the reason for its immobility. The sound of shooting was drawing nearer on the northern bank. While the pace of the feet passing overhead was growing swifter, they seemed to be diminishing in numbers.

Either the wire was tougher than its predecessor, or the Barlow's blade had lost its edge.

'Come on, blast you!' Red gritted, feeling perspiration running from his forehead and down his cheeks. 'Cut through the son-of-a-bitching thing!'

Lead was flying in both direction across the river. Darting a glance to the southern shore, Red saw that the Yankees were forming up in whatever cover they could find and firing over the water. If any of them should see him, he would make an easy target.

Back and forward, back and forward, moved the knife without, apparently, making any impression on the wire fuse.

The last of the feet were coming closer!

So far, the Yankees' attention was directed at the soldiers of the Arkansas Rifles and Texas Light Cavalry. Swinging his gaze in the other direction, Red found that his comrades-in-arms were advancing through the hamlet, or taking up firing positions near the edge of the river.

Nearer came the last of the running feet!

Once they had crossed, whoever was handling the destruction would do what he had to do.

A savage jerk and the Barlow knife slipped through the severed ends of the fuse wire.

Giving a low sigh of relief, Red allowed the two ends and the knife to slip from his fingers. His work was not quite finished. While the barrel could no longer by ignited by electricity, a bullet into it from the southern shore would prove equally effective.

Just as Red was about to draw the keg inwards, yet another soldier's body was pitched from above. Instead of pulling, Red shoved and the barrel tilted from its perch. It landed in the water just after the man had arrived and, Red hoped, the extra splash would not be observed.

Before relaxing and considering how he might make good his escape, the youngster subjected the bottom of the bridge to a careful scrutiny. There were no more fuse wires, nor could he detect any suggestion that other barrels had been set out. So he decided that he had ended the danger of the bridge being destroyed.

And only just in time!

No more men were coming from the northern bank and the last of them had almost gone by his position. In a few seconds, the man responsible for setting off the charges would make his play.

Which raised the point of what Red should do next.

Should he remain where he was until the fighting ended, counting on nobody being able to draw a bead on him?

Or ought he to try to join his companions and tell them of the successful conclusion of his assignment?

Colonel Barnett would want to know for sure that the bridge would not be blown up.

The only trouble being that carrying the news to him could be mighty risky.

So, if it came to a point, would be staying put under the bridge. Once the expected explosion failed to materialize, the Yankees were sure to investigate. Even if Red still held the Russell-Barlow knife, it would be mighty inadequate. against men armed with rifles and several yards away.

A cry of agony shattered the air from above Red and the running thud of the final pair of feet changed into a fumbling stagger. There was a crash of something heavy striking the wooden guard rail and a blue-uniformed figure fell from the bridge. It was bare-headed, the face covered with blood, and wore the dress of a Yankee infantry's first lieutenant.

The officer was still alive. Plunging beneath the surface, he reappeared, flailing wildly in an attempt to keep his head above water.

'Help!' the wounded lieutenant screeched. 'Help me. I can't see!'

Nobody on the banks took any notice.

Watching the enemy officer being swept downstream, his struggles and calls for help growing weaker, Red knew that he would be drowned if somebody did not go to his assistance. Either the effects of the wound, or the blood flowing from it, had deprived the lieutenant of his sight. Whichever was the reason, he could not survive for much longer.

That was, Red concluded, a hell of a lousy way for a man to die.

Wriggling from the inspection beam, Red dropped into the water. Disregarding the danger of being shot by one side or the other, he struck out as fast as he could after the lieutenant. Red wondered how long it would be before a Yankee, or one of his own people, started throwing lead his way. It did not happen, so he concluded that both factions were too occupied in their fighting to interfere with the rescue.

Before Red reached the officer, he sank out of sight. Filling his lungs, the youngster followed. Finding the man, Red grabbed him under the armpits and, kicking out furiously, raised them both to the surface. On his head emerging, he immediately looked around. The current was thrusting him towards the southern bank. With the injured man hanging so heavily, Red doubted if he could hope to cross and reach his own side.

'Come on, feller!' yelled a voice with a Northern accent. 'Fetch him here. We'll help you!'

Swinging his gaze towards the speaker, Red saw a 'Wisconsins'' sergeant and a private running forward. More enlisted men used rifles to give them covering fire. They were on the fringe of the Yankees' line and would probably be part of the flank guard, Red decided.

Another glance across the river assured Red of how little hope he had of reaching his friends while towing his limp and unwieldy burden. So he continued to swim in the speaker's direction, drawing the lieutenant along with a hand cupped under his chin.

Seeing the soldiers continuing to wade forward, Red slowed his stroke and let them come until the water was lapping at their chests. The youngster was thinking fast and had seen a hope of avoiding being identified as an enemy. While his soaking shirt would be unlikely to give him away, the riding breeches were unmistakable evidence that he was not in the infantry. His bare feet might suggest that he was a Lancer who had taken to the water in a hurry to rescue the stricken officer.

So Red continued to swim even after he could have dropped his feet to the bottom. The soldiers reached out, taking hold of the officer and drawing him out of Red's grasp.

'Can you manage, friend?' the sergeant inquired.

'There's another wounded feller out there,' Red replied, trying to avoid sounding like a Texan. 'I'll see if I can help him!'

With that, the youngster turned and swam away.

'Hey!' yelped the private, staring after Red. 'He's wearing riding breeches and he sounded like a Reb. He ain't—'

'You're seeing things!' growled the sergeant, who had made a similar deduction. 'No Texan'd save one of our officers.'

'But—!' the soldier began.

'He saved Mr. Rint here,' interrupted the sergeant. 'So, unless you want to spend the rest of the War cleaning the officers' shit-houses, you'll reckon he's gone to save another wounded feller. Now let's get the hell away from here. The Rebs haven't shot at us yet, but I'd hate like hell to keep tempting them.'

Expecting to be shot at by friends or foes at any moment, Red struck out towards the northern bank of the Ouachita. He took a line that ought to carry him ashore below the fighting. The way he saw it, he had been shot at and taken enough chances for one day.

Directing a look upstream, Red grinned. The bridge was still standing, with only dead or badly wounded Yankees occupying it.

'They've likely tried to blow her up by now,' the youngster thought. 'I wonder what they'll do when they find that they can't?'

CHAPTER SIXTEEN

RIDING alone from the woods fringing the Ouachita River, Dusty Fog was an anxious and worried young man. He wondered what his father and, more particularly, Colonel Barnett would think of the action he had just taken. It was an unusual one, but he felt that he had been justified in sending Company 'C' across the Ouachita River while he returned to make his report.

On reaching the woods with his men, Dusty had ordered them to dismount and continue on foot. That had been a sound move, for riders would have been impossible to control in such terrain. Moving forward, he had found that the Yankees' picket was already making a fighting withdrawal. The arrival of reinforcements had led to them all being killed or captured.

Dusty had learned of Red's departure from Corporal Hassle. So he had dispatched the old timer and Kiowa to see if they could discover what had happened to his cousin. With that taken care of, Dusty had pushed on to the edge of the woods. There, he had halted his men before they could be seen by the Yankes at the hamlet. To have continued the advance would have availed him nothing, except for needlessly killed or wounded men. Instead, he had watched the enemy crossing the bridge.

After the lieutenant who had ably commanded the rear guard was shot and had fallen into the water, the withdrawal had been accomplished. Dusty had waited with bated breath. The moment had come when the Yankees would try to destroy the bridge. Try as he might, Dusty had been unable to locate any trace of his cousin and wondered where Red might be.

When no explosion had happened, Dusty had been relieved and perturbed. Either the Yankees had failed to take the precaution of mining the bridge, or Red had been successful in nullifying their efforts. Yet there was no sign of the young lieutenant.

Kiowa and Hassle had returned with Red's property. From the story they had read in Red's tracks, Dusty knew that he had set off in the way that Dusty had outlined. That the bridge was still standing had suggested that Red had put the scheme to use and had pulled it off.

The question that had nagged at Dusty was, what had happened to his cousin after the conclusion of the mission.

While searching the banks in the hope of learning something about Red's fate, Dusty had given Billy Jack his orders. While the small Texan had known that he must place a whole lot of faith in his lanky temporary sergeant major, he had been satisfied that Billy Jack could be trusted with the work. Leaving his men to cross the river and carry out his scheme, Dusty had returned to the open ground with the intention of reporting to his superiors.

While Dusty believed that his father would approve of his actions, on discovering what had motivated them, he felt less certain of how Colonel Barnett would respond.

An infantryman to the core, Barnett had a reputation for being a stickler where military protocol was concerned. He was also said to have small respect for the abilities of volunteer officers. So he might be disinclined to accept suggestions from a very young and junior first lieutenant; especially one belonging to a volunteer *cavalry* regiment. Even more so when that same lieutenant had already implemented part of the proposals without having awaited their acceptance.

For all that, Dusty believed he had been justified and correct in sending the remnants of Company 'C' across the river and having given them specific orders on how they must act on the other side.

Locating his father was not difficult. Dusty saw Major Hondo Fog standing with Barnett and several infantry officers on the slope beyond the range of the rifles across the river. Guiding his horse towards them, the young Texan examined the battle-ground as they were doing. More than ever, he felt certain that he had acted correctly. He only wished that he could be as sure that Red was alive and well.

The Yankees had made good their withdrawal, Dusty observed, but it had cost them dearly. Yet the price had been lighter than if they had remained in the trenches without the support of the Vandenburg Volley Guns.

From the enemy, Dusty swung his gaze to the Confederate States' force. Making use of the Yankees' deserted trenches, or the buildings of the hamlet, the Arkansas Rifles were shooting across the river. The mountain battery's shells were falling accurately around the 'Wisconsins'' defensive positions. Already the three Companies of the Texas Light Cavalry were heading downstream. They would be going to swim over and either out-flank or take the Yankees from the rear.

Swinging from his saddle, Dusty handed the gelding's reins to the stocky Texas Light Cavalry sergeant who stood some distance from the officers and held two horses.

'You did good, Mr. Fog,' Sergeant Glissade praised. 'What happened to Cap'n von Hertz?'

'A sharpshooter made wolf-bait of him,' Dusty replied. 'Sergeant Major Goering's dead too.'

'It could've been worse,' Glissade commiserated. 'They was three to your one. Like I said, you did good.'

'Gracias,' Dusty said, knowing that he was receiving high praise.

'Your pappy was wondering why you didn't use the *caracole*, like Cap'n von Hertz aimed to,' Glissade went on, a note of warning in his voice. 'Maybe you'd best go and tell him.'

'I'll do that,' Dusty promised and turned away.

Walking forward, Dusty was conscious of the senior officers' scrutiny. His father – who looked like a taller, older, version of himself – showed relief and puzzlement, but the others displayed only the latter emotion. Schooling his face into what he hoped would be an expressionless mask, the small Texan came to a a halt and saluted.

'Lieutenant Fog, Company "C" reporting, sir,' Dusty said to the colonel.

'Where's Captain von Hertz, Mr. Fog?' Barnett demanded, returning the salute.

'He was killed by a sharpshooter while we were taking up our position in the woods, sir,' Dusty explained. "Our scout got the sharpshooter, but he was too late to save the captain.'

'That left you in command, Mr. Fog?' asked one of the infantry majors.

'Yes, sir,' Dusty agreed.

'You did damned well,' Barnett stated. 'Who carried out your assignment?'

'Mr. Blaze, sir,' Dusty answered and continued anxiously. 'Hasn't he reported yet?'

'Not yet,' Hondo admitted, watching the brief play of disturbed emotions on his son's face. Dusty and Red had been inseparable companions for most of their lives. 'I reckon he's safe enough, boy.'

'Where's your Company now, Mr. Fog?' Barnett wanted to know.

'I've sent them across the Ouachita, sir.'

'Under whose command?'

'My sergeant major's, sir.'

'Goering's a sound man, sir,' Hondo commented.

'He was killed in the attack on the Lancers, sir,' Dusty corrected. 'I appointed Sergeant Billy Jack to take his place.'

'He's good and reliable too, colonel,' Hondo declared.

'Why did you send them, Mr. Fog?' asked the major who had spoken earlier. 'And why didn't you go with them?'

'I felt it best that I should report to Colonel Barnett, sir,' Dusty replied. 'But I figured that he'd want a message sending to ask Colonel Gaylord to get to the bridge as quickly as possible.'

'You figured right,' Barnett declared. 'But not at the cost of sending a full Company to fetch him.'

'Only one man, Corporal Cotton will be going, sir,' Dusty

pointed out. 'The rest are waiting to carry out another duty.'

'You've told them to join up with the other Companies, huh Dusty?' Hondo suggested.

'Only if they can't do what I hope they'll be able to do, sir.'

'And what might *that* be?' Barnett growled.

'They'll try to convince the Yankees that our reinforcements are already on hand, sir,' Dusty drawled, retaining a flat, neutrally respectful timbre in his voice. This was the moment when he must lay himself open to recriminations, scorn, maybe even disciplinary action, if his idea should fail to meet with the colonel's approval. 'That might make them more willing to listen to your terms, sir.'

'Terms?' Barnett barked. 'Just what terms might they be, *mister*?'

'I wondered if we – you, that is, sir – could make them an offer—'

'Such as?' Hondo prompted, as his son's words died away and Barnett did not offer to comment.

'Giving them the opportunity to hand over the bridge?,' Dusty began.

'We've as good as got it now!' snorted the infantry major, but none of his companions appeared to share his sentiment.

'Yes, sir,' Dusty conceded tactfully. 'But I thought that we might be able to speed things up.'

'How?' Barnett challenged.

'We could offer them an exchange, sir,' Duty replied. 'Their freedom and an unrestricted passage through our lines for the bridge.'

'The Yankees wouldn't go for that!' growled the major. 'I know damned well I wouldn't!'

'I think the Yankee colonel will, sir,' Dusty contradicted, in the politest possible manner.

'What makes you think that, Mr. Fog?' Barnett asked, looking at the small Texan with added interest.

'The way he pulled back his men as soon as he saw the

Vandenburgs or Lancers couldn't help him, sir,' Dusty elaborated, decided that the question had been a point in his favour. 'Like you said last night, sir; the fact that the Yankees sent such a strong force, and not just a small detail to blow up the bridge, suggests they were supposed to try to hold it for their Army's use. Only I reckon their colonel was more concerned with the lives of his men and didn't aim to throw them away without good cause. I'm betting that, given a chance, he'll be willing to get them away safe. Especially if he believes that they're already close to being surrounded and cut off on the wrong side of the river.'

'The Yankees won't give in that easy,' insisted the major who had already protested. 'I wouldn't in their place.'

'Not even to save your command, what was left of it, from being killed or taken prisoner?' Hondo put in. 'Because that's what's facing the Yankees if they refuse our terms.'

'And if they accept,' the infantry major countered, 'they'll be free to fight against us again.'

'There'll be a lot of our men left alive who'd die trying to take the bridge,' Hondo pointed out. 'Because there's no easy way to do it. Time isn't on our side.'

'And if we give them enough of it, they could come up with a way to destroy the bridge,' another of the infantry officers remarked. 'Mr. Fog's idea could save us all that, if it comes off.'

'We'll give it a try,' Barnett declared, before any further discussion could take place. 'Will you deliver the terms, Major Fog?'

'I will, sir,' Hondo agreed, without hesitation.

'You realize that I can't allow considerations of your safety to influence my future actions if they don't honour your flag of truce and take you as a hostage?'

'I accept that, colonel,' Hondo agreed.

'Very well,' Barnett said. 'Is there anything you need?'

'The loan of a bugler,' Hondo suggested. 'And I'd like to take Mr. Fog with me, sir.'

'Mr. Fog?' Barnett repeated, looking from father to son and back.

'It's his plan, sir,' Hondo reminded the colonel. 'And the experience might come in useful for him in the future.'

'So it may,' Barnett conceded, nodding approvingly as his eyes returned to the small Texan. There was a very capable young man, with a great future. As such, he should be given every opportunity to participate in matters of importance. He looked the kind who would profit by doing so. 'I'll leave how you handle things in your hands, Major Fog. The rest of you gentlemen rejoin your Companies. I want everything ready to launch an assault, but I also don't want any mistakes if the call for a truce is accepted. We'd be getting ready to attack if we were expecting the arrival of reinforcements. So we'd best act as they'll expect us to. Don't you agree, Mr. Fog?'

'Yes, sir,' Dusty answered. 'I had something like that in mind.'

'Then why didn't you mention it?' Barnett inquired.

'I didn't reckon I'd need to, sir,' Dusty admitted.

'It's pleasing to find that at least one young lieutenant credits us old fogies with having a modicum of intelligence, Hondo,' Barnett commented dryly. 'Either that, or your son's a born diplomat. I'll not embarrass *any* of us by asking which you think it is. Go and attend to your duties, gentlemen.'

'I'll not ask if it *was* diplomacy, boy,' Hondo said with a grin, as they went to their horses. 'But I'd admire to know.'

'Colonel Barnett's one smart *hombre*, for a foot-shuffler,' Dusty obliged. 'I reckoned he might see reason, but he wouldn't want too much of it rammed down his throat by a wet-behind-the-ears, fly-slicer luff like me.'

'There's something in that,' Hondo smiled. Then noticing the way in which his son continually darted looks towards the river, continued, 'Don't worry, boy, young Red's all right. I'm willing to bet on it.'

'I hope so,' Dusty replied. 'If he's been killed—'

'It was after doing something that had to be done,' Hondo interrupted.

'But it was *my* duty to do it,' Dusty protested.

'You couldn't do it, through no fault of your own, boy. And Red couldn't have handled the Company as well as you did. You *know* that you made the right decision.'

'Even if Red was killed?'

'*Even* if Red was killed,' Hondo agreed. 'Because the destruction of the bridge would mean that a whole lot more than just Red would die. As it is, boy, once the Yankees accept your terms, we can cross the Ouachita and their main body won't be able to follow us.'

'Yes, sir,' Dusty drawled and, wanting to turn his thoughts from his cousin, went on, 'We'll need a white flag. I'll fetch one of those lances and I've a shirt in my saddle-pouch that'll do for it.'

'*Bueno*,' Hondo answered. 'Go to it.'

Mounting his gelding, Dusty returned to the scene of his Company's fight with the Lancers. Leaning over, he scooped up one of the discarded weapons without needing to halt or dismount. On rejoining his father and Glissade, he produced the shirt and fastened its sleeves to the shaft. At that moment, Sergeant Weather rode up.

'I've got your sabre here, sir,' the non-com announced, handing over the weapon.

'*Gracias*,' Dusty replied. 'Is everything all right with you?'

'Well enough, sir,' Weather confirmed.

'See to the men until I get back,' Dusty requested, sheathing the sabre.

An infantry bugler ran to meet the Texans as they rode down the slope. At Hondo's command, he blew the 'Cease Fire'. The message was relayed by shouted orders and the shooting ended on the northern bank of the river. After a few seconds, the Yankees also stopped using their weapons.

'Let's get going!' Hondo ordered. 'Show them the flag, Sergeant Glissade.'

'Yo!' answered the non-com, accepting the lance and elevating it so the improvised flap flapped in the breeze.

'Keep sounding calls, bugler,' Hondo went on.

With Glissade holding the lance upright and the bugler playing loud calls to emphasize that no surprise was intended, the party advanced. On reaching the end of the bridge, Hondo brought them to a halt. For a few seconds nothing happened. Then a tall, bearded Union infantry officer – whose shoulder straps bore the gilt laurel leaves of a major – strode forward and looked across the river.

'What's on your mind, major?' called the Yankee officer.

'A parlay, major,' Hondo replied. 'Will you meet us at the centre?'

'I will.'

'Can I suggest a truce for thirty minutes, while we're at it, to give us all time to attend to our wounded.'

'I accept that,' the Union major answered.

'This's as far as you and the bugler go, sergeant,' Hondo remarked, as he and Dusty dismounted.

Having handed their reins to Glissade, Dusty retrieved the lance from the sergeant and followed his father. The 'Wisconsins' ' representative walked to meet them, followed by half a dozen soldiers who started to examine the dead and wounded men on the bridge.

'Major Fog, First Lieutenant Fog, Texas Light Cavalry', Hondo introduced, saluting. 'I'm here on behalf of Colonel Barnett, commanding the 1st Arkansas Rifle Regiment.'

'Major Grimsby, speaking for Colonel Middleton, 18th "Wisconsin" Heavy Infantry,' replied the Union officer and returned the compliment. 'May I ask what's on your mind, major?'

'Colonel Barnett sends his terms—,' Hondo began.

'We'll not surrender!' Grimsby stated grimly.

'We're not suggesting that you should. Instead, we're willing to let you come back across the river and offer you unrestricted passage through our lines for all your remaining men.'

'Suppose we say "No"?'

'Then a lot of men are going to die unnecessarily,' Hondo warned. 'You can't destroy the bridge. Nor can you hold it for long enough to let your main body arrive and stop us crossing.'

'That's a debatable point, major,' Grimsby countered, in a flat, non-committal voice. 'The Army of Arkansas—'

'Is still over eight miles away,' Hondo interrupted. 'And not moving fast. Long before it arrives, your regiment will have been wiped out.'

'You won't find *that* easy to do,' Grimsby warned, 'with the width of the river between us.'

'Our reinforcements on the south of the river have already been called on, major. Between us, we've got your regiment cold.'

'You're bluffing,' Grimbsy sniffed.

'Am I?' challenged Hondo, having kept the rim beyond the Yankees covertly under observation. 'Take a look behind you and see how much of a bluff it is.'

Turning, Grimbsy stared at the high ground about three quarters of a mile from his regiment's positions. A startled exclamation burst from his lips at what met his gaze. Lined on the rim were a number of Confederate cavalrymen. In their centre sat an officer, with what looked like a plume of some kind fixed to the turned-up left side of his Jeff Davis hat's brim. Such of the enlisted men who wore that kind of head-gear sported similar decorations. They were, Grimsby knew, the mark of members of Gaylord's Dare-Devils.

'Good going, Billy Jack!' Dusty breathed. 'You'll be disappointed, everything going so right.'

In accordance with his youthful commanding officer's instructions, Billy Jack had made the crossing and succeeded in remaining undetected by the enemy. After faking the plumes on the hats – with Sandy McGraw wearing Red's tunic and hat, having removed the ruined badge, to pose as an officer – the men of Company 'C' had moved to a position from which they could watch what happened at the bridge. Waiting until the parlay was under way, the sergeant had brought them into view.

Seeing the Yankee major staring his way, Sandy took off and waved his hat as if signalling to the Arkansas Rifles.

Then he turned and gave an order which sent Vern Hassle galloping away to the east as if going to report to the main body of the reinforcements.

'Like I said, major,' Hondo drawled, with the complacement air of a man who was holding all the winning cards. 'It's no bluff.'

'Maybe it's not,' answered Grimsby, trying to sound unimpressed. 'But it *could* be.'

'Calling it *will* cost you every man you've got,' Hondo warned. 'Those who aren't killed will be taken prisoner. Even if you'd prepared defences, we'd crush you in the end – And the end would come a whole heap too soon for you to carry out your original mission.'

Watching Grimsby, Dusty could tell that he was affected by Hondo's words and the apparent evidence of how close Gaylord's Dare-Devils were to his regiment. The major's eyes strayed to the dead and wounded on the bridge. Then he looked across the river at the hamlet. From there, he watched the last of the Texas Light Cavalry's supporting Companies as they disappeared into the woodland. They would come over and join with the new arrivals.

'I'll go and see what Colonel Middleton has to say,' Grimbsy promised. 'You'll have your answer in five minutes, Major Fog.'

'What do you reckon, boy?' Hondo inquired, as Grimsby marched stiff-backed in the direction from which he had come.

'He's convinced,' Dusty guessed. 'Question being whether he can convince his colonel. I reckon Middleton'll see reason. There's no sign of them holding Red prisoner, though.'

'He'd not likely be out in the open if they were,' Hondo pointed out. 'We'll ask Major Grimsby about him.'

The five minutes dragged by slowly, with Union soldiers carrying off the wounded and glowering at the two Texans. However, the truce was respected and nothing untoward happened. At last Major Grimsby returned and, although he was trying to hide his feelings, Dusty felt sure that the answer he brought was in the affirmative.

'Colonel Middleton accepts your terms, Major Fog,' Grimsby said quietly. 'If you gentlemen will accompany me, we'll arrange the details.'

Throwing another worried glance downstream, Dusty stiffened. A grin of pure delight and relief came to his face as he watched a horse bearing two riders appear from the trees. In front, guiding the animal, was a Texas Light Cavalry enlisted man. Behind him, without hat, tunic, socks, boots and weapons, sat Red Blaze.

The sight was all that Dusty needed to make his pleasure complete.

CHAPTER SEVENTEEN

THE crossing of the Ouachita River had been accomplished successfully by the Army of Arkansas and North Texas. Having preserved the bridge for their use, they had destroyed it as soon as their rear guard was safely on the southern bank.

On his arrival, General Jackson Baines Hardin had confirmed the terms accepted by Colonel Middleton. Not only had the remnants of the defending force been allowed unrestricted passage, Ole Devil had provided them with medical aid, facilities to bury their dead and transport to carry off the wounded.

Having dealt with that problem and the business of crossing the river, Ole Devil had organized his defences. There would be no further retreat, he had warned his tired but determined men.

Not until the next morning did Ole Devil receive reports from Colonel Barnett and Hondo Fog. Having done so, the tall, lean, hawk-faced general sent for Colonel Blaze and, after a discussion with the commanding officer of the Texas Light Cavalry, passed the word for Dusty Fog to report to him.

By the time the small Texan had arrived, his father had gone to carry out other duties. So Dusty found himself confronted by two of his uncles and Colonel Barnett. They were eying him with blank, hard expressions.

'Lieutenant Fog, reporting as ordered, sir,' Dusty said, halting and delivering a smart salute to the general.

'Let me compliment you on your handling of the Lancers, Mr. Fog,' Ole Devil replied, cold black eyes raking the young blond from head to foot. 'But I hear that you disregarded Captain von Hertz's instructions on how this should be done. He had intended that you should use a *caracole.*'

'Yes, sir,' Dusty admitted.

'You knew that?' Colonel Blaze inquired.

'I did, sir,' Dusty agreed.

'But you didn't do a *caracole*?' Blaze went on.

'No, sir. I didn't think that it would serve our needs.'

'Do you consider yourself a better judge of a tactical situation than Captain von Hertz?' Blaze demanded.

'No, sir,' Dusty replied. 'Probably the captain would have seen that, under the circumstances, a *caracole* wouldn't work. But he was killed before he could change his mind.'

'A *caracole* is sound tactics for men with firearms opposed by Lancers,' Ole Devil remarked, still studying Dusty with what might have been criticism. 'Why not this time?'

'The Lancers were in three ranks, sir,' Dusty explained. 'While we would have shot up the rear one, the other two wouldn't have been affected. They'd've been free to keep going at the battery.'

'So they would,' Ole Devil conceded and the colonels' faces broke into smiles which matched his own. 'You've done very well, Dustine.'

'Thank you, sir,' Dusty answered quietly, but could not conceal his pleasure at the praise.

'Company "C" needs a new commanding officer,' Blaze put in, looking at the general. 'I'd like to promote Mr. Fog to captain and give it to him.'

'I agree,' Ole Devil drawled.

'There is one point, general,' Barnett put in. 'While I accept that M— Captain Fog has carried himself in an exemplary manner throughout the affair, I feel we can't overlook the fact that he disobeyed his superior's orders. With the best of intentions, I'll admit, but to ignore it could establish a dangerous precedent.'

'That's true enough, Colonel Barnett,' Ole Devil conceded and the frosty expression returned to his face – yet with a twinkle in his eyes. 'You can't be let get away with it, young man. So I think that I know a suitable punishment. You'll need a new second-in-command.'

'Yes, sir,' Dusty said, wondering what was coming next.

'Colonel Blaze is promoting Mr. Blaze to first lieutenant,' the general continued. 'And he'll be confirming your appointment of Billy Jack to sergeant major. That, gentlemen, I feel is punishment enough.'

The smiles were back on the older men's faces, matching that creasing the small Texan's features. Dusty wondered what Red and Billy Jack would make of their promotion.

'All right,' Colonel Blaze ordered. 'Go and take over your Company. You're in command now, *Captain* Fog.'

Kill Dusty Fog!

As the world is divided into two parts, Great Britain and its colonies, I dedicate this book to Mike Prorok of Chicago, the Colonial Gentleman.

CHAPTER ONE

THIS'S REAL HELPFUL OF THE YANKEES

The attack came suddenly, unexpectedly and with devastating effectiveness. Certainly the idea that it might happen had never entered 1st Lieutenant Savos' head as he rode along the narrow woodland trail leading to Little Rock, followed by the two lumbering 10-inch siege mortar-wagons and their caisson which formed his platoon.

Earlier that morning his platoon, last in the battery's line of march, had been forced to halt when the near rear wheel of the leading mortar-wagon showed signs of slipping from its axle. On being informed of the mishap, the battery's commanding officer had ordered that Savos' men must correct the fault themselves and follow as quickly as possible. Due to a delay in the arrival of a courier, there had been little enough time for the battery to assemble, load their heavy mortars and march to Little Rock where they were ordered to be present for inspection by the newly arrived General Horace Trumpeter.

So Savos and his men had been compelled to deal with the matter unaided. He suspected that his two 'chief-of-piece' sergeants had conspired to delay the work, ensuring that they would arrive too late to join the ranks of artillery, infantry, cavalry and shiny-butts from the various non-combatant Departments, which even at that moment would be forming up on the open ground at the edge of the town. Neither sergeant had troubled to hide his objections to being uprooted from their comfortable camp as part of the garrison at Hot Springs just to welcome General Trumpeter. He was the latest in a line of Generals sent to lead the Union's Army of Arkansas to ascendancy over the Rebs who held the land south and west of the Ouachita. Or to try; for the predominantly Texas regiments of Ole Devil Hardin, commanding general of the Confederate States' Army of Arkansas, showed a marked, strenuous reluctance to being ascended.

'Can't we make any better speed than this, Sergeant Cragg?' Savos asked petulantly, looking back as he started to ride beneath the spreading branches of a large old white oak that grew at the side of the trail.

'*We* can,' Cragg answered, not leaving his place by the near lead horse. 'It's the hosses 'n' wagon's slow us dow—'

Before the reply ended, the sergeant saw something which drove it out of his mind. Unfortunately, his realization of the sight's implications came a shade too late.

A shape launched itself from amongst the thick foliage of the white oak. Hurling down from the lowest branch, it caught Savos by the shoulders and dragged him from his saddle.

With a feeling of shock, Cragg realized that, although bareheaded, the attacker from the oak tree wore the uniform of a Confederate cavalry officer. There were other significant factors which might have occurred to him, given time; but, even as the realization came, he found himself with troubles of his own. Something hissed through the air. Coming from among the bushes at the side of the trail, the running noose of a rope fell over his head and tightened about his shoulders. Feeling himself being hauled from his horse, he let out a startled yell. He forgot about his officer's predicament and gave his attention to saving himself. Even as he kicked his feet free from the stirrup irons and concentrated on attempting to hit the ground standing up, he saw that he could expect little immediate assistance from his companions.

Unlike members of 'field' artillery batteries, the siege-mortar crews did not ride on the team horses or wagons. Instead, with the exception of the officer and chiefs-of-piece, they marched alongside the heavy draught horses which pulled their weapons. Dressed for the review, they had their short artillery swords slung on their belts. The swords proved to be woefully inadequate.

Men clad in uniforms of cadet-grey, tight-legged breeches with yellow cavalry stripes down the outer seams and knee-high riding boots, appeared on either side of the trail. Some rose from among the bushes, or dropped off over-hanging branches, while others sprang from behind tree trunks.

Unnoticed by the Yankee artillery-men, a rope slanted upwards from the lower limbs of a chestnut tree into those of the big old oak opposite. Leaves rustled where the rope disappeared at its lower end. Gripping it, a tall, wide-shouldered young 1st lieutenant swung out of the foliage. Hatless, he had a thatch of rumpled, fiery hair and a cheery, pugnaciously handsome face. Around his waist, hanging lower than the usual military pattern, was a weapon belt carrying two walnut handled 1860 Army Colts butt-forward in open-topped holsters. Not that he attempted to draw the revolvers. His open legs wrapped around the torso of the open-mouthed, staring second chief-of-piece and the force of his arrival bore the other from his saddle. Dumping the sergeant to the ground, the Rebel lieutenant dropped to land astride him. Around lashed the officer's fist, colliding hard against the non-com's jaw. Going limp, the victim slid limply to his assailant's feet.

Bursting on to the trail without allowing the rope between them to slacken, Cragg's captor proved to be a gangling Confederate sergeant major with a prominent adam's apple and a worried, care-worn face. Despite his melancholy appearance, the sergeant major acted with speed and efficiency. Under the propulsion of his hands, the hard-plaited Manila rope seemed to take life. Two coils rolled forward, dropping one after the other over Cragg's shoulders and further pinioning his arms. Wild with anger, but unable to free himself, he attempted a kick at the approaching Rebel. Down stabbed the miserable Rebel's left hand. Deftly he caught Cragg's rising foot. With a jerk and twist, the sergeant major tumbled the Yankee face down. Before the chief-of-piece could recover his breath, his captor had secured his ankles and completed the job by drawing and lashing his wrists together.

More by luck than riding skill, Savos managed to quit his saddle and land on his feet. Spitting out startled oaths, he thrust his assailant away. In a quick glance around, he learned the full extent of the danger. None of his men carried firearms and all looked to be proving too slow at drawing their swords. Their attackers, on the other hand, held Army Colts, although apparently contenting themselves with taking prisoners, for there was no shooting. From studying the situation, Savos jerked his head around and stared at the figure whose dramatic appearance had sparked off the assault.

Five foot six at most in height, Savos' attacker looked very young. More so when the triple three-inch-long, half-inch-wide gold bars on his stand-up collar and double braid yellow silk 'chicken-guts' up the outside of his tunic's sleeves announced him to be a captain in the Confederate States Army. He had curly, dusty blond hair and was handsome, although not in an eye-catching manner. Savos read a strength and power in the young face that matched the width of the shoulders and slim-waisted development of his small frame. The tunic ended at waist level, without the 'skirt extending half-way between hip and knee' as required by the C.S.A.'s *Manual of Dress Regulations.* A tight-rolled, scarlet silk bandana replaced the black cravat of a formal uniform, its ends trailing over the tunic. While his trousers and boots conformed to *Dress Regulations*, he wore a non-issue gunbelt similar to that of the red-haired lieutenant. In its holsters carefully designed and cut to their fit, two bone-handled Army Colts pointed their butts to the front.

All that Savos saw as he spluttered another curse and started to bring up his fists. Clearly the Rebels did not intend to risk the sound of shots reaching Union ears. In which case, Savos figured that he stood a chance. Having boxed in his Eastern college, he expected no difficulty in felling his small attacker. With the captain in his hands, he could compel the other Rebels to surrender. Rumour had it that they showed more loyalty to their officers than did members of the Union Army, a thing he could turn to his advantage.

However Savos was given no opportunity to put his skill as a pugilist into use. Already the small Rebel was moving closer. Gliding forward, he struck at the lieutenant with lightning speed. The way in which he held his hand, with fingers extended together and thumb bent over the up-turned palm, looked amateurish to one trained in the noble art of pugilism. Yet he had no cause for complaint about the result of the blow. Referring to the impact against his solar plexus in later years, Savos would liken it to being kicked with the sharp hoof of a wounded bull wapiti, or running full-tilt into a sword's blunted point. Such fanciful descriptions did not occur to him at the moment of receipt. With a strangled croak, he doubled over and fell back a couple of steps.

Following Savos up, the captain struck again. Still he did not clench his fist, but chopped the heel of his open hand against the side of the other's neck. Once more the awkward method in no way impaired the efficiency of the attack. On the arrival of the blow, Savos collapsed in a limp pile on the trail.

Clearly the captain did not doubt that his methods would produce the desired effect, for he turned his attention to what was going on about him immediately after striking Savos the second time. A faint grin twisted at his lips as he watched the red haired lieutenant fell the sergeant and spring clear. Turning with his fists raised, the red head glared around as if hoping for a chance to use them. However such had been the speed and surprise of the attack that he found no takers. Already the Yankee artillerymen were standing with raised hands, looking into the muzzles of persuasive revolvers.

After studying the wagons, the captain looked along the trail. He saw that the horses of Savos and the two Yankee sergeants had been caught by the men positioned earlier for that duty. Satisfied that the horses could not give warning by running riderless across the rolling, open land beyond the woods, he turned back to his men. He walked across to where his mournful-featured sergeant major stood with an expression so worried that he and not the Yankees might have been captured.

'Did any of them get away, Billy Jack?' the captain asked, his voice a pleasant Texas drawl.

'Nary a one,' the sergeant major replied miserably.

'All right your side, Cousin Red?' the captain went on.

'We got 'em all, Cousin Dusty,' the red headed lieutenant answered.

'Have them hawg-tied,' ordered the captain. 'I'll go make sure that Yankee luff's* not hurt bad. It's easy to hit just a mite too hard when you use the *tegatana* against the side of the neck.'

Despite his concern, the captain found Savos groaning his way slowly to consciousness. Relieving the lieutenant of his revolver and sword – the officer alone wearing a firearm on his belt – the young Rebel stood back with an air of satisfaction. Hooves sounded and he turned to face a tall red-haired soldier who was approaching, leading three horses and carrying the company's guidon. Spiking the end of the guidon's pole into the ground, the soldier allowed the horses' long, split-end reins to dangle free. Going to the big black stallion on the right of the trio, he took the white Jeff Davis campaign hat from where it hung by its storm strap on the low horned, double girthed saddle.

'Figured you'd need this, Cap'n Dusty,' the guidon carrier remarked, offering the hat to the small blond.

Shaking his head, fingering the side of his neck and groaning, Savos forced himself into a sitting position. Slowly the mists swirled away from before his eyes and he took in the scene around him. Not far away, the small captain stood donning the campaign hat. On its front was a silver badge formed of a five-pointed star in a circle. That meant he was a member of the Texas Light Cavalry. The saddles of the three exceptional fine horses, each carrying a sabre and coiled rope on opposing sides of its low horn, gave added confirmation of the regiment to which the Rebels belonged, the double girths being peculiar to the Lone Star State.

Looking next towards his halted mortar-wagons, Savos saw

* Luff: derogatory name for a young 1st lieutenant.

his men being disarmed or tied up hand and foot. As he swung angrily towards the captain, intending to protest about such treatment, a puff of wind fluttered the Rebel company's guidon and drew his attention to it. The sight of the letter it carried momentarily drove all thoughts of objecting out of his head.

From studying the letter 'C' on the guidon, Savos jerked his head around and stared at the small captain. The man who commanded Company 'C' of the Texas Light Cavalry had a name well-known on the Arkansas battle-front. Yet could that short, almost insignificant-looking captain, not more than eighteen years of age and a young eighteen at that, be the famous Dusty Fog?

Over the past year, Captain Dusty Fog of the Texas Light Cavalry had become much mentioned by virtue of his excellence as a military raider. In fact, many men who had been matched against him ranked the leader of Company 'C' with those two other Dixie masters, Turner Ashby and John Singleton Mosby. The Texans fighting to retain the Toothpick State for the South held Dusty Fog in higher esteem than Ashby or even than the 'Grey Ghost', Mosby himself.

Nephew of Ole Devil Hardin, Dusty Fog was a native Texan. So the other sons of the Lone Star State accorded him pride of place. They boasted of his lightning fast draw and deadly revolver-shooting skill, or told tales about his uncanny ability at barehand fighting. There were few, however, who could have told from whom he had learned his peculiar, yet effective skills in the latter. The truth was that he had been taught the secrets – all but unknown in the Western Hemisphere at that time – of *ju-jitsu* and *karate* by Ole Devil Hardin's Japanese servant, using them to back up his not inconsiderable strength and to off-set his lack of inches.

To the Union soldiers on the eastern side of the Ouachita River, Dusty Fog's name had become synonymous with trouble, misery and disaster. At the head of the hard-riding, harder-fighting Company 'C', he played havoc with the Yankees in Arkansas. He struck when least expected, with the raging fury of a Texas twister and left destruction as great as any caused by a whirlwind in his wake. For all that, many Union soldiers regarded him with open, or grudging, admiration. He was recognized by the majority of them as a courageous, resourceful, yet chivalrous enemy.

Among his other exploits had been the destruction of a vitally important bridge over the Moshogen River. In a way that particular raid could be blamed for Savos' present misfortune. Learning that a Yankee lieutenant was falsely accused of cowardice and desertion for his conduct during the attack on the bridge, Dusty Fog had offered to attend the officer's court martial to give evidence. This had been arranged by Ole Devil Hardin, through the Union Army's top brass. Although he had travelled under a flag of truce, Dusty was compelled on three occasions to defend his life; culminating with his killing General Buller in a duel which the other – who had personal reasons for wanting the lieutenant convicted – had forced upon him.* Buller's death had created a vacancy in Arkansas which Trumpeter had filled and so, indirectly, had caused Savos to leave the safety of the Hot Springs' defences and fall into the Rebels' hands.

After putting on his hat, the small Texan walked towards Savos. There was none of the cocky swagger which might have been expected from one so young and small who held a rank of some importance. Savos became aware of the strength of the other's personality. That was no mere stripling half-pint holding rank because of kin-ship with important Rebels and controlling his men through family influence or the *Manual of Field Regulations*. Much to his annoyance, Savos found himself sitting up straighter as he would when approached by a senior officer of his own regiment.

'Are you all right, mister?' the captain asked.

'Yes – sir,' Savos answered, the honorific popping out of his mouth before he could prevent it. 'Are you Dusty Fog?'

'Captain Dustine Edward Marsden Fog,' confirmed the small Texan. 'None of your men are seriously injured. I'll be leaving you hawg-tied and under guard for a spell, mister; but I'll make sure that one of you can get loose afore we pull out.'

'What're you going to do?' Savos inquired, understanding the reason why his men were being tied.

'I'm figuring on firing a salute for your new general,' Dusty drawled. 'And I don't want you around trying to spoil it.'

'You – you mean that you're go—?' Savos croaked, staring in disbelief at the two squat mortars. Then he turned his eyes to the caisson, knowing what it held.

'Just that,' Dusty confirmed and nodded to where the red-haired lieutenant was approaching. 'Mr. Blaze here'll look to you, but don't try anything *loco*, mister.'

'*Loco* being Spanish for crazy, friend,' drawled 1st Lieutenant Charles William Henry Blaze cheerfully. 'Which trying to escape, or make fuss for us'd be.'

*Told in *The Fastest Gun in Texas*.

First Lieutenant Blaze might have been baptized Charles William Henry, but it was doubtful if even he remembered the fact. His thatch of fiery, ever-untidy hair had qualified him for his commonly-used name 'Red'. Dressed in a similar regulation-flouting uniform to his cousin, it carried two collar bars and a single-braid 'chicken guts' insignia.

Already Red Blaze had built up a reputation for courage, possessing a hot temper and an almost unequalled ability to become involved in fights. Yet Dusty recognized that he had virtues which more than off-set his minor faults, including one which few people noticed. Older senior officers tended to think of Red as irresponsible, but Dusty knew better. Given a job to do, Red became calm and let nothing distract him. Aware of that, Dusty never hesitated to trust Red to carry out any duty he was given.

Leaving his cousin to deal with Savos, Dusty walked over to join his lean sergeant major. As always Billy Jack looked a picture of dejection. The peaked forage cap had never been regarded as a thing of beauty and the one perched on Billy Jack's head increased his general lugubrious appearance. There was nothing smart about his uniform, the three stripes and arc of silk announcing his rank coming almost as a surprise. Yet he was real good with the two Army Colts hanging in the open-topped holsters low on his thighs. Maybe Billy Jack conveyed the impression of always expecting the worst, but Dusty knew him to be a tough, shrewd fighting man and well deserving of his rank.

'We done got these-here stove-pipes, Cap'n Dusty,' Billy Jack announced miserably, nodding towards the mortar-wagons. 'Now I surely hope you ain't thinking of trying what I know you're thinking of trying with 'em.'

'We are,' Dusty assured him. 'Why else did I have you boys learning how to use artillery the last time Uncle Devil took us off patrols to rest up the horses?'

'Just being your usual ornery self,' the sergeant major answered *sotto voce*, then grinned with all the insincerity of a professional politician meeting a rival for office, and went on in a louder tone, 'I allus figured you'd got a right good reason for doing it.'

'And I heard you the first time,' Dusty warned him. 'Damned if I wouldn't bust you to private, but the rest of this bunch're worse than you. Anyways, let's take a look at what we've got. Way that Yankee luff jumped when I said we're fixing to fire a salute for Trumpeter, he's toting along everything we'll need to do it.'

'*That's* what I figured you aimed to do,' Billy Jack wailed. 'It's all your fault he's here, anyways.'

'How come?' Dusty asked, as they walked to the first wagon.

'If you-all hadn't downed that nice ole General Buller, in a duel, for shame, they wouldn't've had to replace him. Now they've done sent along a regular fire-eating, ring-tailer ripper who allows he'll have all us poor lil' Texas boys drove back across the Red River in a month and'll be eating supper at the Governor's mansion in Houston comes early fall.'

Knowing just how much the other's woe-filled tirade meant, Dusty ignored it. For a moment he studied the mortar on the leading wagon, then nodded his head approvingly. Just as he had expected, the weapon was of the same pattern as those used by the Confederate States' Army. So he and his men could set it up, load and fire it with no great difficulty. Whether they could operate the mortars to the best of their potential was another matter. Dusty hoped that they could.

Sent to meet a Confederae agent and collect his information, Dusty had learned of the grand review in Trumpeter's honour. At the first there had seemed to be nothing he and his Company could hope to achieve against the large number of troops who had been assembled. He had ridden in the direction of Little Rock with no greater intention than to learn if Trumpeter had brought fresh regiments, or new, improved weapons along. When his forward scout had brought word of the unescorted mortar platoon, Dusty had seen a chance of intervening. So he had arranged and sprung the trap into which Savos marched so blindly. Even if he could not make use of the mortars, destroying them noisily near Little Rock would serve to show how little the C.S.A. in general and the Texas Light Cavalry in particular feared Trumpeter's threats of driving them back into Texas and capturing the capital city of Houston.

While the capture of the battery had been accomplished easily, using the mortars would still be anything but a sinecure. A month's training with the artillery had taught him the basic principles involved in firing different weapons. But there was much he did not know, particularly about the correct fusing of the mortar shells.

Yet the temptation to make a more dramatic gesture than merely blowing up the mortars was great. Not for Dusty's personal aggrandizement, he cared nothing about that, but as a means of lowering the Yankees' morale. If it could be done—

Letting the thought hang in the air, Dusty went by the second wagon. He climbed on to the caisson and raised the lid of the first chest. Inside lay everything he would need: the round shells, powder charges made up in serge bags, boxes of fuses, lanyards, friction primers. The caisson also carried handspikes, rammers loading tongs and sponge-buckets, all of which his men knew how to use. Most important, to Dusty's way of thinking, was a sheet of paper fastened to the inside of the chest's lid.

'Well now,' the small Texan said, reading the printed instructions listing angles for firing at various ranges and times of the shells' flight at those distances. 'This's *real* helpful of the Yankees.'

'It sure is,' agreed Billy Jack dolefully. 'Now we'll know what we've done wrong when we get blowed up.'

Which, as Dusty knew, was unqualified support for his scheme. Given that much information, they could use the mortars with reasonable efficiency. Certainly sufficiently well for his purposes. So he grinned at his sergeant major and said, 'All right, let's go show our respects to the general.'

CHAPTER TWO

YOU SURE RUINED HIS REVIEW

'THE review's formed up to the north of town and well clear of it,' Red Blaze reported with satisfaction as he rejoined his cousin on the edge of the woodland in which they had captured the Yankee mortar platoon. 'There're none of our folks watching that I could see.'

After securing the prisoners, Dusty had sent Red to join their forward scout, under orders to reconnoitre and learn if the attack could be made without endangering Confederate property or lives. From what the red head had just said, he could continue with the bombardment.

'Make a map of how the land lies,' Dusty ordered, for they were about a mile and a quarter from Little Rock and the rolling nature of the ground hid the town from his view. 'No patrols out?'

'Nary a one,' Red snorted and nodded to where the forward scout lay looking cautiously over a rim about three-quarters of a mile ahead. 'Kiowa's riled, he allows the Yankees're selling him and us short not keeping watch.'

With that he dismounted and, clearing a piece of ground, made a rough map of the area they hoped to bombard. Having completed his task, he collected his big brown horse which had been waiting patiently, ground-hitched by its dangling reins, mounted and rode back in the direction from which he had come.

Dusty studied the map for a moment, then looked towards his departing cousin. In his mind's eye, Dusty pictured the geography of the area. Then he turned and waved the two mortar wagons forward.

'Line them on Kiowa,' he told the men leading the horses.

Although considering themselves the elite of the best damned *cavalry* regiment in the Confederate States' Army, the men detailed to act as gun crews sprang to their work with a will. The novel means of carrying the war to the enemy, combined with a desire to show the new Yankee general what kind of opposition faced him, gave zest to their movements. However, the two sergeants temporarily appointed chiefs-of-piece watched the men and controlled their high spirits.

Guiding the leading wagon, Sergeant Stormy Weather halted it so that its pole yoke lined directly at Kiowa Cotton on the distant rim. Sergeant Lou Bixby brought his wagon around until it stood alongside the other and also pointed in the required direction.

Normally the mortars would have been operated from a bed of stout timbers, to prevent the continued recoil sinking them into the ground and to facilitate altering the alignment or replacing them on the wagons when the time came to move on. Knowing that there would be time for at most three shots, and intending to destroy the platoon's equipment before he left, Dusty did not bother with such refinements. Going behind the wagons, he checked on their alignment. Each of the mortars weighed 1,852 pounds, so he wished to save his men from the exertion of using the handspikes to alter the aim as much as he could.

Satisfied, Dusty told the men to make ready the mortars. Weather and Bixby secured the ropes of the windlass at the rear of the wagons to the horns of the mortars, then unfastened the stout pins connecting the limber portions of the wagons to the rear sections which carried the weapons. While the limbers were being removed and the wagons' slip-ways lowered to the ground, Dusty joined Billy Jack's party by the caisson.

'Dang the luck!' the sergeant major moaned, watching two men lift an eighty-seven-and-a-half pound round shell – raising it between them in the grip of the specially-designed shell-tongs – from the forward of the three ammunition chests. 'The blasted things're filled, so we can use them.'

'Do you know how to?' Dust inquired.

'I figured you just stuck the shell in the hole 'n' hoped for the worst,' Billy Jack answered languidly, taking a long, tapered wooden fuse from a box and studying the time-graduations marked down its length. 'Likely they're all wrong and'll go off in the barrel.'

'Don't you *ever* look on the bright side?' Dusty demanded.

'Sure I do. I 'member the last time real well. It was eight years, three months, two weeks 'n' four days back, come sundown. One of our good borrowing neighbours done fell down our well as he was coming calling.'

'What happened?'

'It warn't the drinking well, so we figured it'd be a plumb

waste of time to pull him out 'n' left him there,' Billy Jack explained, then dropped his pose for a moment. 'Range'd be around a mile 'n' a quarter, I reckon.'

'Near enough,' Dusty agreed. 'Forty-five degrees elevation. We'll give 'em twenty seconds first go and alter it for the next if we're wrong.'

'Should have a big enough target, anyways,' the sergeant major drawled, using the point of his knife to pierce the wall of the fuse at the required graduation. 'Or was you-all figuring on dropping the shells on top of Trumpeter's fool lil Yankee head?'

'I'll settle happy enough for scattering his review,' Dusty answered.

With the fuses cut, he and Billy Jack fitted them carefully into the holes at the bottom of the shells. Ignited by the detonation of the main firing charge, the priming compound would burn down the inside of the wooden tube until reaching the opening cut by the sergeant major. There it would set off the five-pound bursting charge and explode the shell. While it did not work every time, the method gave a reasonable chance of success.

Wasting no time, the crews of the mortars had slid the pieces to the ground and removed the carriers. Selected for their strength, burly men wielded the handspikes and made adjustments to the directions in which the barrels pointed. Due to the care in positioning the wagons, they had little to do before Dusty announced his satisfaction. Removing the wooden tampions from the muzzles, the chiefs-of-piece gave the orders to load. First the powder charges went into the twenty-eight inch tubes and were rammed home. Then the men handling the tongs manoeuvred the shells into position.

Maybe the Texans did not move with the skilled precision of a trained artillery team, but they still carried out their duties at a good speed. Watching them, Dusty saw his earlier decision to have them trained to use artillery weapons justified. At the time it had been merely a means of keeping them occupied during a period when they were resting between patrols. The training was now paying off in that it allowed him to strike at the Yankees.

While the men completed the loading, Dusty looked about him. Two of his men stood some distance away, ready to cut the telegraph wires between Little Rock and Hot Springs and prevent warning of Company 'C's' presence being sent ahead of them. Half-a-dozen more were headed west with the Yankee platoon's horses, for the heavy draught animals would not be able to keep up with the Company's mounts in the event of a hurried departure. The remainder of the Company, less those employed on the mortars, kept watch on the surrounding country.

'Sure hope them fuses work like they should,' Billy Jack said in a tone that hinted he doubted if they would. 'Likely they'll make the shells bust in the barrel. Being so, I'll stand away somewheres safe. Like at the end of this-here lanyard.'

Considering that the eight-foot long lanyard connected to the friction-primer in the right-side mortar's vent-hole, the gloomy prediction failed to worry the men who heard it. In fact Sergeant Stormy Weather hardly looked up from working the lever that tilted the barrel to the required angle of fire.

'All set, Cap'n Dusty!' announced the burly, jovial-featured Weather.

'Ready to go,' confirmed the tall, dapper Sergeant Bixby by the other mortar.

'Let 'em go!' Dusty ordered.

Instantly Billy Jack and Bixby gave sharp tugs at their lanyards, operating the friction-primers. Steel rasped over the highly-combustible priming compound and ignited it, sending a spurt of flame into the powder grains of the main charge which turned rapidly into a terrific volume of gas. Set alight by the burning powder, the fuse began to operate. With a deep roar, the shell vomited from the left side mortar. A moment later, the second ball curved into the air.

Standing on the saluting base, General Trumpeter scowled as he watched the mass of men before him preparing to start the review. He frowned, thinking of the doubt he had seen on the faces of the senior officers under his command when he had spoken to them on the subject of his plans to defeat the Rebels. Maybe the Union Army's superior numbers, weapons and technology was swinging the War more and more in their favour on the other battle-fronts, but that did not apply in Arkansas. There the C.S.A. held firm and showed no sign of weakening. In fact, if the South had been able to send more men and equipment to Ole Devil Hardin, Trumpeter's colonels figured they would be hard-pressed to hold on to the land they had already taken.

In accordance with the policy of the Union's high command, the pick of the troops and weapons were reserved for the Eastern battle-zones. Most of the top brass favoured concentrating on striking down the heart of the Confederacy. After that had been accomplished, Texas – possibly the least affected of the Southern States by the major issues of the War – would be more ready to accept offers to surrender. So Arkansas had become garrisoned by green regiments, or those found wanting in the hard tests of combat. Poorly trained, demoralized by continual defeat, the men before Trumpeter were far from being ideal material for his dreams of conquest and fame. In fact he found himself doubting the wisdom of having so publicly stated his intentions when being assigned to take over the deceased General Buller's command.

Tall, slim, dark-haired, his handsome features were marred by a perpetual expression of arrogant superiority and an air of condescension. He made a fine figure in his smart blue dress uniform. Yet his military service did not extend beyond the start of the War and his background was not West Point but an Eastern civilian college. More politician than soldier, he had attained his rank with the patronage of powerful friends in the anti-slavery lobbies of his State's Legislature and the Federal Congress, aided by a chronic shortage of officers in the Union Army. For many years before the War, the Southern States had supplied the majority of the U.S. Army's officers, most of whom had returned to their homes on Secession. Few of the non-coms showed the necessary qualities to make officers, so the vacancies had been filled by men who at other times would have scorned to join the Army.

One of that kind, Trumpeter had passed rapidly up the promotion ladder, without any great effort or risk. Aware of the possibilities offered by military acclaim when back in civilian life, Trumpeter had sought for a way by which he might reach the public's notice. Buller's death had offered it. There had been some reluctance among the other generals at taking over the unsuccessful Army of Arkansas. So Trumpeter's appointment met with no objections.

On his arrival, he had soon found that he faced a far more difficult task than he had imagined while riding a desk in far-off Washington. However, he possessed ideas that the routine-dulled brains of the career-soldiers could never have produced; two of which were already being put into effect. When they brought results, he would convince the weak-spined jellyfish before him that the Rebels across the Ouachita were no different from the other scum who formed the Confederate States. After which there would be replacements. Trumpeter meant to bring in men whose agreement with his 'liberal' beliefs made them worthy of carrying out his schemes of conquest.

Trumpeter's scowl deepened as he studied the contingent from the 6th New Jersey Dragoons. On first meeting their colonel, he had mentioned his scheme to obtain remounts of a standard equal to that of the Rebel cavalry. Colonel Verncombe had expressed doubts that they could be delivered without strong escorts and would be subject to constant harassment or loss to the raiding Texans. So Trumpeter had not mentioned the plan he had thought out and already set into motion. He had hoped that the results of his brilliant scheme would make their appearance in time for the review, but they had not arrived. When they came, he could confound the doom-predicting Verncombe and—

An eerie double screech rose, growing louder by the second to chop through Trumpeter's thoughts. It was a sound which some of the men present recognized, although their general failed to identify it. Down from the sky curved a black ball and another followed it. Before Trumpeter had time to decide what was happening, the first shell exploded.

By accident, rather than deliberate, planned knowledge, the detonation of the first bursting charge took place at almost the ideal moment for maximum effectiveness. Exploding in the air about fifty yards above the centre of the assembled men, the shell sprayed a hail of .58 calibre musket balls on to them. Screaming and plunging, a horse went down while three men also fell. An instant after the first shell went off, the second burst and added its deadly cargo to that of its predecessor.

Coming so unexpectedly, the two shells threw the whole of the review into complete confusion. While the actual damage inflicted by the flying musket balls was not great, the side-effects proved to be all that Dusty could have desired. The cavalry and artillery suffered most. Caught in the process of mounting, men were flung from their startled, rearing horses. In the case of the cavalry, that meant only animals bolting with empty saddles; but the field artillery saw several of their cannon and caissons being dragged away by uncontrolled, frightened teams.

'Sponge those barrles out real careful!' Dusty warned his men, his eyes on Red who had rejoined Kiowa on the distant rim.

Plunging the sponge on the end of a ramrod pole into a wooden bucket filled with water, a good-looking young private called Tracey Prince heard the words and grinned. He removed the sponge, shook it to get rid of excess water and thrust it into the barrel of the right side mortar to douse any remnants of burning powder. Not until he had checked that all was well did Sergeant Weather give the order to reload. Working just as fast and carefully, Sergeant Bixby's men recharged the second piece.

Seeing Red's obvious delight at the result of the first shots, Dusty made no alteration to the cutting of the second pair of fuses. Nor did he consider that the recoil had thrown the solid weight of the mortars sufficiently out of line to make any major corrections necessary.

Again the mortars boomed as he gave the order to fire. Standing behind them, Dusty saw that one shell was veering away from the other. It would not be far enough out of line to fall into the town, but he decided against chancing a further volley. He had no wish to continue the bombardment, with its indiscriminate slaughter. Having achieved his purpose of bearding General Trumpeter in the other's Little Rock den, Dusty intended to make good his escape. To have ruined the review and retired without loss or casualties would have a greater effect than staying until driven away by the Yankees.

'Stack the rest of the charges and shells around the mortars!' Dusty barked. 'Bring the wagons and caissons up between the stove-pipes. I want everything wrecked when we leave.'

In addition to meeting the agent, Dusty had been told to raid and do whatever damage he could while in enemy territory, so he had the means to destroy the loot completely. Red and Kiowa still remained on the rim, which meant that the Yankees had not yet organized a force to attack and drive Company 'C' away. While his men carried out their orders, Dusty wondered what was happening outside the town.

All was confusion and pandemonium after the arrival of the first pair of shells, Fifty-five seconds later, before any semblance of order could be restored, the third shell burst in the air above the tangled, cursing mass of men. Having heard the banshee wailing of the shells' approach, discipline was forgotten and soldiers of all ranks flung themselves to the ground. Some of the cavalrymen who had managed to retain a hold of their horses' reins let loose and dived for safety. Trying to maintain control over his platoon, a lieutenant of Stedloe's Zouaves felt the wind of a close-passing musket-ball against his cheek. Fortunately for the future peace and security of the Sovereign State of Texas, 1st Lieutenant Jackson Marsden escaped without injury.*

Staring with fascinated horror, Trumpeter saw the second shell falling in his direction. Throwing himself from the saluting dais, he heard the missile explode and musket balls strike the stand he had quit an instant before. Rage filled him as he wondered which Rebel was responsible for the murderous attempt on his life. How-

*The reason why is told in *The Devil Gun*.

ever, he stayed on the ground until sure that no other shells were coming.

Excited and amused by the chaos he saw displayed before him, Red Blaze did not forget his duty. There had been no attempt at organized reprisals and, studying the way the Yankees acted, none would be speedily forthcoming. So he nodded to the tall, lean sergeant at his side.

'I'd best go tell Cousin Dusty what's happened, Kiowa.'

'Yo!' replied the other. 'I'll stay on here a spell like Cap'n Dusty said.'

Nobody, except possibly his mother, would have called Kiowa Cotton handsome. At best he looked like a particularly evil brave-heart Indian warrior hunting for the white-eye brother's scalp. Yet he was a good soldier, well-suited by birth and upbringing for the important duty of guiding Company 'C' on their missions behind the enemy lines. Bare-headed, armed with a Remington Army revolver and bowie knife, he was to stay behind until pursuit was formed and sent after them, then take word of it to Dusty.

Collecting his horse, Red rode back to where Dusty was fitting the end of a coil of quick-match fuse into the hole in a shell. The men had worked fast and everything was as Dusty required by the time his cousin arrived.

'How'd it go, Cousin Red?' asked Dusty.

'You sure ruined his review,' Red replied. 'I haven't seen so much fussing, coming and going and running around since that time you and me brought a skunk to Cousin Betty's birthday party.'

'Let's hope the Yankees don't catch us and lick us the way she did,' Dusty grinned. Tommy Okasi had taught their cousin, Betty Hardin, to be proficient at *ju-jitsu* and *karate*.* On the occasion Red had mentioned, she put her lessons to good use in dealing out summary punishment to the offenders.

'They'll not be fixing to come after us for a spell yet,' Red guessed. 'You scattered the Dragoons and they're the best outfit Trumpeter's got. Need any help here, do you reckon?'

'Nope,' Dusty decided, wedging the cord-like fuse into place. 'Head out with the company. I'll catch up with you.'

Riding off, Company 'C' heard the roar of an explosion and, looking back, saw their leader approaching. Where the Yankee mortar platoon had been, only a large, smoking crater and scattered remnants of wood and metal remained. There was nothing of its equipment the Yankees could salvage.

*Betty's skill is demonstrated in *McGraw's Inheritance*.

CHAPTER THREE

DO I EVER TAKE FOOL CHANCES?

'I BET ole Trumpeter's pot-boiling wild over us getting away from him after busting his reivew,' Red Blaze enthused as he rode with Dusty Fog and Billy Jack ahead of the Company.

'He'll be after our hides for certain sure,' Billy Jack agreed dolefully. 'We should've told that Yankee luff we was Company 'A'.'

'And have Trumpeter get all riled at Brother Buck? For shame,' Red protested. 'Let him 'n' Brother Pete find their own Yankee generals to get riled at e'm.'

After firing the salute in General Trumpeter's honour, Dusty and his men had headed west at a good pace. By night-fall they had crossed the Saline River, making for the narrows which separated Lake Hamilton from Lake Ouachita. Kiowa had caught up shortly after they pulled out at dawn. He brought news that the Yankees had sent out a patrol three-companies strong, but it travelled slowly and would be unlikely to catch up with them. Nor would the garrison at Hot Springs be alerted to their presence. Not only had the telegraph wires been cut, but three long sections were carried off by the Texans. Trumpeter had sent a mounted courier with a message for the garrison commander at Hot Springs. However, Kiowa stated that he would not arrive. The spare horse, bearing a New Hampstead Volunteers' saddle, led by the scout gave confirmation to his statement.

Continuing their journey, and travelling at a speed possible only to master horsemen and first-class mounts, they crossed Garland County, avoiding the hamlets of Jessieville and Mountain Valley. At no time did they see any sign of pursuit, nor had word of their coming reached Hot Springs, for no force came from the town to intercept them.

By mid-afternoon they were riding through the lightly-wooded country parallel with but a mile from the northern shore of Lake Hamilton. The conversation between Red and Billy Jack ended abruptly as they saw the bare-headed Indian-dark Kiowa Cotton approaching from where he had been riding forward scout.

At a signal from Dusty, the fifty-strong main body of the company came to a halt. They needed no further orders, adopting a formation permitting an all-round defence should one prove necessary. The out-riding pickets to the rear and flanks also stopped, maintaining their vigil while awaiting instructions.

'Come across a bunch of fellers with some hosses up there by the narrows, Cap'n Dusty,' Kiowa announced, halting his horse and getting as close to a salute as he offered to anybody.

'Soldiers?' Dusty asked.

'Ain't wearing uniforms if they are. Got maybe a hundred head of real good hosses and two wagons along. There's ten of 'em, toting what look like Burnside carbines and revolvers.'

Digesting the information, Dusty nodded approvingly. Trust Kiowa to bring in all the pertinent details, such as the nature of the other party's armament. Burnside carbines, being single-shot, were not as dangerous as Spencer or Henry repeaters, but, firing metal-case cartridges, could be re-charged faster than a muzzle-loader. Such details were important in the event of a fight. Before Dusty could speak, Billy Jack injected the kind of comment they had come to expect from him.

'Could be a trap, Cap'n Dusty; 'n' when we spring it, they'll jump us and wipe us out to a man.'

'What do you reckon, Cousin Red?' Dusty inquired, ignoring the gloomy words.

'If they're civilians, we'll have to go real careful,' Red answered 'You mind what Uncle Devil told us about steering clear of doing anything the Yankee newspapers can call atrocities.'

Since the start of the War, the Rebels and the Yankees had learned the uses of propaganda. Each side eagerly published stories of the other's atrocities, or blew up minor unsavoury incidents out of all proportion, as a means of stirring their people's patriotic indignation or creating an unfavourable image of the enemy to the rest of the world. Fully aware of how effective such propaganda could be, Ole Devil Hardin had given strict orders to his officers regarding their treatment of Union or non-aligned civilians they came across while on patrol.

'We'll go take a look, anyways,' Dusty decided. 'How does the land lie where they're camped, Kiowa?'

'They're out in the open, clear of the woods. We can get up to maybe a hundred yards of them without being seen. One thing I know for sure. There're no blue-bellies about. I looked real careful and if there is, they're hidden under the water 'n' not breathing enough to make bubbles.'

Which meant that no Union force was watching the party by the narrows, ready to swoop on and destroy any Confederate patrol that made its appearance. However Dusty intended to take precautions.

'I'll come with you, Kiowa. Bring the company along after us, Cousin Red. Don't show yourselves until you figure I need you. And be ready for anything. I'd hate like hell to see Billy Jack get wiped out to a man.'

'It'll come sooner or later, anyways,' the gangling sergeant major replied. 'So don't you go putting yourself out special on my account, Cap'n Dusty.'

What're them fellers doing, Kiowa?' Red asked.

'Making camp for the night, looked like,' the scout answered. 'They don't have any guards out, nor even fellers riding herd on the hosses.'

'They could be guerillas, Cousin Dusty,' Red warned. 'Don't you go taking any fool chances with them.'

'Do I ever take fool chances?' Dusty smiled.

'Not more'n once a week,' Red admitted.

'Trouble being,' Billy Jack put in mournfully, 'you ain't had your go at it yet this week.'

Chuckling and promising to take care, Dusty rode off at Kiowa's side. Red gave the signal which spread the company into a mounted skirmishing line, then led them at a slower pace after his cousin. The main body had covered almost a mile when they saw their commanding officer and scout halt and dismount. Realizing that Dusty meant to study the mysterious party before going closer, Red further reduced the company's speed.

Leaving the horses ground-hitched, Dusty and Kiowa stalked cautiously to the edge of the woodland. Standing behind a stout old oak tree, they looked at the open ground bordering the narrows between the two lakes.

First Dusty examined the pair of wagons, standing with their teams unhitched. They appeared to be ordinary farm vehicles, with plain canopies that were open at the ends. From his position he could see into them. While they carried loads of some kind, they held neither concealed men nor weapons. That reduced the risk of the party acting as bait for a trap, a possibility Dusty had considered.

The horses took Dusty's attention next. As Kiowa had claimed, they were a fine selection. Grazing quietly on the rich grama grass beyond the wagons and men, they stayed together in a way that hinted they had been long in each other's company. An exceptionally fine bay stallion was tethered clear of the others. Clearly the men trusted the horses to remain bunched, for nobody was riding herd on them.

So Dusty turned his eyes to the party gathered at the fire and saw what might be the answer to the lack of care. All but one were poorly dressed and looked like a gathering of town-dwelling manual workers who normally had small contact with horses. That they wore revolvers suspended at their sides – although not in such efficient holsters as the Texans sported – and had Burnside carbines stacked in neat pyramidal piles close by came as no surprise. Most men carried arms when travelling. Deserters, hunted by the military, often had to steal to stay alive. Worse than them, there were gangs of guerillas, who looted and pillaged under the guise of fighting for the Union or Confederacy, to make travelling hazardous. In fact, apart from the exception, the men might fall into one of these categories; although deserters or guerillas normally took greater precautions when in camp.

From all appearances, the exception was the party's leader. He wore a suit of big-city style, derby hat, spats and glossy shoes, but had removed his cravat and collar. The gunbelt about his waist looked out of place when taken with his warm, confiding, sunny cast of features. Short, round as a butterball, he exhibited an air of jovial respectability rarely, if ever, seen among the human wolves who called themselves 'guerillas'.

'Could be Yankee soldiers,' Kiowa remarked after a moment. 'Their cavalry use plenty of Burnsides.'

'Sure,' Dusty agreed. 'But civilians up north can likely buy them.'

While most of the companies manufacturing firearms sought for bulk orders from the military, they augmented their profits by offering their products on the open market. The Burnside was a reasonably good gun, easy to operate and maintain and priced at a level within the reach of civilians. Finding so many of them together might be no more than coincidence. Even the fact that their owners had piled them military-fashion proved nothing, for the men could have seen soldiers doing it.

'What do you reckon then?' Kiowa wanted to know.

'I don't reckon they're blue-bellies disguised to trap us, but we'll play it careful,' Dusty answered. 'You and I'll go to them and hold their attention until the Company gets here.'

Returning to their horses, they mounted. Dusty signalled for Red to keep coming. Then he and Kiowa passed out of the shelter of the trees. A big, burly man standing with the chubby dude saw them appear. Dropping his hand towards the flap of his holster, he growled a warning. Although most of the others showed anxiety, or reached for their revolvers, the dude displayed no alarm. Instead he spoke in a calm, reassuring manner and tapped the left side of his jacket. The words did not carry to Dusty's ears, but he saw the men refrain from drawing their weapons. Although they stood with empty hands, they formed a group behind the big man and scanned the woods beyond the approaching Texans with suspicious eyes.

Only the dude appeared completely unmoved by the arrival of the two Rebels. Leaving his companions, he padded almost daintily in the pair's direction as they halted their horses. While he seemed a mite puzzled – only to be expected when meeting Confederate soldiers so far in Union-held territory – he showed neither animosity nor concern.

'Good afternoon, gentlemen,' the dude greeted in a cultured New England accent, darting a glance beyond them. 'Welcome to our camp. If you wish to have a meal, feel free to join us.' He paused then continued, 'Are you alone?'

'My Company's about a mile back,' Dusty answered, confident that Red would keep the men hidden and not give the lie to the words. He swung to the ground and went on, 'Mind if I ask who you are and what you're doing here?'

'Understandable questions both, sir. My name is Oswald Lomax Hoffinger and I am leading this party of recently-arrived immigrants to join their families in New Mexico.'

'Can you prove it?' Dusty inquired, knowing that Kiowa was watching the men.

'Of course, sir,' Hoffinger agreed. 'I have a document in my pocket, if I may be permitted to produce it—'

'Go to it,' Dusty offered.

For all his pompous manner, the dude had the good sense to give a warning before letting his hand go out of sight under his jacket. Reaching across to his inside breast pocket, Hoffinger brought out a sheet of paper. While opening it and holding it to Dusty, he spoke in a foreign language, addressing the words to his companions as they stood scowling at the Texans.

'I was merely informing them that all is well, Captain,' Hoffinger declared, smiling disarmingly. 'None of the poor fellows speak English and all are concerned by your arrival.'

'Maybe they've cause to be,' Dusty said.

'They have not, sir,' Hoffinger stated before Dusty could do more than glance at the paper. 'In fact you might almost say that I'm helping the Confederate States. I'm taking these able-bodied men away from the fighting. They had been tricked into enlisting in the Union Army, poor fellows, but my organization – you've probably heard of us, the Society For The Preservation of Human Rights—?'

'I can't say I have,' Dusty grunted and started reading.

Bearing the official printed heading of the Department of the Interior, the document stated that O. L. Hoffinger, secretary of the Society For The Preservation Of Human Rights, had permission to escort the 'under-named' men to the Territory of New Mexico and that they and their property must not be taken into service by any officer of the United States' Army. Everything about the paper seemed authentic enough, although Dusty could not vouch for the validity of the signature on it.

'I trust that this explains our position to your satisfaction, Captain,' Hoffinger said when he saw that Dusty had finished reading.

'Not all the way,' Dusty replied.

'Then permit me to clarify it somewhat. Word reached my Society of the scandalous way in which these poor fellows had been treated. Naturally we set about obtaining their freedom as they had been enlisted by fraud. We are not without influence in Congress, and succeeded. Their families had already gone to take up their homes, so it was decided that I should accompany them and ensure that they reached their destination without further interference.'

'How about the horses?'

'Bought before their enlistment, as the means of tilling their farms. We insisted that the Army returned them and once again justice prevailed. How could they plough their land without horses?'

'Mind if I talk to them?' Dusty asked, ignoring the question.

'Feel free— Do you speak German?'

'Nope,' Dusty admitted, studying the men. None of them had Teutonic or Anglo-Saxon features and coloration. 'Are they Germans?'

'From various parts of mid-Europe. Polish mostly. But Mr. Glock there speaks German well enough for me to communicate with them through him.'

Walking towards the fire, accompanied by Hoffinger, with Kiowa prowling alert for danger on their heels, Dusty thought over what he had been told. All the men were of military age and in good health. With an urgent need for extra troops, it seemed unlikely that the Union Army would release potential recruits. Yet they might if sufficient political pressure was brought to bear. The North was infested by 'liberal' organizations for the protection of the 'down-trodden', some of which carried considerable weight in Congress. If Hoffinger's Society was one of the more influential, the Army might yield to its wishes as a gesture of good will. Especially with the men unable to speak English, rendering training them difficult. In one way the number of Burnside carbines strengthened the story. Possibly the Society had obtained a reduction in price by buying in bulk. Having obtained the men's release, the Society would waste no time in reuniting them with their families and might even send one of their senior officials, armed with suitable authority, to act as an escort.

From an officer in the C.S.A.'s viewpoint, Dusty considered that the men would be of less use to the Union as farmers in New Mexico than by serving in the Yankee Army. He could also imagine how the North's newspapers would blow up the story if Hoffinger had told the truth and he took the horses from their owners.

Yet all the horses, particularly the big bay stallion, looked far more suitable for riding than performing the dragging and hauling of farm work.

Then a thought struck Dusty as he approached the big man called Glock. It was a small matter, maybe, but significant in view of Hoffinger's story. New Mexico lay to the west, yet the trace-poles at the front of the wagons were pointing eastwards. While the springy grama grass did not lend itself to retaining tracks that proved otherwise, Dusty doubted if Hoffinger's party would turn their wagons to face the direction from which they had come when making camp for the night.

So far none of the men Dusty approached had shown that they knew his Company was close at hand, but he felt sure that Red was already in position. Which meant he must make his move before Glock's bunch discovered their presence.

Suddenly, giving no hint of his intentions, Dusty stepped close and stamped as hard as he could on Glock's right foot. Letting out a startled howl, the big man hopped on his left leg, clutched at his throbbing toes and acted just as the small Texan hoped that he might.

'What the hell do you reckon you're—!' Glock roared in a language Dusty and Kiowa could understand. chopping off his words as he realized what he was doing.

'Man,' drawled the Indian-dark scout, tensing ready to back his captain's play. 'You sure learned to talk English fast.'

Aware of what he had done, Glock slammed his aching foot to the ground. At the same time, he stabbed his right hand towards the flap of his holster. Behind him, the other men just stood and stared. Even Hoffinger appeared to be shocked into immobility by Dusty's actions.

Dusty knew that Glock would be unable to draw the revolver at any speed, so he decided against gun-play as a means of halting the attempt. While Dusty could easily have fetched out one or both his Colts and shot Glock, he knew doing so might spark off a full-scale fight.

Not that he feared for his own safety. At the first hint of trouble, Red had brought the Company out of the trees. They were now galloping forward, guns in hand, so that the men behind Glock would be wiped out before any could offer more than a token resistance. Taking no pleasure in killing, Dusty did not want that to happen, Especially when there was a more satisfactory way of handling the situation. Without ever having heard of psychology, he guessed that capturing some of the enemy, then releasing them disarmed but uninjured, would carry a greater morale impact than leaving them dead. By treating them so leniently he would emphasize to the captives, and their comrades-in-arms, the superiority of the Confederate States Army in Arkansas.

So Dusty left his guns in the holsters and relied, as he had against Savos, on Tommy Okasi's training. He did not use the *tegatana,* handsword, but brought off one of the even more effective *keriwaza* kicking attacks. Measuring the distance between himself and Glock, he balanced on his right leg and launched his left foot into the air. Curling his toes upwards as far as possible, he flexed his ankle and propelled the ball of his foot with considerable force against the pit of the big man's stomach.

Glock slammed backwards and doubled over. Jerking the hand from the unopened holster, he clutched at his mid-section. Winded and filled with nausea, he was in no condition to defend himself against the continuation of the attack. Following the man up, Dusty drove his clenched right fist in a power-packed backhand swing to the centre of the other's face. Lifted erect by the impact, Glock pitched helplessly into the arms of the men behind him.

From delivering the blow, Dusty whipped his right arm down and over so his fingers grasped the butt of the left side Colt. Already his left hand was curling about the bone handle of the other revolver. Steel rasped on leather, merging with the clicks of the hammers being drawn back to full cock. In three-quarters of a second from Dusty starting his draw, the men into whom Glock had collided were looking down the barrels of his Army Colts. The manner in which he had handled Glock left them almost numb with amazement and he did not intend to grant them time to recover.

'Don't move, any of you!' Dusty warned.

And, in some strange way, he no longer looked small. Instead he gave the impression of possessing size and bulk sufficient to tower above them all. Such was the force of his personality that, taken with his fast-drawn Colts, he prevented the men from attempting to resist.

Knowing Dusty, Kiowa had expected him to do something and had been ready to take a hand when he did. Even as Dusty stamped on Glock's toe, Kiowa had slid out his bowie knife. When Hoffinger made as if to move forward, Kiowa caught him by the scruff of the neck from behind. Bringing the dude to a halt, Kiowa pricked his plump ribs with the clip point of the knife and breathed a savage warning.

'You-all too fat to tangle with Cap'n Dusty.'

'That, I assure you, was never my intention,' Hoffinger croaked, staring in fascinated awe at the result of Dusty's attack.

Releasing the dude's neck, but keeping the knife in position, Kiowa reached around to pluck the Le Mat revolver from Hoffinger's holster. The rest of the Company came up, most of them bringing their horses to sliding halts and lining their weapons at the dude's men. Sergeant Weather led half-a-dozen soldiers towards the unattended horses, ready to control them should there be shooting. The precaution was unnecessary. So effectively did the Texans surround the other party that resistance would have been suicidal.

'Disarm them, Mr. Blaze!' Dusty ordered. 'Billy Jack, take four men and search those wagons.'

'I think that I had better tell you the truth, Captain,' Hoffinger called, being prevented by Kiowa from going closer to the small Texan.

'I was just figuring to ask you to do that,' Dusty replied, watching his orders carried out. 'Let him come, Kiowa.'

Scuttling gratefully away from the Indian-dark sergeant, who he felt wanted only an excuse to take his scalp, Hoffinger came to Dusty's side and dropped his voice in a confiding manner.

'The fact of the matter is, Captain, that we have stolen these horses and deserted from the Union Army and are headed west of New Mexico to start a new life.'

CHAPTER FOUR

LINE FIVE UP AND SHOOT THEM

'DESERTERS, huh?' Dusty grunted, twirling away his Colts.

'From the Union Army, sir,' Hoffinger confirmed. 'This is a carefully planned desertion, hence the spurious document which you thrust into your tunic before testing my men.'

'Why'd you lie about it when we rode up then?'

'Merely to ascertain how the document and story would stand up under the scrutiny of an alert, efficient officer like yourself. I had, of course, every intention of telling you the truth after you had tested my companions' ability to act as newly-arrived immigrants who speak no English. You produced a remarkably effective way of testing them, I must say.'

Every word Hoffinger spoke had a ring of truth to it, while his whole being exuded an aura of sincerity. So much so that Dusty felt suspicious. Yet he admitted that his feelings might stem from antipathy to smooth-talking, portly dudes, or even out of his dislike for deserters.

'That's how it is, huh?' Dusty said.

'Exactly how it is, sir,' Hoffinger confirmed. 'And an officer of your undoubted experience can visualize the effect on the Union Army in Arkansas when words gets out that there has been such a large desertion. More so when the soldiers learn that, in accordance with General Hardin's policy, the deserters were given free passage for themselves and their horses by members of the Texas Light Cavalry.'

'I see. We're going to let you fellers go and take those horses with you.'

'In return for which I will gladly append my signature to a statement that you have done so. When news of it—'

'Drop it, *hombre*!' Dusty snapped, his entire attitude changing to one of cold annoyance. 'You're not deserters.'

'But I assure you we are, sir!' protested Hoffinger. 'We are tired of fighting for a cause in which we no longer believe. So we are going to New Mexico—'

'Then how come your wagons are pointed east?' Dusty countered and looked at Hoffinger's men. 'Are you bunch deserters?'

Sullen faces glared at him and Glock, removing a hand from his bloody nose, answered in a surly tone.

'Yeah. And Ole Devil Hardin allowed any Yankee who deserted could take his guns and hosses with him without having 'em took off him by Rebel soldiers.'

A point which Dusty had been considering ever since Hoffinger had mentioned that they were deserters. Both sides had used such inducements as safe passage through their lines, or offers of homes and employment, to encourage desertion by the other's soldiers and sailors. So Ole Devil had given orders that his men would in no way interfere with deserters from the Union Army.

If Hoffinger had told the truth, Dusty could not confiscate the horses. Capture of the dude's party by the Yankees would be almost inevitable if he did. Dusty could imagine the delight displayed by various Northern newspapers at receiving proof that the Rebels did not keep their promises to deserters. The story would have an adverse effect in Arkansas, where desertion caused a steady drain on the Federal man-power. Even worse to Dusty's way of thinking, it would imply that his uncle – for whom he felt the greatest admiration and respect – could not be relied upon to keep his word.

Once again Dusty knew that he must step warily. Maybe the Yankees, plagued by desertion, had sent out Hoffinger's party to prove that the Rebels in the field did not honour their commanding general's offers of co-operation to deserters. Unlikely, perhaps, but Dusty wanted to be certain before taking any action.

'I reckon that you're guerillas, not deserters!' Dusty stated and looked to where Red stood listening. 'What do you say, Mr. Blaze?'

'They're stinking border-jumpers for sure, sir,' Red answered, judging that an affirmative reply was expected and obliging. 'I can smell it on them.'

'We're deserters!' Hoffinger insisted, seeing his men show signs of concern.

'The hell you are!' Dusty barked. 'They're guerillas, Mr. Blaze.'

'Yes, sir! And Un – General Hardin gave orders that we shot any of 'em we caught. Say now! I heard tell that some of Quantrill's boys had got to arguing which killed best, an Enfield or a Sharps. To settle it, they lined up five prisoners to see how many of 'em each gun'd shoot through.'

'I heard about that,' Dusty said thoughtfully, showing none

of the delight he felt at the way Red had caught on to and improved upon his scheme.

'I was wondering which'd shoot best out of my Henry 'n' these Burnsides,' Red remarked in a speculative manner. 'Seeing's how we're going to kill this bunch, I just might's well find out.'

'Hey now—!' Glock began, but was held back by the Texan guards.

'Go to it,' Dusty said. 'Line five up and shoot them, Mr. Blaze.'

Shock creased the prisoners' faces as Red swung eagerly towards them. The inhuman experiment carried out by members of William Clarke Quantrill's guerilla band had been given much publicity in the North. Clearly all Hoffinger's men had heard and believed the story. Nor did they doubt, looking at him, that Red was not only willing but eager to duplicate the trial on their bodies. Only the dude remained calm. Standing at Dusty's side, he smiled and opened his mouth. Before Hoffinger could speak, Glock came to a military brace and saluted the small Texan.

'We're soldiers, Cap'n,' the big man declared. 'I'm Sergeant-major Glock of the New Hampstead Volunteers and these fellers're from my company.'

'How about that, Mr. Hoffinger?' Dusty asked.

'We are deserters—' the dude insisted.

'Prove it,' Red challenged, 'and fast. I'm wanting to try these guns.'

'I can hardly produce a document from the Army to say we've deserted,' Hoffinger protested.

'Damn it, we're the official escort for these remounts, Cap'n!' Glock yelled, indicating the horses. 'Being dressed this way's part of a fool notion Hoffinger thought out.'

'Can you *prove* that?' Dusty drawled, while Red fingered a Burnside longingly.

'Of course we ca—!' Hoffinger began.

'Show him that paper, you crazy son-of-a-bitch!' Glock roared being restrained from springing forward by the lined guns of the guards. 'They ain't fooling.'

'Damn it!' Red growled. 'I'm tired of this talking. Cut out five of 'em, Sergeant Bixby and send a man for my Henry.'

'No!' Glock bellowed and his men added their voices to the plea. 'Cap'n, he's got another letter, telling the truth about us. It's in the "grape-shot"—'

'You stupid bastard!' wailed Hoffinger. 'Why didn't you call their bluff? Neither of them aimed to go through with it.'

'Didn't we?' Dusty asked. 'Let me have Mr. Hoffinger's revolver, Kiowa.'

'I doubt very much if you did, sir,' the dude answered, knowing that Dusty had read correctly the meaning of Glock's last sentence, interrupted though it had been. 'By the "C" on your guidon, I assume that you are Dusty Fog. Unfortunately I failed to see it in time to announce the fact.'

'Hell's teeth, yes!' Glock spat out. 'If I'd known—'

Ignoring the comments, Dusty examined the revolver. Due to a lack of manufacturing facilities in the South, Colonel Alexandre Le Mat had gone to France to produce his revolvers. Sufficient of them had been smuggled through the U.S. Navy's blockade on the Confederate ports for Dusty to be familiar with their peculiarities. The gun he held was a standard production model. Under the .40 calibre hexagonal barrel was a second shorter and larger tube. At its rear end, this tube acted as a base-pin for the nine-shot cylinder and was, in fact, a smooth-bore barrel designed to fire a .50 calibre 'grape-shot' ball.

However Hoffinger's Le Mat did not carry its lethal secondary load. Inserting the tip of his little finger, Dust eased a rolled sheet of paper out of the 'grape-shot' barrel. It proved to be an authorization for Hoffinger to collect one hundred remounts and deliver them to the U.S. Army of Arkansas' headquarters. In the next paragraph, Sergeant-major Glock and the escort were permitted to travel in civilian clothes. Lastly, all Union Army officers were required to give the party every assistance by order of General Horace Trumpeter.

Watching Dusty read the document, Hoffinger wondered if there was any way in which the situation might yet be saved. Annoyance filled the chubby dude. Not so much at the failure to trick Dusty, although that rankled a little, but because he had made the mistake of under-estimating an opponent's potential. To a man in Hoffinger's profession, such a mistake was inexcusable.

Hoffinger had started life as a petty thief, graduating to the more genteel status of confidence trickster by virtue of his native talents. A man by nature peace-loving, he had avoided active participation in the War. Hovering safely clear of the fighting, he had managed to garner a comfortable living. Circumstances, not unconnected with a supply-contracts swindle in the process of going wrong, made a change of scenery of vital importance. The western 'hinter-lands' had seemed the best choice when good fortune presented him with the chance of getting there and making money without too much work or risk.

It had all begun when he learned that General Trumpeter had obtained permission to purchase remounts from the Pawnee Indians. Officers with considerable experience of conditions in Arkansas had warned that collecting the horses would be fraught with difficulties. In fact, the general consensus of military opinion had been that purchases from that source would be a waste of time and money, with the results not worth the cost. The unanimity of their views merely served to convince Trumpeter that he was right and he looked for a way to prove it.

A keen student of human nature, Hoffinger felt that he knew how to deal with Trumpeter. By sycophantic agreement and professing 'liberal' leanings, the dude had convinced the general that he was the man most suitable to collect the horses. Hoffinger had suggested using a small escort, dressed in civilian clothes and backed by the fake document as a means of tricking any Rebel patrol which met them; although he had been glib enough to make it appear the idea came from Trumpeter. Seeing a way to prove the career-officers wrong, Trumpeter had needed little convincing. If a man like Hoffinger succeeded, the general figured that he would have a powerful weapon to wave in the faces of his critics.

Patriotic fervour had not prompted Hoffinger's actions. He had seen a way out of his difficulties and means to start a profitable career. Up until the meeting with Dusty Fog, everything had been satisfactory. As well as collecting the horses, he had made useful contacts and picked up some easily-sold merchandise. So he had hoped for further missions, with the Army paying his expenses and providing an escort to ensure his safety. At least they had on the first trip. He could not see there being others if he failed to deliver the horses.

'This's about what I'd figured it'd be,' Dusty drawled, folding the paper and placing it with the other 'authorization' in his tunic's inside pocket. 'You'd show it to any Yankee officer who wouldn't accept your "Society" story, I'd say.'

'That is correct, sir,' Hoffinger agreed. 'I might have needed proof that we aren't deserters or guerillas.'

'Likely General Trumpeter reckoned if a civilian could bring in his horses, it'd show his men that us Rebs aren't so all-fired tough or smart after all.'

'I couldn't say about that,' Hoffinger answered tactfully.

'Did you figure anybody's fall for that story you told me?'

'I've always found the more unlikely the story, if it is backed by documentary proof, the more likely it is to be accepted. You might have accepted it yourself if I'd thought to have the wagons turned to face west when we halted.'

'Could be,' Dusty admitted. 'Not having pickets out helped your story, soldiers would have. I'd've thought twice before taking horses from civilians when they'd got what'd read in a Yankee newspaper like a real good reason for needing 'em.'

'What's in the wagons, Billy Jack?' Red asked, seeing the sergeant-major ambling disconsolately towards them, a large buckskin bag trailing in his hand.

'Food, bed-rolls 'n' such in the first 'n'. I've had all their ammunition put on the hosses. T'others toting buffalo hides, Injun moccasins and such—'

'They're mine, Captain Fog!' Hoffinger interrupted. 'And so is that money—'

'This here, Cap'n Dusty,' Billy Jack went on, holding out the bag. 'Found it hid in the second wagon.'

'It's mine!' Hoffinger insisted. 'All I have in the world. I staked all my savings on this collecting mission and that's all that remains.'

'Give it to him, Billy Jack,' Dusty said. 'We don't rob civilians. Let's go take a look at the horses.'

'Why not share a meal with us first, Captain?' Hoffinger suggested. 'We've enough food for you.'

'Thanks for the offer,' Dusty replied. 'That's what we'll do.'

During the meal, Hoffinger studied Dusty and revised his previous ideas. The earlier crude flattery had been aimed at a naïve youngster holding rank by family influence. Now Hoffinger knew better. Young he might be, but the small Texan controlled those hard-bitten veterans by virtue of his personality and achievements.

Looking around, Hoffinger noticed that the Texans continued performing their duties with the minimum of supervision. While he entertained the officers by the wagon carrying his property, Hoffinger saw Billy Jack and Kiowa seated talking amiably to Glock and Corporal Mullitz. Staring at the latter, Hoffinger felt the start of an idea. A long chance, maybe, but infinitely better than no chance at all. Quickly he turned back to his guests, not wanting them to become aware of his interest in Mullitz. During the rest of the meal, he put together the details of his scheme.

'Thanks for the food, Mr. Hoffinger,' Dusty said at last, coming to his feet. 'Have the men get ready to pull out while I look at the horses, Cousin Red.'

'They're all good stock,' Hoffinger put in. 'Except for the bay stallion, that is. He won't be any use to you.'

'Why not?' Red inquired with interest.

'He was sent by a Pawnee chief as a gift for General Trumpeter. But I fear that he is unmanageable.'

'I've yet to see the horse that couldn't be managed,' Red remarked.

'This one can't,' Hoffinger stated before Dusty could speak. 'In fact I'm willing to bet that you haven't a man here who can saddle and ride it, even though the chief assured me it had been saddle-broke and one of his men rode it in from the tribe's horse-herd.'

'You'd bet on it?' Dusty asked quietly.

'I would, sir. And I have a thousand dollars in gold to back my words.'

'A thousand dollars,' Dusty said. 'Against what?'

'The remounts,' Hoffinger told him.

'That's a right sporting bet!' Red snorted. 'The hosses're worth more than a thousand dollars.'

'True,' Hoffinger replied. 'But I have seen the horse ridden and feel that I should be given odds.'

'The hell—!' Red started hotly.

'He's right,' Dusty interrupted. 'If that chief told the truth, he should have the odds. So if Mr. Hoffinger fetches out that thousand dollars, I'll take his bet and give it a whirl.'

Hoffinger held down the delight he felt at Dusty falling into the trap. He did not doubt that the bet would be honoured and, considering how the horse had acted when his men tried to saddle it, was sure that Dusty would fail.

'The money's in my hand, sir,' Hoffinger said, holding out the bag. 'Mr. Blaze will be acceptable to me as stake-holder.'

'We'll let Sergeant-major Glock help him,' Dusty answered. 'Red, tell Sandy to fetch over my saddle while I take a look at the horse.'

Leaving Red to attend to the details, Dusty went to where the bay was tethered. Swinging to face him, it backed off until halted by the rope. Ears pricked and nostrils flaring, it exhibited a nervousness which increased as Sandy McGraw came up carrying Dusty's saddle, saddle-blanket and bridle. A jingle from the latter's bit brought a louder snort and the horse reared as high as the picket rope would let it.

'Put the blanket and saddle down, Sandy,' Dusty ordered in a quiet, gentle voice. 'And take the bridle away with you.'

The guidon-carrier obeyed and as he retired, Billy Jack passed him walking with greater than usual speed.

'Hear tell you've bet you can ride that hoss, Cap'n Dusty,' the sergeant-major said. 'Got to talking to Fritz Glock about it just now. He reckons the Pawnee Chief they got it off allowed it'd been three-saddled. Only neither him nor Joe Mullitz've managed to get a saddle on its back or bit in its mouth.'

'Sounds bad,' Dusty drawled, knowing that 'three-saddled' meant the horse had been ridden at least three times by the man breaking it.

'Don't you sell'em short. They're both thirty-year men and trained as cavalry afore the War. Mullitz was a riding instructor back East.'

'Did he ever serve out West?'

'Neither him nor Fritz from what they told us.'

'That figures,' Dusty said cryptically. 'Let's see if I can win that bet.'

'Ole Devil'll have your hide if you lose!' Billy Jack wailed and, for once, his concern was not entirely assumed, for he knew the stakes of the wager.

'Likely,' Dusty admitted. 'Tell Glock's men I figure the New Hampstead Volunteers're sporting enough not to make fuss and spoil my chance.'

'Sure,' Billy Jack answered. 'And in case they ain't sporting enough, I'll have 'em watched real good.'

Turning his attention to the horse once more, Dusty noticed that its nervousness had died slightly with the removal of the jingling bridle. As he expected, it had on an Indian hackamore and not a U.S. Army halter. The chief difference was that the former had reins attached to a *bosal* – a rawhide loop fitted around the face just above the mouth – instead of a lead-rope.

Although Sandy had removed Dusty's bed-roll and sabre on hearing of the bet, he had left the rope strapped to the saddle horn. Taking it, Dusty walked slowly towards the horse. Snorting and pawing the ground, it watched him suspiciouly. All the time, he kept up a flow of soft-spoken, soothing talk. With the picket rope knotted to the *bosal,* he could not flip his loop over the bay's head. Instead he slid the stem of his Manila rope across the top of its neck. Catching the end of the stem underneath the neck, he quickly formed a running noose and drew it tight.

Naturally the news of the bet had attracted considerable attention. Recalling their non-coms' experiences with the bay, Glock's men waited to see how Dusty would fare. Equally interested, the Texans kept clear of their prisoners and remained alert for trouble. Neither Red nor Billy Jack looked too happy about the affair, being aware of what might happen to Dusty should he lose.

A smile played on Hoffinger's lips as he watched the rope tighten about the horse's neck. Then it wavered and died. Instead of fighting to tear free, the bay stood still. Keeping the rope taut, Dusty backed until he could pick up his saddle and blanket. Still moving unhurriedly, he returned with them in his hand. The horse let out another snort, yet did not fight against the rope. Up close, Dusty set down his saddle. Then he caressed the bay's head with his hands, stroking its nostrils and eyes before taking hold of the head-piece of the *bosal*. Keeping the head steady, he leaned forward and began to blow into its flaring nostrils.

'What's he do—!' Hoffinger yelped, the words ending as Red rammed an elbow into his ribs.

'You try yelling to spook the hoss again,' Red growled in a low, savage tone, 'and I'll raise lumps all over your pumpkin head with my Colt's butt.'

Knowing that his escort meant to carry out the threat, Hoffinger lapsed into silence. Yet, to give him his due, surprise rather than any foul motive had caused the outburst. He had been amazed by the bay's lack of resistance and at Dusty's actions.

After standing by the horse's head for a short time, Dusty took up his saddle. Anticipation bit at Hoffinger, mingled with the thought that something was wrong. Not until Dusty had slid the folded blanket into place did the dude realize what it was. With growing delight, he saw that the small Texan was standing on the right side of the horse instead of at the left. Yet the bay showed none of its usual objections to either the blanket or the saddle, despite the change of procedure. Not even the adjustment of the girths about its belly provoked the kind of savage protests which had met attempts by Glock or Mullitz to saddle it. Instead it stood quietly and allowed Dusty to unfasten the picket-rope from the *bosal*.

'He's not using a bridle or bit!' Hoffinger croaked, watching Dusty slip his right foot into the stirrup iron and swing astride the bay.

'Danged if he's not forgot,' grinned Red, knowing that the *bosal* served as a bit and beginning to realize why Dusty had accepted the bet.

Settling on the saddle, Dusty felt the horse tense itself between his legs. Gripping the reins in his right hand, he cautiously freed his rope. A nudge with his heels sent the bay off in a long 'straight-away' buck. Although it sailed high, it came down without twisting, whirling or the dangerous powerful hindquarter's kick that could drive the base of the rider's spine against the cantle of the saddle. Performed without the refinements, bucking straight-away posed no problems for a man with Dusty's skill. In fact he soon realized that his mount was doing no more than try him out. It continued to crow-hop for a short time. The see-saw motion of the bucking looked spectacular, but required little effort to ride out. Nor did it sustain the fight and it soon began to respond to the messages of the reins.

'I – I don't believe it!' Hoffinger croaked as Dusty rode towards him.

At the same time, the dude knew that his last chance had gone. Even the hope that his escort would take advantage of their captors' preoccupation, jump and overcome them, did not materialize. All Glock's men sat under guard, staring with open-mouthed amazement and apparently frozen into immobility by the ease with which the small Texan had mastered the hitherto unmanageable stallion.

'My bet, I reckon,' Dusty drawled, halting the horse. Swinging his left leg forward and over the saddle horn, he dropped to the ground at the bay's right side. 'Sandy, put my rig back on the black.'

'And see you take it off the bay from the Indian-side,' Red advised, grinning as he took the bag of money from Glock's limp hand.

'*Indian*-side?' Hoffinger repeated.

'Why sure,' Dusty said. 'Didn't you fellers notice that the Indians always saddle-up and mount from the right, instead of at the left like white folks?'

'I didn't,' Hoffinger began. 'From the ri— But that means—'

'Yeah,' agreed Dusty. 'Every time your men tried to saddle it from the left, they spooked it. Trying to use a bit made things worse. Indians don't use 'em.'

'Way you took on,' Red continued, 'I reckon you figured Dusty'd rile it up by putting a rope 'round its neck.'

'I did,' Hoffinger admitted, surprised to learn that the youngster had read his emotions so well.

'An Indian breaks his horse by roping it and choking it down,' Red explained. 'That's rough on the horse and after he's felt it a couple of times he learns better'n fight against a running noose. After the horse gets over being choked down, the Injun fusses it a mite and blows into its nostrils. Damned if I know why, but doing that quietens it down and lets him know the feller doing it's his friend.'

'You still took a risk, Captain Fog,' Hoffinger pointed out. 'Even counting on us not knowing which side to saddle and mount from, the Pawnee chief could have been lying about it being fully saddle-broken.'

'Indians don't do a heap of lying,' Dusty answered. 'And I figured it was near on certain he hadn't, the bay being a chief's gift for General Trumpeter.'

'I'm afraid that I still don't understand.'

'Figure it this way. That chief's got plenty of horses to sell and's likely getting a better price from you than he could any other place—'

'The price is adequate, I admit, but I still don't follow your reasoning.'

'It's easy enough,' Dusty told him. 'The chief wants to keep General Trumpeter friendly and eager to buy more horses. So he sends along a gift. Now he doesn't know how good a rider the general is, so he figures not to take chances. The horse he picks looks good, has some spirit, but's real easy and gentle to ride. That's the way I saw it and reckoned I could win the bet easy. The South can use a thousand dollars in Yankee gold, only I coudn't take it from a civilian by force, now could I?'

'Well, I'm damned!' Hoffinger croaked. 'You've slickered me, Captain Fog!'

'They do say it's hell when it happens to you,' Dusty replied with a grin. 'I want to pull out in fifteen minutes, Cousin Red.'

'Yo!' Red replied and walked away grinning.

Once again Cousin Dusty had pulled it off. Sure Red and Billy Jack knew how Indians trained and mounted their horses; but neither of them had thought out a way to put their knowledge to use. Dusty had done so and gained a large sum of money for which the Confederate States' Secret Service could probably find a purpose. What was more, he had done it in a way which the Yankee newspapers could not call robbing a civilian. Glock and the others were sure to talk of the bet on their return and would be believed no matter how the Union tried to prevent it.

In fifteen minutes, the Company was ready to march. Smiling, Hoffinger held out his hand to the small Texan who had bested him.

'I hope General Trumpeter's not too riled at you for losing the remounts,' Dusty said, shaking hands. 'Tell him from me that we'll likely need them in our retreat across the Red River.'

'That's one excuse I won't use,' chuckled Hoffinger. 'I feel that by now he will be very touchy when that particular stream is mentioned. Good-bye, Captain Fog. With no disrespect, sir, I hope our paths don't cross again.'

'They might if you try to fetch in more of these remounts,' Dusty warned.

'That is a remote contingency, sir,' Hoffinger sighed. 'My continued employment depended on delivering this bunch.'

'I'm real sorry to spoil it for you,' Dusty said. 'But I reckon a feller as talented as you'll find some way of earning his living. *Adios*.'

'That young man is going to annoy General Trumpeter before he's through,' Hoffinger told Glock as they watched the Texans drive the horses into the water.

'He's already done it,' Glock answered, fingering his stomach and grinning with grudging admiration. 'Damned if he didn't fire a salute for the general, Billy Jack told me. Out of two of *our* mortars and right into the middle of a review Trumpeter was holding. Yes sir, Mr. Hoffinger, Trumpeter's going to hate Dusty Fog's name.'

CHAPTER FIVE

WE'VE GOT TO STOP THOSE GUNS!

'THERE'S something up, Mr. Blaze!' growled grizzled old Corporal Vern Hassle, bringing his horse to a sliding halt after returning at speed to the four-man scouting party sent ahead to learn what force of Yankees guarded the Snake Ford of the Caddo.

It was almost noon on the day following the capture of Hoffinger's horses and Company 'C' were travelling south-east as fast as they could manage accompanied by the remounts and heavy draught animals. They had seen no sign of pursuit, but Kiowa kept watch on their back-trail. The previous night, in camp, Dusty and Red had studied their maps and decided where they could best make their crossing into Rebel territory.

Every ford along the Caddo and Ouachita Rivers was guarded by detachments of Confederate and Union troops. In addition, both sides kept patrols moving along the rivers' banks to watch for infiltration by the enemy. On their way out, Company 'C' had crossed at an unguarded stretch of fast-flowing water through which only expert horsemen could pass. Using the same place on their return would be dangerous for they had a large bunch of riderless horses with them. To make a crossing would be a lengthy process and leave them open to attack should a Yankee patrol locate them.

While there had been two fords closer, Dusty had selected Snake Ford. The other two had to be approached across open, level ground with no chance of taking the Yankees by surprise. Snake Ford lay in a wide, winding valley. Being of little military importance, it was held by a company of Stedloe's Zouaves and a platoon of Dragoons. On the other side, a full battalion of Arkansas Rifles could be swiftly brought up to support the Texans in their crossing. The strength of Rifles stemmed from the fact that the ford was in the centre of their regiment's patrol area, rather than concern over holding on to it.

Wanting to make his dash across the river with few if any

casualties, Dusty had sent Red ahead to see if the Yankees were watching their rear. Trained in Indian warfare, Vern Hassle ran Kiowa a close second in ability. He had advanced to make a scout and his return heralded trouble.

'What's up?' Red demanded.

Before Hassle could reply, Red heard the staccato blast of a bugle blowing the 'alarm'. Faint shouts wafted back to the Texan's ears, followed by the crackle of rifle shots.

'That!' Hassle replied. 'When I left, the Arkansas boys were forming up like they're fixing to attack the ford – and there's a battery of cannon on this side.'

'Let's go!' Red barked. 'Is anybody watching this way, Vern?'

'Nope,' the corporal answered; then the four horses were running.

Urging their mounts to a gallop, Red's party raced across the remaining half mile and drew rein just before reaching the rim overlooking the Snake Ford. Dropping from his saddle, Red slid free the Henry rifle from its boot. Before leaving the horses ground-hitched, he told the others to take their carbines and ammunition. Thrusting a box of .44 bullets, taken from his saddle-pouch, into his tunic, Red advanced on foot until he could see the river.

The trail along which they had ridden wound down a gentle slope and across about a quarter of a mile of level ground before entering the water to emerge on the other bank which had the same general features. As the name implied, the Caddo made a S-shaped curve at that point. To either side of Red, the downwards slope extended until it eventually fell in a sheer wall to the water. There was, however, an area of about half a mile down which one could ride to reach the ford.

All that Red had expected to see from his study of the maps. What came as a shock was the sight of the Arkansas Rifles battalion formed up in line of battle and starting to advance determinedly down the opposite slope. That and the battery of Model 1857 12-pounder Napoleon gun-howitzers facing the Rebels on the Yankees' shore. From all appearances, the whole battalion, colours flying and bayonets fixed, were moving to the attack. Their numbers would have been adequate against the normal guard, even if the assault led to casualties from the enemies' rifle fire. The same did not apply when they must advance across more than eight hundred yards of open country, in the face of artillery bombardment, before reaching the river.

Red knew that a well-served Napoleon could fire two aimed

shots a minute, using spherical case or solid shot. When the range shortened, the guns would switch to canister and speed up their rate of fire. Canister, each one holding twenty-seven balls, turned the Napoleons into a kind of giant shotgun and dispensed with the need for taking careful aim. It could not be put into use successfully until the enemy came within three hundred and fifty yards range; but after that every gun in the battery could get off up to nine shots before the attackers reached it. Such a volume of fire might easily wipe out the whole battalion.

Already solid shot was crashing among the advancing soldiers, the Yankee battery commander wisely forgetting spherical case due to the uncertainty of the timing-fuses' operation. Down by the river, the Zouaves and Dragoons crouched in their defensive positions and exchanged shots with the Rifles' skirmishers. So far the Yankee infantry did not fire at the main body of the attackers. Almost half a mile was not a distance over which the average soldier, armed with the U.S. Model of 1861 rifle-musket could be counted on to make a hit.

On marched the Arkansas Rifles, keeping their ranks well despite the canon-fire. In front strode the colour party, bearing the regiment's battle-flag, and officers with drawn swords. The enlisted men carried Enfield rifles at the high-port. It would be several minutes before they were close enough to put the rifles into effective use and all that time the Napoleons would continue to fire at them.

'We've got to stop those guns!' Red snapped.

'You mean for us four to charge down there and do it?' asked Tracey Prince.

'Just three of us,' Red corrected. 'Vern. Take my horse and ride relay to the Company. Tell Cap'n Fog what's coming off here.'

'How about you?' the old corporal inquired.

'We're going to move down the rim, find places to settle in and start to shooting,' Red explained. 'Move it!'

'Yo!' replied Prince and Private Tarp Hayley eagerly, each holding a Sharps carbine. Like Red's Henry, the Sharps were battle-field captures and effective weapons in skilled hands.

Studying the battery as he and his companions passed over the rim, while Hassle hurried off to deliver the message, Red concluded that it had only recently arrived and come hurriedly. He could see no sign of the battery-wagon – which carried tents and supplies for the guns' crews – the travelling forage or six reserve caissons of ammunition which normally accompanied the Napoleons when they moved. While there had been some attempt to conceal the guns behind bushes, the crews had not raised protective earth-works. Nor had the three ammunition chests been removed from the guns' caissons and brought closer to the pieces. So far the crews had fed their guns with charges brought from the limber's chest. Their teams and the Dragons' horses were held among a clump of trees over by the left side wall.

'Fan out and find cover!' Red snapped to Hayley and Prince. 'Don't bother with the Zouaves, go for the gun crews.'

Swiftly they separated and each found a place which he felt suited his needs. Red flattened behind a rock, setting the box of bullets close to his left hand. Three hundred yards lay between him and the nearest cannon. The battery, spaced at around fourteen yards intervals and allowing a further two yards per gun, covered an eighty-two yards front. Which meant even the outer pieces were in range of his Henry or his companions' Sharps carbines.

Grimly Red set his rifle's sights. With the wind blowing towards the Confederate side of the ford, Dusty might not hear the fighting. That meant there would be a delay before help could come. So Red knew what must be done. Unless the guns' rate of fire was reduced, the Arkansas Rifles faced terrible losses. The bellowing of the Napoleons and sight of Confederate soldiers falling told him that.

Taking aim, Red squeezed the Henry's trigger and felt the recoil's kick against his shoulder. Through the swirling powdersmoke, he saw the chief-of-piece for the third gun from the left stagger and fall. Down and up flicked the Henry's lever, throwing an empty cartridge case into the air. Before it landed, Red had swung the barrel and shot the number-one man of the crew. Caught in the act of ramming a solid shot down the barrel, the soldier collapsed and snapped the shaft of the rammer. Until a spare could be brought up, the gun was out of action.

Swiftly Red changed his point of aim, raking the fourth from left gun with half-a-dozen bullets. He hit two men and threw the rest into such confusion that the piece went unfired. From the sound of carbine shots on either side of him, he knew that Prince and Hayley were doing their part in slowing the battery's rate of fire.

Already the artillerymen were beginning to realize that the bullets did not come from the Arkansas Rifles and started to look for their new assailants. All too well they understood the danger to themselves. In the days of its greatest exponent, Napoleon

Bonaparte, cannon-fire and especially canister had been a most deadly weapon to employ against unprotected bodies of troops. While canister was still terrible, improvements in hand-held arms had rendered it less effective and it no longer had the advantage of superior range over rifles. So the Yankees wanted to make the most of the canister before the Arkansas Rifles came too close.

Seeing his men go down, the major commanding the battery swung to look at the slope. In doing so, he inadvertently saved his life. Kneeling behind a rock some thirty yards to Red's right, Hayley had selected the major as his next mark. He touched off his shot just as the officer moved and missed.

About the same distance to Red's left, Prince rested his carbine on the lip of the hollow in which he crouched, sighted and fired. Caught in the head, the number-three man of the far left cannon spun around and with a spasmodic gesture flung away the vent-pick with which he had been about to prick open the loaded serge powder bag to make way for the insertion of the friction-primer. Cursing, the chief-of-piece fumbled in his pockets for another vent-pick, without which the gun could not be fired.

The major raked the slope with his field-glasses and located his attackers. Only three men, but they posed a serious threat to the battery's efficiency. Snapping an order to his orderly, he sent the man racing with a message to the Zouaves' commanding officer.

Watching the orderly, Red guessed at the nature of his mission. Across the river, the Arkansas Rifles were still marching at quick-time with their colonel striding in front of them. Not until within a hundred yards would they make their charge. The harassing of the Napoleons must continue if the charge was to succeed.

Although his Henry still held five rounds, Red rested its butt on the ground and began to reload. Opening the magazine-tube after forcing its spring towards the muzzle, he fed ten flat-nosed .44/28 bullets base first down the tube to refill it. While working, he blessed the fact that he had brought the Henry along instead of his Spencer – also a battle-field capture. The Spencer might be more powerful, but had a slower rate of fire and only a seven-shot magazine.

While Red reloaded the Henry, his companions' single-shot carbines continued to crack. Clearly they were having some effect, for the Napoleons' fire slackened.

'Bunch of Yankee puddle-splashers coming, Mr. Blaze!' called Prince.

'Go for the battery as long as you can,' Red replied, closing the magazine tube and returning to his firing position.

A dozen Zouaves led by a sergeant ran by the guns towards the slopes, but they would have to be ignored until the last minute. Already the Arkansas Rifles had entered the zone in which canister could be used against them. Nor did they show signs of halting while rifle fire beat down the menace of the Napoleons.

With a grim-set face Red poured bullets at one of the centre guns. Watching men go down, he noticed that the piece at the left of the line stood unattended. Clearly he and his men had inflicted sufficient casualties for the battery's commander to concentrate the depleted crew on other guns.

Down below, a Springfield rifle banged. Its .58 calibre ball spattered rock chips from Red's cover. Changing his line of sight, the red head sprayed lead at the Zouaves. He dropped the sergeant and one man, then wounded another before the rest took cover. The speed at which he had fired warned the Yankees that they were facing a good shot armed with a Henry, fastest-shooting rifle of the War. So they flung themselves to shelter instead of carrying out their orders. Once more Red turned his attention to the Napoleons.

When the Texans continued to shoot at his guns, the major sent another message to the Zouave entrenchments. Red saw the Infantry major stare up the slope and hesitate, wanting to retain as many men as possible to meet the Rifles' onslaught. Yet he also saw the danger if the harassment of the battery continued. Its fire had already been reduced to a half and at a time when it should be at its highest. So he gave an order which sent a further twenty men under the command of a lieutenant towards the slope.

Seeing support on its way, the first party of Zouaves resumed their advance. Darting from cover to cover, they ascended the slope. Once again Red began to reload the Henry. Unnoticed by him, a Zouave rose from behind a bush and lined a long-barrelled rifle at him.

Catching a movement from the corner of his eye, Tracey Prince turned his head to take a closer look. He saw the Zouave behind Red and twisted around to aim and fire his carbine. In doing so, he saved his and Red's lives. Even as he moved, another Zouave appeared and took a shot at him. The bullet spanged off the rock where Prince's body had been resting an instant before, but without affecting his accuracy. The Sharps spat and blood masked the face of the man beyond Red. Dropping his Springfield he turned and stumbled blindly down the slope.

On firing, Prince swung to face the threat to his own existence. Standing in plain sight, as the reloading could be done faster that way than when kneeling or prone, the second Zouave went about it with trained speed. Clearly he was a veteran, fully capable of making the best time possible at the tedious business of recharging the obsolete, muzzle-loading Springfield rifle. Already he had withdrawn a paper cartridge from his belt-pouch, torn open its base with his teeth, poured the powder into the barrel, used the covering as a wad and thrust the round ball into the muzzle. Resting the cup-shaped end of the ramrod on to the ball, he drove it to the bottom of the barrel. No less speedily he removed the rod, dropping it once clear of the muzzle, and drew back the hammer to half cock.

Although black powder fouled badly when discharged, firing one bullet did not build up sufficient residue to make thrusting home the next round a difficult process. So in slightly less than twenty seconds after missing Prince, the Zouave was ready to fit a percussion cap on the nipple and try again.

Unfortunately Prince held one of the weapons which rapidly wrote a finish to the cheap-to-produce, easy-to-maintain muzzle-loading rifles with which both sides had been armed at the start of the War.

While turning, Prince had shoved forward the Sharps' trigger-guard. This in turn caused the breech block to descend into its loading position. Like the rifle, the carbine fired a non-metallic cartridge; but he did not have to bite it open. Slipping the bullet into the chamber, he returned the triggerguard to its normal place. As it closed, the knife-edge of the breech block sheared through the linen base of the cartridge. Nor did he need to fumble with percussion caps.

The Maynard-primer, which looked like and acted in the manner of a child's roller-cap pistol, had failed to meet the stringent demands of war. Amongst its other faults, the allegedly waterproof coating had allowed the patches of fulminate to become damp and inoperative. So the United States Army had gone back to the slower, but more certain, individual copper cap for the Springfield. The Sharps used the simple, effective Lawrence disc-primer. Operated by a spring-fed magazine built into the frame, the primer fed percussion discs on to the nipple of the carbine's breech and utilized the falling hammer to place them there as well as igniting the fulminate. In that way, the Lawrence primer did away with capping by hand and increased the Sharps' rate of fire.

Making a snap alignment of the sights, Prince squeezed the trigger. The .52 calibre Sharps bullet tore into the Zouave as he was taking a percussion cap from its box. Twisting around, he fell back out of the Texan's sight.

Hayley set his sights on the number-six man as he lifted a round of canister from the limber of the gun on the right of the battery. Engrossed in his work, the Texan forgot to stay alert. As his carbine cracked, three rifles banged like an echo. All three bullets found their billet in Hayley's body and he died without witnessing the excellent result of his last shot. The short-barrelled Sharps carbine lacked the extreme long-range accuracy of the Company's excellent rifles. At ranges of around three hundred yards, the impact point of the bullet might vary by several inches no matter how carefully it had been aimed. Flying down the slope, Hayley's lead ploughed through the round's paper covering and into the serge bag of black powder. Ignited by the heat of the bullet, the two-and-a-half pound charge exploded. Caught in the blast, the remaining charges in the limber detonated. The numbers five, six and seven crew members disappeared in a flash of raging light and roar of sound. Flung from their feet, the remainder of the gun's crew and of the neighbouring piece stayed down until sure that there would be no sympathetic explosion from the next limber's chest.

After shooting Hayley, the three Zouaves hurled themselves into the nearest cover. They had seen enough of the Texans' deadly shooting not to risk standing exposed while reloading their rifles. Others of their party continued to advance. In the lead, the young lieutenant made for Red's position with his sword in the right hand and revolver in the left.

Pumping lead through the red-hot barrel of his Henry, Red was momentarily dazed by the limber's disintegration. Across the river, the Arkansas Rifles were wavering under the hammering of the Napoleons, reduced though it had been. They also faced the volley-firing of the Zouaves and Dragoons. So Red ignored the danger to himself and concentrated on getting off as many aimed shots as he could at the battery.

CHAPTER SIX

YEEAH, TEXAS LIGHT!

EVEN as Red worked the Henry's lever and tried to remember how many bullets he had fired since last replenishing the magazine, he heard the wild, ringing notes of a bugle blowing the 'charge'. Twisting his head involuntarily towards the sound, he saw Dusty galloping over the rim, followed by most of the Company.

A revolver barked close at hand, its bullet tearing the hat from Red's head. That brought his attention to more pressing matters than admiring his companions' riding skill, or blessing his cousin's timely arrival. Swinging to face the direction from which the shot had come, he saw the Yankee lieutenant looming towards him. Again the Zouave's revolver spat. Its bullet struck the barrel of the Henry and spun it from Red's hands. With a yell of triumph, the Zouave sprang forward and swung up the sword. Red threw himself to one side, right hand turning palm-out to close on the butt of the off-side Colt. Fetching it from leather as he landed on his back, he fired upwards. Caught under the chin by the bullet, the Yankee officer staggered into the path of one of his men who was trying to draw a bead on Red. Thwarted in his attempt and seeing the Rebel cavalry rushing down the slope, the soldier dropped his rifle and fled.

Knowing that he could not join in the charge while afoot, Red holstered his Colt and rolled across to pick up the Henry. He found that the bullet had only glanced off the top of the octagonal barrel. Satisfied that the rifle was operative, he turned his eyes towards the battery once more.

On hearing Hassle's news, Dusty had wasted no time. Signalling in the flanking pickets to increase his fighting-strength, he had left Sergeant Weather and six reluctant men to control the captured horses and brought up the rest as fast as he could. By the time he reached the rim, he had been prepared to launch an immediate attack. Many Confederate cavalry regiments placed their assault emphasis on firearms, but the Texas Light Cavalry always made use of their sabres in a charge. So every man had his reins fastened to the saddlehorn, guiding his horse with his knees while holding a sabre in one hand and revolver in the other.

'Yeeah, Texas Light!'

Loud rang the Texans' battle-shout, mingling with the bugler's spirited rendition of the 'charge', sounding above the drumming of over fifty sets of thundering hooves. Forming a single line parallel to the river, the grey-clad riders urged their horses on with wild, grim determination.

Becoming aware of the new peril, the crew of the number three gun sprang to its trail-bar. Under the profane urgings of the chief-of-piece and battery commander, they lifted the stock of the gun and started to drag its 2332 pounds of tube and carriage around to face the Texans. Red and Prince saw what was planned and turned their weapons towards the gun. Under the combined hail of fire, three men fell and the remainder were prevented from bringing the piece to bear on Company 'C'.

Taking heart at the sight of the cavalry, the Arkansas Rifles raised a cheer. Their line, faltering before the depleted battery's canister, straightened and pressed forward. From a hesitant walk, they swung back into quick-time and built up to a double march into the shallow water of the ford. Down went the bearer of the regimental colour, shot by a Zouave. Although badly wounded, he kept the flag held in the air until another member of the colour guard took it from his hand. Having done his duty, the stricken man collapsed and lay still.

Even as Dusty led his men down the slope, he wondered what had caused such an attack to be launched on the ford. It could be part of some new offensive planned by Ole Devil after Company 'C' had left on their current mission. Yet he doubted if his uncle would permit an unsupported assault.

Not that Dusty devoted much time to idle conjecture. Although Red and Prince had prevented the turning of the Napoleon, Company 'C' did not ride unchallenged. Some of the Zouaves and Dragoons had turned from the advancing Rifles and opened fire on the approaching cavalry. A cry of pain from behind him told Dusty that at least one of the bullets had taken effect.

The ground shook and trembled to the thundering hooves. Best mounted of the Texans, Dusty had drawn slightly ahead of the Company. Suddenly he felt a sharp jolt run through his racing horse and knew what it meant. The big black horse – one of three he had broken and trained – screamed, staggered and started to go down with a bullet in its chest. Instantly Dusty kicked his feet from the stirrups, tossing his right leg up and across the saddle. As the horse crumpled forward, he sprang from its back. His momentum carried him clear, but he was in danger of being ridden down by the rushing men behind him.

Looking back, he saw a riderless horse approaching in the lead of the Company. Twirling away the revolver, he sprang forward to catch hold of the empty saddle's horn and vaulted astride. The leather was slick with the previous user's blood, but he retained his seat and charged onwards. Without any conscious thought on his part, he drew the revolver ready for use.

Springing away from the half-turned gun, the sergeant chief-of-piece rushed at Dusty and lashed out with his short artillery sword. Down flickered the small Texan's Haiman sabre, catching and deflecting the Yankee's blade. Then Dusty lunged, driving his point into the man's chest and dragging it free as the horse carried him by. A revolver crashed from the left, its bullet fanning the air by Dusty's face. Almost of its own volition, the bone-handled Army Colt lined and barked an answer. Hit between the eyes, the battery commander let his smoking revolver drop and followed it to the ground. Hardly aware of having shot the Yankee major, Dusty whirled his horse in a rearing, sliding turn to see where he could best direct his activities.

As always under such conditions, Dusty later remembered only flashes of what followed, brief, flickering cameos from the bloody fight raging on the Snake Ford of the Caddo. While shooting the Yankee major, he saw that the Arkansas Rifles had crossed the river and were engaging the defenders with bayonets. Bodies lay in the water and the down-stream current was tinged a pinkish-red with their blood.

Not far from Dusty, charging forward with his Enfield and bayonet at the ready, an Arkansas Rifles private made for a terrified Zouave drummer-boy. Letting his bugle fall, the boy sank to his knees. At the last moment, the soldier swerved and left the boy kneeling unharmed, with eyes closed and lips moving in a soundless prayer.

An artilleryman lined his revolver at one of the passing Texans. Before he could press the trigger, he was knocked sprawling by Billy Jack's horse. He was not given a chance to recover. Rushing up, the Rebel who had spared the drummer-boy plunged home the bayonet and pinned him to the ground.

One of the Napoleons roared, hurling its charge of canister indiscriminately into the wild hacking, thrusting scrimmage of Yankees and Rebels before it. Blue- and grey-uniformed bodies tumbled together, torn open by the flying 1.5 inch balls from the cannon. Reining his horse alongside it, a Texan sprang from his saddle. He landed on the tube, miraculously keeping his balance while kicking one of the crew in the face and cutting down the chief-of-piece with his sabre. Then he pitched sideways, shot by the lieutenant who commanded the two-piece section to which the gun belonged. An instant later the officer also lay dead, shot in the back of the head by an Enfield bullet.

Sweeping away from the rest of the Company, Vern Hassle and six men descended on the four Yankees who had been detailed to watch over the artillery's and Dragoons' picketed horses. One of the Union soldiers tried to fight. Without slowing his horse, Hassle cut loose with his old Dragoon Colt. He hit the man and hurled him backwards. Another of the horse-minders went down before the last two threw aside their unfired carbines and raised their hands in surrender. Leaving half of his party to deal with the prisoners, Hassle set the others to work calming the Yankee horses and preventing any from tearing free and escaping.

On the edge of the trenches, the Arkansas Rifles' tall, lean colonel and the major commanding the Zouaves fought a savage duel with their swords. Seeing his chance, Colonel Barnett went into a near-classic lunge and spiked his point between the other's ribs. Behind the colonel, a Dragoon sergeant flung up and lined his carbine. Charging in, a mounted Texan almost severed the Yankee non-com's head from his shoulders before he could fire.

As the fight ebbed his way, an artillery lieutenant sprang on to a caisson and jerked up the lid of the forward chest. Drawing his revolver, he pointed it downwards. A fanatical Unionist, he intended to take as many of the hated Rebels with him as he could, without regard for his own men who would also perish. Reining his borrowed mount around, Dusty raised his Colt shoulder high. Sighting on the Yankee officer, he fired – and not a moment too soon. Rocked backwards by the .44 ball, the lieutenant got off his shot. The bullet flung up splinters from the edge of the chest, but did not hit and explode the charges inside it.

Then the fight was over. Assailed from two sides, left virtually leaderless the Yankees discarded their rifles or carbines. Hands shot into the air and yells of surrender rang out. Despite the growing trend in the East towards Southern defeat, the Confederate States' Army of Arkansas had scored another victory on the bloody banks of the Caddo River.

Returning his Colt to its holster, Dusty rode towards where the Arkansas Rifles' colonel stood glaring around. Instead of showing pleasure, or gratitude for Company 'C's' assistance, Colonel Harvey Barnett eyed Dusty with every indication of fury.

'Where the hell have you been, damn you?' Barnett roared as Dusty swung from his saddle.

A slight frown creased the small Texan's face at the furious greeting. After bringing his men on to the scene at such an opportune moment, he felt that he deserved a more civil and reasonable response. Any commanding officer would be shaken after suffering heavy losses, but Barnett's attitude hinted at more than that. From the way he had spoken, it almost seemed that he not only expected Company 'C' to arrive but felt they should have come earlier in the attack.

'Raiding across the Ouachita, sir,' Dusty answered, holding his temper in check and sticking the point of his sabre into the ground to leave his hands free.

'Raiding!' Barnett blazed, face almost white with rage. Then, with a visible effort, he regained control of his emotions. 'I'll speak to you when I've attended to my duties, Captain Fog. And you'd be advised to see to your own.'

'Yo!' Dusty answered, saluting.

Wondering what had caused the colonel to act in such a strange manner, Dusty saw Sandy McGraw approaching. He told the guidon-carrier to retrieve his saddle from the dead horse and handed over his sabre. Walking to rejoin his men, he saw Red and Prince standing on the slope looking at the still shape of Tarp Hayley.

'What in hell're them puddle-splashers doing, Cap'n Dusty?' Billy Jack demanded, coming over. 'They could've got wiped out, attacking that way, if we hadn't happened along.'

'Sure,' Dusty replied. 'Secure the prisoners, see to the wounded, put pickets on the rim to watch for Yankee reinforcements.'

'Yo!' Billy Jack answered.

Half an hour went by and Dusty's orders were well on their way to completion. Red had just returned to report that the Company had lost six dead and eight wounded when Dusty saw Barnett and the Rifles' stocky, middle-aged adjutant, 1st Lieutenant le Branche, approaching. Before they reached the young Texans, the two officers halted and stared up the slope. Having heard no warning from the pickets he had had put out, Dusty turned to learn what attracted their attention. He saw Kiowa and Weather driving the captured remounts and draught horses down the slope. Facing Barnett, Dusty found that the expression of anger had returned to the colonel's features and felt surprised at the reaction. He could not see why the evidence of a successful raid should bring such a response.

'Where did you get those horses?' Barnett demanded, gritting out the words.

'I took most of them from the Yankees out by Lake Ouachita, sir.'

'You mean that you have the audacity to admit you went off on a raiding mission without first reporting yourself to *me*?'

'I beg your pardon, sir?' Dusty said, completely baffled by the comment.

The Texas Light Cavalry rarely received orders to report to a ford's guard before entering Yankee territory. On his present assignment, Dusty had not even made his crossing anywhere near the Snake Ford.

'Damn it, Fog! You're not deaf and don't act the innocent with me!' Barnett raged. 'Were you, or were you not under orders to give my battalion a cavalry screen and support during the attack on this ford?'

'I was not, sir!' Dusty stated flatly.

Soft-spoken the reply might have been, but it held a ring of truth. Barnett stiffened, staring hard at Dusty's face.

'If you weren't, then who was?' the colonel growled. 'And where the hell are they now?'

'I couldn't say, sir. I've been over the Ouachita for six days on a general reconnaisance and raiding mission. It's only by chance that I came back this way and I've seen no sign of any other cavalry unit.'

Being aware, and mostly approving, of Ole Devil Hardin's policy of sending cavalry raiders across the Ouachita, Barnett thought of his own losses and his anger did not lessen. However he no longer blamed Dusty for his misfortunes or the failure of the cavalry cover to arrive. At first, and more so when he had seen the captured horses on the rim, Barnett had suspected that Dusty was sent to support him but had crossed the river on a self-appointed raiding mission.

'My apologies, Captain Fog,' Barnett said. 'I see you aren't at fault. In fact if your men hadn't harassed the battery my losses would have been far heavier!'

'That was Mr. Blaze's work, sir,' Dusty corrected.

'I'll see that you're commended for it, Mr. Blaze,' Barnett

promised, then frowned and went on, 'This whole damned affair's been bungled somewhere.'

'How's that, sir?' Dusty asked.

'This morning I received orders from General Hardin to take this ford by noon today.'

'Why, sir?'

'As a crossing for our troops when we commence an offensive tomorrow.'

Instead of clarifying the matter, the words merely increased Dusty's mystification. Only the day before he had left on the patrol, he had overheard Ole Devil angrily damning the shortage of men and materials which prevented the Army of Arkansas from taking more effective measures against the Yankees. Of course, in six days the situation could have changed. While there had hardly been time for reinforcements to arrive, Ole Devil might be under orders to start a campaign designed to draw Union troops away from the hard-pressed Southern armies in the east.

Yet, knowing his uncle, Dusty doubted if he would order an infantry attack – even by a battalion against the normal company and platoon guard of the Yankees – without ensuring it had the backing of cavalry. Ole Devil did not squander his men's lives in such a reckless manner. Which brought up another point. The Snake Ford was far from an ideal place from which to launch an offensive. Usually the Yankees felt it so unimportant that they maintained only a small guard. It might be no more than coincidence that they had strengthened the defences – or there could be another, more sinister reason.

'When did the battery move in, sir?' Dusty inquired.

'Last night. I must admit that it came as a shock to see them in position, especially when I received the order to attack. If it had come from anybody but Ole Devil, I'd have hesitated to obey without having seen the cavalry—'

'How did the order come, sir?' Dusty wanted to know, for the gist of the colonel's words struck him as significant.

'In the usual way,' le Branche answered for Barnett. 'By a Texas Light Cavalry courier.'

'You accepted it, mister?' Dusty asked.

'Of course.'

'Did you know the courier?'

'I don't recall having seen him before,' the adjutant admitted. 'But they change regularly and he acted in the normal way.'

'Which doesn't mean to say he was genuine,' Dusty pointed out.

Every instinct the small Texan possessed warned him that there was something very wrong with the orders. The possibility of an imposter delivering fakes was not wildly unlikely. Even if the Yankees did not have Texas Light Cavalry uniforms taken from corpses or prisoners, their tailors could easily make one. Both Union and Confederate officers had received their earliest training before the War in the U.S. Military Academy at West Point. The drill, organization and ceremonial of the C.S.A. for the most part copied that of the Union. Some Texans had elected to serve the North when their State seceded. So if an imposter delivered false orders, he would not only dress correctly and know the routine, but could also talk like a loyal son of the Lone Star State.

'Are you saying there's something wrong with that order, Captain?' asked Barnett.

'It's just a hunch, sir,' Dusty replied. 'Those Napoleons happened along at a mighty convenient time and the cavalry support you expected never came.'

Opening the sabretasche suspended from his left shoulder, le Branche drew out several sheets of paper and held the top one to Dusty saying, 'This is it.'

At first glance, and on closer inspection, the order appeared to be genuine. The type of paper used, the printed heading, even the phrasing of the various commands and instructions were faultless. So Dusty looked long and hard at the signature on the bottom.

'This's not General Hardin's writing, sir,' he finally told Barnett. 'It's a real good copy, but that's all it is.'

CHAPTER SEVEN

IT'S OUR TURN TO PLAY TRICKY

TAKING the sheet of paper from Dusty's hand, Barnett compared it with other orders which he knew to be genuine. At last the colonel nodded grimly and admitted that it was a cleverly-contrived fake. Nor did he need to strain his brain to decide what lay behind its production and delivery. Morale was high amongst the Confederate troops in Arkansas and they had complete faith in their commanding general.

As Barnett had been about to say earlier, he would have hesitated to make the attack when his cavalry screen had failed to announce its presence if the order had come from anybody other than Ole Devil Hardin. The forged document promised that the horse-soldiers would be in position and that, backed by Ole Devil's signature, had been sufficient for the colonel.

Expecting the cavalry support promised by their respected general, even though they had not seen it, the men of the Arkansas Rifles' battalion had marched on the ford in the face of the newly-arrived Yankee battery. They might easily have been decimated by the Napoleons. Meeting with a crushing defeat would have shattered the survivors' faith in Ole Devil and the mistrust would have spread through the rest of the Confederate Army under his command. The bloody repulse would also have done much to boost the flagging spirits of the Union Army opposing them.

Which brought up another point – one shocking in its implications. Dusty saw it first, expressing it even as it started to form among his companions.

'Likely the Yankees wouldn't send out just one set of orders!'

A shocked silence followed Dusty's words. The colonel and two lieutenants exchanged apprehensive looks. Perhaps at that moment along the Caddo and Ouachita Rivers other Confederate soldiers were marching gallantly to their deaths, expecting help which would not come.

'Red!' Dusty went on, knowing there was no telegraph communication between the Caddo and Upper Ouachita fords. 'Pick relays of good horses for you, Billy Jack, Kiowa and Vern Hassle. Two of you'll go down-river, two up, as fast as you can push those horses. Warn every ford guard and patrol you come across not to make an attack if they've just had orders to do it.'

'It'll be too late!' le Branche protested. 'That damned son-of-a-bitch left almost four hours ago.'

'We've still got to try,' Dusty replied. 'How many horses had he?'

'Just the one,' le Branche answered. 'And he went down-river.'

'We might catch up with him,' Red decided. 'I'll see if the Yankees've enough good horses along, Cou – Cap'n.'

'Do that,' Dusty confirmed and turned to Barnett. 'Our own mounts've been hard-pushed these last few days, sir.'

'I understand,' the colonel replied and a frosty smile played briefly on his lips. 'Horses aren't like infantrymen, they get tired after a few miles. Use my name as your authority for countermanding the orders, Mr. Blaze.'

'Yo!' Red replied, saluting and swinging on his heel to stride away.

The surviving company commanders of the battalion approached their colonel. Not knowing that the order had been a fake, they scowled at Dusty. Before any of them could speak, Barnett gave them the order to withdraw to their own lines.

'With the colonel's permission—?' Dusty put in.

'What is it, Captain Fog?' Barnett asked, then told le Branche to explain to the three majors why the cavalry support had been delayed in its arrival.

'Why don't we hold this side of the river now we've taken it, sir?' Dusty suggested, ignoring the comments which followed le Branche's explanation.

'I've had heavy losses—'

'My Company's at your disposal until reinforcements arrive, sir,' Dusty offered. 'And enough of them know how to handle a cannon for us to make use of those captured Napoleons. It could be that our Army'll need something to hold the Yankees' attention for a spell.'

'Keep talking,' Barnett prompted.

'With the start he's got, my men aren't likely to catch that feller in time to stop the attacks. After the losses they'll suffer, the ford guards won't be in any shape to fight off determined counter-attacks—'

'That's true,' admitted the colonel and his majors rumbled their agreement.

'So I reckon we should make ready to hold that rim up there,' Dusty continued. 'And make sure the Yankees know that's what we're fixing to do.'

'How do we do that?' asked le Branche.

'By turning loose all the prisoners, including the wounded. I'll have some of my boys make up Indian-style litters for them. Among the horses we give the Yankees to haul the litters, there'll be a fast saddle-mount – by accident, of course.'

'And one of the officers we free'll use it to find the nearest Yankee force and tell them what's happening here,' Barnett finished as Dusty paused for breath. 'With luck they'll come for us instead of attacking the other fords. That'll give Ole Devil time to rush up reinforcements.'

'That's assuming the order's a fake and this's a plot,' put in the major commanding Company 'E', which had suffered heaviest in the attack.

'You've my word that that's not General Hardin's signature, sir,' Dusty answered politely. 'And the whole deal strikes me as the kind of tricky play the new Yankee general would make. I've come across another example of it with these remounts I captured at the top end of Lake Hamilton. Their escort was carrying a fake document.'

'Buller'd never've been smart enough to think of it, that's for sure,' Barnett growled. 'And a series of victories brought about by Trumpeter would set his command off to a good start.'

'Yes, sir, it would,' Dusty agreed. 'Which's one of the reasons why I reckon we should make them fight hard to retake this side of the river, even if he doesn't aim to use the orders as openers in an offensive. That way his men won't think his notion was so all-fired smart after all.'

'They sure as hell won't,' enthused Barnett. 'Damned if we don't give it a whirl, gentlemen.'

'There's another thing, sir—' Dusty began.

'Tell us, Cap'n Fog. You've made right good sense so far.'

'I reckon it's our turn to play tricky. Let's make the fellers we turn loose think that we knew all along the order was a fake, but went along with it so's we could spring our own trap and capture the battery.'

'By cracky, yes!' boomed Barnett. 'They'll blame Trumpeter all the more that way. And, thinking of their own losses, they'll be more likely to overlook how many we had killed. See to the arrangements, gentlemen. Captain Fog, have a man with a fast horse ready to deliver our reports to General Hardin. My own couriers both went to have their horses re-shod this morning before the messenger arrived with that order and aren't back yet. Your man can call in at my regimental headquarters and I'll ask for some help to be sent in.'

'Yo!' Dusty replied, then stiffened to a brace and continued, 'Could your men be told what's happened, sir? That way they won't go to blaming my boys for us not showing up earlier in the attack.'

Barnett sucked in a deep breath, knowing that to follow Dusty's request would mean admitting that he had been taken for a sucker. Yet not to do so might bring trouble in its wake. So he nodded and agreed to pass on the facts to his men. Once that was done, he could only hope that he would redeem himself by making a success of defending the captured strip of territory.

Holding their horses to a fast, mile-devouring half-gallop, Red Blaze and Kiowa followed the trail through the wooded country alongside the Caddo River. They had been fortunate in finding eight Dragoon horses suitable for their mission. It had been decided that Red and Kiowa should head down-river, while Billy Jack and Vern Hassle would carry the warning in the other direction. Behind them, Dusty's plan was already being put into action. They hoped that it would succeed, or Trumpeter's boast of conquering Texas might yet be fulfilled.

All the time they rode, Kiowa kept his eyes darting from side to side. He studied the river's bank with care, but also gave attention to the thick cover on the other side of the trail. They did not meet up with a Confederate patrol, but that was no surprise. The Arkansas Rifles battalion supplied the patrols along that stretch of the river and Barnett had not sent any out after receiving the order to make the attack.

Soon after passing the confluence of the Caddo and Ouachita Rivers, Kiowa brought his two-horse relay to a sudden halt. Reining in his own mounts, Red watched the sergeant drop to the ground and plunge into the bushes lining the river-side of the trail. Wondering what had attracted Kiowa's attention, Red prepared to follow him. Before he could do so, Red had to make a grab at and catch the reins of the sergeant's horses. Unlike Kiowa's usual mounts, the animals acquired from the Dragoons had not been trained to stand ground-hitched and showed signs of continuing along the path.

'What's up, Kiowa?' Red called, impatiently curbing the restless fiddle-footing of the four horses.

'Saw something that looked powerful like a feller's leg in here,' the scout answered. 'And it is one.'

Swinging from his saddle, Red took the precaution of securing the relays' reins to the branches of a sturdy bush. Then he went to join Kiowa and found the sergeant looking down at a body. It was bare-foot, unarmed, with the linings of its pockets turned inside out. Clad in the uniform of a Texas Light Cavalry private, the corpse had two bullets in its back to tell the cause of death. Bending forward, Kiowa rolled the body over and they studied its agony-distorted features.

'I can't mind him,' the scout commented. 'Which I ain't claiming to know every feller in the outfit.'

'He's not one of the regular couriers, that's for sure,' Red replied. 'This looks like border-jumpers' work, Kiowa.'

'Sure enough does. Ain't nobody but a bunch of murdering guerillas'd take a man's boots and turn out his pockets after they've killed him. You want for me to take out after 'em, Mr. Blaze? They're headed for the river.'

'They'll be across it by now,' Red replied and made a wry face. 'I'd best see if he's got anything left to tell us who he is.'

While Red went about the distasteful task of searching the body, Kiowa made a thorough examination of the area. The Indian-dark sergeant paid great attention to the age of the various tracks and formed his conclusions.

'Anything?' Kiowa asked as Red straightened up.

'Nope. We'd best get on our way.'

'Yep,' Kiowa agreed. 'Only there's likely no rush any more. He was killed 'tween three 'n' four hours back. Which means he's likely the son-of-a-bitch with the fake orders. You allowed he'd come down this way.'

'Sure I did, and the time'd be about right,' Red replied, covering the dead face with his bandana. 'Only we daren't count on it being him. Let's ride. He'll have the next ford's guard send somebody out for him.'

Returning to their horses, they freed the reins, mounted and continued with their assignment. While certain that Kiowa had formed a correct estimation of when the man was killed, Red kept them moving at a fast pace. It appeared likely that the impostor with the forged orders had fallen victim to a band of Yankee guerillas, a fate met by more than one lone man riding dispatch. In which case there would be no more unsupported attacks –

unless there should be more than one man delivering the forgeries. Red figured he would rather be sure than sorry.

At last the Texans came into sight of the next ford and reined their horses to a stop. Studying the peaceful conditions which prevailed, Red let out a long sigh of relief. He could see no signs to tell that a battle had taken place recently. In fact from the lack of hostile action on the part of the rival guards, they might have been members of the same regiment camped for some reason on opposite banks of the river.

Keen-eyed as always, Kiowa raked the Yankee's shore and spotted something which he regarded as significant despite the peaceful scene.

'I'll bet it was the feller with the false orders we found back there,' the sergeant said. 'There're half-a-dozen Napoleons hidden over that side and pointed this way.'

Following the directions indicated by his companion, Red located one after another of the carefully-concealed cannon amongst the bushes. They were positioned so that their fire would effectively sweep the crossing.

'No bet,' Red decided and starting his horse moving.

Riding into the Confederate camp, Red reported to the major commanding the guard. After hearing what had happened at the Snake Ford, the major said that the Napoleons had moved into position the previous night. He had received no orders to attack and nodded his agreement with Colonel Barnett's instructions that he ignore them should they arrive. Arranging for the body to be brought in as soon as possible, Red looked across the river.

'If that feller'd got here—' Red breathed.

'Yes,' the major replied. 'It's just what you'd expect a stinking Yankee soft-shell* to try and pull.'

'Sure it is,' Red drawled. '*After* he's tried to pull it.'

Continuing their fast-paced journey, Red and Kiowa made for the next ford. On arrival, they found similar conditions to those at their last point of call. A battery of six-pounder cannon had been brought up the previous night, the pieces being concealed, yet able to lay a cross-fire on the ford. Until he had heard Red's news, the guard commander was at a loss to explain why the cannons had made their appearance. At first he had kept his men stood-to in their defensive positions, which explained why the Texans had not met a patrol between the two fords. The Union attack feared by the guard commander had not materialized and he had been on the point of sending a patrol along

* Soft-shell: a liberal-intellectual.

the river's bank when Red and Kiowa came on the scene. Repeating Colonel Barnett's orders, Red took to his horse once more.

After covering about a mile, the Texans met an infantry patrol travelling towards the ford they had just visited. Halting, Red learned that no orders to attack had been received by the next guard down-river; although it too was now covered by a battery of six-pounders. There had been no reports of trouble, or even artillery movements, from the lower fords. Learning of the incident at the Snake Ford, the infantry lieutenant stated his intention to watch extra carefully for fake couriers. Red warned him to make sure the courier was a fake and, if possible to take him alive.

'I'd sure hate the puddle-splashers to shoot down one of our boys who's riding dispatch, Kiowa,' Red said as they watched the patrol march away. 'There's no need to keep going.'

'We headed back to the Company?' the sergeant inquired.

'Not by what you'd call the quickest way,' Red answered. 'I've been thinking about what Cousin Dusty's trying to do—'

'And?'

'The Yankee'll have at least three batteries against our one – soon's they can get the guns from the other fords to the Snake. Which they couldn't do happen somehow they was to lose all their hosses in the night.'

'They do say Yankees are *real* careless with their stock,' Kiowa grunted and fingered the knife on his belt. 'We could go see if it's true.'

'That's just what we'll do,' Red decided; then a thought struck him and caused a grin to flicker across his face. 'Wouldn't it be a pistol if those guerillas take them fake orders to sell to the Yankee soldiers? I'd give money to see old Trumpeter's face, happen he thought up this fancy twirl-me-round, when he gets his own orders handed back to him.'

CHAPTER EIGHT

YOUR GUERILLA FRIEND KILLED ONE OF OUR SPIES

BEING a man who enjoyed his creature comforts, the Yankee general who had originally captured Little Rock selected a fine old colonial-style house in the best section of the town for his official residence. Ever optimistic, subsequent generals saw no point of seeking other quarters when at any time they might be continuing their advance towards the borders of Texas.

On the afternoon of the fourth day after his grand review had been disrupted and ruined, General Horace Trumpeter paced restlessly about the first-floor front room which had been converted into his private office. Back and forwards he tramped; from the door, passing the large desk in the centre of the room and almost brushing against the drawn-back, heavy drapes of the window in turning. Once he came to a halt by the window, glowering across the balcony into the foliage of the fine old white-oak tree which spread so close to the balustrade. The sight of the tree and the well-kept gardens stretching to the high walls surrounding the property gave him no pleasure that day. Scowling across the lawns and flower-beds, liberally dotted and lined with decorative bushes, he gave an angry snort, then resumed his walking and thinking.

Normally his thoughts would have been directed to the future, planning the country that he intended to build after the War ended. It would be a fine country, where all men were equal – guided and directed, of course, by himself and a carefully selected few of the liberal elite – and worked for the common good. In his day-dreams, he could imagine himself as President, respected by all, receiving the adulation of the masses as the saviour of the Union and creator of a land which was 'all for the people'. They were the dreams first formed as a college student and the War had presented him with an opportunity to bring them to fulfilment.

Such thoughts did not wing their delightful way that afternoon. In tune with his thudding feet, two words repeatedly throbbed inside his head. 'Dusty Fog! Dusty Fog! Dusty Fog!' Even before he had come to Arkansas, Trumpeter had heard the name. He had been one of those who raised their voices in protest against the Texan being permitted to attend and give evidence at Kirby Cogshill's court martial.* For the most part, Trumpeter had put the tales of Dusty Fog's abilities and talents down to nothing more than propaganda by the Confederate States. Trumpeter knew that he could not perform the feats credited to the Texan; which meant that no lesser mortal could do them. Since his arrival in Arkansas, he had seen evidence which would have caused a less egotistical man to change his mind.

The previous night Hoffinger had returned, bringing the news that the first consignment of remounts had fallen into enemy hands. That had been bad enough, but more so when Trumpeter's brilliant scheme to outwit the stupid Rebels had failed so badly. Far worse had been the discovery that the peckerwood† responsible for the loss was the same man who ruined the review.

Thinking back to the difficulties he had experienced in obtaining the money to purchase the remounts, Trumpeter cursed Dusty Fog's name. There would be career officers in plenty willing to crow 'I told you so' when the news of the failure went the rounds. Feeling the pinch financially, Congress would display an even greater reluctance to hand out money that might be put to more spectacular, vote-catching use on the important, successful battle fronts.

No matter how he looked at recent events, Trumpeter could see only one bright spot. Brilliantly conceived, his plan for ruining the morale of Ole Devil Hardin's troops would still carry him through and win the acclaim he desired. Four assaults halted with heavy losses to the Rebels would make impressive reading in the Northern newspapers. More so when it would be remembered, pointed out even by a reporter-friend who had followed him to Little Rock, that before his arrival the Union's Army of Arkansas had known little other than continual defeat.

With the exception of ordering the batteries to the selected fords, the plan had been made and partially implemented before Trumpeter left Washington. Nor had he taken any of his new subordinates into his confidence. Only he and the trusted agent with the forged orders knew of the plan. While Trumpeter told himself that his reticence stemmed from caution and fear of discovery by the Rebel's efficient Secret Service, he knew it was

* How Cogshill repaid Dusty is told in *Cuchilo*.

† Peckerwood: derogatory name for a white Southerner.

because he wanted to be sure of success before announcing that the scheme had been tried.

So, knowing no better, the guards on the fords would regard the opportune arrival of the artillery as proof that their new general could out-think and out-plan the enemy. Such a belief in his omniscience would be of the greatest use in building up his troops' confidence, and holding it until the time came when he could make public the story of how he had tricked the Rebels and paved the way for the conquest of first Arkansas, then Texas.

Glancing out of the window in the course of his perambulations, he saw something which jolted him from his day-dreams. A smirk of triumph twisted at his lips as he came to a halt. Accompanied by a dishevelled, travel-stained 1st lieutenant, Colonel Verncombe came through the front gates. Anticipation tingled through Trumpeter as he watched the sentries break off their salutes to the visiting officers. Having expected reports of the repulses to arrive since noon, he decided that Verncombe must be bringing the first. Probably Verncombe wanted to deliver his congratulations in person. That, from a career soldier, would be a most satisfactory tribute.

Crossing to his desk, Trumpeter forced himself to sit down and assume a calm, passive appearance. When Verncombe arrived, the general wanted him to suspect nothing. That way, the approbation for showing the forethought to reinforce the fords' guard with artillery would be so much more pleasing. Time seemed to drag as he waited. At last he heard feet thudding on the passage beyond the door and he looked down at the papers on the desk. Without raising his head, he called, 'Come in' when a knock sounded. His aide, a tall, slim lieutenant, entered to say that Colonel Verncombe requested an interview.

On being brought into Trumpeter's presence, Verncombe got straight down to business. Almost as soon as he had completed his salute, he started speaking and the words were not in the form of congratulations.

'Did you arrange for fake orders to be delivered to the Rebels on the Snake Ford of the Caddo – general?'

Something in the colonel's tone rang a warning bell in Trumpeter's head. Raising his eyes, he scowled at Verncombe's coldly angry face until the other belatedly added the final word. While Trumpeter rarely remembered military courtesy to his superiors, he expected it blindly and at all times from his juniors. Failing to stare down the Dragoon colonel, Trumpeter stiffened in his chair.

'I don't understand your question, colonel,' Trumpeter said and his voice held a warning.

'It's simple enough – sir,' Verncombe replied, too old a hand to permit his anger to lead him to indiscretion. 'Did the general arrange for false orders to be delivered to the Rebels, causing them to make an assault on our guard at the Caddo River's Snake Ford – sir?'

'What makes you think I did?' Trumpeter demanded cautiously, guessing that something had gone wrong and determined to avoid making any statement which might lay the blame where it belonged, on him.

'Yesterday the Arkansas Rifles launched an attack on the ford and, despite a battery of our artillery having been moved in, took it from us.'

'*Took* it?' The words burst from Trumpeter's lips before he could stop them.

'Yes – sir. The attack was made at battalion strength and with cavalry cover from our side of the river.'

'And then what happened?' the general gritted.

'The guard on the ford and battery of Napoleons were captured,' Verncombe told him, 'after suffering heavy losses.'

Wanting a scapegoat, Trumpeter swung his cold gaze to the Dragoon lieutenant. Although haggard, travel-stained and dishevelled from long exertions, the young officer was not wounded in any way.

'How did you come to escape, mister?'

'I didn't escape—' the lieutenant answered, cheeks reddening at the implications which he read into the question.

'You call me "sir"!' Trumpeter barked.

'I didn't escape – *sir*,' the lieutenant answered, stiffening into a brace. 'We were *all* released by the Confederates. They mostly turn their captives loose out here. Captain Fog even—'

'*Who?*'

Trumpeter almost screeched the word as he leapt to his feet. Dropping back a hurried, involuntary stride, the lieutenant threw a startled glance at Verncombe. Then the young officer stared at the general's shocked, white face. A long thirty seconds went by before the lieutenant could think up and make his reply.

'Ca-Captain Dusty Fog, sir. It was him who took us from the rear and captured the battery.'

'Are you sure it was him?' Trumpeter asked, struggling to regain his pose of imperturbability. He sank into his chair and waited for the answer, hoping against hope that the lieutenant was wrong.

'There's no doubt of it, sir,' the young Dragoon replied. 'It was Company 'C' of the Texas Light Cavalry; although it came as a helluva – a real surprise when I learned who he was.'

'How's that?' Trumpeter spat out.

'I'd always heard he was a giant of a man. But he's small and not more than eighteen at the most. Only when he speaks to you, you forget about him being small. And you should have seen how those Texans jumped when he spoke to them—'

'Yes!' Trumpeter interrupted testily, wondering when last anybody had jumped to obey *his* commands.

All too well the general remembered Savos' and Hoffinger's descriptions of their captor. Each of them had commented at length on Dusty Fog's small size and laid much emphasis on the fact that his personality had caused the captives to forget such minor details as feet and inches of height. It seemed unlikely that there could be three, or even two, Confederate cavalry captains so identical in appearance on the Arkansas battle-front. Much as Trumpeter hated to face the fact, he knew that Captain Dusty Fog had once again been responsible for ruining his plans for aggrandizement.

'They turned us loose, sir,' the lieutenant went on, determined to exculpate himself from the unspoken insult Trumpeter had laid on him. 'Even gave us horses and made litters to carry our wounded. Captain Fog talked to me while his men and the Arkansas Rifles started to erect defences on the rim above our positions. It was he who mentioned the forged orders, sir. From what he implied, the Rebels knew they were fakes, but acted on them to capture the battery and our side of the ford. As soon as we were out of sight of the Rebels, I took the best of the horses and rode as fast as I could to report to Colonel Verncombe.'

'How about it?' Verncombe went on. 'Did you have the fake orders passed out, general?'

Overlooking the fact that the colonel spoke in a manner anything but polite or militarily correct when addressing a one-star brigadier general, Trumpeter shook his head. If Fog had spoken the truth, the Rebels must have suspected the man who delivered the forged document. With luck, he had been killed not captured. At any rate, Trumpeter had no intention of admitting his connection with the abortive attempt, especially to a subordinate officer and career soldier.

'I know nothing about it,' the general lied. 'If the—'

Never had a knock on the door been so welcome to Trumpeter's ears. Turning from Verncombe's accusing eyes, he called for whoever knocked to come in.

'Lieutenant Silverman of the Zouaves is here, sir,' Trumpeter's aide announced on entering. 'He's asked to see you on a matter of extreme urgency.'

'Show the lieutenant in, Mr. Frost,' Trumpeter ordered, only too pleased to be given a chance to dismiss the Dragoons. 'If you gentlemen will excu—'

Before the 'gentlemen' could be sent from the room, Silverman entered. Of middle height, he was stocky, sallow-faced and wore an untidy uniform. Like the Dragoon lieutenant, he gave the impression of having done some hard, fast travelling. Being of 'liberal' persuasions, he had burst in on Trumpeter, wishing to flaunt his success in the faces of the two Dragoon career soldiers who Frost had told him were present. In his left hand, he held three sheets of paper which Trumpeter thought looked unpleasantly familiar.

'Sir!' Silverman said, coming to a halt, saluting and offering the papers almost in one movement. 'While on patrol along the Caddo River, I came into possession of these orders issued by Hardin. He's planning an offensive and has ordered attacks on three fords along the Ouachita.'

Fighting to hold down his emotions, Trumpeter had to force himself to take the papers from Silverman's hand. Then he stared at them as if mesmerized. Without any doubt, as he saw straight away, they were the orders forged with such care and attention to detail at his instigation in Washington. Not until certain that he had composed his features into an impassive, blank mask did the general look at the beaming Silverman. From the expression on the Zouave's Hebraic face, he expected praise and commendation for his actions.

'How did you come by these?' Trumpeter asked, hoping that his voice sounded less strained to the listeners than it did to his own ears.

'From a guerilla I met on the Ouachita,' Silverman explained. 'I was on my way to commence a patrol when I met him. He's a good man who circumstances prevented from enlisting in the Army—'

'What kind of circumstances?' grunted Verncombe.

'I don't think we need concern ourselves with that, Colonel,' Trumpeter put in coldly. 'Go on, Mr. Silverman.'

'As soon as I saw the contents of the orders—' Silverman began.

'You came rushing here with them,' Verncombe finished for him. 'Didn't you think that you should warn the men guarding the fords?'

'I – I sent my sergeant to do that,' Silverman answered sullenly. 'And, anyway, as I had the orders it didn't seem likely that the attacks would be made. So I came here as fast as I could to hand them over to General Trumpeter.'

'You did the right thing, Mr. Silverman,' Trumpeter praised, although he wished that the other had come at a more opportune moment or waited until the Dragoons had left the office before displaying his trophies. 'I'll mark your report to that effect.'

Despite his general's approval, Silverman could see that Colonel Verncombe was less impressed with his brilliant grasp of the situation and prompt action. The Dragoon eyed him coldly and said:

'Mister, I hope for your sake that your sergeant reached the fords in time to give a warning – or that those orders are fakes.'

'Fa – Fakes?' Silverman yelped, thinking of the fifty dollars he had paid for them. "Good man" or not, the guerilla had insisted on being remunerated for his trouble before handing them over.

'It's a possibility, Mr. Silverman,' Trumpeter admitted. 'They may have been put out by our Secret Service—'

'Which means that your guerilla friend killed one of our spies, mister,' Verncombe went on.

'Mr. Silverman couldn't know that, Colonel!' Trumpeter interrupted coldly. 'He acted correctly and in a manner which I approve. We don't know that these are fakes. After all, whoever was killed must have delivered the first set of orders and been allowed to go on with the others.'

'Not necessarily – sir,' Verncombe objected. 'How loyal is that guerilla of your's, mister?'

'I – I've never dealt with him before,' Silverman answered warily. 'But I've heard good reports about him from other officers. He told me that he'd killed the Rebel courier on the other side of the river and I'd no cause to think he lied.'

'Of course, he wouldn't offer you anything that might show the orders were forged, would he?' Verncombe demanded.

'I – I don't follow you, sir,' Silverman muttered.

'If he'd killed a courier on his way to Ole Devil with the forged orders and a report, he'd know they wouldn't be worth anything to him,' Verncombe explained. 'So he wouldn't say anything about it.'

'It's possible,' Trumpeter admitted, willing to clutch at any straw as long as it held the conversation away from his share in the responsibility. 'Did he say or do anything to make you think he might have other documents taken from the courier?'

'No – sir,' Silverman answered, applying the honorific as Trumpeter showed disapproval of its omission by *him* for the first time. 'If he'd had any more, I'm sure he'd have passed them on.'

'Unless he figured he could get a better price somewhere else,' Verncombe sniffed, for he had no illusions about the loyalty or honesty of the average guerilla leader.

'As I said, Colonel,' Trumpeter declared when Verncombe swung to face him. 'I know nothing about forged orders. Perhaps the plan to use them was made in General Buller's time?'

'*You* ordered the artillery to move up,' Verncombe pointed out.

'Yes,' admitted Trumpeter, thinking faster than ever before in his life. 'I found an order left by General Buller for reinforcing the four fords with batteries of artillery and put it through. It was possible that there were developments afoot of which I hadn't been informed.'

Opening his mouth to ask another question, Verncombe closed it with the words unsaid. Already he had gone to the very boundaries of military etiquette and a demand that he be shown Buller's order might lead to his facing a court-martial for gross insubordination. From his wary attitude, Trumpeter had recovered after the first shock at seeing the documents. He could be counted on to know how he might best defend himself against criticism – no matter how justified – by an officer of lower rank.

'You wanted to say something, Colonel?' Trumpeter challenged.

'Only to ask for orders, sir,' Verncombe replied blandly, figuring that if the commanding general could lie he was at liberty to do so. 'Mr. Aston says that the Rebels were making preparations to hold the eastern bank of the Snake Ford. What action does the general plan to take – sir?'

Ignoring the thinly-veiled sarcasm in his subordinate's voice, Trumpeter quickly marshalled the facts and tried to reach a decision. The Snake Ford of the Caddo had little military significance. Two of the reasons for selecting that area had been its lack of importance and distance from the main battle-zone. So, on the face of it, there seemed little need and no urgency to act. For all that, he knew there could be only one answer. As long as the Rebels occupied the eastern side of the ford, they would be a constant reminder of his failure. Not knowing of his thwarted grand plan, people would only remember that his predecessors had at least managed to hold on to the land already captured.

So, regardless of the cost to his command, the Rebels must be driven back to the western bank. Looking at Verncombe's cold, impassive face, Trumpeter saw a chance of taking his revenge on the colonel.

'Your regiment will retake the ford, Colonel Verncombe,' Trumpeter announced with the air of one conferring a favour.

'We'll need artillery support – sir,' Verncombe answered, aware of the general's intentions and the price for failure.

'There are three batteries at the neighbouring fords,' Trumpeter told him. 'I'll give you an order for them. Then you'll have all the support you need.'

CHAPTER NINE

THEY'VE CAPTURED MRS. GREENHOW

GENERAL JACKSON BAINES HARDIN, better known as Ole Devil was a tall, slim, tanned man who sat the chair behind his desk as if riding in full review. Hawk-faced, with eyes that hinted at a sense of humour under the grim mask, he was a different kind of soldier to his opposite number across the Ouachita. Tough, hard as nails, strict without being a blind martinet, Ole Devil Hardin had won the respect of his men on the battle-field and by his interest in their welfare.

Nothing on his face showed his feelings, or that he was studying his favourite nephew carefully, but he nodded in satisfaction as Captain Dusty Fog completed a verbal report on the recent activities of Company 'C'.

It was over a week since the capture of the Snake Ford from the Yankees and during that time Dusty's Company had taken a major part in defending the rim above the river. Ole Devil had been in full agreement with the decision to hold the recovered territory and had acted with characteristic speed. Reinforcements, including trained artillerymen to take over the Napoleons, had been rushed to the Caddo. Their arrival increased the already serious problems faced by Colonel Verncombe. Already the Dragoons had been delayed by lack of artillery support. On their return from delivering the warnings about the forged orders, Red Blaze and Kiowa had crossed the Ouachita and succeeded in running off every horse belonging to the batteries brought up to repulse the attacks which never came. By doing so, they had deprived Verncombe of the cannons at a time when they would have done him most good.

After an unsupported attack at regimental strength had failed, due to the fire from the captured Napoleons, Verncombe had found his men disinclined to take further risks. Just as Dusty had hoped, the story he had started circulated amongst the Dragoons. It caused much discontent, especially from the long-serving career-soldiers, and considerable cursing over the 'college-boy' general's stupidity in trying such an impractical, easily detected trick. The Dragoons were grudging of their lives and unwilling to face death to recapture land that ought never to have fallen to the enemy in the first place.

'By the time they'd got artillery with them, sir, so had we and trained gun crews to man the first battery,' Dusty concluded, then went on after a brief pause, 'Colonel Barnett's handled things real well all the way through, sir.'

'Has he?' Ole Devil grunted coldly.

'Yes, sir. I know he had both of his mounted couriers away at the same time, but he's infantry. Horses don't mean a thing to him.'

'He was fooled by those forged orders—'

'Anybody would've been, sir. You've seen them and know how good they are. The signature on them is so near perfect that *I* couldn't see any difference between it and the real thing.'

'That wasn't what you told Barnett,' Ole Devil pointed out.

'No, sir,' Dusty admitted. 'Only I had to say something that would convince him it was a forgery. So I took a chance on him figuring, me being your nephew, that I'd be able to tell. It paid off— And that he obeyed in spite of the cavalry not reporting to him's a mighty high tribute to *you*, sir.'

Giving a non-committal grunt, Ole Devil looked at the papers on his desk so that Dusty might not see any hint of the pride he felt at his nephew's behaviour. Many young officers would have been determined to grab the fullest amount of glory for themselves from the incident at the Snake Ford, but Dusty's primary interest was to help Barnett out of his difficulties.

'I think we can forget the matter,' the general said gruffly. 'Whatever happens to Colonel Barnett, if anything, is none of your concern, Captain Fog.'

'No, sir,' Dusty replied.

Yet Ole Devil's words had told him that Barnett's career would not suffer as a result of being taken in by the forged order. Having cleared up that point, Dusty wondered why his Company had been replaced at the ford and he had received orders to report as quickly as possible to General Hardin's headquarters at Prescott. With his report finished, he did not expect to be kept waiting long before he learned the reason.

'You've heard of Mrs. Rose Greenhow, Dustine?' Ole Devil asked.

'She's one of our best spies, isn't she, sir?'

'She is,' Ole Devil agreed. Less hide-bound than most Confederate senior officers, he admitted that women spies served a useful purpose; although he did not entirely approve of Southern ladies performing such unpleasant and dangerous work. 'She's coming to report to me with information about Trumpeter and other matters. So I want her collected from Wexler's place—'

'Is she in Little Rock already, sir?'

'She will be by the time you get there, according to my information. She's coming by stagecoach, travelling as a Yankee major's wife on her way to join him. Naturally she doesn't want to stay in Little Rock any longer than necessary. So I want you to travel fast, meet her and bring her here.'

'Yes, sir. It shouldn't be too hard. The Yankees've taken most of their troops along the Ouachita up to the Snake Ford, so getting across'll be easy enough. I'll not take the full Company. A small party can travel faster. Do you reckon Mrs. Greenhow can ride?'

'She can, if what I've heard of her is true,' Ole Devil confirmed. 'But I doubt if she'll be up to your Cousin Betty's standard.'

'That's not likely, sir,' Dusty grinned.

'No, it's not,' the general admitted, for his granddaughter possessed exceptional ability as a horsewoman. 'Pick her horses carefully and don't expect too much and you should get her through. By the way, Dustine, Betty and Georgina Blaze are expected to arrive any day now on a visit.'

'Let's hope they don't get here until after Mrs. Greenhow's gone, sir,' Dusty drawled. 'If they do, she's likely to wind up with another couple of lady spies.'

'Not if I've anything to say about it,' Ole Devil stated, smiling frostily. Like Dusty, he knew the two girls to be high-spirited and likely to snatch at the opportunity to take a more active part in the war against the Yankees. Then he became serious again. 'I don't need to tell you how important it is that Mrs. Greenhow is kept out of the Union's clutches, Dustine.'

'No, sir. Now, with your permission, I'll go and pick the men I want with me. We'll be on our way before sun-down.'

'Thanks for the bay stallion, Dustine,' Ole Devil remarked as the small Texan saluted and turned to leave the office. 'Only you didn't need to send word that it has to be saddled and mounted from the right. *I* know all Indian horses do.'

'I figured you might, sir,' Dusty answered with a grin.

'And you'd better take half of your ill-gotten gambling gains with you,' Ole Devil concluded, also smiling. 'Wexler can probably find use for it.'

Leaving Ole Devil and making his way to Company 'C's' lines, Dusty pondered on the vagaries of a cavalry officer's life. There had been much speculation amongst his men on the subject of their recall. The reasons suggested had ranged from the optimistic, that they were to be sent back to Texas on furlough, through the dramatic, that they would be spear-heading an offensive aimed at driving the Yankees clear back to Washington, to Billy Jack's pessimistic view that they were all to be court-martialled for fraternizing and gambling with the enemy. When Dusty had been asked to guess what quirk of fate took them back to Headquarters, the idea that it was to collect a female spy from the heart of Union territory had never entered his head. Yet, as Ole Devil had warned, the mission was of considerable importance.

Along with Belle Boyd – in whose company Dusty would later go on two dangerous missions* – Rose Greenhow ranked high in the Confederate States' Secret Service. Between them, originally in the face of official antipathy and disapproval, they had built up an organization which had caused the Union Army a great deal of trouble. Despite the objections of various senior officers and members of the Government, the two Southern ladies had more than justified the wisdom of employing them as spies. The Yankees would be most pleased to lay hands on either Belle Boyd† or Rose Greenhow if the chance arose, for both of them possessed information that could all but wipe out the Confederate's Secret Service.

For all that, Dusty felt little concern over his assignment. Without falling into the trap of over-confidence, he felt certain that he could once again cross the Ouachita, pass undetected through the Union-held country, reach Little Rock and return. The way he saw it, as long as Rose Greenhow could handle a horse at least adequately, bringing her to Prescott would present him with no serious problems or difficulties.

Ordering a protesting, but obedient, Red Blaze and Billy Jack to take charge of the Company, Dusty selected his escort. Kiowa Cotton, Corporals Vern Hassle and Sandy McGraw expressed their delight on finding that they would be accompanying Dusty instead of remaining in the safety of the regiment's camp at Prescott. Stifling Red's and other members of the Company's reasons for inclusion in the party, Dusty kept his destination to

*Told in *The Colt and the Sabre* and *The Rebel Spy*.

† More of Belle's history is told in *The Bloody Border* and *The Bad Bunch*.

himself. He made his arrangements with the speed born of experience.

The journey to the rendezvous passed without incident or alarm. Each of the party rode a two-horse relay and the corporals also led a mount apiece to be used by Rose Greenhow on the return trip. Wanting to make the best possible speed, they carried only the bare essentials. Sabres and carbines had been left behind, although Dusty had brought along his Henry rifle. Their bedding was restricted to a single blanket and poncho, with a spare taken for Rose's use. For food they would rely on pemmican,* the nourishing 'Indian-bread' which could be easily carried, and anything that came their way. Dusty had with him two more items, a Union Army cloak-coat and officer's fatigue cap, but they were for a practical purpose rather than added luxuries for his comfort.

Travelling fast, for their mounts were the pick of the Texas Light Cavalry's extensive remuda, they had seen no Union troops. At night-fall on the day after leaving their headquarters, Dusty left the corporals and horses hidden in the wooded country half a mile to the east of Little Rock. Dressed in the cloak-coat and fatigue cap, the former hiding his uniform and armament, Dusty went forward on foot. Devoid of any disguise, Kiowa drifted along like a shadow on Dusty's heels; ready to fade into the darkness should they meet anybody.

Approaching a wooden building on the outskirts of the town, Dusty became even more cautious. While a lantern hung by the back door, its light turned down to a feeble glimmer, he took no chances. Not until Kiowa had scouted the area and announced all was clear did he go closer. Satisfied that nobody was spying upon him, Dusty crossed to the door and knocked.

'Who's there?' called a querulous voice.

'Lieutenant Oakland, 3rd Cavalry,' Dusty replied.

A lock clicked and the door inched open as a thin, sharp, mean-featured face peered out at Dusty.

'Come in, lieutenant,' said the owner of the face, opening the door. 'A man in my position has to watch who he lets in at night. Those Rebel scum've threatened to kill me.'

Grinning slightly at the greeting, Dusty stepped into the work-room of an undertaker's shop. For all his comments, Hugo Wexler was the head of the Confederate States' Secret Service in Arkansas.

Small, slender, dressed in sober black, Wexler looked the part

*One recipe for making pemmican is given in *Comanche*.

of a successful undertaker. In many ways his appearance and occupation helped his work as a spy, but he had another, more valuable asset. Back in the early days of the abolition issue, he had decided that a physical clash between the North and the South could not be avoided. Firmly believing that each State should have the right to secede from the Union if its policies proved incompatible with those of the Federal Government – the major issue of the War, although the abolitionists recognized and used the propoganda value of freeing the slaves as their excuse for entering into hostilities – Wexler had sought for a way to serve the South. Becoming a member of the Radical Republican faction in Arkansas, he had succeeded in convincing them of his complete devotion to their cause.

Facing the derision and hostility of his own people had not been easy, but Wexler held on. At the outbreak of the War, he had 'fled' to safety with the other Radicals and returned to resume his business in Little Rock on the heels of the victorious Yankee Army. Everything about his background made him ideally suited to gather valuable information for the South. It had been due to his efforts that Ole Devil Hardin had known the Union Army's weaknesses; a knowledge which allowed him to halt the Yankees' advance on assuming command in Arkansas.

'You should ask for a guard from the Army, Mr. Wexler,' Dusty remarked in a loud voice.

'We're alone, Captain,' Wexler answered, pleased with the way his visitor remembered to take precautions. 'And I've bad news for you. They've captured Mrs. Greenhow.'

'The hell you say!' Dusty spat out. 'How did it happen?'

'You remember the dude who you took the remounts from?' Wexler asked.

'Sure.'

'He was at the stagecoach depot, waiting to leave on the stage that brought Mrs. Greenhow in. As you can imagine, he's not been over-popular with Trumpeter since his failure. Well, it seems that he'd known her in Washington. She's a striking woman, very beautiful and not easily forgotten. Anyway, he recognized her and saw his chance to regain Trumpeter's favour. Before I could contact her, he had fetched the Provost Marshal and denounced her.'

'Damn his orney lil hide,' Dusty said quietly. 'I near on took him along with us, but I didn't reckon he could've swum a horse across the narrows between the lakes. What happened?'

'I must say Mrs. Greenhow was good,' Wexler replied. 'She

looked shocked and angry, demanded to see the commanding general and for her husband to be informed. It didn't do any good, they took her with them.'

'Where're they holding her?'

'In one of the basement cells at the town's jail. It's mainly used for a military prison now.'

'What force does Trumpeter have guarding her?'

'Just the normal jail guard and a woman brought in to act as matr—' Wexler began, then he stared hard at the *big* young Texan who was one of the few people who knew of his secret second identity. 'You can't be thinking of attempting a rescue, Captain Fog!'

'I was sent to collect her,' Dusty answered. 'If there's any way it can be done, I aim to make a try.' He paused, then went on, 'How's her being captured hit you and your boys, Mr. Wexler?'

'She knows we are in Arkansas, but not much more than that,' Wexler replied. 'She doesn't know any of our names.'

'She's still got to be set free if it can be done,' Dusty stated.

'Damn it, I know that!' Wexler snapped. 'It's *you* I'm thinking about.'

'How do you mean?'

'Mean – Lordy lord! Haven't you heard—?'

'About what?'

'How Trumpeter feels about you after the way you've been cutting up since his arrival in Arkansas.'

'Billy Jack did warn me that I'd go riling him,' Dusty admitted with a grin.

'*Riling* him!' Wexler croaked, raising his eyes to the roof and shaking his head. 'You steal two mortars and shell his grand review, scattering it to hell and gone and make him a laughing-stock in front of the civilian population. Then you capture his remounts and he can't get money to buy any more. If that's not enough, you spoil his plan to discredit Ole Devil, causing him to look an imcompetent fool to his men; who don't believe it when he says that he knows nothing about the forged orders. And then you run off the horses from the three batteries of artillery he was relying on to push you back across the Caddo before Ole Devil could reinforce you—'

'That last was Cousin Red, not me,' Dusty objected cheerfully.

'This's serious, Captain Fog!' Wexler snapped. 'More serious than you know. Trumpeter has sent out an order to all his commanding officers. It made a stir amongst them and they say it's without precedent. I've seen a copy of it and it says, "No matter how it is done, capture or KILL Dusty Fog!" Captain, the word "kill" is in capital letters.'

'Yes sir!' Dusty drawled. 'Don't you ever tell him, but ole Billy Jack was right. I *have* riled Trumpeter up.'

'Damn it, Captain!' the agent yelped. 'He means every word of that order – and with most of his officers, it will be "kill", not "capture"!'

A half smile played on Dusty's lips and he seemed unconcerned by the threat to his life. Not that he discounted its danger. There were many Union officers in Arkansas with reason to hate him and who would be willing to carry out their general's order given half a chance.

'I'll just have to go extra careful,' Dusty remarked. 'But I'm going for all of that.'

'I've told you the dangers,' Wexler said simply.

'Why sure,' Dusty agreed. 'Which I'm not fixing to charge the jail-house at the head of Company 'C', sabres drawn and flags flying. But we both know that we've got to get Mrs. Greenhow out if we can.'

'That goes without saying.'

'Then let's figure out how we can do it. How's she guarded?'

'With just the normal jail-house staff right now. A sergeant and six corporals—'

'No more than that?' Dusty breathed.

'They're trained men, from Army stockades.'

'Which means they'll be tough, mean, but not too smart,' Dusty commented. 'As long as that's all the guard on her.'

'It is, although they brought in the wife of a sergeant to act as matron,' Wexler answered. 'Trumpeter has stripped the town's garrison to give strength to a massive assault on the Snake Ford, he's even emptied the cells of prisoners for it. Don't look so worried, I've already sent warning to Colonel Barnett that it's coming.'

'Just seven men,' Dusty said quietly. 'And a woman, maybe. I'd've expected more than that.'

'In addition to being short of men in the town garrison right now, Trumpeter believes that Mrs. Greenhow's capture is a secret,' Wexler explained. 'Probably he also assumes that, even if we found out, we'd never expect him to put a Southern lady into a common jail-house. So he doesn't want to attract attention by increasing the guard.'

'That figures,' Dusty admitted. 'Tell me all you know about the jail; how it's guarded, the routine the guards follow, when they get fed and how, everything that might help. Maybe we can think up some way to get her loose.'

'I hope we can,' Wexler said sincerely.

'There's another thing we've got to think about,' Dusty warned. 'Trumpeter won't like it one lil bit if we bring it off. He'll want blood and it'll be the Lord help you happen he found out who you are.'

'That's a chance I have to take,' Wexler answered. 'Risking being found out is something I've come to live with.'

While Dusty accepted that, he knew a successful rescue would rouse Trumpeter to such a pitch of fury that the Yankees were going to hunt as never before for the people responsible. While Rose Greenhow's freedom might be of considerable importance to the South, so was Wexler's. Somehow, Dusty could not think how right then, he must find a way to divert suspicion from the little undertaker if the rescue bid should be brought off.

Suddenly a thought came to Dusty, driving the concern he felt for Wexler's safety momentarily from his mind.

'Say, not long back I read something in a Yankee newspaper about stockade guards being in trouble with the soft-shells.'

A frown creased the undertaker's brow. He did not answer for some seconds, then he realized what Dusty meant.

'That's true, they were and still are,' Wexler finally agreed. 'I didn't bother to report it to General Hardin, it didn't seem important enough.'

'I don't know about that,' Dusty drawled. 'It may just be important enough to help us prise Mrs. Greenhow loose from that old jail-house.'

CHAPTER TEN

HE NEEDS TEACHING RESPECT FOR HIS BETTERS

DISREGARDING the scowls of the other enlisted men present, Sergeant Bernie Slasser and Corporal Dick Pope swaggered into the Birdcage Cafe for their supper. Although the owner secretly wished that they would go elsewhere, he stood by their usual table and greeted them politely. Big, burly, with brutish faces and close-cropped hair, they wore Burnside hats and infantry uniforms; but every soldier in the room knew to which branch of the Army they belonged. Stockade guards had never been selected for charm of personality and understanding natures. Alertness and caution had become a way of life with the pair. Their hands never strayed far from the twenty-six inch long oak batons dangling from loops and balancing the holstered revolvers on their belts. Aware that every man in the room most likely hated their guts, the knowledge caused Slasser and Pope no concern.

'It's a nice night, gentlemen,' greeted the owner, grinning with patent insincerity.

'You're getting your share of it,' Slasser grunted, hanging his hat on the back of a chair and sitting down. 'We'll want a meal to take back. Nothing fancy and don't hurry it. If it's not ready, the fellers we relieve can fetch it.'

'I understand, sergeant,' the owner replied truthfully. 'Do you gentlemen want your usual?'

'It's no worse than any of the other hawg-wash you serve,' Pope growled and, after the man had left, grinned at his companion. 'Did you see that Southern gal?'

'Not enough,' Slasser answered. 'We can go take a look later. Sarah'll've gone then.'

'It'd be best if we waited until we knew what the Man* has to say about her first,' Pope suggested cautiously. 'He's wetting his pants on the hour about correct procedure since the top brass sent out that damned order about how we treat the prisoners.'

* The Man: in this case, the Provost Marshal.

'There's only one way to treat a prisoner,' Slasser spat out. 'Rough.'

Pope darted a quick glance around, as if wishing to make sure that nobody had heard his companion's comment. Then he let the subject lapse and the arrival of their food prevented Slasser from resuming it. While eating, their alertness never left them. Continually flickering their eyes around the room, they gave the impression that they were studying the soldiers to select the ones most likely to fall into their hands. Neither of them showed any great interest when, at the conclusion of their meal, a seedy-looking civilian sidled over to their table. Poorly-dressed, prone to giving a hacking cough at regular intervals, he was assistant to one of the sutlers who followed and traded with the soldiers.

'Sergeant—' the man began, bobbing his head ingratiatingly after a preliminary cough.

'What's up, Hacker?' Slasser demanded.

'Air that bounty on deserters still getting paid?'

'Sure,' the sergeant agreed, interest replacing his frown. The Union Army offered a reward of a hundred dollars to anybody who was responsible for the capture of a deserter. 'Why?'

'Nothing,' Hacker replied, starting to turn away. 'I was just ask—'

Shooting out a big hand, Slasser caught the civilian's thin arm and crushed it. 'Where is he, Hacker?'

'I – I—' the man answered, then he gave a resigned shrug. 'He's in here.'

'Which one?' Pope inquired.

'See that short runt sat near the front door?' Hacker answered, without looking at or indicating the person he meant. 'He's the one. Used to be with Custer's outfit. Owed my boss money, which's how I 'member him.'

Without displaying too obvious interest, the two stockade guards turned and studied the man in question. Small, though well-built, young, with a bare head of curly blond hair, he wore a collarless shirt and poorly-fitting cheap civilian suit. For the most part, he looked like an ordinary youngster from the working-class section of the town. Only one thing pointed to Hacker's statement being correct. His boots, which showed from under the table, were of better quality than the rest of his wardrobe indicated. There was another sign which the experienced pair could recognize. While waiting for his food to arrive, the youngster kept his head bent forward except when darting flickering, furtive glances around the room.

'Why'd a deserter come here to eat?' Pope asked.

'Likely he thinks this's the last place anybody'd expect to find a feller who's gone over the hill,' Hacker offered.

'Them's cavalry boots he's wearing, Popey,' Slasser went on. 'Even if he ain't a deserter, it'd be interesting learning where he got 'em. Let's go over and see what he's got to say for his-self.'

'You won't forget it was me's pointed him out, will-ya?' whined Hacker as the non-coms came to their feet and put their hats on.

'We'll not forget,' Slasser promised, winking at his companion. 'If he's a deserter, we'll see the right thing's done.'

Seated at the table with his back to the wall, Dusty Fog watched the by-play between the civilian and the two soldiers. Nothing about him showed that he was aware of their scrutiny and interest. As a waiter placed a steaming plate of stew before him, he grinned and tensed. The first stage of Mrs. Greenhow's rescue had begun.

As always, Wexler had proved to possess plenty of vitally important information about the current situation. Admitting that he had expected Dusty to attempt a rescue bid – and ready to try himself if the other had not arrived that night – the undertaker had already gathered in details of the woman's incarceration. He had previously collected a thorough working knowledge of the jail's routine in case it might one day be needed. Working from what he had been able to tell Dusty, a daring scheme was concocted. There had been little enough time to arrange its details, but so far everything was going correctly.

Surreptitiously watching the soldiers drawing closer, with Hacker following on their heels, Dusty measured the distance between them with his eyes. Give them their due, they were putting on a mighty good act. Neither showed any obvious interest in him and they were acting in a casual manner as if merely leaving the cafe. An unsuspecting victim might have been fooled by them. Aware of what was going on, Dusty made ready to play his part. None of the other occupants of the room were watching the stockade guards right then, but Dusty figured that he ought to be able to draw attention their way.

In a casual-appearing gesture, Dusty rested the palms of his hands under the edge of the table. Then he glanced up and down and jerked back his head in a startled manner, as if suddenly becoming aware of the two non-coms bearing down on him. Catching his cue with the skill of a professional actor, Hacker went on with the next part of the scheme. In addition to being a sutler's assistant, he was one of Wexler's most trusted agents.

'That's him for certain sure, sergeant!' Hacker yelled. 'He's over the hill from Custer's outfit!'

Letting out an annoyed grunt, Slasser lunged forward. He had hoped to be within reaching distance before the 'deserter' realized the danger, but Hacker's shouted comment ruined his chances of doing it. So he advanced, meaning to reach over the table and grab the small young man. Despite being alerted, he could hardly escape. The wall prevented him from backing away.

Not that Dusty meant to try escaping in that manner. Instead he heaved upwards with his hands, throwing the table over. His aim could hardly have been better if he had practised the move for days. Shooting off the inclined surface, the plate of stew distributed its hot contents over the front of Slasser's tunic. Nor did the damage end there. In falling, the edge of the table cracked against the shin-bone of the sergeant's forward leg. Going by the screech Slasser let out, the impact caused him considerable pain.

Having dealt with Slasser in a most satisfactory manner Dusty came to his feet. For his plan to succeed, he had to make what seemed a determined attempt to escape, but without antagonizing Corporal Pope. So he contented himself with evading the other's hands and resisted the temptation to deliver a *karate* attack. Ducking by Pope, Dusty ran towards the door. Bounding forward, Hacker thrust out his right leg to trip and bring the small Texan sprawling to the floor.

'Fix the bastard good, Pope!' Slasser bellowed, hopping on his sound leg and massaging the injured shin. 'Tromp him into the ground!'

Elbowing Hacker aside, Pope held down an inclination to carry out his sergeant's instructions. All around the room, feet shuffled, chairs scraped and men stood up hurriedly to obtain a better view of what was happening. Refraining from driving his boot into Dusty's body, Pope bent to grip the collar of his borrowed jacket and jerked him erect. Seeing the burly guard raise the small youngster and slam him against the wall, an angry, menacing growl rose from the on-lookers. Only a few of the closest soldiers knew what had started the fuss, but their attitude mirrored that of the remainder. Maybe they had little sympathy with deserters, but they actively hated and despised the stockade guards.

Knowing how the enlisted men felt, Pope decided to do no more than haul his captive upright. Pope might be as hard, tough and unimaginative a roughneck as ever guarded military prisoners, but he possessed sufficient sense to see the danger. If he should start to work the small 'deserter' over with feet or fists, the crowd would intervene. There were men present only seeking the opportunity to tangle with members of the stockade guard, yet they formed the least serious threat to his way of thinking. Others would be just as eager to witness an incident that could be reported to those 'liberal' Congressmen who took an interest in and gave protection to the 'under-dog'. Under the prevailing conditions, Pope had no desire to antagonize the latter group of his audience.

Mouthing obscenities, Slasser prepared to fly in the face of popular opinion. Hot stew soaked and clung to his tunic, while pain throbbed through his shin. Added to that was the knowledge that almost every man in the room revelled at the sight of his injury and humiliation. It all served to rouse his never too amiable temper to a furious pitch.

For the first time, Dusty wondered if the plan was going wrong. Seeing the big sergeant looming at him, he hoped that nothing had happened to keep Wexler from carrying out the part assigned to him. Crouching against the wall with an attitude of numb terror, Dusty prepared to launch a devastating *karate* attack to protect himself. To do so would ruin the rescue bid and endanger his own safety.

Even as Dusty tensed to drive up his foot, he saw the front door open. So did Slasser, and recognized the two men who entered. With a feeling of baffled frustration, the sergeant scowled at the newcomers and revised his intention of teaching the 'deserter' an immediate and painful lesson. Neither Trumpeter's aide, 1st Lieutenant Frost, nor that mealy-mouthed soft-shell undertaker would stand by and watch while he battered the small son-of-a-bitch to a pulp.

If Frost had been alone, he would have ignored the disturbance he heard while passing the Birdcage Cafe. The place was a hang-out for enlisted men and going in without an escort to quell the trouble could be dangerous. Unfortunately he had just met Wexler and the undertaker insisted that they should investigate. Knowing that Wexler possessed some influence, even in military circles, Frost dare not refuse. Reluctantly he opened the door and stepped inside.

When Frost saw the men responsible for the noise, he realized the advantages of intervening. Firstly, another soft-shell stood at his side. Knowing how he would act in similar circumstances, he believed that Wexler would enjoy making an adverse report to General Trumpeter if he failed to protect the small victim. Secondly, he had the typical liberal-intellectual's hatred of those whom he regarded as the tools and implements of authority. While willing to make use of the stockade guards for his own ends, he despised them at other times. Third and most important, to prevent Slasser from attacking the terrified youngster would raise Frost in the esteem of the watching enlisted men. One never knew, during some future election men in the crowd might remember the incident and be persuaded to vote for him.

So Frost fixed Slasser with a cold glare, wanting to remind the other that a lieutenant was backed by the disciplinary powers of *The Manual Of Field Regulations*, and barked, 'What's all this?'

'We've been told this bastard's a deserter,' Slasser answered, coming to a surly, grudging brace. 'Was going to ask him about it when he jumped us and tried to escape.'

'Did good at it, too!' called a voice from the crowd.

'Are you a deserter?' Frost asked Dusty as Slasser swung around furiously in an attempt to recognize the speaker.

Knowing that the small Texan's voice might spoil the deception, Hacker was prepared to give confirmation. The need did not arise. Wanting to prove that they had not acted hastily, Pope stepped forward and threw up a smarter-than-usual salute.

'Sure he is, lieutenant, sir,' the corporal declared and pointed to the floor. 'Look at them boots. They're U.S. cavalry issue.'

A point with which Dusty could not have truly argued, considering they had been looted from a Yankee convoy. While he had borrowed the civilian clothing from a store of such things kept by Wexler, he had retained the boots as offering proof of Hacker's accusation.

'They're cavalry boots, no doubt about that,' Frost admitted. 'Who told you that he's a deserter?'

'Hacker there,' Slasser muttered.

'Now that ain't entirely right, sergeant,' the gaunt man objected, then faced Frost and bobbed his head in a respectful manner the officer found most gratifying. 'I only said he *looked* like a feller I knowed in the 7th Cavalry, sir. My boss'd know for certain sure, but he's out of town for a couple of days.'

Dusty made a feeble escape to free himself from Pope's hand, taking care not to be too violent or to hurt the other, and quitting when he was banged back against the wall. Looking what he hoped was sullenly and guiltily at Frost, Dusty tried to will the other into reaching the correct decision.

'Have you ever seen this youngster around Little Rock, Mr. Wexler?' Frost inquired.

'Well, I can't be sure,' Wexler dithered. 'But I don't recall ever seeing him. And, even if he is a local boy, where did he get those boots from?'

'There's that,' Frost admitted and looked at Dusty. 'What have you to say?'

'Nothing!' Dusty mumbled, trying to avoid sounding like a Texan. 'Lemme go.'

'Not without a better account of yourself than that!' Frost snapped. 'Take him to the cells and hold him, sergeant. We'll see how a night there loosens his tongue.'

'Yes, sir!' Slasser replied, with more enthusiasm than he had shown since Frost entered the cafe.

Catching hold of Dusty's right arm, Slasser held it firmly while Pope fanned his hands over his person in search of weapons. Finding none, he gripped Dusty by the other arm. Holding him between them, the guards led him to the door.

'I hope that nothing will happen to the young man, Mr. Frost,' Wexler remarked in a carrying voice. 'There are so many stories about how prisoners are treated in the stockades.'

'Not in our stockade!' Frost protested. 'He won't be harmed as long as he behaves himself.'

Letting out a low grunt that might have meant anything, Slasser opened the door and they hustled Dusty through it. On the sidewalk, the sergeant slipped his baton free and hefted it almost lovingly. His leg still stung sufficiently to act as a reminder of his grievance. Baring his teeth in a mirthless grimace, he glared viciously at Dusty.

'All right, you short-growed son-of-a-bitch,' the sergeant snarled. 'Now I'm going to beat the—'

More cautious than his companion, Pope kept his eyes on the building they had just quit. As he had expected, he saw Frost and Wexler watching them through a window. While he did not particularly care what happened to Slasser, he figured that he might be held jointly responsible should the other make an unprovoked attack upon their prisoner.

'Not here, damn it!' Pope warned. 'They're watching you. That stinking son-of-a-bitch Frost'd break us both if you laid a hand on him.'

'Yeah,' rumbled Slasser, returning the baton to its sling. 'Only what happens when there's no witnesses's another thing. He needs teaching respect for his betters, Popey, don't he?'

'Could be,' Pope grunted, without his usual enthusiasm for such a pleasant pastime. 'Let's get him down there. The boy's're waiting to be relieved.'

In the cafe, Wexler watched the men lead Dusty off along the street. So far everything had gone according to plan, although he wondered what Dusty had thought about the delay in his arrival. It had been all for the best. Seeing Frost coming in his direction, Wexler had waited for him. While Slasser might have held off his attack in the presence of an influential local 'soft-shell', he was more likely to refrain if he saw an officer. There was something further for Wexler to do before he had finished with Frost.

'Would you care for a meal, Mr. Frost?' the undertaker offered. 'I was going to the Grand Hotel for supper, why not join me?'

'That's good of you, Mr. Wexler,' Frost replied. 'I don't mind if I do.'

Unnoticed by Slasser or Pope, although expected by Dusty, Hacker came from an alley alongside the cafe. For once the thin man did not cough, but moved in silence as he followed the guards and their 'prisoner'. Keeping his distance and acting in a normal manner, Hacker tailed them to the main square on the far side of which the jail-house was situated. Up to there Hacker had found no difficulty in trailing along behind the trio. Only a few people used the square and they were all on the opposite side. So he continued with extra care and remained undetected. From what he could see, there would be no chance of following beyond the building next to the jail. It was the City Bank and a lamp inside its farther window threw light across the sidewalk. Not wishing to pass through the illuminated area, Hacker came to a halt and stepped into the mouth of the bank's side alley. From his position, he could see the big building which served as a court as well as housing prisoners. Most of it lay in darkness, unoccupied for the night, but a lamp hung over the side door and a light showed at one of the windows towards the rear.

Standing like a statue in the darkness, Hacker watched the sergeant and corporal escort Dusty to the side door. It opened at Slasser's knock and they hustled the small Texan inside. When the door closed, Hacker sucked in a deep breath. Captain Fog had got that far. The most dangerous part of the rescue bid lay ahead.

Never had time gone so slowly for Hacker. At last the door opened and men came out. Although not five minutes had elapsed since Dusty's disappearance into the jail-house, it seemed far longer to the gaunt man. Counting the uniformed figures as they emerged, Hacker took a heavy leather purse from his jacket's pocket. Tossing it into the air and catching it, so that it gave off a faint jingling sound, he looked around to make sure that he was unobserved.

'What a way to treat good money!' he mused and skidded the purse along the sidewalk until it halted on the edge of the lighted area. 'They can't miss seeing it there. I should pitch horseshoes that good.'

With that he withdrew deeper into the alley. Flattening himself against the bank's wall, he listened to the heavy feet thudding on the sidewalk. The sound drew closer and Hacker could hear men talking as they walked. Knowing they were the guards relieved by Slasser and Pope, he strained his ears to catch their conversation.

'To hell with helping Slasser work that runt over,' were the first audible words to reach the listener. 'Not after what the Man told us.'

'He's set on doing it regardless,' another of the party went on. 'Well, that's up to him and Pope.'

'Popey won't help him,' declared a third. 'And if Slasser does it—'

'You can bet he will, after what that runt did to him,' stated the first speaker. 'Whooee! I'd've loved to see it.'

'If he does it, somebody else'll be wearing the sergeant's bars comes noon tomorrow,' continued the third guard, in a tone which implied that he expected to be the 'somebody'. 'Slasser's riled enough to— Hey, what's this on the sidewalk?'

'It's a purse,' announced the first speaker as the feet came to a halt. 'A good heavy one at that.'

'Feller it belongs to must've dropped it when he come out of the bank,' guessed a fourth voice. 'What'll we do with it?'

'If he's that damned careless, he don't deserve to get it back,' stated the third guard. 'So let's us poor, deserving gentlemen share it between us.'

Apparently the idea met with approval. Moving out of the light, the guards gathered in a bunch at the mouth of the alley and shared out the contents of the purse. With that done, they continued on their way discussing how they would spend their 'lucky' find. Watching them pass from sight and listening to the sounds of their passing fading away, Hacker figured that another item of the plan had been successful. In possession of a twenty-dollar windfall each, the guards would be unlikely to hurry their return to the jail.

'That all of 'em, friend?' whispered a voice from behind Hacker.

Stifling a yelp of surprise, for he could have sworn that he had the alley to himself, Hacker whirled around and reached under his jacket. He could not see the speaker, so did not draw the Deringer concealed in the waistband of his trousers. Just as he decided that his ears had played a trick on him, he heard a faint chuckle and saw a slight movement at the rear of the bank.

'Who is it?' Hacker breathed.

'Kiowa,' replied the tall, lean shape which came on noiseless feet from the shadows. 'I'm Cap'n Fog's scout, mind me?'

'I do *now*!' Hacker answered. 'You near on scared me white-haired.'

'Didn't figure shouting, or singing "Dixie" 'd be the thing to do,' Kiowa drawled. 'Have they all pulled out of the jail?'

'All the men have, I counted five of them,' Hacker replied. 'But the woman, the one they're using as matron, may still be there.'

'Likely Cap'n Dusty can tend her needings if he has to,' Kiowa said. 'Now you'd best get going. I'll sort of keep watch down by the side of the jail house and stop any of those five yahoos coming back too early.'

CHAPTER ELEVEN

YOU AIN'T KILLED HIM, HAVE YOU?

'WHAT the hell—?' gasped the guard who opened the door at Slasser's knock, staring at the sergeant's stew-smeared tunic. Then, seeing the anger on the three-bar's face, he stood aside and let them bring in their 'prisoner'. 'Who've you got there, serge?'

Swiftly Dusty looked around and took note of his surroundings. They were standing in what must be the entrance hall of the building. Most of it was in darkness, but lamps illuminated the section by the side door through which he had entered. Off to his left, the stairs leading down to the basement were also well-lit. Men came from a room at the rear of the building. Four of them, wearing their hats and weapon belts like the one who had opened the door. Apparently the room served as their quarters, for Dusty could see two beds beyond its open door. The sergeant's wife who had been hired as a matron did not make her appearance.

Before Dusty could worry about the matron's non-appearance, Slasser thrust him into a chair by the table at the left of the door and snarled a warning that he had better stay put, or else! Having no intention of doing otherwise with the full complement of guards present, Dusty crouched in the chair trying to look terrified. His eyes went to the table. On it lay a pen, inkpot and the Guard Report Book in which details of prisoners accepted or discharged were entered.

'He's a stinking deserter is who,' Slasser snarled. 'And a real feisty one. Needs teaching proper respect for his betters and I reckon we're the boys to do it, don't you?'

Watching the men, Dusty saw that they understood the sergeant's meaning. He also read worry, concern and blank refusal on the coarse, hard faces. Even without knowing of Frost's and Wexler's intervention and interest in the small 'prisoner', the five men wanted no part in the respect-teaching.

Self-preservation rather than common humanity caused their hesitation. Every one of the five enjoyed the privileges being a stockade guard brought and had no desire to be returned to their original regiments. They figured that it could happen if they took a part in beating up the small youngster.

Recently there had been incidents in which stockade guards had inflicted brutal beatings without cause on prisoners. Such things had always happened, of course, but the guards concerned had been careless. Their victims had been men with important friends. So word of their treatment had reached influential circles. Questions had been raised in Congress, while the 'liberal' newspapers thundered demands for investigations and the prevention of further assaults. Such was the heat of public protest that the Union Army's top brass had given strict and definite orders to all Provost Marshals regarding the future conduct of the guards.

Dusty Fog possessed the supreme quality of a fighting cavalry officer, the ability to take advantage of any prevailing set of circumstances. Knowing something of the stockade situation, from conversations with captured Yankee soldiers and from Union newspapers gathered during raids, he had seen how they might make use of it. According to Wexler, Slasser had the reputation for being a sadistic brute who took pleasure in ill-treating prisoners. Such a man would not easily change his ways, no matter what instructions he received from the Provost Marshal. Especially if his temper could be roused in some way.

So the incident at the Birdcage Cafe had been planned; although Dusty had not expected the table to fall in such a satisfactory manner and was prepared to use feet or knees to achieve his end. Figuring that Slasser would then be determined to extract a savage revenge, Dusty had avoided stirring up the same desire on Pope's part. Wexler's 'timely' arrival had been to ensure that the beating-up did not take place immediately, or out on the street. It had worked and Dusty found himself inside the jailhouse. Now he was gambling on the other five guards being reluctant to endanger their careers by helping Slasser to work him over. If that happened, he felt sure the sergeant would be the more determined to do it without their assistance.

A very long, for Dusty at least, thirty seconds ticked by. The five guards shuffled their feet, exchanged glances with each other and Pope, but avoided meeting Slasser's cold eyes. Growing more impatient by the second, the sergeant unbuckled his belt and removed his tunic.

'What about it?' Slasser demanded, tossing the tunic on to the table and adjusting the belt about his middle. 'Who's going to help me?'

This was the decisive moment. In a very short time Dusty would know if his rescue attempt stood any chance of succeeding – or whether he would be fighting for his life against the combined attack of several larger, heavier and stronger men all trained in rough-house self-defence.

Sure he and Wexler had made arrangements against the latter eventuality. If all had gone as it should, Hacker would have followed him to the jail and would carry a warning to the undertaker if the five guards did not leave within five minutes of his arrival. Maybe Wexler could not do his part by persuading Frost to visit the jail. Even if he did, they might arrive too late to save Dusty from injury.

'You know what the Man told us—' one of the five mumbled.

'The Man—!' Slasser spat out.

'He way out-ranks *you*,' growled a surly-faced red-head who considered himself next in line for promotion. 'So I ain't doing it!'

Looking at the others, Slasser saw that the blank refusal had caused them to make up their minds. All could remember the grim emphasis with which the Provost Marshal had spoken on the subject of mis-handling prisoners. Unlike the sergeant, they had no cause to dislike the small 'captive'. So they all affirmed their non-compliance.

'Get the hell out of here, happen you feel that way!' Slasser snarled, face reddening with anger. 'All of you can go.'

'Come on, boys,' said the red-head. 'How about the food for that Reb gal?'

'It wasn't ready when we left the Birdcage,' Pope answered. 'One of you'll have to bring it with you.'

'There's no call to rush back with it,' Slasser continued, not wanting witnesses – particularly the red-haired corporal – around while he dealt with the small prisoner. 'Where's Sarah?'

'She's gone home for the night,' the red-head replied, making for the door. 'If that gal wants anything, one of you'll have to tend to her.'

With that, the men trooped out of the building. Pope closed and locked the door behind him, then turned with the expression of one who knew that he faced an unpleasant duty.

'Come on, Popey,' Slasser said in a cajoling tone. 'Let's put this short-growed son-of-a-bitch away for the night.'

'It shouldn't take two of us,' Pope answered, having been made extra wary by the refusal of the other five guards. 'You take him down.'

'What if he jumps me?' Slasser inquired.

'If that happens, it's between you and him,' Pope replied. 'I won't see it happen, but I'll take your word that's what he did.'

'Have it your way,' Slasser sniffed, knowing he could count on the corporal to give the right answer when questioned later. 'I'll see to his needings.'

With that he shot out his right hand to grip Dusty's collar. Jerking the small Texan out of the chair, he grinned a little. Hell, a runt like that would be easy meat. In fact two of them would probably reduce the fun by finishing him off too quickly. Catching Dusty's left wrist from underneath, Slasser deftly turned the trapped arm into a hammerlock position. The move was made with the swift ease of long practise. Experience had taught the sergeant that the combined hold was the best way for a single man to control and make a prisoner walk in a required direction.

Allowing himself to be guided to the wooden steps leading to the basement, Dusty kept alert without resisting. He was ready, if Slasser was to hurl him down the stairs, to try to break the force of his landing. Yet he doubted if the man would do so. Slasser wanted the pleasure of battering him to a pulp and to do it while he could still feel the blows landing.

So Dusty looked around him as he went down the stairs. Ahead of him, at the other side of the basement, were a line of ordinary open cells made out of steel bars. With a feeling of relief, he saw that they were unoccupied. No other prisoners had been brought in since Trumpeter released those already held to take part in the attack on the Snake Ford.

That raised the point of where the Yankees were holding Mrs. Greenhow. Once again Wexler had provided the answer. Turning his head to the right, Dusty studied the two rooms used to house female or dangerous male prisoners. Completely enclosed, they had solid wooden doors fitted with peep-holes and secured with double bolts but no locks. Only one of the doors had its bolts closed, so that would be the cell holding the Confederate lady spy.

Having satisfied himself on that score, Dusty gave thought to his escape. He could see well enough, for the basement was lit with hanging lamps. Once he reached the floor, he could make his move.

The moment Dusty felt the hard stone of the basement under his feet, he changed from passively yielding to dangerously active. Alert for the first warning sign, he was ready when Slasser slackened his grip ready to commence the beating. Instantly Dusty stepped back with his left foot, until it was alongside and pointing to the rear of the sergeant's right boot. Taking his weight on the right leg, Dusty pivoted his body to the left and used its motion to free his trapped arm. Before Slasser had become fully aware of the danger, Dusty drew the bent arm from behind his back. Snapping it upwards and twisting his palm to face his assailant, he pulled the wrist from the other's fingers.

Up to that point Dusty had displayed only a frightened, unresisting obedience. So the sudden transition to aggression took Slasser completely by surprise. Having already loosened his hold, he could not prevent the trapped wrist from slipping out of his grasp. Instinctively he tightened his grip on the collar, which was what Dusty wanted him to do. Pressing his left forearm and shoulder against Slasser's right arm, Dusty used the leverage he exerted to throw the other off balance. While he could not apply sufficient pressure to throw the sergeant to the floor, Dusty opened the way for a continuation of the attack. Drawing back his right arm, Dusty ripped a punch into his captor's solar plexus. Due to his own awkward position, he could not strike with his full power. The blow landed hard enough to bring a grunt of pain from its recipient. While it also caused him to release Dusty's collar and take an involuntary step to the rear, it did not incapacitate him.

Swiftly Dusty brought up his right foot in a stamping kick aimed at Slasser's body. Showing considerable speed for so bulky a man, the sergeant snapped his hands down and caught the rising leg by its ankle. With a twisting heave, he pitched Dusty across the basement. Slasser failed to appreciate that his efforts alone did not cause the small Texan's flight through the air. Feeling his ankle trapped and the first warning twist at it, Dusty applied a counter learned from Tommy Okasi. Thrusting up with his other leg, he added force to the sergeant's heave and went with it. Long training at *ju-jitsu* and riding had taught Dusty how to fall on even hard surfaces. Covering his head with his forearms, he curled his body into a ball and lit down rolling. The wall halted his progress and he used it to force himself upright.

'Try to escape, would you?' Slasser roared, loud enough for the words to reach Pope so that they could be repeated later as 'proof' that he had acted in self-defence.

Something about Dusty's attitude as he rose warned Slasser of danger. No other prisoner had managed to escape from the collar-and-hammerlock take-down hold. Yet the small man had done so— Or was he small? Standing in that half-crouched position of readiness, he gave the impression of size and deadly, latent power. Maybe he called for stronger measures than mere bare hands.

Sliding the baton from its belt loop, Slasser gripped it in his right hand and moved forward. He looked as big as a bull buffalo, dangerous as a winter-starved grizzly bear and meaner than a stick-teased diamondback rattlesnake. Rushing forward, he revised his opinion. Despite the quick way in which he made his feet, the small 'deserter' seemed dazed and unready to resist. Disinclined to take chances, but not wanting his victim to lose consciousness too quickly, Slasser raised the baton. Down it whistled in a blow calculated to strike Dusty's collarbone and either break it or leave it numbly inoperative.

Although Dusty looked dazed, he had never been more alert. Guessing what his attacker intended, he waited until the club began its downwards swing before thrusting himself sideways along the wall. Swinging around before Slasser regained control of the baton, Dusty snapped another side-kick. His boot thudded against Slasser's right bicep, but not hard enough to put the muscle out of action. Knowing better than to go in close, Dusty made no other attack. He wanted room to manoeuvre, so sprang away from the wall and turned ready to take the offensive.

Once again Slasser displayed his speed. Swivelling in a fast turn, he spat a curse and lunged towards the small Texan. Out licked the club, in a round-house swing powerful enough to crush Dusty's skull if it had landed. It missed, but the sergeant whipped it across in a snapping back-hand slash directed at the side of Dusty's head. While launching it, Slasser reached a decision. Much as he hated to admit it, the small 'captive' was proving too much for him.

'Pope!' the sergeant bawled at the top of his voice. 'Get the he—!'

Realizing the danger, Dusty moved in. He shot his left foot out to the left, bending his right leg and ducking his head and torso underneath the arc of the baton's swing. Feeling the wind of the stout oak club's passing stir his hair, he flung up his left hand to block and hold off its return. Hearing Slasser start to shout, he knew that he must finish the sergeant before Pope put in an appearance. It seemed that providence had offered him a way of doing so.

In turning, Slasser had halted with his feet spread apart. From his crouching posture, adopted to evade the blow, Dusty was ideally placed to take the advantage offered to him. Drawing back his right fist, he propelled it forward and, this time, was in a perfect position to strike. Driving up with the full force of the small but powerful frame behind them, his knuckles smashed into Slasser's testicles.

Numbing agony tore at the burly non-com. It was a torment that numbed the mind and tore into his vital organs. Chopping off, the yell for help turned into a croaking bawl of anguish. The baton fell from his limp fingers and he was helpless, unable to think of defending himself against Dusty's next actions. For, wanting to render the sergeant *hors de combat* before Pope arrived the small Texan did not content himself with merely striking the blow.

From impacting on Slasser's lower body, Dusty's right hand flashed up to join the left. They both closed on the trapped wrist, turning the sergeant's hand palm-upwards. At the same time Dusty spun on his heel so that he stood with his back to Slasser. Levering the arm against its elbow joint, Dusty bent his torso forward and catapulted the man over his shoulder. Turning in the air, he came down hard on to the stone floor. Dusty thought that he heard the pop of breaking bones as Slasser landed. It was a sound that would have gladdened the hearts of many prisoners who had suffered under the burly sergeant's baton, boots and hard fists.

Following Slasser down, Dusty noticed that his head tilted over at an unnatural angle. The sound he had heard must have been caused by the other's neck breaking. Jerking open Slasser's holster, Dusty slid the revolver from it. He could not remember when the smooth, hand-fitting curves of an Army Colt's butt had last felt so comforting. The sergeant was out of the deal, but that did not mean the game had been won. Dusty still had Pope to deal with; a point very quickly brought home.

'Did you shout, serge?' called the corporal from the hall above.

All too well Dusty knew what that meant. When no answer came and Pope could not hear the sounds of Slasser working on the prisoner, he was certain to investigate. So Dusty looked around for a way in which he might silence the second guard. Although he had taken Slasser's revolver, it did not supply the answer. The sound of a shot might be heard outside the building. Nor did hiding in the main line of cells present a better solution; their barred walls offered no concealment. For a moment Dusty thought of hiding in the room next to where he hoped to find Rose Greenhow. The trouble being that it was the obvious place for him to go.

'What's doing down there?' asked Pope, sounding a mite worried.

Figuring that time was running out, Dusty saw the ideal hiding-place and wondered why he had not thought of it straight away. Darting across to the stairs, he ducked into the triangular cavity beneath them. Used to store the jail's brooms and buckets, the space was large enough for his purposes. More than that, the wooden steps had no fronts. Dusty found that he could see and, more important, reach through the gaps between the steps.

Almost as soon as he had taken his place, he heard Pope's footsteps drawing nearer. Slipping the Colt into his waistband to leave both hands free, he drew in a deep breath and let it out gently.

'You ain't killed him, have you?' the corporal demanded anxiously, sounding almost directly above the waiting Texan. 'If you have, I'd— What the hell—?'

Clearly Pope had just received his first view of Slasser's sprawled-out body. Dusty wondered what he made of it. Expecting that he would find Slasser standing over the still, possibly lifeless, figure of their 'prisoner', learning that the sergeant was the victim must have come as a hell of a shock. The footsteps halted as Pope took in the scene. Faintly Dusty heard the rasp of steel on leather, which meant that the corporal had drawn his revolver, and he waited for the sound of its hammer going back to full cock. The feet resumed their movement without it coming. Either Pope had forgotten a basic precaution, or he held a double-action weapon which did not require cocking before it could be fired. Whichever reason applied, the corporal came down the stairs at a good speed.

'Keep moving, damn you!' Dusty breathed, hands raising towards the gap on a level with his eyes. 'Don't start figuring out where I'm at!'

Almost as if he had heard and was willing to oblige, Pope continued to hurry down the stairs. Remembering the small size of their prisoner and his apparently meek acceptance of capture, the corporal was astonished by what lay below. Not until half-way to the bottom did he start to realize that he could not locate the second party in the drama.

The realization came just a moment too late.

Seeing Pope's right foot descend on to the step in front of him,

Dusty reached through the gap with both hands. Already stepping forward with his other leg, the corporal felt his leading ankle seized in a powerful grip but could not stop himself advancing. Jerking back hard on the captured limb, Dusty contrived to throw Pope off balance. With the corporal's wail of shock and terror ringing in his ears, Dusty opened his hands. Carried forward by his impetus, Pope hit a lower step with one foot then pitched on across the basement.

Released by its owner, the revolver sailed through the air. Hardly daring to breath, Dusty watched its flight towards the cells. It landed on the floor, bounced and struck one of the doors but did not fire.

With no control of his limbs, Pope landed erect and continued to move. Flailing desperately, his arms tried to grab at the air in an attempt to stop himself, but to no avail. Still travelling fast, he crashed head-first into a cell. The top of his skull rammed against one of the steel bars with a sickening thud and he crumpled limply on top of his revolver.

Dusty leapt from the cavity, running towards Pope. Although he went prepared to use boots or hands to complete the silencing, he saw that neither would be necessary. Blood and something grey were oozing from the corporal's head, spreading evilly on the floor. The way had been opened for Dusty to set Rose Greenhow free.

CHAPTER TWELVE

THEY'VE TAKEN ALL MY CLOTHES

SATISFIED that he need not worry himself further about the two guards, Dusty still took precautions. Raising Pope's unresisting body, he retrieved the revolver from beneath it. He examined the gun, recognizing it as a double-action Starr Army model; which explained why the impact against the bars had not caused it to fire. However the force of the collison had damaged the base-pin and thrown the cylinder out of line, so it would be of no use to him.

Dropping the revolver, Dusty rose and crossed the room. Glancing at the stairs, he drew back the bolts and opened the door behind which he hoped to find Rose Greenhow. Light flooded into the small cell, giving Dusty his first view of the woman he had risked his life to rescue. She stood in the centre of the cubicle, blinking a little but tense and alert.

'Who are you?' she demanded in a voice as brittle with menace as the spitting snarl of a she-bobcat preparing to defend its young.

In her mid-thirties, Rose Greenhow was a tall woman with a statuesque, magnificently curved figure. Dusty was left in no doubt on that score. Her milk-white shoulders and arms were naked as she hugged at the coarse grey U.S. Army blanket wrapped around her torso. Ending at knee-level, leaving her perfectly-formed bare legs and feet exposed to his gaze, it emphasized the swell of her bosom, slender waist and richly contoured hips. Black hair, somewhat dishevelled at that moment, framed a strikingly beautiful face with proud, defiant, hazel eyes. Surprise showed on her patrician features as she stared at him, mingled with suspicion but giving no hint of fear.

'Captain Fog, Texas Light Cavalry, ma'am,' Dusty replied and as Wexler had warned him that she would want proof that he was speaking the truth, went on, 'Simon Oakland helped me to get in here so that I could rescue you.'

'I don't know what you mean,' the woman declared, looking at the small, insignificant youngster in the ill-fitting civilian clothes. 'In fact, I still don't know why I have been subjected to this scandalous treatment. When my husband hears what has happened—'

Nothing about her showed that she recognized the name of the man who was to have made contact with her and helped her to reach Ole Devil Hardin. In fact, despite speaking with the accent of a well-bred Southern lady, she sounded genuine in her reaction. There was one thing that made Dusty sure that he had not made a mistake. Clearly she had been disturbed by the sounds of the fight in the basement, even if she could not see it. Looking behind him, her eyes took in the two motionless guards sprawled on the floor. If she was, as she claimed, the wife of a Yankee officer imprisoned by mistake, she ought to be screeching her head off for help.

'We've no time to waste, ma'am,' he warned, drawing the Colt from his waist-band and offering it butt forward to her. 'It's full-capped and loaded. Can you use it?'

Despite her caution, Rose Greenhow desperately wanted to believe a rescue bid was in progress. Yet she knew that the Yankee Secret Service might be trying to trick her. Looking from the revolver to Dusty, she thought fast. If the enemy had faked the escape, they would have selected a more credible 'rescuer'; one whose stature made him capable of felling the pair of guards. The small man had said he was Captain Fog of the Texas Light Cavalry. He spoke like a well-educated Texan, and she had heard stories of Dusty Fog's bare-hand fighting prowess. Everything depended on his response to her next words.

'I leave such violent things to my cousin,' she said, not touching the gun.

'Oakland allows that Miss Boyd's real good with that fancy *ivory*-handled *Navy* revolver *David* Dance made up special for her,' Dusty answered, knowing that he was facing a test and supplying the information given to him by Wexler.

All Rose's suspicions went as she listened to the emphasis Dusty placed on certain words. While a Yankee might guess which cousin she had meant, the small Texan knew the maker, type and furnishings of Belle Boyd's revolver. That information could only have come from somebody deep in the Confederate States' Secret Service. The details he had given were not of the kind which might have been extracted under torture from a captured spy.

So she accepted Dusty as genuine. Then she saw the quizzical manner with which he was studying her. Thinking fast, she realized that one of his facts had not been entirely correct. Only a small thing. It could have been a mistake – or he might be doing a little testing on his own account.

'David Dance may have carved the handle,' she said. 'But it was George who made the gun.'

'Yes, ma'am,' Dusty agreed. 'David's the wood-worker of the family.'

'I'm sorry, Captain,' Rose went on. 'In my line of work one takes few things at their face value.'

'It's a good way to be, ma'am. I'm a mite that way myself,' Dusty drawled, confirming her suspicion that the wrong name had been deliberate. 'I've settled the guards, but their *amigos* might come back any time. We'd best get moving.'

'That won't be easy,' Rose pointed out, gesturing at the blanket. 'They've taken all my clothes.'

'The hell you say!' Dusty ejaculated. 'That's one thing me and Wex – Oakland never figured on. Do you reckon they're upstairs in the guards' quarters?'

'I doubt it. When that Yankee pig of a Provost Marshal had me stripped, he said he would take my clothes to headquarters and make a thorough examination of them. Much good that will do him. All my information is in my head.'

At that moment Dusty was not greatly interested in how Rose carried her information. Silently he cursed the lack of foresight which had caused them to overlook the possibility of the Yankees taking Rose's clothes. All too well he realized the difficult position her state of undress placed them in. Maybe the blanket served to retain some semblance of her modesty, but it would be completely inadequate for what lay ahead. Even if she could walk barefooted and unnoticed through the back-streets, it would be impossible for her to make the long, hard, fast ride to safety clad in such a manner. Nor could Wexler help. Wanting him to have as good an alibi as possible, Dusty had arranged to head for the Ouachita without meeting him again. Wexler would spend the time until the escape was discovered in the company of Frost, so Dusty could not contact him.

As Rose joined him at the cell's door, Dusty looked around the basement in search of inspiration. His eyes went to the two motionless shapes on the floor, then swung speculatively back to the woman. From what he read on Rose's face, her thoughts were running along similar lines to his own.

'Can you use this, ma'am?' Dusty inquired, offering her the Colt again.

'If I have to.'

'Then take it and watch the stairs. I'll get you something to wear. Which I sure hope you're not a choosy dresser, ma'am.'

'That depends on what I'm dressing for,' Rose smiled, wondering how she had ever thought of her rescuer as being small. 'I'm sure that I can manage with what you have in mind, under the circumstances.'

Taking the revolver from Dusty's hands, Rose watched him cross the room. Pausing for a moment, he studied the two men and decided that Pope – being slightly smaller than Slasser – was the better suited to his needs. At that the corporal's clothing would be far too large for Rose, but they had nothing else for her to wear. Glancing over his shoulder, Dusty saw that she had turned her attention to the stairs. Grim determination creased the beautiful face and she handled the Colt with calm competence as her ears strained to catch any warning sounds which came from the entrance hall.

Knowing that he could rely on the woman to keep a good watch, Dusty knelt at Pope's side and started to undress him. With a wry, distasteful twist to his lips, he unfastened the raw-hide laces and removed the ankle-length Jefferson-pattern shoes. Under them Pope had on a pair of almost new, thick grey woollen socks far superior to the usual stove-pipe* variety issued by the Quartermasters' Department. Taking them off, he thrust them into the shoes and unbuckled the baton-loaded belt. Then he raised Pope into a sitting position, leaning him against the bars of the cell, trying to prevent the blood from running on to the tunic.

Leaving Dusty to work without interruption, Rose maintained her watch on the stairs. Nothing happened to alarm her and at last the small Texan stood up. Carrying a bundle of clothes and a pair of shoes in his arms, he rejoined her. Rose could not hold down a smile as he approached. In addition to the Union-blue coloured garments which she had expected, she noticed one of red flannel material. Glancing by Dusty, she discovered that Pope lay as naked as she had been before wrapping herself in the blanket. Turning her eyes back to her rescuer, she was surprised to see him blushing.

'They're not the clothes for a lady, ma'am,' Dusty apologized.

* So called due to their alleged resemblance in shape to the elbow of a stove-pipe and because after about forty-eight hours' wear the socks, like the pipe, had a hole at each end.

'Only it'll be a rough ride back to our lines and I figured you'd need them.'

'Anything will be a welcome improvement, Captain,' Rose assured him. 'Will you put them on the bed for me, please?'

'Sure, ma'am,' Dusty agreed.

'Then, if you'll keep watch, I'll dress as quickly as I can,' Rose continued, wiping off her smile so as to avoid embarrassing him.

Entering the cell, Dusty dumped his burden on the bunk. Almost snatching the revolver from Rose's hand, he scuttled through the door. She smiled, wondering if the threat of armed enemies would have made him depart so hurriedly. Still smiling, she dropped the blanket and picked up the long-legged red flannel drawers.

None of the clothing fitted her, which came as no surprise. The trousers hung baggily, but with the suspenders tightened and waist-belt taken to its last notch, they stayed in place. Even with the thick socks on, the ends of the trouser legs tucked into the uppers and the laces drawn as tight as she could manage, she felt that she had her feet inside a couple of packing boxes. However the shoes served their purpose and ought to stay on unless she tried to be to active.

'How the mighty have fallen,' Rose sighed ruefully as she buttoned the loose-fitting tunic, thinking back to the days when she had been known as the best-dressed hostess in Washington's glittering social whirl. 'I'd hate for Cousin Belle to see me like this.'

Shuffling from the cell, she joined Dusty at the foot of the stairs. In passing, she noticed that he had taken the time to find a blanket and had covered Pope with it.

'You sure look elegant, ma'am,' Dusty grinned, looking at her and holding out the corporal's weapon-belt with the baton hanging from it. 'There's only one last touch needed. There's no revolver, but I'd keep the club if I was you.'

'Yes, it will help my disguise,' Rose agreed. 'I should imagine that ordinary soldiers try to avoid stockade guards. So if any of them see it, they won't come too close. What I need now is a hat.'

'Pope must've left his upstairs,' Dusty suggested. 'Let's go and look.'

The entrance hall was deserted when they reached it. Leaving Rose to collect the hat, Dusty made for the side door. He intended to look outside, but the open Guard Report Book caught his eye. Thinking of what Wexler had told him about Trumpeter's reaction to his activities, Dusty started to smile. If any member of

Company 'C' had seen that smile, they would have known that their leader was planning some fresh devilment to torment the Yankees. Sliding the Colt into his waistband, he went to the table.

Tucking stray curls under the brim of a Burnside campaign hat she had found, Rose emerged from the guards' room. She saw Dusty return the pen to the inkpot and straighten up from the table. Wondering what he had been doing, she joined him. A gurgle of delight broke from her as she looked at the book. While waiting, he had filled in the section marked *REASON FOR ARREST OR RELEASE.*

'To be returned to her loved ones,' Rose read, 'by order of General Jackson Baines Hardin, C.S.A. Signed, D. E. M. Fog, Captain, Texas Light Cavalry.' While amused, she felt that she should give a warning. 'Trumpeter will be fit to be tied when he sees this.'

'Likely, ma'am,' Dusty admitted. 'Which's why I've done it. A man in a temper's judgment gets clouded. He quits thinking straight and acts rash. So I want for him to know who rescued you.'

'He'll still realize that you must have had local help.'

'Yes, ma'am. Only, way he feels about me already, I'm figuring he'll be wanting *me* even worse than the fellers who helped.'

'Trumpeter's a vindictive, vicious man, Captain Fog. There's no telling what he might do to take his revenge on you. Take care in future and *don't* fall into his hands.'

'I'll try extra hard not to, ma'am,' Dusty promised and took the key from the lock.

Opening the door, Dusty looked out. Nobody was in sight, so they left the building. Wanting to make things look as normal as possible, he closed and locked the door behind them. Then they walked along the alley towards the rear of the building. Just as they passed through the light thrown by the guards' room's window, they heard footsteps behind them.

'Hold it up there, corporal!' barked an authoritative voice.

Looking back, Rose saw two men at the mouth of the alley. She recognized both of them. The one in the uniform of a Union Army captain and carrying a bundle wrapped in a blanket was the Provost Marshal. At his side, looking a mite distressed and perturbed, waddled Hoffinger.

'Best do what they say, ma'am,' Dusty whispered. 'If we run now, they'll raise the alarm. Let them come real close.'

Slipping free the baton as she turned, Rose held it concealed at her side. Dusty had not drawn the Colt after filling in the column of the book, but made no attempt to touch it. Everything depended on them retaining the element of surprise. They stood far enough beyond the window's light to be indistinct shapes rather than identifiable figures. Given just a smidgin of good Texas luck, the approaching men would not discover their mistake until close enough for him to deal silently with them.

'Where're you going and what's that kid doing around here?' the captain demanded, striding unsuspectingly towards what he assumed to be one of the stockade guards and a local youngster.

Looking at the figures, Hoffinger felt a growing, uneasy suspicion that one of them seemed familiar. Not the corporal, although there was something odd about 'him', but the civilian. For some reason, the way the smaller shape stood facing them appeared to strike a chord in Hoffinger's memory.

Small!

That was the word needed to trigger off the dude's realization of the truth. Dusty Fog had stood in just such a manner, apparently relaxed but at coil-spring readiness, just before launching his attack on Glock.

'It's DusTY FO—!' Hoffinger yelped, his voice rising higher as the certainty of the suspicion grew.

The recognition had not come quickly enough. Already the two men were in the darkness beyond the window and close to the waiting couple. Although it had been Dusty's intention to silence the Provost Marshal first, he changed his mind in a hurry. Hoffinger must be prevented from making any more noise.

Mentally cursing the lousy turn of fate that had brought the chubby dude to the jail-house, Dusty sprang forward. With the speed that allowed him to draw and shoot a Colt in less than a second, his right hand stabbed in Hoffinger's direction. A thumb and four powerful fingers closed about the dude's throat, sinking in and tightening with a force that paralysed his vocal cord. Even as Hoffinger's words chopped off, Dusty's left hand reached for the Colt in his waistband ready to deal with the Yankee officer.

The need did not arise. For a refined, well-bred Southern lady, Rose showed a remarkably quick grasp of the situation and moved with commendable speed. Seeing Dusty leap at and silence the dude, she devoted herself to the Provost Marshal. In fact, recalling the humiliation suffered at his hands during the search and removal of her clothing, she found satisfaction in being given the chance to settle accounts with him.

Bringing up the baton, she lunged and drove its tip hard into his solar plexus. With a croak of pain, he dropped the bundle and jerked backwards. Rose followed him, swinging the baton around. Crashing on to the captain's head, which was encased in a silk-braided fatigue cap, the blow tumbled him to the ground.

'And Cousin Belle couldn't have done it neater,' Rose told herself. Then, hearing a sound from the rear of the alley, she turned with the baton lifting to strike.

Dragging the croaking Hoffinger after him at arm's length, Dusty also turned. He recognized the tall, lean shape looming through the blackness and spoke a warning, 'Don't hit him, ma'am. He's one of mine.'

Judging by his captain's tone that some explanation of his presence might be called for, Kiowa decided to avoid making it if he could. Instead he acted as if he had been obeying orders.

'Thought I heard somebody coming 'round the back, Cap'n Dusty. It war only a cat when I got there.'

With a heave, Dusty propelled the half-strangled Hoffinger towards the scout. Catching the front of the dude's jacket in his left hand, Kiowa held the point of his knife to the centre of the fancy vest.

'Keep him quiet!' Dusty ordered. 'How's the captain, Mrs. Greenhow?'

'He looks better now than when we last met,' she replied and the tension she felt made her continue. 'For the Good Lord's sake call me "Rose". You make me feel old, saying "ma'am" and "Mrs." '

'Yes, m – Rose,' Dusty grinned, looking at the Provost Marshal and deciding he would be no danger for some time. 'Let's go.'

'How about him, Cap'n?' Kiowa inquired, shaking Hoffinger who was too busy trying to recover from the strangling grip to protest.

For a moment Dusty hesitated and Hoffinger's life hung in the balance. If Dusty had given the word, Kiowa would have driven his knife home. Two things saved the chubby dude, Dusty's aversion to cold-blooded, unnecessary killing and the fact that he saw a way of making use of the man.

'Bring him with us,' Dusty ordered. 'But if he tries to make fuss, or shout to anybody, kill him.'

'That's easy enough done,' drawled Kiowa, deftly twirling his captive towards the rear of the building. Transferring his hold to the back of Hoffinger's coat collar, he pricked the bowie knife at the spot where its blade could most easily reach the kidneys.

'Start your feet moving, *hombre*. Do like Cap'n Dusty says or I'll leave you here permanent.'

Remembering Kiowa as vividly as Dusty from their last encounter, Hoffinger did not doubt that he would obey his captain's order. So he had no intention of causing trouble, or trying to warn any members of the garrison they chanced to meet that Rose Greenhow had escaped.

'This's the Provost Marshal, Dusty,' Rose remarked, stirring the unconscious officer with her toe. 'Perhaps he was coming to collect me.'

'Or set you free, figuring it was all a mistake,' Dusty answered, picking up the bundle. 'This feels like it's got clothes and shoes in it.'

'They'd know Hoffinger didn't make a mistake,' Rose told him. 'There was a knife-bracelet and a ring that would tell them who I am. Come on, we'd better get away from here.'

An unprotesting Hoffinger allowed himself to be hustled through the back streets. Nobody saw the party and they reached the outskirts without being challenged. As he walked, he wondered why Dusty had ordered that he be brought along. Not to be killed that could have been done just as easily by the jail-house and was against the small Texan's chivalrous nature. Certainly not as a hostage, to be traded for their freedom if they were caught. Dusty Fog, and more particularly Rose Greenhow, knew the Yankees would never make such a *trade*.

'Why have you brought him, Dusty?' Rose inquired and Hoffinger listened with interest. 'Will you release him when we get to the horses?'

'No, ma – Rose. I'm going to take him with us to Prescott.'

'Because he denounced me to the Yankees? If so, I assure you that I've no desire for revenge. It was my own fault that I was recognized. I felt so sure that nobody in Arkansas would recognize me that I didn't travel in disguise.'

'Revenge's not what I'm figuring on. Like you said at the jail-house, Trumpeter's going to know I had help from somebody in Little Rock. So I'm fixing to let him know who it was.'

'I don't—' Rose began, then gasped out, 'Hoffinger!'

'Yes'm. There's going to be a rumour started that he's one of our spies. Old Trumpeter's going to be reminded of a few lil things. Like how we knew where to find the remounts and how we come to be on the Snake Ford at just the right time after we'd met Hoffinger. Time we're through, Trumpeter'll be certain that Hoffinger's been working for us all along.'

'You've hit it!' Rose enthused. 'He'll even think that Hoffinger denouncing me was part of a plot to make him look foolish when I escaped. He's egotistical enough to accept that we'd do it just to have him removed from command, for fear of his brilliance.'

Listening, Hoffinger felt a shudder run through him. Once those rumours started to circulate, he was a doomed man in Little Rock. Remembering Trumpeter's delight at capturing the notorious Rose Greenhow, he could imagine the reaction when the general heard of her escape. Hoffinger's disappearance would seem like conclusive proof of guilt. Ironically, he had asked to accompany the Provost Marshal, on hearing that the officer intended to interrogate Rose, hoping that his presence would prevent her from being brutally ill-treated. Not that his good intentions – even if Trumpeter had known about them – would save him. The general would show him no mercy. In fact Trumpeter would not want him taken alive so that he could testify to how he had deceived the most brilliant brain in the Union Army.

'Fetching him along's going to slow us down some, Cap'n Dusty,' Kiowa warned. 'We don't have a relay for him to use and we're late starting back as it is.'

A point which Dusty had been considering since deciding how to use Hoffinger. The need for speed had prevented him from bringing more than the bare minimum of horses for his party. Rescuing Rose had consumed valuable hours that ought to have been spent in heading for the safety of the Ouachita River. Expecting to start back almost immediately, he had planned the journey accordingly. Slowed down by being unable to use the full potential of the two-horse relays, dawn would find them far from the wooded country where he had hoped that they could hide during the day. However he had to balance that against the chance to remove all suspicion from Wexler. Dusty thought that the opportunity justified the risk.

'We'll take a chance on it,' he told the others.

CHAPTER THIRTEEN

HE'S LEFT ME AFOOT SO'S HE CAN ESCAPE

JUST as Dusty feared, sun-up found them traversing rolling but open country. So they kept moving, with Kiowa ranging ahead of them, keeping to the low land and avoiding sky-lines if they could.

On rejoining his men, Dusty had changed back into his uniform. The bundle had held Rose's clothing, but she retained the borrowed outfit except for donning her own shoes. Everything had been ready for their departure. Pausing only long enough to tell Hacker – who had met Dusty's group on the edge of town – of the scheme to incriminate Hoffinger, they had moved out. The alarm bell had sounded before they had covered a mile, warning them that Rose's escape had been discovered. No pursuit came close, nor could the news be passed ahead. Seeing Dusty returning with Rose, Sandy McGraw had found and cut the telegraph line to the south-west.

Towards noon they were travelling along the bottom of a large valley. Ahead of them, Kiowa peered cautiously over the rim of the left-hand slope. Ducking down his head, he turned his horse and galloped back to his companions.

'There's a Yankee patrol coming this way, Cap'n Dusty,' the scout announced. 'Once they top that rim, they'll see us for sure.'

'No place to hide, either,' Dusty replied, looking around. 'How many of them and how far off are they?'

'Twenty or so, look like 3rd Cavalry to me. About half a mile off.'

'Too many to fight,' Dusty decided. 'There's only one chance. I'm going to make a stab at drawing them away from you.'

'You?' Rose gasped.

'Yes'm. I haven't ridden my black all night and I'll bet he's got the legs of any horse in the Yankee Army. When they see me, they'll give chase – Especially if they know who I am.'

'That's for sure,' Kiowa growled, for Dusty had passed on

Wexler's information during the night. 'After Trumpeter putting out that order about you, every blue-belly officer in Arkansas'd give his right arm for a chance to get you.'

'How can you be sure they'll recognize you, Dusty?' Rose inquired.

'Vern's going to tell them,' Dusty answered. 'If you'll do it, Vern, that is. Could be you'll wind up in a Yankee prison-camp—'

'Allus did want to see what one of them looked like,' the old corporal drawled laconically. 'Just what've you got in mind?'

Quickly Dusty explained his scheme. Watching the men, Rose saw that they showed no hesitation in accepting it. Even Hassle, who might end up as a prisoner-of-war, gave his agreement.

'How about Hoffinger?' Rose asked.

'Have no fear, dear lady,' the dude answered. 'By this time I am branded as a Confederate spy. My life depends on reaching your side of the Ouachita River. I will do nothing to impede our escape.'

'See you don't,' Dusty ordered. 'Go with Kiowa, Rose. And Kiowa, *you* keep going no matter what happens to us.'

Leading a twenty-strong patrol of the 3rd Cavalry, 1st Lieutenant Koebel saw a rider coming over the ridge up which he and his men were about to ascend. Even as Koebel realized that the newcomer was a Confederate cavalry captain, a second figure followed him. On foot, the man wore the uniform of a Texas Light Cavalry corporal. He was short, white-haired and clearly very angry.

'Come back with me hoss, blast ye!' the old corporal screeched, bounding after the captain.

Suddenly the Confederate officer became aware of the 3rd Cavalry patrol's presence. Reining his horse in a tight turn, he let out a yell, raked it with his spurs and sent it racing away at a tangent to the north-east. The corporal drew his right hand revolver, firing a shot in the direction of his departing superior.

'Take six men and get after him, sergeant!' Koebel barked. 'Remainder, draw pistols and follow me.'

While his sergeant gave chase to the fleeing captain, Koebel led the rest of the patrol up the slope. From all appearances, the old Rebel non-com was too filled with indignation at the officer's desertion to see the danger.

'Blast your stinking hide, Cap'n Fog!' the corporal bellowed in a carrying voice. 'You come back here!'

Until he heard the name spoken by the furious old-timer, Koebel had intended to go over the rim and see if more of the enemy were in the vicinity. Instead he brought his horse to a rump-scraping halt. His men also stopped their mounts, amused by the ancient Rebel's antics.

'Who did you say he was?' Koebel demanded, hoping that he had heard correctly. 'Who is he?'

Glaring around him, Vern Hassle howled in well-simulated exasperation and flung down his smoking revolver. Although his right holster was empty, the discarded Colt had belonged to Slasser. Stamping his feet in a paroxysm of wrath, he shook his fists in the air.

'Blast that Dusty Fog's hide!' Hassle raged. 'He's left me afoot so's he can escape.'

'Was that *Dusty* Fog?' asked one of the soldiers.

'Of course it b—!' Vern began, then stared wildly around as if the true nature of his position had just struck him. 'Now look what he's done! I knowed I shouldn't've come on this scout with him!'

Ignoring the excited chatter which rose from his men, Koebel hurriedly revised his plans. To hell with going over the rim, there would be nothing on the other side. It was obvious what had happened. Fog had somehow lost his horse while on a mission accompanied only by the corporal. Typical of an arrogant Southerner, he had taken the aged non-com's mount. On seeing the patrol, Fog had deserted his companion and fled. If the rest of his Company had been close by, he would have attacked instead of running.

While there might be gaps in Koebel's logic, he refused to see them. From all he had heard, whoever captured or killed Dusty Fog would stand high in General Trumpeter's favour. The man responsible could expect promotion and further recognition from the grateful commanding general – and Koebel had sent his sergeant after the fleeing Rebel instead of going himself.

'Guard this feller, corporal, you two men!' Koebel ordered, the words tumbling out in his haste to get started. 'Come on, the rest of you. After him. I'll give a month's pay to the man who brings him down.'

Already primed with excitement, the soldiers needed no further encouragement. Setting their horses into motion, they galloped at a reckless pace towards the rest of their party. Watching them go, the Yankee corporal gave a disgusted sniff and swung from his saddle.

'Rest your butt-ends,' he told his companions. 'They've got a long ride ahead of them. Shed the gunbelt, old timer.'

'Won't I just!' Hassle answered, complying. 'To hell with fighting for the South, happen that's how an officer treats me!'

'All officers're sons-of-bitches,' grinned one of the privates, holstering his Colt as he dismounted. 'Look how Koebel's rid off and left us.'

'I hope he enjoys the ride,' the second soldier remarked, dropping his gun into leather as he watched the chase. ' 'Cause I'm betting that's all he gets. That hoss of Fog's runs like a pronghorn antelope in a hurry.'

'Fog's hoss!' Hassle yelped. 'That's *my* danged hoss!'

And, tossing his gunbelt to the Yankee corporal, he launched into a magnificently profane discourse on the subject of Dusty's behaviour, morals, ancestry and possible fate. All in all it proved to be a fine performance and the Yankees listened with considerable amusement, not noticing that the rest of the patrol went rushing away from them. Hassle watched the departure, straining his inventive powers to find ways to keep his guards occupied. At last he paused for breath, standing snorting like a mossy-horned bull.

'That's was sure beautiful to hear,' chuckled one of the privates. 'It'll be a real pity to waste you on them prison-camps' guards.'

'Danged if I ain't pleased to be going to one,' Hassle answered, rubbing his hips. 'Trouble being, I've drawed on next month's pay and 'twouldn't be right not to go back and work it out.'

'Don't see as you've any other choice, pop,' the Yankee corporal said, letting the barrel of his Colt dangle downwards and shaking Hassle's gunbelt.

Still rubbing at his sides, the old timer moved his hands behind his back in a casual-seeming manner.

'Could argue about that, son,' he said and the right hand appeared holding the second of his revolvers which had been tucked into the back of his breeches. Cocking the hammer, he threw down on the other two-bar and continued, 'Let it drop peaceable. I'm mortal bound to dee-cline your offer.'

'And I'm here to see he gets that chance!' Sandy McGraw announced, rising from the top of the slope with Dusty's Henry rifle aimed at the Yankee privates.

Staring into the muzzle of the old Dragoon Colt, the Yankee corporal stood still. Before he could line his revolver, the Dragoon would put lead into him. He flickered a glance at and estimated the rest of the patrol were too far away to hear the sound of shooting over the thunder of their horses' hooves. Then he looked at his companions. Faced with a Henry repeater, they showed no inclination to take chances.

All of the trio had served long enough in Arkansas to know of the Texas Light Cavalry's skill with firearms and chivalrous treatment of prisoners. Deciding that they would be killed if they resisted, but released unharmed should they surrender, they followed the sensible course. Letting his revolver and Hassle's gun-belt drop to the ground, the corporal joined his companions in raising their arms.

'I reckon we've been slickered,' the corporal said, eyeing Hassle with a mixture of annoyance and admiration. 'Now what?'

'Soon's we've took your guns, you boys can get going,' the old timer replied. 'We wouldn't want you to be toting all that extry weight while you're walking – Which you will be. We'll be needing your hosses.'

'So'll you be walking, for a long spell, happen Cap'n Dusty gets to know what you called him,' Sandy declared, feeling relieved.

If the ruse had failed, he would have started shooting in an attempt at preventing the patrol from crossing the rim. So would Vern, while Dusty turned and charged to the attack. In that event, their chances of survival would have been slight.

Holding his black stallion to a gallop, Dusty turned in the saddle to see if his scheme was working. To his satisfaction, he found that the second portion of the patrol had swung off the ridge and were coming after him. That meant they had not reached the top, or seen Kiowa leading Rose and Hoffinger to safety. With only three men guarding him – and not doing a very good job of it – wily old Vern Hassle ought to escape, backed by Sandy and the Henry. Dusty knew that he could rely on the two corporals not to make their move too early.

Much as he would have liked to watch until Hassle escaped, Dusty faced the front and concentrated on the work at hand. The horse he rode had speed, endurance and was in the peak of condition. While making his arrangements, he had transferred every piece of equipment to the second of his relay, retaining only the clothes he wore and his gunbelt to add weight to his saddle. Being lighter than the majority of his pursuers, a superior rider to them all and far better mounted, he felt sure that he could eventually leave the Yankees behind.

However, he must not do so too quickly. First he had to lure them well clear of his companions. That would call for careful judgment, keeping close enough to encourage them to continue the chase, yet at a distance where they would be unlikely to hit him with their revolvers. Also he must try to nurse his horse so that it kept something in reserve in case of emergency.

From the cracking of shots that mingled with the drumming of hooves from behind him, Dusty concluded that some of the Yankees were trying to hit him. None of the bullets came close enough for him to be aware of their passing and he had no intention of returning the fire.

After covering about a mile, Dusty twisted cautiously around. Without disturbing his balance on the black's back, he studied his pursuers. Already the two sections had mixed together, which meant those from the rear party had driven their mounts extra-hard to catch up. The gap between Dusty and the leaders remained about the same, but the rest were beginning to string out. Poorer riders and weaker horses were already feeling the strain.

'Keep coming, you Yankee gentlemen!' Dusty gritted, turning forward. 'The further you follow me, the better Mrs. – no, she said I could call her "Rose" – the better her chances.'

Koebel for one had no thought of calling off the pursuit. Raking with his spurs, he goaded his lathered mount to greater efforts. Anxiety gnawed at him as he passed among the sergeant's party. He hoped that none of the shots being fired would hit the Texan before he had assumed command once more. Avid for the prestige, and promotion, that would come from carrying out Trumpeter's unusual order, he gave no thought to the strain he was imposing upon his horse. Instead he forced it to stride out faster. Man after man fell behind him and at last he ranged himself alongside his sergeant. Glancing over his shoulder, the non-com stiffened as he recognized the officer.

'What's up?' the sergeant demanded, starting to rein in and wondering if they had fallen into a trap, with a large force of Texas Light Cavalry following to spring it on them.

'Keep going!' Koebel yelled back. 'Get him. It's Dusty Fog!'

Which explained almost everything, particularly the officer's display of frenzied eagerness, to the experienced non-com. Trumpeter's order regarding Dusty Fog had aroused much speculation amongst the enlisted men. A long-serving soldier, the sergeant understood Koebel's motives. Equally aware of the benefits to be gained, the three-bar urged his horse on with renewed vigour.

Another mile was covered, without the distance between pursuers and pursued changing. No matter how the Yankees spurred their horses, the small Texan remained just as far ahead.

A vague suspicion began to creep over the sergeant and he remembered how he had once seen a fox run before a pack of hounds to lead them from its cubs. Maybe Dusty Fog was drawing the patrol away from something, or somebody, of importance. If so, he was succeeding. Looking back, the non-com saw that at least half of the patrol had already been forced to halt and the remainder straggled well behind.

'It's no use!' the sergeant shouted. 'We'll kill the horses trying to catch up with him!'

From his mount's uneven gait, Koebel knew the man spoke the truth. Yet he refused to give up the attempt when the chance of promotion and acclaim rode less than a quarter of a mile ahead.

'Keep after him!' Koebel croaked, slamming his spurs brutally against the heaving flanks of his horse. 'We'll get him ye—'

The stabbing of the spurs proved Koebel's undoing. Gamely trying to respond, the horse missed its footing, staggered and fell. Pitching over its head, the officer landed hard and skidded along the ground.

Taking warning from Koebel's fate, the sergeant brought his mount to a stop. Without a backwards glance, he dropped to the ground and snatched the Springfield carbine from the saddle-boot. Breathing hard, he sank on to his right knee. With his left elbow supported on the raised knee, he still found the exertions of the gruelling ride prevented him from taking aim. Try as he might, he could not stop the barrel wavering in tune with the expansion and contraction of his struggling lungs. More in hope than expectancy, he squeezed the trigger at a moment when the sights lined on Dusty. It was a gesture of desperation. Clearly the bullet had no effect. Giving a resigned shrug, the sergeant stood up. Before he could reload, the small Texan would be out of range.

Other members of the patrol came up and reined in their lathered, leg-weary horses, watching Dusty continue to ride away. Booting his carbine, the sergeant went to Koebel's side. Bending, he examined the officer and decided that Koebel could count himself a lucky man. While his shoulder and arm had been broken by the fall, its result might easily have been fatal.

'Are we going after him, serge?' a soldier gasped.

'The hell we are!' the non-com replied; but did not mention that he now believed they should never have started the chase.

'We'll rest the hosses, do what we can for the luff, then head back and see what's on the other side of that ridge. Only,' he finished to himself, 'by now we'll likely be way too late.'

A point with which Dusty was in complete agreement as he twisted his torso and looked back. Satisfied that the patrol would not trouble him again, he allowed the black to slow down. Rose ought to be safe by now, so Dusty dismounted and gave thought to making good his own escape.

At about the same time that Dusty found himself free to make for the Ouachita River, Lieutenant Frost tiptoed nervously into his commanding general's presence. Seated at his desk, Trumpeter raised a haggard face and stared at his aide.

'The search of the town's finished, sir,' Frost reported. 'Nothing's been found. No word from the patrol we sent out towards the Arkadelphia section of the Ouachita.'

'They won't do any good!' Trumpeter spat out. 'You should have sent out more than one patrol.'

While organizing the pursuit of Rose Greenhow and her rescuers had not been Frost's responsibility, he knew better than to raise the point. Brought back to the general's residence by the clamour of the alarm bell, Frost had found considerable reluctance amongst the rest of the staff to report Rose's escape to Trumpeter. It had fallen on Frost to break the news that the general's prize captive – whose arrest would divert attention from the unfortunate incidents of the lost remounts and Snake Ford – had been set free.

Frost had thought that Trumpeter would suffer a heart-seizure on reading Dusty Fog's entry in the Guard Report Book. Hurling the book at the wall, Trumpeter had cursed and raged like a madman, but had done nothing to take control of and correlate the hunt for the woman. Stripped of men for the assault on the Snake Ford, the garrison could not do a thorough job and hold the town against possible Rebel attack.

'I'd never have suspected Hoffinger—' Frost began, then realized that the comment had not been the most tactful he could have made.

'He's to be shot on sight!' Trumpeter snarled. 'All of them are!'

'Yes, sir,' Frost replied in a flat, neutral tone that still implied his doubt that the chance would arise.

Sinking his head on to his hands, Trumpeter ignored his aide. Thoughts churned and tumbled across the general's mind. All too clearly he could see the diabolical plot worked by the Rebels to discredit him. They were afraid to have a man of his superlative brilliance in a position of importance. While he had been tied to a desk in Washington, he was innocuous to their hated cause. Put in command of the Union's Army of Arkansas – last area of Confederate supremacy – his guiding genius would mean a turning point for the North. So the Rebel scum had conspired to bring about his removal.

Of course nobody had suspected Hoffinger. Getting him into Trumpeter's confidence had been almost clever. Thinking back, the general recalled that it was Hoffinger's idea to collect the remounts in that unorthodox manner. He could also have learned of the forged orders and been prepared to give the information to his companion-in-evil *Captain* Dusty Fog. If the two incidents did not prove sufficient to remove Trumpeter, they had arranged for the 'denouncing' of the woman as Rose Greenhow. Then, after the general had reported her capture to Washington, conspired with members of the garrison to set her free.

They thought that they were smart, but they underestimated the man against whom they pitted their feeble wits. Soon, very soon, they would learn their mistake. Maybe not so soon in the case of Hoffinger and the woman. The Rebel Secret Service would move them to a place temporarily beyond his reach. Not so the other participant in the vile plot. Dusty Fog would remain in Arkansas; a living reminder pointing the finger of scorn at Trumpeter. Something must be done about that and Trumpeter knew what it was to be.

'Who can get in contact with the guerillas, Mr. Frost?' the general asked, raising his head.

'A few of the officers know members of different bands, sir,' Frost answered.

'Get as many who can reach guerilla leaders as you can,' Trumpeter ordered, picking up his pen and drawing a sheet of official paper towards him. 'And do it quickly!'

CHAPTER FOURTEEN

TRUMPETER'D ADMIRE TO SEE YOU DEAD

'BELIEVE me, Betty, Georgina, being a spy is a terrible life,' Rose Greenhow told the two girls as they approached the big house which served as the combined headquarters of Ole Devil Hardin's staff and the Texas Light Cavalry. 'Oh, I know it sounds romantic, gay and noble, but it isn't. You have to do things which sicken you; let men you despise paw and maul you to win their confidences, lie, cheat, steal – even kill. I've done all that and hated every minute of it.'

Seven days had gone by since Rose's release from captivity. Her escape, after passing the 3rd Cavalry patrol, had been uneventful. Guided by the corporals and Kiowa, she had crossed the Ouachita and spent a worrying twenty-four hours until Dusty joined them. Changing into her own clothes, she had delivered her information to Ole Devil and now waited to return to the East. She had been made welcome and treated as a honoured guest by everybody, although there had been a certain hostility on the part of Company 'C' until Dusty had returned unharmed.

Since their arrival, small, petite, black haired and beautiful Betty Hardin and slightly taller, buxom, blonde and pretty Georgina Blaze had devoted much of their time to trying to enlist, with Rose's aid, as spies. From the first, she had attempted to dissuade them from the idea and, with her departure imminent, increased her efforts. Looking at the eager young faces, she wondered if they took her words to heart. Betty appeared to be partially convinced, but Georgina seemed as determined as ever to join the Confederate States' Secret Service.

Situated on the edge of Prescott, the house had been built with its front away from the town. From its porch, one could look across the gardens to the rolling, wood-covered hills. The nearest slope rose about half a mile away, covered with bushes and trees that still offered feeding terrain for an occasional Kansas whitetail deer.

A black horse stood saddled and ground-hitched in front of the main entrance and Ole Devil Hardin strode from the house with Dusty Fog at his side. Seeing the woman and girls coming towards them, the general threw a frosty grin at his nephew.

'Good afternoon, General,' Rose greeted.

'Mrs. Greenhow,' Ole Devil answered, directing a cold stare at the girls without it having any visible effect. 'I hope these two young misses haven't been bothering you.'

'On the contrary,' Rose smiled. 'I find them most refreshing and delightful. They remind me of when I was young.'

'That's strange,' Ole Devil growled. 'They have just the opposite effect on *me*. May we expect you at the ball tonight, Mrs. Greenhow?'

'You must come,' Betty insisted, black eyes twinkling. 'Why grand-papa gets quite lively when he throws away his walking-cane and takes the shawl from his tired old shoulders.'

An explosive snort broke from Ole Devil, but a smile played on the corners of his lips. Possibly no other person would have dared make such a comment.

The ball was to celebrate the successful conclusion of the Snake Ford affair. While strengthening the defences on the rim, Colonel Barnett had also been preparing for the inevitable time when the Union Army assembled such force that they would sweep the Confederate soldiers back by sheer weight of numbers. He had held on, defeating lesser attacks while cavalry patrols harassed the Yankees' flanks and rear, until receiving Wexler's warning of the massive reinforcements approaching. Then, in accordance with Ole Devil's orders, had made ready to withdraw.

After a night's artillery bombardment, Colonel Verncombe had launched an attack at strength in the grey light of dawn. Leading his men forward under heavy cannon fire from across the river, he had been puzzled by the lack of response from the Confederate positions ahead. Neither the captured Napoleons in their protective earthworks nor the figures in the trenches responded to the sight of the advancing enemy. Verncombe had soon learned why this was.

During the night, the Confederate defenders had fallen back to their own side of the river. They left behind dummies armed with useless, rusted rifles and wooden models of Napoleons for the Yankees to capture. Made at Barnett's instigation, the decoys had been moved in under the cover of darkness over four nights and were substituted without any report of it reaching Verncombe. Furious at having been tricked, the assault force continued its advance; only to be halted after heavy losses at the river's eastern edge. Seeing the impossibility of crossing the ford in the face of such heavy, concentrated and determined opposition, Verncombe wisely refrained from making the attempt.

So the Union's Army of Arkansas felt no pleasure at retaking the strip of territory. Maybe the Northern newspapers would enthuse over the success and probably regard it as the prelude to Trumpeter's promised advance into Texas, but the men concerned knew better. Once more they held the east side of the Snake Ford, but could go no farther; and taking it had cost many lives without the consolation of a corresponding number of Rebel dead. They were even denied the weak pleasure of retaking the captured Napoleon battery.

Ole Devil considered that there was cause for celebration. Making Barnett the guest-of-honour would be a public demonstration that the general did not blame him for accepting the forced order.

'I'll be honoured to attend, General,' Rose said. 'If you will promise me a dan—'

Two shots cracked from the slope in the background, one deep followed almost immediately by another lighter in pitch. Breaking off her request, Rose joined the others in looking for signs of who had fired.

'They came from up near the top, sir,' Dusty said, pointing. 'I can't see anything for the bushes.'

'It could be somebody from the regiment out hunting,' Georgina suggested.

'Could be,' Dusty admitted dubiously. 'The first sounded like a heavy rifle, but the other was a Henry.'

'I loaned Kiowa *your* Henry, Dusty,' Betty put in. 'He's promised to fetch a couple of tom-turkeys in. That could have been him.'

'It could,' Dusty agreed. 'I reckon I'll ride up there and take a look.'

'Do that, Dustine,' Ole Devil confirmed. 'Its probably nothing, but we may as well be sure.'

Suspicious by nature and upbringing, Kiowa Cotton never entirely relaxed his vigilance. Even while returning from a successful turkey hunt, so close to his regiment's camp, he remained alert for any unusual sounds or sights. Coming across the fresh tracks of a single horse, he gave them a close scrutiny. Made about an hour before, they followed a route which struck him as curious and significant. Whoever rode the horse had taken pains to select an inconspicuous route. While a clear trail lay close by and could be seen from different points, the rider had kept clear of it.

Of course he might be one of Wexler's men delivering a report and wishing to keep his identity a secret. Or he could be a Yankee soldier on a scouting mission. Whatever his motive, Kiowa figured that the man rated investigation.

Dropping the bodies of two turkeys to the ground, the sergeant rode forward. Indian-bred, the horse he sat moved with an almost wild-animal silence. Kiowa knew the country around Prescott well enough to pin-point his exact location. If the mysterious rider continued in a straight line, he would arrive on the slope over-looking the headquarters building.

A slight movement from ahead brought Kiowa to an immediate halt. For a moment he could see nothing out of the ordinary. Then another movement drew his attention to it. Slowly the shape of a horse, standing amongst the bushes some distance away, came into focus. Only a flicker of an ear had betrayed it, for its dun coat merged well with the shadows. Without its involuntary movement, Kiowa might have ridden closer and alarmed it.

Dropping from his saddle, Kiowa slipped the Henry from its boot. He left his horse ground-hitched and darted forward on foot. Making use of every bit of cover, he moved in an arc that ought to keep him from disturbing the dun. Silently he climbed up the ridge, slipping through the head-high clumps of buffaloberry bushes until he passed over the top. Then he caught his first glimpse of the horse's owner.

One glance told Kiowa that, whatever he might be, the man had no innocent purpose. Big, gaunt, with a wide-brimmed hat, clad in fringed buckskins with pants tucked into unpolished riding boots, he lowered a small telescope through which he had been studying the front of the distant house. Coming to his feet, a powder-horn suspended from his left shoulder, he thrust the telescope into his waist-band. Then he picked up the long Sharps 1859 rifle and advanced like a hunter stalking his prey.

Unless Kiowa missed his guess, the prey stood outside the big house. Even at that distance, the sergeant could make out the shapes on the porch. With the aid of his telescope, the man would have identified them.

Working with Dusty Fog had taught Kiowa to think before acting. If the man intended to kill somebody at the house, discovering who and why was mighty important. So Kiowa neither spoke nor fired at the intruder. Instead he moved forward, meaning to take a living, talking prisoner if he could. Before he had taken three steps, he felt the breeze, up to then blowing directly into his face, veer to the left. It would be carrying his scent to the man's waiting horse. An animal so well trained would have learned other lessons than merely standing like a statue. Sure enough, even as Kiowa realized the danger, the horse cut loose with a loud snort.

Instantly the man whirled around. Seeing Kiowa, he continued raising the rifle which was already swinging towards his shoulder. He moved fast. Far too swiftly for the sergeant to dare take chances. With the Sharps lifting to point at him, Kiowa flung himself sideways. Accurate as it might be at long ranges, the Sharp's length and weight made it clumsy and awkward to manoeuvre at speed. Going down in a rolling dive, Kiowa snapped the Henry into line and fired. His shot came as an echo of the Sharp's deep boom. Lead screamed over the sergeant's head in testimony to the nearness of his escape. His own bullet tore into the man's chest, ploughing up to burst out at the back.

Throwing the Henry's lever down and up, Kiowa saw the man turn, hunch forward, drop the Sharps and fall. The sergeant rose, advancing cautiously with the repeater ready to speak at the first hostile move. Extending his left foot, he rolled the man over. For a moment the other's eyes glowed hate, then they glazed and the gaunt body went limp.

'Now who the hell are you?' Kiowa mused. 'And what'd you come to do?'

A question which Dusty repeated almost word for word on his arrival.

'What do you reckon, Kiowa?' he went on, looking at the body.

'He was watching the house through that telescope, then started to move in for a shot at one of you who was outside.'

'Nobody would want Cousin Betty or Cousin Georgie dead,' Dusty said. 'Which means he was after Uncle Devil or Mrs. Rose.'

'You was there, 'long with the others,' Kiowa pointed out, 'And Trumpeter'd admire to see you dead.'

'Hell, I'm not that important so's he'd send a sharp-shooter special to get me,' Dusty protested. 'Mrs. Rose, maybe. Or even Uncle Devil, but not me.'

'He was after one of you, that's all I know,' Kiowa drawled. 'I've been through his pockets, ain't nothing in 'em to say who he is.'

'Back-track him, see where he's come from,' Dusty ordered. 'I'll have him and his horse taken in. Maybe Mrs. Rose can help out when she sees him.'

On learning of the reason for the shooting, Rose expressed her interest and suggested that she should supervise the search. Waving aside her apologies for interfering, Dusty admitted that it had been his intention to ask her do so. Accompanying the small Texan to the barn farthest from the house, she set to work. Drawing aside the blanket which covered the man, she looked at his face.

'I don't know him, but I don't pretend to know every member of the Yankee Secret Service,' she said. 'You've had him stripped, that's good. While I start on his clothes, check under his arms, between his legs, in the cheeks of his arse and among his hair. You can discount him having anything in his ears or mouth, or up his nose, he wouldn't carry documents concealed there for any length of time.' She made a wry face and went on, 'Maybe I should have had Betty and Georgie come help me. Then they'd really know what a spy has to do.'

'If you'd rather, I'll do the searching,' Dusty offered.

'No,' Rose answered. 'This's work I've been trained to do.'

From what Dusty saw, after following her instructions about searching the corpse, Rose had learned her lessons well. No detail was too small for her to examine. First she crushed every article of clothing between her fingers, held close to her ear so that any faint crackle of concealed paper could be detected, then checked the thickness of the cloth in case another piece of material bearing identification was stitched between the layers. The hat was studied inside and out, the sole, heel and upper of each boot ripped apart, the waist and gunbelt torn to pieces. Brought along at Rose's request, the armourer stripped the man's weapons to bare essentials and the saddler gave the horse's leatherwork an equally thorough going over. Even the telescope was dismantled to be scrutinized. The dun horse received as careful a search as had been given to its master.

'Nothing,' Rose announced, after the powder horn had been emptied and split open to expose its interior. 'I'll stake my life that 'he's carrying nothing to identify him— And yet I've never known a Yankee agent not to.'

'If he'd've had anything, you'd've found it,' Dusty praised, coming over from where he had been washing his hands and arms after the messy business of examining the horse. 'Could he be a U.S. Army sharp-shooter sent to kill you?'

'It's possible,' Rose admitted, showing her pleasure at the compliment 'From what Kiowa told you, the man had been watching the house for some time.'

'That's what he said and he can read tracks real good. The feller watched the house until you met us outside, then moved forward to start shooting. Which means he was after one of us. If he'd just wanted to kill at random, he wouldn't've waited. There were fellers moving about all the time. I figure he was after you, or Uncle Devil.'

'Some of the Yankee Secret Service would like to see me dead, I admit. But it's not likely they'd go at it that way. Killing Devil would throw your Army into confusion, perhaps. Not for long, but long enough to let the Yankees launch an offensive before he could be replaced. Except that "Oakland" would have warned us if a move of that magnitude was planned. It couldn't be kept a secret.'

'Not from Wex – Oakland, anyways,' Dusty agreed.

'There's another alternative, Dusty,' Rose said. 'Trumpeter could have sent the man after you.'

'Kiowa reckoned that,' the small Texan replied. 'Hell, he couldn't want revenge bad enough to risk a sharp-shooter* just to get it. Even if the feller was a sharp-shooter that is.'

'He wasn't on that slope just to admire the scenery,' Rose objected.

'Do you reckon he's Army?'

'There you've got me, Dusty. That buckskin shirt, his trousers and gunbelt could have been bought anywhere west of the Mississippi. The boots are cavalry issue, so is his undershirt, which doesn't mean much as they can be bought easily enough. The hat could have been picked up north or south of the Mason-Dixon line and is old enough to have been bought before the War. It doesn't help us.'

'That's a Rocky Mountain saddle and the horse's range-bred,' Dusty went on. 'It's not carrying a brand of any kind.'

'Neither his rifle nor revolver have U.S. Army proof-marks,' Rose told him.

'Sharp-shooters mostly buy their own rifles,' Dusty replied. 'And a whole mess of fellers, especially from out West, fetched their revolvers along when they joined the army.'

'It's puzzling,' Rose sighed, thinking of one solution to the mystery but dismissing it as unworthy of serious consideration. 'So we can only wait and see if Kiowa learns anything.'

* Sharp-shooter: Civil war name for a sniper.

'That's about all,' Dusty agreed, reaching much the same conclusion as Rose had and not mentioning it for similar reasons. 'Anyways, I don't reckon there'll be another try until whoever sent him learns he didn't make it. Sharp-shooters aren't so plentiful or easy come-by that they'd chance losing more than one at a go.'

'Talking of going,' Rose gasped as she glanced through the open doors of the barn. 'It's long gone time we went and dressed for the ball.'

Turning, Dusty let out a low whistle of surprise. He had not realized how long the search had taken. Night had fallen and already the big house was glowing with lights, while the activity about the place warned that the festivities would soon commence. So he told their assistants to clear up the barn, allowing Rose and himself to go to change their clothing. Rose had been fitted out with dresses on her arrival and had even managed to find a gown suitable for the occasion.

For Dusty's part, he knew that the casual, comfortable uniform worn on patrol would not meet with official approval that night. Reluctantly he made his way to the quarters he shared with Red, meaning to don the correct full dress. On his arrival, he found his striker waiting. Dick Cody had spent most of his adult life attending to Army officers' welfare. While proud of his current charge, he did not approve of the way Dusty ignored the *Manual of Dress Regulations*. Nothing pleased Cody more than to watch his officer going forth in a double-breasted, skirted tunic, embellished with a black silk cravat, white gloves, trousers instead of riding breeches, correct accountrements and sabre.

'I'm sure pleasured that you changed your mind, sir,' Cody greeted.

'How's that?' Dusty asked.

'About attending the ball in your dress uniform.'

'What else would I wear tonight?'

'But Miss Georgina came and said you'd decided to go in your skirtless tunic and riding breeches, sir,' the old striker explained, looking bewildered.

'She must've been joshing you,' Dusty replied. His cousin knew of Cody's feelings about the matter of uniform and was not averse to a joke.

'Joshing or not, sir,' Cody answered indignantly, 'she took them with her. And your hat, boots and gunbelt.'

'*Gunbelt!*' Dusty snapped. 'Damn it, Cousin Georgie's gone

way too far this time. I'll pound some sense into her fool hide, see if I don't.'

'Yes, sir,' Cody agreed enthusiastically. 'She sounded so sincere that I didn't doubt that you had sent her.'

'I hope she sounds that way when I get through with her,' Dusty growled. 'What damned fool game is she playing?'

Before Cody could express an opinion, they heard a disturbance from the town. Somebody shouted a warning which mingled with a revolver shot. Then another shot cracked, followed by more shouting; this time from several places.

'It coming from Main Street, sir!' Cody stated.

'Sounds like it,' Dusty agreed. 'I'd best go and see what's happening.'

CHAPTER FIFTEEN

I'LL KILL HIM WHERE HE STANDS

'IT'S working, Cousin Betty!' Georgina Blaze enthused as she strode along the centre of Main Street dressed in Dusty's uniform, hat, boots and gunbelt. 'We're taking them all in.'

'Out here in the street, maybe,' Betty answered. 'It won't be so easy in good light. You know, Cousin Dusty's not going to like you walking around in his uniform.'

Smaller than Georgina, Betty had borrowed clothes from one of the drummer-boys. In the hope of making her disguise more acceptable, she carried his drum on her back. Gripping its V-shaped sling in her left hand, she looked along the almost deserted street. Lights showed in a number of buildings, from many of which came the sounds of people enjoying themselves. Ahead was the Shenandoah Hotel, its porch and hitching rail deserted despite the noisy evidence of revelry from within.

'Why he won't mind me borrowing his old uniform,' Georgina protested, trying to sound more confident than she felt. 'Will he?'

'He'll not be pleased,' Betty guessed. 'I surely hope Tommy hasn't shown him that *yoko-guruma* throw he taught me.'

'That—?'

'*Yoko-guruma*,' Betty repeated. 'It means lateral wheel or something and it's a dilly.'

'It sure sounds that way,' Georgina smiled. 'And if we can walk the length of Main Street, then get by the guards to the ball dressed like this, it will show Rose we're smart enough to be spies.'

'Or convince her more than ever that we're not,' Betty replied. 'It's a *loco* trick – and before you get into a tizz, I agreed to try it.'

A man came from an alley opposite to the hotel, slouching towards the girls. Medium-sized, stocky, he wore civilian clothes of sober colours and kept his right hand behind his back. At the same moment, the door of the Shenandoah's barroom opened and Hoffinger stepped on to the porch. Halting, the chubby dude looked in each direction along the street. Seeing the man approaching the two uniformed figures, he stiffened slightly. For a moment he studied the girls, then his eyes went to something about the man which could not be visible to them.

'Air you Cap'n Dusty Fog?' asked the man from the alley.

'I am,' Georgina agreed, making her voice sound husky.

'Look out!' Hoffinger screamed, leaping forward.

The warning came too late. Hearing Georgina answer in the affirmative, the man brought his hand into view. Shock momentarily numbed the girls, causing them to ignore Hoffinger's warning; for they saw the hand held a long-barrelled Army Colt that lifted to line at Georgina. Muzzle-blast flared redly on the night-darkened street as a .44 bullet spun from the revolver to drive into the blonde's left breast. Cocking back the hammer swiftly, the man started to swing the barrel towards Betty. Then he heard the thud of Hoffinger's feet and turned to meet what might prove a greater danger than the diminutive 'drummer-boy.'

Anger filled Hoffinger, wiping away his love of peace. Recklessly he plunged from the sidewalk, striding determinedly towards the man. He gave no thought to the consequences of his actions, or his inadequacy to deal with an armed man. Since his arrival in Prescott, he had convinced his abductors of his pacific intentions and complete lack of desire to escape. So they allowed him to roam around unattended and his jovial nature had won him many friends. Popular he might be in all walks of the town's society, but not sufficiently trusted to be allowed to carry a gun. Being unarmed did not prevent him going forward.

Coming around fast, the man slanted his Colt in Hoffinger's direction. Aware that he could not reach the other in time to prevent him shooting, the little dude hoped that he might buy the second girl – whom he recognized despite her disguise – the opportunity to run to safety.

Only Betty did not run. Born of a fighting stock, spirited and self-reliant in her own right, she recovered rapidly from the shock of the attack. More than that, she saw Hoffinger's peril and knew that he would die unless something was done in a hurry. Flashing up her hands, she gripped the drum with the intention of ridding herself of it to be free to help her rescuer. Even as she raised it over her head, she saw a better use for it than hurling it aside. Swinging it high, she took a stride towards Georgina's assailant.

With death staring him in the face, Hoffinger saw something rise into the air behind the man. Then, accompanied by a dull boom, the other's head disappeared inside Betty's drum. Again the Colt roared, but surprise had caused its barrel to be deflected and its bullet tore a furrow through the hotel's name-board instead of into the dude's chubby frame.

Ducking his head, Hoffinger butted into the man as he tried to remove the drum. At the same moment, Betty smashed her interlaced-fingered hands into his kidney region from behind. The impact bore the man backwards, despite Betty's blow, and he went down with Hoffinger on top of him. Mouthing curses, the little dude flailed inexpertly at his victim. On the street, doors were flung open as people appeared to investigate the disturbance. Bursting out of the hotel's barroom, Billy Jack and other members of Company 'C' swarmed forward. Still striking out wildly, Hoffinger felt himself gripped and dragged upright.

'Ease off, Ossie!' Billy Jack growled, clinging to the dude's right arm. 'We'll tend to him.'

Slowly Hoffinger's fighting rage died away. Looking around, he saw the man firmly held by Sergeant Weather and Sandy McGraw. Then the dude's eyes turned to where Betty knelt at her cousin's side.

'Oh Lord!' the black-haired girl was sobbing. 'What have we done? What *have* we done?'

Everything was in confusion as people milled around and asked questions, or stared in bewilderment at what they saw. Billy Jack's lackadaisical pose left him and for once he showed why he held the rank of sergeant major in the Texas Light Cavalry's elite Company 'C'.

'Quiet it down!' he roared. Then, as silence fell, he turned to Hoffinger and spoke in a gentler tone. 'What happened?'

'I – I don't know,' the dude admitted, struggling to think and quieten his churned-up emotions. 'The – I saw – the young ladies – knew she wasn't Captain Fog – saw his gun – I shouted, but it was too late.'

Which left a lot unexplained, but helped Billy Jack to understand a little of what had happened. He knew Georgina to be a practical joker, which might account for why she was wearing Cap'n Dusty's clothes. Seeing her lying there had given the sergeant major a hell of a shock. Now he realized that her disguise had, for some reason, brought tragic results.

The crowd opened up to let Dusty come through. Striding forward, expecting to find there had been a quarrel ending in gun-play between the participants, he slammed to a halt. For a moment he could hardly credit the message of his eyes. Then he moved forward, dropping to one knee at Betty's side. One glance at Georgina told him that she was beyond help. Blood still spread slowly on the left breast of the borrowed tunic, but he had seen enough of wounds to know that she was dead.

'What happened?' Dusty asked and the listeners could hardly recognize his voice.

Twisting around, Betty flung herself into Dusty's arms and sobbed a reply;

'He – that man – asked Georgie – 'Are you Cap'n Dusty Fog?' – and when – when she said she was – she – he – he shot her.'

An ugly, menacing rumble rose from the crowd, directed at the man held by the non-coms. It died away as Dusty glared around. Then the small Texan looked at the prisoner and sucked in a deep breath.

'He asked Georgie if she was me,' Dusty said quietly, 'and shot her when she said she was.'

'Y-Yes,' Betty gulped, shocked by his tone into momentarily forgetting her horror and grief.

'Then it looks like he got the wrong one.'

Saying that, Dusty gently freed himself from Betty's arms. Just as gently, he removed the gunbelt from Georgina's body. In a silence that could almost be felt, he strapped on the belt and fastened the tips of the holsters to his thighs. Moving clear of the girls, he addressed his men.

'Turn him loose and put a gun in his hand!'

'Cap'n—!' Billy Jack put in and he did not intend to continue with one of his usual unmeant doleful warnings or complaints.

'Do it!' Dusty snapped. 'Or I'll kill him where he stands!'

Billy Jack nodded to Sandy and Weather. As they released the man, the sergeant major took out his right hand Colt. Sobbing for breath, the man fell back against the hotel's hitching rail. Slowly Billy Jack walked forward and thrust his Colt into the man's right hand, then stepped aside.

'All right, *hombre*,' Dusty said. 'You want to kill Dusty Fog. Well, I'm him. Get to doing it.'

Almost recovered from the effects of the combined attack, the man stared numbly at the *big* Texan. Everything about Dusty filled the man, hard as he was, with a gnawing terror. Cold merciless retribution as certain as the hangman's noose showed on the young face. The powerful figure stood poised like a cougar waiting to spring, hands held out from its sides with fingers slightly crooked ready to close about the white handles of the holstered Colts. That was no man he faced, but a machine, a deadly highly-developed machine with just one purpose – to kill him.

'N-No!' the man croaked, finding himself unable to throw the gun away.

'Count to three, Billy Jack,' Dusty ordered – and it was an order, despite the cat's purr gentle way he spoke. 'By three, he'll use that gun or die.'

'One!' Billy Jack said, for he could no more resist than the ashen-faced killer could toss aside the Colt. The rest of the crowd stood as if turned to stone, oblivious of the people who came from the big house, conscious only of the scene before them.

'Two!' Billy Jack counted.

'No!' a woman's voice shouted. 'Dusty. No!'

Face pallid and raging with emotion, Rose Greenhow ran along the street ahead of the party from the ball. She had heard from a Negro maid of the girl's idea to impress her and planned to surprise the would-be spies on their arrival. Waiting with members of the guard to capture them, she had heard the shooting. On learning from where it originated, Rose had an almost clairvoyant idea of what had happened. Sending a man to notify Ole Devil of the trouble, she set off to look into it and prayed she might be wrong. All too soon she knew how right she had been. No humane considerations motivated her call to Dusty. The man cowering against the hitching rail could answer questions – but only if he stayed alive.

'Three!' Billy Jack said.

'Captain Fog!' Rose screamed in the same breath.

At the sergeant major's word, Dusty's right hand moved. All the long, hard hours of practising his draw, backed by the carefully considered design and excellent workmanship of his gunbelt, permitted him to fetch out the long barrelled Colt with blinding speed. He had never moved faster than at that moment. Out came the revolver, its hammer drawn back by his thumb and trigger going to the rear under the pressure of his forefinger as the seven-and-a-half inch 'civilian pattern' barrel* turned towards its target. Straight as if pulled by a magnetic force, Dusty's Colt lined at the man's head.

And did not fire!

With the trigger depressed to the full and thumb quivering

*The normal Army model had an eight inch barrel.

on the verge of freeing the hammer, reason returned to the small Texan. A concerted gasp rolled from the spectators. Letting out a moan, the man dropped Billy Jack's revolver and turned to sob into his arms against the hitching rail.

'Clear the street, all of you who aren't involved!' Dusty ordered, lowering the hammer and returning the Colt to its holster.

Like snow before a fire, the crowd melted away. There were at least two officers senior in rank to Dusty present, but they withdrew like the rest. By the time Billy Jack had retrieved his Colt and the man's revolver, only the people directly concerned with the incident remained. Ole Devil arrived fast, accompanied by Colonel Mannen Blaze, Dusty's father and others of the family.

'What's happened, Dustine?' the general demanded while the women moved towards Betty and the body.

Slowly, fighting down her grief, Betty rose and faced the men to repeat in more detail the story she had told to Dusty. At its end, the Texan senior officers turned to Hoffinger.

'My thanks, sir,' Ole Devil said.

'I – I was too late,' the dude mumbled, seeming to have shrunk into himself and showing none of his usual urbane poise.

'You saved Cousin Betty's life,' Dusty put in. 'With your permission, Uncle Devil, I aim to let Trumpeter know that Mr. Hoffinger's not a traitor—'

'Trumpeter!' croaked the killer, turning from the hitching rail and drawing every eye his way. 'It was Trumpeter who offered the reward to any man who could kill you, Cap'n Fog.'

'What was that?' Ole Devil barked, striding forward.

Rose and Dusty beat the general to the man and the small Texan said, 'Tell it fast and all!'

'It's true!' the man croaked, reaching inside his jacket. 'I've got the letter he sent to—!'

'Let him take it out!' Ole Devil ordered as Sandy and Weather sprang on to the man and grabbed his arms. Taking the folded sheet of paper which the killer produced, he read it. 'Well I'll be damned!'

'Look at it, Hondo!' Colonel Blaze said, after receiving and studying the paper. 'It's damnable.'

Looking like a taller, older version of Dusty, Major Hondo Fog read the message. Without comment, he handed it to Rose.

'To whom it may concern,' Rose read aloud. 'I, Horace Trumpeter, General Commanding the United States' Army of Arkansas, will pay the sum of one thousand dollars with no questions asked, to any man who produces proof that he has killed the rebel and traitor who calls himself Captain Dusty Fog.' She paused, then continued, 'It's signed by him and marked with his official seal. Who are you?'

'Ike Smith,' the man, to whom the question had been directed, answered. 'I was one of Toby Mattison's boys—'

'A lousy border-jumper!' Billy Jack ejaculated.

'Who else knows about this letter?' Rose demanded, ignoring the comment.

'Nobody's far's I know. I saw Toby get it and when he didn't tell us what it was I snuck it from him.'

'Is there a big, gaunt Westerner in your gang?' Rose asked. 'He wears a large grey hat, buckskin shirt and trousers, cavalry boots. Rides a dun gelding and uses a Sharps rifle.'

'Sounds like the feller in Stegner's bunch, the one they call Rocky Mountains,' Smith answered. 'He allows to be a better'n fair shot with that rifle.'

'And *that's* why we didn't find any identification!' Rose said. 'He was a guerilla trying to collect the bounty.'

'I wondered if he might be one,' Dusty confessed. 'Only I knew no lousy guerilla'd come after any of us just to serve the North.'

'The same thing occurred to me,' Rose admitted. 'But it seemed so unlikely – Why didn't I speak. We could have been on guard—'

'You weren't to know,' Ole Devil told her gently. 'None of us could imagine a general of the United States Army would stoop to doing it.'

'I *should* have realized!' Rose insisted. 'All along I've known Trumpeter was a rabid radical, the kind who'd break if he found himself under any strain. I ought to have guessed it was possible he'd hire men to kill Dusty.'

'Nobody blames you, Rose,' Hondo declared; then his face clouded. Before the War, he had fast been gaining a name as one of the most shrewd peace officers in Texas. During that time he had developed the habit of looking at any incident from all its angles. Doing the same on the Prescott street, he reached an ugly conclusion. 'If Trumpeter sent those bounty notes to Mattison and Stegner, he'll have passed them to the other guerilla bands.'

'And it's likely that they'll be trying to claim the reward,' Rose went on.

'That's how I see it,' Dusty remarked in the same quiet voice with which he had ordered Billy Jack to arm Smith.

'It'll have to be stopped!' Rose stated. 'Grant wouldn't allow it if he heard of Trumpeter's actions.'

'Grant's a long ways off,' Dusty pointed out. 'Time we can get word to him, could be somebody else'll have been killed in mistake for me. No ma'am, Rose. There's only one man who can stop that bounty quick enough to do any good. The feller who's offering it.'

'*Trumpeter!*' Rose gasped, staring at the small Texan as she began to understand what he meant.

'Yes'm. And I'm fixing to give him a chance to earn his own bounty.'

'He'd never cancel the offer!' Ole Devil said, then realization struck him. 'You mean that you're going to face him down?'

'Yes, sir,' Dusty confirmed.

'Not alone you won't!' Red Blaze declared. He had arrived with the others and listened to the conversation while comforting Georgina's mother. 'The whole Company, the whole *regiment* comes to that. 'll be with you.'

'They won't,' Dusty contradicted. 'Just me and four men're going.'

'Who're the other *three*?' Red wanted to know.

'Billy Jack, Kiowa happen he's back in time, Vern Hassle—'

'I'll volunteer, Capn' Dusty,' Sandy McGraw announced, beating Sergeant Weather to it by a split second.

'You, Sandy,' Dusty confirmed. 'This's no chore for a married man, Stormy. You'll run the Company as acting sergeant major while we're gone.'

'Dusty, you can't—!' Rose protested.

'Those bounty letters won't be done with until one of us is dead,' Dusty replied. 'Already one innocent girl's been killed because of them. There could be others. So I'm going to stop them.'

'What're we going to need, Cap'n Dusty?' asked Billy Jack.

And then the sergeant major, Red and Sandy realized that permission for the mission to proceed had not been given. So they turned their eyes towards Ole Devil. As always, he thought first but came to a decision without a waste of time.

'You think you can achieve something, Dustine?'

'I'm going to try,' Dusty stated. 'I won't take chances, sir. I want to get to Trumpeter too bad for that.'

'What do you think, Hondo?' asked the general. 'He's your son.'

'And he's set on going,' Hondo replied. 'There's no way, short of hog-tying him, that'll stop him. And I know that, whatever he does, it'll be thought out carefully, not rushed at blind.'

Which agreed with Ole Devil's summation. He had already made up his mind, but had needed the extra seconds to steel himself for giving the permission that might send two of his nephews and three good soldiers to their death. The fact that they would go with or without authority provided him with some small consolation; and he knew that something must be done to stop the guerillas acting on the bounty offer.

'Good luck, Dustine,' he said. 'If there's anything you need, ask for it.'

'Let me go with you, Dusty,' Betty put in. 'Please. Lord! I could have talked Cousin Georgie out of this foolishness, but I didn't try. I'll go mad if I don't do something.'

Looking at Betty, Rose felt that she must speak. This was no naïve girl filled with ideas of how glamorous a life she might have as a spy. Betty had matured, grown up, changed in the minutes since Georgina had died. While aware of how dangerous the mission would be, Rose felt that Betty deserved a place on it and might be of assistance.

'Take her, Dusty,' Rose begged. 'I'd come with you, but I don't ride well enough and would slow you down.'

Betty and Dusty faced each other, standing withouut speaking for several seconds. He knew that she would accept his refusal, but that things would never be the same between them again. So he nodded his head and said, 'You can come.'

CHAPTER SIXTEEN

GENERAL TRUMPETER, MEET CAPTAIN DUSTY FOG

PATROLLING outside the eastern wall of General Trumpeter's residence was not a duty Private Sloan regarded with enthusiasm. Unlike on the other three sides, no gates pierced his part of the wall. So he could not stop and chat with the stationary sentries. The duty would have seemed less onerous if there had been any logical point on keeping watch that side. In addition to the ten-foot stone wall around the property, the nearest dwellings – a pair of smaller houses some fifty yards away – had been commandeered and were occupied with Union personnel. Anyways, who the hell among the Rebs would figure on sneaking in and killing old 'Bugle-horn' Trumpeter. Fact being, from the hash he had made of things since his arrival, the Confederate States Army ought to be real keen to leave him in command.

Just about the only consolation Sloan could find came from his clothes. No longer did Zouave regiments wear fancy copies of frog-eating French uniforms, but dressed like honest-to-God American soldiers. He preferred even a forage cap to the Zouave fez. Over his infantry uniform, he wore an overcoat with a shorter cloak than that sported by cavalrymen. Around the coat was his well-polished cartridge-box belt, with leather sling, passing diagonally from the cartridge box on his right hip to the left shoulder, cap box, bayonet scabbard and canteen; although Sloan could not see the point of carrying the latter.

The sound of footsteps drew his attention to the gap between the adjacent houses. Bringing his rifle and bayonet to the required position – in case it was the officer-of-the-day making rounds, rather than expecting to need the weapons – he gave the prescribed challenge.

'Halt. Who goes there?'

'Now you-all don't think lil ole me's a Johnny Reb soldier, do you?' answered a feminine voice.

Peering through the darkness, Sloan made out the figure of a girl coming towards him. Small, dainty, wearing a sleeveless white blouse and a skirt of glossy black material, she walked with an attractive hip-sway. Lowering his rifle, Sloan grinned. Every enlisted man knew that the officers entertained ladies – a *very* loose definition – in their quarters, regardless of Regulations. So he saw nothing suspicious about her presence.

'Where you going, gal?' Sloan demanded, figuring he had best not ask where she had been.

'Home,' she replied. 'Don't you-all tell me it's not allowed.'

'It's after curfew,' Sloan pointed out. 'I'm supposed to holler for the sergeant of the guard.'

'If you do, he'll only take me off someplace and – scold me a lil,' the girl purred. 'Now a big, strong, handsome gentleman like you won't let that happen to me, will you?'

'What do *I* get if I don't?'

'A kiss – for starters.'

Figuring that he could take the chance, even if no more than a kiss came out of it, Sloan leaned his rifle against the wall. Then he took a stride forward and put his arms around the girl's waist. From what he felt, she wore nothing under the blouse. She was warm, inviting, yielding to the force of his charm. As he lowered his face, she brought up her hands to his shoulders. Savouring in anticipation the coming kiss, he became aware that three men in uniform were approaching from the gap through which the girl had appeared. They were cavalry soldiers, going by their uniforms, but no *Union* cavalry wore gunbelts of that kind.

Even as Sloan's grip slackened, the girl slipped her right leg between his spread apart feet. At the same time, she thrust up her hands. The bases of her palms rammed with some force under his chin. Bright lights blazed briefly before Sloan's eyes. Deftly the girl hooked her advanced leg behind his left foot as the force of the double blow caused him to retreat. Tripping, he fell backwards and his skull smashed into the wall as he went down.

'Nice going, Cousin Betty!' Dusty Fog complimented, as he, Kiowa and Billy Jack sprang forward.

'Is he dead?' Betty Hardin inquired worriedly, watching the gangling sergeant major kneel by the sentry's motionless body.

All too clearly Betty saw what Rose Greenhow had meant about the unpleasant nature of a spy's work. There had been nothing gay, romantic, or noble in tricking the sentry, necessary though it might have been.

When Kiowa had returned, saying he had back-tracked the dead guerilla for five miles without learning anything, Dusty's party made ready to travel. With Betty wearing boy's clothing and all non-essentials left behind, they had made a fast but uneventful ride from Prescott.

Leaving Red and Sandy to guard the horses and, when the time came, cut the telegraph wires, Dusty took Betty and his men into Little Rock. Visiting Wexler, Dusty found him preparing to send a warning about Trumpeter's bounty offer. On learning of the events in Prescott, he put all his knowledge at Dusty's disposal. Not only had he made a very accurate map of the general's residence, but he gave a complete description of its staff and the manner in which it was guarded. With that done, he had continued to tell of the most recent developments.

Since Rose Greenhow's escape and learning – through rumours started by Wexler – of Hoffinger's 'treachery', Trumpeter had become suspicious and uncommunicative; which explained the undertaker's delay in discovering the offer had been made. Not even the officers who had delivered the notes knew of the contents. On learning of the general's actions and obtaining one of the letters, Wexler had arranged for it to reach Colonel Verncombe. Little love was lost between the Dragoon and Trumpeter. Knowing Verncombe to be the most senior officer under the general, Wexler had hoped that something might come of the colonel learning such an offer had been made.

Disinclined to wait in the hope that something *might* happen, Dusty had decided to go on with his plan. From what he had learned, he considered the eastern wall offered the best point of entry – if its sentry could be removed in silence. Rather than chance stalking the man across the open ground, he had arranged for Betty to act as a decoy. Warned of what she might need by Rose Greenhow, Betty had brought along suitable clothing. Consisting only of the blouse and skirt, borrowed from a girl who knew Billy Jack very well, the weight of her disguise had been negligible and proved its worth. Picking a time shortly after the sentries had been changed, she had done all Dusty required. The way she had handled Sloan was her own idea, backed with the training received from Tommy Okasi.

'He'll live,' Billy Jack answered, unbuckling Sloan's cartridge belt.

'You're nearest his size,' Dusty told the sergeant major. 'Get dressed *pronto* and start walking his beat.'

'I allus knowed you aimed to bust me,' Billy Jack complained as he drew the cartridge-box's sling over the sentry's head. 'Only I never figured it'd be to private in the *Yankee* Army.'

'And a puddle-splasher at that,' Betty went on, smiling weakly. 'Why I'm shamed by your meanness, Cousin Dusty.'

Glancing at his cousin, Dusty grinned. Often he had seen new recruits on their first dangerous mission relax and gain confidence from Billy Jack's gloomy wailing. Betty appeared to have thrown off her worry and concern, caused by the way she had deceived the sentry.

While Dusty kept watch, Billy Jack removed Sloan's accoutrements and overcoat. He donned the garments himself, leaving Betty and Kiowa to rope and gag the unconscious sentry.

'How'll I do?' Billy Jack inquired, putting on the Yankees kepi.

'You'll get by, happen you keep your boots out of sight,' Dusty replied.

Yankee infantry wore trousers and Jefferson bootees, but the overcoat was too short to hide the discrepancy.

'You could walk kind of scrunched up,' Betty suggested.

'If that'd've been Cap'n Dusty,' moaned the sergeant major, 'He'd've told me to cut a foot or so off my legs.'

'I *had* thought of that,' Betty assured him, 'but it would take too long.'

'Let's go!' Dusty ordered. 'You all know what to do. If I'm not back to you three minutes after any shooting starts, I'll be dead, so get away.'

'Yo!' Kiowa answered, with as near emotion as he ever showed, moving to stand with his back to the wall.

Dusty placed his right foot in the sergeant's cupped hands and thrust upwards with his left leg. Assisted by Kiowa's lift, he rose and swung himself on to the garden wall. Lowering himself on the other side, he dropped into the garden. There he crouched against the wall, searching for signs that his arrival had been detected. Wexler had claimed that no sentries patrolled inside the grounds, but precautions cost nothing and kept a man alive. Certain at last that he was undetected, he began to move across the garden.

Passing amongst the bushes, Dusty pictured what his companions would be doing. Beyond the wall, Betty and Kiowa were dragging the sentry away while Billy Jack walked the beat. Then the girl would return, ready to stand and talk with the sergeant major if the north or south wall sentry happened to look. Out with the horses, Red and Sandy waited for sounds of shooting before cutting the telegraph wires. To do so earlier might prevent a routine message from going out. That would alert the Yankees, for cutting the wires was a regular habit of the Texas Light Cavalry when on patrol in Union territory.

On reaching the corner of the house, Dusty looked along its front. He saw nobody and kept moving. Once he had to creep on hands and knees beneath a window, with Yankees officers talking inside the room, but he reached the big old white oak which – if Wexler's description had been correct – reared before the window of Trumpeter's office.

The gnarled condition of the trunk offered sufficient foot-holds for him to climb the twelve foot or so to the lowest branch. By keeping on the house's side of the trunk, he avoided detection by the main gate's sentries. Once in the branches, he moved fast. Nor did reaching the general's balcony prove difficult. Stepping from a branch on to the stone balustrade, he saw a chink of light glowing from the centre of the drawn drapes. That meant the room most likely had occupants. However its windows were open, relieving Dusty of the task of forcing an entry.

Advancing on silent feet, Dusty looked through the tiny gap in the drapes. Going by the single star on the epaulettes of the man standing by the desk, Dusty had found General Trumpeter's room. The other's actions caused him to wait instead of entering. Slipping a .32 calibre metal-case cartridge into the cylinder of a Smith & Wesson No. 2 Army revolver, Trumpeter pivoted its barrel down to connect with the frame. Even as Dusty prepared to step through the drapes, a knock at the door changed his plans. With an almost furtive, guilty air, Trumpeter cocked the revolver and placed it in the open right hand drawer of the desk. Dusty felt puzzled by what he saw. Surely a brigadier general, even if he was a soft-shell appointed for political rather than military reasons, ought to know better than leave a cocked revolver lying around.

'Come in,' Trumpeter called, without closing the drawer.

A young lieutenant entered, the one-eighth of an inch gold cord down the outer seams of his trouser leg showing him to be a member of the staff. Behind him came a big, burly man wearing the double-breasted jacket and eagle-insignia of a colonel. Even without the buff facings of the uniform, different in shade to the normal calvalry yellow, Dusty recognized Colonel Verncombe of the 6th New Jersey Dragoons. He had seen the colonel from a distance on more than one occasion during the fighting at the Snake Ford.

'You can go, Mr. Frost,' Trumpeter said and Dusty thought that he detected a signal pass between the general and lieutenant.

'What do you know about this?' Verncombe demanded, stalking to the desk as Frost backed from the room and closed the door.

Without looking at the sheet of paper thrown before him, Trumpeter scowled at his visitor and replied, 'There's still a difference in our ranks, Verncombe!'

'To hell with rank!' Verncombe barked, tapping the paper with his right forefinger. 'Did you put this damnable thing out?'

'What if I did?' challenged Trumpeter and sat down.

'It's monstrous, that's what. A general in the United States Army using his official position to settle a personal vendetta.'

For a moment Trumpeter did not reply. His eyes flickered in the direction of the door and Dusty formed the conclusion that he expected somebody to arrive. Then the general swung his gaze back to Verncombe. In a casual-seeming gesture, Trumpeter inched his right hand towards the open drawer.

'Watch your words, Verncombe!' Trumpeter spat out. 'Your conduct is mutinous – and not for the first time.'

'If my conduct is mutinous, I'd like to know what you call your own,' the colonel blazed back. 'Having young Fog murdered by some stinking guerilla won't excuse your mistakes.'

'Have a care, Verncombe!' Trumpeter snarled, speaking loud and darting another glance at the door. 'You'll go too far!'

Suddenly everything became clear to Dusty. Now he understood why Trumpeter had loaded the revolver and placed it cocked in the open drawer. The exchange of signals between the general and Frost, taken with the interest in the door and over-loud comments gave the game away. Unless Dusty missed his guess, Trumpeter planned to kill Verncombe and had done so before the other produced the damning bounty offer or spoke mutinously.

What was more, Dusty knew why. After so many failures Trumpeter must be under heavy fire from Washington and in danger of losing his command. So he planned to use an old method of worming out of difficulties. Select a scapegoat, someone who could be blamed for all the failures. And who better than the most senior colonel in the Army of Arkansas. Accuse Verncombe of everything – after he was dead and unable to refute the charges – and escape the consequences.

There might even be a more personal reason for selecting Verncombe. Whatever small credit accrued from the Snake Ford affair had gone to the colonel. Everybody knew – and Trumpeter knew that they knew – Verncombe had done well in straightening out his superior's muddles. So the general had every reason to hate the burly, competent Dragoon.

Dusty understood the whole situation; including that he must intervene or see the colonel murdered. From all appearances, Verncombe was too angry to see his danger and was headed for a carefully laid trap.

'Howdy,' Dusty said, stepping quickly through the drapes and letting them fall back into place. If anybody outside had seen the flicker of light, they ought to be unaware of its cause. Or too uncertain to think it worth investigating.

'What the—?' Trumpeter gasped, staring goggle-eyed and jerking his hand from the drawer. Shocked by the sight of an armed Confederate cavalry officer in his office, he continued with almost inane gravity. 'Who are you?'

Verncombe did not need to ask. Small the newcomer might be in feet and inches, but he gave the impression of far greater size. More than that, the colonel had seen Dusty during the brief Snake Ford campaign. A cold, sardonic grin twisted at Verncombe's lips; but he made no attempt to draw the revolver from his waistbelt holster despite Dusty's empty hands. Instead he turned his eyes to the general and performed the introduction with almost correct formality.

'General Trumpeter, meet Captain Dusty Fog.'

'F-Fog!' Trumpeter repeated and could not prevent himself from asking, 'What are you doing here?'

'I've come to make you call off those guerillas who got your bounty notes,' Dusty replied.

Silence fell on the room, except for Trumpeter's laboured breathing. Sitting rigid in his chair, he stared as if mesmerised at the small Texan, without saying a word. It was left to Verncombe to break the silence. Even he needed a good thirty seconds to recover from finding himself in such an unbelievable situation. Through it all Dusty stood just inside the room. Legs slightly apart, he balanced on the balls of his feet and every fibre of his being stayed tuned ready for instant action. Having answered Trumpeter's question, he waited for the next move to be made.

'And if he won't?' Verncombe inquired at last.

'He'll do it, colonel,' Dusty answered, sounding gentle as a summer breeze. Yet under the soft-spoken words lay a greater menace than could have come from the screamed-out threats of a lesser man. 'He'll do it – or see if he can do better against me than Buller did.'

There the Yankee officers had the whole matter laid before them as plainly as if the small Texan had spoken volumes in explanation. Either Trumpeter rescinded his offer of the reward, or he faced Dusty Fog with a gun in his hand. Still the general did not speak and once more Verncombe took up the conversation.

'You know about this letter then?'

'I know,' Dusty agreed. 'Because of it, a girl of seventeen was murdered.'

'How do you mean?' Verncombe demanded.

'A guerilla had one of the letters and figured to collect the bounty. A cousin of mine, a young, pretty girl, colonel, got dressed in one of my uniforms and walked through Prescott wearing it for a joke— Only she didn't get all the way through. The guerilla saw her and, it was dark, figured he'd found me. He walked up and shot her.'

'The hell you say!' Verncombe breathed and glared at Trumpeter.

The words broke Trumpeter's spell and he jerked himself upright in the chair. Up to then the shock of being confronted, in the supposed safety of his own residence, by the cause of his misfortunes had held him immobile. Seeing his subordinate's cold contemptuous scowl jolted him back to reality. While aware of the peril, he also figured that it might help him out of his difficulties.

'Take him prisoner, Verncombe!' Trumpeter commanded.

'You put that bounty on him,' the colonel replied, little realizing that he was approaching another trap. 'I don't need the money, so do your own dirty work – if you've got the guts.'

A flat refusal, or even any hesitation to obey, was what Trumpeter had hoped would happen. Now he had the excuse he wanted to kill – no, carry out a justifiable execution of Verncombe. It would merely be an extension of a plot hatched earlier that day. The major difference was that the colonel had come unbidden instead of being sent for.

Everything had been arranged before Frost had arrived to say that Colonel Verncombe wanted an interview. After leaving them together, the aide was to go to the Provost Marshal and say that he feared trouble from the 'drunken' Verncombe. On reaching Trumpeter's office, they would hear voices raised in anger. Then, as they burst in with drawn guns, Trumpeter would take the Smith & Wesson from the drawer and shoot Verncombe dead. With a court martial threatened over his failure to keep Rose

Greenhow a prisoner, the Provost Marshal would be inclined to accept any version of the incident given by his general.

Dusty Fog's presence would form only a slight impediment to the plan. He could not know of the revolver being so handy in the drawer. Anyway, he would be fully occupied with the two officers when they arrived. Possibly he would kill one of them, if the stories of how fast he could draw a gun were true. If so, Trumpeter hoped his aide would be the victim. Frost knew too much and would want more than a mere promotion to captain for his share in the Dragoon colonel's death. Fast Fog might be, but one of the two was sure to get him while he shot the other.

First however, the stage must be set and the scene prepared.

'Take him, Verncombe!' the general bellowed, glancing at the door.

'Why don't you do it?' countered the Dragoon.

'Damn it, I'm not armed!'

No harm in fostering that illusion. A Texan, full of the idiotic chivalry of the South, would not fire on an unarmed man.

There it was!

The handle of the door turned slowly. Outside Frost and the Provost Marshal were waiting, guns drawn ready for use and the Texan still stood with empty hands.

'This is the last time, Verncombe!' Trumpeter shouted. 'Take him. That is an order!'

As the door flung open and the two officers burst in, Trumpeter grabbed at the Smith & Wesson.

CHAPTER SEVENTEEN

HE'S HEADING FOR THE WEST WALL

EVERYTHING might have gone as Trumpeter hoped, but for three unforeseen circumstances.

First: Dusty expected Frost to return and figured that he would not come alone. He even guessed at the aide being accompanied by only one man. While Trumpeter wanted 'proof' that he had acted within his rights, too many witnesses would be dangerous. One man, carefully selected, would tell a convincing story. The more involved, the greater the risk of confusion in their evidence.

Second: the small Texan knew about the hidden Smith & Wesson, so he was not fooled by the general's protestations of being unarmed.

Third: and most important: Trumpeter had no conception of the lightning speed and ambidextrous dexterity with which Dusty could handle his guns.

Rushing into the room with their revolvers held ready for use, Frost and the Provost Marshal found a different situation to that which they had expected. They skidded to a halt, staring at the small figure by the window. Quicker than Frost to recover his wits, the Provost Marshall started to move his gun around towards the officer wearing a uniform of Confederate grey.

Across flashed Dusty's hands, passing each other and working in perfect unison. The matched Colts swept from their holsters, angling outwards. Flame ripped from both barrels at almost the same moment; less than a second from when his hands began to move.

At the door, Frost saw Dusty partially disappear behind two swirling clouds of burned black powder's smoke from which sparked red spurts of flame. Just realizing the implications of what he saw, the aide felt a savage impact against his shoulder. Pain roared through him and he spun around, screaming, to fall into the passage beyond the door.

Still turning the barrel of his Colt, the Provost Marshal saw the same as Frost. A moment later he died. The bullet from Dusty's second Colt struck him between the eyes. In going backwards, he fired his revolver. Dusty felt the breeze of its lead passing his face.

Bringing the Smith & Wesson ready cocked from the drawer, Trumpeter started to point it in Verncombe's direction. Although he guessed the other's intentions, the colonel stood without a movement. Amazement twisted the satisfaction from Trumpeter's features as he saw his 'rescuers' struck down by Dusty's bullets. Suddenly, shockingly, he realized that the small Texan had ruined another of his carefully-made plans. Fear, fury and self-preservation drove Trumpeter to react. Mouthing wild curses, he forgot Verncombe and tried to line the revolver on the greater danger.

Cocking his Colts, Dusty twisted his torso towards the desk. Like extensions of his will, the long barrels directed themselves to the Yankee general. First left then right hand revolver roared, coming so close together that the detonations barely formed two separate sounds. Trumpeter's head jolted as if struck by an invisible hand. The force of the two bullets' arrival lifted him backwards. Disintegrating under his weight, the chair on which he had fallen let him sprawl lifeless to the floor.

Again Dusty drew back the hammers of his guns, although he did so as an instinctive, trained reaction rather than by conscious thought. Turning, he brought the Colts in Verncombe's direction. The colonel stood with open hands dangling loosely at his sides, but Dusty knew it was not fear that kept him out of the fight. Career-soldier and man of honour, Verncombe could understand why Dusty had taken such a desperate chance. More than that, the colonel hated the deed which had caused the small Texan to come and face Trumpeter. As far as Verncombe was concerned, the War did not exist at that moment.

'Leave the letter,' Verncombe said as shouts of alarm and running feet sounded in the passage.

'Sure, colonel,' Dusty replied, lowering the hammers and twirling away the Colts. 'Thanks.'

With that the small Texan turned and stepped through the drapes. Two strides carried him across the balcony. His work in Little Rock was done. With Trumpeter dead, Verncombe would rescind the offer of a reward for Dusty's death. Now he must try to escape.

Down at the main gate, the two sentries faced the house, gesticulating and talking. If they had seen Dusty come through the drapes, they gave no sign of it. He stepped on to the balustrade and jumped into the tree. Landing on a branch, he climbed rapidly downwards. Just as he had hoped, all the activity was in the house. While men dashed to investigate the shooting, they stayed inside the building. That had been something Dusty had relied upon – or hoped would happen – when making his plans.

Who could blame the Yankees for not realizing what had happened? Nobody could have foreseen that a Rebel would dare break into the private residence of the general commanding the Union's Army of Arkansas.

Swinging from the lowest branch, Dusty dropped to the ground. He landed running, darting to the nearest of the decorative bushes and making for the east wall.

In Trumpeter's office, Verncombe had moved towards the end of the desk. He looked at the first of the men to enter the room and barked, 'See if there's anything you can do for the general!'

Knowing that Trumpeter was beyond all human aid, the colonel sprang to the window. Passing through the drapes, he allowed them to fall back into place behind him. Striding along the balcony, he looked around. Drawing his revolver, he lined and fired it downwards.

'Over there!' he roared as the sentries ran towards the house. 'He's heading for the *west* wall!'

Satisfied that he had diverted the search, for he guessed which way Dusty had come into the grounds, Verncombe returned to the window and blocked the other men's path as they tried to emerge.

'Thanks again, colonel,' Dusty breathed, continuing his swift, crouching run through the garden.

Approaching the wall, he saw that its top had changed shape. Two strange elongated humps lay on it. They stirred as he drew nearer and Betty's voice came from one of them.

'Jump, Dusty!'

Leaping up, Dusty felt his outstretched arms caught in Betty's and Kiowa's hands. Aided by the girl's not inconsiderable strength, the power of the sergeant's wiry frame took the strain of his captain's weight. Bracing his feet against the wall, Dusty walked up it. From the top, Dusty and his helpers dropped down to where Billy Jack was discarding his borrowed disguise.

'Over there, *pronto*!' Dusty snapped.

Not until running towards the wall of the next building did Dusty notice that his cousin had been thinking of herself. The skirt was gone, leaving her legs clad in riding breeches and boots;

which Dusty knew she had been wearing all the time. However, she had the unconscious sentry's tunic on; its sleeves either rolled up or cut off to the desired level. Dusty wondered which of them had realized that the blouse's white material showed up in the dark and would draw attention to its wearer.

The time was not suitable for Dusty to satisfy his curiosity. Already men from the adjacent house, disturbed by the shooting and noise from the general's residence, were coming to investigate. Fortunately they made so much noise that it drowned out the sound of the Texans running feet. Flattening themselves against the wall of the building nearest to the edge of town, Dusty's party watched soldiers streaming by. The men went towards the front entrance of Trumpeter's house, so missed seeing the four figures. Nor did the rear wall's sentries do better, their attention being concentrated on the inside of the grounds.

'Are you all right, Dusty?' Betty asked as they hurried away from the houses.

'Sure,' he replied.

'How about Trumpeter?' Billy Jack inquired.

'He's dead,' Dusty answered.

'Figured he might be,' drawled the sergeant major. '*Now* we'll have another fire-eater coming out here looking to make life miserable for us.'

'I thought you enjoyed being miserable,' Betty pointed out.

'I do,' Billy Jack confessed, then brightened up a little. 'I never thought of it like that. Things ain't so bad after all.'

'It's lucky that feller on the balcony got all twisted around like that,' Kiowa remarked. 'He sent them sentries off the wrong way.'

'*Real* lucky,' Dusty agreed.

The truth about Verncombe's 'mistake' could ruin the colonel's career, so Dusty would never tell what had really happened.

Nobody saw them leave town. Behind them the alarm bell clanged, but they rejoined Red and Sandy, mounted their horses and rode south-east without hearing any sound of pursuit.

In Trumpeter's office, Verncombe looked at the assembled staff officers. All of them knew him and most of them respected him as a competent officer and good man.

'It was Dusty Fog,' the colonel told them and picked up the sheet of paper. 'He came as a result of this letter which the general had circulated amongst the guerilla bands.'

While the letter passed from hand to hand, accompanied by

startled or angry exclamations at its contents, Verncombe explained how it had been the cause of Georgina Blaze's death.

Sitting on a chair in the corner of the office, having his shoulder bandaged, Frost watched and listened. It quickly became obvious that the senior officers present, the ones whose opinions counted in the final analysis, felt revulsion at the letter and disagreed with its purpose. Sick with pain and anxiety, he gave thought to saving his own skin. Deciding that his only hope lay in transferring the blame, he sought for a way of doing it.*

By the time the note had been read, the officer-of-the-day and sergeant-of-the-guard arrived to report that the search of the grounds had been without result. The officer was under the impression that the intruder had gone to the west, then doubled back behind the house to go over the east-side wall. The sentry from that section had been found, stripped of his overcoat and tunic, bound and gagged, against one of the adjacent buildings.

While that information was being digested, a breathless soldier dashed in to say that every telegraph wire out of town had been cut. Wexler had supplied men to help with that part of Dusty's plan.

'That's Fog's way all right,' growled the Quartermaster's Department colonel, bitterly aware that he would have to produce wire to replace the missing lengths. Like all members of his Department, he hated parting with any kind of stores.

'Orders, sir?' prompted the Town Major, looking at the senior officer present – and, with Trumpeter dead, acting commanding general of the Army of Arkansas.

'First we must rescind this bounty offer,' Verncombe stated firmly. 'I want that starting *now*, without any delay, and completed as quickly as possible.'

Mutters of agreement followed the words. None of the older officers wanted it even thought that members of the United States Army condoned Trumpeter's behaviour in placing the bounty. So they saw the urgency to make a public retraction.

'Next we'll organize a search of the town,' Verncombe went

*Frost later declared that Trumpeter and the Provost Marshal had conspired to murder Verncombe, but insisted that he had been an innocent pawn and had intended to warn the colonel. While nobody believed his story, it could not be disproved and it came in useful as a means of avoiding a too-close examination of Verncombe's conduct after the shooting. Wishing to disassociate themselves from Trumpeter's actions, the Union's high command were anxious for the affair to pass over without complications.

on. 'I want patrols ready to leave at dawn. They'd never pick up Fog's trail in the dark.'

'It will give him a good start over our men,' the officer of the day protested. 'We should alert the garrisons between here and the Ouachita River so that they can get out searching parties.'

'That's true enough,' agreed the Town Major, an infantry officer with no clear idea of the difficulties involved in doing so.

Thinking of the superb riding skill and excellent horses of the Texas Light Cavalry, Verncombe doubted if any man in his command could reach the garrisons before Dusty Fog and his party were safely by them.

'Select your best courier, major,' the colonel ordered. 'Send him off as quickly as you can.' He raised his eye piously towards the roof and continued, 'I sure *hope* he gets there in time.'

The Devil Gun

CHAPTER ONE

DESERTER—AND TRAITOR

Ten months ago 2nd Lieutenant Jackson H. Marsden had been honour cadet of his year at West Point Military Academy. Only three months back he received a commendation for his handling of the rearguard action when the Federal forces met with a bloody repulse at Poison Springs. It had been but two weeks since his company commander gave Marsden a strong hint that he was marked for early and rapid promotion. Now he was a deserter and in the next few days, a week at most, would also be a traitor.

Yet it must be done. Loyalty to his country, or rather to the division of his country that he chose to serve, could not stand against the horrible results of the plan he chanced to discover. No man who lived out West—even a man in his early twenties—could fail to be deeply disturbed when contemplating the full meaning of that plan. The fools who spawned the scheme could have no idea of its full and true implications. Or they were so blinded by their bigotry and hatred of the Confederacy that they did not care what terrible and hideous situation their scheme bore in its wake. Marsden did not know which, ignorance or bigotry, accounted for the actions of the men behind the scheme, nor did he greatly care. All he knew was that he must do something to prevent the scheme's completion.

Born into a family of career soldiers, the decision to desert and become a traitor did not come easily. Already he had lost two brothers and several cousins in the bitter fighting of the Civil War. From his earlier days he had been trained in discipline and loyalty, taught that he must do his duty. He served well, putting aside his disappointment at being assigned to the 8th 'Stedloe's East Coast' Zouaves, an infantry regiment, when he hoped for a place in a cavalry unit, and gained distinction if only in the little-publicised campaign to bring Arkansas back into the Union.

At last he came face to face with a situation not envisaged in any military textbook; something militarily and morally wrong—as far wrong as it was possible for inexperienced human beings to get—and he knew he must do something to correct the wrong.

Merely seeing his commanding officer and laying the facts before him would not do. Serving as one of the few regular officers in a volunteer regiment, Marsden knew how slight was the bond between himself and the volunteer officers. While Colonel Stedloe might be a brilliant businessman and showed some courage in action, he could hardly be expected to see all the ramifications of the scheme to which he gave his consent. A regular officer with experience in the West would have discarded the scheme when Captain Castle and Lieutenant Silverman presented it. Stedloe not only accepted the scheme, but gave it his full support and blessing. If he saw any lack of enthusiasm from his regular officers, he probably attributed it to jealousy, for little love was lost between the career soldiers and the amateurs who joined only to fight the South. Perhaps Marsden could have killed the scheme, but he was out of camp on outpost duty during its conception and the other three lacked experience on the frontier, so could not offer objections. In fact, seen with inexperienced eyes, the scheme had much to commend it and its successful conclusion could do much to not only hasten the end of the War, but also might easily bring about Union victory. The commanding general, no career soldier, would view it in that light.

Marsden, lacking support from his own kind, spent a sleepless night. By dawn he reached a decision. Say nothing to anybody, not even to Rory McDougal, West Point companion and fellow career lieutenant in the Zouaves, he took his horse from the lines, used the ferry across the Arkansas River and rode west towards the Ouachita Mountains. That had been the previous morning and by now his absence must have been noticed. Of course Rory would cover up for him as long as possible, thinking he had gone to visit a charming young 'lady' of their acquaintance. Rory would never suspect Marsden of going over the hill, deserting, and might lay his disappearance to action by a fast-riding troop of Southern cavalry making a strike to beard the Union Army in its Little Rock den. Maybe some of the volunteer officers would be suspicious, suspicion came naturally to their kind. Even now a search might be organised with the intention of bringing him back.

The thought brought misery to Marsden. No matter how this affair came out, his career in the Army was finished. A court martial, dismissal from the service at least, more likely a firing squad, awaited him—even if the Confederate Army believed his story and did not hold him as a prisoner of war.

With the Ouachita River ahead, apprehension by Union forces grew less while still remaining a possibility. Although the victory at Prairie Grove in December 1862, the capture of Arkansas Post, battle at Helena and fall of Little Rock in '63 put the Union in possession of all North-Eastern Arkansas, they made little progress in gathering the rest of the state from Confederate hands. In fact the Union's defeats that year at Poison Springs, Mark's Mill, Pine Bluffs and Jenkins' Ferry had prevented further conquest of Arkansas. So the land between the Arkansas and Ouachita Rivers belonged to neither side and was the scene of many bloody skirmishes. The nearer one came to the Ouachita, the less chance of meeting Union forces; yet this also added to the chance of detection should one meet a Union patrol. So close to the Ouachita a lone officer would attract attention. While the Zouaves had given up their flashy uniforms—copied from the French-Algerian troops which gave them their name—and dressed as did most of the Union Army, it would take experienced men only a close glance to know that Marsden belonged to the infantry. No foot-soldier would be so close to the Ouachita River without written authority from his colonel, and certainly would not ride without an escort. If seen by a Union cavalry patrol, Marsden knew he could not think up a convincing story enough to prevent its commander taking him back for investigation and Colonel Stedloe was smart enough to guess at the reason for his lieutenant's presence on the river.

So Marsden rode slowly, keeping to low ground and avoiding sky-lines, alert all the time for hostile presences. Wending his way through the rolling, open country, he saw no sign of other human beings. However, he could not risk crossing at a ford or shallow stretch for such might be under Union surveillance. Knowing the Confederate cavalry's skill as raiders, the Union forces concentrated on preventing crossings of the Ouachita rather than attacking the rebels beyond the river, and kept watch on places where an easy crossing might be made.

Soon he came to the wooded country bordering the Ouachita and, with the sun beginning its downward slide towards the western horizon, rode along the river bank searching for an available crossing place. At last he found a spot that might satisfy his needs. The tree-dotted banks dropped steeply on either side, the river forming a long, deep, slow-moving pool between them and offering no difficulty to a skilled man. Having seen no sign of life on either bank for the past hour, Marsden decided to make his crossing.

Before starting the descent, Marsden swung from his saddle, took out his field glasses and made a careful search of the surrounding country. He was a tall, slim young man, yet gave the impression of strength, with black hair and a ruggedly handsome face. As a result of his pretence of going to Little Rock when leaving camp Marsden wore his black Burnside felt hat, its right side turned up and fastened with his State's coat of arms insignia, the bugle badge of the infantry on its front, together with the regiment's number, and black plume curling up the right side. Instead of his comfortable field uniform, he wore a single-breasted dark blue frock coat with a stand-up collar; a sword belt carried his straight infantry sword and an Army Colt in a closed-top holster. Dark blue trousers with a one-eighth of an inch stripe of sky blue—the colour of the infantry—and well-shone Jefferson shoes completed the outfit. Not a dress a man would wear when riding on lawful patrol in no-man's-land between the Arkansas and Ouachita rivers.

All Marsden's early training had been concerned with cavalry work, so he knew how to handle a horse during swimming. First he stripped off his clothing and wrapped it carefully in his poncho. Strapping the protected bundle firmly to the saddle, he swung afork his bay horse and eased the animal down the slope. In a well-organised crossing, the horse would have been stripped of its saddle, the latter being ferried across along with the rider's property, but Marsden had to make do as best he could. He knew a horse was a powerful natural swimmer capable of carrying even a fully equipped man on its back for some considerable distance, so the bay would not be impeded or endangered by the saddle.

Not for the first time Marsden found himself blessing his lessons in horsemanship as a boy, for they enabled him to select a fine mount and gave him the confidence and ability to handle the horse in any conditions. Before the horse took three steps down the slope, Marsden knew he would need all his ability. Not only did the slope prove to be deceptively steep, but the earth under the horse's hooves gave little support and began to shift beneath the animal. Feeling the horse's hooves churning and sliding, Marsden used all his skill to keep the bay under control and prevent it from a panic which might bring about a helpless slide down the slope at an ever-increasing speed.

Down went the man and horse, still a cohesive unit, with Marsden guiding his mount as well as he could, keeping it clear of the trees which grew on the slope. It said much for his skill on a horse that he kept the bay from crashing into any of the trees, although he grazed his bare legs on more than one occasion.

An instant too late Marsden made a shocking discovery. The slope fell away in a sheer drop of some twenty feet instead of coming down at an angle to join the river; something which could not be seen from the top of the bank. Man and horse saw the danger at the same moment. Throwing back his weight in the saddle, Marsden hauled back on the reins in a vain attempt to stop the downward slide. Then, seeing he could not halt the slide, he gave the horse its head. With the moving earth carrying it onwards, the horse gathered itself and launched out from the edge of the fall, as if trying to leap across the width of the Ouachita.

For a moment it seemed to Marsden that he and the horse hung suspended in the air, then the law of gravity took hold and they plunged down towards the river. Even as he gave a silent prayer that there might be enough water to break their fall, Marsden kicked his feet from the stirrup irons and thrust himself clear of the horse. Side by side they struck the water and Marsden felt himself going down, the icy chill biting into his naked body as the green-looking river swarmed over him. Deeper and deeper he went, until his feet hit the rocky bed of the river. He bent his knees, then thrust with his feet, propelling himself up towards the surface, Above him, he could see the bay's legs and body, with its reins trailing down. Marsden kicked out with his legs, driving himself forward and chancing a kick from the bay's churning hooves as he reached towards the reins. If the bay once got clear, he could not hope to catch up with it, strong swimmer though he was. The horse had been winded by the fall, but seemed to be recovering. Even as Marsden's hands closed on the slick leather of the reins, he felt the horse starting to swim. Then Marsden's head broke the surface. Desperately he clung to the reins and succeeded in slowing the horse sufficiently for him to swim close. A grab with his freehand caught hold of the bay's mane and he drew himself nearer to the horse.

Marsden found himself on the upstream flank of the horse, but realised that his mount had turned towards the shore they just left. While that was only to be expected, Marsden wanted to cross the river. When a horse swims, only its head remains in plain view, the rest of the body being just below the surface; so Marsden knew that the reins could not be used in steering the animal. He drew himself forward until the saddle partially supported his weight and while in that position managed to knot the reins in such a manner that they would not trail down and entangle the bay's legs. With that done, he slipped back into the water, clinging to the mane with his left hand. Scooping up a handful of water with his right, he splashed the bay's face. Twice he did this before the bay started to swing away from the east bank of the river. Not unnaturally the horse showed some reluctance to leave the land which lay so close to it, but Marsden continued splashing until he had his way and the bay's head pointed west. The current was negligible in the deep hole and so Marsden had no difficulty in keeping the horse pointed straight across the river. He found much the same formation of land at the other side, a sheer wall rising some twenty to thirty feet at the water's edge.

'We'll just have to take a chance, horse,' he said gently and looked around.

As far as he could see, the wall continued for at least half a mile in either direction. The question arose of which way to go. After a moment's thought, Marsden allowed the horse to turn its head downstream. They might as well take advantage of what little current flowed through the deep pool, Marsden decided.

After the first shock of contact, the water was not too cold, but Marsden knew he must get out as soon as possible. With the sun setting, the temperature of the river would drop. Even now, the west bank being in shadow due to the setting sun, he could feel a chill creeping through him and knew it would become far worse as night set in.

Not for almost a quarter of a mile did any sign of relief come and even then it offered small comfort. A crack in the face of the wall led down to a shelf of dry rock which thrust out into the water. Eagerly the bay made for land and Marsden made no attempt to prevent it. Hooves sliding on the wet rock, the horse drew itself up onto solid ground and Marsden gratefully hauled himself out in the bay's wake.

Once ashore, the young officer looked around him and studied his position. The rocky out-crop on which he stood made a shelf some thirty feet long and fifteen wide, and the crack in the wall clearly went all the way to the top. This latter was proved by the animal dung which lay scattered about the rock, although no tracks could show upon such a hard surface. Marsden, a keen hunter, examined the different droppings with interest, recognising wapiti, Kansas whitetail deer and black bear faeces. Only the first and last of the trio interested Marsden at that moment, for a whitetail could climb where no horse might follow. However, Marsden figured he ought to be able to take as sure-footed a horse as the bay anywhere either a bulky bull wapiti or a black bear managed to walk.

On further examination a chilling fact became plain to Marsden. The bear's droppings appeared to be much fresher than he cared to think about. While the black bear might not be as dangerous as a grizzly, meeting one in the confines of that crack would be mighty hectic for a man armed only with a sword and revolver.

Thinking of his weapons recalled to Marsden his state of undress and caused him to unstrap and open the poncho-wrapped bundle. Apparently the poncho's rubberised cloth fulfilled its manufacturer's advertising boasts, for none of the clothing gave any sign of dampness as he took them out. Using his undershirt as a towel, he dried himself swiftly and then dressed. With his weapon belt around his waist, the holster's top opened to allow easy access to the revolver butt, Marsden felt a little more contented. He checked on the bay's saddle, mounted and urged the horse up the steep slope of the crack.

Although the climb proved difficult, and called for skilled co-ordination between rider and mount, it did not bring out the added hazard of the black bear. Once out of the crack, the going proved much easier. Finding a slightly level piece of ground which offered grazing for his horse, Marsden dismounted. Already night had fallen and he decided to care for the horse before continuing with his search for a Confederate unit to which he could surrender.

With the bay grazing and its saddle-blanket hung out to dry, Marsden found himself with nothing to do but think; and with the thoughts came back misery. Crossing the Ouachita had been the end of any chance to withdraw from his plan. Up to then a fast ride would still have carried him back to safety and his absence could be put down to visiting Betty Mayhew in Little Rock. He knew he could rely on her to agree that he had been with her the whole time. At most Stedloe would have awarded his errant shavetail with a week of Officer of the Day duties. However, the time when Marsden could return had now passed. Nor, when he thought of the effects of Castle and Silverman's scheme, could Marsden turn back even if he knew for certain he would not be punished in any way for his absence.

The feeling of misery drove Marsden to forget his plan to stay in the small clearing until dawn. He checked the saddle-blanket and found it to be dry enough for use. So he saddled the bay, mounted and rode off into the darkness. Holding his bay to a steady walk, he topped the west bank of the Ouachita and set off towards the rolling mountains.

Two hours went by without any sign of human beings. Marsden kept his horse at a steady walk and used his eyes. Just as he was thinking that it might be as well to halt for the night, he caught a glimpse of something red in the blackness to his right. Halting his horse, he turned his gaze in the direction but saw nothing. He wondered if his eyes might be playing tricks on him, but backing his horse a few steps brought the red glow into sight once more. A fire glowed among trees about half a mile or more away. From its appearance, Marsden concluded that its makers had no wish to be located. That in itself meant little. No troops on active service would willingly give away their position. However, it could mean danger. A raiding band of Union cavalry were likely to take precautions with their fires and Marsden knew he must not ride blindly. Capture by the Union now meant certain and immediate death. No patrol raiding in enemy territory would burden itself with a deserter who clearly intended to search out and hand himself over to the enemy.

Only by winding about and keeping his eyes fixed on the partially hidden glow of the fire did Marsden manage to head in the required direction. At last he decided he could chance going no closer on his horse. Still he could not see what manner of people used the camp and so intended to make his scout on foot. Fortunately for him, the wind blew from behind him and towards the camp. There was no chance of his horse getting wind of any mounts the campers might have, and betraying Marsden's presence by whinnying a greeting to its kind.

After securing the bay to a tree, Marsden moved forward on foot. Anybody in that area of the Ouachita Mountains would most likely be a belligerent from one side or the other. Maybe Marsden would have sufficient luck to come into contact with a Confederate unit commanded by a man who would see the full import of his news and waste no time in directing him to the commanding general, or somebody who could make arrangements to halt Castle and Silverman's scheme.

Moving through darkened, wooded country in silence was no time for idle thought. Every instinct must be directed to the silent placing of feet and ensuring that nothing caught or rattled against the surrounding trees and bushes. Marsden threw off his thoughts and concentrated. From odd glimpses gained during his advance, Marsden decided that the camp must be set in a fair-sized clearing surrounded by thick bushes; an almost ideal location in that it offered good cover to the occupants and almost hid their fire from sight.

On silent feet Marsden eased closer to the camp, coming to a halt at the side of a large bush. Gently he parted a couple of branches and peered through the gap. At one side of the clearing stood a couple of lines of good horses, yet they had no guard watching them. A couple of bell tents, and a trio of hospital pattern tents were scattered about the clearing in a most unmilitary manner. Those two sights gave Marsden a warning that he must not fall into the hands of the people in the camp, even before he saw the occupants.

CHAPTER TWO

DAVID O. DODD'S SISTER

Crouching in his position behind the bush, Marsden turned his eyes to the occupants of the camp as they gathered about the fire. Not one of the party wore a uniform of any kind—unless he counted the occasional Union overcoat or tunic. In 1864, even with the U.S. Navy's blockade slowly strangling the South, the Confederate Army still kept its men in some semblance of uniform. The ten or so men around the fire wore head-dress ranging from coonskin caps to a good quality Burnside officer's hat, and sported civilian clothing as diverse as the head-wear. Only one thing had they in common, every man wore a pair of revolvers at his waist. None of them had shaved and all looked mean, cruel, vicious in the light of the flames. Marsden ignored the single woman at the fire, giving her hardly more than a single glance and discarding her as one of the usual type of camp-follower to be found with such a band.

'Bushwhackers!' he mused. 'I'd best get the hell out of here.'

During the War many bands of irregulars fought on both sides; if fought was the correct term for their activities. Unattached to any formal military organisation, the bush-whackers of the South and the Red-Legs of the Union looted and raided in the name of patriotism. Despised by the formal forces of the North and South, the various bands of irregulars ranged the strife-torn land, avoiding the real fighting. Even if Marsden knew which side claimed the party's so-called allegiance, he must not fall into their hands.

Even as the thought came to Marsden's head and he started to turn away, he heard the startled chatter of a disturbed bird. The soldier brought his head around towards the sound and saw a dark, human shape looming towards him. With no time to draw a weapon, Marsden shot out his fist, driving the gauntlet-covered knuckles full into his attacker's face. Although he changed the attacker's advance to a hurried retreat, Marsden knew he was not out of danger. He sensed rather than saw the second man coming in from the rear with arms widespread to grab him. Back shot Marsden's left arm, propelling the elbow savagely into the chest of the second attacker, bringing a gasping croak of pain and sending him stumbling away.

Surprised yells rose from the camp, but Marsden ignored the sounds. Just as he prepared to plunge away into the trees and make a dash for freedom, he saw yet a third bearded shape materialise close at hand. The fire's light glinted momentarily from the butt-plate of the carbine held by the third man as it swung up and drove down again. Too late Marsden tried to avoid the blow. His foot slipped and he felt the carbine's butt contact with the side of his hat. The force of the blow sent Marsden sprawling through the bushes and into the camp clearing where he landed on his knees. Snarling, gibbering almost in his rage, the first attacker crashed forward through the bushes after Marsden and launched a kick at the officer's head. Although Marsden tried to avoid the lashing boot, he only partially succeeded. He managed to move himself sufficiently far forward that his head missed the impact of the kick, but took it in his ribs instead. Pain knifed through Marsden and he pitched over, rolling on the ground.

Men sprang forward, catching Marsden by the arms and dragging him to his feet. Snarling curses through blood-dripping lips, the first attacker prepared to resume his assault.

'Let me at him!' screeched the man. 'I want to see his blood.'

'Now jest you hold it up there!' growled a commanding voice, and at its sound the man drew back.

Dazedly Marsden turned to look at the speaker. It figured, the big, burly man wearing the Burnside hat and good-quality clothing was sure to be the leader of the bushwhacker band. Swaggering forward, the man jerked a contemptuous thumb at Marsden and turned to the carbine-armed attacker who slouched forward on moccasin-clad feet.

'Done saw him sneaking down on the camp,' the man said without waiting for the obvious question. 'Me'n the boys moved in on him. Done sent Milky to collect his hoss, Ashley.'

A sick, sinking feeling hit Marsden as he heard the name. While not as famous, or notorious, as Bloody Bill Anderson, George Todd or William Clarke Quantrill—possibly due to their presence in a more publicised section of the fighting area—Wick Ashley's reputation was known to people in Arkansas. It was not a reputation to hearten a man unfortunate enough to fall into Ashley's hands.

'Drag him closer to the fire so's we can see what we got, boys,' Ashley ordered.

'Wonder if there's more of 'em about?' asked the sentry, resting his Perry carbine on the crook of his arm.

'You'd best go see, Thad,' suggested Ashley.

'Reckon I had at that,' agreed the man and faded off into the bushes.

Walking back to where two of his men stood supporting and restraining Marsden by the fire, Ashley looked the young soldier over as a farmer might study a prize bull.

'Fancy sword, cost good money,' Ashley grunted and stepped forward to open Marsden's holster. 'New Army Colt too.' He reached out to feel the material of the uniform, then examine the epaulets. 'That's good broadcloth, and I'll swan if these doo-hickey ain't solid gold. Boots's hand-made too. Yes sir, boys, I reckon we caught us a good one there. I'll just bet his folks'll pay up without asking twice to get him back. Might even have enough cash-money back at his camp to have it done his-self and save time.'

Among their other nefarious acts the irregulars ran a profitable side-line in offering such prisoners as they felt wealthy enough a chance to pay ransom for their freedom. Many of the bands had contacts on the enemy side who could notify the prisoner's friends or relations and arrange for the delivery of the ransom money. It seemed that Ashley possessed such a contact, for he showed complete confidence and did not need to think about disposing of his prisoner.

Cohesive thought returned to Marsden, forcing him to stand still instead of struggling against the restraining hands while his pockets were emptied. A snap of fingers and cold scowl caused one of the searchers to pass Marsden's well-filled wallet to Ashley. Looking into the wallet, Ashley ran an appreciative finger across the paper money it held. Marsden tried to struggle as a stocky, bearded tough hauled out his father's watch from under the tunic, but the men holding him tightened their grip and kept him immobile.

'Allus wanted a gold watch,' grinned the man and turned to Ashley. 'It's my turn to take first pick at his gear.'

'Have I argued?' inquired Ashley and the man held the watch to an ear before stuffing it away into his pocket. Ashley swung his attention back to Marsden. 'How's about it, soldier boy. You got anybody'd pay to get you back safe and well?'

'I—I've got to be taken to a Confederate unit,' Marsden answered.

'We're a Confederate unit, boy,' scoffed Ashley.

'I mean regulars.'

'Now ain't we good enough to suit you?' sneered the bushwhacker leader.

'I tell you, man, it's imperative that I reach a regular Confederate Army unit without delay.'

'Sure you do. You're one of their smartest officers. All the rebs wear these blue uniforms nowadays.'

A guffaw of laughter rose from among the men, but the girl turned from where she had been stirring stew in a pot at the fire.

'He might be a Confederate spy, Ashley,' she said, coming towards her leader.

For the first time Marsden gave his attention to the girl, for her voice came as a surprise. She did not speak in the coarse, strident tones of the usual cheap harridan one found among the irregular camp-followers. Nor did she have the tone of a rich, well-bred Southern belle. Her voice came somewhere between the two, like the daughters of small businessmen, storekeepers and the like Marsden met in the various Arkansas towns. The girl was bare-headed, her reddish brown hair hanging to just above her shoulders and curling out at the ends, showing signs of care not often seen among camp-followers. While not beautiful, she had an attractive face, one that might have looked merry and friendly in normal times but now had tight lips and cold, hostile brown eyes. The face was tanned by the elements, but showed no signs of being degraded by a life of debauchery.

She stood about five foot six and the clothes she wore tended to reveal rather than hide her figure. A tartan man's shirt, a couple of sizes too large for her, still showed that she possessed a mature figure, while the levis pants she wore hinted at the rich curves and shapely legs underneath. High-heeled riding boots almost completed the picture. No cheap, flashy jewellery spoiled her healthy, wholesome appearance, but a Tranter revolver was thrust into the left side of her waist band, its butt pointing inwards. Marsden formed an impression that the gun might be much more than a decoration.

Clearly Ashley respected the girl's opinion, for he turned towards her.

'Reckon he might, Jill?'

'He's riding alone,' answered the girl. 'Or we'd have heard from Thad by this time if there was more of them about.'

'You could be right, gal,' purred Ashley and turned to Marsden. 'Are you a spy, feller?'

Marsden did not reply immediately, wanting time to think out his words. The man who had taken Marsden's watch stepped forward and drove his fist savagely into the young officer's belly, knifing the breath from his lungs and causing him to try to double over.

'You answer up when Ashley asks you something, boy!' the man warned.

'Keep back and leave him a chance!' snapped the girl called Jill. 'He can't talk if you keep hitting him.'

'Yeah?' began the man sullenly. 'Well——'

'You pay Jill mind, Whit!' barked Ashley. 'Stand back there and leave me do the questioning.' Ignoring his man, Ashley looked to where Marsden, still firmly held, tried to rub the pain out of his stomach. 'How about it, boy. Are you a spy?'

'You—you might say that,' agreed Marsden hopefully.

His hope went crashing to the ground.

'Well, if you are,' Ashley grinned, 'I'll bet the Yankee Army'd pay right well to lay hands on you.'

Marsden could have groaned at his mistake. The War meant only profit to men like Ashley, they were not moved by patriotic feelings. Mentioning that he might be a spy had been a wrong move, as Marsden now realised. It would have taken some time for Ashley's agent to make contact with the Zouaves and start the negotiations for the ransom and during that time a chance of escape could present itself. Far less time would be needed to contact any Union outfit with the view of selling a Confederate spy. The agent would not even need to locate a specific unit as in the case of a legitimate captive; in fact, if Marsden judged correctly, the agent probably knew exactly the right person to see when offering a prime piece of loot for sale.

'If he is a spy——' the girl put in, just a hint of worry creeping through her voice.

'The Yankees'll pay well enough to have him delivered,' interrupted Ashley. 'Or if they don't—well, I reckon his gear'll bring in something. He sure won't be needing it again.'

A bellow of laughter greeted the remark, but Marsden noticed that the girl did not join in with her companions. Standing slightly behind the men, her eyes met Marsden's and an expression of doubt crept on to her face. The arrival of the man with Marsden's horse brought an end to further talk. A swarm of bushwhackers descended on the bay, eager hands grabbing out at the saddle-bags in search of loot. However the band retained some discipline, for the men holding Marsden did not relax their hold and a watchful hard-case with a rifle stood to one side ready to end any escape-bid.

After watching that nothing of real value escaped him, Ashley swung towards the men holding Marsden and snapped, 'Clamp on those leg-irons in the Sibley and leave him safe.'

The men holding Marsden knew their work and had sufficient strength to enforce their will on him. Swiftly they dragged him into the nearest Sibley tent, slung him to the ground and clamped on the leg-irons before he could make a move to prevent it. A pair of handcuffs followed, securing his wrists, the whole being coupled together by a chain long enough to allow him to sit up, but not stand erect. Marsden knew that kind of restraint, having seen it used on military prisoners, and was aware of the futility of trying to escape.

After securing Marsden, the men left the tent and he lay on the bare ground, as helpless as a chicken. Outside the flames leapt and flickered, showing against the tent's walls.

Plates and cups rattled, talk and laughter reached Marsden's ears and he knew the men must be at their evening meal.

Time dragged by and at last the tent's flap raised. The girl entered, a plate of soup and mug of coffee in her hands. However, before coming within reach of Marsden's arms, she laid down the mug, took out her revolver and placed it in the doorway. Not until that had been completed did she advance and kneel by Marsden's side. Deftly she helped him into a sitting position and laid the plate on his lap.

'You'll have to make do with just a spoon, and there's no bread,' she told him. 'It's bear stew, that's all the meat we have. Thad downed a bear back on the bank of the Ouachita this afternoon.'

'Look, Miss, you have to believe me,' Marsden said in a low voice. 'It's vital that I should reach a Confederate outfit. The lives of thousands of people depend on it.'

'Are you a spy?'

For a moment Marsden thought of lying, although his upbringing and training revolted at the idea. He knew he could not make a lie that sounded like the truth and so shook his head.

'No. At least, not in the way you mean.'

'Best eat that food while it's still warm,' Jill said, her voice cold.

'You have to believe me——' groaned Marsden.

'Believe you?' spat out the girl. 'Why should I believe anything you say? You're a Yankee and I'm David O. Dodd's sister.'

Marsden knew the name and felt sick despair rising in him, for he knew he could expect little sympathy from the sister of a man—a mere boy of seventeen—whom the Union Army executed as a spy shortly after their arrival in Little Rock. However, he determined to try.

'I'm no spy——'

'Nor was my brother. He was just a fool kid who thought he was a man. The information he gathered had no importance and he had no way of passing it to our troops even if it was important.'

'He had maps of our installations, the supply park——'

'I could expect a Yankee to excuse his kind,' Jill snapped, and started to rise.

'Listen to me, Miss Dodd!' Marsden put in, almost spilling

the plate of stew as he tried to reach out and catch her arm. 'Please listen!'

The girl had started to draw back, but something in Marsden's voice halted her and turned her eyes from the Tranter at the tent's door to his face once more.

'I'll listen, but I'm not saying I'll believe a word of it.'

'I'm not denying that I'm a Union officer and that I'm loyal to the North. But I learned something important and I must tell it to a Confederate Army officer.'

'What did you learn?' asked the girl.

'Two members of my regiment have a——'

Suddenly the girl swung her head towards the door, turned back to Marsden and said, 'You start eating, mister.'

Before Marsden could make a reply, the tent's flap lifted and Ashley peered in suspiciously.

'You're taking long enough, Jill,' he said.

'Maybe you'd like to feed him,' the girl answered.

'What was you talking about?'

'Feller reckons he has something real important to tell, something that might save a lot of our folks.'

'Has, huh?' grunted Ashley. 'What is it, Yankee?'

Marsden thought fast and knew that he must not speak of his knowledge to the bushwhacker. Not even the dreadful meaning of the scheme would change Ashley's attitude and knowing of it would give the bushwhacker something of saleable value. Maybe Ashley could evaluate the true worth, offered in the right place of Marsden's knowledge. Colonel Stedloe might pay well to have word of the scheme suppressed until after its successful completion and would not want too close an investigation into Marsden's desertion. No, it would never do to let Ashley learn what brought him over the Ouachita.

'Come on, mister,' the girl said. 'Tell us about it.'

'Well—It's—I——' Marsden forced himself to stutter and fumble like a man caught unaware or detected in a lie. 'It's real important.'

'I just bet it is,' boomed Ashley. 'So important that you reckoned Jill might set you free to slip away.'

'You lousy, stinking *Yankee*!' Jill spat out, catching up the coffee mug and hurling its contents into Marsden's face.

While not boiling, the coffee proved hot enough to make Marsden rear up and tip over backwards. The plate of stew tipped from his knees and fell to the ground as he went. Jill turned and stormed out of the tent, scooping up her Tranter in passing and without a backward glance.

Bending down, a grinning Ashley helped Marsden sit up. 'You shouldn't've tried that, soldier-boy. Jill's a smart gal, but she could fall for a good-looking feller like you. Only she'd blow your head off as soon as look at you for wearing a Yankee uniform. Like to tell me what *did* bring you over here?'

'I'm on a scouting mission,' answered Marsden, trying a bluff. It missed by a good country mile.

'In full dress and alone?' grinned Ashley. 'Naw, I don't reckon so. You're on something important, just like you told Jill.'

'Maybe I just got tired of fighting and want to surrender.'

'Can't say as I go a lot on that, boy.'

'You could find out by handing me over to the Confederate Army. After all, you are fighting on their side.'

'Sure I am,' replied Ashley. 'Only I'm fighting for me. I don't give a damn whether they free the slaves or keep 'em as they are. Made good money before the War both running slaves to the North and setting 'em free, and sending 'em back to their owners for the reward. Only reason I support the South's so that if they win I'll be able to go on making money the old way.'

'How do your men feel about that?'

''Bout the same as me. They'd rather ride with me and make money than be in some army outfit.'

'And Jill Dodd?'

A cold, warning scowl came to Ashley's face. 'Jill hates you Yankees for what you did to her brother. If some reb regiment'd have her, she'd be wearing a grey uniform and fighting. Only they won't have a woman, so Jill rides with my outfit. She might have listened to you just now, but she won't any more. Anyways, I'm fetching Thad in and putting him to guard you. Thad's a mountain man, mighty sharp-eared, and he'll be told not to let anybody talk to you.'

It seemed that Ashley did not entirely trust his female member. Anyway, he had no intention of allowing her to make further private conversation with his prisoner.

'How about some food?' asked Marsden.

'Jill's the cook, she might be mean enough to throw away

what's left of the stew rather than have a Yankee eat it,' Ashley answered. 'Now why don't you tell me what brought you across the Ouachita. I'm going to learn one way or another when we get you back to our main camp, it'll be easier on your hide to talk friendly.'

'I'm just a deserter,' Marsden insisted.

Coming erect, Ashley shrugged. 'It's your hide, boy. Only Thad's a mighty persuasive feller when he has to be. Think on it. Don't rush, you got all night.'

CHAPTER THREE

DEATH OF A BUSHWHACKER

Although he doubted if he would, Marsden slept at least some of the night. One of the bushwhackers brought him another plate of stew and mug of coffee soon after Ashley left, but the girl did not make another appearance. With the meal finished, Marsden was left to himself although the black silhouette on the tent's wall showed that Thad stood guard outside. Sheer exhaustion brought sleep to him at last, even though his chains forced him to adopt an uncomfortable position.

Dawn's grey light showed through the tent as Marsden opened his eyes. Outside, from what he could hear, the bushwhackers were awake and preparing to break camp. Voices and laughter reached his ears. Then the tent shook violently and began to collapse. The mass of canvas and central support pole came clattering down on him and he started to struggle, as well as he could in the chains, to extricate himself. Something round and hard prodded into his side, sending a wave of pain through him.

'Come on, Yankee!' whooped a voice. 'Wriggle harder.'

Marsden forced himself to lie still rather than give more cause for amusement to the men around the fallen tent. Outside, some half a dozen bushwhackers, including the man who felt Marsden's hard fist the previous night, gathered around. Raising his rifle, the man thrust it down hard at the mound which marked Marsden's position.

'Wriggle, Yankee!' whooped the man, as well as he could through his swollen lips. Again he thrust the rifle's muzzle down. 'Come on, make a move to get——'

Suddenly the man felt a violent push which sent him staggering away from the tent. Jill Dodd, flush-faced and angry, glared at the others of the taunting group and pointed down with a quivering finger.

'Get that tent pulled off him!' she snapped.

'We was only funning, Jill gal,' answered one of the men.

'Uncover him!'

'He's only a Yankee!' objected the man Jill pushed.

'He's a human being!' the girl answered hotly. 'And he's going to be treated like one.'

'There's some'd say you was going soft on that Yankee,' stated the man. 'Or maybe that you're forgetting what they did to your brother.'

'I'm not forgetting anything!' Jill blazed back, the Tranter sliding into her hand. 'If you want, I'll kill him right now. But if not, he'll be treated like a human being and not humiliated.'

Slowly one of the men bent down, gripped the canvas and started to draw it from Marsden. Some of the others helped, uncovering the young lieutenant. Jill Dodd had a unique standing among Ashley's bushwhacker band. There had been other women who followed Ashley, but they were no more than cheap prostitutes who found making a living impossible due to the War and came to earn their keep with their bodies. Jill rode as a serving member of the band. Only once, soon after she joined them, had an attempt been made to treat her as a normal camp-follower. The man who made the attempt died with a .36 Tranter ball in his belly and the remainder of the band took the hint. There were no further attempts on Jill's virtue. In the six months or so that she rode with the band, she proved herself able to handle a horse and shoot with the best of them and gained Ashley's confidence until he came to regard her as his second-in-command. None of the men around the tent doubted that Jill would shoot their prisoner, or that she meant to enforce her orders to them in the same manner if they disobeyed.

Always a late riser, Ashley appeared at the door of his tent and glowered across the camp.

'What's all the fuss?' he bellowed. 'Why in hell haven't you started to break camp?'

Thad opened his mouth to answer, but the words did not come. Instead the man stared past his leader, made as if to raise his Perry carbine from the crook of his arm, thought better of it and stood still. His actions brought every eye towards the two uniformed figures who stepped from among the bushes and advanced towards the centre of the camp.

Clearly the new arrivals belonged to some crack Confederate regiment, for their uniforms, though travel-stained, were of excellent material and cut. The taller of the pair, a gangling bean-pole who topped the six-foot mark and had a miserable, careworn face, wore the usual kepi, cadet grey tunic—with a prominent Adam's apple showing through its stand-up collar—yellow-striped cavalry breeches tucked neatly into high-legged Jefferson boots. Instead of the usual weapon belt, he wore one of brown leather, broader and lower on the hips than normal, with a pair of walnut-butted 1860 Army Colts in open-topped holsters, the holster bottoms secured to his legs by thongs. From the triple bars and arc of silk, denoting rank of sergeant-major, on his sleeves, that man must have more to his make-up than showed in his face and general manner.

Turning his eyes from the sergeant-major to the second soldier, Marsden bit down an exclamation of surprise and hope.

On the face of it, the second man did not seem to be worthy of Marsden's interest. Even the term 'man' might be thought an over-statement when applied to a male person not long gone eighteen, and not large-grown for his age. Even with a white Confederate version of the Burnside hat —without one side turned up and devoid of a plume—on his dusty blond-haired head, the second man clearly stood no more than five foot six. However, his shoulders had a width that hinted at strength and tapered down to a slim waist. Cool grey eyes looked from a tanned, handsome, intelligent young face, yet he did not give the impression of a swaggering half-pint who used his rank and social position to enforce his will on others. The uniform he wore set off his build, although it did not entirely conform with the Confederate Army's *Manual of Dress Regulations*. While the jacket had a stand-up collar, bearing the triple half-inch-wide, three-inch-long strips of gold braid of a captain, its wearer replaced the official black silk cravat with a tight rolled scarlet bandana. The double-breasted jacket bore the necessary double braid rank insignia on its sleeves and double row of seven buttons, but it ended at the waist, being without the prescribed 'skirt extending to halfway between hip and knee,' His riding breeches and boots had clearly been made to measure. Like his sergeant-major, the young captain wore a brown leather weapon belt, however, the two white handled Army Colts rode butt forward in their open-topped holsters and not so low hanging as the other man's.

'Release that man,' ordered the small captain, the drawl in his voice confirming Marsden's thoughts of his place of origin even without the lieutenant needing a second look at the hat badge—a five-pointed star in a circle.

'He's our prisoner,' Ashley replied, darting looks around him and seeing only the silent woods.

'He's an officer of the Union Army,' stated the captain. 'I'll take him out of your hands.'

Pleasure at his rescue was mingled with doubt and concern as Marsden turned his head in an effort to see what support the two soldiers had to enforce their demands. He saw nothing but the trees and bushes which surrounded the clearing. Surely the two men had not been fools enough to come unsupported?

Ashley seemed to think so. After another quick glance around, he started to raise a big right hand, meaning to grip the front of the small captain's non-regulation tunic.

'Just who do you reckon you are, you short——' Ashley began.

Out and up stabbed the captain's left hand in a move almost faster than the eye could follow. He caught Ashley's thumb neatly, his own thumb resting on the trapped member's second joint and fingers curling around, using leverage and counteracting pressure in a manner which threatened to snap the gripped bones. On securing his hold, the captain turned Ashley's palm upwards and at the same time raised the trapped hand. In an attempt to relieve the extreme pain caused by the hold, Ashley allowed his hand to bend inwards and twisted so he stood with his back to his captor. Moving a pace to the rear, but retaining his hold on the thumb, the captain raised his right leg, placed his foot against Ashley's rump and, releasing his grip, pushed hard. Ashley shot forward, stumbled, and went to his knees, mouthing a mixture of curses and orders to his men.

'Hold it right there!' ordered the sergeant-major, backing his words with a Colt in both hands.

The angry curses which rose from the bushwhackers died again. So interested had they been in watching Ashley's abortive attack on the captain that none saw the gangling non-com produce his weapons. However, all took in the sight of the lined Colts and discarded any ideas that might be forming on the matter of taking reprisals against the rash intruders.

Twisting around, still on his knees, Ashley studied the situation. First to strike his notice was that the sergeant-major's full attention was fixed on his men. Next he observed that the captain had not as yet drawn his weapons.

'Which of you's Ashley?' asked the captain.

Already Ashley had one hand on the butt of his fancy Remington revolver. From the way he saw it, the two soldiers had made a deadly error in tactics. The moment that bean-pole non-com tried to turn his guns towards Ashley, the rest of the band would pump him. With a holstered gun, the captain could not draw lift, aim and shoot before being swamped under. Satisfied on that point, Ashley jerked out his Remington and started to raise the gun shoulder high so he could take aim.

Instantly, even as Ashley started to pull his gun, the captain moved. Faster than the eye could follow, the left hand flashed across and closed upon the curved white grip of the right-side Colt. The moment the gun came clear of leather, its user's forefinger entered the trigger-guard and already his thumb drew back the hammer. Nor did he take the time to lift the Colt shoulder high. His legs moved, halted to place him squarely facing Ashley, the knees slightly bent. Elbow almost touching his belt buckle, Colt no more than waist high, the captain fired his first shot. From first movement of the hand to crash of the shot took less than a second, but at the end of that time Ashley died with a .44 bullet in his head.

So swift had been the small captain's action that it took everybody in the clearing—with the possible exception of the lean sergeant-major—completely by surprise. Not for several years would Ned Buntline and his fellow-writers publicise the speed with which some Western men could draw and shoot a gun. At the start of the War, Arkansas was so far past the frontier days that such superlative skill with weapons ceased to be a necessity of life and none of the bushwhackers knew just how fast and deadly a man raised in the West could be. Even Marsden, reared as he had been in New Mexico, felt surprised, for such speed and ability was the exception rather than the rule.

On the shot, almost before Ashley's body hit the ground, grey-clad soldiers dressed in the manner of the sergeant-major stepped from cover all around the camp. The guns held by the newcomers quelled any hope the bushwhackers might had had for avenging their leader's death.

Holstering his Colt, the captain pointed to Marsden and said, 'Release him!'

The words jolted one of the bushwhackers into action. Taking out the necessary keys, he walked to Marsden's side and unlocked the handcuffs, then removed the leg-irons. Slowly and stiffly, Marsden came to his feet. He stood working his arms and legs to get the stiffness out of them, touched his sore ribs and then rubbed his aching belly. All the time, he studied the bushwhackers. Finding the man he wanted, Marsden strolled over and held out his right hand.

'I'll have it back,' he said.

'Sure, mister,' gulped the man and reached for his inside pocket to take out Marsden's watch.

Taking the watch, Marsden slipped it back into its usual place. Then his left hand bunched into a fist and shot forward to drive into the man's stomach. Marsden struck hard, his fist sinking into the man's belly, doubling him over in a croaking mass of pain and dropping him to his knees.

'That's enough, mister!' barked the captain. 'Take charge of the prisoner, Mr. Blaze.'

A freckle-faced, pugnaciously handsome young lieutenant, his hat shoved back to show curly, unruly fiery-red hair, moved forward. While Mr. Blaze understood Marsden's feelings, and could guess that the Yankee lieutenant had been rough-handled by the bushwhackers, he also knew that the irregulars must be given no chance of grabbing a hostage.

'My apologies, sir,' Marsden said, stepping away from the bushwhackers and turning to the captain. 'I was just exchanging gifts.'

'Likely, mister,' the captain answered dryly. 'Take two men, Red, go with the lieutenant and collect all his gear.'

'Yo!' answered the redhead and grinned at Marsden. 'Just point it out and we'll get it back for you.'

'That jasper there's wearing my weapon belt, most likely

has my Colt in the holster, but I don't see my sword anywhere.'

'Now don't you worry none about *them,*' smiled the redhead, but it was a cheery smile not a malicious leer. 'We'll take care of them for you.'

Marsden nodded. For the moment he had almost forgotten that he was now a prisoner of war. 'I expect so,' he said. 'Ashley there had my wallet.'

After seeing Marsden started on his task of recovering the property looted from him, the captain gave his attention to the bushwhackers. Or rather Jill Dodd brought his attention to them by stepping forward and speaking.

'What about us?' she asked. 'Why have you come here?'

A momentary flicker of surprise crossed the captain's face as he heard Jill speak, but he made no comment about such a girl's presence among the bushwhackers.

'You all know that after Quantrill's raid on Lawrence, Kansas, the Confederate and Federal Governments outlawed unofficial raiding bands?' he said.

'General Chetley never objected before,' Jill pointed out.

'General Chetley isn't in command any longer. By order of General Jackson Baines Hardin, all irregular groups are to disband or join the regular forces and take service in the Army of the Confederate States.'

'And if we don't?' snapped Jill.

'Also by order of General Hardin, any group continuing to stay in operation after warning by an officer of the Confederate Army will be treated as hostile and shot on sight.'

'Damn it to hell!' Jill shouted. 'We're fighting the Yankees too. Why only two weeks back we were over the Ouachita raiding their outposts.'

'Sure,' agreed the captain, his voice suddenly cold and grim. 'You hit a couple of outposts and stirred up an area into which one of our patrols went to destroy an important supply depot. The Texas Light Cavalry lost some good men, and missed their chance through you. That's why I've been out with a patrol looking for Ashley.'

'We didn't know,' Jill gasped.

'And most likely wouldn't have cared either,' growled the captain. 'I found your main camp, burned it down.'

'You did *what*?' hissed the girl.

'That's right, I burned it down. I found evidence there

that Ashley had been trafficking in prisoners of war—and I also found property belonging to a group of Southern sympathisers who were attacked and robbed.'

A look of shock came to Jill's face at the words. 'That must have been when Ashley sent Thad, myself and six of the men on a scouting mission. I didn't know about the attack on our people. But I can't believe he would do such a thing.'

'I can show you evidence,' the captain told her. 'There were four in the party killed. Two more badly wounded and the only woman wished that she had been killed.'

'Is that why you shot Ashley?'

'I shot him to prevent him killing me, but knowing he was Ashley doesn't make me feel any worse. Now, ma'am, I'll get on with my business,' said the captain, and he turned his attention to the watching bushwhackers. 'All right, you have your choice, enlist in the army, or return to your homes.'

'By cracky, cap'n,' Thad said, stepping forward, 'fellers's can move as neat as your boy're worth siding. I'll come with you, if I can. Maybe you wouldn't've found it so easy to get our look-out happen I'd been there instead of guarding the Yankee soldier-boy.'

'Kiowa there'd've took you like the rest, *hombre*,' remarked the sergeant-major, indicating a tall lean, Indian-dark sergeant, and speaking as if discussing the crack of doom.

'Drop it, Billy Jack,' ordered the captain. 'You'll ride with us when we leave, soldier. Any more of you?'

Feet scuffled and glances were exchanged, but none of the other bushwhacker males offered to give up their free life for the discipline and danger of fighting in a formal outfit.

'I'll go with you,' Jill announced.

'We've no place for a woman, ma'am,' smiled the captain. 'If I was you, I'd go back home.'

'*Home?*' Jill spat the word out as if it tasted bitter as bile. 'My home is in Little Rock.'

'Then come with me to Hope and I'll find you accommodation.'

'Like hell! I'll make out on my own, thank you very much.'

With that Jill turned and stamped angrily away. The captain watched her go, gave a sad shake of his head and swung back to the men.

'Collect your horses and gear, all of you!' he barked. 'Remember this. If I see any of you in a bushwhacker band again, I'll order my men to shoot.'

Turning, the captain walked over to where Marsden stood with Red Blaze. One of the bushwhackers looked at the sergeant-major and asked:

'Reckon he'd do it?'

'Mister,' answered the lean non-com. 'When Cap'n Fog says a thing, you'd best believe him, 'cause he sure as hell aims to do it.'

'Is he *the* Cap'n Dusty Fog?' breathed the bushwhacker almost reverently.

'There's not two of 'em,' admitted Sergeant-major Billy Jack miserably. 'And you'd best get moving afore he decides to take you all in and find out who rode with Ashley when them Southern folks was killed.'

'Captain Fog?' Marsden gasped, feeling foolish at repeating the small Texan's introduction, but unable to think of anything more adequate to say. 'This is a pleasure and an honour, sir.'

It was also, although Marsden did not mention the fact, the best piece of luck to come his way since he first heard of Castle and Silverman's plan.

Over the past year Captain Dustine Edward Marsden Fog's name had risen to prominence, until many folk ranked him equal to the great Colonel John Singleton Mosby as a fighting cavalry leader. Some even claimed that Dusty excelled Mosby in the art of light cavalry raiding. To the Union Army, Dusty Fog's name spelled serious trouble. At the head of his troop of the Texas Light Cavalry, he struck like lightning, caused havoc like a Texas twister, and disappeared like sun-melted snow only leaving more damage in his wake. Although only eighteen years old, Dusty had caused more than one Union veteran cavalry commander to wonder whether he knew his trade after all. Yet not only did Dusty Fog's name stand high as a raider, he was also a chivalrous enemy and no man need fear falling into his hands.

However, the latter consideration did not entirely account for Marsden's relief and pleasure at discovering his rescuer's identity.

'You'd better explain how a Union infantry lieutenant comes to be on this side of the Ouachita. Or did they take you on the other bank?'

Marsden smiled. No officer on fighting service would wear dress uniform, a point Dusty appeared to have noted already.

'I crossed the river to find you, sir,' Marsden explained. 'Well, not you exactly, but a Confederate outfit, preferably one from Texas.'

'You'd best explain that, mister,' Dusty said. 'Only leave it until we're on the move. I don't think there'll be any more trouble from this bunch. And I want to get back to camp as soon as I can.'

Ten minutes later the soldiers departed and the bushwhackers gathered in a disconsolate bunch.

'What do we do now?' asked one man.

Nobody appeared to have any suggestions until Jill moved forward. 'Bury Ashley, then break camp,' she ordered. 'We'll strike west and across the Texas line until this blows over. Then we'll start raiding again. Nobody's going to stop me fighting the Yankees.'

CHAPTER FOUR

MARSDEN'S INFORMATION

On leaving the bushwhackers' camp, Dusty and his troop escorted Marsden to the town of Hope by the shortest possible route. During the ride Marsden managed to convince Dusty of the importance of his business without going into details of Castle and Silverman's scheme. For his part, Dusty studied Marsden and assessed the other's character, deciding that such a man would not lightly become a deserter and traitor. So Dusty accepted the other's word and promised an immediate interview with General Ole Devil Hardin on their arrival at the regiment's headquarters.

The Texas Light Cavalry were encamped around the large, stately home of a wealthy Union supporter who fled when the flames of war grew in Arkansas. While riding through the smart, tented lines, Marsden found himself studying the excellent dress, equipment and spirits of the men. All appeared to be well-dressed and armed, also to be better fed than their Union opposites beyond the Ouachita. A party of men who passed Dusty's troop, each leading a packhorse loaded with beer and wapiti meat, gave Marsden an indication of the way the Texans fed. Southwest Arkansas might not be rugged frontier any more, but it still held vast herds of game; and should these fail the resources of Texas lay close at hand. Naturally the Confederate forces in Arkansas lived well.

Another reason for the well-being became apparent with a little thought. The Texas Light Cavalry might be a volunteer regiment, raised and financed by wealthy Texans, but its officers had seen combat before the War. A few served in the Texas War of Independence in 1836, others during the Mexican War of 1842, and most against either Indians, *Comancheros* or other Mexican bandits. So the officers possessed *practical* knowledge of fighting that few Easternbred volunteers had had a chance to gain. The rank and file of the regiment consisted of men who could ride and shoot almost as soon as they could walk, were trained and skilled in all the arts of cavalry warfare.

'Take over, Cousin Red,' Dusty told his second-in-command on their arrival at the horse lines. 'Unless you'd rather escort Mr. Marsden to see Uncle Devil.'

'Who, *me*?' yelped Red Blaze, who tried to keep as far away from his uncle as possible. 'No, sir, Cousin Dusty. I'll see the troop, *you* go visit Uncle Devil.'

'Tell my striker to have Mr. Marsden's gear taken to our quarters, Red,' Dusty ordered, handing his horse's reins to his guidon carrier. 'This way, Mr. Marsden. We'll likely find the General at headquarters building.'

A coloured servant took the two young officers' hats as they entered the big, Colonial-style white house. The servant had been in the former owner's employment but left behind when his master fled and took service with the new occupants.

'De General's in conference in de library, Cap'n Dusty, sah,' the servant explained. 'Got your pappy, Colonel Blaze and another colonel-gennelman with him.' He rolled his eyes warningly. 'If Ah was you-all, Ah'd steer clear of him, sah.'

'I have to see him, Henry,' Dusty replied.

'Well. Ah has done warned you, sah. Don't you say Ah didn't.'

With that the Negro turned and waddled away, shaking his head sadly in contemplation of the folly of the younger generation.

For all his brilliance as a cavalry leader, and abilities in other directions, Dusty hesitated a moment before raising his hand to knock on the library door. From inside the room, now converted to Ole Devil's office, came an angry bellow which Dusty knew all too well.

'But damn it to hell, John don't those foo—the General Staff back East realise I'm fighting a war here too? I'm not asking for much——' The voice died away as Dusty, sucking in a deep breath, knocked on the door, then resumed with, 'Come in, damn it. Don't stand beating the door down.'

'Mister,' breathed Dusty, opening the door. 'Your information had best be *real* important.'

With that he ushered Marsden into a big, book-lined room.

The four men at the desk in the centre of the room all looked at the new arrivals. Hondo Fog, senior major of the regiment, looking like an older and taller version of Dusty; bulky but iron hard Colonel Blaze; lean, ramrod straight, hawk-faced Ole Devil Hardin; the other colonel, a man of just over medium height, well-built, handsome, black haired and giving a hint of a cavalryman's build even though seated in a chair; all sat eyeing the two young officers coldly. Marsden only just held down a gasp as he recognised the younger colonel. That was the Grey Ghost, John Singleton Mosby himself. Yet Mosby mostly served farther east and should not be in Arkansas, unless——

'I'm in conference, Captain Fog!' growled Ole Devil scowling at his favourite nephew as if Dusty was a copperhead Southern supporter of the Union.

'Mr. Marsden requested an interview with you, sir,' Dusty replied. 'He says it's a matter of extreme urgency, sir.'

The mention of Marsden's name drew all but Mosby's attention to the young Yankee. Giving a nod, Ole Devil told Marsden to come up and state his business.

'I hardly know where to begin, sir,' Marsden said after marching smartly to the desk and throwing up a salute fresh from the pages of the drill manual.

'Try at the beginning, Mr. Marsden,' Ole Devil suggested. 'How did you come to be captured?'

'I found Mr. Marsden held prisoner at Ashley's camp, sir,' Dusty put in.

'Which doesn't explain how he got there.'

'The bushwhackers caught me while I was looking for a Confederate outfit to which I could surrender, sir.'

Marsden saw a slight stir among the men, read added interest in their scrutiny and drew in a deep breath.

'Why did you want to surrender, mister?' asked Colonel Blaze.

'I learned of a plan to cause the withdrawal of most, if not all, of the Texas troops from the Army of the Confederate States, sir.'

'And?' prompted Ole Devil.

'The plan calls for arming the Comanche, Kaddo and Kiowa tribes, sir.'

'That plan was suggested two years ago, mister,' Ole Devil said coldly. 'I believe the idea was to supply the Indians with worn-out flintlocks in return for their assistance at fighting the Southern forces in Texas. It fell through when somebody pointed out that they wouldn't confine their activities to the Confederate Army, or even just to Southern sympathisers.'

'This is a different plan, sir,' Marsden insisted, marvelling a little at Ole Devil's knowledge of Union affairs. 'The people putting it through——'

'Grant and Sherman would never authorise it,' objected Ole Devil.

'They know nothing about it, sir. Nor will they until the plan is brought to a successful conclusion. Faced with a *fait accompli*, one resulting in the withdrawal of all Texas troops from the conflict, it would hardly be politic for even Generals Grant and Sherman to object.'

Looking around the table, Marsden guessed he had made his point. Texas put some 68,500 men under arms in the Confederate forces, skilled fighting men. Its beef herds helped feed the South. Along its coast-line lay many ideal spots where blockade-running ships could land vitally needed supplies. If anybody made a plan which caused all that to be withdrawn from the Confederate cause, not even the two senior generals in the Union Army would dare to openly criticise the methods used by the plotters.

'And you think a few flintlocks will bring the three tribes together?' asked Dusty.

'Not flintlocks,' Marsden answered. 'Three hundred Sharps' breechloading rifles, ten thousand linen cartridge rounds—and the services of an Ager Coffee Mill gun.'

'An Ager Coffee Mill gun?' repeated Dusty.

'Yes. It's a——'

'Mister, I know what it is,' Dusty grunted.

Machine guns, repeating firearms, had long been a military dream and nightmare. A few types had made their appearance during the Civil War. The Confederate Army made use of the William Rapid Fire gun, an effective one-pounder repeating cannon. On the Union side, the Barnes and Ripley guns were tried, but the Ager Coffee Mill gun proved to be the only practical model—the Gatling not having made its debut at that date—and offered the Yankees a deadly addition to their armoury. Deadly, but not perfect, as Dusty pointed out.

'It's got its bad points, mister. If you fire it at over one hundred and twenty rounds a minute, it burns the barrel out.'

Surprise at Dusty's knowledge prevented Marsden from remarking that the Confederate Army possessed no arm, not even the Williams gun, capable of equalling the Ager's rate of fire. Instead he said:

'Think of the effect such a gun would have upon men who know only weapons that need reloading after each shot.'

'That's a good point, Mr. Marsden,' Ole Devil stated and a low rumble of agreement echoed his words. 'You mean that the men behind this scheme mean to present an Ager to the Indians?'

'Yes, sir, and instruct them in its use.'

'How did you come to learn of this scheme, Mr. Marsden?' asked Hondo Fog.

Starting with his return from outpost duty, Marsden told the men everything about his discovery and decision to desert and bring word to the Confederate troops.

'Couldn't you have informed your own higher authority?' Mosby inquired.

'I doubt if General Thompson would object to it, sir,' Marsden replied. 'And it would take too long for word to reach General Sherman. You see, the plan has already been put into operation.'

'When?' snapped Ole Devil, sitting forward in his chair.

'The wagon with the rifles and ammunition left eight days ago. The Ager was taken after them on the day before I returned from outpost duty. That was how I learned of the scheme. Castle is my company commander and when I came to report I heard he had left camp. So I started asking questions and learned what he was up to.'

'And they can contact the Indians—without leaving their scalps on some coup-pole?' Ole Devil asked.

'They think so, sir. Castle and Silverman wouldn't willingly go into any danger. Their rendezvous with the arms wagon is where they meet a Union agent who trades with the Indians and can contact the old man chiefs of each tribe.'

'His name?'

'I'm not sure, sir. The best I could learn was that they call him the Parson or something like that.'

Suddenly Mosby thrust back his chair and came to his

feet. He stepped around the desk, halting to face Marsden. Looking straight at the lieutenant's face, Mosby started a line of questioning the other expected.

'Just why are *you*, an officer of the Union Army, telling all this to us?'

None of the Texans spoke or offered to intervene. The same question had been in their heads, although possibly they could guess at the answer. However, Mosby, coming from Virginia—a state long past the days of Indian raids—might be able to make a more unbiased inquiry into Marsden's motives. Mosby had been a member of the Bar before the War and so knew how to question a suspect.

'I was raised in New Mexico, sir,' Marsden replied. 'I've seen Indian work.'

An answer which could possibly have satisfied men who also knew the results of Indian warfare. Mosby did not appear to be convinced.

'So you now expect General Hardin to make arrangements to quell this Indian uprising?'

'Yes, sir.'

'By sending troops from his command to do it?'

'I hadn't thought of how he might handle the affair, sir.'

'But if he does send, say a battalion, from the regiment, it might alter the balance of power in the Union's favour.'

Marsden did not answer. All too well he knew how delicately balanced was the situation in Arkansas. Hardin's force numbered less than the Union troops and only their superior tactics and fighting ability prevented the Yankees from advancing and sweeping the state back under Federal control. The loss of even one battalion, acted upon by the Union forces, could see the Confederates pushed out of Arkansas.

'Well, Mr. Marsden?' demanded Mosby.

'I don't quite follow your question, sir,' Marsden answered.

'Let me put a supposition before you, mister. Suppose this is a plot, not to arm and raise the Indians in Texas, but to create discord, uncertainty and alarm among the Texans in General Hardin's command?'

'If that had been my intention, sir,' Marsden said hotly, 'I'd have told Captain Fog of it in the presence of his men so that they could spread the word among the troops.'

'Mr. Marsden,' Ole Devil put in. 'Do you give us your word that you are not trying to trick us in any way?'

'I do, sir.'

Standing rigid to attention, Marsden met Ole Devil's frosty black eyes without any sign of flinching. He wanted to look at the others, try to read their thoughts, but knew that any attempt to do so might be construed as a sign of guilt. At last Ole Devil gave a nod and glanced at Mosby.

'One thing still puzzles me, Mr. Marsden,' the Grey Ghost remarked, but much of the brusque note had left his voice. 'This plan wasn't made during the past ten or so days. How come you didn't know of it earlier?'

'I'm a career soldier, sir. There's little common bond between us and the volunteer officers. They wouldn't let me in on anything of this nature in case I could offer concrete reasons why it would be ill-advised.'

'Ill-advised!' Blaze snorted. 'Arming the Indians would be rank lunacy.'

'Just how did you learn of the scheme?' Mosby asked, ignoring the outburst.

'My suspicions were aroused, sir,' Marsden answered and a faint grin came to his lips. 'A bottle of whisky is a finer inducement to talking than torture, sir, properly used.'

Mosby resumed his seat and looked around the circle of tanned Texas faces, with great attention to Ole Devil's expressionless mask. Taken with the news Mosby brought from the East, Marsden's information could be a terrible menace to the Confederate cause. It was Ole Devil's assumption of command that brought the Union advance in Arkansas to a halt, his leadership and tactics which held a superior force back beyond the Arkansas River. Through Ole Devil's actions, a large Federal army, badly needed elsewhere, must stay in Arkansas. With that knowledge in mind, Ole Devil requested reinforcements, one regiment each of infantry, cavalry and artillery, and Mosby had just brought word that the General Staff could not spare the men. Having seen, and heard, Ole Devil's receipt of the news, Mosby wondered how the other's feelings towards the Confederate States might be affected in the light of the new development. After all, Ole Devil *was* a Texan and of all the Southern states, Texas had the least interest in one of the basic causes of the War.

'Just how serious do you regard the situation, General?'

asked Mosby when nobody offered to continue the conversation.

'It could be very serious,' Ole Devil admitted.

'Maybe Kiowa could tell us what chance there is of the tribes merging, sir,' Dusty put in. 'He's lived among the Kiowa, his mother was one of them, and he'll maybe be able to help.'

'Can he keep his mouth shut?' growled Ole Devil.

'If he says "good morning" he's being real talkative, sir,' grinned Dusty.

'Go get him then, Dustine. Take a seat, Mr. Marsden.'

'Dusty!' Mosby put in as the small captain turned to leave. 'While you're out, find my escort. Ask Sergeant Ysabel to report to me.' He turned back to the desk. 'Sam Ysabel knows the Comanche, married Chief Long Walker's daughter. He could know something.'

'Sam Ysabel, huh?' grunted Colonel Blaze.

'Do you know him?' grinned Mosby.

'I've heard of him. Used to be a border smuggler. Ran a good line in duty-free Mexican wine—or so they tell me.'

The latter part of the speech came as Blaze remembered his pre-war post of justice of the peace in Rio Hondo County, and as such he should not be aware of the quality of a smuggler's goods.

'He's a damned good scout. Only one I have that's better is his son, Lon.' Mosby remarked, ignoring Blaze's statement. 'It's a pity the boy isn't here, but he went out with a patrol after a bunch of Yankees who caught and tortured a couple of our men.'

On leaving the house, Dusty headed straight for the post sutler's building. He figured the conference had taken long enough for his troop to be dismissed and knew where to find the men he wanted. The sutler used one of the property's out-buildings and furnished it with a bar counter, tables and chairs gathered from unmentioned sources. Inside, a man could purchase such luxuries and necessities of life as the owner managed to gather, and generally relax from military discipline.

As Dusty expected, his sergeant-major and sergeant sat with a group of senior non-coms, one of them a man Dusty knew, but who did not belong to the Texas Light Cavalry.

'Gentlemen,' Dusty greeted as he walked to the table.

'My apologies. I'd like to see you outside, Billy Jack, Kiowa. You, too, Sergeant Ysabel.'

Instantly the three men rose, although Sam Ysabel did not have a reputation for adhering strictly to discipline. Outside the sutler's store, Ysabel gave Dusty a broad and admiring grin.

'Billy Jack's just been telling me about what happened when you went over the Moshogen to give evidence at that Yankee shavetail's court martial,* sir,' he said. 'Haven't seen you since then.'

'Billy Jack talks too much,' Dusty answered. 'You and Kiowa are wanted at the General's office.'

'That means trouble,' groaned Billy Jack. 'You just see if it don't.'

'Likely,' Dusty grinned for he was not fooled by his sergeant-major's pose. Under that lachrymose exterior lay a tough, capable and intelligent fighting man. 'Go tell Cousin Red that we'll maybe pull out in a hurry.'

'Yo!' replied Billy Jack and swung away from the others.

During the return to the house, Dusty took time to study the father of a man who would one day be his real good friend. At that time Dusty had not met Loncey Dalton Ysabel, better known as the Ysabel Kid, but had come into contact with the Kid's father once before.

Ysabel looked much the same; tall, well-built, powerful. Black-Irish and Kentuckian blood flowed through his veins, a fighting mixture without peer. He moved with a long, free stride, yet set his feet down lightly and in silence. An old Dragoon Colt hung at his right side, a James Black bowie rode his left hip in a Comanche medicine sheath. However, in time of war, unless Dusty missed his guess, the Sharps breech-loading rifle would form Ysabel's chief defence and offence tool.

Neither of the sergeants asked any questions on their way to the house, and followed Dusty into Hardin's office. Inside, Dusty saw that time had not been wasted while he fetched the non-coms. Maps were spread out on the desk and the Confederate officers stood around it, while Marsden sat at one side, silent and obviously hiding his thoughts.

*Told in *The Fastest Gun in Texas.*

'Come in, gentlemen,' Old Devil told the non-coms. 'Mr. Marsden, tell them what you told us about this scheme to arm the Indians.'

Although he watched their faces as he talked, Marsden could see no sign of emotion, no hint at whether Ysabel or Kiowa believed him. Only once did either make any interruption. Following Marsden's mention of the Union agent who promised to gather the tribes, Ysabel asked:

'Would that feller's name be the Deacon, mister?'

'I—— Yes, that's it. The man I was questioning didn't talk too well when he reached that point and all I could make out was some kind of preacher.'

'Know the Deacon, Hon—Major?' Ysabel asked of Dusty's father.

'Can't say I do.' Hondo Fog had been local peace officer in the Rio Hondo before following Ole Devil to fight for the Confederacy.

'Naw. Most likely you wouldn't. He steered clear of places where the law was enforced. Was a trader, whisky, muskets, powder, lead, steel war-axes, he dealt in the lot.'

'Could he arrange a meeting with the old man chiefs of each tribe, Sergeant?' asked Ole Devil.

For almost a minute Sam Ysabel did not reply. He exchanged glances with Kiowa, scratched his bristle-covered jaw and nodded.

'Sure, General,' he answered quietly. 'I reckon the Deacon could.'

CHAPTER FIVE

THEY HAVE TO BE STOPPED, CAPTAIN FOG

Silence fell on the room after Sam Ysabel's words, for none of the Texans doubted his knowledge of Indian affairs. Ysabel belonged to the hardy brotherhood who pushed into the wild, unexplored country with the desire to see what lay beyond the next hill. Unlike the settlers who followed in their wake. Ysabel's kind befriended the Indians, adopted their ways, learned their traditions and thoughts. Such a man could be expected to estimate the chances of Castle's scheme working with more accuracy than any settler. After a moment, Ysabel expanded on his statement.

'The Deacon knows enough of the old man chiefs to call all three tribes together, General. But he'd need some mighty strong medicine to make 'em listen to him.'

'Three hundred rifles like your Sharps and ammunition would give him a good starting point,' Ole Devil pointed out.

Ysabel looked down at his rifle. At that time the Model 1859 Sharps could claim to be the finest rifle in general use. Neither the Henry nor Spencer repeating rifles could equal its range, accuracy or dependability, and ammunition for both was difficult to obtain.

'Yes, sir,' admitted Ysabel. 'Spread out among the right folks in each tribe they'd gather a whole heap of support.'

'Don't forget the Ager, sir,' Dusty put in.

'I'm not likely to forget it, Captain Fog!' Ole Devil barked.

'You mean one of them Ager Coffee Mill guns, sir?' asked Kiowa.

'The men behind this scheme are taking one to the meeting and intend to offer it as support to the raiding parties,' Ole Devil replied.

'What would its effect be, Sam?' Mosby inquired.

'Big medicine, Colonel,' Ysabel answered soberly. 'Just about as big as you could get. They'd think it was a Devil Gun. I tell you, one good victory with that thing backing 'em and those Yankees'd have every Indian in the whole damned state painting for war.'

'As bad as that?' asked Blaze.

'Worse,' grunted Ysabel. 'Even such of the old man chiefs who wanted to stay out of it wouldn't have any say with that thing siding the war-shouters.'

'We have to stop the Ager falling into Indian hands, sir,' Dusty stated.

'Yes, they have to be stopped, Captain Fog,' agreed Mosby. 'The question is how do you stop them.'

'Prevent them from contacting the Indians,' Dusty suggested.

'To do that, you have to find them,' Blaze pointed out. 'Did you learn either their rendezvous, or the meeting place with the Indians, Mr. Marsden?'

'No, sir. The informant collapsed into a drunken stupor before I learned either. Each party slipped through the Ouachita Mountains, avoiding your patrols, and were to meet somewhere on the Red River.'

'There're a hundred crossing points on the Red,' Hondo growled. 'We can't cover them all. And Texas's a whole heap too much land for us to start combing it to find a small party.'

'What escort did the two parties have, Mr. Marsden?' asked Ole Devil.

'One mounted company of Zouaves were taking the wagon to the rendezvous, but the Deacon claimed he could handle the situation better without so many men and so the escort was to return when the meeting was made.'

'Why send them separately, Mr. Marsden?' Blaze put in.

'The Ager hadn't arrived and a messenger from the Deacon arrived with news that he was expecting representatives from each tribe to visit him. He wanted something to show the Indians when they arrived. So it was decided to send off the arms wagon immediately. Castle and Silverman, in civilian clothing, were to follow with the Ager on a light artillery mount. They had a guide to take them through your lines.'

Ole Devil might have commented that lack of men prevented him from making accurate coverage of the Ouachita Mountains, but did not bother. Nor did Mosby need any explanation, for he specialised in slipping through the enemy's lines and knew how it could be done, especially in mountainous land.

'It doesn't help us much to know where the rendezvous might be,' the General commented. 'They'll have passed that point now.'

'Just thought of something, General,' Ysabel said. 'A thing like this, getting the three tribes together I mean, calls for a special medicine place. You don't just ask Comanche, Kiowa and Kaddoes to meet up and forget all the years of war in any old place.'

'Sam's right, General,' Kiowa agreed. 'It has to be some place that the Great Spirit keeps for his-self.'

'Kind of sacred ground,' continued Ysabel. 'All the tribes have them. Places where enemies can meet and talk things out without needing to watch for sneaky games. A medicine place'd be the only location you could gather Comanche, Kiowa and Kaddo without getting trouble.'

'Where would such a place be?' asked Ole Devil.

'Can think of half a dozen scattered about Texas,' Ysabel replied. 'There's one on the Sweetwater, another on the Colorado.'

'They'd be too far south,' Dusty guessed, consulting the maps. 'The Yankees need something close at hand.'

'How about the joining of the Salt and Clear Forks of the Brazos?' Kiowa put in. 'That's an old medicine place.'

'I reckon you hit it, Kiowa,' Ysabel enthused, looking at the spot to which the lean sergeant pointed. 'The Deacon knows that country pretty well.'

'It's a touch close to Fort Worth and Dallas,' objected Ole Devil.

'Over a hundred miles from the nearest, and Indian country at that,' Ysabel replied. 'No, sir. Was I asked, I'd say that's our place.'

Once again all the men gathered around and studied the maps. To experienced soldiers, the true meaning of the insignificant spaces upon the paper stood plain and clear. A thumb and forefinger might span from the Red River to the fork of the two tributaries of the Brazos, but all knew how many actual miles lay between the points.

'With four days lead, they'll be over the Red now,' Hondo pointed out. 'But with wagons they'll be travelling slow. We might send a battalion——'

'I can't even spare a company, not and hold out here in Arkansas,' Ole Devil answered. 'And a company would travel too slowly to intercept them.'

'A small party could move fast enough, sir,' Dusty put in.

'How small?' asked Ole Devil.

'I thought myself, Kiowa, Billy Jack and two more would do,' Dusty said. 'A party that size, mounted on the pick of our horses, could cover between thirty and forty miles a day even without taking remounts from any Confederate outfit we happened across.'

'It's getting on for three hundred miles to that fork, Dusty,' Hondo warned.

'Yes, sir, but if we're lucky we'll catch the Yankees before they reach it. How many men'll be with the wagons, six, ten, a dozen at most. The Indians wouldn't stand for many more than that. With surprise at our back, I reckon we can handle them.'

Ole Devil sat back in his chair, the impassive mask dropping onto his face and warning all who knew him that he was thinking. Every man present understood the problem facing the grim-faced General. His orders were to prevent further Union advance in Arkansas, and if possible regain the territory already taken. While he could hold the Yankees beyond the Arkansas river and prevent their gaining more land, he needed every man to do so. Despite Dusty's youth, he was a valuable fighting leader and a man not easily spared. To let Dusty go, even with only four men, would seriously weaken Ole Devil's precarious hold on the delicately balanced position. Yet to refuse would be just as disastrous. Once the Indians took to the warpath, there would be no stopping them short of using considerable force. Nor would the blood-crazy, coup-seeking braves differentiate between soldier and civilian, or between man, woman and child. The Indians, would ravage Texas from north to south, leaving the country, already weakened by the number of men away at the War, a burning, bloody ruin. Ole Devil knew the result of such an Indian uprising and also realised that every Texan serving the Confederate Government would want to return home to defend, or avenge, his family once the news spread.

So Ole Devil had to balance the temporary loss of a good officer against the possibility of the South losing thousands of badly needed soldiers. There could only be one answer.

'Who do you want with you, Dustine?' he asked. 'And before you say it, I can't let Mr. Blaze go with you. I need one of you to lead your troop.'

'You'd best take Sergeant Ysabel, Dusty,' Mosby put in. 'He knows the country——'

'And I'm kin to Long Walker, top war chief of the Comanche,' Ysabel finished for his commanding officer. 'It's a pity Lon's not here, Long Walker's his grandpappy.'

Like many of his kind, Sam Ysabel had taken an Indian wife; unlike some of the frontiersmen, he remained true to the Indian girl and grief at her death sent him from the Comanches, although he stayed in touch with them.

'Be pleased to have you, Sergeant,' Dusty said. 'And for the other man——'

'May I be the other man, sir?' Marsden put in.

All the Confederates in the room looked at the young Union officer. He read a mixture of surprise, inquiry, suspicion even in the various faces.

'Why, mister?' asked Ole Devil.

'My people are causing the trouble, sir. I'd like to help put it right.'

'If you fall into Union hands, you'll be shot, boy,' warned the grim-faced General, but an almost gentle note crept into his voice.

'I will whether I see it through or stay here, sir, in the end.' A man who acted as Marsden had could expect death at the hands of his own people. He knew and accepted that fact before he started out for the Ouachita. However, he wanted to see through the thing he started. Knowing the risks they took, he stood a fair chance of never coming back and preferred that to bringing shame upon his family.

Dusty smiled. 'We'll be travelling light, real light, sir. Mr. Marsden's an infantry officer, does he think he can stand the pace?'

'I trained for cavalry almost from birth, sir,' Marsden answered.

'Then you can come along,' Dusty promised. 'With your permission, sir, I'll start making my preparations. We'll pull out at first light in the morning.'

Although they might be able to leave earlier, Dusty knew it would be better to utilise the rest of the day in making sure they had the best horses and preparing for the long, hard ride ahead.

After Dusty's party left the room, Mosby turned to Ole Devil. 'Do you think we can trust Marsden, sir?'

'I know we can,' Ole Devil answered. 'Haven't seen the boy since he was ten, but he's his father's son.'

'How about it, Dustine?' queried Ole Devil.

'You know his family, sir?'

'You might say that, Colonel Mosby. I served with his father in the Mexican War, General Marsden is Dustine's god-father and young Marsden there is my god-son. They named him Jackson Hardin for me. Now, gentlemen, we'll see what we can do to get my god-son out of the mess he's in. You're a pretty good lawyer, John. Is there a precedent for his action?'

'If there is,' Mosby replied after a moment's thought, 'I can't think of it.'

'Or me,' admitted Ole Devil. 'I think that we'll have to try direct methods. Hondo, can you take down a letter to General Philo Handiman, we'll send it under a flag of truce to the nearest regular Yankee outfit, they'll pass it on to Philo in Washington.'

Not knowing that his future was under consideration, Marsden resigned himself to his fate. In an attempt to stop himself thinking of his ruined career and possible fate, he studied the scenes around him. First thing to strike his eye was that the Texas Light Cavalry's camp showed none of the casual slovenliness he associated with volunteer outfits. Next of interest being the amount of Union Army gear on view. Tents, leatherwork, arms all bore the mark of Union make, even though the voices around the camp sounded Texan.

'You look surprised that we're living so well, mister,' Dusty remarked.

'I am, sir,' admitted Marsden.

'We couldn't do it relying on our own folks' supplies. Apart from the uniforms, we mostly draw on the Yankees for anything we need.'

A faint smile came to Marsden's lips at the small captain's words. Something told Marsden that the forthcoming trip would be an education for him and that he might gain knowledge of use in his career. The smile went as Marsden realised that in all probability he no longer had a career or a future.

Telling the two sergeants to grab a meal, then report to his tent and bring Billy Jack, Dusty took Marsden to his quarters in the officers' lines. Another of Marsden's illusions went as he found that the wedge of tents had been stockaded and gave every hint of permanency.

'We aren't going anywhere,' Dusty remarked in answer to the other's comment on the permanent nature of the quarters. 'Not unless it's back over the Arkansas.'

The tent proved to be spacious, although not luxuriously furnished. However, it compared favourably with Marsden's quarters with the Zouaves. Dusty shared the tent with his second-in-command and Red Blaze sat on one of the beds, his jacket off, Marsden's weapon belt lying next to his own. A pair of saddles rested on burros, wooden racks like inverted A-shapes. One glance told Marsden that the Texans might use many Union items, but they stuck to their range rigs. The saddles had double girths and the type of low horn only rarely seen in New Mexico. A coiled, thirty-foot rope hung on one side of each saddle's horn, with the slings for carrying a sabre at the other side. From the saddles, Marsden turned his attention to the arms leaning against the burros. As the Spencer carbine did not come into use until after the War started, he concluded the pair in the tent must be battlefield captures.

From the Spencers, Marsden turned his eyes to the sabres and saw something that interested him. He wondered how he could satisfy his curiosity.

'Everything all right, Dusty?' Red asked.

'Sure. Have a bed brought in for Mr. Marsden, he's our guest.'

The order aroused no comment from Red. Among the regular officers of the Union and most of the Confederate brass the rules and chivalries of war were still honoured. A captured officer could expect decent treatment and certain privileges.

'I'll tend to it,' Red promised. 'His weapons are here, I left them until you told me how to dispose of them.'

'You can let him have them back. He'll be riding out with me in the morning.'

Once again Red refrained from asking questions, although he clearly showed his surprise. Never before had Dusty taken a captive to a prisoner-of-war camp, his time being too fully occupied for him to be spared on such an unimportant detail. Nor did the return of the weapons lessen Red's perplexity. While a regular Union officer's sword might be returned to him by his captors, no Confederate would willingly part with such a highly prized item as an 1860 Army Colt; the most highly thought-of handgun to have made its appearance in the War.

At last Red could hold his curiosity no longer. 'What's on, Cousin Dusty?'

'I've a chore to handle, Mr. Marsden's going along.'

'Taking the troop?'

'Nope. Just Billy Jack and Kiowa.'

'Can you tell me about it?'

'Later maybe,' Dusty replied. 'Have you ate yet?'

'No, thought I'd wait for you.'

'As soon as we've washed up, we'll go and grab a meal then. Care to take first crack at the wash-bowl, Mr. Marsden.'

'Thank you, sir,' Marsden replied.

'I'll go tell the striker to bring more water,' Red said, rising and walking from the tent.

Restlessness drove Marsden to make conversation and he sought for something to talk about.

'That's not regulations, is it, sir?' he asked, indicating the jacket Dusty removed and placed on the second bed.

A grin came to Dusty's face. 'A shavetail called Mark Counter, in Sheldon's outfit, started the no-skirt jacket and the idea caught on. I find it better for work than the authorised undress uniform.'

Then Marsden recalled the thing which interested him on his arrival. Crossing the tent, he looked at the sabre on one of the burros.

'May I, sir?' he asked, reaching towards it.

'Feel free,' Dusty replied.

At West Point and since, Marsden had always heard that the Confederate Army possessed poor swords. Shortage of material due to the blockade of Southern ports, lack of skilled tradesmen and forging facilities prevented the rebels from owning decent weapons. However, the pair of swords in that tent showed excellent workmanship and proved to be of Southern manufacture; no Union company would use the letters C.S.A. in the hilt pattern of its produce.

The sabre Marsden examined had sharkskin-covered grips secured with gilt wire, and its blade sported a stopped blood gutter and an additional thin, deep channelling on both upper sides of the blade for added flexibility and strength. On examination, Marsden found the blade's steel to be as good as any from a Union force. He hefted the sabre, noting its razor-sharp edge, and found he did not care for its balance.

'A fine blade, sir,' he said, returning the sabre to its sheath.

'The Haiman Brothers made it for me,' Dusty replied. 'A thirty-two-inch blade instead of thirty-six, and a shade lighter than the artillery sabre.'

Now it had been pointed out to him, Marsden saw the difference in length between the two sabres.

'Do you find yourselves at any disadvantage using it against arms of the conventional length, sir?' he asked, and regretted the question as soon as the word left his mouth. A small man in a large man's world might resent any comment or hint at his lack of size.

'Nope,' Dusty replied with a grin. 'It only means that I have to get closer to the other feller than he gets to me.'

Apparently Dusty took no offence. Suddenly Marsden realised that Dusty Fog accepted his lack of inches and, very sensibly, made no attempt to carry the full-length cavalry sabre in an effort to hide his small size. Looking first at the sabre, then at Dusty, Marsden wondered how well the small Texan could handle the weapon. Before he could go into the matter, Marsden saw Dusty's striker, a cheery young Negro, arrive with water.

'All right, mister,' Dusty said. 'Let's wash, go have a meal, then we'll get everything ready for pulling out in the morning.'

CHAPTER SIX

MR. MARSDEN PICKS A HORSE

'Like I said,' groaned Billy Jack as Dusty finished telling him of their latest assignment, 'trouble.'

'Sure,' agreed Dusty. 'We'll need the pick of the horses. I want a real good mount for Mr. Marsden.'

The mournful pose left Billy Jack and he nodded, then continued with his preparations.

'Carbines?' he asked.

During his meal at the officers' mess Dusty had given some thought to the matter of armament. On such a ride every ounce of weight counted and he balanced the value of taking along carbines and ammunition, giving his party weapons with a longer range than their Colts, against the extra loading of the horses.

'Just sidearms,' he answered. 'We're not fighting unless we're forced. Fifty cartridges, powder flask and twenty round ball per man.'

'Huh, huh,' grunted Billy Jack. 'Packhosses?'

'Two, carry food for the mounts and jerked meat. We're travelling light.'

'Like to take my old rifle along, Cap'n,' Ysabel put in.

Dusty studied the big Sharps for a moment. Men like Ysabel felt lost without a rifle handy, regarding it almost as a part of their own body. Knowing the independent nature of Ysabel's kind, Dusty took the request as quite a compliment. Not that he intended to allow that to sway him in any way. His party might find use for a rifle and Ysabel was the best man to handle it.

'Take it, Sergeant,' he authorised. 'No more than fifty rounds though.'

'Yep,' agreed Ysabel. 'Won't need no cartridges for my belt gun. I allus use loose powder and round ball.'

'I'll leave it to you,' Dusty answered.

'Jerked meat, coffee, sugar do for food?' asked Kiowa.

'That and anything we can pick up on the way,' Dusty replied.

Watching the others, Marsden realised that all knew their business and had ridden on many missions of a dangerous nature. The questions and orders were merely routine, for each man knew his part.

'Let's go and see about your horse, Mr. Marsden,' Dusty suggested. 'Billy Jack, head down and tell Sergeant Granger I want him to put the remuda in the big corral.'

'Yo!' replied the gangling non-com and was about to depart when Dusty joined him and said something in a voice too low for the others to catch. 'I'll tend to it, Cap'n Dusty.'

'Leave the food side to you, Kiowa,' Dusty went on and the sergeant left on Billy Jack's heels.

'Need me for anything, Cap'n?' asked Ysabel.

'Come down to the corral with us,' Dusty suggested. 'If you're ready, Mr. Marsden, we'll go see about collecting your horse.'

Although not a member of the party, Red Blaze had been present. He rose from his bed and prepared to carry on with his duty of escort to Marsden. Knowing that the Union possessed a reasonably efficient spy network even in Arkansas, Dusty took no chances of news of his mission leaking out. While in camp Marsden would be treated as a prisoner-of-war and kept under escort. Dusty knew he could rely on his cousin to keep quiet about the mission and so asked Red to be Marsden's escort even though the redhead held a higher grade of rank than the prisoner.

Dusty did not appear to be in any great rush to reach the corral. Strolling leisurely through the camp, he and Red kept up a friendly conversation with Marsden and did nothing to prevent the Union officer from examining his surroundings. At last they reached the horse lines. All around them, the never-ending business of cavalry soldiers went on. Men cleaned up the picket lines, led horses to water, saw to feeding their mounts. To a casual, inexperienced observer everything might have seemed to be in wild confusion, but Marsden saw the disciplined purposefulness of the scene. One thing he noticed was that the officers and sergeants clearly trusted their men to carry out the assigned work without constant supervision. That was understandable. Born in a land where a horse was far more than a means of transport, being an absolute necessity of life, the men of the Texas Light Cavalry knew better than neglect their mounts.

Never had Marsden seen such a fine collection of animals. Nor did his admiration decline when he approached one of a series of big pole corrals. Already a number of horses had been driven into the corral and, although they belonged to the regiment's reserve of mounts, Marsden noticed their glossy coats and general signs of good health.

'Take your pick,' offered Dusty.

Sensing a test of his horse-knowledge and judgment, Marsden swung himself up to sit on the top rail. Once there he started to examine the horses with careful eyes and knew straight off that no easy task lay before him. All the horses showed well-rounded frames that told of perfect condition and looked as hard as exercise and training could make them.

At last Marsden saw what he wanted. While not the biggest horse in the corral, he decided to ask for the sorrel gelding with the white star on its face. Everything about the sorrel pleased him. Its head gave an impression of leanness, although with good width between the eyes, which were set well out at the side and promised a wide range of vision; depth through the jaw, the lips clasped firmly over the teeth and the nostrils flaring well open. That head ensured good breathing capability while the erect ears pointed to alertness. Of course, Marsden knew the old dealers' claim that one did not ride the head; but a good head, all things being equal, usually meant a good horse. The sorrel's neck had sufficient length and strength to give a good carriage to the head. A short back, level from the dip behind the withers and a well ribbed-up frame offered a firm base for the saddle, while the powerful loins, fore-limbs and legs hinted at power, stamina, speed and agility.

Several of the horses showed up almost as well, but the sorrel possessed an undefinable something which made Marsden select it.

'I'll take that one,' he said, indicating the horse.

Almost before the words left Marsden's mouth, Billy Jack swung up alongside him. The sergeant-major held a sixty-foot-long Manila rope in his hands, a running loop dangling ready. Up and out whirled the loop, flying through the air to drop around the sorrel's neck. The throw had been so swiftly and neatly made that Marsden turned towards Dusty meaning to comment on it. A smile played on Dusty's lips, mirrored on the faces of Red and Billy Jack. Suddenly Marsden knew that the sorrel was placed among the other horses, on Dusty's whispered orders, as a test of his knowledge.

A momentary irritation rose in Marsden's thoughts. In addition to being at least three years older than Dusty Fog, he had attended West Point and was not just some volunteer who held rank because his uncle happened to be the commanding general. Then sober thought wiped out the irritation. Dusty was embarking upon a desperate and dangerous assignment, also upon a very long and arduous journey. One could not blame him for taking no chances.

'That's a good horse, mister,' Billy Jack remarked, drawing in on his rope. 'Only I wouldn't let the Yankee General, Custer, catch you riding it.'

'Why?' Marsden asked, watching the calm way the sorrel accepted the rope.

'It used to belong to him.'

Then Marsden remembered that among his other exploits Dusty had led a raid on the 7th Cavalry's camp and drove off a fair number of the regiment's mounts. Knowing something of Custer's taste in horses, Marsden decided that possibly the sorrel had been one of the General's personal mounts.

'Reckon you'd best use one of our saddles, Mr. Marsden,' Dusty suggested as Billy Jack led the sorrel from the corral.

'Had one fetched down for you, mister,' Billy Jack called over his shoulder. 'It's there on the rail.'

Sensing something out of the ordinary in the air, a small knot of soldiers hovered in the background. On seeing that Marsden went towards the rail-hung saddle, an air of anticipation ran through the watching men. All wanted to see what kind of a horseman the Yankee shavetail might be. With his army's reputation to uphold, Marsden hoped that he might put on a good display. However, he had never used a double-cinched range saddle and wondered if he could handle it correctly.

'Here, Yankee,' a voice said. 'I'll lend you a hand.'

Turning his head, Marsden looked towards the speaker. All in all the approaching man did not strike Marsden as being the type to voluntarily offer assistance. He was a tall, burly young man with a sullen truculent face and wore the uniform of Mosby's Rangers. However, Marsden knew that appearance could be deceptive and so raised no protest. Not that the soldier intended to burden himself to any great extent, for he took the blanket and left Marsden to handle the saddle. Not that Marsden objected, as he liked to saddle his own horse.

Walking to the sorrel, the soldier went around it, halting on the side away from Billy Jack and in a position that hid him from the watching men. He took his time in getting the blanket into place, slipped a hand under it to ensure its smooth, unwrinkled fit, then let Marsden swing on the saddle. To one side of the group, Sam Ysabel glanced at the horse then turned his eyes to study Marsden's helper.

While saddling the sorrel, Marsden took the opportunity to study the animal. It showed no objections at receiving the saddle, although it moved restlessly when he first put the rig on. Clearly the sorrel was used to being saddled and ridden, however it might want to debate the matter of who ran things when it felt Marsden's weight for the first time. Not that Marsden felt worried, he reckoned he could hold his own in that kind of company.

With everything set, Marsden gripped the saddlehorn, placed a foot in the stirrup iron and swung upwards. Cocking his leg over, Marsden settled his weight down in the saddle. Instantly the sorrel gave a shrill scream of pain and took off in a wild leap. Only by a grab at the horn did Marsden prevent himself from being thrown. He came down hard on the saddle once more after being raised clear out of it, landing just as the horse's feet touched the ground again. Another scream of pain burst from the horse and it took off once more. Marsden could not imagine what was happening. He did not for a moment believe that Dusty misled him or gave him an outlaw horse. No horse could have fooled Marsden so completely as to its character. Yet the sorrel seemed to be almost crazy as it bounded and leapt, squealing on each leap's completion.

Dusty threw a glance at the burly soldier who helped Marsden, then turned and raced to where a saddled horse stood ready for use in an emergency—a simple precaution when handling spirited animals that might be snuffy through lack of work. Taking off in a bound, Dusty leap-frogged over the horse's rump, landed in the saddle, caught up the reins and started the animal moving. A second rider, a man returning from some duty, sent his mount racing towards the wildly leaping sorrel so as to give assistance.

Bringing his horse alongside the sorrel, Dusty yelled a warning to Marsden and hoped the other knew what to do. Marsden still stuck on the horse despite his amazement at its behaviour. True he expected some trouble, but nothing so serious as the wild fit of bucking. He knew that somehow each time he slammed down into the saddle, the impact brought on another spasm. Yet there was no way he could dismount short of leaping clear and chancing a broken leg. Then he heard Dusty's yell and saw the small captain loom alongside, coming in very close. At the same moment a second rider appeared at the other side, crowding in on the sorrel.

'Now!' Dusty yelled as he extended an arm towards Marsden.

Grabbing out, Marsden hooked an arm around Dusty's shoulders and felt the Texan's hand clamp hold of his belt. Then he kicked his feet free of the stirrups and felt himself dragging over the saddle. A moment later he hung suspended from Dusty and the sorrel drew away from them still bucking. Leaning from his saddle, the second rider managed to catch the sorrel's trailing reins and brought the animal to a halt.

Once clear of the sorrel, Dusty set Marsden down on the ground. Swinging from his saddle, Dusty left the horse to its own devices and strode towards where the sorrel stood fighting its reins. Dusty took the reins and started to calm the horse, speaking gently and holding its head down. Hearing a burst of laughter, Dusty threw a cold, ominous glare at the Mosby man who had helped Marsden.

When the sorrel calmed down and stood still, although shivering, Dusty moved alongside it and started to loosen the saddle-girths. Running forward, Marsden helped to strip off the saddle. With an angry gesture Dusty reached under the blanket and brought something out. Marsden looked down at a small iron ball with four knobbly lumps of pyramid-shape rising from it.

'So that's what made him buck!' Marsden breathed. 'But I don't——'

'I do!' Dusty growled and swung from Marsden to walk to where the burly Mosby man stood wiping his eyes and still laughing. 'Did you put this under the sorrel's saddle blanket?'

With an effort the soldier stopped laughing and the truculence returned to his sullen features. 'Sure I did. Figured to see how well the Yankee shavetail could ride a hoss.'

Which, as any member of the Texas Light Cavalry could have warned the soldier, was most definitely not the manner to use when answering a very annoyed Captain Dusty Fog.

'Damn you, Heimer!' Sam Ysabel bellowed. 'I'll——'

'I'm handling this, Sergeant!' Dusty cut in.

It had long been Heimer's boast that he showed respect only for Colonel Mosby and he objected to having a short-growed kid-officer from another regiment mean-mouthing him.

'So I shook the shavetail up,' he scoffed. 'Hell, he's only a Yankee——'

'Walk that horse until it cools down,' Dusty ordered quietly.

'Like he——'

Heimer's words chopped off abruptly as Dusty moved forward to insist on obedience to orders. Out and up drove Dusty's left fist, sinking with some force into the pit of the unsuspecting Heimer's stomach. Knowing his own size and reputation as a rough-house brawler, Heimer never thought the small captain dare lay a hand on him. So the blow, anything but a light one, took him completely by surprise. Grunting, he went back on his heels, took a pace to the rear and doubled over. Dusty whipped up his other hand, swinging it around so that the knuckles caught the offered jaw with a crisp thud.

Lifted erect by the punch, Heimer staggered back several feet before he managed to catch his balance and come to a halt. Then he gave an enraged bellow, lowered his head and launched a charge calculated to flatten a much larger man than the grim-faced officer who so rough-handled him.

'We'd better stop him!' Marsden gasped and started to move forward.

'Leave be, Jack,' answered Red Blaze, clamping hold of

the other's arm and restraining him. 'Dusty won't hurt that feller none.'

At which point Marsden began to see that his fears had been misplaced.

Instead of side-stepping the other's rush, Dusty waited for it. However, before Heimer struck him, Dusty's hands shot out and clamped hold of Heimer's jacket just below the armpits, arms locking against the man's bent-forward body and holding it. Moving fast, Dusty pivoted his hips slightly to the left and started to fall backwards. Suddenly Dusty hooked his right foot behind Heimer's left leg and pressed his left boot against the front of the other's right ankle. Heimer howled as his feet lost all control. By using Heimer's momentum, Dusty changed the charge into a head-long tumble. While a good horseman, Heimer did not have time to break his fall. He felt himself falling, let out a wail and landed with a crash upon his back.

Bounding up, Dusty went forward, bent and laid hold of Heimer's jacket front. With a heave, Dusty fetched the winded man to his feet and then heaved him into Sam Ysabel's waiting arms.

'See he tends to the sorrel, Sergeant!' Dusty barked. 'And if it isn't fit for use in the morning I'll stuff his pants with these damned burrs and ride him on a cannon until he wishes his mother and father never met the one time they did.'

Gripping Heimer by the scruff of the neck, Ysabel shook him savagely. 'You hear that, boy?' he growled. 'Well you'd better believe it. Happen that hoss ain't fit to be rid Cap'n Fog'll surely do what he says.'

While he claimed to be tough, and could not be counted among the world's brighter intellects, Heimer knew enough to call a game quits. He did not know how the small captain managed to handle him with such comparative ease, but his every instinct warned him that Dusty could most likely repeat the process, or maybe even find a rougher and more painful method next time. Nor did he offer to raise objections to Sam Ysabel's handling, for the big sergeant had a direct, blunt and very effective way of enforcing his demands. So Heimer, limping slightly, went to the sorrel took the reins, and started to walk it.

'How the hell did he do that?' Marsden asked a grinning

Red, while Dusty spoke with Ysabel. 'I know a few wrestling tricks, but that——'

'Uncle Devil's got a servant,' Red explained. 'Most folks reckon Tommy Okasi comes from China, but he claims to hail from some place called Nippon. Well, ole Tommy knows a mighty fancy way of fighting they use back to his home. Taught Dusty near on all he knows.'

Then Marsden remembered how Dusty handled the bushwhacker, Ashley, and decided that wherever that Tommy Okasi feller came from, his way of fighting sure gave the small Texan a powerful edge over bigger and stronger men.

After a thorough walking session, Heimer returned with the sorrel and stood apprehensively by while Dusty and Marsden inspected the animal's back. While they found that the metal burr had made a small indentation where it pressed on the sorrel's back, both men realised that no permanent or serious damage had been done—which was fortunate for Heimer.

'He'll do,' Dusty told the young man. 'Throw the saddle on him again so that Mr. Marsden can ride him.'

Although the horse fiddle-footed a little on being mounted, it soon settled down and showed signs of regaining confidence in its rider. When Marsden returned from making a circuit of the corrals, he knew he sat a horse capable of carrying him through the long and hard journey ahead.

CHAPTER SEVEN

BUSHWHACKER RAID

By half-past nine in the morning Elizabeth Chamberlain knew that she and her small escort were utterly and completely lost. All around them rolled the Arkansas hill country, with not a single identifiable mark. Nowhere could she see any sign of the convoy in which she travelled from Fort Downey, one of the posts established by the Union to hold the eastern half of the Indian Nations against the rebels.

A second, less palatable, thought struck Liz—as she preferred to be called. If it came to a point, she might well blame herself for her present position. Instead of allowing the soldier at her side to concentrate on driving the buggy, she insisted on showing her views on equality by engaging him in conversation and straightening him out on various matters. While talking, they must have taken a wrong turning and, followed by three of the mounted escort, wandered away from the convoy. March discipline had not been good and the line straggled badly in the darkness, so their absence would not be discovered until dawn at the earliest.

At first Liz stubbornly refused to believe that she could make such a mistake and when she did both she and the escort failed to do the obvious thing and stay where they were until a search party came for them. Instead they tried to retrace their steps and in doing so became more completely and utterly lost.

'How about it, Miss Chamberlain?' asked one of the escort, a youngster in his teens. 'What d'you reckon we ought to do?'

Liz thought furiously. Despite the liberal views gained by association with some of the new type of Union Army officers, she could not shake off the habits and training of a lifetime. Being the daughter of the men's colonel, she felt that it rested on her shapely and beautiful head to steer them out of trouble. Her only major problem remained how she could do it.

'Could stop here and wait for a search party,' the driver of the buggy suggested. 'They'll be looking for us.'

'No,' Liz replied. 'We'll make for that high ground and see if we can catch sight of our party.'

None of her escort thought of questioning her decision. Obediently the driver headed the buggy up the slope at his right and the other men followed. Liz sat in silence, trying to remember something told her, or overheard, in the past.

'I suppose we're in Union-held territory,' she suddenly remarked.

'The convoy had to pass pretty close to reb country,' the driver replied. 'That was why we moved over-night. Sure hope no reb patrol sees us.'

'There's worse than reb army patrols about,' one of the escort stated. 'I was with a supply train that got jumped by that Captain Fog of the Texas Light. We'd stopped for water and them rebs just seemed to come up out of the ground. We didn't have a chance so the shavetail told us to throw down our guns. Them rebs never fired a shot, just took the wagons, all our horses and guns. Treated us real good. It's not their soldiers that worry me, it's them bushwhackers who're the mean ones.'

Actually Dusty Fog had not been responsible for the raid in question, but his name had become so well known that every Yankee hit by the Texas Light Cavalry gave him credit for the affair.

On reaching the top of the slope, Liz's party halted and began to scan the broken, rolling, bush-dotted land for some hint of where they might find their convoy. Nothing met their eye except the thinly wooded Arkansas hills, rolling slopes broken by ravines and gashes, ideal country for hiding in, but no comfort when lost on possible enemy ground.

Low-growled curses reached Liz's ears as the escort fell slightly away from the covered-over buggy and discussed their situation. She became suddenly and chillingly aware of her own position as a lone, unprotected, attractive young woman with a quartet of scared young men who had little chance of contact with the opposite sex.

A small, dainty hat perched on Liz's head. Being at the stage where defiance of conventions seems the only way of life, she wore her straw-coloured hair cut short and boyishly around her truly beautiful face. The clothes selected for the journey, white frilly bosomed shirt, black jacket, tan divided skirt and dainty black riding boots, clung to a shapely body, emphasising the rich curves. All in all she must look as desirable as water in the desert to those four young men. If they once panicked and decided to desert, they might also——

Liz's thoughts died away as an uneasy feeling came over her. Once, in her sixteenth year, she had been at her father's militia camp and, believing herself to be alone, stripped naked to swim in the cool waters of a stream. While swimming, she became conscious of the feeling that somebody was watching her. A search of the area revealed nothing, but later she learned that a party of soldiers had been on a nearby ridge, studying her through a telescope.

The same feeling crept over Liz again, but although she searched the area, she saw no sign of possible watchers. Then she remembered the thought which had nagged at her on the way up the slope. More than once she had heard men talk of the importance of not appearing on a sky-line when in hostile country. Now she sat in a buggy, out in plain view on a rim.

'Nothing,' said the driver. 'They must have missed us by this time.'

'We'll go back into the valley,' Liz answered. 'Keep going until we find water, then make camp. The convoy's scout ought to be able to track us.'

Once again the men obeyed her. On reaching the foot of the slope, they turned and continued their journey along the rough trail. Ahead lay the mouth to one of the ravines which split into the slope, bush-dotted, rock-covered and somehow menacing. With each stride of the horse, Liz felt her apprehension growing and the belief that somebody watched them increased.

Even as Liz opened her mouth to mention her thoughts to the driver, shots crashed from the bushes at the side of the trail. Liz saw two of the escort pitch out of their saddles. Beyond the men, bearded shapes showed among the bushes, guns roaring in hands.

'Bushwhackers!' yelled her driver and grabbed for the buggy whip.

He needed no such inducement to speed. Spooked by the sudden noise, stink of gunpowder and blood, the harness horse lunged forward and started to run, almost jerking the wheels from the ground as it hit leather. More shots came. Holes appeared in the canvas cover of the buggy, but none of the lead struck home. The last member of the escort proved less fortunate. Caught in the head and chest by bullets, the soldier slid down from his spooked horse and landed limply upon the ground.

Tearing by the mouth to the ravine, Liz saw more shapes; this time mounted on horses. Wild yells rang out and the horsemen gave chase, charging their mounts out of the ravine. One fact began to register in her mind. The attackers wore civilian clothing. No matter how poorly made it might be, the regular Confederate soldier always wore a uniform.

The riders, four in number, raced their horses after the speeding buggy and Liz knew it would be only a matter of time before they caught it. In fact their fast saddle mounts closed the gap with the harness horse rapidly. Shots were fired, but none hit the buggy.

Before they covered two hundred yards, Liz saw a rider coming up on either side of the buggy. The man at her side started to raise his revolver, gave her a second glance, grinned wolfishly and urged the horse on. At the other side of the buggy, a second rider came up. Desperately the young driver tried to yell that he surrendered. Coming in close, the bushwhacker fired once. Jerking under the impact of a .36 ball, the driver let whip and reins slide from his fingers, then he slumped forward in his seat.

Bringing his horse alongside the buggy animal, the bushwhacker tried to lean over and grab its reins. Failing, he gave a snarl, drew his revolver and fired down. A scream burst from the stricken harness horse. Its forelegs buckled under it and it went crashing down, sliding along the ground. Liz let out a cry of pity and fear. Desperately she grabbed at the side of the seat, clinging on with grim determination. Although it lurched wildly, the buggy remained upright. The driver's body toppled from its place, but Liz managed to stay in her seat.

Dust churned up, horses snorted as they came to sliding halts around the buggy. Liz saw men advancing with guns in their hands, heard surprised comments as they saw her clearly for the first time.

'Yeah,' grinned the man who shot the horse, speaking through a fist-damaged mouth. 'That's why I didn't drop her and shot the hoss.'

'Never seed such obliging folks,' another went on, eyeing Liz's body in a predatory manner. 'Get sky-lined so's we know they're about. Then dog-my-cats if they don't come along towards us instead of going away and make us chase 'em.'

'Now you just take your eyes off *her*, Tibby!' warned the first speaker. 'Why for d'you reckon I shot the horse?'

Sick terror bit into Liz at the words and the way the man leered in her direction. She had no weapons, not even a Derringer or one of those new-fangled, light-calibre, metal-cartridge Smith & Wesson revolvers which were becoming popular among Union officers. Even the buggy whip lay some distance away and far out of her reach.

Grinning evilly, the man started to move forward. Hooves drummed and Liz saw a couple more riders tearing along the valley bottom. Much to her surprise, she realised that one of the newcomers was a woman. Nor did that one offer to halt her horse and dismount. Instead, the girl kept her mount moving, causing the bushwhacker to jump back hurriedly. With superb skill, the girl halted her mount and glared at the men. Liz could barely believe her eyes, but the men actually appeared to be sheepish and perturbed by the girl's cold stare.

'You damned fools!' Jill Dodd hissed. 'You crazy, stupid idiots!'

'They're Yankee soldiers,' the fist-damaged man replied sullenly.

'And her?' Jill snapped.

'We didn't know she was with them.'

Looking to where some of the bushwhackers were searching the bodies of their victims, Jill yelled a warning.

'Just take their guns and ammunition. You know what *he* told us.'

Liz gave her rescuer a longer and more penetrating stare, wondering how such a girl came to be riding with a bunch of murderous bushwhackers. Glancing back along the trail Liz saw one of the men push a watch back into a soldier's pocket and another removing ammunition from the driver's pouch. With a shock, Liz realised that all her four companions were dead.

'You murdered them!' she gasped.

'Killed,' Jill corrected, slipping from her saddle. 'They're Yankee soldiers and we're Confederates.'

'They were only boys!' Liz went on.

'They were older than my brother when the Yankees murdered him,' Jill answered. 'And wearing arms and uniforms.'

'If your brother was riding with this bushwhacker——' Liz began.

'He wasn't!' Jill interrupted. 'All he did was——'

'Hey, Jill,' called one of the bushwhackers. 'Reckon we'd best be moving?'

'It'd be lost,' she replied. 'A party this small wouldn't be travelling alone and their friends'll be looking for them. Get the Yankees' horses and we'll move.'

'How about that Yankee gal?' grinned the man.

The question set Jill something of a problem. She had not intended to make any more raids and was scouting when the noise of her men's gunfire brought her back on the run. Now she found herself with a prisoner. The obvious solution would be to leave the other girl to be found by her friends, but Jill saw that such an idea might not prove so easy. Firstly, that small party must have become separated from the main body and hopelessly lost or they would not have been heading into Confederate-held territory. So the search party might fail to find the girl. Another point Jill conceded was that one or more of her own men might slip away from the band, if she left the girl behind, and return to do what Jill had already prevented once.

'She rides with us,' Jill stated. 'At the first town, we'll turn her loose and she can be sent back to her own people.'

'Be best, only I don't like being slowed by no buggy,' the man answered.

'Can you ride, Yankee?' asked Jill.

'I can,' admitted Liz, then stared defiance. 'But I've no intention of doing so.'

'Bring a horse for her!' called Jill.

Collecting one of the dead men's horses, a bushwhacker brought it to where the two girls stood facing each other. Liz decided to make as much difficulty as she could, delaying the bushwhackers' departure in the hope that a Union search party arrived and saved her.

'I won't mount!' she insisted.

'You'll mount!' Jill told her. 'Or I'll damned soon make you!'

Fire flashed in two pairs of eyes as the girls glared at each other. They both crouched slightly, fingers crooking ready to grab at hair. Then Liz became aware of the way the male bushwhackers started to gather around. She read anticipation and sensual delight on each face as they watched the girls and waited for the next development. Suddenly a feeling of revulsion hit Liz and she knew she could not make a physical resistance to the other girl's demands, not with those men standing, waiting and watching every move. They would like nothing more than to see two girls fighting and she did not intend to degrade herself by so doing.

'All right,' she said. 'I'll ride. Can I take my travelling case with me?'

'Sure,' answered Jill, sounding just a shade relieved at not being forced to tangle in a hair-tearing cat-fight with the Yankee girl. 'You can take along a small bag, but we'll have to leave the rest of your gear here. If some of your folks're out looking for you, they'll find it.'

All too well Jill realised the precarious nature of her position. During the two days since Ashley's death, she led the band by the force of her personality and because none of the men showed any qualities of leadership. One wrong move, a single mistake, a temporary set-back, would see the band break up and Jill deserted, if nothing worse. So she allowed Liz a face-saver out of gratitude for not being forced to take the showdown to a conclusion.

Going to the buggy, Liz walked to the rear and drew aside a cover to expose a small trunk and a box made to be strapped to a saddle. She took the latter, it contained toilet articles, a change of underclothing and a couple of blouses; all she would need during the next few days. If the bushwhackers kept their word, she could expect to be free in two days at the most and the Confederate soldiers would give her unrestricted passage to her own people.

'This's all I need,' she told Jill.

'Heck!' Jill said, and a man joined them. 'Strap this on the bay's saddle.' After the man went to obey his orders.

Jill turned back to the other girl. 'Now listen good to me, Yankee. I stopped Guthrie abusing you just now. But if you try anything foolish, or make fuss for us, I won't be able to hold him back a second time. You think on it.'

Liz thought on it, thought long and hard as she mounted the dead soldier's horse. Among other things, she wondered how a girl like Jill came to be riding with the bushwhackers and what gave her such a hatred for the Yankees. Once moving, Jill kept her horse alongside Liz's mount, but made no attempt at conversation. In a hollow they collected a string of half a dozen packhorses and then continued their interrupted journey.

During the ride Liz could not help noticing the cautious manner in which the bushwhackers rode. Scouts went out ahead, behind and upon both flanks and the rest of the party kept to low ground as much as possible. She wondered what made the party so nervous when traversing Confederate-held territory. After they had covered about two miles from the scene of the ambush, something else happened to give Liz more food for thought.

The flank scout on the left suddenly whirled his horse and came racing down to the main body. Riding to meet the man, Jill listened to his low-spoken message. To Liz it became clear that the other girl did not like what she heard. Turning, Jill galloped back to the halted party.

'Hold it here,' she ordered. 'And keep those horses quiet.'

Then an idea came to Liz. The scout must have seen a search party from the convoy; one of considerable force from Jill's concern. If she could get up the ridge, or even create enough noise, help would be rushing towards her. For a moment she sat trying to think of the best way to achieve her ends. Perhaps a sudden thrust of heels into her horse's flanks might carry her through. Before Liz could make the move, a signal from Jill brought two men to her side and the bushwhacker girl moved her horse in front of the trio, bottling any way out.

'They're too far away,' Jill commented. 'And if you try screaming, the boys will quieten you.'

One glance at the leering faces of the men told Liz that the quietening would prove mighty unpleasant. Any attempt at escape would bring a bullet into her at best. The party from which they hid could not arrive in time to save her.

So, having no desire to throw her life away, she sat quietly until the scout, who returned to his position, gave the signal for them to move on again.

Once on the move, Guthrie kept his horse alongside Jill's mount and Liz listened uncomprehendingly to their conversation.

'Reckon it was him still after us?' asked the man.

'Could be,' Jill agreed.

'What about when he finds them Yankees back there?'

'They're soldiers and we only took horses and guns.'

'And her!' Guthrie spat out, jerking a thumb towards Liz.

'We couldn't just leave her behind.' Jill answered. 'She might not've been found. He'll understand that.'

'Reckon he'll give us a chance to explain?' asked the scared-looking man.

'Look!' Jill hissed. 'You know my idea was to keep moving west, cross the Red and lay up in Texas for a spell. *You* had to hit those Yankees while I was out on scout. Now dry off and keep those horses moving. He'll not come too far after us and we'll be safe over the Red.'

Sullenly Guthrie dropped back and Jill rode ahead without speaking to her prisoner. Liz began to wonder which Union Army officer caused such concern among the bushwhackers. During the War, only General George Armstrong Custer's name went out as a Union cavalry leader—and his fame rested on rash, but fortunate, chase-taking that, with plenty of luck, seemed to come off—certainly no Federal officer in Arkansas possessed a reputation likely to scare such a hardened bunch of roughnecks. She decided against asking any questions and the journey continued.

Towards sundown the party crossed the Red River and entered the State of Texas. However, once over the small ford, Jill insisted that they push on for a time. Not until four miles lay behind them and the moon rose palely in the sky did she give the order to halt and make camp. They had followed a small stream which joined the Red below the ford and their stopping place lay in open ground with the stream at the foot of a slope, forming a wide, deep pool. Having halted, Jill set her men to work. She had some caring for the leg-weary horses, others making a fire and starting to cook a meal, one more set about erecting a shelter tent.

'We'll be using that,' she told Liz. 'Look, I can either

have you chained, or I'll take your word that you won't try to escape in the night. Which is it?'

Liz gave quick thought to the matter and replied, 'I'll give you my word.'

'Come and eat then,' Jill accepted. 'It won't be fancy, but it's filling.'

With the meal over, the two girls retired to their tent. Neither undressed and they made their bed with Union Army ponchoes and blankets, using the earth for a mattress. Jill refused to talk much and Liz felt too tired to make any great conversational efforts. She saw that the other girl slept with the Tranter revolver gripped in her hand and felt instinctively that the move was not a pose to impress her.

Liz spent a restless night, but made no attempt to break her word. At dawn she found that the bushwhackers intended to make a late start, resting their horses after the hard work of the previous day. She stuck close to the tent, not caring to face the barrage of stares which greeted her every appearance. Time dragged by and towards noon heard Jill give the order to prepare to move.

'We'll be pulling out in half an hour,' Jill remarked, entering the tent. 'I don't know where the nearest town is, but we'll find it and leave you safe.'

'Up there!' yelled a voice. 'It's him!'

Instantly pandemonium reigned outside the tent. Men shouted curses, then the girls heard hooves drumming. Turning, Jill saw her band leaping afork their mounts and scattering in panic. In their haste, the men discarded belongings, left behind saddles even. Jill looked downstream and saw an approaching party, recognising the man in the lead. Panic always proved infectious and the girl prepared to dash to one of the abandoned horses to make good her escape.

Even as Jill reached her decision, Liz took a hand in the game. From the noise, Liz guessed that the man the bushwhackers feared had arrived on the scene. It seemed that he came too late, for the male members of the band were making good their escape. Liz determined that the rebel girl would not get away. With that thought in mind, Liz hurled herself across the tent. Locking her arms around Jill's waist, Liz sent the other girl crashing through the tent's flap and brought her to the ground outside.

CHAPTER EIGHT

A PROBLEM FOR CAPTAIN FOG

Riding the borrowed sorrel, Lieutenant Marsden sat in the centre of the line of men moving across the rolling Texas range country some two and a half miles beyond the Red River. To his right Dusty Fog sat afork a magnificent black stallion, a big, fine looking animal which turned Marsden almost green with envy. Beyond Dusty, Sam Ysabel rode a big strawberry roan stallion which looked even meaner than all hell and matched the black's seventeen hands of grace and power. On Marsden's left came Billy Jack, then Kiowa, each sitting a big black horse of a kind only seen ridden by field-rank officers in the Union Army. All in all they were a superbly mounted body of men.

The reason for riding in line abreast with Marsden at the centre did not imply distrust of his motives. In line, only the leading horse had an unrestricted view of the ground it must traverse and each succeeding animal moved in air polluted by those preceding it.

Since leaving the Texas Light Cavalry the previous day at just after dawn, Marsden had already received several lessons in the art of long distance fast travel by horse. He also knew the reason for Dusty's strict inspection of saddlery and animals—with great emphasis on the state of each horse's shoes, to the extent of having every animal re-shod—and found himself admiring the young captain's attention to detail.

Dusty insisted that they wait until dawn had broken sufficiently for his party to see clearly as they saddled up the horses. After the first two hours at a fast trot guaranteed to wipe out any snuffiness the horses might feel, Dusty called the first halt. Not that the men rested during the halt. Instead they examined and made necessary adjustments to packs and saddles while allowing their mounts to clear themselves and graze.

From then on the remainder of the day had been pure hard work. Alternating between riding at a trot and walking, leading the horses, the men covered mile after mile. Every hour brought a halt, the first and second short and giving the horses time to blow, but on the third hour long enough for the men to off-saddle and let each mount's back dry off, then the horses were grain fed and allowed to graze before being saddled and moved on. In that manner, they covered around forty miles the first day and, as long as the horses held out, ought to make at least thirty more each day by using the same methods. If so, they should reach the Brazos River's fork area in time to organise a search for Castle's wagons.

Moving on that morning, the party made good time until they approached the Red River ford selected by Dusty as best suited to their purposes. Sam Ysabel had been ahead to scout the small ford and he sat back from the edge, keeping under cover when the others arrived.

'Bunch went across last night, Cap'n,' he reported. 'Fair-sized party. From the sign they kept going, followed that stream there west.'

Kiowa rode by the others and went to the river's edge, looking down at the tracks. Turning, he said, 'Be about fifteen of 'em, some packhosses. One of 'em's a purty lil gal.'

'Don't see no footprints,' Ysabel remarked.

'Never yet saw a danged Comanche's could read sign,' answered Kiowa with a faint mouth movement that passed as a broad friendly grin in his circle.

'Danged Injun varmints,' Billy Jack put in, enjoying the inter-tribal rivalry expressed by the two sergeants.

'Ashley's bunch of bushwhackers?' guessed Dusty. 'Looks like they didn't listen to me. Let's cross.'

'And 'fore ole Kiowa here swells up and busts a gut with all this funning,' Billy Jack went on to Ysabel. 'We trailed Ashley's bunch for so long that even I can pick out their hosses' tracks.'

'Paleface brother got heap big mouth,' grunted Kiowa, 'Side with Comanches too. I——'

'Move over!' Dusty ordered.

All levity left the men and they advanced as a unit ready

to fight. The water came barely to the level of the stirrup irons and the river's bed offered a firm, safe footing so that the party experienced no difficulty in making their crossing. Nor were they opposed during the crossing and on the other side continued their journey. They followed the same line as the bushwhackers had the previous night.

'Smoke up ahead,' Ysabel said, pointing. 'Soon know if our Kiowa brother can read sign or not.'

'Likely,' Dusty replied. 'It's on our line of march and I don't want to waste time going around. Remember the arrangements happen we get jumped by Yankees—even Kiowa can make a mistake.'

Among other things before leaving the Texas Light Cavalry's camp, Dusty made arrangements for action should they be attacked. Not wishing to make a fight unless forced, he planned well and Marsden admitted that the small Texan thought of the best way to handle the situation.

The reference to a bushwhacker band left Marsden feeling puzzled. After the raid on the Kansas town of Lawrence, both Union and Confederate Governments disowned the various irregular bands and ordered a cessation of all guerilla activity. From the direction they took, Marsden concluded that Dusty meant to visit the bushwhacker camp. Of course, if the smoke ahead proved to be no more than the bushwhackers', Dusty's party did not need to make a detour; and Marsden knew that every mile saved was of vital importance on their mission.

Topping the rim brought the camp into sight at a distance of almost half a mile. From all appearances the bushwhackers were preparing to move out. Men saddled horses, packed up their gear, but as yet had not struck the one tent erected.

Even as the party started down the slope, a bushwhacker saw them. His reaction came as something of a surprise to Dusty's party. Letting out a yell and pointing up the slope, the man dropped his bundle and raced towards the horses. Other men stared, yelled and instantly the camp took on the appearance of an overturned ant's nest. The bushwhackers dashed in all directions, discarding their property. One man tried to mount his horse, forgetting that he had not tightened the cinches. When the saddle slipped off, the man made no attempt to recover it. Instead he bounded afork the horse's bare back and set his spurs to work. Like leaves blown by the wind, the bushwhackers started their horses galloping in every direction, except towards Dusty and his men.

'What the hell?' asked Ysabel.

'Reckon they think we're still after 'em,' answered Billy Jack.

'There's more to it than that,' Dusty objected. 'They must've——'

Two shapes erupted from the tent, chopping off Dusty's words half said. While he recognised one as the bushwhacker girl, he had never seen the other. Even at that distance Dusty could see the excellent quality of the second girl's clothing and guessed, if her actions proved anything, that she did not belong to the bushwhacker band.

'Land-sakes!' Billy Jack ejaculated, staring at the girls. 'Just look at them go. They're worse'n a pair of Kilkenny cats.'

Just what Liz expected Jill to do when tackled, she had not thought about. It may be that she thought her rescuers were so close that help would speedily be on hand to subdue the rebel girl. However, having laid hold on Jill, Liz found herself in a similar position to the man who caught a tiger by the tail, then found that he could not let go.

Taken by surprise, Jill went down with Liz clinging to her waist. Landing on her side, hurt and wild with a mixture of fear and fury, she acted instinctively. She drove back her upper elbow, catching Liz in the face and bringing a squeal of pain. A savage writhe brought Jill around to face her assailant. Blood from Liz's nose splashed down on to Jill's face as the rebel girl's hands drove instinctively for hair. On top, Liz screeched again as the top of her head seemed to burst into painful fire, taking her mind off the hurt of her nose. Like Jill, Liz had never been engaged in physical conflict—childhood scuffles excepted—but her own instinct for self-preservation took over. Even as Jill arched her back and rolled Liz over, the Union girl's hands found hair and she drove her head forward to try to bite.

On the ground the two girls twisted and rolled over and over, oblivious of the fleeing bushwhackers or approaching party. Hands alternated at tearing hair, grabbing and nipping flesh, swinging wild slaps and punches; legs waved, kicked, curled around each other, with Liz ignoring the way her skirt rode up to expose the white flesh over the top of her black stockings.

So wild with pain and fury did the girls become that neither realised they were rolling towards the bank of the stream. Vaguely they heard hooves coming towards them and faint shouts reached uncomprehending ears. Seeing the danger, Dusty sent his horse bounding forward. Before he reached the struggling girls, they tipped over the edge of the bank. Locked in each other's arms, ignoring the bumps and jabs of the hard ground beneath them, they went rolling down the slope. Not until they plunged into the water did either girl realise what had happened. Their wails of shock died into soggy gurgles, for at that point the stream formed a large pool with sheer sides, as they plunged into the water and disappeared beneath the surface.

Shock caused the girls to separate, the sudden chill of the water winding them and causing them to forget their fury. Breaking the surface some distance from each other, soaking, winded and dazed, the girls stood for a moment. Then their eyes met and recognition began to return. Slowly Jill put the back of her hand to her lips and looked at the blood on it. Gasping for breath, Liz reached up to shove back her wet hair. Then each girl started through the waist-deep water towards the other, ready to resume hostilities.

'Well dog-my-cats!' Billy Jack gasped admiringly as he topped the slope and looked down. 'Iffen they ain't coming to taw again, my name's——'

'Let's have 'em out,' Dusty interrupted, and unstrapped his rope. 'I'll take the bushwhacker gal, Billy Jack.'

'Don't leave me no choice, Cap'n Dusty,' grinned the sergeant-major, his own rope coming free.

Almost together the two ropes flew out and down, nooses dropping over the girls' heads and down below the level of their shoulders. Startled yells left feminine lips as they found their forward progress halted and arms pinned to sides while still some distance apart.

'Haul 'em in!' Dusty ordered.

Springing from their horses, Marsden, Ysabel and Kiowa ran to the ropes. After securing his rope to the saddlehorn, Billy Jack dropped to the ground and went to assist Marsden hauling Liz out of the water and up the slope.

'Now this here's what I call real fishing,' grinned Billy

Jack, watching the two squealing girls hauled up the slope towards him.

'I wouldn't want to put either of them in a glass case on a wall though,' Marsden answered.

Before they reached the top of the slope, surprise, exhaustion and realisation of pain forgotten during the wild, thrashing mêlée, drove all thoughts of further aggression from the girls. Seeing the men above her, Jill became aware of her position and wondered what her fate would be at the hands of the grim-faced young captain who killed Ashley. Dusty Fog must have been hunting for her band and would have found the bodies of the ambushed Union soldiers. If so, he knew that the bushwhackers went against his orders and continued their operations.

With the fight over, reaction bit sharply into Liz, more so than affected her opponent. Sobbing, she sank to her knees and on the rope being taken from her shoulders, covered her face with her hands. Pain nagged at her; bruises gained during the roll down the slope throbbed dully; where teeth, feet or hands connected on flesh each sent a separate sting through her and her hair roots seemed to be on fire. In that condition, she could not think and so missed the surprising detail of seeing a Union lieutenant in company with the Confederate soldiers.

'Tend to them, Kiowa,' Dusty ordered. 'Rest of you see to the horses. We'll make this our noon halt.'

Kiowa had learned Indian-style medicine from his mother and gained something of a reputation as a curer of minor ailments. Stepping forward, he opened his saddle-bag and took out his medicine kit, then went towards the girls. One glance told him that neither had sustained serious injury during the fight and also that Liz needed his services far more than did Jill.

'Just let me take a look at you, ma'am,' he said gently.

At another time Liz might have objected to submitting to treatment by a man like Kiowa. In her present condition, she wanted help and willingly accepted its offer on receipt. With surprising gentleness, Kiowa drew the girl's hands from her face and bent forward to look at the blood-trickling nose.

Forcing herself to her feet, Jill walked slowly to where Dusty stripped the saddle from his big black stallion.

'I don't see why you're hunting us down like this,' she stated, holding her torn shirt together as best she could. 'They were Yankee soldiers, and the boys only took their guns and horses.'

'You've lost me, ma'am,' Dusty answered, swinging the saddle clear. 'Who were Yankee soldiers?'

'The bunch Guthrie ambushed back in Arkansas. We saw your troop while we were pulling out and heading for Texas after the ambush.'

'Not my troop, ma'am,' Dusty corrected, although he now saw the reason for the bushwhackers' flight on seeing him. 'Who's the girl?'

'She was with the Yankees. I didn't know what Guthrie aimed to do, I was out on scout when they saw the Yankees and made their hit. Then I couldn't leave the girl alone. Brought her along and was going to leave her in the first town we found.'

'How is she, Kiowa?' called Dusty.

'Mite shook up, but nothing broke or hurt too bad.'

'I didn't start the fight,' Jill put in. 'And I wouldn't've let anything happen to her.'

'I believe you,' Dusty replied. 'Only you should have taken my advice and left that bunch. They're not fighting the Yankees.'

'They would have been,' Jill insisted. 'I aimed to reform the band in Texas, get men in it who wanted to fight.'

'That's what the army's for,' Dusty said. 'Have you any dry clothes?'

'Sure.'

'Go change into them. See if you can get your prisoner into something dry.'

'What do you intend to do with me?' asked Jill.

'Lady,' admitted Dusty, 'that's something I haven't figured out yet. Go get dried off and changed.'

Turning, Jill walked away. She went to where Liz sat on the ground and looked down. Almost with relief Jill saw that the Yankee girl seemed to be recovering and in no danger. A little stiffly, she offered to fit Liz out with dry clothing. While Liz first thought of refusing, she realised—through her exploring fingers—that her blouse had suffered damage in the fight and that she needed to get out of the wet clothing. So, just as stiffly as Jill offered, Liz accepted.

Thought had returned to Liz with Kiowa's ministrations and she looked about her, seeing much that was puzzling. The bushwhackers had all fled, but from Confederate, not Union soldiers; and a small party at that. Then Liz became aware of Marsden and wondered at his presence. At first she thought he might be a prisoner, yet knew of no prisoner-of-war camp in Texas. Also no prisoner would be under the escort of a captain and three senior non-coms.

Still pondering on Marsden's presence, Liz followed Jill into the tent. While accepting the other's offer of dry clothing, Liz maintained frigid silence and Jill did nothing to help. Opening her war-bag, Jill produced two shirts and a couple of pairs of men's pants, remarking that she had nothing else to offer. Liz opened her travelling case and took out dry underwear and a towel.

While stripping off her clothes. Liz could hear enough to tell her that the men were tending to their horses. As she started to dry herself with the towel, she caught the sound of voices; one a southern drawl, the other a northern accent. Apparently the two officers were in conference and she strained her ears to catch what they discussed.

'So the bushwhacker girl brought the other one with her.' The small man with the southern drawl was speaking. 'Showed good sense in doing it too. The other girl might never've been found—or one of the bushwhackers gone back to her.'

'You believe the girl intended to release Miss Chamberlain?' asked Marsden, having recognised Liz as an acquaintance from Little Rock's army social circle.

'Sure. That girl's no bushwhacker slut,' Dusty replied. 'And she'd a hold on that rabble or Miss Chamberlain'd've been raped before now.'

'Thing now is what do you aim to do with them?'

'How's that, mister?'

'We can't leave them here,' Marsden pointed out, then went on. 'Could find a town, like the girl intended.'

'There's none around and we're too far north for the main Texas-Arkansas trails,' Dusty answered.

'If the girl can control her men, leave them both here,' Marsden suggested.

'And if the men don't come back?'

'Reckon they won't, sir?'

'Nope. They'll figure that I've taken the girls with me and destroyed the camp. So the girls will have to come with us.'
'Can they stand up to the pace?'
'Mister,' Dusty said quietly but grimly, 'they'll have to stand up to it. You know as well as I do what's at stake.'
'Yes, sir,' agreed Marsden. 'Couldn't we leave them at either Dallas or Fort Worth?'
'It'd take us a day out of our way. We don't have a day to spare, mister.'
'Then let one of the men——'
'I'd thought of it. But there's nobody I can spare. Even without being short-handed if it comes to a fight, and needing them to deal with the Indians. Sam Ysabel's our best man with the pack animals and Kiowa's got the medicine skill if we need it. And Billy Jack can cold-shoe a horse as well as many a blacksmith. It just won't do, mister.'
'How about me?' asked Marsden.
'You're no plainsman, mister,' Dusty answered. 'And you'd not get far travelling through Texas in *that* colour uniform. No, mister, those girls will have to take their choice. Stay here and chance being found—or come with us and stick the pace. There's no other way and too much at stake for me to do otherwise.'
Watching Dusty, Marsden felt sympathy with the other's position and knew just what moral fibre it needed to make such a decision. Reared in the strict Southern tradition, Dusty did not lightly toss aside his training on the subject of women's treatment. However, the small Texan had to balance two lives against the chance of preventing an Indian uprising which would bring death, or worse, to thousands of men, women and children.
'Go pick the best two horses from the bushwhacker remuda,' Dusty ordered. 'I want the rest of their stock scattered and all this stuff destroyed if the girls agree to come along with us. See to it, mister.'
In the tent Liz looked at Jill who donned a pair of men's long-legged red-flannel underwear.
'Who is that small captain?' she asked.
While he might have broken up her bushwhacker band, Jill still felt considerable pride in the small Texan's reputation as a Confederate soldier.
'Captain Dusty Fog,' she answered a shade pompously.

Liz tossed aside her towel and started to dress. Thoughts churned in her head as she slipped on the dry underclothing. She knew Dusty Fog's reputation and felt certain that something very important lay behind the captain's presence so far from the battlefields of Arkansas. The scrap of conversation she heard confirmed her belief and she felt cold anger well inside her as she realised that the Union officer must be a traitor. He seemed to know her, which meant they must have met. Swiftly Liz finished dressing, feeling uncomfortable in men's clothing. She stepped to the door of the tent and raised the flap a trifle.

'Jackson Marsden!' she breathed.

While visiting in Little Rock, Liz had met Marsden and heard him mentioned as a promising career officer. Only something of great importance would turn such a man into a traitor. From what she overheard, the mission the men rode on was of vital significance with time its essence for success.

Ever since the death of the soldiers, Liz had felt guilty, blaming herself for them getting lost in the first place. Now she saw a chance to partially make amends. She would go with the Texans and do everything in her power to make sure that their mission did not succeed.

'I'd like to see you ladies outside when you're dressed,' Dusty called, standing outside the tent.

A smile played on Liz's lips. Captain Fog thought his problem with herself and the other girl was over—she aimed to see that it had only just begun.

CHAPTER NINE

A CLASH OF WILLS

'You must understand, ladies,' Dusty told the girls. 'I refuse to allow considerations of your sex to slow me down. If you come with us, it is on the understanding that you obey my orders and accept my conditions. We'll be covering between thirty and forty miles a day and that's rough on a *man*.'

Looking around her, Jill gave a shrug. Although Dusty had not mentioned the nature of his mission, she knew it must be very important for him to lay down such terms to a pair of girls. She decided that she could make a sacrifice for the Confederate States.

'I accept your conditions, Captain Fog,' she said.

'Do you, Miss Chamberlain?' asked Dusty.

'Yes,' Liz replied.

Something in the girl's voice drew Marsden's eyes to her and he felt puzzled by her mild acceptance. Although he did not know her too well, Marsden figured Liz to be an intelligent young woman. In which case she must know of the importance of the Texan's mission—although not the details of it. He knew her to be almost fanatically loyal to the Union, due in some measure to the kind of friends she made among the intellectual Southerner-hating set of volunteer officers. So Liz should be protesting, demanding immediate return to her own people and relying on Southern chivalry to get her way; or at least trying to delay the party's departure by argument. The manner in which she surrendered to the inevitable worried Marsden.

Taking advantage of the delay, Billy Jack and Sam Ysabel had cooked a meal from the bushwhackers' supplies and the party ate well. After the meal, Dusty set his men to work. Jill helped saddle the horses while the men fitted the pack saddles on the baggage animals, but Liz stayed out of the way. Instinctively Liz knew the moment for defiance had not yet arrived and so remained meekly obedient.

Before moving out, Dusty saw that all the bushwhackers' property was destroyed and their remuda scattered. He did not intend to leave them the means to reorganise should they return to their camp-site.

'From now on you tend to your own mount, Miss Chamberlain,' he said.

'Of course, Captain,' she replied.

'Mount up, then. You'll ride at my right, Miss Chamberlain, you at the left, Miss Dodd.'

Jill swung astride her spirited buckskin gelding and Liz mounted the kettle-bellied bay mare assigned to her, feeling just a trifle self-conscious and aware that she filled out her borrowed pants rather well. However, none of the men appeared to be interested in how she looked and she concentrated on handling her horse.

On moving out from the destroyed camp, Liz found herself with Dusty at one side and Marsden upon the other. She realised that she ought to be showing some interest in his presence.

'May I ask how you come to be here, Mr. Marsden?' she asked. 'Are you a prisoner?'

'No, Miss Chamberlain,' Marsden replied.

'Then what are you, a traitor?'

'You might say that,' Marsden agreed.

A low hiss left the girl's lips and anger glowed in her eyes. 'Do you think betraying your country and your honour is worth the monetary gains you receive?'

'I'm not doing it for money,' Marsden replied.

'Then why do you, a supposedly loyal Union officer, betray your own country?'

'Because——'

'He has a good reason, Miss Chamberlain,' Dusty put in. There was no point in letting the girls know the true nature of the assignment. Even now there might be a chance of a south-bound party to take the girls off his hands, in which case they probably would talk and he did not wish to start panic among the people of Texas.

'I'd like to hear it,' Liz snapped.

'Maybe you will, one day,' answered Dusty.

Sensing that further questions would be ignored, Liz let

the matter drop and concentrated upon handling her horse. Holding to a steady trot, the party covered three miles before Liz saw a chance to put her delaying tactics into operation.

'Dismount and walk,' Dusty ordered.

Every eye turned to Liz as she remained in her saddle when all but she and Dusty swung to the ground.

'I won't!' she stated. 'I refuse to walk!'

She took a gamble on her knowledge of southern chivalry. With the camp back on the stream destroyed, and no sight of human habitation from one horizon to the other, the men would not leave her behind. So she aimed to delay them by argument, stir up trouble among them. If Dusty Fog allowed her to ride, it would make discontent among the others. Also riding would tire her horse—to be fair, she took no pleasure in the thought of inflicting suffering upon her mount—and she knew the speed of the party could be no faster than the pace of the slowest member.

So Liz prepared for a clash of will with Dusty Fog, looked forward to testing him and learning just how far she might go.

Edging his horse towards Liz's mount, Dusty suddenly reached out and gripped her by the waist. Like many people when first coming into contact with Dusty, Liz failed to appreciate the powerful nature of his frame. Taken by surprise both at Dusty's prompt action and his strength, Liz felt herself lifted, swung from the saddle and lowered to the ground.

'I still won't walk!' she shouted and flung herself into a sitting position on the ground.

Dusty did not even give the girl a glance. 'Sergeant-major!' he snapped. 'Take Miss Chamberlain's horse.'

'Yo!' Billy Jack replied.

'I refuse to walk!' Liz warned, conscious that every eye was on her.

'Give me the word and I'll drag her along by the hair, Captain,' Jill said.

'Move out!' Dusty ordered, ignoring the girl's suggestion.

Only Jill failed to obey the order immediately. As the men stepped off, she stood for a moment, throwing glances first at Dusty, then towards Liz. Although town-raised, Jill had heard often enough of the dangers of being left afoot on the open plains of Texas. Since leaving the camp, the party came across several large bunches of half-wild longhorned Texas cattle and Dusty warned that such animals feared only a mounted human being; and the cattle were but one of the dangers to a girl afoot.

'Don't be a fool, Yankee,' she urged. 'Captain Fog's not bluffing.'

'And neither am I,' Liz replied grimly.

Giving an angry snort, Jill started to turn. Then she gave a shrug, drew the Tranter—picked up by Billy Jack at the camp—and offered it butt forward to Liz.

'Here, you're more likely to need it than I am.'

For once in her life Liz felt at a loss for words. Taking the Tranter, Liz watched Jill turn and walk away leading the buckskin. Setting her teeth grimly, Liz prepared to call Dusty Fog's bluff.

'You can't just walk away and leave her,' Jill said, catching up with Dusty.

'It's her choice,' he replied.

Like Liz, Dusty knew the clash of their wills had begun. While he could appreciate her motives and admire her guts, he refused to be swayed from his purpose. If he showed weakness, Liz would come to expect it. For the sake of his mission, he must break the girl's defiance and aimed to do it.

Nursing the Tranter as she sat on the ground, Liz watched the party walking away from her. Not one of them gave a sign of being aware of her absence and she set her face in an expression of determination. Slowly she looked around and a feeling of awe crept over her as she studied the vast, open, rolling miles of land around her. Apart from the party walking away, she could see no sign of human life, not so much as a far-distant smudge of smoke hinting at a house's presence.

A momentary fear crept into her as she realised how precarious her position would be if the small Texan refused to back down. For hundreds of miles all she could expect would be deadly danger. The buffalo wolf, the black bear, even the mountain lion under certain conditions, could be dangerous to a lone traveller. Nor would many of the human beings she might meet prove any more of a blessing. She had escaped rape at the hands of the bushwhackers once, but what if they found her alone and without Jill Dodd's protection? True Liz held a gun, but she knew just how little defence it would give in her unskilled hands.

'Take hold of yourself, girl,' she told herself. 'He'll break and come back for you.'

'Keep moving, Miss Dodd,' Dusty growled as Jill slowed her pace and started to turn her head. 'Don't look back!'

Jerking herself around, Jill turned a worried, pleading face towards the small Texan. 'You can't just desert her, Captain.'

'And I can't waste time on her little games either,' Dusty replied.

'Is what you're doing so important that it's worth the life of an innocent girl?' Jill demanded hotly.

'Take my word, Miss Dodd,' Marsden put in. 'It is important.'

'How would you know?' Jill snapped, her smouldering hate of Union supporters driving her on.

'Because Mr. Marsden gave up his career, and that's as important as his life to him, to bring us news that started this mission,' Dusty growled.

'Then you *are* one of our spies,' the girl gasped.

'No, ma'am!' Marsden replied.

'Then why——' Jill began, stopping speaking when she realised that she could not make herself continue with the question of why he turned traitor.

'Because Mr. Marsden learned something real important, Miss Dodd,' Dusty explained, and Jill writhed at the scorn and fury in his voice. 'Something that, unless stopped, will cost thousands of innocent men, women and children their lives. That's why he turned "traitor" and came to us.'

Contrition bit into the girl and she looked at Marsden. 'I'm sorry. More sorry than I can tell you.'

'Forget it, Miss Dodd,' answered Marsden. 'And remember that Captain Fog is doing what he must.'

'Couldn't you have told the Yank—Miss Chamberlain about your mission, Captain?' asked Jill. 'Surely if she knew how important——'

'She might not try to delay us,' Dusty admitted. 'But I can't risk taking time to explain and then have her cause me more trouble to delay me.'

'Would she still try if she knew?' Jill said.

'Put yourself in her place,' Dusty answered. 'Suppose

you learned something that put you in a position to help the South to victory. Would you try to do it?'

'Of course.'

Even after so short a time Dusty had come to know enough about Jill to make an argument she would understand. He wanted to stop her talking about Liz and reckoned that such an argument might bring off the desired result.

'So would Miss Chamberlain,' he said, cementing the idea in Jill's head. 'And that's why I won't let her delay us.'

Suddenly Jill realised what a strain Dusty must be under at having to make such a decision. Being born and raised in Texas, he knew even better than Jill the dangers to a person left afoot on the range. Jill set her teeth, fixed her eyes on the forward horizon and fought down her desire to look back. Flickering glances at the men on either side of her she read their concern from the tight-set faces. Only the knowledge of their mission and the respect they felt for their leader kept them walking on, leaving Liz behind, as Dusty ordered.

With growing disbelief and anxiety Liz watched the party continue to walk away. A quarter of a mile separated them and grew on to the half-mile mark. Every step they took, Liz expected to see them halt, look back, possibly one of them return to plead with her for a change of mind. Yet each step saw them going further from her, increasing the distance with relentless precision.

A movement to her right caught the corner of her eye. Swinging around, she saw a small band of pronghorn antelope stepping daintily through the bush-dotted range about two hundred yards away. Even as she looked, something startled the animals and they broke in a wild, scattering, leaping flight. Liz felt a momentary panic, wondering what spooked the antelope and knowing she could not equal their speed should the unseen menace come her way.

'He'll turn back soon,' she told herself, but with less conviction than on the last occasion she used the sentiment.

At that moment her eyes caught another movement. Turning, she gave a low cry of horror and stared at a diamondback rattlesnake all of three foot long as it glided through the buffalo grass some yards from her. Liz came hurriedly to her feet. The vibrations of her rising halted the snake, bringing it into a defensive coil while the interconnecting horny caps which formed its rattle giving out their vicious buzz-saw warning. Choking down a little sob, Liz started to walk as fast as she could after the departing party.

'That's a might stubborn lil gal, Sam,' Billy Jack remarked after they had covered something over half a mile since leaving Liz.

'Sure,' agreed Ysabel. 'Only this time she's met somebody a damned sight more stubborn.'

If Dusty heard the men, he ignored them. Mouth set in grim, determined lines, he fought down his inclination to turn back. However, one of the party had not been under Dusty's kind of discipline long enough to stick rigidly to obedience of orders. Having fought down the inclination as long as she could, Jill chanced a quick glance to the rear.

'She's coming after us!' Jill said, letting out a gasp of relief and showing neither jubilation nor derision at Liz's defeat.

'Keep your eyes to the front and stay marching,' Dusty growled.

Catching the faint note of relief in Dusty's voice, Jill felt no resentment at his brusque tone. Was it her imagination, or did Dusty slow his pace? She could not be sure. With a woman's instincts, she saw beneath the stony exterior and grim determination, reading Dusty's feelings at the course of action forced on him. Whatever business took him west, it must be mighty important to make him treat a girl as he had Liz. A shudder ran through her as she remembered what Dusty said about the thing he must stop costing thousands of innocent lives. While she could not imagine what it might be, she felt the growing urgency with which Dusty pressed on to the west and knew he meant what he said.

Behind the party Liz increased her pace to a fast walk. Her cheeks reddened a little as she wondered what kind of reception the others would give her. Probably they would mock her. That little rebel slut was going to—— The weight of the Tranter stopped that line of thought and Liz remembered just how much she owed to Jill Dodd.

Going down a slope which took them out of Liz's sight, Dusty looked at his party. 'Halt!' he called. 'We'll rest up here for a spell.'

'I need it,' Jill groaned.

'The hosses get the rest, ma'am,' grinned Kiowa. 'We work.'

'Billy Jack, tend to Miss Chamberlain's horse this time,' Dusty ordered.

'Yo!' the sergeant-major replied. 'Get your hoss's nose-bag out of the saddle-pouch, Miss Dodd. Sam'll give you the grain.'

Clearly the men knew their duties, for none needed telling what to do. Each of them took his horse's nose-bag from the saddle-pouches and Sam Ysabel led the way to one of the pack animals. Carefully he opened one of the grain sacks on the right of the pack saddle and started to pour a quantity of food into each bag as it was offered to him.

'Round the other side, ma'am,' he said as Jill came up in her turn.

For a moment the order puzzled Jill, then she realised that the load must be balanced if the horse's back was to be kept free from injury. Jill did not know it, but a difference of as little as two pounds in the weight of the packs could injure the horse. However, of necessity, Sam Ysabel had learned the pack train trade very thoroughly and could gauge a balance with his eyes as well as many men would do with a set of scales.

Taking the feed-bag to the buckskin, Jill happened to glance inside as she prepared to place it into position. She saw something brown among the grain and reached in to extract a small ball of what appeared to be wood.

'What're you doing, gal?' asked Billy Jack as she prepared to toss the object away.

'I found it mixed in with the grain,' she explained.

'Sure. We put it there. It's meat.'

'Meat?' Jill gasped. 'But horses don't eat meat.'

'Don't set down and carve a pot-roast, ma'am,' agreed Ysabel. 'But the Comanches learned way back that slipping some small balls of meat in with the other food helps a hoss to keep going when it's travelling fast.'

'Get those nose-bags on there,' Dusty called. 'Buckle it up good and tight, Miss Dodd, so he doesn't have to toss his head to get at the grain and lose most of it.'

Removing her horse's bit, Jill fixed the nose-bag in position and drew it up tight. The horses had been allowed to drink when crossing a small stream some three hundred yards back and the buckskin started eating as she drew on the bag. After caring for her own mount, Jill looked around to see if she could help with any of the others. Finding that the men had cared for all the stock she gave thought to her own needs.

'I've got to go into the bushes,' she remarked, and Dusty nodded.

'Let me take your horse, Miss Dodd,' Marsden offered.

Jill's fingers brushed against Marsden's as she handed over the reins. A tingling sensation ran through her and she lifted her eyes to his. Then she remembered that the Yankees had murdered her brother and tried to fight the feeling down. Turning, she walked hurriedly up the slope and into a clump of bushes near the top. Since joining the bushwhackers, most of her toilet arrangements were made in a similar manner. Then she always kept her Tranter handy and felt uneasy at the thought that the gun was in Liz's hands. However, she guessed that the Texans would respect her privacy and went out of sight to attend to her business.

With set face and grim bearing, Liz walked down the slope towards the men. Jill came from the bushes adjusting her waist belt and Liz braced herself for the first of the expected taunts.

'I'll take the Tranter, Yankee,' Jill remarked in a neutral tone. 'And if you want to go, I'd go now, Captain Dusty'll be wanting to move off real soon.'

Handing Jill the gun, Liz disappeared into the bushes and soon the two girls walked side by side down the slope. Although Liz's back remained stiff with defiance, she found none of the expected derision. A feeling of pique hit her, a touch of disappointment, as she found she could not even feel like a martyr suffering at the hands of a vicious enemy.

Looking around, Dusty saw that his force had everything ready to move and so gave the order to march. Liz swung into her saddle and wondered at the sense of security the touch of leather and presence of the rest of the party gave her. Quick thought warned her not to try any more delaying tactics right then. When they made camp for the night might offer greater opportunities. However, her annoyance at being ignored—when she had worked herself up to take derision if not actual abuse—drove her to pick on somebody. Marsden, in his Union-blue uniform, provided her with the best target.

'Mr. Marsden,' she said. 'Didn't you command the rear-guard action at Poison Springs?'

'Yes, ma'am.'

'You handled it magnificently, so I heard. There were many rebel casualties,' she went on in a carrying voice, then turned to look at Kiowa. 'Were you at the action, Sergeant?'

'No, ma'am,' Kiowa answered.

'Were any of the Texas Light Cavalry?'

'Three companies.'

'Did you see any of them, Mr. Marsden?' Liz asked.

'If you mean, did he help kill any of our outfit,' Dusty put in coldly. 'I'd say it was likely. A soldier's duty is to kill his enemies. Only we're not fussing with him for what happened in the past.'

A flush crept over Liz's face as she realised that she had instinctively made a move to split up the party, and saw it fail. Once more her anger turned on Marsden. 'I fail to see why a man like you turned traitor and renegade!' she snapped.

'You leave him be, Yankee!' Jill shouted across Dusty. 'He must've had real good reason.'

'He had, ma'am,' agreed Billy Jack. 'If Castle gets them Injuns——'

'Billy Jack!' Dusty roared, but knew that the damage had been done. 'That's why we're heading west in such a hurry, ma'am. Two of your officers are trying to stir up an Injun uprising in Texas.'

'Carney Castle's scheme!' Liz gasped. 'I heard him mention it. Why it would bring about the withdrawal of all the Texas troops from the rebel army. You lousy traitor, Marsden. You told the rebs——'

'Keep in line, Dodd!' Dusty barked as Jill started to swing her horse with the intention of resuming hostilities. Turning back to Liz he continued, 'Mr. Marsden knows what such an uprising would mean. Understands the cost in innocent lives. The men behind the idea don't, or they'd never have started it.'

'You rebels have used Indians to do your fighting for you,' she pointed out.

'Pike's Cherokee Brigade,' agreed Dusty. 'That's not the same thing——'

'Why?' spat Liz. 'Because they sided you rebs——'

'No, ma'am. Because the Cherokee aren't Comanche, Kiowa or Kaddo.'

'They scalped our dead on the field at Pea Ridge,' Liz reminded him.

'They did, ma'am,' Dusty answered. 'Which's just what I mean. The Cherokee are tamed Indians. They've lived white-man fashion for years. Most of 'em are Christians, send their kids to school. Yet when they went to war, they went right back to the old ways and started scalping.'

'Cap'n Dusty's right, ma'am,' Ysabel put in. 'Them Cherokee're tamed Injuns and like lap-dogs alongside buffalo-wolves when took with Comanches, Kiowas and Kaddos like the fool Yankees're trying to stir up. At least our Cherokees stuck to killing and lifting hair from Yankee *soldiers*.'

'Those hostiles Castle plans to stir up, ma'am,' Dusty said quietly. 'Once they get started, they'll not leave a living white in Texas.'

'And a thing like that won't just stay in Texas. Word'll go out and every hostile across the country'll paint for war,' Ysabel warned grimly. 'There'll likely not be a white man, woman or child left alive from the Red River to the Pacific. That's why we're headed west.'

Liz relapsed into silence and thought of what the men told her. Although she knew little about Castle's scheme, she had met the man. Thinking back, she remembered hearing him discuss the effects of an Indian uprising in Texas. The with-drawal of the Texas troops could bring victory for the Union. Castle made it clear that such an uprising would need to be controlled, the Indians held in check and directed only at profitable targets. Of course, the rebels would try to stop such a plan, nor would they hesitate to try to blacken the Union's name by pretending the situation was far more serious and endangered the life of their people. Naturally the Texans would try to make her believe in the danger. She refused to be swayed from her purpose and determined to help the Union cause by doing all she could to prevent Dusty Fog's party interfering with Castle's war-winning scheme.

No chance presented itself during the rest of the day's

march. Liz walked slowly to the camp-fire after tending to her horse at the end of the day. As she sat down, a thought struck her. She would stay awake and when all the others slept release and scatter the horses.

CHAPTER TEN

YOU'RE PLAYING A GAME, MISS CHAMBERLAIN—DON'T

'Come on, Yankee,' said a voice, while a hand shook Liz's shoulder and jarred through her sleep. 'Time to be up and doing.'

Cold grey light met Liz's eyes as they came open. Stifling a low groan, for the ground proved a far less satisfactory mattress than her bed at home offered, she forced herself up on one elbow and peered around sleepily. The men gathered around a fire and held plates, while a coffee pot bubbled on the flames.

'You sure slept well last night,' Jill went on, with a friendly smile. 'Why even afore we set camp, you'd gone off. Didn't disturb you, not that we could have.'

'So much for my big idea!' thought Liz, tossing aside the blankets and rising stiffly. It seemed that she slept through the night instead of laying awake until a chance presented itself for her to free and scatter the horses.

'Here, I'll lend you a hand to pack your bedroll,' Jill offered. 'You can't eat until it's done.'

'Thanks, reb.' Liz answered, suddenly feeling ravenously hungry and sniffing at the aroma of cooking meat that wafted from the fire.

With the bedroll packed ready for loading, Liz walked with Jill towards the fire. It came as something of a surprise to see a smile on Dusty Fog's face.

'Good morning, Miss Chamberlain,' he greeted. 'How do you feel?'

'I'd like a hot bath and a buggy to ride in,' she found herself replying, 'but apart from that I'm fine.'

'You can have the hot bath, happen we find some warm-water springs,' Dusty told her with a grin. 'But buggies're something we're long out of.'

'So much for Southern hospitality,' she sighed, but her voice held no anger or bitterness.

'Comes the end of the War, ma'am,' Dusty answered, 'happen you're in the Rio Hondo country, I'll fix you with a buggy that's soft and comfortable as swan's down, rig you a bath too, but you'll have to take it by yourself.'

'I should hope so, for shame,' she chuckled.

Suddenly she thought how incongruous the situation had become, for her to be standing exchanging pleasantries with a man who only yesterday deserted her and whose vitally important mission she intended to ruin if she could.

'Sure hope these pronghorn steaks are all right, ma'am,' Billy Jack said, handing her a plate. 'I'd rather have it hung for a couple of days, but Cap'n Dusty allows there's not time for that. Eggs aren't bad though.'

'Pronghorn? Eggs,' she breathed. 'But where——'

'Sam got one last night,' Billy Jack explained. 'Pronghorn I mean.'

During the meal, an idea began to form in Liz's mind for making trouble among the party. However, before she could make a move towards starting, Dusty saw that she had finished eating and gave orders to prepare for moving.

'Can you manage, ma'am?' asked Ysabel as she walked towards her saddle.

Seeing Kiowa hovering in the background, Liz shook her head. 'I—I'm not sure if I can.'

'Sergeant Ysabel!' Dusty barked. 'Tend to your duties. Kiowa, help him. Mr. Marsden, help the ladies—only don't pamper them.'

'Yo!' Marsden replied.

'Go help the Yankee, Mr. Marsden,' Jill suggested as he came in her direction. '*I'm* not so milk-soft that I can't saddle and tend for my own horse.'

In her desire to stifle a growing tolerance and liking felt towards at least one Yankee, Jill said the right thing. Annoyance glinted into Liz's eyes and she forgot her pose of the meek, near-helpless female in the presence of strong, reliable men. Taking up her saddle and bedroll, she stamped indignantly towards the mare. Determination to show the rebel that anything a Southern girl could do, a Yankee could do better, drove her to forget her plan and also the aches in her saddle-stiffened body.

On reaching the horses, she found that releasing them in the night would not have been such an easy task. The Union Army always picketed their horses, the Texans preferred to give their mounts a certain amount of freedom to move and graze. All the men's mounts had chain hobbles on their fore-legs, a leather cuff buckled around each leg over the pastern joint and connected by a short swivel chain which let the animal move around at a slow walk in order to pick good grazing. To remove the hobbles in the dark would take much time and could only be done with some noise.

Liz found the bay and Jill's buckskin secured in a different manner, though not one easier to remove than the chain hobbles would be. A loop of rope encircled the mare's neck secured with a bowline knot that rested on the left shoulder. From there the rope went down to be taken in a half-hitch around the ankle joint of the left hind leg and carried back up to join and knot about the neck looped in a manner which raised the hoof about four inches above the ground.

'Didn't have any spare gear along, ma'am,' Billy Jack apologised as she glared pointedly at his horse's fore feet. 'Had to use a scotch hobble on you ladies' mounts. Watch that half hitch on the legs. It stops the horse kicking free, but it's surely hell to get off.'

After freeing the mare's leg, Liz prepared to saddle up. While taking up her saddle-blanket, she saw another chance to delay the party; although not one she cared to use. However, she must put loyalty to her country before her dislike at inflicting deliberate suffering upon her horse. She knew the purpose of the blanket, to give protection and padding to the horse's back against the weight and pressure of the saddle. To do this correctly, the blanket must be raised slightly off the back-bone and withers and also, very important, laid flat on the back without wrinkles. Taking up the blanket, she made sure that the underside held a ridge of raised material which would chafe and rub into the mare's body, making her back sore.

Just as Liz put the blanket on, she felt a violent shove and heard Jill's contempt-filled voice at her side.

'Land-sakes, Yankee, don't you know a damned thing? Here, let me put your saddle on for you.'

Hot anger flared up in Liz, reddening her cheeks and brought her fingers into a hair-grabbing crook. Before she could move, a hand caught her arm and she turned to glare fury up into Marsden's face.

'Drop it, Miss Chamberlain,' he warned.

'I don't know what——' Liz began.

'Stop this playing at being the saviour of the Union.'

'*Playing!*' she gasped.

'Playing!' repeated Marsden coldly. 'You're playing a game, Miss Chamberlain—Don't. Captain Fog won't let you delay him. If he'd seen what you just did, he'd maybe have given you what you deserve.'

Despite herself, Liz felt a shudder run through her, for she knew the punishment meted out to a soldier who negligently or deliberately allowed his horse to get a sore back. He was stripped naked and strapped into the saddle, then made to ride that way until he knew how the horse felt. Glancing to where Dusty saddled his black stallion, Liz wondered if he would treat her in such a manner and decided he might. She wondered if perhaps he might have been telling the truth about the ultimate result of Castle's plan. Then she gave an angry shake of her head. No, Dusty Fog only made up the story of wholesale Indian slaughter of innocents as a way of playing on her emotions and gaining her co-operation. A man with Castle's sense of social conscience and belief in the rights of the individual would never chance any scheme that might endanger innocent lives.

Snarling that she could handle the mare without further help, Liz thrust by Jill and continued the saddling.

Once again the party continued with its westwards march and the girls learned just how rough such a trip could be. Alternately riding and walking, the halts spent checking hooves, condition, saddlery or feeding and watering the horses, Dusty led his party and covered over thirty miles each day. With each passing mile, his hope of meeting a south-bound party to whom he might deliver the girls grew less and less. Since the War took so many men from Texas, people tended to concentrate in or around the towns and cities and did little travelling. So, although he hated having to subject the girls to such continuous effort, he continued to hold his pace.

And it was an effort for both girls, although Liz felt the effects more than did Jill. While healthy and used to an open-air life, Liz found a vast difference between taking a long ride in the morning and making thirty miles a day with the care of her horse awaiting her attention at the end of the trip. Under those conditions she found little time for plotting further delaying tactics. In fact, during her scant leisure hours she felt no inclination to waste time in planning ideas that would need further bodily effort to carry out. Her life became a continuous struggle against weariness and pain as unused muscles protested and stiffened under the strain. When in camp, she finished her work, ate her food and dropped into her blankets to sleep like a log. Only Liz's determination not to let the rebel girl see her give way kept her moving when her body screamed to be let collapse on the ground and move no more.

Due to her life with the bushwhackers, Jill felt the strain somewhat less than did Liz; not that Jill found keeping up the pace easy and often had to use Liz's presence as an inducement to keep going.

The men did what they could to ease the girls' burden, but all had more than enough work on their hands and both Jill and Liz were compelled to attend to much of the care and attention their horses needed.

Three days went by, long, hard days, and with each Marsden found his admiration for the Texans' skill as horsemasters growing. He watched everything and learned much that would be of use to him in his career as a soldier. From the range-wise men he learned which plants and roots possessed medicinal value, what certain animal signs meant in the way of finding food and water on the open plains. Everybody in the Union Army knew that the end of the Civil War would mark the beginning of westward movement onto the Great Plains home of several hostile Indian tribes. With the knowledge he gained on the trip, Marsden knew he could be of the greatest use in the future campaigns. Such a thought always brought on a fit of brooding as he remembered that he no longer had a career as a soldier. While he cursed the men who formed the Indian-uprising plan, he laid no blame on his present companions, for they took no part in his decision to desert and become a traitor.

Possibly only Jill knew how Marsden felt and of his fears for the future. As the days went by, it became a convention that Marsden helped Jill as much as his own duties allowed. The other men vied with each other to assist Liz with her horse management, but grinned, winked and stood aside to let Marsden lend Jill a hand.

'Tell you one thing, Jackson,' Jill remarked on the evening of the third day as they stood by the horses and watched Liz hobble slowly towards the camp. 'That Yankee gal's got guts.'

'So have you,' he answered.

'I'm doing it for the South,' Jill told him. 'If those yahoos stir up the Indians, the Yankees might win the War.'

Suddenly Jill became aware of a slight tension come over the young man at her side. Seeing him glance down at the trail-dirty Union-blue sleeve of his jacket, she realised what her words meant to him. By his actions he had given up his career and ruined himself. Now she stood like a damned fool, rubbing salt in his open wounds. Contrition flooded over her. Reaching for his hand, she led him from sight of the camp. They came to a halt in a depression which hid them from view. Turning to face Marsden, Jill looked up at his unshaven face.

'Lordy, Jackson,' she said. 'I'm sorry for what I just said——'

His hands found hers, clasping them and drawing her to him, feeling the warmth of her body against his. Next moment they were in each other's arms.

'It's no good!' Marsden moaned, trying to free himself.

'Why?' asked Jill, drawing back. 'Because I'm a reb and you're——'

'Because I've no future. Nothing to offer you.'

'And what if I tell you I don't care?'

'They'll court martial me when I go back, Jill,' Marsden tried to explain, reading the anger that grew in her eyes. 'I'll be broken even if they don't have me shot as a deserter and traitor.'

'You don't have to go back,' Jill pointed out.

'I have to, Jill.'

'Why?' she insisted.

'I took an oath at West Point and broke it. I have to go back when this is over.'

'And what about me?' she asked, her voice brittle.

'Jill!' Marsden groaned. 'I just have to go back.'

'To the Yankees?'

'To my people.'

Jill tore herself from his hands, glaring her fury at him. In her pent-up emotional state it seemed that he had tried to take advantage of her. She blamed him for making her forget the reason she hated the Yankees and turned her fury on him.

'You lousy *Yankee*!' she spat, then turned and fled back to the camp.

Black despair welled over Marsden as he watched the girl go. Suddenly he knew just how much Jill had come to mean to him. He wanted Jill to be his wife, loved her for her many good qualities, wished to share his life with her. Only he could offer her no life.

Dropping his hand, Marsden opened the flap of his holster and curled his fingers around the butt of the Colt.

'That's no way out, Jack!' Dusty's voice warned from behind him.

Turning, Marsden saw the small captain walking towards him and growled, 'Did you——'

'By accident. I'd been taking a scout around and came back at the end of it. You're too much of a man to take that way out—even without what it would do to the girl.'

'I've nothing to go on, for.'

'It's your decision,' Dusty said calmly. 'One thing though, Jack. Don't rush it.'

With that Dusty swung around and walked towards the camp. Marsden stood for a long time before he angrily thrust down the Colt, closed the holster flap and followed on Dusty's heels.

If anybody at the camp noticed a change in Jill and Marsden's attitude, they made no comment. Watching the girl, Marsden wanted to go to her, tell her he would stay in the South. Pride and his sense of duty prevented him from doing so. For her part, Jill also wanted to apologise, to beg Marsden's forgiveness, yet she, too, had a stubborn streak of pride. If either one had made the slightest move towards the other, they would have been plunged into a sea of reconciliation—only neither offered to make the move. So they sat silent, morose and letting the rift between them grow wider and wider.

Possibly Dusty would have tried to mediate, to bring Jill and Marsden back together, but he had much on his mind. He never continued marching until the sun set but always called a halt while enough light remained for his party to see their way to tending to the stock. How successful the policy proved showed in the excellent condition of the horses. While a little thinner, all still looked in fine shape and showed no signs of weakness.

Following their usual routine, the senior non-coms gathered around Dusty as he unfolded his map to calculate their day's journey and mark off the ever-decreasing distance to the ring drawn around the Salt and Clear Forks of the Brazos. Usually Marsden would have been in the group, but that night he sat in black despair by the fire which Jill, again following routine, built ready for preparing a meal. None of the men noticed that for once Liz lay awake and watched them, listening to every word they said.

'We'll be about here, I'd say,' Dusty stated, tapping the map. 'Put the Sulphur behind us this afternoon. Ought to cross the Sabine around noon tomorrow and be on the East Trinity the day after. I'd say four more days ought to see us in the area.'

'Just thought, Cap'n,' Ysabel put in. 'The Deacon runs a spread on the East Trinity, ranch, supply house and store.'

'Whereabouts?' asked Dusty.

'I'm not sure,' Ysabel admitted. 'Only heard him talk about it.'

'They might have called in there, Cap'n,' Billy Jack suggested.

'Might,' admitted Dusty. 'If we see any sign of the place, and it's not too far off our line, we'll scout it. If not, we push on. I don't reckon we can start hoping for much until we cross the West Fork of the Brazos, but we'll expect it after the Denton.'

'And if we haven't called the play right, Cap'n?' asked Billy Jack, never one to look on the bright side.

'I'm trying not to think about that,' Dusty answered, trying to sound as if the responsibility sat lightly on his shoulders. 'If we're wrong, there'll be a couple of Indian prophets without honour in their country. Here, put the maps in your saddlebags for me, Billy Jack. Kiowa, let's give the stock a last look over before dark. Sam, take Mr. Marsden and see what you can scare up between you for supper. Miss Dodd, make the coffee, please.'

Watching the men go about their duties, Liz wished that

she felt less tired and could raise the energy to try to lay hands on the map. Even now she did not know their destination and guessed that the map would tell her that. Perhaps if she could destroy the map, she could—— Still thinking on that line she drifted off to sleep.

At dawn Liz awoke to a feeling of difference and for almost a minute could not think what brought about the change. Then she realised that the nagging stiffness which usually accompanied her waking had gone. She wanted to leap from the blankets, dance, throw cartwheels like a kid. Only the thought of what her relief from stiffness meant prevented her from displaying her pleasure. She could now go ahead with her plans for disrupting the party.

However, the chance to obtain the map did not present itself and Liz could not think of any other move. Before breakfast finished, she could see that the men knew of her improved condition. Even if she had not seen it at breakfast, Liz knew it later, for Dusty pushed on at a better speed.

The party crossed the Sabine River more than an hour before noon and kept up a good pace. At two o'clock in the afternoon, Liz rode between Jill and Billy Jack wondering if she might manage to get the plans that night, or if she could stir up some other kind of trouble. Maybe she could take advantage of the rivalry shown by the non-coms when helping her to set them at each other's throats? Or she might exploit the obvious differences which caused Jill and Marsden to quarrel.

Ahead of them, the ground dropped away in a steep slope and they steered a course to take them along its top. All around lay the open, rolling land Liz had come so used to seeing. She wondered what would happen to her should she carry out a successful plot to prevent Dusty Fog carrying out his orders.

As if in answer to Liz's thoughts, something went 'splat!' against her left ear and a spurt of dirt erupted from the ground ahead of her horse. She had never heard the sound of a close-passing bullet. The others all knew the sound, even without the following crack of a rifle, and all started to swing around to see who shot at them.

CHAPTER ELEVEN

THEY'RE ONLY LOUSY REBS

Sam Ysabel brought his huge roan around in a rump-scraping, dime-small pivot turn that would have made a British polo player's eyes sparkle in admiration; and he did it by heel pressure alone, his hands being occupied by transferring the Sharps rifle from the crook of arm to butt-cudled against his shoulder.

Even as Liz saw the line of blue-uniformed figures on the top of a slope some three hundred yards away, recognising them as salvation and the means to end the Texans' mission, she heard the bellow of Ysabel's rifle. Up on the slope, the firer of the first shot slammed backwards under the impact of Ysabel's .52 calibre bullet and flopped limply to the ground.

A wild yell, like the sound of hounds clamouring around a treed cougar, rang out from the Union troops. Yelling an order to charge, their leader sent them boiling down the slope in a wild rush; but he did not take the lead as one might expect. Instead it seemed that he allowed as many of his party as possible to come between himself and those gun-handy Texans before allowing his horse to move forward.

Elation, pleasure—and just a touch of disappointment—filled Liz as she watched the soldiers charging down. Soon she would be among her own kind again and able to tell them all she knew of Dusty Fog's mission. Yet in a way she would miss the cheerful uncomplaining companionship of the Texans, for she had found herself growing to like them despite her political feelings. She expected the Texans to dismount and make a fight and realised that she might be in the thick of flying lead very soon, but the thought did not frighten her.

'Scatter!' Dusty yelled, almost as an echo to Ysabel's shot.

Only Liz of the party did not know what the order meant. When laying his plans for the journey, Dusty prepared his men for just such an emergency. Having no intention of risking the success of his mission by fighting a superior-numbered enemy force if he could avoid it, he had planned accordingly. On his command, the party dissolved into fast-moving, fanning-out segments. Leading one packhorse, Billy Jack started his mount running along the top of the slope, with Jill at his side. Marsden gave the girl one piteous glance before urging his sorrel and packhorse off on the heels of Kiowa's running black and Kiowa led the third packhorse as they cut off to the right. Swinging down his rifle, Ysabel brought the roan about in a half turn and set it galloping at an angle to Kiowa's right, going away from the Texan. Last to leave the field, Dusty headed his black stallion towards the slope. Even as he went, Dusty saw Liz following Billy Jack's section and wondered what game the girl played this time.

Liz's original movement after the others was involuntary. Used to travelling with the rest, her mare obeyed its herd-instinct and lunged forward on the heels of the departing horses. Even as she reached down on the reins, meaning to halt her mare and join her approaching companions-at-arms, a thought struck Liz. Clearly the Confederates did not intend to make a fight, and with that much of a lead they ought to be able to outride those clumsy-looking Union soldiers. So if she could only delay the rebels, her people might take them. At that moment Liz remembered the maps Billy Jack carried. They might be of the greatest help in locating the remainder of the Texans in case of an escape.

Eagerly she urged her mare after Billy Jack and Jill. The little mare proved to be a flier. Carrying less weight, and unencumbered by a trailing packhorse, Liz's mount closed up to and came between Billy Jack's and Jill's. Then she started to edge her mare towards the packhorse which in turn moved in against Billy Jack's black and urged it towards the edge of the slope.

'Get over, J——!' Billy Jack started to yell, turning his head. The words trailed off as he saw Liz, not Jill, at his side.

When making arrangements for Jill's inclusion in the escape groups, Dusty had not included Liz. Should the party separate, it would be because they met a Yankee force among whom Liz, as a Union supporter, could be safely left. So Billy Jack felt a momentary surprise at seeing Liz. Then he guessed what she aimed to do. His black's hooves churned the earth on the very start of the slope. If it once went over, he knew it would stumble or be forced to slow down to such an extent that he fell into the hands of the Yankees.

Liz read the expression on the lean non-com's face and felt disgusted with herself. Thinking back to all the little kindnesses shown her by Billy Jack, she hated to be acting in such a treacherous manner. A few more inches would see him go over the edge of the slope—only she could not make herself continue. Before she could swing the mare clear, Liz felt her hat sent spinning from her head and two hands dug into her hair from behind, pulling at it, dragging her backwards out of the saddle. Her horse lost stride, a shriek of pain burst from her lips, then Billy Jack passed her and his black swung away from the edge of the slope.

'Keep going, Billy Jack!' screamed Jill's voice from close behind Liz.

On seeing Liz's attempt to ride Billy Jack off the level ground, Jill wasted no time. She urged her buckskin closer to the other two, leaning over to send Liz's hat flying, then lay hold of her hair. Billy Jack turned slightly in his saddle and saw the girls' horses slowing down. Even without Jill's advice, he would not have stopped, for he knew Dusty's orders on the subject. On hearing of Dusty's plans for such a situation, Jill agreed that she must be sacrificed rather than endanger her escort and stated that she would be reasonably safe in Union hands provided she knew nothing of the Texans' plans. So Billy Jack kept his horse running, the pack-animal keeping pace at its side, and left Jill behind.

While holding rank as captain, and serving in a regiment which saw considerable action, Marty Wilson had so far avoided contact—and its risks—with the enemy. Sometimes he had been heard to boast that the rebels might be brave enough when bullying some poor Negro, but showed a great lack of courage when faced with armed Union men. However, he never really believed that theory and expected a stiff fight on sighting his quarry. With that thought in mind, Wilson made sure that he let his men lead the charge on the Texans. Much to his surprise, he saw the rebels separate into fleeing groups after one of their number shot down the guide who brought the party overland from the Red River.

'Split up!' he yelled wildly. 'Get after them. Kill 'em!'

Although his men felt the exhilaration of the chase and the heady joy which came from the sight of the fleeing enemy, obeying Wilson's order did not come easy. Members of Marsden's Zouave regiment, they had been formed into a mounted company in an attempt to answer the mobility of the Texas Light Cavalry; but they lacked the Texans' experience on horseback. Showing none of the Texans' rapid disintegration, Wilson's company split apart and one group took out after each segment of Dusty's party. Due to lack of foresight and planning, Wilson found himself with his sergeant, a burly, sullen hard-case called Fitch, and only two men. Taking the easiest course, he led his small group down with the intention of pursuing the girls and Billy Jack.

Wilson's party watched Jill tackle Liz and the girls go sliding from their horses to the ground where they tangled in a wild-hair-tearing tangle of waving arms and thrashing legs. Instantly all thoughts of chasing Billy Jack were forgotten. The men slid their horses to a halt, laughing, whooping out encouragement and profane advice to the struggling girls. Bringing his mount to a sliding halt, Wilson looked back.

'Get after hi——' he began.

The words died off as he recognised one of the fighting girls. Even through the trail-dirt and dishevelled coating, Wilson made out the features of Liz Chamberlain. He wasted no time in wondering how she came to be involved in a hair-yanking brawl with another girl on the North Texas plains. Remembering that her father had considerable influence, both financially and politically, he reluctantly decided he must end what looked like developing into a promising fight.

'Pull them apart, Sergeant!' he ordered.

A scowl came into Fitch's face at the words, then he grinned and dropped out of his saddle. Moving forward, he watched the girls struggle to their knees still clinging to each other's hair, then grabbed Liz by the arms from behind. One of his men had also dismounted and caught Jill in a similar manner. Pulling backwards, the men managed to separate the girls, but it took all their strength to prevent a resumption of hostilities. Liz stopped struggling first and stood with face flushed and breasts heaving as she stared at her rescuers.

'Quit it, gal!' the soldier holding Jill yelled, and shook her hard.

Sanity returned to Jill, warning her of the futility of struggling. She relaxed and stood gasping for breath, glaring defiantly at Wilson as he swung out of his saddle.

'Are you all right, Liz?' he asked.

Liz looked at the medium-sized, sallow-faced young man and found difficulty in recognising him. Not because he looked much different from her last meeting, Wilson never looked clean or tidy even when in full dress, but because she had met so many people on her visit to Arkansas.

'I'll live,' she replied, touching her left eye with a finger tip and wincing.

'What're you doing here? Who's that girl?'

'Her name's Jill Dodd,' Liz answered guardedly.

'A rebel?' growled Wilson.

'Yes, I am!' Jill put in, shrugging the man's hands from her and glancing hopefully towards the buckskin which had come to a halt some yards away.

'We'll take her along with us,' Wilson stated and looked to where Billy Jack faded off into the distance. 'There's no chance of catching him now, Sergeant. We'll go on to the Deacon's place. The guide told me how to find it last night.'

'Do your men know where to find you?' Liz inquired, as the second private rode after her mare and the buckskin.

'Yes,' replied Wilson—a slight pause which made Liz eye him suspiciously. Wanting to take her mind off the subject, he pointed to where Jill's Tranter lay on the ground. 'We'd better take that with us.'

The man behind Jill grabbed her again as she started to move forward and Liz went to pick up the revolver. Thrusting the Tranter into her waistband, she smiled at Jill.

'I'll return it when we part, reb,' Liz promised.

'That's a good hoss,' Fitch growled, eyeing the buckskin avariciously. 'Too good for a rebel slut to——'

'He's too much horse for you, Yankee,' Jill spat back.

'Yeah?' the sergeant grinned. 'Well, I'll——'

'Take your own horse, Sergeant!' Liz ordered coldly.

Turning his eyes towards the girl, Fitch prepared to snarl a refusal. However, Wilson backed Liz with his own command and Fitch slouched to his leg-weary mount.

On moving out, Jill strained her ears for sounds of shooting that would mean the Yankees had caught up with her friends. She heard nothing and concluded that the rest of the party must have made good their escape. Not that it surprised her when she came to consider the poor condition of the Yankee horses and inexperience of the captain.

Just how ignorant Wilson was showed in the fact that he never once offered to dismount and walk to rest his horses. Riding on at a slow trot, he led his party due west. During the ride Liz learned what brought Wilson to Texas. Although he approved of Castle's plan in theory, it contained too much danger for his liking. So he contented himself with commanding the escort to the Red River. After seeing the arms and Ager gun over into Texas, Wilson prepared to make a fast ride to the safety of his own lines. On his way back, the civilian guide met him with orders from Colonel Stedloe. Marsden had deserted, taking news to the rebels. Guessing what Ole Devil Hardin would do, Stedloe sent orders for Wilson to follow Castle's party and use his company to protect it. Instead of following the wagon tracks of Castle's party, the guide led them towards the Deacon's ranch; he showed as much reluctance as Wilson had to going into the Indian council area. Fate intervened, bringing them into contact with the enemy and Wilson considered his duty well done.

Night had fallen when the party rode towards the deserted ranch buildings. Being Eastern-raised, Wilson had the horses taken into the barn instead of using the corral. Only Liz's example made the men care for their horses before going to the ranch house in search of food. However, nothing Liz could do prevented Wilson from locking Jill in a small saddlery-store in the barn. He said it was to keep her out of the men's way, but Liz suspected that Wilson had a blind bigoted hatred towards the Southerners and was merely taking his spite out on the girl.

'I'll have food sent to you, reb,' Liz promised and even managed a smile as she looked at the othe's dirty face. 'And I'll send along some hot water and soap.'

'You need it yourself,' Jill answered, eyeing Liz's unkempt appearance, now blackened eye, but unable to hold any hate against such a game girl.

However, when the door closed, Jill looked around her prison and felt like crying. The room was small, its walls stout and the window heavily barred—to keep out marauding black bears rather than prevent a prisoner escaping, but too strong for her to attempt anything against.

Time dragged by, Liz came with hot water, soap, a towel and Jill's other clothing, standing by while the rebel girl washed and changed.

'I'll bring you some food as soon as I can,' Liz told Jill as she prepared to leave the room. 'And we'll return you to your people first chance we get.'

'Bring that lamp out with you,' Wilson called from the barn. 'She might try to use it to burn her way out.'

Figuring that Jill just might make such an attempt, Liz picked up the lamp and carried it out of the room. Left alone, Jill made herself as comfortable as possible and sat thinking of the past few days. A chink of light showed under the bottom of the door, for Liz insisted on leaving the barn well illuminated to help guide any of Wilson's men who might be in the vicinity.

Time dragged slowly by. Outside the room, the horses in their stalls moved restlessly, chomping hay or stamping their hooves. Jill felt very tired and decided to try to settle down and sleep. Then she heard steps approaching the door, heavy and uneven-sounding steps which worried her. The lock clicked and the door jerked open. Leaning against the door's jamb, his face twisted in the slobber-lipped sneer of a bad drunk, Fitch looked Jill up and down.

'Come on out'f it, gal,' he ordered in a whisky-slurred voice. 'Me 'n' you's going to have some fun.'

As he often received visitors who did not wish to discuss their business in the presence of the hired help, the Deacon lived in a small, one-room cabin separated by several yards from the bunkhouse. Wilson and Liz sat at the table in the room, having just finished a meal she made for them. Although Liz wished to go and feed Jill, the man insisted on talking. Liz felt concerned for, on taking a meal to the soldiers, she learned that Fitch had found a couple of jugs of corn liquor. The men all appeared to have taken their share of the potent stuff, but Wilson made no attempt to halt their excesses. Guessing he had made a mistake in the girl's eyes, Wilson sought to divert her by discussing the business which brought him to Texas.

'Things could go bad wrong if the Texans escape and

catch up with Castle,' Liz remarked, after explaining her presence in Texas and telling all she knew.

'Yes,' Wilson agreed and, wishing to exculpate himself, went on, 'I could've commanded the chase if I didn't have to stop and look after you. But you know what ignorant fools these men are.'

Ignoring the latter part of Wilson's speech, Liz warned, 'I've an idea that Captain Fog knows the rendezvous.'

'He can't. Why not even I know that for certain. Only the Deacon and Castle know where they're meeting the Indians. We didn't let any of the regulars know, so Marsden couldn't have told the rebels that. I always knew we couldn't trust those lousy regulars.'

'Jack Marsden claimed he deserted because the scheme endangered thousands of innocent lives. Is that true?'

'No!' Wilson spat out.

'But all the Texans seemed to be so sincere, and two of them have lived among the Indians. They say that the braves will attack indiscriminately, killing civilians, women, children——'

'So?' growled the captain. 'They're only lousy rebs.'

For the first time Liz began to gain an inkling of the mentality of men like Wilson. While preaching tolerance, his kind were capable of the most vicious, bigoted intolerance against anybody who did not blindly fall in with their way of thinking or follow their beliefs.

'But if there is dan——' Liz began.

Her words chopped off as she heard a shrill scream from the barn. Instantly Liz forgot her argument. Turning, she dashed across the room, tore open the door and raced towards the open doors of the barn. Wilson followed on her heels, catching up with her just as she reached the barn's door. Both halted, looking to where Fitch held Jill pressed against the side of a stall, his hands tearing open the struggling girl's shirt front.

Only for a moment did Liz wait for Wilson to order his sergeant away from the other girl. Wilson made no such attempt, fearing to push a point where he might have to clash with his sergeant. True, Wilson had behind him all the might and weight of the *Manual of Field Regulations*—and did not hesitate to use its powers in an area where backing waited to enforce his will. However, he knew that he possessed no such backing in Texas and must stand on his own feet. So he declined to interfere when Fitch, noted as mean when wet, might refuse to obey him.

'Leave her be, Sergeant!' Liz shouted. 'Make him, Wilson!'

Twisting his leering face towards his superior officer, Fitch gritted, 'All right, Wilson, make me.'

Fury etched itself on Wilson's face and his hand went to the hilt of the straight infantry sword he wore. He lacked the courage to draw the weapon, even though his sergeant no longer wore a weapon belt.

Liz sprang forward, drawing Jill's Tranter from her waistband—and thanking the Lord that she had not put the gun aside when she changed.

'Let go, right now!' she hissed.

Something in her voice brought Fitch's eyes to her. What he read on her face caused him to release Jill, letting her fall sobbing against the wall. For a moment Fitch stood scowling uneasy defiance, but he could not meet the scorn and fury in the girl's level stare. Letting out a lurid curse, Fitch turned and slouched out of the barn.

'I'll deal with him in the morning,' Wilson promised, his voice a shade weak.

'Will you?' sniffed Liz and went to Jill's side.

Watching Fitch fade off into the darkness, Wilson felt a sense of inadequacy at Liz having done something beyond his power to achieve. For Wilson to know that someone could better him brought hatred against the one who did better. However, he felt it would be imprudent to show his hatred openly to Liz, so turned it against Jill instead.

'Maybe she knows where the rebs plan to meet up again after scattering,' he said, pushing by Liz and tilting Jill's face upwards by gripping her chin. 'Do you know, reb?'

Jill found herself faced with a different situation, one which did not scare her as much as the threat of rape by a drunken brute. So she kept quiet. Wilson shook her head from side to side savagely.

'Where'll they meet?' he yelled.

'Go to hell!' Jill answered.

Viciously Wilson swung his other hand, lashing it forward then back across Jill's face and rocking her head from side to side. Again he repeated the demand for information and received the same reply.

'That's enough!' Liz shouted.

Mean-minded and untrustworthy himself Wilson imagined everybody to be cut in the same mould. Suspicion came easily to him and he saw danger in Liz's words. Without giving any warning, he swung around and slapped the Tranter from her hand, then thrust her aside. Turning back to Jill, he lashed another slap across her face. Dazed by the blows and previous rough handling, Jill collapsed to her knees. Wilson loomed above her, his sallow face contorted with fury and sadistic delight at inflicting pain.

'Where are those stinking rebs?' he almost screamed, and when no answer came from the girl, drew back his foot.

CHAPTER TWELVE

COME ON, BRAVE MAN—TRY ME!

A heave, a scrabbling of hooves, then Dusty Fog and his black stallion made the top of the steep ridge. Turning, Dusty looked down and back to where a quarter of a mile away his pursuers urged their leg-weary, jaded horses after him. From the look of the long Springfield rifles slung across their shoulders, he judged them to be mounted infantry. In the Union Army even the volunteer cavalry outfits were armed with much shorter carbines of one kind or other. By the way the men sat their horses, he reckoned they would be unable to make the difficult climb which he had just accomplished. After leading them a chase of five miles, he decided that it was time he lost them anyway and went about his business.

Although he could have ridden clear away from his pursuers in less than a mile, Dusty held his black down to a pace which kept the Yankees believing they would overtake him at any moment, while leading them further and further away from their companions. At first the state of the land drove him south-east, but at last he began to make a long, looping half circle towards the west and now he headed in the right direction again.

Unshipping his Springfield and bringing his horse to a halt, one of the soldiers aimed and fired a shot. Where the bullet went was anybody's guess, but it came nowhere near Dusty. Grinning, the small Texan drew back a little from the rim and flattened down to offer a smaller target while watching the Yankees approach the foot of the slope. The corporal in charge of the section started to urge his horse up the slope and although the animal responded gamely, it could make no headway. Nor did any of the others do better.

'Here endeth the first lesson,' mused Dusty and slipped back from the rim. 'I don't reckon they'll bother me again.'

Returning to the stallion, Dusty took the reins and started to walk. He led the horse for some way until he found an area which offered him shelter from unfriendly eyes. At the foot of a bush-dotted valley, he stripped off the black's saddle and allowed the horse to roll while preparing to water and feed it.

When the horse had cooled down from its exertions, Dusty took his canteen and tipped the contents into his hat's crown. Taking the bit from its mouth, he allowed the horse to drink its fill. With that done, he unpacked the nose-bag from the saddle-pouch ready to start feeding. One of the reasons Dusty did not bring carbines on the mission had been because the weapon's boot made an ideal receptacle for an emergency feed of grain. Tipping the golden drops of concentrated energy from the boot into the nose-bag, he set up the stallion with a better feed than he himself would have until he joined up with the rest of his party. While the black first ate its grain, then grazed on the ankle-deep buffalo grass, Dusty watched his back trail. He saw no sign of the Union soldiers, nor did he expect to.

An hour later Dusty rode on again. Although he kept constantly alert, he saw nothing of friend or foe. That did not surprise him, for he knew his men would scatter far across the range and lead their hunters as he had done. The Yankee officer in command of the company was going to have the hell of a chore rounding up his men again when the Texans finally shook them off.

Although he never cared to risk his horse by riding in darkness, Dusty kept going for a time after night fell. In this he was helped by the fact that the big black stallion showed considerable skill at travelling in the darkness. He believed himself to be safe from any pursuit, but wished to cover as many miles as possible towards the rendezvous with his men. Using the instinct gained during a lifetime on the great Texas ranges, and steering his course by the stars, Dusty continued to move towards the west.

Topping a rim, he saw lights down to his left. A small ranch's buildings, he guessed. Maybe the Deacon's place near the East Trinity. If not, Dusty stood a better than fair chance of finding Confederate supporters at the buildings. Possibly one or more of his party might be present.

With the possibility of the place belonging to the Deacon,

Dusty did not ride blindly and noisily towards the buildings. He saw no sign of life around the place, apart from the lights in the barn and showing from windows of two of the other buildings. Nor could he see horses in the corrals.

Dusty was still almost a quarter of a mile from the buildings when he heard a girl's terrified scream ring out. Almost without conscious thought, Dusty drew his left-hand Colt, clicking back the hammer under his thumb. Even as he prepared to put spurs to the black's flanks, he saw the front door of one building jerk open. Liz burst into sight, racing towards the barn and behind her sprinted a Union Army officer. Watching the girl and Wilson dash into the barn, Dusty felt concern for the welfare of Billy Jack and Jill. Maybe his loyal sergeant-major had been killed or captured. He decided to move in on foot. If Billy Jack was held prisoner, then he must be rescued. If not, well the fates would take care of things from then on.

Before Dusty could dismount, he saw a burly sergeant leave the barn. From the way the man walked, Dusty figured him to be toting a fair load of corn liquor. It did not require the second-sight of a Comanche witch-man to guess at the cause of Jill's screams. Dusty hoped that Liz arrived in time to save Jill from the drunken Yankee.

The presence of the Yankee officer hinted at there being a Union force on hand, or at least an escort. Knowing how he would act under similar circumstances, spending a night in hostile territory, Dusty thought that there might be sentries posted around the place. He reached the corral without any alarm being given and prepared for a dash towards the barn. Looping the black's reins over the corral rail, Dusty found his eyes on the sabre. If the Yankee had guards out, he must deal with them silently. Cold steel made a mighty effective silencer. While the 1860 Army Colt might be as fine a revolver as made to that date, it lacked the more robust qualities which made its descendants—particularly the 1873 Model P Peacemaker or the 1911 Government Model automatic pistol—such handy clubs when empty. Striking a blow with the barrel of the Army Colt could only be done with the serious risk of snapping the loading lever's retaining catch, or damaging the cylinder which, unlike fitted on later models, had no top strap covering and protecting it. The Haiman sabre had no such defects. A blow from its hilt would stun a man, while a thrust of its point to the kidney area was certain to drop a man in such agony that he would be unable to cry out in the few seconds of life left to him.

Drawing the sabre, having holstered his Colt earlier, Dusty darted across the open space. Voices came from the barn. Shouted demands for information in a male voice. Dusty also heard Jill make some answer, then the sound of slaps and more yelled questions. Just as Dusty burst into the barn, he saw Wilson slap the Tranter from Liz's hand, then turn to shout at Jill.

'Where're those stinking rebels?' Wilson screeched, drawing back his foot for a kick.

'Right here,' Dusty told him.

Letting out a startled yelp, lowering his foot hurriedly and turning, Wilson swung around to face Dusty. For a moment Wilson's hands quivered ready to rise in surrender, then he saw that Dusty appeared to be alone and held a sabre instead of a Colt.

During his time in college Wilson had learned fencing. In fact he became very good with a blade, having found that such gave him access to the company of the rich students he hated for having more money than himself. Taking in Dusty's small size and apparent youth, Wilson decided that victory would be certain enough for him to risk his valuable neck in a fight. Then he noticed the gunbelt and matched Colts and a momentary fear gripped him. However, he knew the chivalrous nature of the Southerners and doubted if the small Texan would draw a gun if challenged to fight with swords.

'You'd best surrender, reb,' Wilson warned. 'If not I'll cut you down.'

'Like you did to Jill?' asked Dusty. 'Come on, brave man —try me!'

Something in Dusty's manner gave pause to Wilson's actions. Wilson tried to tell himself that he could not trust Dusty to fight fairly, but he knew that fear held him from making a move. Then he thought back to his college successes and decided he could risk a sword fight against the obviously much younger and smaller man, provided the other kept his guns out of it.

'You'd shoot me down if I tried,' Wilson sneered. 'I'm not wearing a gun.'

'That's a sword at your side,' Dusty pointed out. 'Pull it and use it. Only you'll find it harder than slapping a gal around.'

Liz had darted to Jill's side and knelt by the rebel girl, arm around her. Looking up, Liz watched Wilson draw his sword and ran the tip of her tongue across her lips. All too well she knew of his skill with the sword and wanted to warn Dusty, to give the small Texan a chance to make an escape. Before the words came, she saw they would be too late.

Out slid Wilson's sword, its thirty-four-inch blade glinting under the barn's light. In height, weight and reach Wilson held all the advantages. He looked forward to an easy victory; to killing the small Texan, for he had no intention of accepting a surrender. Perhaps his men would hear the noise and come to investigate. If so, he wanted them to see him killing, or having killed, a rebel officer. Then those sullen, mutinous scum would be more amenable to his orders. He could arrest and punish Fitch for daring to show disrespect to him.

Studying the way Wilson assumed the on-guard position, Dusty guessed that the other knew more than a little about the use of a sword and studied the Hungarian style of sabre work. Dusty favoured the French school, having learned fencing from a New Orleans master. As in everything he set his mind to, Dusty learned his fencing lessons well and kept up his practice by training with the other officers of the Texas Light Cavalry.

Up lifted Wilson's sword blade in the first move of the salute. Immediately Dusty began a reply—and Wilson changed from the salute to a vicious cut across at Dusty's exposed right side. Liz let out a low, angry gasp at the treacherous move, expecting to see Dusty go down with his ribs slit open.

Wilson's move failed for one reason. From what he saw of the other, Dusty had not expected courtesy or fair play. So, while he replied to the salute, Dusty stayed alert for just such a move. In a smooth flicker, the Haiman's blade came down, engaged the foible of Wilson's sword and deflected it. From where Dusty sent the point of the sabre licking out in a thrust. Only by making a hurried, unorthodox and startled leap to the rear did Wilson avoid taking Dusty's point in the belly.

Catching his balance, Wilson met Dusty's attack. If Wilson

expected to rely on his superior reach to keep Dusty back to a distance where the Texan's attacks depended solely upon ripostes, making an offensive action following a successful parry, he was disappointed. Instead of standing back, Dusty drove forward, fighting well within Wilson's reach and cramping his prearranged moves. Wilson knew how he would be fighting matched against a taller man and could not conceive that any brain might devise another method. In a very few passes he learned that Dusty did not intend to blindly follow his lead in the way they fought.

Liz and Jill stayed where they were, watching the fight. Of the two, Liz understood more fully the high standard of the sword-play shown by the two men. After a few passes Liz became lost to the true implications of the fight in studying the beauty and grace of the movements and the skill of the participants. Having seen a great many fencing matches, and knowing something of the game herself, Liz realised just how good both men were. Wilson had speed, a devastatingly fast beat, could bind his opponent's blade and take it out of line, then make his own move, be it lunge, cut or feint, with startling rapidity. Yet for all that, Liz became slowly aware that Dusty was the superior man. It became clear that Dusty did not fluster in the face of speed. Dusty knew that speed alone could not assure success. In fact, on a couple of occasions Wilson's speed almost brought him to grief when he made a very fast one-two attack and found his blade coming back into closed line from the second disengage before Dusty moved. Both times only Wilson's skill saved him from a wound, but he knew that he had met his match with a sabre.

In desperation Wilson changed styles, going in point first as if handling a training foil or duelling sword. Instantly Dusty adopted the same method of fighting and, despite the sabre's awkwardness in such work, showed that he excelled at that form of fighting too. The master who instructed Dusty in fencing was a French-Creole and never considered the sabre to be a gentleman's weapon. One learned to use the sabre well, of course, and it did have uses in mounted warfare, but a gentleman much preferred the more artistic and skilful use of the point instead of slashing with a cutting edge. So the master insisted that his pupils became fully conversant with the finer points of sword work and again Dusty proved a most adept pupil.

Just how adept showed when Dusty began to drive the other back across the barn, the lightning fast point of his sabre coming time after time within a hair's-breadth of catching Wilson's body. Once again the Yankee was forced to revert to a slashing attack. Desperation lent him the courage of a frightened rat and he launched an attack which forced Dusty to retire towards the door of the barn. Sweat poured down Wilson's face and he found difficulty in breathing. Dusty, being fitter and in better condition, showed less signs of distress and knew that it would be only a matter of minutes before he could terminate the fight. However, he knew he might not be spared those minutes. At any moment the Yankee sentries might hear the sound of steel against steel and come to investigate.

Timing his moves just right, Dusty feinted to Wilson's head in the start of a compound attack. Up rose Wilson's arm in an attempted parry and too late he realised his mistake. At just the right moment Dusty's feint changed to its true purpose and came down in a cut at Wilson's body. Shining steel glittered as it drove across to bite through Wilson's clothing and inflict a painful gash in the man's side. Wilson screeched like a stuck pig as the blade bit home. Although the wound was not serious, he dropped his sword and stumbled backwards to fall against the wall of a stall. He hung there, eyes wild with fear and mouth opening to beg for mercy.

'Dusty, behind you!' Jill screamed.

Fitch had returned to the bunkhouse in a smouldering humour and found the two soldiers in that stage of drunkenness when they could be persuaded to take any kind of action. Setting to the task, he soon had the soldiers ready to go with him to the barn. Wilson had never been popular with the men under him and neither objected to teaching him a lesson as a prelude to taking and having fun with the girl. Collecting their rifles, each man fitted on his bayonet as a means of quietening any objections Wilson might show. Then they headed for the barn. Fitch watched them go and a drunken sneer came to his face. Once they dealt with Wilson, they would be mutineers and he had the right to kill them. After that the girls would be his until he chose to leave. He intended to show that officer's daughter where she came off, it ought to be fun.

Not until almost at the barn did the two soldiers realise

anything was wrong. Neither had heard the clash of steel and did not recognise the sound. However, when they approached closer to the open doors, they saw Wilson in the final stages of his fight. The sight of the cadet-grey uniform of Wilson's attacker drove all thoughts of mutiny from their heads. Even as Dusty began his compound attack, the soldiers charged forward to help out their officer.

If they had come in side by side, making a concerted rush, the two men would have had Dusty at their mercy. In the heady exhilaration of the prospect of a fight, mingled with whisky consumption, they made a race of their attack and one proved fleeter of foot than the other.

Howling a wild shout, the first man launched a thrust at Dusty's body. He gave the small Texan no chance to use the sabre and only Dusty's swift-sidestep caused the blow to miss. Carried on by his own momentum, the soldier rushed forward. He felt a hand clamp hold of his shirt front, saw Dusty slipping backwards under him, contact with a boot that rammed into his belly. Then the soldier lost all knowledge of the subsequent happenings. He had a vague knowledge of losing his balance and felt the foot against his belly giving a powerful shove. Instantly the room appeared to whirl around and he saw the floor rushing towards him. The rifle clattered to the floor as Dusty performed the *tomoe-nage* stomach throw of ju-jitsu and sent the soldier sailing into the air. Taken by surprise, with his reflexes slowed through whisky-drinking, the soldier could do nothing to break his fall. Down he crashed, landing head first on the hard-packed earth floor of the barn. A dull pop sounded as the neck bones broke and the soldier's limp body crumpled to the ground.

By that time his companion had arrived. Roaring with rage, the second man raised his rifle and sent the bayonet driving down at Dusty's recumbent body. With a rolling twist of his hips, Duty avoided the thrust and the bayonet's tip shattered on impact with the ground. Even while performing the *tomoe-nage* Dusty retained his grip on the sabre. Twisting back, he drove upwards in what would have been a thrust if aimed at the body. Instead the sabre passed between the man's legs and its razor-sharp blade sliced into the soft flesh of the inner thigh to sever the femoral artery. Blood followed the sabre from the gash in a rushing flood. The soldier had but thirty seconds to live.

Dusty received no respite. Even as he started to rise, and while the stricken soldier lurched blindly away, Dusty saw yet another menace to his life. Still carrying the stone jug, Fitch arrived on the scene. With a snarl of rage, he sprang forward. Ignoring the gun at his belt, Fitch swung the jug around like a club and struck at the small Texan's head. Only just in time did Dusty duck. He had just made his feet and moved his head down quickly. The jug brushed Dusty's hat in passing and he took a fast pace to the rear before launching a backhand cut which laid open Fitch's belly like an axe-split melon. Fitch stumbled backwards, guts pouring out of the terrible wound. Behind Dusty, Liz screamed, covering her face with her hands to shut out the terrible sight.

While just as shocked and horrified as Liz, Jill saw something which made her forget, momentarily, the nausea which arose in her. Wilson made no attempt to help his men at first, but stood cowering against the wall. Nor did the sight of the first two deaths affect him. Being entirely self-centred, like all cowards, Wilson cared nothing for the men under him. All he knew was that he had a chance to save his own miserable life. On the ground not far from him lay Jill's Tranter and, while Dusty met Fitch's attack, Wilson screwed up sufficient courage to go forward to grab the weapon. Knowing his lack of skill with a revolver, Wilson moved forward, meaning to get so close that he could not miss.

Taking the scene in, Jill knew she must do something to save Dusty. Close at hand a pitchfork leaned against the wall. She had tried to reach it when Fitch made his rape attempt. Unhindered by other hands, she caught up the fork and sprang forward. Pure blind chance directed the prongs of the fork into just the right place, for Jill struck without conscious effort. Wilson was just lining the revolver at Dusty's back when he felt a sudden, excruciating agony bite into him. Arching his back, Wilson triggered off a wild shot. Dusty whirled around, sabre ready for use, and saw Wilson crumpling forward. The Yankee crashed to the ground at Dusty's feet, the shaft of the pitchfork rising from his back. One glance told Dusty what caused the instant collapse. Either by design or accident, Jill sent its prongs into Wilson's kidneys and ended his murder attempt.

Dusty knew he must waste no time. Although both girls

appeared to be on the verge of hysterics, he had more important things on his mind. At any moment the rest of the Yankee party would arrive, attracted by the shot. He must be prepared to fight his way clear and make for the black. Could he leave Jill and Liz behind? Would they be safe in the hands of the leaderless party. From what Dusty had seen of the sergeant and soldiers, and smelled on their breaths, discipline must be lax. If the rest of the party had also been drinking, maybe not even Liz would be safe among them.

Thinking of the girls caused Dusty to look for their horses. Only four other mounts stood in the stalls alongside the buckskin and mare. Maybe the whole of the Yankee party lay around the barn. Dusty decided to take a chance on his guess proving correct.

Gently he led the girls from the barn and into the cool night air. Possibly because she had seen violent death more than once with the bushwhackers, or maybe because the victims were Yankees and not good specimens at that, Jill recovered control of herself before Liz regained a hold.

'Are there any more of them, Jill?' Dusty asked.

'Only those in the barn,' she finally managed to answer. 'I ki——'

'Easy, gal,' Dusty put in as her words trailed off. 'Let's get Miss Chamberlain to the house. Say, did they get Billy Jack?'

Jill caught Liz's eye and read pleading on the other girl's face. Neither of them knew for sure how Dusty would react when he heard of Liz's action. Possibly he might leave the Yankee girl behind when he rode on. Nothing Liz could think of would be worse than being left alone in that place of death. Jill realised that at last she had a Yankee almost pleading with her, silently begging for help.

'My horse stumbled, Captain,' she stated. 'I yelled to Billy Jack to keep going and he did, just as you ordered.'

'Huh, huh,' Dusty grunted. 'You girls go up to the house. I'll do what I can in the barn. Make up a meal for me, please, Jill. We'll pull out after we've rested.'

CHAPTER THIRTEEN

THIS'S WHAT THEY'LL TURN LOOSE

The East Trinity River lay almost an hour's ride behind Dusty Fog and the two girls. Overhead the sun began to dip down past its noon height. Up on a rim stood a magnificent specimen of longhorn Texas cattle. Big, black, nine hundred pounds of powerful frame, with a six-foot spread of needle-pointed horns capable of gutting a black bear or impaling a cougar gracing its head, a bull of the first water. Giving a deep-throated bellow, the bull swung around and passed over the rim from sight. Dusty brought his horse to a halt and a wistful grin twisted his lips.

'Whooee!' he said. 'I bet he's a mean one. If the good Lord made anything more cross-grained, stubborn, ornery or vicious than a Texas longhorn, I sure've never seen it. One of 'em'll charge you after you've hauled it from a bog-hole; run a hoss ragged chasing it; hunt the worst cover it can find; damned near burst your teeth trying to chew its meat when it's dead. But it sure makes a real pretty sight when you've been away from home for a spell.'

Liz stared at Dusty in surprise. After seeing him fight and watching the calm competent, efficient manner he handled the problems of the march, she had thought him to be hard, de-humanised almost by the life war forced him to lead. Now she saw him in a different light. That coldly confident young man felt homesick and must be thinking of his folks, his home in the Rio Hondo country.

'Your family must have many slaves for you to give up so much, face such dangers, live such a life that you can keep them,' she commented.

'There's no slaves in the Rio Hondo country, only a few coloured folks and they're all free.'

'Then why did you——' Liz began.

'Come on now, Miss Chamberlain,' Dusty interrupted with a smile. 'You know that the slavery issue's only one reason the South fought. A mighty good one for the Yankees to use. It's making your soldiers feel mighty noble to believe they're fighting to free a lot of bad done-by slaves. Only most slaves live just as well as a white worker up north—and nobody's thought of what they aim to do with all the Negroes when they're set free.'

'If Texas isn't a slave state, why did they fight?' Liz insisted.

'There are some slaves in Texas,' Dusty admitted. 'Down on the coast you'll find a few, but I don't think there're ten men in Texas who own enough slaves to need an overseer. Nope, slavery's not what brought Texas into the War.'

'What then?' asked Liz.

'We figure that each State is a sovereign government. Fact being that idea goes right back to when the original thirteen States combined. The States formed to be of mutual benefit to each other. Way we see it, if our State doesn't like the way things are run, then it should be allowed to pull out.'

'Cap'n Dusty's right on that,' Jill asserted.

'Sure,' Dusty said. 'Another thing Texas didn't like was the way the Union asked us to join, gave us promises and then sold us down the river.'

'How do you mean?' asked Liz.

'We were told to disband the Rangers and did it believing the Union would give us armed protection against the Indians and the Mexicans. That aid never came. It gave the Secessionists fuel to burn and they stirred up folks. Uncle Devil decided, and it wasn't an easy decision, that we fought for the South.'

'And you don't believe in slavery?' Liz insisted.

'No, ma'am. Only I sure as hell can't see how throwing thousands of Negroes out into the world and telling them they're free folks will solve their problems. I read about riots in New York a few years back; white folks objecting to slaves sent north by the underground railroad* coming into town and grabbing their work. If——'

* Underground Railroad: Organisation for smuggling freed slaves to Northern States.

'Dusty!' Jill gasped, for the first time dropping the formal 'Captain' in her agitation and pointing ahead of them.

On following the direction of Jill's point, the discussion on the coloured people problem became forgotten. A puff of smoke rose into the air from the side of a distant hill, closely followed by two more.

'Indians?' Liz gasped.

'You might say that,' grinned Dusty, 'Sam Ysabel's as near to an Indian as a white man can come.'

'I don't understand,' Liz gasped.

'It's part of the plan we made for if we had to split up,' Dusty answered. 'I made no rendezvous. Told Sam Ysabel to outride his hunters, make sure he had a clear area around him and then send up smoke. The rest of the party gathered in on the smoke when they saw it.'

'Then none of you but Sam could know where the others would gather,' Liz said. 'How about if he was caught?'

'If Kiowa hadn't seen Sam's smoke three hours after noon on the day after we split up, he was to send up the smoke. Only I didn't expect any trouble. I've yet to see Yankee cavalry that can outride those boys of mine.'

'No bunch as sorry mounted as that lot back there could,' Jill stated.

'I'm sure I saw a rider a moment ago,' Liz interrupted. 'Yes. There. Look!'

Turning their eyes, Dusty and Jill saw a distant rider. The girls could see nothing more than that, but Dusty grinned and said, 'Billy Jack.'

Almost as if he heard the words, Billy Jack swept off his hat and waved it over his head. Instead of riding towards them in a straight line, however, Billy Jack continued forward, approaching the others on a diagonal course which also kept him headed on the required route to the west.

A momentary fear hit Liz as she watched the man approach them. No matter what Jill had told Dusty, Billy Jack knew the true reason for her capture by the Yankees. Nor would he be likely to forget Liz's attempt to ride him over the slope and deliver him into Union hands.

'See you get clear, Cap'n,' Billy Jack remarked, although Liz felt his eyes studied her coldly.

'There's times I don't know how you get so smart and

all-seeing, you old goat,' Dusty answered. 'Have any trouble in shaking your lot?'

'I may as well tell you, Captain Fog,' Liz put in stiffly. 'I tried to get Sergeant-major——' she paused as she could not remember ever hearing Billy Jack's surname. 'I tried to cause the sergeant-major's capture. Jill stopped me and that was how she came to be in Union hands.'

'I sure hope the Yankees pulled you pair apart a mite gentler than we did,' Dusty answered.

Two pairs of eyes turned to him as the meaning of Dusty's words struck the girls. Suddenly both realised that he must have seen everything before taking his horse over the top of the slope.

'Then you knew all along about Liz trying to have Billy Jack captured,' Jill gasped.

'Saw some of it,' agreed Dusty.

'Tell you though, Cap'n Dusty,' Billy Jack put in. 'Miss Liz was pulling her hoss back even before Jill jumped her.'

'And she only did what I would've done in the same position,' Jill went on.

'Reckon she did,' Dusty grinned. 'All right, swing down and let's start walking for a spell. That is unless Miss Chamberlain figures to sit down for a spell.'

'I tried *that*,' Liz reminded him. 'It didn't work then and I doubt if it would now.'

'How did your lot go, Billy Jack?' asked Dusty as they started walking.

'Easy enough. I could've rid them out of sight in less than a mile, but I allowed to give 'em some work to do. Lost them in some rough country down south a piece. Say, how come you tied in with the girls?'

Dusty explained and Billy Jack listened with a grin. A wistful gleam came into the sergeant-major's eyes when Dusty mentioned tangling with the Yankee captain and Billy Jack promised himself that he would hear the full story from one of the girls as his captain gave only the bare details and omitted any reference to either his duel with Wilson or battle against the other members of the enemy party. All Dusty mentioned was that he tangled with the Yankees, then after a meal left the ranch; neither girl wished to stay there through the night with the bodies in the barn. After covering a couple of miles from the Deacon's place, Dusty and the girls camped for the night and moved on at dawn.

Alert and watchful, the party continued to head west. They made their way towards the hill from which the smoke rose, although after the brief puffs no sign of human life showed. For all any of the party saw, they might have been the only people in the whole of the North Texas range country. While approaching the hill, they saw no hint of Sam Ysabel's presence and Liz, for one, wondered if some hitch had come to Dusty's arrangements. Barely had the doubt come than Ysabel rose from cover behind a large rock. Rifle across his arm as usual, he came down the slope and for once his impassive face showed emotion. Grinning his relief, he advanced towards the others.

'Howdy, Cap'n, folks,' he greeted. 'See you made it.'

'Looks that way,' Dusty agreed, also grinning. 'You alone here?'

'Sure. Likely Kiowa's got his-self all lost. Them Kiowas never could find their way around.'

'Have any trouble shaking your bunch?' asked Dusty.

'Nope. I took off a way and lost 'em in some cedar brakes down thataways. I reckon they're still lost. Been here sooner, but my roan threw a shoe.'

'Isn't there any sign of Ja—Kiowa yet?' Jill put in.

'Why not say "Jackson," reb?' Liz interjected. 'It'll be as easy and we all know who you mean.'

A red flush crept into Jill's cheeks and she glared at Liz, but her concern for Marsden's welfare prevented her from making any comment. Instead she turned and looked expectantly at the big sergeant with pleading in her eyes.

'None I've seen,' admitted Ysabel. 'Let's get the hosses out of sight. And don't you worry none, gal, he'll show up real soon.'

Turning, Ysabel walked off and the others followed him to a pleasant, well-concealed valley with a small stream meandering along its bottom. The roan and packhorse stood grazing on the stream's bank and Dusty told his party to off-saddle and rest their mounts.

'I'll go back and keep watch, Cap'n,' Ysabel suggested. 'Haven't seen any sign of Injuns, but they do say that's the time to watch out for 'em.'

'So I've heard,' Dusty drawled. 'Only you'd best come

back and lend us a hand with the shoeing. That damned roan's got meanness in him.'

Ysabel gave out with a deep cough of laughter. 'If you reckon the roan's mean, you should see my boy Loncey's white. The ole Nigger hoss of his makes my roan look as peaceable as a preacher at a ladies' sewing-bee.'

Although Dusty thought that Ysabel exaggerated a mite, the day would come when he saw the truth of the big sergeant's words.

Billy Jack finished tending to his horse and turned to go towards the pack-animal. However, Jill turned from her buckskin and called, 'Just get the pack off, Liz and I'll see to the horse while you handle the shoeing.'

While seeing that the suggestion would save time, Billy Jack wondered if he could trust Liz not to try further delaying tactics. Liz saw his hesitation and made a quick decision. Walking to Billy Jack, she looked him straight in the face.

'I'll give you my word that I won't make any trouble,' she said.

'That's good enough for me,' he replied.

On opening the pack, Billy Jack struck a serious snag. He knew that Dusty planned to push on as soon as the shoeing was completed, leaving Kiowa to follow their tracks on his arrival at the rendezvous. So the discovery Billy Jack made did not please him and he doubted if it would make Dusty feel any delight.

'I can't start shoeing yet, Cap'n,' the sergeant-major announced. 'Got the buffer, drawing knife and rasp, but the shoeing-hammer and pincers are with Kiowa. Sam's pack-hoss had the nails though and his shoes are in his saddle-pouch.'

'We'll just have to wait for Kiowa then,' Dusty replied.

To do so meant a delay, but Dusty knew it was unavoidable. Every horse carried a set of ready-made shoes for just such an emergency, but replacing one called for the correct tools. When arranging the packs, Dusty had had to share out the loads equally between the three load-carrying horses. Shoeing equipment weighed far heavier for its bulk than did grain or human food, so he shared Billy Jack's kit among the three animals. The system failed due to the unforeseen circumstances of a horse throwing a shoe after the party split up for a time to avoid any enemy attack.

Listening to the men talk, Liz knew that a delay to their march had come. She should have been delighted, but somehow could not raise any pleasure at having her work done for her. Since listening to Wilson's comment when she mentioned the danger to innocent civilians, she wondered if Castle's plan might be as ill-advised as the Texans claimed.

Dusty told the girls to grab some rest when they finished tending to the stock, then he left the valley and walked up to where Ysabel kept watch among the rocks. Looking across the range, Dusty could see no sign of Kiowa and Marsden.

'You say you've seen no sign of Indians, Sam,' he said.

'Nary a sign, Cap'n.'

'Is that good or bad?'

'Bad as a riled-up diamondback cornered in a barrel. Saw a big bunch of buffalo back a piece. Found signs that Indians had jumped 'em further on, couple of days back. Old men and squaws had done the killing.'

'And?' Dusty prompted, although he could guess.

'Hunting's men's work. Only time they leave it to the squaws's when there's war-medicine in the air,' Ysabel explained.

'That's what I figured,' Dusty said quietly. 'We could've called our guess at the council place right.'

'Could have,' agreed Ysabel.

'Wonder if Kiowa and Jack Marsden made it,' Dusty remarked after a pause.

'If the bunch after 'em were no better mounted than them who took after me, ole Kiowa could outride 'em,' Ysabel guessed. 'And young Marsden rides real good—for a Yankee.'

'Real good,' agreed Dusty. 'I don't like the delay though.'

Not until shortly before sundown did Kiowa and Marsden make their appearance. Jill tried to stand back, act cold and distant, but failed. Giving a relieved gasp, she flung herself into Marsden's arms.

'Let's have the horses tended to,' Dusty remarked.

'I'll see to Mr. Marsden's,' Liz promised, 'or the packhorse, whichever you want, Captain.'

'The choice's your own, ma'am,' Dusty told her with a grin. 'How's that for Southern hospitality?'

Leaving Liz to handle Marsden's sorrel, Dusty helped Billy Jack to unload and unpack the packhorse's load. While waiting for Kiowa's arrival, Billy Jack had prepared the roan for being re-shod. Due to Dusty's foresight in having each horse fresh-shod before leaving the regiment, much of Billy Jack's work had been done and he only needed to ensure that the horn grown since the last shoeing be removed and the bearing surface for the reception of the new shoe made level by judicious use of the rasp. After that, he nailed a cold shoe into place and finished his work.

Knowing Billy Jack's skill in such matters, Dusty left him to his work and joined Kiowa at the fire. With the horses cared for, Liz knelt at the fire preparing a meal for the men. She listened to the conversation out of simple curiosity, not because she sought some information useful in spoiling Dusty's arrangements.

'Saw some Indian sign down to the south,' Kiowa remarked. 'Couple of sizeable bunches headed north-west. Then we come across a bunch of young Kaddo bucks and hid out from 'em. That's why we came in so late.'

'Those Kaddos headed right for the council grounds?' asked Dusty.

'Reckon so,' admitted the lean sergeant. 'We called it right, Cap'n.'

'Looks that way. Say, where's Jill and Jack Marsden?'

'Need you ask,' smiled Liz.

'Reckon not,' Dusty admitted with a grin. 'Only I hope they don't stop out there spooning too long. We've some fast moving to do to make up for the delay.'

Next day the party pushed on at a fast pace, riding and walking to such purpose that they made all of forty miles. Nor did they slow down the following day. The party crossed the Elm Fork of the Trinity just below its junction with the Denton and passed over the Trinity's West Fork so as to make camp on the southern tip of Lake Bridgeport. That night first the girls, then the men, grabbed a chance to swim in the lake, wash off the travel dirt and try to soak away the ache of hard travel. Dawn found them moving across what today is Jack County. Having found Indian sign, fresh and headed west, Dusty now kept Ysabel out ahead as scout and Kiowa brought up the rear. The rest of the party kept together, still travelling fast but now using caution and even more alert for trouble. Dusty no longer feared trouble from the Yankees, but he knew the Indians would be a far more serious menace than any Union soldiers.

'What are those?' Liz asked, pointing to several circling black dots in the noonday sky, as she walked at Dusty's side and led her mare.

'Turkey buzzards,' he answered. 'Hovering over an Indian kill, maybe.' For all his light tone, Dusty gave the turkey vultures another glance before directing his gaze towards Ysabel. Seeing the sergeant halt, turn and wave, Dusty went on. 'Mount up. Keep back a piece, you girls.'

Leaving the other two men to guard the girls, Dusty urged his horse to a faster pace and joined Ysabel on top of a rolling fold of land. A low hiss of anger left Dusty's lips at what he saw below on the other side of the slope. Side by side, Dusty and Ysabel rode down the slope towards what had once been a peaceful, neat little cabin. When Dusty told Liz that the circling turkey vultures could be hovering over an Indian's kill, he meant a buffalo, elk, or maybe a long-horn butchered for meat. What lay before him was not so innocent.

By the corral lay the naked, mutilated shape of what had been a burly white man, the mangled flesh giving no hint as to which of the many holes and gashes killed him. Not far away the gutted body of a large dog sprawled in death.

'Why the hell do they have to carve a man up like that?' Dusty growled. 'I wonder who he was.'

'Dutchy Ritter, Cap'n,' Ysabel replied. 'I know his dawg. He was a horse-trader with a wife and two kids.'

'When did it happen?'

'Towards evening yesterday, I'd say. Don't get it though, Dutchy allus got on with the Comanches and this's Comanche country.'

Dusty did not reply. Riding to the house, he swung from his saddle and walked to the shattered door. Only by an effort could he force himself to enter the building, for he guessed what he would find inside. Through necessity Dusty had become accustomed to seeing death, but he was pale under his tan as he returned to the open again. He expected the sight in the room to be bad, but not quite *that* bad.

By the time Dusty emerged, the remainder of the party had come up. Liz, face set and pale, eyes fighting to avoid looking again at the grisly things by the corral, dismounted and walked towards the house.

'Is this Indian work?' she asked, her voice hoarse and strained.

'Yes, ma'am,' Dusty replied.

'Was he alone?'

'No.'

Listening to Dusty's flat, cold, one-word reply, Liz knew something far worse than the horror at the corral lay in the building. Much as she wanted to turn and run, Liz knew she must see the inside of the cabin. Setting her teeth grimly, she walked by Dusty and before he realised what she meant to do had passed through the door. A low cry left her lips at what she saw. The two children, a boy and a girl, were bad enough, their small bodies battered and mutilated—but the worse horror hung half in, half out of the bed. In life it had been a pretty woman and carrying an unborn child. The face was unmarked. A hideous gash laid the throat open to the bone. Yet there was even more. The woman's belly had been ripped open and the unborn child's body trailed on to the floor by her side.

'This's what they'll turn loose all through Texas,' Dusty said quietly.

For a moment Liz stood staring around her. Then she gave a low moan, turned and collapsed sobbing into Dusty's arms. The cabin seemed to be whirling around, heaving up and down before Liz's eyes and everything went black.

Blue sky greeted her when she recovered. Jill knelt at her side and the rebel girl's face showed concern. To one side Dusty stood talking with Ysabel, and Liz caught the words.

'So it was Kaddo work,' he said.

'Sure. Young bucks headed for the council and took a chance to gather some loot,' Ysabel agreed. 'I didn't figure Comanches'd jump Dutchy, he got on with 'em.'

'I should have stopped Liz going in there,' Dusty stated.

'Should have,' agreed Ysabel. 'Only now she knows what Castle's scheme'll mean.'

'Yes,' Dusty said flatly. 'Now she knows. Let's go help the others with the burying.'

CHAPTER FOURTEEN

WE OWE YOU THAT MUCH, MR. MARSDEN

'We're too late, Cap'n,' Sam Ysabel told Dusty quietly. 'They've beaten us to it. Arrived this morning.'

Sitting to one side of the small Texan, Liz listened to the words with a cold chill of apprehension. She had talked little since the finding of the ravaged ranch and her face showed haggard lines not entirely due to fatigue. Watching Dusty, she wondered what he would—or could—do in view of Ysabel's news. They had reached the upper tip of Lake Sheppard and made a hidden camp in the pine woods just below where the Brazos flowed into the lake. On arrival, Dusty sent Ysabel out on a scout of the area, from which the sergeant had just returned and brought the worst possible news.

Liz wondered how Dusty must feel, having ridden so far, planned so well, and to find that he came on the scene just a few hours too late. It must be a bitter blow. Yet she could see no chance of preventing Castle's scheme. Four men and two girls—yes, two, for she intended to give all her help to stopping the uprising—could do nothing against a large camp of Indians who had the backing of an Ager Coffee Mill gun.

'How much do you know?' Dusty asked.

'Caught me a Kaddo buck as he was out hunting,' Ysabel answered. 'He got around to talking after a spell. The big council's fixed for tonight. Then the Yankees'll be showing off their Devil Gun, which's what they're calling the Ager.'

'Is it much of a camp?' asked Billy Jack, mirroring Liz's thoughts.

'I'd put it at around fifty each of Comanches, Kaddos and Kiowas. Few Wacos, smidgin of Attacapas from the coast, and I'd swear to there being some White Mountain Apaches out of New Mexico.'

'But how did they all get to hear of the council?' Liz put in.

'Now that's a right smart question, ma'am,' Ysabel answered. 'I've lived among the Comanches, am a member of the Dog Soldier Lodge, but I don't start to pretend I can explain half the things I've seen Injun medicine-men do.'

'The meeting's set for tonight, you say, Sam,' Dusty said.

'Yep. The chiefs have seen the rifles and only want showing how the Devil Gun works.'

'The arms wagon is in the camp?'

'Nope. The Deacon's not that *loco*, Cap'n. He's got it stashed down in the woods on top of the big bend the river makes afore it forks apart. Meeting's right down at the bottom of the bend's loop.'

'Many men with the wagon, Sam?' Marsden inquired as he sat at Jill's side.

'The two Yankees, Deacon, his right bower, Cracker and three more. Reckon the Deacon'll take Cracker along when he goes with the Yankees to the Council, seeing's how he don't speak Spanish, and Spanish's the only language that they all understand.'

'Leaves three with the wagon then,' Billy Jack stated. 'At least we'll stop 'em getting the rifles, Cap'n Dusty.'

'And the Injuns'd still ride. More so to get them back. Especially when they see what that Ager'll do,' Kiowa informed him.

'If we could only get into that council——' Dusty began.

'We can,' Ysabel replied. 'Least I can. I'm a member of the Dog Soldier lodge and can go to any council called for the tribe.'

'Even in your army uniform?' asked Dusty.

'Got my medicine boot for the Sharps, with that it don't matter how I dress. Long Walker's there and he's my friend. If I know him, he don't want this war. He's an old-time Comanche and won't hold with riding alongside Kaddos, much less with Wacos or them coast Attacapas. With him there, I can walk into that council.'

'Can you take me in with you?'

For a long moment Ysabel did not reply. Then he nodded his head. 'There's one way. If you and I were blood brothers, I could take you along.'

'Then you'd best make me your blood brother,' Dusty said.

'Have you a plan, sir?' Marsden asked, watching Dusty intently.

'Call it a fool notion, mister,' Dusty replied. 'I've learned a few things about Indians during this journey. Enough to take a chance on spoiling the Devil Gun's medicine.'

Although a painful death awaited him if anything went wrong with Dusty's plan, Billy Jack did not hesitate to ask, 'How many of us're going, sir?'

'Only Sam and I,' Dusty answered, and stifled the low rumble of objection with a gesture. 'Mr. Marsden, you'll take Billy Jack and Kiowa tonight and either bring away that arms wagon, or destroy it. Either way, it must not fall into the Indian's hands.'

'And the girls, sir?' Marsden said.

'They will remain here, hidden,' Dusty ordered, and looked at Liz as she made a start at protesting. 'No arguments, Miss Chamberlain. Neither of you are trained or suited for the work ahead. I want you to remain here with the pack animals. If we haven't returned at dawn, or if you hear anything to suggest that we won't be coming back, strike out to the south along the river. Ride as you've learned during the journey and when you find white folks start to spread the word of what's happened up here.'

'Very good, Captain,' Liz replied.

'We'll get through, if we can,' Jill promised, trying to hold concern out of her voice as she clung to Marsden's hand.

'Best show us how the land lies around the wagon, Sam,' Kiowa suggested.

Squatting on his heels by the fire, Ysabel used his bowie knife's point to clear a patch of earth on which he drew a rough, but fairly accurate map of the arms wagon's location. Using his knowledge of such matters as a guide, he pointed out the easiest route by which to make an advance towards the clearing in which the wagon stood and mentioned the snags one might expect.

'Only thing I can see's going to be whether Mr. Marsden and Billy Jack can move quiet enough through the woods in the dark,' he concluded. 'Them boys guarding the wagon know Injuns and won't be sleeping on the job.'

'How about it, Mr. Marsden?' Dusty asked.

'I've hunted deer, sir.'

'Deer don't shoot back and take your scalp, mister,' Ysabel remarked, but his voice stayed friendly. 'You'll have to move *real* quiet through the woods so's to get up close——'

'And then cross about twenty yards of open ground to reach the men,' Dusty interrupted, bringing up a point the other overlooked. 'They'll have to be taken quietly. I don't want the Indians at the council alerting.'

'There's no chance of waiting until the guards sleep, sir?' asked Marsden. 'They might all go to sleep at the same time.'

'In *Injun* country?' Ysabel grunted. 'I tell you, mister, these fellers know the game. They're still alive and they've been in hostile country most of their growing lives.'

Silence dropped on the men for a moment as they began to examine the difficulties of the situation.

'I could get to the edge of the clearing without 'em hearing me,' Kiowa stated. 'But it's moving in on them that'll make the fuss.'

'What we need is a diversion,' Marsden put in.

Liz had sat listening to the talk, her brain working furiously in an attempt to help out with the problem. An idea came to her and she looked at Jill for a moment before speaking.

'Perhaps Jill and I could cause the diversion you need,' she said and explained her idea.

'It might work,' Dusty admitted.

'Won't it be too dangerous for—the girls, sir?' Marsden asked.

'Mister, they're living in danger,' Dusty answered. 'But it's going to take some slick timing to bring it off. And there's another thing——' At this point his words trailed off and he sat for a few seconds thinking out the idea which came. 'There's one way we could play it,' he finally remarked.

None of the three men guarding the arms wagons cared for the thought of sitting within two miles of a sizeable Indian camp while in possession of such desirable loot as three hundred Sharps rifles, with ammunition, percussion caps and Maynard tape primers to feed the said weapons. True the various tribes gathered for a peaceful council, but some of the younger bucks might take it into their heads that the top of the big bend of the river did not count as sacred ground and so could be raided with impunity.

So the trio stayed alert, ears strained to catch any deviation from the normal night noises. While the men might lack formal schooling, and their morals left much to be desired, all knew one thing very well; how to stay alive in hostile country. The normal night noises did not disturb them, but a fresh sound came to their ears and brought them to their feet at the small fire on which their coffee pot stood.

'Hosses,' announced the lean, bearded man. 'Coming this way.'

'Only two of 'em,' remarked the short, stocky man.

A moment later all three heard the faint click of steel striking rock, although less keen ears would have failed to catch the sound.

'Shod hooves,' growled the third of the guards.

No Indian ever rode a shod horse. Even should he take a white man's horse as loot, the Indian ripped off the valuable metal shoes for his own use.

'Get out of sight!' snapped the bearded man. 'Hit the wagon, Smokey. You go in the bushes, Will.'

Neither questioned the bearded man's right to give orders. Turning, the short man hurried across the clearing and took cover in the bushes on the very edge of the area illuminated by the fire. Moving just as fast, the third man went to the rear of the wagon, swung himself up and disappeared inside. The bearded man threw a glance at the Volcanic rifle which rested against his saddle, then he looked towards the picketed team and saddle horses at one side of the clearing. Finally he sank on his haunches at the fire, drawing his Navy Colt and resting it on his knees.

Nearer came the horses, following the rough trail made by the Deacon on previous trading visits to the bend of the river. If the riders aimed to sneak up on the camp, they showed poor judgment or mighty poor faith in the guards' abilities. Making no attempt to ride quietly, the newcomers came closer, although still out of sight.

'Hello the fire!' called a female voice.

'Who is it?' a second woman's voice went on.

A few seconds later the man found himself gazing at a pair of dishevelled, pretty girls who rode slumped wearily in their saddles. His eyes took in Jill's torn shirt and the fact that she needed one hand to hold the cloth together. From there he gazed with frank interest at Liz, whose blouse had lost a sleeve and hung ripped open down its side, while her skirt was torn from hem almost to hip and showed an expanse of bare white leg as she rode astride.

'Th—Thank God!' Liz gasped. 'You're white men. We've been lost for hours until we saw your fire.'

Rising, the man eyed the girls suspiciously and made no attempt to holster his gun. 'Where'd you come from?' he asked.

'We were travelling to Fort Worth with a party from the Indian Nations,' Jill answered. 'Only we lost them last night.'

'Get down,' the man growled.

Instinctively he knew something to be wrong, although he could not quite put his finger on it. Certainly the girls looked weary, untidy and scared enough to have been lost for some time. Maybe——

At that point he lost interest in the matter. Liz started to swing her leg over the saddle and dismount, but the torn hem of her skirt caught on the horn and hung there. A squeal of embarrassment left her lips as she lowered her foot to the ground and found her leg exposed to view.

When dressing for her part in Dusty's plan, Liz donned the clothing damaged in her first fight with Jill and augmented it with a pair of very daring drawers of a kind actresses, but few of Liz's class, wore. She thought the effect might be increased by the extra exposure the drawers offered as opposed to the more ladylike long-legged variety a proper young lady wore. From the way the bearded man's eyes bulged out, she knew she'd made a wise decision.

'I—I'm caught up,' she told the man pathetically.

Watching Liz, Jill could barely hold down a chuckle. Give her her due, the Yankee girl could sure act. She looked as helpless as the heroine of one of the melodramatic plays put on by travelling theatrical troupes; although they never showed their legs in so daring a manner during mixed or family shows. Certainly the bearded man had no suspicions as he started forward to help free Liz's skirt.

Nor, it appeared, had the other two guards. In an age when a woman's exposed calf drew gasps of indignation, or interested stares, depending on the sex of the observer, men like that trio would not hesitate to take a closer look at as much exposed female limb as Liz offered to view.

Dropping from the wagon, Smokey walked towards the girls. He failed to see why Rogers should have all the fun. So did Will, for he emerged from the bushes and started to hurry across the clearing. In his haste, Will failed to notice a dark shape rise behind him and follow on his trail with the silent, deadly purpose of a cougar stalking a whitetail deer. In one respect Will might have counted himself fortunate. While awaiting the girls' arrival, Kiowa watched Will's arrival in the bushes. Knife in hand, the Indian-dark sergeant stalked Will and had been on the point of silencing the other when Will left cover to lend a hand with Liz's predicament. Silently, Kiowa glided out of the woods after Will and only the other's preoccupation with viewing Liz's legs prevented his normally keen senses from detecting his danger.

Although as absorbed in the view as his two friends were, Rogers could not help but feel that he missed an important detail. Not until he had almost reached Liz did he realise what was wrong. While the girls showed signs of hard travelling, their horses appeared to be fresh.

'What the——' he began.

At which point Billy Jack and Marsden burst into sight from either side of the trail down which the girls appeared. Guns in hand, they sprang forward, covering the startled guards.

'Freeze, boys!' Billy Jack requested.

Rogers let out a low snarl and his hand stabbed down at his gun. Jumping her buckskin forward, Jill swung up the hand she kept hidden from the guards. In it she held her Tranter and she put the gun to good use. Up rose her hand and, powered by a strong arm, slammed the barrel of the gun downwards on to Rogers' head. Giving a low grunt, the man buckled at the knees and went down.

Exposed to the guns of the newcomers far more than Rogers had been, Smokey raised his hands in surrender. While a shot might alert the boss' party at the big council, Smokey knew its bullet would end his life; and he did not feel in the mood for noble self-sacrifice right then.

Across the clearing, Will reached hipwards. He figured himself to be far enough from the soldiers to take a chance and also that they could not see his movement. Even as his fingers closed around the butt of his gun, his instincts told him that he was not alone. The feeling received confirmation when something sharp pricked his spine just at the point where the kidneys could best be reached by an exploratory knife.

'Let's keep it quiet, *hombre*,' growled an Indian-savage voice in Will's ear. 'Just walk forward slow and easy.'

A hand removed Will's gun, tossing it aside, and he walked forward slowly.

'It worked,' Liz announced proudly, freeing her dress and letting it drop into something like a respectable position.

'Never thought it wouldn't,' Billy Jack replied as he advanced to disarm the other guards.

Nor had he, for he possessed great faith in the planning ability of the small man who led him. Dusty's idea worked smoothly. To give them a chance to approach the camp undetected, Dusty told Marsden and Billy Jack to ride behind the girls and drop off the horses just before reaching the clearing. In that way they avoided a long, difficult stalk through the woods with the danger of making some noise to warn the guards. How well the plan worked showed as the Deacon's men lost their weapons without a shot being fired or an unnecessary noise made.

'Tie them securely, Sergeant-major,' Marsden ordered, and wondered if the man would obey him.

'Yo!' Billy Jack replied.

While Marsden might be a Yankee, Billy Jack had received Dusty's orders to let Marsden command the party and the lean non-com needed no more than that. Swiftly but thoroughly Billy Jack and Kiowa roped their prisoners' hands and feet. With that done, Kiowa grinned at Liz.

'How's about showing us how you got these jaspers watching you, when we get back to the regiment, ma'am?' he asked.

'I thought you saw just now,' she answered, trying to think if she had ever seen the impassive man smile before.

'I did, only a feller can allus learn if he sees a thing done enough.'

'Sure can,' Billy Jack chuckled. 'Let's hitch up the wagon and pull out.'

'Say,' Kiowa drawled as they led the team horses into position. 'These rifles will sure come in handy for our infantry.'

'They sure will,' Billy Jack agreed.

Suddenly Marsden realised what the words meant. If the Texans took the arms wagon back to Arkansas, the rifles would be used against the Union Army, probably to kill members of his regiment. A grim, tight expression came to his face.

'We'll throw the rifles and ammunition over that cliff into the lake,' he said. 'There's nearly thirty foot of water under it Sergeant Ysabel said as we passed it. The Indians will never recover them from there.'

An angry objection rose to both Texans' lips, but died unsaid. For the first time in days they remembered that Marsden served the Union. Yet they also knew what his presence meant to the people of Texas. Billy Jack and Kiowa exchanged glances, then the sergeant-major nodded.

'We owe you that much, Mr. Marsden,' he said.

'How about the prisoners?' Marsden asked, to conceal his gratitude and relief.

'We'll turn them loose. With the guns gone, they'll know what to expect if the Indians lay hands on them,' Kiowa replied. 'Wonder how Cap'n Dusty's doing?'

CHAPTER FIFTEEN

LET THEM KILL ME WITH THEIR DEVIL GUN

In many ways the Ager Coffee Mill Gun was a fine weapon, far superior to the Barnes or Ripley guns which preceded it and better, more reliable than the Billinghurst Requa or Vandenburg Volley gun. The model in Castle and Silverman's possession stood on a light artillery mount, but lacked the protective shield fitted to some models as defence for the gunners against return fire by the enemy. Single-barrelled, .58-in. calibre, it derived its name from the resemblance its operating parts bore to the coffee-grinding mills of the day.

Standing to the left of the gun, Lieutenant Silverman fed another handful of loaded chargers into the hopper-shaped magazine on top of the gun. The sallow-faced, large-nosed stocky lieutenant made sure each charger went in correctly, for both he and his partner in the scheme knew they must not let the Indians see the gun jam.

Captain Castle, at the gun's right side, twirled its cranking handle at less than the fastest possible speed. Far from a source of supply, he wanted to conserve powder, shot and chargers as much as possible. While the guns fired slowly, it still exceeded anything the Indians had ever seen. Mutters of awe rose all around the halfcircle of watching chiefs and braves as the gun continued to crash, spewing its used chargers around the tall, slim, lean-faced captain's feet.

At last Castle stopped turning the handle, although several rounds still remained in the hopper. By the time he had turned towards the Indians, he found their usual impassive masks looking at him and he read nothing on their faces. Running a tongue tip over his lips in a nervous manner, Castle turned his gaze to the two civilians who stood on his right. Tall, gaunt, clad in the garb of a circuit-riding preacher, the Deacon's sombre features showed as little expression as the Indians'. He stood with legs braced apart, an eight gauge, twin barrelled shotgun held down before him in both hands. Next to the Deacon lounged a lean, long-haired, dirty, mean-faced man in smoke-blackened buckskins, but the gunbelt around his waist and the holstered Army Colt were clean and cared-for.

An elderly, stocky, powerfully built Comanche chief growled out a question and Cracker turned to Castle.

'Long Walker says the Devil Gun eats much powder and shot. Can you get more?'

Bending down, Castle lifted one of the used chargers and held it for the chief—one of the most powerful and influential present—to see. The charger proved to be a steel tube with a place in its bottom to accommodate a percussion cap. Taking the powder flask and moulded lead bullet from Silverman's reluctant hand—the lieutenant hoped to heighten his prestige by demonstrating how to load the charger, but Castle did not intend to allow anyone to share his glory. The captain showed the Indian how easily the Devil Gun's appetite could be appeased.

'Tell the chief that we will have powder, lead and fresh charges brought as we need them,' Castle ordered Cracker. 'We have enough for an attack upon both Fort Worth and Dallas, after we have proved our claims for the gun on some smaller objective.'

While Cracker interpreted, Castle stood thinking of his great scheme. Once the Indians rose, there would be no stopping them and they would wipe out the hated rebels. That ought to bring the Texans fighting in the Confederate Army home with a rush, but they would not arrive in one party and the Indians ought to be able to swamp, then exterminate each body of men as it returned. That loss of man-power would so weaken the South that it must surrender. Castle wished there was some way the Indians could be turned loose though all the Southern States so as to leave none of the rebels alive.

At that point of his day-dream, Castle became aware of a stir among the assembled Indians and a startled gasp from Silverman. Bringing his eyes in the direction everybody stared, the Union captain let his mouth drop open at what he saw.

Two men walked from the darkness which surrounded the area lit by large fires. Not just two men, but a pair of Confederate soldiers, a captain and a sergeant, in uniform. Unlike the two Union officers, who showed a voluntary untidiness beyond that of hard travel, Dusty Fog looked smart; for Jill and Liz had worked hard all day to clean up the signs of the journey from his clothes. To show their 'good faith' the two Yankees attended the meeting without weapons. From what Ysabel told him. Dusty retained his gunbelt as a sign that he respected the others present and expected them to be able to trust him among them while armed.

Up lunged a Kaddo brave, lifting the Hawkens rifle from his knees. Before he could make a move, one of his companions caught his arm and pointed to the fringed, decorated buckskin boot which covered Ysabel's rifle.

'This one is called Ysabel!' boomed Long Walker in a warning voice. 'He is a member of the Dog Soldier lodge as his medicine pouch shows.'

Which meant that the big white man had a right to attend the council and anyone who objected chanced the wrath of the most feared of all the Comanche war lodges.

'And the other?' asked Plenty Kills, main chief of the Kiowa.

'This one is a great war chief of his people,' Ysabel answered in Spanish. 'He is my blood brother, we cut wrists and mixed blood.'

And that gave Dusty the right to be present.

'What do you want here?' Lone Hunter of the Kaddo asked.

For the first time in his life the Deacon panicked. Knowing his fate at the hands of his fellow-Texans should his betrayal become public news, he prepared to take the easy way out, relying on the Devil Gun's medicine to quieten any Indian-raised objections to his breach of hospitality.

'They're spies!' he screeched and started to lift his shotgun. 'Get 'em!'

Instantly Cracker sent his right hand stabbing towards the butt of his gun. He knew Sam Ysabel could never remove the long medicine boot from the Sharps in time to take a hand, which left only that rebel captain to be handled.

An instant behind Cracker's move, Dusty sent his hands crossing to the white handles of the matched Army Colts in a flicker of movement almost faster than the eye could follow. Three-quarters of a second later the two Colts crashed in Dusty's grip, their shots sounding so close together that no man, not even the most quick-eared Indian present, could tell the sound apart. Caught between the eyes with a .44 bullet, the Deacon pitched over backwards, his shotgun still not raised high enough to fire. Colt still in leather, Cracker rocked, spun around and fell even as his boss went down.

A low mutter arose from the watching Indians, but interest and not anger prompted it. Every man present was a brave-heart warrior with a name for being a bone-tough fighter from soda to hock. The quickest and most effective way to gain their attention was to display superlative skill in the handling of any kind of weapon. Every man present realised they watched a master hand demonstrate his talent in the business of killing enemies.

'This one is called Magic Hands,' Ysabel boomed out as Dusty holstered the guns. 'He comes to the council to listen and speak.'

Long Walker looked around the party of leading chiefs with whom he sat. First Plenty Kills, an old friend of the Comanche chief, nodded in agreement. Not to be out-done in courtesy and adherence to tradition, the other chiefs gave their complete assent to Dusty's continued presence.

Remembering what Ysabel told him about Indian etiquette, Dusty turned to Castle and saluted.

'Carry on speaking, sir,' he said.

Confusion and distrust showed on Castle's face as he received Dusty's permission and watched the small Texan walk over to sit among the chiefs. Then he saw a way out of the predicament.

'I can't speak Spanish.'

'Sergeant Ysabel will interpret for you,' Dusty countered.

'I said all I meant to before you came,' Castle snarled.

'And I heard you,' Dusty replied. 'With your permission, sir, I'll speak to the council now you're through.'

Once more a low rumble went around the assembled Indians. Tradition meant much to them and they respected a man who showed courtesy to an enemy. All would listen to Dusty the more willingly now he had shown his knowledge of their ways.

Stepping forward, Dusty looked around at the sea of impassive brown faces. After a moment's thought to prepare himself for speaking in Spanish, he began to address the council.

'The blue-coat chief says you should attack the settlements. You have tried before and many brave-hearts now roam the land of the spirits. He says many of our men are away, fighting with his people. That is true, but they can return soon and will come bringing many wheel guns——'

'You have the Devil Gun!' Castle yelled, for Ysabel had been translating Dusty's words for the Yankee's benefit. In doing so Castle committed a breach of council etiquette, he should have waited for Dusty to finish before speaking.

'The Devil Gun is only one. We have many wheel guns,' Dusty went on.

Again Castle burst in. 'The Devil Gun is here. The grey-coats' wheel guns are far away.'

While Ysabel turned Castle's words into Spanish, Dusty thought up an answer.

'This chief thinks much of the Devil Gun's medicine. But has he showed you proof that its medicine is good?'

'I fired the gun.' Castle answered edging nearer to the trap Dusty set for him. 'All men here saw its power.'

Like a flash Dusty cut back with. 'All men heard noises. But children in their games make noises and do no harm.'

'You've seen the gun work!' Castle yelled.

'But you have not seen it kill!' Dusty pointed out and he walked slowly around to halt some twenty feet before the muzzle of the gun. 'Let them kill me with their Devil Gun—if its medicine is strong enough to do so.'

Although Castle knew no Spanish, he understood Dusty's gesture without needing Ysabel's explanation. A quick glance around the council showed him a tense expectancy and he knew that he must accept the Texan's challenge. On the face of it everything was in Castle's favour. He stood at the side of the gun still, its firing handle close to his hand. All he need do was reach forward, grip and move that handle to send a bullet into Dusty's stomach. Such a simple thing to do.

And then Castle remembered how the Deacon and Cracker came to die!

They too thought they had an easy task on their hands. Almost as if it happened again. Castle saw the way the small Texan's hands moved to draw, shoot and kill the two renegades.

When Castle conceived his scheme, he saw himself following in the wake of the attacking Indians, using the Ager from a safe distance and taking no chances. Running risks with his valuable life did not enter his calculations. He planned to stay alive to reap the acclaim and benefits the successful end of the plan would bring. Only he would not do so if he tried to reach the gun's firing handle.

'It's your turn to handle the gun, Herbie,' he told Silverman.

Shock, fear and suspicion mingled on Silverman's face at the words. Silverman had a mean-minded, mistrusting nature, and also a very broad streak of caution. Killing people without a chance did not worry him, but trying to kill a man who could move as quickly as Dusty did, brought a muck-sweat of apprehension to the Union lieutenant.

'It was your idea,' he hissed back at Castle. 'You do it.'

A rustle of movement ran through the council as the two Yankees hesitated to display the Devil Gun's medicine. Through it all Dusty stood still, hands at his sides, face showing complete assurance that should Castle make a move, Dusty knew he could beat it. After almost two minutes Dusty took his plan a step further. Slowly he reached down and unfastened the holsters' pigging thongs from around his legs.

'Perhaps the Devil Gun's medicine does not work against armed men,' he said.

Shocked disbelief etched itself upon Ysabel's usually impassive face as he saw, though could hardly believe, what Dusty aimed to do. Ysabel's agitation showed even more as he gave a low-growled warning.

'You'll have to go through with it if you once start, Cap'n.'

'I aim to, Sam,' Dusty replied and unbuckled his belt. 'I aim to.'

With that, Dusty tossed his guns to one side and stood empty handed before the yawning muzzle of the Devil Gun. However, he gave the impression of being ready to dive after and grab his guns should Castle make a move.

Sucking in his breath, Castle took a chance. He lunged forward, reaching for the firing handle with his right hand, the left swinging the gun on its lateral traverse. Crouching slightly, Castle aimed the Ager's barrel downwards so that it moved in line towards where Dusty's gunbelt lay. Around turned the handle, flame spurting out—to strike nothing but earth.

Dusty had not dived for his guns—he never meant to do so. At Castle's first movement, Dusty went forward in a rolling dive, straight towards the left side of the Ager. While Castle swung the gun towards the right, Dusty passed from its range of fire and to comparative safety.

Letting out a yell in which fear and fury mingled, Silverman sprang from his place at the loading hopper to land kneeling at Dusty's right and grab down at the Texan's throat with both hands. Castle, filled with concern for his safety, and mortification, plunged around the Ager and prepared to launch a vicious kick at Dusty from the other side.

Realising that he must deal with Silverman first, Dusty went into action long before Castle made his move. Even as Silverman's hands reached his throat, Dusty's left leg rose and its knee smashed into the Yankee's ribs. A grunt of pain burst from Silverman and his hold relaxed slightly. Up shot Dusty's right arm, passing between Silverman's as it aimed towards the other's face. Instead of clenching his fist, Dusty kept the fingers extended and held together, thumb bent across his palm in the *nukite* piercing hand of karate. The tips of his fingers stabbed hard under Silverman's nose, catching the philtrum collection of nerve centres. Although unable to put all his power behind the blow. Dusty still brought about a rapid release of his throat and left himself free to handle Castle's impending assault.

Rolling over on to his left side, Dusty struck around with his left arm. He used the *uraken* back-fist blow to hit and deflect Castle's kicking leg. On the heels of the *uraken*, Dusty's right hand stabbed forward to catch Castle's raised ankle and heaved to unbalance the Yankee. Drawing up his left leg under him, Dusty lashed out a snap kick with his right that just missed Castle's groin and sent him reeling away.

Dusty began to rise, conscious of the admiring mutters from the watching Indians. Before he made his feet properly, Dusty saw Silverman come in with a swinging fist. Unable to avoid the blow, Dusty took it and went crashing into the Ager's wheel. Springing forward in a concerted rush, Castle and Silverman each grabbed hold of Dusty's jacket front with one hand while smashing the other into his face or body. Unable to retreat, Dusty threw up his left hand in a sweeping-block move, its edge chopping into Castle's arm and preventing the fist reaching his face. At the same moment Dusty drove back his right arm, to use a pressing-block that held Silverman's attempt to hit his stomach. Such was the strength of Dusty's small frame that he held both bigger men's blows, actually pinning Silverman's hand against the lieutenant's body with his blocking blow. Releasing hold of Dusty's jacket, Castle sprang back to try another line of attack.

'Hold him, Herbie!' he yelled.

If it came to a point, Dusty held Silverman; for his pressing-block kept the other's disengaged arm immobile. Castle came in, throwing a savage right at Dusty's head. Pivoting to face the danger, Dusty retained his pressing-block on Silverman and knocked aside Castle's blow with his left arm, following it with a smashing jolt of his right elbow into the Yankee captain's chest. Croaking in pain, Castle staggered backwards and gave Dusty a chance to deal with Silverman. Like a flash Dusty delivered a kick to the rear, stamping his boot heel against Silverman's shin. So quickly had everything happened that Silverman's brain could not cope with the situation and issue orders. The impact of Dusty's boot against Silverman's leg prevented the need for thought. With a yelp, the stocky lieutenant released his hold and hopped away on one leg.

Leaping forward, Castle swung a roundhouse blow towards Dusty's head. Dusty saw the danger, ducked under the punch, sank a right into Castle's belly and jack-knifed him over. Driving up his knee, Dusty caught Castle's down-dropping face and jerked him erect. Whipping across his left Dusty smashed home a punch which spun the Yankee around and sent him sprawling to the ground in front of the Ager gun. Before Dusty could make a move to handle any further developments, Silverman leapt in from behind him and curled arms around the small Texan in a full nelson hold. Fear and desperation lent strength to Silverman's arms and Dusty grunted as the hold sent pain knifing into him.

'Carnie!' Silverman screeched. 'Do something!'

The words bit through Castle's spinning senses and as his eyes regained focus they rested on a possible salvation. Not far ahead of him lay the Texan's gunbelt, its white-handled Colt burden showing like providence to Castle's eyes. Ignoring his companion's cry, he flung himself forward, hands reaching towards the butt of the nearest gun.

Once again Dusty had thought faster than his enemy. Recognising the danger, he prepared to handle it. First he must free himself, and he knew he could not do it quickly enough by matching arm strength with Silverman. So he did not try. Drawing forward his body, Dusty propelled it back, driving his buttocks into Silverman's lower belly with enough force to cause an immediate release. Moaning, Silverman reeled backwards and Dusty ignored him for the moment.

Bounding forward, Dusty reached the Ager. He took quick sight and whirled the firing handle even as Castle's hands hovered over the butt of the nearer Colt. Loud in the night rose the chatter of the Devil Gun's repeated explosions; flame belched from its barrel. A line of dust-spurts rose, creeping closer to Castle's body. He turned a horrified face towards the gun, mouth dropping open and trying to speak. The bullets crawled closer and closer, throwing up dirt as they ploughed into the ground. Then no more dirt rose. Castle jerked as the first bullet struck his body. Five more .58 balls tore into him before Dusty could halt the Devil Gun's fire. Torn almost in half by the lead, Castle's lifeless body pitched over and lay still.

Dusty left the gun, whirling to meet any attack Silverman launched. Although a good three inches taller and much heavier than Dusty, Silverman lacked the guts to continue the fight. Turning, he started to run—and made a fatal mistake. While the Indian admired and respected a brave man, he had nothing but contempt for a coward. Giving a low, disgusted grunt, one of the watching braves bounded up as Silverman approached. Out thrust a buffalo lance, its point ripping into Silverman's body. The stocky lieutenant let out a croaking scream and fell, writhing out the remainder of his life and shedding his blood upon the Texas plains he had hoped to redden with the gore of the Southerners he hated.

Leaning on the side of the Ager gun, Dusty fought to regain his breath. He heard the rumbling approval of the watching Indians and saw Sam Ysabel springing towards him. Regaining his breath, Dusty waved Ysabel aside and faced the assembled tribal chiefs.

'The Devil Gun's medicine is bad,' he stated. 'It did not protect the blue-coats.'

'But it killed well,' Plenty Kills remarked, pointing to Castle's body.

'It killed the man who would have used it, not me,' Dusty pointed out. 'And should you take it to war, the same would happen to you. The blue-coat lied when he said the Devil Gun would bring you victory. We have wheel guns which could shoot from far away and smash it. And if you ride to war, which tribe takes the Devil Gun?'

There Dusty posed a problem to the Indians. No one tribe would willingly allow any other to be in possession of such a deadly weapon. Talk welled up. Hostile glares passed among the various tribal enemies. Not for five minutes could Ysabel make himself heard to put forward his flash of inspiration. At last silence fell and all eyes went to the big, burly sergeant with the war lodge sheath on his rifle.

'Who owns the Devil Gun now the blue-coats are dead?' he asked, but gave his audience no time to answer. 'Among all true men the brave who counts the coup takes the loot and keeps it. Of course among the poor-spirited people like the Tejas,* such is not done.'

Put that way, no Texas Indian with pride in the honour of his tribe could object to Dusty retaining ownership of the Ager; not when watched by critical members of the other tribes. If only one tribe had been present, its members might have chanced the wrath of the Great Spirit at failing to give a warrior his due, and killed Dusty to gain possession of the Devil Gun. As Ysabel well knew, no race-proud Indian would lower his tribal honour by doing so before witnesses from another nation.

'What do you do with the Devil Gun, Magic Hands?' asked Long Walker in good English.

'It's medicine is bad,' Dusty replied. 'No true man wants such a thing to fight for him.'

'You fixing to take it with us, Cap'n?' Ysabel inquired, bringing Dusty his gunbelt.

Much as the South could use such a weapon, Dusty knew

* Tejas: Texas tribe noted for friendship with the white men.

what he must do. To take the Ager would be asking for trouble. He knew that once clear of the council area one of the tribes, or a bunch of name-making young braves from it, might decide to take the gun for the use of their own people. If Dusty attempted to return to Arkansas with the Ager, he could expect trouble all the way.

'See if there is any powder in the caisson, Sergeant,' he said.

Without another word, Ysabel turned and went to where the Ager gun's caisson stood. The caisson, a two-wheeled ammunition carrier fitted with the necessary parts so a team of horses could be harnessed to it, proved to hold two twenty-five-pound kegs of du Pont black powder, spare chargers and moulded bullets. Taking out the kegs, one of which had been opened, Dusty placed it under the wheels of the gun. Next he used some of the contents of the open keg and lay a trail of powder from the full keg to some twenty feet away. Returning to the Ager, Dusty set the used keg at the end of the trail, making sure a continuous line of powder ran to it. He walked back to the end of the powder trail, accepted the match offered by Ysabel and rasped it alight on the seat of his pants. Nobody spoke, not one of the Indians moved, as they watched Dusty place the flame on the end of the powder trail. Flame spurted up, crawling along the ground until it came to the two kegs. Loud in the night came the roar as some thirty pounds of black powder exploded. For a moment the watching Indians were blinded by the glare. When their eyes cleared again they found the Devil Gun to be wrecked beyond any hope of repair.

'Reckon that's that,' breathed Ysabel, relief plain in his voice.

'Like you say, Sergeant,' Dusty answered. 'Now all we have to do is get out of here.'

'That'll cause no fuss,' grinned Ysabel. 'Just look at all them chiefs rushing up all excited to meet you.'

Watching the slow, dignified manner in which the chiefs rose and walked towards him, Dusty found it hard to imagine anything less rushing or excited in appearance.

'That's all rushing and excited?' he asked.

'Sure is,' agreed Ysabel. 'For Injuns that is. Usually they'd sit back and let you make first move.'

'You fight well, Magic Hands,' said Long Walker, halting before Dusty and offering his hand to be shaken white man's fashion. 'Aiee! You might be a Comanche.'

'Never have I seen such a way of fighting,' enthused Plenty Kills, not to be out-done in the matter of showing respect to a great warrior.

'It was a remembered fight,' Lone Hunter went on, 'and would have been the greater if the blue-coats fought better.'

A rumble of agreement rose from the other chiefs, but all made it clear that they did not blame Dusty for any discrepancies the fight showed. Then came promises that no concerted, inter-tribal action would be made against the whites in Texas.

'But the young men will still raid,' warned Long Walker in the apologetic tone of one who explains an obvious point to a social equal. 'That is always the way. How else can the young man make his name as a warrior, or win trophies to buy many squaws? It is a pity you can have but one woman, Magic Hands. You would have many white maidens wanting you to buy them.'

'It is no pity,' stated Plenty Kills. 'If Magic Hands had plenty squaws, they would give him many sons like himself and the white-eyes could then drive us from our lands with ease.'

The compliments continued, each chief trying to excel the others in their praise for a brave fighting man who might one day be a potential enemy. Standing before the chiefs, Dusty tried to stay impassive and hide his pleasure at the praise. He felt grateful that none of his kin or brother officers heard some of the things said in his praise.

Finally each chief gave his word that none of his people would impede Dusty's party during their return to Arkansas.

'Ask them for a relay of horses, Cap'n,' Ysabel suggested. 'Then I can go on ahead of you to tell General Hardin how things've turned out.'

While Dusty had thought of the possibility of sending a man ahead with his report, he hesitated to ask Ysabel to take the task. It meant an even more hard and gruelling ride than the trip out and Dusty wanted a volunteer to make the journey. Having his volunteer, he made the request. Eagerly the chiefs offered the pick of their horse herds and Ysabel selected three fine, powerful horses which, along with his roan, ought to be able to cover fifty miles a day given anything like reasonable conditions.

The next morning Dusty and his small band turned east, following the wake of the faster-travelling Ysabel and leaving the Indian council to disband. Although Dusty did not hear of it until many years later, a picked escort of Comanche Dog Soldiers trailed his party from a distance ready to lend a hand should any other tribe break its word.

With each day of the journey to the east, the Texans grew more relaxed and cheerful at the thought of returning to their friends. Liz gradually threw off the shock of seeing the Indian-massacred family and tried to raise Marsden's spirits, without much success. Each day Marsden grew more quiet and disturbed, for the return to Arkansas meant that he must face his own kind and stand his trial as a traitor. In love with Jill, wanting to make her his wife and devote his life to making her happy, he knew that he stood but little chance of being allowed to do so.

CHAPTER SIXTEEN

MARSDEN'S FATE

Lieutenant Jackson Hardin Marsden never stood trial for either desertion or treason. On his return to Arkansas, he was taken under a flag of truce to the Ouachita River and passed into the care of a colonel from the U.C. Adjutant-General's Department. After a thorough interrogation of Marsden, reading a bulky letter sent by General Hardin, and interviews with Liz Chamberlain and Jill Dodd, the colonel took Marsden to Little Rock, from where the lieutenant found himself detailed to join a west-bound supply train and transferred to a cavalry regiment serving in the Montana Territory. With Marsden when he went, travelled Mrs. Marsden; until recently Jill Dodd, Confederate sympathiser, ex-bushwhacker band member and hater of everything to do with the Union. Far from the civil conflict, she managed to make her husband happy; and even forgot her old hatreds.

What brought about the Union's remarkable leniency towards Marsden?

A number of things.

First, Ole Devil Hardin's report of the affair reached General Handiman at the Adjutant-General's Department and from him went to Sherman, Grant and finally into President Lincoln's hands. The latter, great man that he was, saw the full implications and cost in innocent lives of Castle's scheme. He also visualised the effect word that such a scheme had been tried might have upon world opinion. At that time the United States strove to improve its public image—although the term had not then come into use—in the eyes of the European countries. The United States' prestige had dwindled in Europe after a U.S. Navy ship stopped a British merchantman on the high seas and forcibly removed several accredited Confederate ambassadors and other officials. Feelings ran high in Britain at the breach of diplomatic immunity and insult to her flag, and the United Nations feared that what was then the greatest power in the world might swing its weight fully behind the Confederacy. Even now the situation hung in a delicate balance. Should word of the attempted arming of Indians and endangering of innocent civilians leak out, the Confederate propagandists in Europe would have fuel to burn against the Union. Ole Devil hinted in his letter to Handiman that any attempt to court martial Marsden would see the full facts placed in the hands of various European military observers who visited the combat zones.

After some deliberation, a decision came down that Marsden had acted for the best. Colonel Stedloe of the Zouaves received a letter which left him in no doubt of how the top brass regarded his permitting the scheme. In the same package came orders transferring Marsden to the Eighth Cavalry who kept the peace with—or against—the Indians in Montana Territory. The order was dated the day before Marsden deserted, turned traitor—and helped save thousands of men, women and children from death at the hands of Indians inspired by the evil medicine of the Devil Gun.

THE END

J.T. EDSON OMNIBUS VOLUME 2

BY J.T. EDSON

The Ysabel Kid is one of J.T. Edson's most vibrant and colourful characters. Half Comanche, half Irish, the Kid was raised as a Comanche brave. From his Irish father he learned superb rifle skill, and from Dusty Fog he learned how to be a fighting man on the OD Connected Ranch. Dressed in black, riding his white stallion, the Ysabel Kid is a character no one can ever forget.

Here are three stories, all featuring the Ysabel Kid – COMANCHE; SIDEWINDER; OLD MOCCASINS ON THE TRAIL

0 552 13603 4